THE

MISER OF SHOREDITCH:

OR,

THE CURSE OF AVARICE.

AN

ORIGINAL HISTORICAL LEGENDARY ROMANCE

Of the Fifteenth Century.

BY PECKETT PREST, ESC.

" Content is wealth, the riches of the mind,
 And happy he who can the treasure find;
 But the base miser starves amidst his store,
 Broods o'er his gold, and griping still for more
 Sits sadly pining, and believes he's poor."

DRYDEN.

LONDON:
PRINTED BY R. BEARD, CRAVEN BUILDINGS, CITY ROAD.

1855.

NOTICE.—On Monday next will be published an entire new Historical
Tale, entitled SCHAMYL; or, THE WILD WOMAN OF CIR-
CASSIA.—With startling facts connected with the Illustrious
Warrior that will rivet the attention of all readers.
It will be closely printed in two page columns, in smaller
type wich will contain a great amount of reading.

———————————

PRICE ONE PENNY—No. 2 GIVEN GRATIS WITH No. 1—IN A NEAT
WRAPPER.
To be had of all Booksellers.

THE MISER OF SHOREDITCH

NEAT WINES CALEB COSEY

AN ORIGINAL HISTORICAL LEGENDARY ROMANCE, OF THE SIXTEENTH CENTURY.

"Content is wealth, the riches of the mind,
And happy he who can the treasure find;
But the base miser starves amidst his store,
Broods o'er his gold, and griping still for more,
Sits sadly pining, and believes he's poor."

DRYDEN.

CHAPTER I.

YE OLD TANKARD OVER AND AGAINST YE VILLAGE OF FYNESBURIE.

THE RIVALS.

OUR Tale commences about the year 1560, when the now populous locality of Finsbury was a village. What is now the City Road was one of the most lonely and unfrequented places in the suburbs; the nobility had their town residences in Aldgate, and Hogs-den (Hoxton), was quite an aristocratic part of the town. And a clean, old-fashioned, quiet hamlet was that same village of Fynesburie, bounded by green fields and intersected by shady lanes, winding their way towards Shoreditch, which at that time was a place of great traffic, and, as at the present day, devoted to business, albeit its shops and warehouses had but an unpretending appearance, and its highways and byeways, its nooks and corners, courts and alleys, were none of the most inviting description.

Over and against the village above-named, and near the locality now called Worship Street, stood a quaint old hostelrie, known by the sign of " The Tankard," much frequented by persons in the neighbourhood, and kept by a stout, jovial-looking wight, yclept Master Caleb Cosey, whose rubicund visage plainly showed his propensity for his own beverage, the flavour of which was much palated by his customers, and in which they sometimes indulged to an unlimited extent.

The aspect of the locality to which our tale refers, at the time of which we are writing, was indeed wondrously different to what it is at present.

The only semblances of roads near Fynesburie were the old Roman Road, now called Old Street Road, and the Bridle Road, now the Curtain Road, stretching from "The London Apprentice," an ancient tavern standing upon the site of the present house of that sign at the entrance of the old town of Hogs-den. Around was a wide extent of fields, lanes, and marshes, dangerous to wander through after nightfall, with a solitary house or cottage scattered here and there, extending in one direction to " Islyntone," and in the other, taking in the heaths and downs of Mary-the-Good (Marylebone), to the wood of Saint John. But to our tale.

It was May-day, bright and lovely, the May-pole reared its gay head in front of the Old Tankard; and from an early hour, numerous persons of almost every rank were assembled to do honour to the cheerful season, and Master Cosey was full of business.

Shakspeare says that it was impossible to make the people sleep on May morning, and this eagerness " To do observance to the morn of May," was not confined to any particular rank in society, but royal and noble personages, as well as the vulgar, went out a " Maying " early in the first morning of the month.

Chaucer says, " on that day forth goeth alle the Court, bothe moste and leaste, to fetche the flowris freshe, and braunche and bloome;" and Stowe says that, " In the month of May, the citizens of all estates, in every parish, or sometimes two or three parishes adjoining together, had their several Mayings, and did fetch in May-poles with divers warlike shows, with good archers, morris dancers, and other devices for pastimes all the day long ; and towards evening they had stage plays, and bonfires in the street."

King Henry the Eighth and Queen Katherine partook of this diversion, and rode a Maying from Greenwich to the high ground at Shooter's Hill, accompanied with many lords and ladies. Here they were received by two hundred tall yeomen, all clothed in green, with green hoods, and bows and arrows. One of them personating Robin Hood, as captain of the band, requested the King and all his company to stay and see his men shoot; to which his majesty agreeing, Robin Hood whistled, and all the two hundred discharged their arrows at once, which they repeated on his whistling again. Their arrows had something placed in the heads of them which made them whistle as they flew, and altogether made a loud and uncommon noise. The gentleman who assumed the character of Robin Hood then desired the King and Queen, with their retinue, to enter the greenwood, where, in arbours, made with boughs, intermixed with flowers, they were plentifully supplied with venison and wine by Robin Hood and his men.

Such were the sports on May-day morn, at the period to which we refer.

Among the guests assembled before the Old Tankard were several of the wandering tribe, who had been for some time encamped in the green lanes adjacent, and who seemed fully resolved to enjoy themselves on this occasion, if we except one of them, a young female, who sat apart from the rest, gloomy, thoughtful, and silent.

The Gipsy-girl, Mabel as she was called, did not appear to be more than twenty years of age, but an expression of heavy care and anxiety was visible on her dark but handsome features, and the same depressing feeling partly dimmed the lustre of her fine black eyes. From this abstracted mood no one sought to arouse her, and her companions having freely partaken of the beverage supplied to them by mine host of The Tankard, waxed exceedingly merry, and presently burst forth into the following rude chorus, in tones that were pleasing, if not strictly musical—

> Merry Gipsies all are we,
> Who so jovial, who so free?
> Caring not where'er we roam,
> In every clime we find a home.

> 'Neath the old oak's leafy shade,
> In the bonny greenwood glade;
> Our tents we pitch, with pleasure rife,
> Then hey for a wandering gipsy's life!
> Hey, for the merry, merry gipsy's life!

Having concluded this vocal display, the gipsies retired into the house, Mabel not offering to follow them.

" Ah! " observed Master Cosey, addressing himself to the persons present; " as I was saying, neighbours, there is nothing like drinking to keep soul and body together. It is the want of good liquor that drives so many persons mad, for, when the clay is not properly moistened, is it at all wonderful that it should become *cracked* ?"

The guests laughed, and at that moment the voice of a man was heard singing in a merry mood at a short distance off. " Eh! by-the-bye," ejaculated Caleb, looking in the direction from whence the sounds proceeded; " here comes one of the best customers to the Old Tankard—Master Timothy Tapcan, the tinker, and, as usual, in a glorious state of insobriety, as he calls it. He's a wet soul and I honour him for it. Ah, Timothy," he added, as the tinker made his appearance, staggering, " here thou art then, and in thy cups as usual."

" Why," faltered out Timothy, " marry, and I do begin to think that I am a leetle bit toxicated. I feel in a state of all-overishness topsyturvyness like. I-I have had a fall which has deranged my internals. Caleb, bring me a tankard of your very best, or I shall swoon."

" Aye, marry will I, Master Timothy," said the worthy host ; " for there is nothing like drinking.—Steady, steady."

Having led him him to a seat, he departed to execute his order.

"Now," observed the tinker, "I dare say they think I'm ine-ine-briated; but I never do that sort of thing. I am as sober and temperate a man as need to be. It's nothing but love that make me act as I do. I want to enter the salubrial state of hymen. Ah! here's the medicine which will cure all complaints," he added, as Caleb returned; "I say Caleb, you know my Abigail, Abigail Allspice I mean, the waiting maid of Miss Constance Welborn of the old Grange near Hogs-den, where I am now going; isn't she a lovely creature? Here's her health. There's rare merry making at the Grange, to celebrate the birth-day of Miss Constance; and I can tell you a secret, Caleb."

"A secret?"

"Aye, Constance Welborn is going to be married next Monday-week."

"Marry, and is it even so?" said Cosey.

"Yes, it is," answered the tinker; "I heard all the particulars yesterday. It's all over with poor Master Evelyn Heartwell; it seems the young spark's ruined, so Sir Milford Welborn has broke off the match."

"Ah!" tis well;" muttered Mabel to herself, and a smile of satisfaction passed over her features, and she continued to listen attentively.

"Poor Evelyn!" ejaculated Caleb. "Then who's to be the husband of Constance?"

"Oliver Dalton, to be sure."

"Well, I am not sorry for that, because he's a liberal-hearted youth, and one of my best customers."

"Well, I am then;" remarked Timothy; "I don't half like that Oliver. If he's not a scoundrel at heart my name's not Timothy Tapcan. Nobody knows who he is, what he is, or where he comes from. He happened to save the old gentleman's life, when he was attacked by robbers, and that established him in his favour. Besides poor Evelyn Heartwell is a good lad; he has been unfortunate, and so far as the word of a respectable travelling tinker will go, he's welcome to my affluence to persuade Sir Milford to accept him as the husband of Constance."

"Never!" exclaimed Mabel, vehemently, and starting up; "the maiden may possess his heart, but his hand must never be her's. I Mabel, the wandering gipsy-girl, say so."

"Bless me Mistress Mabel," said the tinker, "and what can you have to do with the business? Any one might be inclined to think that you had a sneaking regard for the young man yourself."

"Hold! loquacious idiot!" exclaimed Mabel, sternly, and she again retired to a remote corner and sunk into meditation.

"Well;" observed Timothy, "that's not very civil, certainly;—but I declare here comes the very man we have been talking about. How pale and careworn he looks."

Evelyn Heartwell (who was a fine, handsome young man, but with a melancholy expression of countenance,) now slowly approached the spot, and sunk disconsolately on a seat, without taking any notice of the persons present.

"Lost! ruined!" he sighed; "beggared in fortune; scorned by the world; rejected by the haughty uncle of her whom my soul adores, I am indeed a wretched being. Poor Constance, thou alone art faithful."

He hastily persused a letter he had in his hand,—pressed it to his lips, and then added;

"Dear, dear girl; yes, I will indeed meet thee to-night;—sigh my last farewell on thy bosom, and then bear myself from thy presence for ever. The wide ocean shall in future be my home, and when the wild tempest tosses about the frail barque, I will fancy I hear thy gentle soothing tones in the voice of the storm, and smile at its terrors. I cannot help thinking of old Jasper Scrimpe, the miser. He has appointed me to meet him at his house in Shoreditch this evening ; that house whose doors have ever been closed to the poor and needy. 'Tis strange, what can he want with me ? However, I'll attend him."

"Ahem!" cried Caleb Cosey, advancing towards him at that moment, and bowing obsequiously ;—"Welcome, Master Evelyn Heartwell to the Old Tankard. The best hostelrie for miles round. Capital old wines. What shall I have the honour to bring you?"

"A glass of water !" replied Evelyn, abruptly.

"Water! water?" exclaimed the astonished Caleb ; "awful idea!"

"Away! away!" cried the young man impatiently.

"Excuse me, but—"

"I hate impertinence,—begone!"

"But what shall I bring you?" again urged the indefatigable host.

"Civility and attention when you come this way again ;" was the laconic answer.

"Humph !" muttered Caleb to himself; "he's a stubborn fool, that's evident. But come along, Timothy, let's into the house and enjoy ourselves. Nothing like drinking." Thus saying, he departed, followed by the tinker, and Mabel advanced towards Evelyn, who starting, recognised her.

"Mabel the gipsy-girl, here ?" he exclaimed.

"Yes," she replied, in melancholy accents, "the gipsy wanderer feels a sad pleasure in following in your path, and in listening to the tones of your voice Misfortune has overtaken you, and—"

"You pity me ?"

"Pity you !" she repeated ; "oh, how much more ardent is the sentiment I entertain towards you ; you love the fair Constance of the Grange, and that thought is madness to my soul !"

"For Heaven's sake, what mean you?"

"Oh, canst thou not read it in my looks ? Think you that the wild child of the forest glade is insensible to the tenderest emotions that can animate the human breast ? But mark me, Evelyn, scorn and indifference may excite other passions in my bosom, and—but no more—farewell, and when distance perchance may separate us, remember that there is one who loves you yet more fondly then it is possible for Constance Welborn to do."

Fixing upon him a look of the most indescribable tenderness and emotion as she uttered those words, the gipsy-girl hurried away.

"I'm astonished !" ejaculated Evelyn ; "too well do I understand thy feelings !"

He again seated himself at the table, and resting his head on his hands, became lost in thought.

Oliver Dalton had now arrived at the spot. He was a young man of graceful exterior, and gaily attired, but the expression of his features bespoke a wild and reckless disposition. He was too busily occupied with his own thoughts at first to notice Evelyn.

"Bravo ! bravo !" he ejaculated ; "Fortune smiles once more upon me ; this money that I have duped the fools out of at the gaming table, will enable me to support the character. I have assumed and to cozen still further the foolish old baronet. Ah, the gipsy Luke, the thief, the mur—no, that name must be erased from my vocabulary. Well, after all, here I am, professing to be the very paragon of honour and virtue, and talking love and sentimentality to one of the loveliest of her sex ;—the wedding day fixed, and—ha, ha, ha, Luke, this is better then following the beggarly fortunes of the gipsy tribe."

"Oh, Constance, dear Constance !" sighed Evelyn. The tones of his voice smote the ears of Oliver, and turning, he observed him.

"Ah!" he muttered; "my rival here? Should he have overheard me. I know not how it is, but whenever I look upon him I cannot help shuddering, while a sensation thrills at my heart for which I cannot account. Poor fellow!—his power is at an end now. It is almost too contemptible to finally trample on a worm; yet do I so heartily hate him that I delight to taunt him. Good day to thee, Master Evelyn," he cried aloud; "I greet thee."

"Oliver Dalton!" exclaimed Evelyn.

"Aye, your *friend*;" replied the former sarcastically.

"Your friendship is gratuitous;" returned Evelyn, contemptuously; "I am not *your* friend."

"Humph! and why not, good Evelyn?

"The man who would be Evelyn's friend, must first prove himself possessed of honour and virtue."

"Nay, you are sarcastic, Heartwell;" remarked his rival; "but I bear you no malice, though you did seek to rival me in the affections of Constance Welborn."

"Rival *you*!" repeated Evelyn, indignantly.

"Aye, but it is all past now. I am too happy to day to quarrel with any one. The baronet has fixed the day for my union with Constance, and—"

"Heartless villain!" said Evelyn, aside. "Oliver Dalton!" he added, passionately.

"At your service;" replied Oliver, with mock politeness. "Nay, now, be cool. Come, we will be merry to day I am resolved; so be seated, and—"

"Oliver Dalton!" interrupted Heartwell. passionately; "arouse not my anger. You are planting a dagger in my heart let me begone —oh, Constance!"

He sank overpowered by his feelings, on a seat.

"Ah!" observed Oliver; "that's the wisest plan; oh, we shall soon understand each other and be friends. What ho!—host!"

Caleb quickly attended the summons.

"Wine! wine!" demanded Oliver; "the best your hostelrie can produce."

"Attend to you like a flash of lightning," replied Cosey; "nothing like drinking!—wine unlimited;—what liberality.'

"My raillery galls him," said Oliver, aside; "tis glorious revenge."

Caleb now returned with the wine.

"Now, Evelyn, my friend, drink," said Oliver.

"Psha! arouse yourself from this melancholy; why man, you look as dull and cheerless as a November day. Come, drink I say."

"No, urge me not; I am not disposed to drink, especially with Oliver Dalton."

"In spite of all," remarked Oliver, "I will not be angry with you. I say you shall pledge me a toast, and that shall be my future bride, Constance Welborn!"

"Constance!—my Constance!" cried Evelyn, starting up passionately; "Oliver Dalton, come you here to insult me?"

"Is it then an insult," demanded his rival, "to endeavour to persuade you to drink towards the health of one of the most lovely of women, and whom you once pretended to love?"

"*Pretended* to love! Shameless slanderer, you come to triumph o'er my misery."

"Base-born wretch!" exclaimed Oliver, fiercely ;—"outcast and beggar as thou art."

"Can I endure this?" said Evelyn; "I'll hear no more! Villain!" and unable any longer to control his feelings, he struck Oliver violently.

"Ah!" cried the latter furiously, "a blow! Oliver Dalton struck by a reptile like Evelyn Heartwell. Revenge! revenge!"

He sprang upon him as he spoke, and snatching Evelyn's dagger from his belt was about to plunge it in his breast, when Caleb and Timothy darted from the house and interposed between them.

CHAPTER II.

THE RECOGNITION.—THE OLD GRANGE NEAR HOGSDEN. —SIR MILFORD WELBORN AND CONSTANCE.

"Gentlemen, gentlemen," said Caleb Cosey, "has my excellent old wine proved too strong for you, that you are going to kill one another?"

"Oliver Dalton," said Evelyn, sternly, "for the present you have escaped my just evenge, and I leave you to the utter contempt of your own worthlessness. Villain!"

"Stay, vain boaster!" exclaimed Oliver, fiercely, and he was about to follow, when Caleb detained him.

"Now, now, don't be rash, good Master Oliver," said the old man. "You'd better stay and cool your courage over another flask of my excellent old wine, Nothing like drinking for a man that's in a passion."

"Confusion!" exclaimed Oliver, when Caleb and Timothy had departed; "to be struck by this upstart! But I will have revenge. This dagger, bearing his name on the blade, may serve me."

At that moment his eye fell upon the letter from Constance, which in the struggle Evelyn had accidenally dropped. It contained the following words:

"Dearest Evelyn, in spite of every danger, I will meet you to-night at ten in the Lover's Walk. Ever your's, Constance."

"By Jove!" ejaculated Oliver, "this is fortunate. I will be at the place of assignation. Now, Evelyn Heartwell, dearly shall you feel the vengeance of Oliver Dalton!"

As he thus spoke, he hastily thrust the billet into his pocket, and with a look of mingled satisfaction and determination, he hurried from the spot. He had not proceeded far, however. when he again paused, and as a dark expression of malignity overspread his features, he muttered:

"Each step I take, my eagerness for vengeance increases. I will back to my house to provide myself with the means to execute my plot, and then to meet my rival at the place of assignation."

He paused, and ruminated for a minute or two, and then added :—

"I have often thought that, could I by some means or other contrive to get at the coffers of old Jasper Scrimpe, the Miser of Shoreditch, as he is called, it would be an excellent thing for me, under existing circumstances. They say that he is immensely rich, the old curmudgeon, while I am but a poor needy adventurer at the best. The old house he inhabits, I think, might be easily entered, and one bold effort might secure me all I want. I must e'en consider of this."

While Oliver Dalton was thus soliloquising, a man of the most uncouth and suspicious appearance had, unobserved, stolen cautiously behind him, and with folded arms and listening eager ears, stood and watched him.

He was one of the gipsies who had followed him from the Old Tankard, and had evidently some sinister design in view. He was a fellow as ungainly in aspect as he was miserable and rugged in personal appearance, and such a ruffian as it would

not be very agreeable to meet unarmed in a lonely spot. Oliver was about to proceed on his way, when this unprepossessing individual unceremoniously started
before him and obstructed his progress.

"How now, fellow!" exclaimed Oliver, sternly, "why dost thou cross my path?
What would'st thou with me?"

"Charity, good sir, charity," replied the man in a whining tone.

"Away!" cried Dalton, "I have nothing to give."

"Ah!" exclaimed the fellow, starting, "that voice; marry, and methinks I
have heard it before!"

He rudely thrust his gaze into the face of Oliver, and then added:—

"'Tis,' tis Luke Stanton!"

At the mention of this name Oliver turned pale, and trembling, as he eyed the
forbidding features of the gipsy more narrowly, he ejaculated:—

"Confusion!—my former associate, Sampson Brayling! I'm lost!"

"Oh, no, my runaway," returned Sampson, sarcastically; "thou'rt found. So
thou thought'st to slip thine old friends for ever, did'st thou?"

"Do not detain me, Brayling," ejaculated Oliver, in confused and agitated
tones; "if I am seen in company with thee, I'm ruined. I will meet thee, again,
at midnight, here, anywhere, or—"

"Oh, no," said the ruffian, resolutely; "we part not so easily."

"Villain! thou would'st not, dare not—"

"Ha! ha! ha!" laughed Sampson, scornfully, "come, come, Luke Stanton, no
nonsense,—you know me, and I know you; we are old friends, and I cannot think
of parting with you so soon."

"What shall I do?" said Oliver, aside. "For mercy's sake, detain me not;"
he added, aloud; "I will not betray you, I swear—"

"Betray *me*!" repeated the gipsy, fiercely; "you dare not; you would but place
your own neck in the halter. I know more then you suspect, and now that I have
found you I mean to profit by my knowledge. You are the young squire, as you've
called yourself, and have duped old Sir Milford to give you the hand of his fair
niece. 'Tis well;—myself and my companions will invite ourselves to your wedding, Luke Stan—Oliver Dalton, I mean. Ha! ha! ha!"

"You would not betray me?" said Dalton, fearfully.

"Not if we can make a better bargain by keeping your secret," was the reply.

"What would you?"

"Money to be sure."

"Money I have none."

"What!" ejaculated Sampson, ironically;—"a squire, and no money? You
have not bettered your fortunes, then, by turning gentleman. No matter I can
accompany you to Sir Milford's; doubtless he will accommodate you with a few
broad pieces, till you get your remittances, Oliver Dalton!—Ha! ha! ha!"

"What shall I do to escape?" thought Oliver.

"Here," he said, tossing a purse to the gipsy; "take that and begone. 'Tis all
I have at present, but I will meet you in a day or two. Be secret; know me not,
and I will reward you."

"Humph!" replied Sampson, weighing the purse in his hand; this will do by
way of a beginning, but I shall want more soon; so you had better meet me and
the rest of the tribe at our encampment in the green lanes of Fynesbnrie, or we
shall not be too bashful to call at the Grange for you. Good bye, Luke Stan—
Oliver Dalton I mean. Ha! ha!"

And fixing upon him a malicious, sarcastic, and triumphant look, Sampson Brayling hurried from the spot, leaving Oliver in a state of the utmost confusion, chagrin, and fear. For a few minutes after the ruffian Brayling was gone, he stood and reflected; and it was quite evident from his contracted eyebrows, quivering lips, and

the general expression of his countenance, that he was anything but pleased at the meeting, and that Sampson Brayling had hinted at certain facts, and alluded to several circumstances of the past that were anything but palatable to him.

"Curses light on this misfortune!" he exclaimed; "Now shall I have to pander to all the extortionate demands that those fellows may think proper to make, or they will betray me. This meeting with Sampson Brayling at such a juncture is most inopportune, and distracts and bewilders me. What is to be done? However, I must make up my mind to extricate myself from the difficulties by which I am surrounded at all hazards. Let me but secure the hand of Constance Welborn, and I will find some ready means to quiet the dogs. Now to business."

Arousing himself as well as he could, Oliver Dalton proceeded on his way, and was soon lost to sight.

    *   *   *   *   *

The Old Grange, as it was called, stood immediately in the vicinity of the town of Hogsden, and nearly on the site of what is now called the Whitmore Road. And a fine, stately mansion it was, nearly covered with ivy, and having pleasant gardens and orchards withal, with golden corn-fields adjoining, and commanding a picturesque view of the pretty and romantic village of Isylyntone.

The mansion had been erected in the early part of the fifteenth century, and had been for many years the residence of Sir Milford Welborn, Baronet, a gentleman of large wealth, who, with much kindness and urbanity of heart, possessed many unfortunate weaknesses of disposition, as will be shown in the course of our tale. He was a widower, and had no one to whom to devote his regard and attention but an orphan niece, who had been brought up under his protection from the earliest period of childhood.

Constance Welborn! what a beauteous maiden was she; so fair, so gentle, so loving, and so loveable; with a mind as amiable as it was cultivated; and a soul which never harboured a thought which angels need blush to acknowledge. To see her was to admire, and to know her was to idolize.

On the evening of the day on which our story commences, Abigail Allspice, the loquacious waiting-maid of Constance, entered one of the rooms of the Grange in a great bustle, and chattering to herself all the way as she came, said:

"Well, I have executed my love mission to poor Evelyn Heartwell, and have invited my dear little Timothy Tapcan to meet me here. Heigho! what a strange thing this love is; it will not leave us pretty young girls alone. But here comes my young mistress."

Constance now entered the room, with an expression of the deepest melancholy imprinted on her countenance, and advancing to her maid, said:

"So, Abigail, you have returned. Say, did you see my poor Evelyn?"

"Oh yes, Miss," answered Abigail; "poor young gentleman, he did look so pale; but when he had perused it, his eyes brightened up—you know he has very pretty eyes; something like my Tim's, only not quite so sparkling."

"A truce with this, Abigail," said Constance, impatiently, "did he say that he would meet me?"

"Yes, Miss; he kissed the letter, pressed it to his heart, called you an angel, and said he would be sure to be in the Lover's Walk at the time you appointed."

"Alas! poor Evelyn," sighed our heroine; "it may be our last meeting."

"Heigho!" ejaculated Abigail; "what a very cutting thing this love is to be sure."

At that moment the voice of Sir Milford was heard below, and at the sound of it Constance trembled and turned pale.

"There's your uncle returned, Miss," said Abigail.

"He is ascending the stairs," observed Constance; "leave me, Abigail."

"Oh, my uncle," said Constance, in melancholy accents, "how my heart sinks when I hear your footsteps approaching; formerly it leaped for joy at the sound of your voice, and I would rush to your arms, eager to obtain the approving kiss. But you loved me then, and Evelyn too, and bright was the sunshine of our hopes; alas! how sad is the change."

She sank into a chair, overpowered by the emotions that swelled at her heart, and buried her face in her hands.

Sir Milford now entered the room, and looking around him, said:

"Now, now, Constance—Constance, wench, where—oh, there she sits, moping and fretting as usual. Come lass, arouse thee, and no longer give way to those sad thoughts. Constance, I say."

"Sir—uncle—" faltered out our heroine, rising confused; "I beg pardon, but—"

"Nay, child," interrupted Sir Milford, in more tender accents, "this gloomy bearing pains me to witness. Come, come, put on one of those pretty radiant smiles with which thou wert wont to delight me. Why, if you give way to this fretting you'll make but a dull wife methinks."

"I hope, my dear uncle," replied Constance, in a timid voice, and the crimson blushes mantling in her cheeks, "the time is far distant when I shall be put to the test."

"Indeed, Constance," returned Sir Milford, "the time is not far distant. I've settled it all this very day, and next Monday week you will become the bride of Oliver Dalton."

"Oliver Dalton!" repeated his niece with a shudder.

"Yes; why do you always evince such disgust at the bare mention of his name?"

"Alas! my dear uncle, I know not; but there is something about that man which makes me view him with horror; but to think of him as my husband—oh, I dare not."

"Dare not!" repeated her uncle, angrily; "but I tell you girl that you must. I am resolved that no other but Oliver Dalton shall be your husband. He has won my esteem; besides, did he not save my life? Tut, tut, girl, isn't he a comely youth? And—and by all my hopes I swear that you shall have him."

"It is my duty to obey you, sir," sobbed poor Constance; "and though my heart break in the effort, you shall never find me shrink from it."

"Well, well," said the baronet kindly, and taking her hand, "that's a good girl; so you must cheer up and think no more of Evelyn Heartwell. He's a good-looking lad to be sure, but then he must have been improvident to lose all his money, and the niece of Sir Milford Welborn must never be sacrificed to a spendthrift. Goodbye, Constance, good-bye. Oh fear not but marriage will cure you of all those vagaries."

He kissed the pale cheek of his lovely niece as he thus spoke, and then retired from the room and left her to the anguish of her own thoughts.

"Alas!" she sighed, "he remains inflexible. There is no hope for Evelyn, and I am wretched. But I must prepare myself or I shall be too late to meet him. Heaven help us both."

And with a melancholy air she retired from the apartment.

CHAPTER III.

JASPER SCRIMPE, THE MISER OF SHOREDITCH.—THE MEETING.—
CONSCIENCE.

He was an old man—a very old man—of attenuated form, shrivelled cadaverous countenance, a skin like parchment, contracted brows, small, restless eyes, and with a few grey hairs strewed over his head. No one had ever seen a smile upon that unprepossessing countenance; no one had ever known him to utter a kind word to any one; no one respected him—all hated and despised him.

Such was Jasper Scrimpe, the Miser of Shoreditch !

The house, or rather hovel (for it deserved no other name) which the miser inhabited, was old and ruinous; situate in a wretched court or alley near the present Eastern Counties Railway, and in the midst of miserable, squalid beings, whose very looks denoted dissipation and crime. It was a matter of some astonishment that old Jasper should venture to locate himself among individuals of character so questionable; but so it was—no one offered to molest him—they seemed to view him as one of themselves, and suffered him to plod on his wretched, slimy way without interruption.

Nothing could exceed the gloomy, dirty aspect of the Miser's dwelling; the walls were black with age, and tottering from decay, and the different casements were thickly encrusted with the dirt of many years accumulation. In fact it was a fit residence for one who made himself a blot upon humanity, and who brooded in gloom and avarice over his ill-gotten riches. The only being old Jasper Scrimpe had about him was a man who acted as his factotum, and who had resided with him from boyhood. He was called Toby Taper, and his miserable, slender, starved appearance fully corresponded with his name. It was quite evident that neither Toby nor his master fared very sumptuously, and certainly no sensible individual would envy the situation of the Miser's man.

It was night, and old Jasper Scrimpe sat in a dark and miserable room at the back of his house, counting his gold, depositing it in old canvas bags, and with eager eyes gloating o'er his fast accumulating wealth. The glimmering light, emitted by a small lamp, cast a sickly glare upon his cadaverous features, and only served to render the gloom and wretchedness of the place more visible. For a moment he glanced suspiciously around, as though he was fearful that some one might be watching him, and then he again applied himself to his task, chuckling and muttering to himself all the time.

"More gold ! more gold !" he ejaculated; " oh, how the glittering pile increases. I am rich and hap—; no, I am not happy. Conscience with voice of thunder, roars in my ears and makes me wretched."

He paused; a shuddering sensation shook his frame, and an expression of terror and remorse overspread his features.

" Of what use is this gold to me ?" he resumed in a hoarse, dismal voice; " Every coin has been purchased by blood—the blood of my nearest of kin—the good and innocent, and has it not brought upon me misery and despair in the midst of all my ill-gotten wealth ? Why what a poor crawling wretch am I—shunning the very light of day, and looked upon with disgust and loathing by my fellow-creatures. The demon's at work again! I'll go forth and reveal my crimes! I'll surrender myself to justice! I'll resign my gold!—distribute it among public charities—feed the hungry, clothe the naked, and endeavour to make my peace with heaven! I'm mad! I'm mad! Fool! can I end this torture by death? No, no, that would be but to rush upon an eternity of horror. I canno:, dare not, dare not die!"

Overpowered by the conflict of his feelings, the wretched old man sunk back in his chair, and covering his face with his hands, reflected for a time in silence and in bitter anguish.

"Let me be calm," he said at length; "the time approaches which I appointed for Evelyn Heartwell to meet me. 'Tis strange that I, who never before knew what pity or compassion were, should now feel my heart warm towards this friendless youth. I know not how it is, but whenever I look upon him there's something seems to tell me that my fate is involved in his."

He was startled at this moment by a knock at the door, and he hastily concealed his gold just as Toby Taper entered the room.

"How now, knave?" demanded his master, in a harsh and angry tone, "why do you thus intrude?"

"Pr'ythee, good master," returned Toby, "are we not going to have supper? I'm so hungry."

"Hungry, varlet!" cried old Jasper; "thou liest! Why 'tis not more than six hours since thou ate a most extravagant meal!"

"An extravagant meal!" cried Toby; "bacon rinds and cabbage leaves, and of that scarcely sufficient to bait a mouse-trap. I feel as full as if I'd swallowed a snow-ball. Pr'ythee, good master, do relieve my wants or I shall certainly be compelled to eat my jerkin. Oh, I'm so hungry!"

"Out upon thee for a shameless glutton! Thou 'rt getting fat and corpulent, and gross withal. I must e'en lower thy diet, for indulging thee so much of late has rendered thee indolent, sleepy, and saucy!"

"Lower my diet!" ejaculated Toby, with a shudder; "Oh dear, surely it is not possible to do that, unless you feed me from the bellows. Why I'm so thin and genteel already that people have a great difficulty to see me; I cast no shadow before me—I have not substance enough to do that; and I'm called the shadowless man. I must not venture out on a windy day without a couple of weights attached to my person to keep me on terra firma. Oh, I'm so hungry."

"Greedy dog!" exclaimed his master; "wouldst cram that voracious maw of thine to surfeiting? Wouldst ruin me? Have I not fed and clothed thee like a gentleman, in slothful indolence, from a child, ungrateful as thou art?"

A knock at the outer door prevented the old man from proceeding with his harangue.

"'Tis Evelyn," he said; "show the youth into my presence, and harkye, let me hear no more of thy grumbling, or I'll put thee on low diet for a month."

"The heartless old skinflint!" muttered poor Toby to himself, as he quitted the room; "he has certainly a design upon my life. Oh, I'm so hungry!"

In a few minutes he returned, ushering in Evelyn Heartwell, and he then left him and the Miser to themselves. Evelyn cast a hasty glance around the gloomy and wretched place, and then awaited for Scrimpe to begin.

"Thou'rt punctual, young man," he said; "be seated."

Evelyn bowed and obeyed.

"My business with thee is brief," continued the Miser; "thou'rt unfortunate?"

"Alas, good sir," replied Evelyn; "I am wretched."

"I pity thee! I pity thee!"

"Thanks, thanks, good Jasper," said the young man; "your commiseration for the misfortunes of your fellow-creatures does honour to your head and heart, and well becomes your grey airs."

"Bah!" exclaimed Scrimpe, impatiently; enough of this; "I hate flattery. Thou'rt ruined?"

"Beggared!"

" And did misfortune bring thee to it ?"

" It did—it did; for heaven knows how hard I struggled with adversity to maintain a respectable position in society."

" His words move me," said the Miser, aside; " and there is something in his voice and features that—but, psha!—I'm wandering. I believe," he said aloud, " that the late Master Heartwell was not your father, young man?"

" He was not," answered Evelyn; " but I must ever revere his memory and that of his excellent wife, for they received me as a foundling when an infant, and ever acted as the most affectionate parents to me."

The Miser looked at him narrowly as he thus spoke, and a strange expression passed over his features.

" Thou lovest the fair Constance Welborn, dost thou not ?" he interrogated.

" To distraction!" replied Evelyn.

" But her uncle has resolved to sacrifice her to another—is it not so?"

" Alas!" answered the youth; " 'tis too true."

" And what think'st thou of doing ?" inquired Jasper.

" To morrow it is my intention to enter on board a ship, and in the service of my country seek to win myself an honourable station in life, and if possible, to forget that such a being as Constance Welborn ever existed."

" A noble resolution, lad," remarked the Miser approvingly; " but thou must not want for money; thou'lt need it."

Evelyn looked at the wretched old man before him with more astonishment than ever; but Scrimpe averted his gaze, and seemed to experience some strange emotion.

" Oh, where shall I find a helping hand ?" said Evelyn.

" Here," replied Jssper; " take this pocket-book, it contains a sum sufficient for thy wants for some time to come. Take it, and may heaven prosper thee!"

Evelyn took the pocket-book, and was completely lost in amazement.

" Oh, generous sir," he said.

" Nay, nay," interrupted Scrimpe, " thank me not; I am unused to gratitude. Take it, and then when thou art in a foreign land, in thy prayers, do not forget the wretched miser, Jasper Scrimpe. He needs them."

" Good old man, hear me ?"

" Away," said Jasper, peremptorily; " I would be alone."

Evelyn hastily grasped the old man's hand, and he then hurried him out of the room, and returned to his seat, and remained for some minutes wrapped in the most gloomy meditation.

" So, then, Jasper Scrimpe," he soliloquised, at length; " for the first time in thy life thou hast performed a benevolent action. My heart feels light and buoyant, and as it never did before. Oh, how pleasant must be a life of virtue, if this one simple act of benevolence can impart such happiness. But I must to my secret hoard in the Lovers' Walk, and conceal part of my treasure. It might not be safe here. Ah! how little does the traveller suspect the golden hoard that is secreted there. ut 'tis getting late and I must begone."

He now put on a large cloak, in the lining of which were several large pockets. In those he deposited two or three bags of money, and then prepared to take his departure from the house.

" What ho, Toby !" he called; " Toby, thou varlet !"

Toby Taper slowly obeyed the summons, and with a most doleful expression of countenance.

" How now ?" demanded his master, in an angry tone; " why dost thou not hurry when thou hear'st me call, knave ? Hast been asleep ?"

" Asleep!" repeated Toby; " ah, no; I'm too hungry to sleep. I had half a mind to make a meal upon my finger ends, and—"

"Out upon thee for a greedy, ravenous churl, as thou art," interrupted the old man; "an' thou hadst thy will thou wouldst soon empty my larder altogether, and e'en eat me out of house and home."

"His larder!" muttered Toby to himself; "a small cupboard, double-locked, and which contains nothing but mouldy crusts, well-picked bones, intended to make soup of, and a small portion of rotten cheese. But even that would be a luxury to me, if I could only get at it. I'm so hungry!"

"What art thou muttering to thyself?" demanded Scrimpe; "grumbling as usual, discontented varlet as thou art. I tell thee what, Master Toby, I have been too liberal and indulgent a master to thee, and this is the return thou makest me for it. What would'st thou do if I were to turn thee adrift upon the wide world to seek for a living? Where couldst thou hope to fare so sumptuously as thou dost in my house?"

"Sumptuous fare!" repeated Toby, aside; "why the turnspit dog is a perfect prince to me."

"Beware, beware, rascal," said the old man. "Evelyn Heartwell has quitted the house, has he not"

"He has," answered Toby. "God bless him!" he added, aside.

"Did he ask any questions on retiring?" asked Scrimpe.

Toby replied in the negative.

"'Tis well," observed the Miser; "but I must begone. Toby see to the security of the house during my absence, and mind that thou dost not go to sleep, as thine overloaded stomach might induce thee to do. Thou mayest expect me to return in about a couple of hours. Mind me."

The old man now quitted the room, and the closing of the door showed that he had retired from the house.

"Thank heaven he is gone," ejaculated Toby; "the stingy old knave; he will starve me to death if I remain with him much longer. Heaven bless Master Heartwell, for he has made a man of me to-night. As he left the house he slipped a silver piece into my hand, and now while my old master is away I will have a hearty meal, if I never have one again. How shall I lay out this sum of money? I never was so rich in my life before. I will lay every farthing of it out in victuals, and won't I have a sumptuous repast for once, for I'm so hungry! Blissful thought! I can scarcely contain myself. Now for a glorious feed!"

With these words poor Toby Taper hastened on his errand.

CHAPTER IV.

The Lovers' Walk.—The Gipsies.—The Robbery.—The False Accusation.

The Lovers' Walk was a pretty secluded spot near the romantic fields of Isylyntone, and much frequented in the bright days of summer. Ye Old Queen's Head, in the immediate vicinity, was also a goodly hostelrie, well supported by the public in those days, and even patronised by her Majesty Queen Elizabeth, when on her hunting excursions. It was in the neighbourhood of the Lovers' Walk that the gipsies, introduced in the first chapter of our tale, were encamped.

About the centre of the Lovers' Walk was an ancient tree of large dimensions, and the umbrageous foliage of which spread around to a great extent, forming a pleasant shade from the scorching heat of the noon-day's sun, and much frequented by young people especially.

Singular as it may appear to be, it was in the trunk of this tree that old Jasper Scrimpe had for some time concealed his secret hoard, in a large tin box deposited in the earth in such a manner that it seemed to be perfectly secure from discovery, and, he considered, would be much more secure than in his own house. Here every night, and sometimes every morning, when he thought it likely there would not be any one to watch him, the old man would wend his way to add to his glittering treasure, and thither he bent his steps on the night to which we allude.

The moon was shining brightly, and all was calm around. The gipsies had disposed themselves in various ways near the spot—some in their tents, and others reclining on the grass, or engaged with their companions in mirthful conversation. The gipsy-girl, Mabel, stood in an attitude of deep thought at a short distance apart from them, and Sampson Brayling watched her every now and then with a jealous and suspicious eye. At length he advanced towards her, and gently tapping her on the shoulder, said:

"Why so dull, Mabel ? and why dost thou not make thyself sociable with the rest of the tribe as thou wert wont to do ? Now would I give a trifle were I able to penetrate thy thoughts."

"And what boots my thoughts to thee ?" coldly demanded Mabel; "they concern not thee nor thy companions, therefore trouble thine head with thine own business, and leave me to myself."

"Humph!" returned Sampson, "thou art getting crabbed and sour, Mabel, like some ancient beldame. But I guess the cause; the youth Evelyn Heartwell has made a powerful impression on the wandering gipsy-girl's heart, and—"

"How know you this, busy meddler ?" hastily interrupted Mabel; "has a word ever escaped my lips that could have revealed the secret of my breast ? And yet," she added, after a brief pause, "why should I seek to conceal it ? Why should I fear to acknowledge it ? Yes, yes, Evelyn Heartwell has indeed won the affections of the wretched Mabel.

As the gipsy-girl, Mabel, thus spoke, a tear trembled for a moment in her fine black eye, but with a sudden feeling of pride she dashed it away, and evidently wishing to avoid further conversation, she was moving from the spot, when Sampson Brayling detained her.

"How now ?" she demanded haughtily, "what wouldst thou with me ?"

"I would speak a few words with thee upon this important subject," replied Sampson.

"Wouldst pry into all the secrets of my breast?" said Mabel.   "Inquisitive;—but thou may'st e'en save thyself the trouble."

"Why shouldst thou prefer this boy, Evelyn Heartwell, to one of our own tribe?" asked Brayling.   "He loves thee not."

"Alas, alas!" sighed Mabel, and again a tear glistened in her eye.   "Too well do I know that.   'Tis the painful conviction of that which corrodes my heart, and renders me wretched.   Oh! could the poor gipsy-girl excite in his breast one tender and affectionate feeling towards her, the Grand Empress on her imperial throne, might fairly envy her happiness."

"Pshaw!" exclaimed Brayling, impatiently; "hast lost thy senses, Mabel? Where is now that proud and independent spirit that once distinguished thee? Arouse thyself girl, and deign not to own thine heart the slave of one who views thee with scorn and indifference."

"With scorn!   With indifference!" repeated Mabel, and her bosom swelled, and her eyes appeared to flash fire;—"No, no, no, 'tis not in Evelyn Heartwell's nature to harbour such a feeling towards any of his fellow-creatures; if I thought it were so, my detestation for him would be as great as is now the love I bear him.   Base libeller, thou wrongest the character of Evelyn, and—but," she added in milder accents, and seeming to recollect herself, " pardon me Brayling, if the excitement of my feelings on this particular subject should cause my wayward tongue to run riot against thee.   From the earliest days of childhood, when I found myself among the wandering tribe, I have been accustomed to look upon thee as a father, for I never knew one but thee; and though thy manners are generally uncouth and repulsive to others, thou hast ever been most kind to me, and I honour thee for it.   Pardon me, Brayling, pardon me."

And the beautiful girl knelt at the feet of the rough gipsy-chief, as humble as a child, and fixed upon him such an expressive look of feeling that might have moved even the most insensible heart.   And Sampson Brayling could not remain callous to the appeal.   He gently raised the gipsy-girl from her suppliant posture, and while a ray of tenderness dawned upon his stern and sun-burnt features, he said:—

"Poor girl, poor girl, I pity thee;—yes I, Sampson Brayling, the Wolf as I am commonly called, from the bottom of my heart, pity thee, and will watch o'er thy welfare even at the hazard of my life.   Thou hast done me but justice girl, in the respect thou hast acknowledged for me, for I regard thee, and have ever done, with the same affection as if thou wert my own offspring; and therefore would I fain eradicate from thy breast that unfortunate and hopeless passion which thou hast suffered to take possession of it.   Evelyn Heartwell is good, is generous, and honourable, but thou knowest full well that he loves Constance Welborn to adoration and that she returns his passion with equal ardour and enthusiasm."

"And therefore do I hate her;" returned Mabel, hastily: and again the tumult of her feelings shone forth in the expression of her countenance and general demeanour.

"But she is fair and gentle, Mabel," rejoined Brayling, " and merits thine esteem, not thine hatred.   And mark me girl;" he added, gently grasping her wrist, and fixing upon her an ambiguous and mysterious look;—"thou must banish this unlucky passion from thy bosom; for I tell thee that it is criminal for thee to love, as thou dost, the youth called Evelyn Heartwell!"

"Ah! what mean those mysterious words?" cried Mabel, eagerly, and fixing upon Sampson Brayling a look of the utmost astonishment and incredulity—"Explain thyself Brayling; for thou hast created in my breast a certain feeling which I cannot comprehend, and for which I am at a loss to account."

"Oh, Mabel;" returned Sampson; " scorn not my warning, for it concerns thy future weal or woe.   Oh, did not stern necessity, for the present, control my tongue, how marvellous and startling is the tale which I could reveal to thee."

"Thou triflest with me;" observed Mabel, impatiently; "thou hast excited my most ardent curiosity, and now refuseth to gratify it. Keep me not in suspense."

"Be content;" said Brayling, "and be sure that I trifle not. I have already hinted as much as I am permitted to do at present. I tell thee, girl, and believe me I speak the truth, even if Evelyn Heartwell loved thee with all the fervour that thou lovest him, thou might'st esteem him, as 'twould be thy duty to do, but nature would forbid that thou shouldst become his bride. But enough of this for the present. Thou hast heard my warning, and if thou studiest thine own welfare,—

No. 3.

if thou wouldst not bring a curse upon thyself, and the hand of the youth who holds possession of thine heart, thou wilt not neglect it. But I must rejoin the tribe."

"Stay, Brayling;" ejaculated the gipsy-girl, "one word with thee in explanation, I pray."

But he was gone, and had rejoined his companions, leaving poor Mabel in that state of suspense and agitation of mind that may readily be imagined.

She pressed her hand upon her forehead, and for a few moments stood absorbed in deep thought, while her bosom throbbed with various and powerful emotions.

" What fearful and mysterious meaning doth his words convey ?" she soliloquised, " I am lost in doubt, perplexity, and amazement. It is criminal for thee to love as thou dost, the youth called Evelyn Heartwell!—Torturing ambiguity !—What strange fears and suspicions doth it excite in my breast ?—But will this captive heart suffer me to heed the warning ? Ah, no! it may entail misery upon misery upon her,—it may be productive of the greatest horrors that can attend humanity, it may be vain and hopeless, but never while the purple current of life shall continue to circulate throughout her veins, can the gipsy-girl cease to love, nay to worship Evelyn Heartwell.—And yet," she added, after a brief pause; "too soon he may have quitted these shores, and I may no more behold him.—Agonising thought! Oh, were he but the companion of my wanderings, my partner in the greenwood-shade, or leafy dell, so that I were only permitted to gaze upon him, and to listen to the beloved tones of his voice, methinks, though I could not hope to secure his heart, that I could be happy and content. But now—ah, me! I am wretched,—very, very wretched."

Thus saying, and while deep sighs escaped her bosom, the Gipsy-girl moved disconsolately from the spot, and apart from her rude companions.

It was a lovely night; the chaste moon cast her silvery beams on all around; a gentle breeze fanned the air, and softly agitated the leafy foliage of the tall and stately trees, and rendered the hour altogether most pleasant refreshing.

The Lover's Walk was silent, calm, and tranquil, and not a single individual was to be seen in that secluded place, though in an earlier part of the evening it had been thronged by all classes of society, anxious to avail themselves of its cool shade, after the heat of the day, which for the time of year, had been unusually intense.

It was near the time that the lovers had appointed to meet, but neither of them had yet made their appearance, when Oliver Dalton arrived on the spot.

His form was closely enveloped in a large cloak, and his hat was so slouched down over his brows, as partly to conceal his features. He cast an anxious glance around him, and then advanced further into the Walk.

" All is still," he said; " my victim has not yet arrived. I am prepared to meet him. This pistol will quickly quiet him for ever. I will e'en seat myself here, and watch his approach."

With these words, he took his seat immediately beneath the tree, in the trunk of which Jasper Scrimpe had for some time concealed his glittering treasure; and awaited impatiently, and with dark and guilty thoughts, the arrival of Evelyn, fully determined that he would that night gratify his deadly revenge, and rid himself of a rival whom he so mortally detested.

He had not been there many minutes when he was aroused by an approaching footstep, and he eagerly cast his eyes in the direction from whence the sound proceeded.

" Ah!" he ejaculated, " some one comes this way. Should it be he I seek.—No, as I live, and my eyes deceive me not, 'tis the old Miser, Jasper Scrimpe. What can bring him to this spot at such a time of night ?—Would that I had known that the old rat had quitted his hole, it would have been an excellent opportunity for me to have paid a visit to his coffers. But soft, he comes this way ; his step is cautious and stealthy, and portends something mysterious. I'll conceal myself, and watch this strange adventure."

He stepped cautiously behind the trunk of the tree as he spoke, and the Miser immediately arrived at the spot, and pausing when he had got near the tree, looked anxiously around, to be certain that he was not watched.

"All's safe!" he muttered to himself. "No one observes me;—now to my secret hoard. Oh, how little doth the eye of suspicion penetrate the golden treasure this ancient tree conceals. But I must be quick."

He parted the brushwood that choked up the opening in the trunk, and then taking from under his cloak a small dark lantern, which he had brought with him, he put his head in at the hollow, and groped and looked anxiously about.

"My wealth is all secure as when I la t beheld it;" he said, with a chuckle of satisfaction. "Now go ye there, and rest with thy golden companions."

As he uttered these words he took the different bags of gold he had brought with him from his pockets, and gazed at them eagerly.

"One—two—three—four!" he ejaculated; "all is safe!--Ha! ha! ha!--Oh, how my wealth increases. But now to conceal it!"

He was about to deposit the bags of money in the trunk in the tree, when Oliver Dalton accidentally coughed; the old man started round and discovering him, in a frantic voice, exclaimed:—

"Ah! I am betrayed!—discovered!—wretch!—villain!--prying sychophant! thou shalt not have my gold! My arm is yet strong enough to resist thee. Miscreant! robber!"

And in the overwhelming excitement of his feelings, the wretched old man grasped Oliver by the collar.

"Rash old idiot!" cried Oliver, fiercely, "let go thy hold!--I am a desperate man!—Yield up thy money!"

"My gold! my gold!" shrieked Jasper, and his eyes seemed to flash fire with the intense excitement of his feelings, while he clung to his money-bags with even still greater tenacity; my gold! my gold!—Never, while I have life!"

A desperate struggle now ensued, and it was wonderful that so aged a man as Jasper Scrimpe could maintain it with the strength he did.

"Thy gold! thy gold!" again demanded Oliver, determinedly.

"Villain!" replied the old man, "I will die first!"

"Fool!" exclaimed Oliver, savagely, "Take then thy choice!—Die!"

In a moment, he drew forth the dagger which had belonged to Evelyn, and plunged it in the old man's side, who sunk bleeding and insensible to the earth.

Oliver Dalton stood and contemplated the guilty work of his hands for a minute or two in silence; and having then secured the bags of gold, was about to examine the secret hoard in the trunk of the tree, when he was interrupted by the sounds of approaching footsteps, and he hastily concealed his booty beneath his cloak.

"Confusion!" he said; "some one approaches, and should I be discovered here, I am lost!—I must begone with all speed, and return for the remainder of the treasure at the earliest opportunity. Rest thou there!" he added, throwing the blood-stained dagger by the unfortunate miser; "that dagger bearing his name, will cast immediate, and confirmatory suspicion upon Evelyn Heartwell, and my thirst for vengeance will be amply satisfied. But I tarry."

He hurried away as he spoke in an opposite direction, and Evelyn now arrived at the spot.

"The hour of appointment is now some time past," he observed, "and yet Constance has not yet arrived. Surely some accident must have occurred to prevent her. My spirits are unusually depressed to night, and the most dismal forebodings haunt my mind. I feel as though some terrible calamity were about to befal me. Psha! let me not give way to such weak and childish feelings."

At this moment a low groan broke forth from the unfortunate Jasper Scrimpe, and Evelyn started with astonishment and alarm, and gazed in the direction from whence it appeared to proceed.

"Ah!" he exclaimed, "what dismal sound was that? Surely it was a groan; as if from some person in agony."

He advanced a step or two forward, and at that moment the full light of the moon revealed to him the form of the Miser, stretched upon the earth.

"Ah!" he cried;—"a bleeding form; some dreadful deed has been committed."

He raised the form of the poor old man from the earth, and gazing more earnestly in his features, recognised them, and, with mingled feelings of astonishment and horror, exclaimed:—

"Gracious powers!—Can I believe the evidence of my senses?—It is the poor old Miser, Jasper Scrimpe!—Oh, who hath done this hellish crime?—He still breathes; it may not yet be too late to save his life. Let me convey him to the gipsy encampment, where I may procure assistance."

He was about to do so, when Oliver Dalton, accompanied by Sir Milford Welborn and several other persons, arrived at the spot, and instantly surrounded him.

"See!" exclaimed Oliver, "a dreadful crime has been perpetrated, and view the criminal in—"

"Evelyn Heartwell!" cried the persons present, in a breath.

The unfortunate youth was astounded at this dreadful accusation, and could not utter a word. Oliver now picked up the dagger, and having examined it, said:—

"And see, here is the most damning confirmation of his guilt, this blood-stained dagger bears the initials of Evelyn Heartwell!"

"Horror! horror!" groaned the distracted young man;—"I'm lost! lost!"

"Wretched youth!" said Sir Milford, sternly; "what could tempt thee to this inhuman deed?"

A loud shriek was now heard, and Constance darted wildly in among the persons assembled—was about frantically to rush to the arms of the unhappy Evelyn, when Sir Milford prevented her.

"Hold!—hold, Constance!" he peremptorily commanded; "he is a robber and a murderer!"

"No, no, no;" shrieked the distracted maiden; he is innocent! by Heaven he is innocent!"

At that moment the Miser gave some signs of returning consciousness, and fixing his dim gaze first on the wretched Evelyn, he exclaimed in hoarse tones:

"Robber! murderer!—ah! art thou still here?—Give me back my gold! give me back my gold!"

"Oh, God!" groaned Constance, and she immediately fainted in the arms of her uncle.

"I triumph! I triumph!" said the villain, Oliver, aside.

CHAPTER V.

THE PRISONER.—SORROW AND DESPAIR.—THE GIPSY-GIRL.—THE ATTACK
ON THE OLD ROUND HOUSE AT ISYLNTONE.—THE ESCAPE.

IT would almost be impossible, adequately, to describe the sensation which the event, recorded in the previous chapter, excited. There were those among the persons assembled, and they were not few, who from the high opinion they had hitherto entertained of the character of Evelyn Heartwell, and the esteem in which they had held the unfortunate young man, who would gladly, in their own hearts, have acquitted him of the serious crime laid to his charge; but all his circumstances, so far as they had transpired, were so black and condemnatory of him, that, however painful it was to their feelings, they could not but entertain the strongest suspicions of his guilt.

The words of the Miser, (who had now again become insensible)—Evelyn being discovered in the position he was, and apparently struggling with the old man; the dagger stained with fresh blood, and bearing his initials ;—his ruined and desperate situation, which would appear to have urged him on to the deed;—and then his silence, (for horror had completely dumbfounded him,)—surely these were facts sufficiently powerful to prejudice the case against him, and though there were many who pitied him for having been driven by the sharp thorns of poverty and despair from those paths of rectitude and honour, which they believed him previously to have pursued, it was impossible for them to do otherwise than condemn him, and to execute the crime of which he was suspected to be guilty; and therefore the triumph and the exultation of the villain, Oliver Dalton, was the more complete.

A solemn silence of a minute or two ensued, which was at length broken by the hapless accused himself. Suddenly he seemed to arouse, as if from a dream, and struggling violently to release himself from the hands of those who held him, while indignation and an expression of conscience flashed from his eyes, he exclaimed :—

"Unhand me ! I am innocent ! Oh, surely there is no one present, (unless it be that man)," pointing to Oliver Dalton; "for you have all known me from a child, who can believe me guilty of this foul and revolting crime !—It was accident which brought me to the spot at the critical moment. By all my hopes of Eternity, I declare most solemnly that I am not the guilty wretch circumstances would make me appear to be. Oh, Sir Milford Welborn, I pray thee be cautious what you do. But surely you cannot, in your heart, although, unfortunately, I know I no longer possess favour in your eyes, you cannot believe me to be a miscreant so deeply steeped in turpitude. For the sake of your poor innocent maiden, whose warmest passion, I am convinced, is so closely interwoven with mine own, I do beseech you to be charitable and merciful in the conclusions at which you may arrive on this painful subject."

Oliver Dalton bit his lips, and a dark frown passed over his features.

"You hear him, Sir Milford," he said; "the daring, the presumptuous villain. Even in the midst of his guilt, he boldly acknowledges his unholy passion for your fair niece, and would, through her, attempt to excite your sympathy, and hoodwink your reason. Can hypocrisy, and shameless effrontery further go ?"

"Traducer !—liar !" cried Evelyn, fiercely; "you are the insidious fiend who is the cause of all this; and, if you have a conscience to appeal to, it must acquit me of the villainous deed which you would endeavour to fix upon me."

"Wretched young man;" observed Sir Milford, " the violent observations thou hast just made use of, so far from serving to exonerate you from the guilty charge, only tends to strengthen suspicion against you.   The facts, so far as they have gone, speak trumpet tongued against you, and must be fully, calmly, and carefully investigated.   Let him be conveyed before Sir Thomas Overton, the worthy magistrate. Bear the unfortunate old man, Jasper Scrimpe, to the Queen's Head, in the village which is the nearest house, and see that he lack not every assistance that his case may require.   The wound he has received may not be mortal, and his evidence, on some future occasion, will be of the utmost importance."

The latter part of these instructions were immediately obeyed, and the Miser was conveyed to the Queen's Head without delay; whither poor Constance, (who was still insensible), was also borne, accompanied by her maid, Abigail Allspice, who had arrived at the spot.

On beholding her taken away, the distracted Evelyn became the more frantic and violent, and struggled desperately to release himself from those who had seized him, in order that he might snatch one farewell embrace from that beloved being whom he might never behold again.   In this effort, something fell from his bosom on the ground.   It was the pocket-book which he had received from the Miser, the same evening, at his house in Shoreditch.

Oliver Dalton hastely picked it up, and examined it; and while an additional look of triumph passed over his countenance, he exclaimed :—

"Behold, here is fresh and satisfactory proof of Evelyn Heartwell's guilt.   This pocket-book, containing money, and which bears the name of Jasper Scrimpe !"

"That pocket-book !" cried Evelyn; "'tis mine !—'Twas given to me by the unfortunate old man, only about a couple of hours since, at his own house, whither I went by his own appointment."

"A very likely thing," remarked Oliver, with a malicious grin, " that Jasper Scrimpe, the Miser, should open his sorbid heart so much as to make large presents of money to almost a stranger."

"No," said Sir Milford; "the assertion carries a falsehood on the face of it. The guilt of the wretched Evelyn Heartwell is now made more manifest.   But this delay is unnecessary:—away with the prisoner before Sir Thomas Overton."

The persons who held him were about to do so, when a man, whose curiosity nad prompted him to examine, about the trunk of the old tree, suddenly came forward, and presented to Sir Milford several pieces of gold which he had picked up from the ground.

"This, no doubt, is part of the booty taken from the unfortunate old man;" said the baronet;—" see, there is a hollow in the trunk of the tree, from which the underwood seems lately to have been disturbed.   An idea struck me.   What brought Scrimpe hither at this time of the night, if it was not to conceal his money ?   May there not be more hidden in the hollow ?   Let a search be made."

"Confusion !" muttered Oliver, aside; "I am partly thwarted.   I have lost the principal opportunity I was so anxious for."

The search commenced, and the miser's hidden treasure, which consisted of a large sum in gold, speedily brought to light, and at the sight of which the rage and disappointment of Oliver increased.   This, Sir Milford took charge of, and the unhappy Evelyn, having by his exertions completely exhausted himself, offered no further resistance, but was hurried from the spot, followed by the villain, Oliver Dalton; and Sir Milford Welborn hastened to the Queen's Head, to see to the necessities of his niece.

On his arrival at the village inn, which the " Old Queen's Head," as it is now called, was in those days, Sir Milford found that Constance was restored to con_ sciousness, but her mind was in the most distracted state, and seemed likely to be productive of the most serious consequences.

The scene which followed was of the most distressing nature. She raved of Evelyn,—condemned those who had been so ready to accuse him, and again and again, in the most vehement terms asserted her conviction of his innocence of the base crime laid to his charge. Sir Milford, by every argument and persuasion he could make use of, endeavoured to soothe her, but with little or no success; and, after about an hour passed in this manner, he conducted her, almost broken-hearted, to the Old Grange.

The miser had received every attention, and although he remained in a state of insensibility, and unfit to be removed, the wound that he had received was pronounced to be not of a dangerous nature, and it was thought that, with proper care, he might soon be restored to convalesence.

The unfortunate Evelyn was quickly conveyed before the magistrate, Sir Thomas Overton, and the evidence fully gone into against him; but, although it appeared most conclusive, he thought it necessary to remand him till such time as old Jasper Scrimpe could appear.

Evelyn was confined for the present in the old Round-House, at Islington. It was a crazy old building, which seemed very ill adopted to hold any one in security, and it stood near Ball's Pond, and immediately on the site of the present turnpike-gate. It was surrounded by fields, and at some distance in an opposite direction, might be seen the summit of Canonburie Tower, with which so many interesting historical records are associated.

On being left alone in the gloomy dungeon of the Round-House, Evelyn, whose brain was hot and feverish, and whose mind was bewildered and distracted, threw himself disconsolately on a seat, and became completely lost in the tumult of his torturing thoughts.

So dreadful and sudden was the change which only a few short hours had wrought in his situation that it appeared like some horrible dream, and he could scarcely believe in its reality; and when he thought of all the circumstances, which appeared so black against him, and the agony of mind Constance must be enduring, —his heart sunk within him, and he abandoned himself to despair.

"And has it indeed at last come to this?" he soliloquised, as he paced the cell to and fro', with disordered steps;—"Was it not enough that I should be reduced to poverty and misery, and that all my hopes of ever possessing that beloved being to whom my very soul is devoted, but that I must now be accused of a crime at which my nature revolts. To be branded as a thief and attempted assassin!"— Horrible thought!—I shudder as it occurs to me, and the burning blush of shame and indignation glows upon my cheek. Oh, what a cruel fate is mine. Wretched, wretched Evelyn, it would have been better for you, had you never been born."

He beat his breast in the agony of his feelings as he thus spoke, and remained silent for a few minutes.

"But," he resumed; "will Constance, believe me guilty?—Can she suppose me capable of a crime so foul?—Ah, no! she loves me too fondly, and places too much confidence in my strict integrity and honour to do so. But still circumstances are so strong and suspicious against me, that even her confidence may be shaken, and doubts and apprehensions may haunt her mind. That thought tortures me more than all. And yet, Providence will surely not entirely desert me, but will make my innocence manifest, and drag the real culprit forth into the light of day. Heaven forbid that I should accuse any one wrongfully, but something seems to convince me that this is all the work of Oliver Dalton's hands. He is a villian who is capable of almost any crime, however atrocious; of that I am satisfied. The mortal hatred he bears me;—his anxiety to get rid of me;—the malicious looks of triumph he fixed upon me; the dagger belonging to me, stained with the Miser's blood, and which he must have obtained possession of in the struggle which took place between us at the Old Tankard, all serve to strengthen that suspicion. The miscreant! and shall he be permitted to triumph in all his diabolical designs, to the misery and destruction of his innocent fellow-creatures? I cannot believe that he will, but that justice will at last overtake him. But, alas! what evils may he not effect before that takes place? And he is the destined husband of Constance. Her doom is sealed; and even should I escape from the fate which is now impending over me, can I be otherwise than one of the most wretched beings in existence?—To know that her, my soul's treasure, is sacrifised to such a miscreant; that all those bright hopes she had for so many years so fondly cherished, are for ever blighted, would be sufficient of itself to drive me to madness, and I tremble even to contemplate it."

Again he paused, for the violence of his emotions choked his utterance, and his agitation, so far from abating, increased every minute.

Drearily the hours of that fatal night passed away, and sleep never closed the eyes of the unfortunate prisoner, for his mind was too much disturbed by the harrassing thoughts that beset it.

The next day arrived, but brought him no relief. There was nothing whatever to revive his hopes; all was darkness, misery, and despaire.

From his jailor he was enabled to gather some particulars, and amongst the rest, he ascertained the real situation of Jasper Scrimpe, and to learn that the wound he had received being so slight a one, he was likely to recover. This afforded him some gratification, not only on the old man's account, but on his own, for surely when he should be restored to his proper senses, he could exonerate him from the heavy charge which was now brought against him, and probably reveal who was the real guilty party.

"Oh!" he ejaculated; "could I but fairly and firmly establish my innocence of this heinous crime, I would care not what fate might befall me. It would be the greatest consolation to poor Constance, in the midst of all her troubles, to know that I am not the guilty wretch I was suspected to be; and she could still cherish my memory in her heart. Blissful thought!—But I know her gentle and affectionate nature too well, and the strength of the love she bears me, to believe that, under any circumstances, she could ever cease to do so. Dear Constance; why should cruel Fate thus wage war against two hearts so fondly united?—Would it not have been much better had we never met?—It would, it would; for then we both might now have been happy. But," he added, after a brief pause, "it is useless to murmur at the decrees of Providence, and we none of us know what is in store for us. I will still endeavour to encourage hope, and to bear my present misfortunes as becomes a man."

He became somewhat more composed as he uttered these words; but still he found it impossible to divest his mind altogether of the gloomy and torturing thoughts that haunted it, and many were the dismal forebodings that beset his brain.

The morning wore heavily and tediously away, and the afternoon was far advanced, when he was aroused from a deep lethargy into which he had sunk, by hearing the sound of footsteps approaching the cell in which he was confined. An unaccountable feeling of agitation crossed his mind as he listened, though it was probably only the jailor, and he awaited with the greatest impatience for the opening of the door. He was not long kept in suspence.

The door of his cell was suddenly thrown back on its hinges, and the rough features of the jailor appeared, conducting a light, fragile, but graceful female form; there was a faint cry; and the next moment Evelyn clasped his beloved but unfortunate Constance to his heart.

Yes, to see that hapless youth on whom her whole soul's affections were rivited; for whom she would willingly have sacrificed anything, nay, even life itself, she had braved her uncle's displeasure, and taking advantage of his absence from the Grange, had, with trembling footsteps, bent her way to the place in which he was confined; confident, as she felt, of his entire innocence of the fearful crime of which he was accused.

Our pen hesitates to describe the affecting scene which followed. For several minutes neither of the lovers could find strength sufficient to articulate a single word, but sobbed, as though their hearts would break upon each other's bosom;

No. 4.

and, in spite of all his manly efforts to suppress it, the big tear trembled on the cheek of the wretched prisoner; while, as he gazed on the pale, anxious, but beauteous face of the faithful and devoted being whom he strained to his heart, he felt as though madness was about to seize upon his brain. The jailor, after gazing at them rudely for a few seconds, retired from the cell, but remained within sight to watch their actions, and to listen to the conversation that might pass between them.

"Oh, Constance, dear, dear, Constance!" at length ejaculated Evelyn, in a melancholy voice, and gazing into her face with an intensity of feeling which words are inadequate to pourtray; "and hast thou indeed ventured to visit the distracted Evelyn in his gloomy cell, branded as he is with the name of a felon, and believed to have attempted the life of a fellow-creature?—What amiable condescension! what charitable feeling, and generous devotion! Oh, God! that we should thus meet!"

"Evelyn," sighed the poor girl, looking up in his face with the most ardent affection, and the tears streaming from her eyes; "what a dreadful calamity is this!—Why should the wrath of Heaven thus pursue us?—This terrible blow;—alas! it will surely break my heart. But thou art innocent!"

"By all my hopes of Heaven I am," replied her lover solemnly and vehemently; "Oh, Constance, the words thou hast just now uttered convince me that thou believest me to be so, and a weight is removed from my heart which was almost too overwhelming for endurance. Thou most generous and beloved of human beings, do not believe me guilty. the abandoned, the inhuman wretch I am suspected to be, and severe as the trial is, I will bear it like a man. Bless thee, Constance, bless thee!"

"Evelyn," ejaculated our heroine, becoming somewhat more composed, "dear Evelyn; for, in spite of everything, and let cruel Fate will it as it may, thou art still, and ever must be, dear to me; surely thou couldst not suppose that I could entertain the dark and hideous suspicion against thee!—I should indeed be unworthy of thy love could I do so. But still the fearful evidence is strong against thee;—the blood-stained dagger bearing thine initial;—the money found upon thee;—the words of the wounded man;—oh, these are circumstances that distract and bewilder my brain; and fill my mind with dismal apprehensions, almost too torturing for endurance. For Heaven's sake, if thou canst do so, explain."

"Alas! Constance," answered her lover, "Fate seems to have conspired against me, and I shudder when I think of the black array of evidence against me, and how great must be the prejudice already created in the minds of the public against me; still do I not despair, in spite of all this, that I shall surmount every difficulty, and at last be able clearly and satisfactorily to establish my innocence. Oh, depend upon it, it tis he villain, Oliver Dalton, who is at the bottom of all this! he is the guilty wretch who has caused so much misery, and

aring me the mortal hatred that he does, seeks, by every means in his power, to work my destruction.

"Oh, God!" groaned Constance; "can it indeed be so? Evelyn, base even though I believe him to be, thou must have stronger proofs than mere supposition, ere thou dost thus accuse him."

"Constance," said Evelyn, "I am not rash or hasty in the conclusions at which I have arrived. The longer I reflect upon all the circumstances, the more satisfied am I that my suspicions are well founded. We had met yesterday afternoon by accident, at the Old Tankard, where the cowardly scoundrel took the opportunity to taunt and insult me, and to express his exultation at his approaching union with you. He mocked at my misery, and derided my poverty;

he triumphed o'er the annihilation of my hopes, and heaped upon me every opprobrious epithet that his malice could invent."

"Oh, cruel, cruel!" sighed the damsel.

"Aye, Constance." said Evelyn, "it was base, unmanly;—it was the conduct of a ruffian, and as such I resented it: thou wilt not blame me for so doing, I am certain. A desperate quarrel ensued, which came to blows, and, in the struggle, he obtained possession of my dagger, which I did not discover till after we had parted."

"Ah!" ejaculated Constance, as a terrible idea flashed upon her mind; "but proceed—proceed."

"It was with that dagger that the attempted murder of the old miser was evidently effected;" observed Evelyn; "whose hand then but Oliver Dalton's could have done the deed?"

"Horrible thought," exclaimed Constance; "can it be? And am I doomed to become the bride of such a man!"

"Oh, never, never!" cried Evelyn; "Heaven surely will not permit so monstrous a sacrifice."

"I will resist it with all the fortitude and determination that I can summon to my aid," replied our heroine firmly. "Oh, Evelyn. believe me, though Fate should ordain that we may never come together, and even though this may be the last time we may be permitted to behold each other, under any circumstance my heart shall remain constant to thee; fondly shalt thou ever be treasured in my memory;—no other man can, or shall, ever possess the love of Constance Welborn!"

"Blessed words!" cried Evelyn, againing straining the lovely girl to his bosom, and pressing sweet kisses on her blushing cheeks; "they are as heavenly music to my ravished senses. Confident that the heart of my adored Constance remains faithful to me, methinks I can bear all the misfortunes with which it may please the Almighty to visit me, with fortitude and resignation. Bless thee, bless thee, dearest Constance, for the fond assurance thou hast given me!"

"Believe me, unfortunate Evelyn, I have spoken as my heart dictated;" returned Constance; "but still, in spite of all my efforts to subdue them, dark thoughts and suspicions will arise to my distracted imagination. Oh. Evelyn, how came that pocket book, containing money to a considerable amount, and bearing the name of Jasper Scrimpe, in thy possession?"

"Indeed, I told the truth," answered Evelyn; "I met the old miser accidently yesterday morning. He stopped and spoke to me, and evinced a degree of kindness and sympathy towards me which I did not think was in his cold and callous nature, and appointed me to meet him at his house in the evening. I went; he inquired minutely into my present circumstances, and my future designs, and it was then that he gave me the pocket-book and the contents that was found upon me."

"Strange," remarked Constance, "strange indeed, that so hard and insensible a heart should be moved in such a manner. But oh, Evelyn, though I, from the very bottom of my soul, believe thee entirely innocent, alas! I am bound to acknowledge that the circumstances look black and suspicious against thee. The words of the old man, when he recovered his senses;—oh Evelyn, they still seem to ring in mine ears, and drive me almost to madness; how canst thou explain them."

"Alas!" replied her lover; "it was a terrible mistake of the poor old man's which he will no doubt, be able satisfactorily to explain should he be restored to consciousness. His eye first fell on my countenance, and, in the confusion and agony of his feelings at the moment, he imagined me to be the guilty party. But that accusation will be recalled, it must be recalled, and every explanation given.

Oh, my beloved Constance, fear not, for though my position is a critical one, and dreadful is the trial I have yet to undergo, I feel confident that I shall pass through the ordeal firmly and triumphantly."

"God grant that thou mayest indeed be enabled to do so, my unfortunate Evelyn;" said Constance, fervently; "and that happiness, in spite of the dark clouds that now obscure the horizon of thy destiny, may again be thine. But—"

At that moment she was interrupted by the jailor re-entering the cell, and abruptly intimating that the interview had continued long enough, and that it must now cease. Again, and again, did the hapless lovers embrace, and sighs of the most poignant anguish escaped their bosoms; but at length Constance gently disengaged herself from his arms, and fixing upon him one last, tender, farewell look, was led by the jailor from the cell.

Evelyn being now again left to himself, and to all the misery of his own torturing thoughts, sunk disconsolately on a seat, and abandoned himself to despair.

Still the interview he had just had with Constance, had afforded him great relief, and imparted consolation to his mind. She believed him innocent—he was convinced that her heart was faithful to him; and even under all the dreadful circumstances by which he was surrounded, he could not but experience a feeling fast approaching to happiness.

Our heroine had not been gone more than half an hour, when Evelyn again heard footsteps approaching; the door was once more opened, and the jailor re-appeared ushering in a female.

It was the gipsy-girl, at sight of whom Evelyn started with amazement.

"Thou can'st retire," she said, haughtily to the jailor; "there is nothing to fear."

"Humph!" growled the jailor, sullenly; "I know not that. However, thou hadst as well make the best use of thy time, for thy interview must be brief."

With these words he quitted the dungeon, and the gipsey-girl advanced nearer towards the wretched prisoner, while there was a peculiar expression in her eyes, which made him feel anything but comfortable.

"Mabel!" said Evelyn, with a look of astonishment; "how is this?"

"Aye," returned Mabel, with a half sarcastic look: "no doubt Evelyn Heartwell considers the poor wandering gipsey-girl far more bold than welcome in thus visiting thee. Nevertheless, thou mayest find my services valuable to thee."

"Mysterious girl;" said Evelyn, "and is it commiseration in my misfortunes that has brought thee hither?"

"It is;" answered Mabel, "Oh, who can more sincerely pity thee than the poor hopeless being who stands before thee?—"

"Then you believe me innocent?" said Evelyn.

"I know thee to be so;" she replied. "But we must talk low, for caution is necessary here. Read this."

As Mabel thus spoke, she put a slip of paper into Evelyn's hands, on which he eagerly read the following lines:—

"All is in readiness;—the gipsies are your friends;—in a few minutes the Round-House will be attacked, and your rescue effected. Evelyn Heartwell must be saved at all hazards."

"I'm astonished!" exclaimed Evelyn, "is it possible that what is here promised, can be accomplished?"

"It will be an easy task," replied Mabel; "Sampson Brayling and his comrades seldom fail in anything upon which they have fixed their minds. Are you prepared to avail yourself of their friendly assistance?"

Evelyn hesitated for a minute or two.

"And should I do so," he said at last; "will it not appear like an admission of my guilt?"

"Fear not;" returned Mabel, "that shall ultimately be clearly shown to be erroneous. Thou hast no time to hesitate, for I expect them here every minute, and then thou must be prepared to act with firmness and promptitude. Behold, here is the means of self-defence, shouldst thou require it."

With these words Mabel, to the increased amazement of Evelyn, took from beneath the ample cloak, in which her form was enveloped, a sword, and a brace of pistols, giving him one of the latter, and retaining the other herself.

"Strange being;" ejaculated our hero, gazing upon the handsome and intelligent countenance of the gipsy-girl with the deepest interest; "and why dost thou thus concern thyself for me?"

"Simply," she replied, and, at the same time she fixed upon him a look which was sufficient to penetrate his very soul; "simply, because I love thee!—Aye, Evelyn, candour ever marked the character of Mabel, and therefore does she unhesitatingly declare that her poor heart owns thee for its lord and master; though too well she knows that thou can'st make no return for her love, and that thou viewest her with scorn, if not with absolute hatred."

"Nay, Mabel," remonstrated Evelyn, "say not so, for thou dost me an injustice. I admire thy generous and affectionate character;—I esteem thy virtues—I could even regard thee as a sister, but anything more, I cannot!"

"Ah!" cried the gipsy-girl, joyfully, and her bright eyes sparkled with even more than their usual lustre; "as a sister then, be it so; and oh, will not Mabel ever cherish towards thee, even though distant climes may separate us, a sister's love!"

At that moment there was a confused noise heard outside, at which Mabel started, and listened.

"They have arrived." she said, "and the attack has commenced. Prepare yourself, Evelyn!"

The noise increased, and presently the door was burst open, and the jailor entered, evidently in a state of great consternation.

"We are betrayed!" he exclaimed, with an oath; "a ruffianly band have attacked the Round-House; they doubtless seek to rescue the prisoners."

"Aye," replied Mabel; "and they will achieve their object, thou mayest depend upon it, Master Flint. Come Evelyn, we may as well at once depart, and join thy deliverers."

"Ah!" exclaimed the jailor, staring at her with a look of astonishment, and appearing, for the first time, to recognize her; "'tis Mabel the gipsey girl! Fool that I was not to know her before, and to refuse her admittance; for I should then have been certain that some act of treachery was in contemplation. Insolent! thou'lt have to pay dearly for this; but at least I'll cage thee!"

He was about to advance to seize her as he uttered these words, when Mabel, suddenly drawing a pistol from beneath her cloak, and levelling it at him, with a determined look, held him at bay; (for Flint was armed with no more than a short dagger), at the same time Evelyn rushed to her side, and stood ready to protect her.

"Back! back! man;" cried Mabel; "unless thou would'st fain make worms-meat before thy time. Come, Evelyn, let us away!——"

Flint uttered a fearful malediction, and was again about to approach Mabel and Evelyn, notwithstanding the words of the former, and the threatening attitude of the latter; when they hurried from the cell, and securing the door after them, to his surprise and chagrin, the surly jailor found himself a prisoner!

CHAPTER VI.

THE FLIGHT OF EVELYN AND THE GIPSIES.—HAMPSTEAD AND HIGHGATE IN
THE OLDEN TIME.—THE ANCIENT HOUSE ON THE BORDERS OF FINCHLEY
COMMON.

FOR a few minutes, Flint, the jailor, stood astounded and confused, so sudden and
unexpected had been the whole affair altogether.

"S'death!" he exclaimed at last, "the girl has completely entrapped me, and
made me a prisoner in my own cell.   A pretty disgrace I shall get in through
this business.   O, Martin Flint, Martin Flint, that thou should'st ever live to be
thus outwitted by a woman!—Hark!—the rascals are hard at their work; and
unless assistance is speedily procured, the culprit will escape.   What, ho, there!
—release me ;—help! help!"

The noise and confusion outside the cell now increased, and presently the door
was burst open, and two or three men, who were connected with the prisons, and
who were all of them bleeding from the rough treatment they had received from
the Gipsies, rushed into the place.

"A pretty piece of business this, Master Flint;" observed one of them; "the
infernal rascals have drubbed us to our heart's content, and unless we procure immediate assistance to pursue them, they will effect their escape with the prisoner.
Come! come!—let us not delay a moment, or we may consider ourselves no better
than dead men, every one of us!"

"Curses light on this disaster, and the daring rascals who are the cause of it!"
cried Flint, "but let us begone; should we gain aid, it may not yet be too late
to turn the tide of affairs."

They waited to say no more, but hurried from the cell, and from the Round-
House into the main road, but when they arrived there the coast was quite clear,
and they were left at a loss to imagine what direction the Gipsies, with Evelyn
Heartwell, had taken.

In the meantime the fugitives were making the best of their way, and already
had got to some distance from the Round-House.

Evelyn and Mabel, on leaving the cell in which the former had been confined,
found the Gipsies, and the few persons who were attached to the prison, hotly
engaged.   But the latter were soon overpowered by the superior number of their
enemies, and fled in confusion, and Evelyn was hurried by his deliverers from the
prison into the open air.

It was now dusk, and there was not a person to be seen as far as the eye could
stretch.

"Oh, Brayling, interrogated Evelyn, "why should'st thou make this bold and
dangerous adventure in my favour?"

"Ask no questions;" answered the Gipsey-Chief—"the hour is favourable to
our designs, and there is no time to be lost.   Come, come away!"

Evelyn attempted not to elicit any further information, and a large cloak being
thrown around him, the better to conceal his person, they moved with all
rapidity from the place, and, hurrying across the fields to some distance, at length
arrived at the green lanes that led towards Hampstead and Highgate.

Here they found a waggon waiting, as if to receive them, and the driver of it having greeted Brayling familiarly, Mabel and the other gipsies departed another road, and Sampson and Evelyn entered the waggon, which then moved sluggishly on its way, the sturdy waggoner whistling an old country ditty by the side of his team.

"So, thanks to our lucky stars," said Brayling, for the first time breaking slience; we have so far succeeded in our designs, and have given the fellows the slip, after well dusting their jackets for them."

" But why should'st thou hazard so much for my sake Brayling?" inquired Evelyn.

" Simply because I know thou art innocent of the crime with which they charge thee, and I wish to save thee ;" replied the Gipsey.

" But, alas!" returned Heartwell, " will they not misconstrue my flight into an admission of my guilt?"

" And let them do so, if they will ;" observed Brayling; "and conscious as thou art of thine innocence, thou must endeavour to bear up against the scandal, with the patience and fortitude of a man, till such time as a favourable change may take place in the dark destiny which now pursues thee.

" Alas! I fear that time will never arrive ;" answered the young man, in melancholy accents, " for fate, cruel fate, seems to have marked me for continued misfortune. But tell me Brayling, why should'st thou take such an extraordinary interest in the welfare of me, who am almost a stranger to thee ?"

" Thou art no stranger to me, boy ;" said the Gipsey, emphatically, " I have known thee well from the earliest days of childhood, even before thou did'st know thyself."

" How !—what meanest thou ?" said Evelyn, with a look of surprise.

" It would not do for me to enter fully into explanations for the present," replied Brayling?—" suffice it to say that I know thee well, and that thy real name is not Evelyn Heartwell."

" Most true, most true ;" said the latter, " and I never knew my parents. All connected with my origin is at present involved in a deep and impenetrable mystery."

" Which fear not, time will warrant ;" said Brayling. " Thou art unfortunate, and I pity thee."

" Oh, thank thee, thank thee," said Evelyn ;—but Mabel ?"

" Ah !" replied his companion, "she loves thee, but beware how thou sufferest her to make any other impression upon thine heart, but one of esteem; for it is fraught with more danger than thou can'st anticipate."

" Oh no, it is impossible that I can ever love any one else but Constance Welborn ; but she, alas, can never be mine !"

" Thou knowest not that."

" Is she not destined to become the bride of Oliver Dalton ?"

" The villain !—but despair not, Evelyn ; thou must for a time part from her, and seek thy fortune in other lands, for which I promise thee thou shalt not lack the means. The wars now require brave hearts, the British Navy needs good men, and true ; I know that thou hast the courage to fight for thy sovereign and thy country ; such, then, must be thy future destination, and fear not but that the black and tempestuous clouds that now obscure thy fate, will be dispersed, and thou wilt experience that happiness and prosperity thy merits so richly entitle thee to."

" Brayling ;" observed Evelyn; " thy language and the sentiments thou hast just expressed, astonish, me."

" Doubtless they do so ;" answered Sampson, " for they are not exactly in keeping with the character of the uncouth Gipsey Chief. But I was not always what thou now see'st me."

"But the part thou hast taken in thus rescuing me from prison, will, I fear, bring thee and the rest of thy tribe into trouble;" said Evelyn.

"Oh, fear not;" replied Brayling, "we will avoid falling into the clutches of our enemies."

The conversation now dropped, and Evelyn became absorbed in the different thoughts that took possession of his mind. The waggon had by this time arrived at the romantic and salubrious village of Hampstead, with its pretty cottages scattered here and there, its fine old rustic church, and, at different intervals, a stately mansion, the country residences of some wealthy citizen. The night was serene and tranquil, and the bright beams of the moon silvered all around. The feelings of Evelyn became somewhat soothed, by the calm beauty of the hour, and he endeavoured to hope for the best, notwithstanding the numerous dangers and difficulties by which he was at present surrounded.

Slowly they reached hilly and ancient Highgate, which in those days was even a more picturesque and delightful place than it is now. Indeed, it was one of the most beautiful for miles around the metropolis.

At the "Old Mitre," then a truly inviting road-side country inn (albeit, it retains much of its pristine simplicity and comfort at the present day), the waggon stopped to bait the horses, and here Brayling and Evelyn alighted to partake of some slight refreshment.

"How much further have we to proceed ere we shall arrive at the place of our destination?" inquired Evelyn with some anxiety.

"No great distance;" replied his companion; "only as far on as Finchley, on the borders of the Common."

"And why there?" asked Evelyn.

"Because it is the most convenient and secure place for you to remain concealed, till we can make final arrangements for your escape from England," returned Brayling.

"'Tis strange that thou should'st put thyself to all this trouble for my sake," observed Evelyn.

"Thou would'st not feel surprised didst thou but know all," answered Sampson. "I have powerful motives for all I do. But fear not, I am sincere, and every care and attention shall be paid to thee."

"I will place every confidence in thee," said Evelyn, "for thy conduct hitherto is sufficient to assure me that thou wilt not seek to deceive me."

"That opinion is no more than is justly due to me;" said the Gipsey, "but come, we must see about departing."

Evelyn readily gave his assent, and they then re-entered the waggon, and re-sumed their journey.

"Oh, what will poor Constance think of my escape?" said Evelyn, after a long pause, during which he had been deeply wrapped in painful thought.

"Can she be otherwise than gratified at thine escape from present danger?" demanded Brayling.

"But the dreadful anxiety she will naturally be in, as to my present situation."

"She shall be duly apprised of it;" returned Sampson.

"And shall I have an opportunity of seeing her again, probably to bid her a last adieu?"

"Compose thyself, for that shall be contrived if possible."

"Oh, do but that;" said Evelyn, anxiously, "and thou wilt indeed prove thyself to be sincerely my friend."

"Sampson Brayling never makes promises that he does not intend faithfully to perform;" returned the Gipsey.

Evelyn cordially and gratefully pressed his hand, and then once more relapsed into silence.

In due time the waggon arrived at "The Old Mud-House," at Finchley, a name which the present house retained, till within the last few years. Here Evelyn and his companion again alighted, and Brayling, turning to the waggoner, and putting some money into his hand, said :—

"We part here, friend :- -mind and be cautious upon this business. Farewell."

"Good night, master," replied the waggoner ; and Brayling, taking the arm of Evelyn, hurried him towards the Common.

They uttered no conversation, for both of them appeared to be too much occupied by their own thoughts, and a few minutes more sufficed to bring them to the end of their journey, as Evelyn imagined, for they stopped before a spacious building, which stood by itself, in a most lonely spot, and immediately on the borders of the Common, which, even in flood of bright moon-light that glowed upon it, in that calm and peaceful hour, looked gloomy and cheerless.

No. 5.

Evelyn looked with the most anxious curiosity up at the building, and could not help being struck very forcibly by its venerable and gravely imposing aspect. Sampson Brayling watched him narrowly, and with a peculiar expression of countenance, but said not a word.

It was indeed an interesting building, very ancient, built of stone, turreted with small pointed casements,—a cumbrous gothic porch—massive oak doors—and completely covered with ivy. For many ages had that old house evidently stood there, bidding defiance to the destructive hand of time, and shunning the society of all other buildings. A death-like stillness reigned around it (which was only interrupted at intervals by the mournful gusts of wind that swept across the Common), which rendered its appearance, if possible, still more solemn. However, to a man in the situation of Evelyn Heartwell, its grave aspect, and lonely retired locality could not fail of being in unison with his feelings.

"Our journey here ends;" said Brayling, at length breaking the silence he had for some time maintained.

"And is this the house in which I am to remain concealed?" eagerly interrogated Evelyn.

"It is;" answered his companion.

"To whom does it belong?"

"To no one in particular now;" returned the Gipsey; "it has been deserted many years, no one claims it, everybody shuns it, for it is said that some fearful crime was committed in it long since, from which time it has been abandoned; and two old friends of mine, Matthew Smelton and his wife Peg, have been allowed to hold undisturbed possession of it."

"'Tis strange;" remarked Evelyn; "and know you no more of its history?'

"Probably, I may;" replied Brayling, seeming to wish to avoid the subject; "but this is not the time to relate it. Come, we tarry."

They having arrived at the portal, Brayling raised a ponderous knocker, and the sound reverberated hollowly through the ancient building. A pause of a few minutes ensued, and Sampson Brayling was about to repeat the knock, when a light was seen through the crevices of the door, and the feeble voice of an aged man demanded "who was there?"

"It is I, Master Smelton:" returned Brayling;—"so open the door, and that quickly."

"Aye, aye, Master Sampson;" replied the old man; "be not in a hurry, for I am not quite so active as I was some forty years agone."

Another brief pause ensued, when the bolts of the door were withdrawn, and the thin, feeble, and attenuated figure of Matthew Smelton made its appearance. He started back slightly on observing a stranger in the person of Evelyn, but was soon re-assured by a significant look from Brayling, who, taking the arm of our hero, and urging him forward, said :—

"This is my particular friend, Master Smelton ; he is frowned upon at present by Wayward Fate, and therefore, I know that I need say no more to recommend him to your kindest consideration and hospitality."

"Right, right, good Master Brayling;" said the old man; "thou hast estimated my good will at its proper value; this youth is thy friend,—he is our brother, I can see by the expression of his features, and therefore that is indeed sufficient to enlist my warmest sympathy in his favour. So in, my good friends, and welcome."

Re-assured by the observations of the old man, Evelyn followed his companion into the house, and preceded by Matthew, entered an ancient apartment on the ground floor, where the old man having handed Evelyn and Brayling a chair each, said:—

"Here, welcome, welcome, my friends ; thou need'st refreshment, and marry thou shalt have it too, the best that the old house at Finchley can afford. What, ho! dame, dame!"

Matthew rang a hand bell as he uttered these words, and in a few seconds an old woman tottered into the room, and seeing Evelyn and the Gipsy dropped a low curtsey.

"Dame," said her husband, "Master Brayling, our old friend, has brought this stranger hither, who being in trouble claims the sympathy and hospitality which I know full well thou wilt not refuse him. Quick, then, and place before them the best fare thou hast in the larder."

"Aye, marry will I," replied the old woman with a look of the utmost kindness ;—"thou art right welcome my old friend, and as for thee, gentle sir, thou shalt receive every kindness and consideration from myself and my husband."

"Thank you most cordially, my excellent old friend," remarked Evelyn, "I am indeed in sore difficulties, which Heaven knows, are not of my own seeking, and throw myself at the recomendation of my friend, Sampson Brayling, upon thy hospitality."

Peg, as she was familiarly called, returned no answer to these observations, but having again dropped a curtsey, quitted the room.

"Remember, Matthew," said the Gipsey, when the old woman had retired, "that this business requires the utmost secrecy ;—and my companion must remain thy guest for an indefinite period; and I claim for him your best attention during his sojourn here."

"Master Brayling may depend on me ;" replied old Matthew Smelton, "and that this young man shall be cared for, with the same attention as if he were mine own son."

"A word in thine ear,"—said the Gipsey-Chief, drawing him aside and detaining him in conversation for a few minutes, at the conclusion of which, Matthew nodded assentively, and fixing upon Evelyn a look which expressed the deepest interest, said :—

"From what our friend Sampson has just now intimated to me, thou hast a double demand, young man, upon my sympathy and good services, and I tender them with all sincerity and kindness of feeling. Make thyself quite at home, and as much at thine ease as thou possibly canst whilst thou remainest here, and rest satisfied that thy sorrows and misfortunes shall be held sacred by Matthew Smelton and his dame."

"Most heartily do I thank thee, old man, for the feelings thou hast now expressed towards me ;" returned Evelyn. "I am indeed at the present time one of the most unfortunate and calumniated beings in existence; but Heaven can bear witness that I deserve not the cruel destiny which now pursues me."

"I do believe thee ;—I do believe thee ;" said the old man, "and pity and commisserate thee."

The old woman now re-entered the room, bringing in the refreshments that she had been instructed to procure, and of which both her and Matthew most heartily invited them to partake. There was an expression in the countenances of the aged couple, and a warmth and candour in their demeanour, which prepossessed them in the favour of Evelyn, and he began to feel somewhat more at his ease ; though the remarkable change in his situation, the whole events of the last two or three hours, what had past between himself and Brayling ; the anguish of mind which he was certain his beloved Constance was enduring, together with the dreadful uncertainty of the fate which was yet in store for him, continued fully to occupy his thoughts and to distract and agitate his mind.

His curiosity was much excited by what little Brayling had told him respecting the old house into which he now found himself introduced, and the air of mystery and solemnity that prevailed about it, and he could not but feel anxious to learn some further particulars about it, but after what the Gipsey had said, he felt convinced that it would be useless to question him any further upon the subject at present.

Sampson having spoken a few words aside to Matthew and his wife, they nodded assent to the observations he had put to them, and retired from the room.

CHAPTER VII.

EVELYN'S SITUATION IN THE OLD HOUSE.—OLD MATTHEW SMELTON BECOMES SOMEWHAT COMMUNICATIVE.—THE MYSTERY.

EVELYN and his companion partook slightly of the repast which the good dame had brought them, and then another brief pause ensued, which was at length interrupted by Sampson Brayling observing :—

"Thou seest, Evelyn, that so far I have kept my word with thee, and I trust that if thou didst entertain any doubts of my sincerity before, they should by this time be removed."

"Oh, yes, my friend;" replied our hero earnestly, and pressing his hand most cordially within his own ;—"I do indeed place every confidence in the warmth and integrity of thy motives towards me, and believe me, my heart beams with gratitude for the services thou hast already rendered to me ;— services that I had no right to expect from one whom I supposed to be almost a stranger to me. Again do I beg to express my heartfelt thanks to thee."

"Nay, nay, Evelyn," returned Brayling ;— "gratified as I am for thine acknowledgments, still do I not require any superfluous thanks for that which I have done. Believe me I have secret and powerful motives for my conduct, that will be hereafter explained."

"I cannot exactly fathom thy meaning, Brayling ;" remarked Evelyn, fixing upon him a look of anxiety ; "but this old house?"

"Aye, I am fully aware," said Sampson, "that thou art eager to be made acquainted with some further particulars appertaining to it, but for the present thou must e'en suspend thy curiosity. Let it suffice for thee to know that here thou art secure from the most vigilant eye of those that may seek to discover thee ; though I would advise thee to be most prudent and cautious, and not to divulge more than is absolutely necessary of thine affairs to Matthew and his wife, though, as I have before told thee, I place the utmost reliance on their friendship and sincerity. They have the strongest reasons for acting in obedience to my wishes, since they have experienced much benefit from the services I have rendered them. But old people thou knowest are apt to talk thoughtlessly, and from which much mischief often arises. Remember that here thou must be known only by the name of Reuben Grangeforth."

"Enough ;" said Evelyn; "thou mayest be sure that, for my own sake, I will not fail to act with all due precaution ; but will my dear Constance be made aware of my present safety?"

"I have pledged thee my word that she shall ;" answered the Gipsey ; "and that ought to be sufficient to satisfy thee."

"Again do I thank thee, Brayling, from the very bottom of my soul ;" observed Evelyn ;—"to know that Constance will be relieved from the anxieties and apprehensions that must at present distract her gentle bosom, will indeed remove a great weight from my troubled mind. But how long shall I have to remain here?"

"That is uncertain ; it may be for two or three days only.

"And I presume that thou art now about to leave me?"

"Aye," replied Sampson; "as thou must be aware, business will call me away from thee to night; but to-morrow, in the course of the day, thou mayest expect to see me again. Remember what I have said; be of good heart; know Sampson Brayling for thy warmest and most decided friend, and fear not."

Evelyn was about to make some reply when he was prevented from doing so by Matthew Smelton re-entering the room.

"I crave thy pardon, Master Brayling, and thine, my young friend, for this intrusion;" said the old man; " but I was anxious to know whether there was anything thou didst require?"

"No, Matthew;" answered the Gipsey; "no more than again to recommend to thy care and attention this youth, Reuben Grangeforth. For myself, time presses and I must depart."

"I regret that thou art compelled to deprive us of the pleasure of thy company so soon;" but then of course, thou knowest thine own business best. As for this young man, Reuben Grangeforth, as thou call'st him, I cannot but repeat my best wishes toward him, and assure him that he shall have no just cause to complain of the conduct of old Matthew Smelton."

"Enough;" observed Brawling; "1 know that I can trust to thee. So, farewell;—to morrow thou mayest expect to see me again."

"Farewell my friend," said our hero, shaking him by the hand;—and the old man lighting a lamp from the one on the table, escorted Brayling from the room, and Evelyn heard the outer door close heavily after him. The sound fell hollowly and dismally on his ears, and, leaning his elbow on the table, and resting his head upon his hand, he sunk into a melancholy lethargy or reverie, and in which mood the old man found him, on his return to the room. He stood for a few moments and contemplated him with feelings of the deepest interest, and did not offer to interrupt him; but at length in tones of sympathy and kindness, he said;—

"Come, come, my good master Reuben Grangeforth, thou must endeavour to arouse thyself from this melancholy state of dejection, and though the troubles that at present may obscure thy destiny may be severe and hard to bear, thou should'st still try to look forward to the future with hope and confidence. Come, come, cheer thee, cheer thee!"

"Alas, my aged frends," replied our hero, with a sigh; "thou canst, methinks, form but a faint idea of the troubles that now beset me, or thou wouldst not talk thus. I am one of the most wretched of human beings, and my heart sinks within me, and the darkest despair settles upon my mind, when I think of the dreadful dangers and difficulties by which I am surrounded, and which I fear there are no means of my being able to surmount."

"Ah! well-a-day!—well-a-day!" ejaculated Matthew; "and is it even so?— Then do I indeed sincerely pity thee. Think not that I seek to be inquisitive, or to pry into the secrets of thy breast, but are the misfortunes that now beset thee, and bear thee down, of thine own seeking?"

"Oh, no;" replied Evelyn; "the all just God above us knows that they were not; but that they were unforseen and unavoidable on my part. But pardon me, my good friend, my mind is too disordered to night to bear the fatigue of conversation, and I would fain retire to rest, if thou wouldst be so kind as to accommodate me."

"Even be it so, if thou wilt;" returned Matthew; "and after a sound night's rest, may the morning find thee in better spirits. Follow me, Reuben, and I will conduct thee to the chamber which my dame has prepared for thee."

Evelyn bowed consent, and the old man taking up the lamp, led the way out of the apartment.

Having traversed the gothic hall, they ascended a wide oaken staircase, consisting of several winding flights, and terminating in a spacious gallery, the walls of which were decorated old paintings, partly in decay, and covered with dust. Here and there the grim portrait of some ancient warrior, only partially revealed by the faint and flickering light from the lamp which Matthew carried, made our hero start, and caused a dismal and superstitious feeling to come over him.

The old man led his companion to the end of this gallery, and stopped before a large oak door, which he unlocked from a bunch of keys he had brought with him, and they entered a spacious and lofty chamber, which had a gloomy and cheerless appearance, notwithstanding a fire was blazing in the grate.

The furniture was old, cumbrous and rickety, and did not seem to have been used for some years before. The only means of light admitted to this dismal room, was from a couple of small pointed casements, and they were so overgrown with ivy, and encrusted in such a thick coat of dust, that they were of very little use. Evelyn could not help involuntarily shuddering as he gazed around him, which Matthew observing, said :—

" I must acknowledge, Master Reuben, that this old chamber does not present one of the most cheerful or prepossessing aspects in the world; but it is the best that could be got ready for thee at so short a notice. It contains, however, an excellent bed, and I hope thou wilt be able to obtain a comfortable night's repose, which may serve to refresh thee, and to revive thy drooping spirits. Good night, and peace be with thee."

" Good night;" responded Evelyn; and the old man retiring from the chamber, he was left to himself. Throwing himself into a ponderous chair, which was placed before the fire, he abandoned himself to the conflicting and dismal thoughts that pressed so heavily on his mind, and which the melancholy aspect of the chamber, was not at all calculated to dissipate.

"What a strange, sad, and wayward fate is mine;" he soliloquized; " and surely it is more than the fortitude of any individual can enable them to bear up against. What will be the result of it, Heaven only knows, but yet I fear that I am destined to experience many still greater troubles and vicissitudes. Am I not now a wretched wandering outcast, dependant even for a shelter and the common necessaries of life upon the bounty of strangers?—I am,—I am;—and how sickening and degrading is that thought! Alas!—dear Constance, how terrible must be the thoughts that rack thy gentle bosom, when thou reflectest on the fearful situation in which I am at present placed, and the probability of the ignominious though unmerited fate which yet awaits me?—I shudder with the most uncontrollable horror even at the bare idea. Oh! God! oh, God! surely I have not deserved this!"

He struck his forehead in an agony of despair as he gave utterance to these words, and again relapsed into silence, his eyes glaring wildly and vacantly upon the fire before him, whose glowing embers his disordered imagination conjured up all kinds of frightful images.

Then he suddenly started to his feet, and took another survey of the old apartment in which he was; and the sight tended in no way to dissipate the oppressive feelings that held possession of him. His eye, however, fell upon an oaken door at the further end of the room, which he supposed to open into another apartment, and he advanced nearer to examine it but found it was so strongly secured on the other side, as to resist all his efforts to open it. He felt somewhat disappointed at this, for his curiosity was excited, and he returned to his seat, and once more became lost in silent meditation.

The old clock in the hall striking the hour of eleven at length aroused him, and reminded him that it was time for repose;—and fastening the chamber door, after having committed himself to the care and protection of Heaven, and invoked a blessing on the head of his beloved Constance, he retired to bed.

Notwithstanding the fatigue and excitement, however, that he had undergone during the day, painful thoughts were too busy in his mind to suffer him for some time to go to sleep; and he lay restlessly tossing about in the bed, in a state of agitation, which the reader will be well able to imagine.

At length, nature being completely exhausted, he sunk into a kind of doze, but from which he was quickly aroused by a mysterious and rumbling noise, as if of the falling of heavy furniture, and which seemed to proceed from that apartment, into which the door which he had previously noticed opened. He started up in the bed, and by the aid of the light which was still burning in the lamp on the table, gazed eagerly towards it, but saw nothing which could in any way explain the mystery. He reflected for a few minutes, but was at a loss to imagine what could have been the cause of what he had heard;—but that he had not been dreaming he was thoroughly convinced.

While he was thus deliberating upon the subject, his attention was drawn to another noise which evidently proceeded from the same room, and which he now could not possibly be mistaken.

This noise sounded like a number of heavy footsteps, pacing the room backwards and forwards in the utmost confusion.

Filled with amazement and curiosity, Evelyn jumped hastily out of bed, and hurrying to the door, listened attentivly. The same sounds continued for a few seconds.

"Who's there ?"—demanded Evelyn, in a loud voice.

The noise instantly ceased, and no answer was returned. Evelyn again tried the door, but he found it still to be secured in the same manner as before.

"'Tis strange, and unaccountable," he muttered to himself : "what can it all mean ?—Now if 1 were at all prone to the weakness of superstition, I might be induced to believe that this was the effect of supernatural agency. I am completely unable to conjecture the cause of what I heard ; I must therefore endeavour to wait patiently till the morning, and see whether old Matthew can unravel the mystery."

Having come to this determination, and hearing no repetition of the noise, he once more returned to bed, and after a few minutes he again sunk into repose. But his sleep was far from being refreshing, disturbed as it was by strange and fearful dreams, and he felt relieved when the first blush of day peeped in at his chamber.

He arose, and having dressed himself, paced the room backwards and forwards with folded arms, and reflecting deeply upon the singular adventure of the night before. While he was thus occupied there was a knock at the chamber door, and, opening it, old Matthew entered.

The old man greeted him kindly, and informing him that breakfast was ready, if he wished to partake of it at that early hour, invited him below. He also made particular inquiries as to how he had rested.

"Very indifferently indeed ;" replied our hero ;—"but I have two or three questions to put to thee, Matthew, which I hope thou wilt not decline to answer me."

" Name them, Master Reuben," said Matthew, with some degree of hesitation, and fixing a peculiar look upon him ; " and if it is in my power I will answer them."

" The apartment into which that door opens," said Evelyn, pointing to it."

"I never yet saw ;" added Smelton, " although I have inhabited this old house for five and twenty years."

" How ?" said Evelyn, with a look of astonishment and incredulity ; " is it possible ?"

" It is true ;" returned Matthew ; " the door was secured in the same manner you see it is now, when I first came to reside here, and I never felt courage to force it."

" And why so ?" eagerly demanded Evelyn.

The old man hesitated, and seemed rather confused,—but at length replied :—

"Why, thou see'st, Master Reuben, there is a strange mystery connected with that chamber, which I cannot explain.   I have often been most anxious to penetrate the secret, and yet a kind of awe,—a sort of feeling, which I am at a loss to describe, has ever come over me, when I approached that chamber, and withheld me.—But let us below, Master Reuben, where, strengthened by a hearty repast, we can the better discuss this subject."

"With all my heart;" replied Evelyn, and he followed the old man from the room and down the stairs, into the ancient apartment where himself and Sampson Brayling had been introduced on the previous night.

Here they found the old dame busily engaged in arranging the breakfast table, and she greeted our hero in the most cordial manner, which he returned with equal politeness.

Having partaken of the morning's repast, after some trifling conversation, in which Evelyn joined with the best grace he could, though his mind was too busily occupied with subjects of a more important description, the old woman retired, and Matthew and his young guest were left to themselves.

"We can now talk freely, and undisturbed;" remarked the old man ;—"the questions thou hast put to me, Rueben Grangeforth, and the observations thou hast made use of, convince me that thou hast some strong motives for so doing. Was thy rest disturbed?—Didst *hear* anything from that mysterious old chamber?"

Evelyn replied in the affirmative, and then related to Matthew Smelton all that had occurred on the previous night, and the astonishment and curiosity it had naturally excited.   The old man listened to him with much attention ;—during the time he was relating the particulars, he frequently shrugged his shoulders, and when he had concluded, said :—

"Ah !—ah, well-a-day !—'tis strange,—'tis most marvellously strange.—I am not inclined to be superstitious,—but still the extraordinary noises thou hast described to have proceeded from that old room, Master Reuben, and which, times and oft, I have heard myself, are almost enough to make one believe that the place is haunted by some troubled spirit.   Certain is it, if all the old legends that are related of this ancient building be true—and, in good truth, I am inclined to believe in many of them, years since this house, and probably that very room, from the manner in which it has for so many years been secured, was the scene of some fearful tragedy, now buried in the dark records of the past, but which time may probably bring to light."

"You say that you have resided here for five-and-twenty years ;" observed Evelyn,—"to whom did this house belong previously ? "

"Thou'lt pardon me, Reuben," replied his companion ;—"thy curiosity, I own is only natural,—but I have particular motives for secresy upon that important subject, and, therefore do I decline to gratify it."

"Well, my good friend," returned our hero,—"I have no wish to appear prying or inquisitive; but all that you have said the more excites my wonder. This house then had been abandoned before you came to it ?"

"It had, for many months;" answered Smelton ;—"it's former occupants were gone no one knew whither,—and the persons who resided in the vicinity avoided it with dread, and on no account whatever would they approach it after nightfall."

"And why not ? " interrogated Evelyn.

"Because they looked upon it as the scene of some awful crime ;" replied Matthew, " and imagined that a curse rested upon it, and upon all those who should be bold enough to venture within its precincts."

"And yet yourself and your wife have had the courage to reside within it for so many years ? " observed Evelyn, with a look of astonishment.

"True;" replied the old man;—"it may appear strange to thee, Reuben, but it was necessity that compelled me to do so."

"And your right of occupancy has never been questioned?"

"Never!"

"'Tis most extraordinary;" said Evelyn;" I am at a loss to fathom the mystery."

"Doubtless thou art;" coincided Matthew, "but time may probably unravel it."

"And are these all the particulars you know of this old building?—" asked our hero.

"All that I am permitted to relate at present;" answered Matthew.

"But that old chamber, so carefully secured for such a number of years;" observed Evelyn; "and about which such a mystery hangs; what should prevent your entering it, and ascertaining the cause?"

No. 6.

"Oh, not for worlds!" returned the old man, with a look of terror; "for the love of Heaven, young man, do not hint at such a thing, for God only knows what evil consequences such a daring act might be productive of. Whilst thou remainest here, I pr'ythee do not question me any more upon the subject, for I confess that it annoys and disturbs me. Above all do not let thy curiosity supersede thy prudence and reason."

"Thou mayest depend upon me, good Matthew Smelton;" answered our hero; "I am thy guest,—seeking here, for a time, an asylum from danger, and thou shalt find that I will not abuse thine hospitality and kindness."

"'Tis well;—'tis well;—I do believe thee," said Smelton, pressing his hand;—"the dame shall prepare for thee a chamber in another part of the house to night.—But pardon me; I have some little business which requires my attention, and I must leave thee for a time. In the next room thou wilt find some curious old volumes, the perusal of whose pages may happily serve to wile away the time. Fare thee well, till I see thee again."

Having thus delivered himself, old Matthew made his exit from the room, and left our hero to his own meditations, of the nature of which the reader can form a pretty good idea. He pondered for some time over all that Smelton had said, and almost wondered that the mystery of such an old building as that where he now was, should excite such an interest in his mind. However, he could not exactly divest himself of it, and he felt anxious to become acquainted with more than Matthew had yet divulged to him.

After some time passed in thought, he entered the anteroom which the old man had mentioned, and found that it presented rather a more cheerful aspect than the others he had seen, and the furniture was of a more modern description. There were several volumes of books arranged on a shelf on one side of the room, but the mind of Evelyn was too disturbed to suffer him to read, and he walked to a lofty window which descended to the floor, and looked on to the Heath.

It was a dull, hazy morning, and the cheerless aspect of all around, was in complete unison with the thoughts and feelings that occupied the mind of Evelyn at that moment. He stood in silent rumination for a few minutes,—retired from the window, and, sinking into a chair, wretched and depressed, abandoned himself to his own gloomy reflections.

"And such,"—he ejaculated, suddenly rising from his seat,—" and such is the cost of an existence in this sublunary world;—endless cares, unmerited wrongs, —scorn, hatred; but, worse than all, base, hateful hideous calumny; the grandest, the most sublime works of the Supreme, distorted, abused and monstrously outraged to fit men's wicked-designs upon the peace and welfare of their fellow-creatures. Why, what a very fool am I in the estimation of these worldlings!— A thing, an insect, a mere football, to be kicked and buffeted about at their mere will and pleasure.—A wretched outcast;—a wandering beggar, bearing a criminal's odium, and dependant upon the charity and kind consideration of strangers, even to preserve me from a criminal's doom, what have I to tempt me to cling to life? 'Tis but the work of an instant, and this degrading state of moral slavery may be ended, and the soul emancipated from its thraldom. Why should I hesitate?"

His feelings worked up to a pitch of the greatest excitement, as these dismal thoughts occured to his mind, he laid his hand on his pistol, and Heaven only what, in the frenzy and agitation of the moment he might have been tempted to do, had he not fortunately been arrested in his purpose by old Matthew abruptly entering the room.

Matthew noticed the excitement of his countenance and demeanour, and said :—

"Pr'ythee, good Master Reuben, what ails thee?—Thou art strangely agitated, me thinks."

"Oh, Matthew;" returned our hero, in the most dismal accents :—"I am indeed sick at heart. Torturing thoughts drive me to distraction, and the troubles that beset me defy my strength of endurance."

"Nay, my poor youth," said the old man, "thou must not thus abandon thyself entirely to those dismal thoughts. Still hope for the best,—hope for the best."

"Alas! old man," replied Evelyn; "didst thou but know all the melancholy facts connected with me, thou wouldst not talk thus. However, I take thy advice in the same spirit with which I am convinced it is tendered, and thank thee for it, though much I fear it will be impossible for me to adopt it. The more I reflect upon all the terrors of my situation, and the critical position in which I at present stand, the greater, the more absolute becomes my despair."

"Oh, say not so, Master Reuben;" observed Matthew;—even though Fortune frowns to day, to-morrow she may wear her brightest smiles."

"Alas, I fear, never again for me;" sighed Evelyn; "my doom is sealed;—untoward fate seems to have marked me for its victim."

"Unfortunate youth;" ejaculated the old man, in accents of commiseration; "how does it grieve me to hear thee talk thus. Would that I could do anything that might alleviate the anguish of thy mind, how gladly would I exert my poor abilities in so good and worthy a cause."

"I thank thee sincerely, my good friend," returned Evelyn, "for thy sympathy; but indeed it is past all human aid to ameliorate my sorrows. Would that I were dead."

"Oh, forbear, young man;" said Matthew, solemnly; "forbear to give way to such dismal ideas. Thou art yet but in the spring-tide of life,—and though the path thou art at present destined to tread be dark and dreary, thou knowest not, when the gloomy clouds shall have dispersed, what bright prospects may open before thee. Again I say, still hope for the best."

Evelyn shook his head mournfully, and returned no immediate answer.

"Ah! see!" said the old man, suddenly nudging his arm, and directing his attention towards the window. Evelyn looked from it, and beheld a tall and graceful female form, standing a few yards from the house, and gazing intently upon them.

"'Tis Mabel, the Gipsey girl;" said Evelyn, "what brings her here?"

"Doubtless she has something to communicate to thee," replied Matthew."

"Heaven grant that it may be good news."

"Alas! I dare not hope that;" said our hero; "but pr'ythee admit her, good Matthew."

"Aye, marry will I," returned Matthew, "for I am deeply interested in the fate of that poor child of the wood and the wild, about whose history a mystery hangs, which time may perhaps unravel;—and I am always glad to see her."

Mabel now made a sign of recognition, and, moving towards the house, Matthew retired from the room to admit her. In a few minutes he returned, ushering her into the presence of Evelyn.

"I pr'ythee good Matthew," said Mabel, "leave us for a while :—I would talk a time with Reuben Grangeforth."

The old man bowed and retired.

CHAPTER VIII.

MABEL'S LOVE.

"MABEL ;" said Evelyn, when they were alone ;—"what brings thee here ?"

"To bring thee such intelligence as thou mayest be anxious to hear," replied Mabel ; "but the poor Gipsey-girl I suppose is not welcome to thee."

"Nay," returned Evelyn, in his kindest accents, and taking her hand ; "say not so,—for indeed thou wrongest me by such a supposition. That I possess thy warmest sympathy I am well convinced, and Mabel must therefore be always welcome to me as my dearest friend."

"*Friend !*" said the Gipsey-girl, with a sigh.

"Aye," returned Evelyn ; "art thou not so ?—But Brayling, how is it that he has not come ?—"

"Business prevents his doing so ;" answered Mabel ; but he sends to thee his best wishes, and bids thee be of good cheer, for he will exert himself to the utmost for thy welfare."

"I do believe him ;" answered Evelyn, "and must ever feel sincerely grateful to him for the extraordinary interest he takes in the fate of such an unfortunate being as myself. But my escape, has it not caused a great excitement ?"—

"Thou mayest be certain of that ;" replied Mable ;—"but in this old house thou art safe ; and with proper precaution, it will be impossible for thine enemies to discover thee."

"But Brayling and the other Gipsies, have they escaped the danger they incurred by the service they rendered me ?" enquired our hero.

"Fear not for them," answered Mabel ;" the Gipsey tribe always know how to provide for their own safety in cases of emergency. Before daylight this morning they had abandoned the green lanes, and are now safely encamped in the Wilderness, near the Old Road that leads to Shoreditch and Kingsland."

"Ah ! that is well ;" said Evelyn ;—"tell me, hast thou heard anything of old Jasper Scrimpe ?"

"Yes ;—his wound was only trifling, and no doubt he will soon be restored convalescent."

"Heaven grant that he may;" ejaculated Evelyn ;—"for then surely, if there is any sense of justice in his stony nature, he will exonerate me from the base charge which is brought against me."

"He shall be compelled to do so ;" said Mabel, "or 1 am much mistaken."

"But my dear Constance ;" sighed our hero ; "oh, what must be the anguish she is now enduring. How terrible must be her anxiety at my escape, and at the uncertainty of the fate which has befallen me."

"Fear not ;"—returned Mabel,—"Constance Welborn will be informed of thy safety."

"When ?—when ?"—eagerly interrogated Evelyn.

"To-day."

"Ah ! say you so ?—That kind assurance is indeed a relief to my troubled mind. Beloved Constance !—I—"

"No more," hastily interrupted Mabel, in an agitated voice, and at the same time a bitter expression of jealousy and regret, overspread her handsome features ;—"no more ; lest thou should'st turn the current of my feelings against thee. Thy words when thou alludest to *her*, are as daggers to my heart."

"How Mabel!" said our hero; "canst thou marvel that I speak thus of one whom I so fondly, so devotedly love?"

"Ah!" cried Mabel, and her bosom seemed to swell with the power of her emotions;—"it is the knowledge of that which tortures my mind, and racks my brain to madness. Thou lovest Constance Welborn, Evelyn, even in the midst of the annihilation of all thine hopes of ever possessing her for a bride, thou canst not eradicate that fatal passion from thine heart, and therefore could I loothe and hate her."

"Hold!—hold, Mabel;" said our hero;—"thy words shock me;—they are unworthy of thee. Surely thou canst not hate one so fair and gentle as my poor Constance."

"She holds possession of that heart of which I would reign the supreme mistress;" returned the Gipsey-girl;—"and therefore she must have the hatred of Mabel."

"Forbear, Mabel," said Evelyn, "language such as that to which thou hast just now given utterance, I must not, dare not listen to."

"Ah!" sighed Mabel, in the most melancholy tones, and tears trembling in her eyes, "'tis even so, Constance Welborn is the sole object of Evelyn's thoughts and anxiety; and the poor humble Gipsey-girl must be despised, neglected, detested."

"Nay, nay, Mabel;" replied Evelyn, in soothing accents;—"say not so, for indeed thou dost me an injustice. Have I not promised to love thee as a sister? more I cannot offer thee. Come, come, be calm, and endeavour to stifle this unfortunate passion in thy breast."

"Oh, Evelyn,"—said the Gipsey-girl, in a mournful voice, and fixing upon him a look of the most expressive meaning;—"'tis easy for thee to advise, indifferent as thou art to the unfortunate being before thee. But oh, didst thou but know the real passions that rend this aching heart towards thee, thou wouldst not marvel at the violent feelings to which I have given utterance; thou wouldst pity me."

"I do indeed pity thee, poor girl;" said our hero, fervently.

"I merit it, I merit it, Evelyn;" returned Mabel, eagerly;—"for I am the wretched slave of a hopeless passion which I cannot control. From the first moment that I beheld thee, my whole soul has been devoted to thee; my thoughts by day and my dreams by night have been of thee;—oh, it is impossible that Constance Welborn can ever love thee with half that intensity of feeling that I do; and even now I would willingly lay down my life to serve thee."

"Mabel," observed Evelyn, "I know, I am thoroughly convinced of the good feelings thou dost entertain towards me, and thou hast my most fervent gratitude and esteem in return for them. More I cannot promise thee. But thou must endeavour to banish this unfortunate passion from thy breast and to view me only as thy brother. Had I never known Constance Welborn, my heart must have yielded to thee, for I can read the character of thy mind, as in a book, and know that that mind is the receptacle of every virtue."

"Oh, woe's the day then, which first introduced thee to that girl;" said Mabel, bitterly; "for it has made this poor being wretched for ever. But why should thou still encourage a passion which is now entirely hopeless? The fiat of thy fate is sealed. Constance can never be thine; she must ere many days have elapsed, become the bride of another; why then shouldst thou not seek to banish her from thy thoughts, and yield to that fond being who is ready to make any sacrifice for thy sake?—Oh, who can possibly feel for thee the same affection as Mabel, the Gipsey-girl? and who could feel half so happy as she would be, if thou wert the companion of her wanderings in the woodland glade, the forest wild, or verdant meadow?—come then, dear Evelyn, and—"

"Hold!—hold, Mabel!" interrupted our hero, "I must not, dare not listen to this. It would be cruel and unjust for me to encourage hopes that can never be realised."

"Thou dost then reject my love?" said Mabel, haughtily; "thou despisest my overtures, and look upon me as a thing of scorn."

"No, no, Mabel;" hastily returned Evelyn, "Heaven forbid that I should be so uncharitable as to do so. But remember the warning of Sampson Brayling, remember his words :—It is *criminal* to view Evelyn Heartwell with any other feeling than that of esteem."

"Ah! woe is me;" sighed the poor girl, "I do indeed too well remember those mysterious words; they have rung in my ears ever since he gave utterance to them, and I have in vain racked my brain to endeavour to understand the meaning of them. Alas!—what a dismal fate is mine, and for what am I still reserved? Oh Evelyn, though thou canst not love me, is not thine heart moved in pity towards my sufferings."

"It is, it is indeed, Mabel;" answered our hero, in tones of sincerity and compassion; "But struggle against thy feelings, and seek to arouse thyself from this state of melancholy and despair. These clouds will soon pass away, and thou wilt yet be happy."

"Happy!"—replied Mabel, and a deep sigh escaped her bosom, which shewed the bitter anguish of her heart;—"Ah! no!—happiness can never more be the lot of Mabel; it would be madness to expect it, now that all those fond hopes which she once ventured to encourage are for ever annihilated. In future life will be an insupportable burthen to her, and the sooner she is rid of it the better."

"Oh, talk not thus, I implore thee;" remonstrated Evelyn; "but rather seek to look forward with hope and resignation. But this conversation is far too painful, and I pr'ythee let us change the subject."

"Be it so;" returned Mabel, in tones of regret; "since I see that it is so obnoxious to the feelings of Evelyn Heartwell. But I have delivered all the information I have for thee, and must now depart."

"So soon?" said Evelyn; "I was in hopes thou wouldst bear me company in this gloomy place, for an hour or two."

"My society can afford but little gratification to Evelyn Heartwell, methinks;" replied Mabel, coldly; "besides I have other business which will admit of no delay. Thou wilt see Brayling in the morning."

"'Tis well;" said Evelyn; "for in truth, I am most anxious to do so;— Heaven grant that he may then be able to bring me some favourable news of my beloved Constance."

"A slight expression of anger passed over the countenance of Mabel, as she replied :—

"Why is that name ever foremost on thy lips, in my presence? Thou knowest full well the torture it imparts to my breast, and therefore doth it seem to gratify thee to make use of it."

"Oh, no, Mabel," returned our hero; "indeed it is not so; thou judgest wrongfully, and I conjure thee to banish all such ungenerous and fallacious ideas from thy mind. I should heartily despise myself if I thought I could for a moment be guilty of anything so thoroughly mean, uncharitable, and contemptible."

"Alas!" sighed Mabel, and she again fixed her bright and languishing eyes with the utmost tenderness and affection upon the countenance of Evelyn;— "would to heaven that I could forget that there was such an envied being as Constance Welborn in existence; or that thou couldst banish her from thy memory. Her's is the image which haunts my imagination, arrayed in all the seductive blandishments of youth and beauty, and goads me on to jealousy and hatred, sleeping or waking."

"Thou hast promised me, Mabel," said Evelyn—"thou hast promised me that thou wouldst endeavour to stifle this hopeless passion in thy breast ;—to do away with all those rancourous feelings towards that poor girl who merits them not, and to love me only as a sister should love a brother. Come, come, thou wilt not be worse than thy word, I am satisfied : thou wilt evince the fortitude and generosity of thy nature, by adhering to thy promise, wilt thou not ? Constance deserves not thy jealousy or hatred, but, on the contrary, thy warmest esteem and compassion. She too, I know, for my sake, and the services thou hast rendered me, will ever view thee with a sister's love."

"I seek not her love ;" replied the Gipsey-girl, bitterly ; "it would be an insult to my feelings, for well do I feel convinced that the proud spirit of the peerless beauty must ever make her view the poor forlorn wanderer of the lonely wild, with scorn and loathing."

"Oh, how much thou wrongest her by such a supposition, Mabel ;" said Evelyn ; "thou knowest nothing of the tender nature of Constance Welborn, if thus thou judgest so harshly of her character. Oh, would that I could eradicate all such unjust prejudices from thy breast."

"And would," said Mabel, anxiously ;—"oh, would that I could induce thee to forget her, Evelyn. Why still cherish a passion which is frowned upon by fate, and which circumstances have now rendered entirely hopeless ?"

"And thinkest thou, Mabel," returned Evelyn ;—"thinkest thou that this heart can ever prove faithless to her whose most tenderest feelings are for me ? Thinkest thou that my circumstances, however discouraging, can ever alter the sentiments that I now entertain towards her ? I should indeed consider myself unworthy of the name of a man, and deserving of all the misfortunes that could befal me, if I could suffer such a change to come o'er me, and leave that fond being to mourn over my base deceit and ingratitude. No, Mabel, fate may ordain that we shall never come together, but our hearts are too strongly, too fondly cemented for anything to disunite them."

"Ah, me !" sighed the poor girl; "'tis even so ; and what hope is there then for Mabel ? All her fondest wishes are totally wrecked, annihilated, and what other prospect is there before her, but to be tossed about on a sea of troubles— to be exposed to all the shoals, the rocks, and the quick-sands of despair ?"

"For Heaven's sake, Mabel," ejaculated her companion, impatiently, "let us drop this disagreeable subject which is so torturing to us both. We have already indulged in it too far, and it appears that all the arguments we may possibly make use of cannot be productive of any beneficial result. Let us try to view everything at present around us with unprejudiced eyes, and to trust to Providence for our future destiny."

"Too well do I know my future destiny," replied Mabel, with a mournful look; "since the heart of Evelyn Heartwell can never be mine."

Our hero was prevented from returning any answer to these melancholy observations by a knock at the door, and Matthew Smelton again entered the room.

"It glads me to see thee, Mabel ;" said the old man ; "for I know well the honest warmth and sincerity of thy character, and I honour and esteem thee for them. Thou art most welcome."

"No," replied Mabel, coldly ; "thou knowest not the character of the Gipsey-girl; it is a strange anomally, a labyrinth of contradictions, which will defy thee or others properly to understand or to penetrate. But enough of this; the thoughts and feelings of Mabel can concern thee not, and must ever be sacred to herself."

"Pardon me, Mabel;" said Matthew, "I wish not to appear bold or impertinent, for Heaven knows that the friendly feelings I entertain towards thee are earnest and sincere. But a truce with this. Thou hast travelled far, and must require some refreshment, which I will instruct my old dame to immediately place before thee."

"No;" answered Mabel; "I need nothing. I have performed my mission, and now must begone."

"Marry, and thou hast made but a short visit;" said the old man; "I was in hopes that myself and Master Reuben Grangeforth would have had the pleasure of thy company for an hour or two."

"It must not be;" she returned; "I have other and more important business to attend to, which cannot be neglected. Farewell. Reuben Grangeforth, thou wilt remember what I have said, and if thou values thy safety, thou wilt be cautious, and not expose thyself at the window looking upon the common, as I saw thee this morning. Farewell."

"Adieu, Mabel;" replied our hero, warmly pressing her hand, "I do thank thee for the interest thou takest in my welfare, and my best wishes go with thee."

Mabel sighed, returned no answer, and fixing upon him a sad and expressive look, abruptly quitted the house.

"Poor girl," observed old Matthew, when she was gone; "I cannot help feeling the deepest interest in her fate, for I am certain that she possesses a heart that would do honour to any human being whatever might be their position in society."

"True;" said Evelyn, "her mind, I am convinced, is imbued with every sentiment of virtue and integrity; but care, sorrow, and anxiety, I fear are no strangers to her, and I pity her."

"Aye;" remarked Matthew; "she is worthy of it; but there is a strange ambiguity about her character and general behaviour, which I am at a loss to penetrate."

"Knowest thou anything of her history?" asked Evelyn.

"But little," replied Matthew, "there is a mystery about her origin which has ever created my greatest curiosity. Sampson Brayling first introduced her to the gipsies when but a child. Rough and uncouth in his general demeanour to others, he has ever acted with the tenderness and affection of a parent towards her, and I am satisfied that he knows more about her than he thinks proper to divulge."

"'Tis strange;" said Evelyn; and he then changed the topic of conversation. The day passed over without anything occurring worthy of being recorded in these pages. Like those that had preceded it, it was a gloomy and miserable one to our hero, and old Matthew in vain exerted himself to arouse him from the melancholy thoughts that beset his mind.

CHAPTER IX.

TIMOTHY TAPCAN EVINCES HIS HUMANITY.—JASPER SCRIMPE.—THE CURSE OF AVARICE.

TIMOTHY TAPCAN had paid his daily visit to The Old Tankard, at Fynesbury, and was returning home, humming to himself an old and favourite Bachanalian song, when finding himself before the house of Jasper Scrimpe, in Shoreditch, he suddenly paused and reflected. It was getting dusk, there were few persons about, and the old hovel of the Miser, and the surrounding quaint, old fashioned

buildings, had a gloomy and a cheerless aspect, which was anything but in accordance with the season of the year,—the "merry month of May."

"I cannot think for the life of me," said Timothy,—" what makes me sing, for I am very low spirited. Poor Miss Constance is quite distracted at the critical situation of Evelyn Heartwell, and that, of course, makes my dear Abigail most melancholy. What a sensation the escape of Evelyn has caused to be sure ; and it strikes me they will not catch him again in a hurry. Poor young fellow, I feel certain that he is innocent, and so that old hunks, Jasper Scrimpe, could prove if he liked. But he's no more humanity in his compositon than my soldering-iron. This is his house, and an elegant mansion it is. But it is a fit hovel for such a mercenary old rat as he is. Ah ! here comes his man. What a **very** refined and *fine*-drawn specimen of humanity he is to be sure."

No. 7.

Poor, half-starved Toby Taper now arrived at the spot, and was busily engaged in greedily gnawing a large bone, which had anything but a savoury and tempting appearance.

"Why, Toby ;" observed Timothy ; "surely wonders will never cease. Thou art eating, man."

"Yes ;" replied Toby ;—"I am luxuriating myself. Oh, this is a treat !—Don't I enjoy it ?—My old Master had dropped off to sleep, so, as I was so very hungry, I thought I'd go forth on a voyage of discovery. I met a dog with this bone in his mouth; it's a sin to see good victuals devoured by dogs, so I *boned* the bone from him, and a rich banquet it makes me."

"Poor Toby!" said Timothy, compassionately; "'tis hard to have to fare with the dogs. Marry, thou hast not a very delicate appetite."

"Delicate!—" replied Toby; "no, forsooth, and thou would'st not have a very delicate appetite, me thinks, Master Timothy, if thou didst fare as *unfairly* as I do. Why, what dost thou think? Now my old master is ill, he feeds me upon nothing else but the remains of his barley-water, and water-gruel, and he has made me take physic six times because he says that I'm so gross with living so high, and that will restore my blood to a proper state of purity."

We are thus particular in recording these facts, which may appear trifling, because we have a desire to place every trait in the peculiar character of the wretched Miser, Jasper Scrimpe, in the most prominent light, before the reader.

"Why, the rascally old curmudgeon!" exclaimed Timothy Tapcan, indignantly; "I only wish I had my will of him: I'd soon bring him to his senses, I'll warrant. I am not rich, thou knowest, Toby, but I have a bumping heart, and never shall it be said that Timothy Tapcan could see his fellow-man go hungry or a-dry, while he had a coin in his pocket to relieve him. Here, Toby, is a silver-piece for thee;—take it,—take it, and I only wish that thou couldst multiply, it into a score."

Thus saying, the kind-hearted Tinker placed the money in his hand, and poor Toby gazed at it with mingled feelings of delight, astonishment, and gratitude.

"What!" he cried;—"Timothy, this from thee?—Oh, here's a day's luxury provided for me! Thou art a good fellow, Timothy,—a generous fellow;—a—a—a noble fellow, and I thank thee a thousand times!"

"Enough my *fat* friend?" returned Tapcan, with a smile; "thou art welcome. But how is thy miserable old master?"

"Oh, the injuries he has received are only trifling;" replied Toby; "and I have no doubt he will soon be quite well. But he's more crabbed and sour than ever, and is continually lamenting over the portion of money he was robbed of."

"And does he still think it was Evelyn Heartwell who robbed him, and made the attempt upon his life?" asked Timothy.

"Why;" returned the Miser's man; "he wavers very much upon that subject. One thing is quite certain, namely, that Evelyn Heartwell did meet him by appointment that fatal evening, for I let him in ; and Scrimpe acknowledges that the pocket book, with its contents, was given to the youth by himself. Poor Evelyn Heartwell, he is a good young man, and I am convinced that he is innocent. But the old fellow is awake by this time, I dare say, so, I must in. Good evening, Master Tapcan, and again I heartily thank thee for me. A silver coin! Oh, I shall never be hungry again!"

Having thus spoken, poor Toby Taper unlocked the street door, and entered the house.

"Ha! ha! ha!" laughed Timothy; "poor Toby! but I think I will e'en return to the Old Tankard and refresh my inward man."

He was about to depart, when he suddenly encountered Abigail, who had been on an errand from the Grange.

"Oh, my dear Timothy," said Abigail, "is that you?"

"Yes, my beautiful!" answered her lover. "And ain't I delighted to see thee? Oh, Abigail, how charming thou dost look to be sure; thou becomest more lovely every day. It's no use: on the word and honour of a Tinker, I must have a kiss."

He immediately suited the action to the word, evidently not much to the displeasure of Abigail.

"Oh!" ejaculated Timothy, "that was delicious."

"La! Timothy," said Abigail, blushing; "how rude! I declare you quite shock me."

"I can't help it," he replied, "its a natural propensity I've got, and I know the women like it. But how's thy good mistress, my dear Abigail?"

"Ah, poor young lady," answered Abigail, compassionately, "she is almost broken-hearted, and enough to make her, uncertain as she is of the fate of Evelyn."

"Then she has heard nothing of him?" interrogated Timothy.

"Ah, no," replied Abigail, "though I most fervently hope that he is in present safety, and likewise that he will quickly be exculpated from the heinous charge which is brought against him, and the real guilty party may be brought to justice."

"Amen!" said Timothy Tapcan, "to that wish do I respond most devoutly. It is a sad job, my dear Abigail; but we have no cause to be melancholy you know. That delicious kiss has quite invigorated me. Abigail, thou art an angel."

"Ah, Timothy!" returned the blushing damsel, "I'm afraid thou art trying to flatter me, and only seek to make me vain of myself."

"On the word and honour of a Tinker," replied her lover, with mock solemnity, "thou wrongest me, Abigail. Thou art the apple of my eye; the core of my heart; the sunshine of my hopes, and the pearl of my affections."

"Lor, Timothy," said Abigail, "how you talk; upon my word you make me blush. Ah! you men are such flatterers. But after all the vows you have uttered, Timothy, and the promise you made me, only yesterday, that you would purchase the wedding ring in a tangent, much I fear you are going to deceive me."

"Deceive thee, Angelic!" cried the amourous Tinker, "the bosom of Timothy Tapcan swells with indignation at the thought! Oh, Abigail, how canst thou thus suspect mine honour? But I say my dear, canst thou not admit me to an hour's chat with thee this evening at the Grange?"

"Oh, yes, Tim," replied Abigail, eagerly, "if you will only now accompany me, I've got something so nice for you."

"No! you don't say so."

"Yes," continued Abigail; "a beautiful pigeon pie, which I made on purpose for you."

The Tinker was deeply affected, and placed his hands upon his stomach.

"Pigeon-pie!" he repeated,—delicious; my mouth waters at the thought!"

"Jugged-hare, gooseberry pasty, and turtle soup!"

"Jugged-hare?" exclaimed the enraptured Timothy, smacking his lips; "gooseberry pasty, turtle-soup! Heavenly names! I only wish poor Toby Taper, the Miser's man, could be one of the party! Come along, my dear, kind-hearted, Abigail; I have much to say to thee."

And throwing his arm lovingly round the slender waist of his mistress, the gallant Tinker hurried her away from the spot.

The dusky shadows of evening had fallen on all around; the noise and bustle of the day was past; few persons were to be seen abroad at that hour, in (even in those days), the densely populated neighbourhood of Shoreditch. The day had been anything but cheerful; the air had been remarkably cold for the season, with fitful gusts of piercing wind, and drizzling showers at intervals;

and now a dead lull rested upon the aspect of nature, which seemed to portend something fearful. Now and then might be heard a vulgar exclamation from some noisy roysterer, staggering from the tavern where he had been carousing, but that was quickly silenced by the nightly Watch, and all was again hushed in dull and gloomy repose.

But there was a scene still more dreary and cheerless than the one we have just been describing, and that was the miserable room occupied by the wretched Miser, Jasper Scrimpe! Black, and dilapidated walls, denuded of plaister in many places, and exhibiting the bare brick-work; cracked, and worm-eaten flooring-boards, that creaked and trembled with the slightest foot-fall; a dirty ceiling, which surmounted all, like some dark, threatening storm-cloud; broken casements, with filthy rags crammed into the apertures, through which a portion of the light of Heaven might otherwise have been admitted to the place; a small, glimmering taper, fast wearing away; a rusty grate, long a stranger to even the phantom of a fire; squalid poverty, in all its most hideous deformity; griping penury in its most sickening aspect—these were the principal characteristics of the Miser's room! The most fertile imagination could not, by any possibility, depicture a mere wretched scene, and that den, too, the receptacle of one who bore the human form! With what mingled feelings of disgust, pity, shame, and regret, must the spectator have turned away from the contemplation of such a scene.

Oh, Avarice! grasping, sordid avarice; to the understanding thou art the most debasing of passions, and the most deleterious to happiness. It is that degrading, that accursed passion, which exhibits a humiliating picture of human nature, and impressively illustrates the undeniable truth, that wealth cannot grant ease to its possessor, but, on the contrary, fills him with the most alarming fears for the safety of this imaginary good, and suggests the most consolatory reflection to forbearing poverty, whose unequal share in the distribution of wealth is more than counterbalanced by the comparison.

"It is presumed by philosophers,"—says an eminent writer, "that the most important study for the improvement of mankind, is man; and knowledge cannot be more profitably acquired, than in perusing those true examples of human life, recorded in the vicissitudes and incidents presented impartially to the mind, with the direction of truth for their application to our own lives and actions, for imitation or avoidance. In this view, however elevated or depressed the hero of the tale may be, some useful instruction may be gained, as we find ourselves more or less interested in his transactions. In relating the splendid actions of ambitious heroes, little can be adopted or imitated by the most numerous class of society; but, in relating events concomitant with the most miserable penury, a lesson is produced, fraught with wisdom, the purport of which is to show in what small estimation riches are in the eyes of the Supreme, who wisely and equally condemns to human distress, the miser that scrapes, and the spendthrift that scatters."

But to our tale.

Propped up by pillows in an old arm chair, alone, silent, and wretched, tortured by all the horrors that a guilty conscience can inflict, agonized by all the bitter feelings that disappointed avarice can engender, and inflamed by all the malicious passions of revenge,—sat Jasper Scrimpe !

And a pitiable object was that guilty old man to gaze upon. His face was more ghastly than ever; his features pinched and distorted with the anguish of his mind and body ;—his eyes wild, and lighted with an unnatural fire ;—his shaggy eye-brows contracted, and his lips compressed. Since the night of the fatal event in the Lover's Walk, ten years seemed to have passed over his head, and a mountain of care to have been added to the weight upon his breast.

The old clock in his miserable hovel struck the hour of nine,—and the Miser started, and looked fearfully and tremblingly around him.

The expression of the old man's features at that moment, painfully showed the mental sufferings he was enduring, and the wild lament of mingled passions that struggled in his breast, and held their empire over and distracted his brain. A nervous sensation shook his limbs, and he started and trembled at the least sound; but, notwithstanding the terrors he evinced, it was quite evident that the basest passions of his nature still held a predominant sway in his guilty breast, and that he brooded over the exciting occurrences of the last few days with feelings of rage and deadly malice against the individual who had committed the outrage upon him, which at present confined him to his miserable room; but more especially did he lament the loss of that ill-gotten money of which he had been robbed, and the discovery of the place in which he had hitherto concealed his treasures.

Sir Milford Welborn had frequently visited the old man in his wretched hovel since the occurrence, and restored to him the gold which had been discovered in the hollow of the tree. He had also questioned him narrowly upon all the circumstances of that fatal and eventful evening, with the hope of eliciting the truth. But, strange as it may appear, Jasper still persisted in asserting that it was Evelyn Heartwell who was the criminal, and it did not seem likely that that erroneous and unfortunate impression would be easily eradicated from his mind. The escape of Evelyn added to his excitement and retarded his recovery, for his narrow and malignant soul thirsted for revenge, and there was no punishment which he could think sufficiently severe for one who he imagined had acted with such base ingratitude towards him.

On the night of which we are writing the Miser was even more restless and agitated than usual; and again and again he started at the least sound, and glaring wildly round the room as strange and bewildering thoughts rushed upon his brain, in a voice which showed the inward working of his feelings, he exclaimed, as a shuddering sensation came over him—

"Oh, these torturing feelings of fear, anguish, and remorse, they still keep gnawing at my heart like hungry vultures. They prey upon my brain, and drive it to frenzy! For what have I hoarded up my gold and made it my idol? To create for myself an endless source of misery and anxiety, worse than the torments of perdition! Oh, that I could recal the past, restore those to life whom I have so basely wronged, and become again poor and happy. Fool! why should I repent, when all the world conspires to rob me? No one pities me; all mankind look upon me as a thing of disgust and loathing. Hark!" he added, fearfully, as the noise of footsteps on the stairs sounded in his ears, "some one approaches! The wretches come again to plunder me of my gold. But they shall not have it, no! I am but a weak, feeble old man, but still I will protect my gold!—I will protect my gold!—Hark!"

The sounds approached nearer and nearer, and the guilty old man stood, with eyes wildly gleaming, his emaciated form dilated, and altogether worked up to a pitch of the most painful excitement, when the room door was slowly opened, and Toby Taper entered the room, yawning.

"Oh," said Jasper, smiling, "it is thou! Thou hast come at last. Rascal! why dost thou neglect me, now that I am so ill, and unable to help myself? Is there any one in the house?"

"No one but ourselves, good master," replied Toby, "and those imbecile rats and mice that will so pertinaciously infest our dwelling, in spite of the warning of empty cupboards that is constantly before their eyes."

"But," ejaculated Scrimpe; "are the doors all barred and bolted?"

"Yes, dear master."

"What's the time?"

"But now it struck nine o'clock!"

"Nine o'clock! and where hast thou been till this time?"

"Watching to thy safety, kind master."

"Come hither," said the Miser peremptorily. Toby approached fearfully, for no doubt he expected a cuff from the bony fist of his master; and the latter, after eyeing him most suspiciously, passed his finger across his lips.

"Thou liest, varlet!" he said passionately, "there is grease upon thy lips! Thou hast been eating!"

"'Twas only a stale bone, good master," replied Toby, "eating! ah, I only wish I had the chance to eat. But 'tis so long since I performed that operation, I am afraid I should fail, even if I were to try. Pr'ythee, charitable master, do put me to the test."

"Thou hast been feasting that over-fed belly of thine again, I say;" observed Jasper, angrily. "Darest thou deny it, knave?"

"'Twas only a stale bone, I repeat;" returned Toby, "one which I found. 'Twas not one of those thou hast in keeping for our Winter's supply of soup. Does my poor belly look as though it were over-fed? Oh, I'm so hungry!"

"Out of my sight, dissatisfied glutton!" cried his master. "But mind that thou art within hail to attend my summons."

"Yes, kind, benevolent master;" said Toby, going, "Oh," he added, aside, "that I'd the opportunity to invest this capital with which Timothy Tapcan has furnished me, in provender. I'm so hungry!"

He quitted the room, and Jasper Scrimpe having again seated himself in his arm-chair, gradually sunk off into a restless doze.

CHAPTER X.

THE WILDERNESS.—THE MISER'S DREAM.—AN UNWELCOME MEETING AND ITS RESULTS.

THE excitement which the events in the Lover's Walk, the accusation of Evelyn Heartwell, and his subsequent escape from prison, had caused in the public mind, so far from abating, was hourly on the increase; and various and conflicting were the conjectures that were formed upon the subject. There were many who had known Evelyn for years, and who had formed the highest opinion of his character, that sympathized with him and maintained his innocence of the foul deed that was laid to his charge; but the majority of persons, with that uncharitable feeling which unfortunately is too often inherent in the human breast, were prejudiced against him, and believed him guilty; and to such individuals as these, his escape was a source of much annoyance and disappointment.

The anguish of mind which poor Constance was enduring, and the terrible state of doubt and suspense in which she was kept by the uncertainty of what had become of Evelyn since his escape from prison, and the fate which might ultimately await him, may be readily conceived. It was in vain Sir Milford tried all the arguments he could make use of to tranquillize her feelings; she was completely inconsolable, and kept herself almost constantly secluded in her own apartments, refusing to see any one but her faithful attendant, Abigail, and evincing the greatest horror, emotion, and unmitigated disgust whenever the name of Oliver Dalton was mentioned. In fact, he had no particular wish to enter her presence while her mind was so powerfully excited; and he wavered between doubt and fear as to what might be the ultimate result of his diabolical designs. More than all he dreaded Sampson Brayling, who he feared might betray him, in which case he knew that his ruin was inevitable. Strange as it may appear, notwithstanding it was well-known that the escape of Evelyn Heartwell had been effected by the gipsies, and that in all probability he was still under their protection, very little trouble had been taken by the authorities to discover them, they having, of course, abandoned their old place of encampment; and although they had not taken the trouble to retire far (an act of boldness and imprudence on their part), there did not seem to be any probability of their being interrupted for the present, at any rate.

At the period of which we are writing, the old Roman Road, leading from Kingsland, Hackney, and Shoreditch, and now known as the Old Street Road, was, as the reader may well imagine, a very different locality to what it is at present. Wild, dreary, and lonely, with only a few houses scattered here and there, with no tavern nearer than the "London Apprentice," at the entrance to the ancient town of Hogsden, and abutted on every side by large fields, dismal lanes, and the unwholesome marshes of Holywell Mount; few persons cared to venture there after nightfall; for daring highway robberies and murders were of frequent occurrence; every facility for escape being afforded in the neighbourhood. 'Twas there that even the king himself, Henry VIII., one Christmas Eve, attended by two of his courtiers, was waylaid and robbed, and no doubt, he and his companions thought themselves fortunate that they did not get worse mal-treated into the bargain.

At the western extremity of this road was an intricate wood of small extent, stretching only as far as the Gate of St. John's, and known as the Wilderness. The site is now occupied by the Charter House, and Wilderness Row. In this place were the gipsies at present concealed.

It was night, and Sampson Brayling alone—his person concealed beneath the ample folds of a large mantle, and a hat slouched over his brows, had suddenly left the Wilderness. No one knew the errand he was going upon, though, from observations that had fallen from him, it was believed by his companions that he had something of importance in contemplation, and they awaited his return with no little degree of impatience and curiosity.

We must now return to the dwelling of the Miser, who still dozed in his arm-chair, while Toby was in attendance upon him.

"He still sleeps," said Toby, "I only wonder that the thoughts of his gold allows him to sleep at all; I dare say he dreams about it though. I, too, sometimes have my *golden* dreams; but, alas! I wake to a *penniless reality*, and with the addition of an hungry belly."

Jasper now moved, and starting from his chair, in wandering accents exclaimed—

"What sound was that?—Where am I?—Bar all the doors!—Guard well the treasure it has cost me so much crime and trouble to accumulate!—There are thieves in the house!—I hear their stealthy footsteps approaching;—they seek again to rob me of my gold!—What, ho! Toby! Toby, I say!"

"I am here, good master;" said Toby, approaching him, humbly.

"Ah! ah!" said Jasper, "thou art too officious, knave; why art thou skulking here? begone!"

"Yes, dear master!" replied Toby, as he vanished from the room.

"Psha!" said Jasper, when he was gone, "It was but my disordered imagination. I have slept and have been dreaming. Oh, that I might never sleep again to be haunted by such visions as those that have this night disturbed my troubled fancy; even now the remembrance of them harrows up my soul, and chills the blood in my veins with horror. Methought I was wandering through a strange and glittering labyrinth—a maze of avenues supported by pillars of marble, and surrounded by a dome of crystal—piles of golden ore were heaped up in hugh masses on every side, upon which the rays of the sun streamed with effulgence—turn my eyes whichever way I would, they encounter nothing but gold—in bewildering profusion—and at the end of one of the avenues rushed a torrent of the same liquid precious metal—oh, how I laughed and chuckled as I gazed enraptured around me, and cried—"All, all this is mine! Who is now so rich as Jasper Scrimpe?" Eagerly I rushed to gather the golden treasure, when a shock, like that of an earthquake, shook the place—terrific peals of thunder reverberated above—frightful shrieks and noises resounded in the air—the glittering pile around me changed to hideous faces and unnatural, ghastly forms, that grinned and scowled upon me—and the golden torrent was turned to liquid fire, whose intense heat scorched my quivering limbs—appalled, frenzied, I sought to escape but could not—my heart was ready to burst its boundaries—my eyes seemed starting from their sockets—my brain was maddened—the spell of sleep was broken—I!—I!—Oh, mercy!—mercy!—what will be the wretched Miser's doom!"

Overwhelmed with agony, the miserable old man sunk upon his knees and raised his hands and eyes towards Heaven. A loud knocking at the street door aroused him, and he started with the greatest alarm to his feet.

"Ah! what mean those sounds?" he cried, "I am betrayed! my crimes are revealed; 'tis the officers of justice come to apprehend me!"

The wretched man was interrupted in his wild ravings by the hasty entrance of Toby Taper, the expression of whose features was not at all calculated to quiet the old man's apprehensions.

"How now?" he demanded; "What has occurred? Speak quick, on thy life!"

"A strange man," replied Toby, "wrapped in a large cloak, and with not one of the most amiable of countenances, waits below, sir, and demands to see thee upon important business. He will not be refused."

"Ah!" cried Jasper, alarmed, "a strange ruffian, and in my house? Rascal! how darest thou admit him?"

"Because, good master, I could not help myself," replied Toby, "he would not be refused, he would come in."

"Coward!" returned his master, "and is this the care thou takest of my welfare and safety? Why didst thou not put forth all thy strength and oppose him?"

"*My strength!*" repeated Toby, "now, do I look like a second Hercules? Why, I have no more strength than a titmouse, and the mere sight of a clenched fist is little better than sudden death to me. It's all very fine to talk about four stone of skin and bone opposing fourteen stone and a half of flesh, bone, and muscle, to say nothing of an ugly-looking cut-throat knife, and a brace of horse-pistols; but I should very much like to know who's to do it?"

At that moment the gruff voice of the unwelcome and mysterious visitor was heard grumbling outside, to the following effect, and the tones startled the Miser, and added to his alarm:

"A murrian seize ye!" the man ejaculated, "is a gentleman upon important business to be kept waiting here all night in this rat's den? Marry then, I must e'en introduce myself."

"There!" observed Toby, fearfully, "thou hearest, dear master. He is coming this way. Heaven preserve us!"

"Villain! thou hast betrayed me!" fiercely exclaimed the old man, suddenly seizing poor Toby by the throat, and fixing his small, penetrating eyes upon him with a mingled expression of rage and alarm. "Thou art colleagued with this ruffian to plunder me; but old and feeble as I am, I will not resign my dear-earned gold but with my life! rascal!"

"Master! dear, kind master," cried Toby, struggling violently in the wretched Jasper's grasp, "Oh!—oh—I'm choking!"

Sampson Brayling, disguised, now rushed hastily and unceremoniously into the room, and released Toby from his master's hold, who staggered to a chair, over-powered by his emotions, and stared at the Gipsey aghast.

"Miserable old dotard;" said Sampson, sternly; "wouldst add one more crime to the dark catalogue already on thy conscience? Wouldst murder the poor fellow whom thou hast e'en brought to death's door by griping starvation? Begone!" he added, speaking to Toby.

"Oh, most gladly;" said Toby, as he hastily quitted the room; "I never was so frightened in all my life."

"So," remarked Brayling, looking at Jasper with mingled feelings of malice and contempt;—"so, this is Jasper Scrimpe, the man who rolls in riches and pines in sordid misery: why, what a foul blot art thou upon humanity; what a

No. 8.

poor, despicable wretch art thou! everyone looks upon thee with disgust and loathing; all shun thee as a pestilence!"

"Ah! those bold and piercing words!" ejaculated the Miser, in a hoarse voice, and rising, and staggering towards the Gipsey Chief. "Ruffian! what means this daring intrusion? Comest thou to rob me?"

"Fool!" returned Sampson, sternly;—"I covet not thine ill-gotten wealth, even were it to save me from death.—I would not touch that dross—every coin of which thou hast purchased by fraud, injustice,—and bloodshed!"

"By bloodshed!" repeated the old man, in tones of agony and remorse;—"Oh, horror!"

"Aye!"—continued Sampson,—"with the blood of thine own kindred, Gerald Aubrey!—"

"Ah! that name!" exclaimed Jasper, starting and glaring more wildly on the gipsey, as a strange convulsive shuddering seized upon his limbs;—"Stranger, on thy life repeat it not;—the walls have ears—and—and—oh, my brain!—"

"Thou knowest I know thee, wretched old man;—" said Sampson emphatically.

"For mercy's sake, who art thou!—" demanded Jasper, in a faltering voice; "and what cursed ill-fortune brings thee hither?—"

"Thou'lt know that soon enough;" replied Brayling; "'tis many years since we met before. But come nearer;—look closer into my features;—time may have somewhat changed them; but I dare say it has left sufficient traces for thee to have the pleasure to recognise them."

As Sampson uttered these words, he threw off his cloak and hat, and stood revealed to the astonished and terrified old man.

"Death! death!" cried the latter, in accents of the utmost alarm;—"'tis Sampson Brayling!—Lost!—Ruined!—Thou comest to denounce me! I read thy malicious purpose in thy looks!—Oh, open, Earth, and hide me from the appalled gaze of mankind!—Shield me!—Shield me from the avenging wrath of Heaven!"

And with a burst of convulsive agony he covered his face with his hands, and tottered again to the chair, whilst Sampson watched him with scorn and exultation.

"Hark ye, Jasper Scrimpe;" he said, grasping his wrist; "Jasper Scrimpe, as thou think'st proper to call thyself; my business with thee is brief, but it must be to the purpose. No doubt thou thoughtst me long since dead, and that thy guilty secret was secure; but thou seest that I still live; and thou knowest full well that at any time I have the power to expose thee to the horror, disgust, and execration of the world, as a mur—"

"Oh, hold!—hold!" cried Jasper, interrupting him with intense agony. "Hold! I implore thee! Do not mention that dreadful word, which would turn my heart to marble, and freeze the hot blood which now circulates throughout my veins to ice. Oh, mercy!—mercy!"

"Mercy!" repeated Sampson, scornfully, "mercy to such a heartless, mercenary, sordid wretch as thou art?—Darest thou to sue for it, and to him whose miserable poverty thou didst take advantage of to make him the tool, the instrument of thy villany? What, does thy conscience at length sting thee, Jasper Scrimpe? 'Tis fit it should, and torture thee to madness."

"Oh, forbear!—forbear!" gasped forth the old man.

"Ah!" replied Brayling, with increased feelings of exultation, "this sight is as food to the soul of Sampson Brayling. I see thy terror in thy blanched cheeks; thy quivering lips, and trembling limbs. Thou knowest, old man, that one word of mine could place thy neck in the halter!"

"No, no, no!" cried Jasper, fawningly. "Mercy, mercy, good Stephen Brayling! Thou shalt have gold! I will share my wealth with thee, make thee as rich as myself, but thou wilt not bring the poor old man to misery and shame?"

"And canst thou expect mercy who never shewed it to others?" again demanded Sampson. "But on one condition only will I consent to grant thee yet a little longer respite from the gallows."

"Oh, name it, good Sampson," said the Miser, eagerly. "Name it, I do beseech thee?"

"Thou must immediately do justice to the unfortunate Evelyn Heartwell," observed the Gipsey, "he whom thou wilt know better anon. Thou must fully exonerate him from the foul charge which is so erroneously brought against him."

"Ah, the ingrate!" exclaimed Jasper; a deadly expression of malice flashing from his eyes, and distorting his features. "He robbed me of my gold!—he sought my life, and—"

"'Tis false!" interrupted Sampson, "false as thou art black in crime. Evelyn Heartwell is innocent; thou art labouring under a delusion, old man!"

"No, no, no! Did I not see him? Did I not denounce him on the spot? No, I cannot, I will not acknowledge him innocent!"

"Enough, obstinate old man! then thou knowest thy doom. This instant I go to consign thee to that justice thou hast for so many years escaped!"

As he thus spoke, Sampson was about to retire abruptly from the room, when the Miser fearfully detained him.

"Hold! hold! for the love of Heaven!" he cried, "spare me! I—I—I will do anything—anything thou mayest demand! I—I will forgive Evelyn!—I will proclaim his innocence, and—"

"Aye, but I must have more than thy bare word."

"What more wouldst thou?" interrogated old Jasper, in a tremulous voice.

"This paper," replied Brayling, producing a document from his bosom, "thou must affix thy signature to it."

"That paper! What are its contents?"

"Ask no questions," returned the Gipsey, sternly, and walking to the table and pointing to the writing materials. "Thy signature, if thou wouldst save thy life!"

"Yes, yes!" faltered out the wretched old man, tottering to the table, "I—I will, good Sampson Brayling. There—there, tis done!"

"Yes, it is done!" said the Gipsey, triumphantly, and snatching up the paper. "Evelyn Heartwell will be saved! And now, Jasper Scrimpe, I have thee fast! Thou art completely in my power. I congratulate you on the pleasant prospect before thee; the prison walls, with the gallows in the perspective! Fear not, but we shall quickly meet again. Ha, ha, ha, I triumph! I triumph!"

He hastily quitted the room, and left Jasper completely paralysed and horror-struck.

"Gone!" he exclaimed, starting, and looking round, "gone! what have I done? Signed my own condemnation? Horror palsies my heart! A death of shame and ignominy is before me! My brain's on fire! Oh, help!—Toby! —quick!—quick!"

He rang a hand-bell violently as he spoke, and Toby quickly made his appearance.

"Oh, my good, kind master,,' he said, with mock solicitude, "how ill you look; whatever can be the matter? Oh, dear, how sorry I am to see thee so! The heartless old starve-mouse!" he added, aside, "ugh."

"I—I am faint," said Jasper, feebly, "I—I am ill! thine arm! lead me to my chamber, oh!"

"Yes," replied Toby, taking his arm, "my poor, affectionate—confounded—old master!" he muttered to himself; as he led Jasper from the room.

CHAPTER XI.

OLIVER'S FIRST SCHEMES OF VILLANY.—THE DISCOVERY IN THE OLD HOUSE.

THE bright moon shed a silvery light upon the spacious and tastefully arranged gardens attached to the Old Grange at Hogsden, and all was still around, when the gates at the back were opened, and Oliver Dalton, and Black Will, as he was called, one of the gipsies, stole cautiously in, and looked suspiciously around them.

"The coast is clear;" observed Oliver; "here we may confer in safety. Thou dost then enter fully into all my designs, Will?"

"Have I not told thee so;" said the fellow; "if thou art afraid to trust me, why, say so at once, and there's an end of the business."

"No, no, Will;" returned Oliver, hastily, "thou dost not understand me. I place every confidence in thee, since thou hast abandoned Sampson Brayling and the other gipsies, whom I have cause to fear. As I was telling thee, the excitement which this affair of the old Miser has caused in the feelings of Constance Welborn, has induced Sir Milford to postpone our marriage to an indefinite period; in the meantime I'm resolved not to be idle. The treasured wealth of Jasper Scrimpe is a tempting booty. He has it now in his house; one bold effort, and 'tis mine."

"Aye, and that without much difficulty, Master Oliver," said his ruffianly companion; "that is, if thou dost not object to reward me handsomely for the assistance I am willing to render thee.'

"Fear not," replied Oliver; "thou shall be rewarded to thine heart's content."

"Enough," said Will; "then the task is easy. I have procured keys that I know will open the doors of Scrimpe's house, and, when once we have effected an entrance, our success is certain."

"It is," coincided Oliver; "to-morrow night, then—"

"We will accomplish the business," rejoined Will.

"Be it so;—" observed Oliver; "there is no occasion for delay. But hark!—what sounds are those?"

It was a female voice of the most plaintive sweetness, which proceeded from one of the lower rooms of the hall, singing the following simple song, to the words of which Oliver and his rude companion listened with the most breathless attention:—

"Oh! the memory of the past,
 How it steals upon my brain
Recalling joys too bright to last,
 In golden visions once again.
When I wander'd in the wild-wood,
 Or climbed the daisy-covered hills;
In the rosy morn of childhood,—
 Would that happy time were still.
  Oh, the memory of the past,
   Flushes o'er the busy brain;—
  Recalling joys too bright to last,
   In golden visions once again.

All around me, fair and gay,
 Bloom'd my devious path to cheer;
One enchanting Summer-day,
 My mind knew then no winter drear.
Oh, that bliss like this should perish,
 Would such joys I could renew;—
Still fond memory shall them cherish,
 And fancy bring them to my view:
  Oh, the memory of the past,
   Flushes o'er the busy brain;
  Recalling joys too bright to last,
   In golden visions once again."

The voice ceased; and even the miserable heart of Oliver Dalton could not help being moved by its melancholy sweetness.

"'Tis Constance ;—" he said ;—"she comes this way ; away, Will ;— I will meet thee in an hour."

"Remember!" said Will, significantly, as he departed. Oliver retired back, as Constance, in a melancholy mood, entered the gardens from the house.

"How torturing is the suspense," she said. Oh, Evelyn, where art thou ? And what is the fate which is yet in store for thee ?"

She was interrupted by the sudden appearance of Abigail, from the house.

"Oh my dear young lady," said the loquacious maid, "I'm so glad I've found thee. I and my dear Timothy were walking near the Wilderness, at the end of the Old Road, when we met Sampson Brayling, the gipsy, who gave me this letter for you, and told me to make all hast to deliver it to you."

"Ah !" ejaculated Oliver, aside ; and he listened.

"Ah !" said Constance, eagerly taking the letter ; "this may remove my doubts and fears. Leave me, Abigail." The maid curtseyed and retired.

"My hand trembles," said Constance, as she opened the lettter; "my hand trembles, and my heart throbs at double its wonted pace.

She read the note, which contained only the following few words :—" Thy lover is in safety. Meet me to morrow morning at day-break, in the Wilderness, and I will conduct thee to him.—BRAYLING."

"Oh, merciful Providence, I thank thee!" cried Constance, "fervently clasping her hands ; "I will not fail to be there !"

"No more will I, thou mayest depend on't," said Oliver, aside, exultingly.

Constance turned, and discovering him, hastily concealed the letter in her bosom in confusion.

"Oliver Dalton here ?" she said with aversion.

"Yes, sweet Constance," replied Oliver, coming forward, "and sincerely it grieves me to see thee so sad."

"Hold, sir," said Constance, haughtily. "Thy sympathy is mockery to me, and I decline it. Good night !" And she abruptly re-entered the house.

"Humph !" said Oliver ; "freezingly cold, certainly. No matter, proud damsel ; methinks thou will soon have reason to alter thy tone. I have heard that which gratifies me. In a few hours Evelyn Heartwell shall be again a prisoner, and then my vengeance will be accomplished. I triumph. Now to meet my worthy colleague, Black Will."

With these words, Oliver Dalton hastily quitted the gardens.

Our heroine, on leaving the gardens, retired to her own apartment, where she pondered again and again over the brief note she had just received from Sampson Brayling, and which excited in her bosom mingled feelings of hope and anxiety.

"Dear Evelyn,—" she ejaculated ;—"art thou indeed safe; and shall I again behold thee; alas !—I dread, yet am I so anxious for the interview. Oh, what can be the future destiny in store for thee !—why should the cruel fates thus conspire against us ?" Again she paused and reflected.

"How shall I contrive," she said, "to leave the house at so early an hour to-morrow morning? and should my father discover my absence, how can it be accounted for? It may also appear imprudent of me to trust myself to the care and honesty of such a man as Sampson Brayling ; but surely after the service he has already rendered to Evelyn, he will not attempt to deceive me. No ; even at every risk, I will attend to his appointment."

With the most melancholy feelings, she imagined the sufferings which her lover had undergone since the fatal events in the Lover's Walk ; and the deep sympathy she felt for him far exceeded the sorrow of her own breast. Filled with these conflicting thoughts, she retired to her chamber, and anxiously awaited the arrival of the morning, having enjoined Abigail not to fail to call her at an early hour.

In the meantime, the hours of Evelyn Heartwell passed drearily away, at the old house on the Heath, and he received but little relief from the society of Matthew Smelton, notwithstanding the old man expressed the deepest sympathy for him, and evinced the utmost anxiety to ameliorate the care and anguish of his mind.

Sampson Brayling had visited him in the course of the day of the evening of which we are now writing; and though in other respects his manners were ambiguous and reserved to his anxious inquiries respecting Constance, he informed him that she was, as he might well anticipate, in a most disconsolate and anxious state of mind; but that he might rest himself satisfied; for, although he might not be able, neither would it be prudent for him to seek a personal interview with her at the Old Grange, he would watch his opportunity to communicate with her through the means of her faithful attendant, Abigail, and, if possible, obtain for them an interview.

The heart of Evelyn throbbed violently at this thought, and for a moment, a ray of melancholy pleasure dawned upon his agitated bosom. But it was only transient; the difficulties that surrounded him presented themselves most vividly to his tortured imagination, and again his mind sunk with anxiety and despair.

After Brayling had taken his departure from the old house, Evelyn, who felt but little interest in the society of Matthew Smelton, retired to the appartments that were appropriated to his own use, during the time he had been there, and gave himself up to the free indulgence of the melancholy thoughts that would, in spite of all his strenuous efforts to banish them, obtrude themselves upon his mind.

The day had been anything but cheerful or calculated to dissipate the ennui which depressed the spirit of our hero, and the evening set in heavy and dreary. There was no moon, not a star deigned to twinkle in the thick and gloomy sky; everything upon which the eye of Evelyn rested, as he gazed from the casement of his chamber, bore a most cheerless aspect, and to the morbid feelings which at that time agitated his mind, seemed to portend some fresh approaching calamity, which his disordered imagination pictured in various forms. He tried his utmost to shake off this melancholy impression; but all his efforts were unavailing; they rather increased than abated; and the gloom of his chamber, and the sullen silence that reigned throughout the building, and was only interrupted at intervals by the mournful gusts of wind that swept across the wide common, on the borders of which, as has been before stated, the lone house stood, served but to add to the misery and despondency of his feelings.

On a shelf in one corner of the room were a few old volumes of books, upon miscellaneous subjects; and he hastily glanced over their contents, thinking they might probably serve to wile away the time until he should feel disposed to retire to rest; but he saw nothing in them to rivet his attention, or to divert his thoughts from the melancholy subjects that engrossed them; and he was in the act of returning them to the place from which he had taken them, when something fell from the dusty shelf, where they had no doubt for many years been deposited, with a rattling noise, on the floor.

He took up the lamp, and stooping to examine what it was, he discovered a large bunch of rusty keys lying at his feet, and which from their appearance did not seem to have been used for many years.

He looked at these with some curiosity, though why such a trifle should interest him, he was at a loss to conceive. He reflected for a minute or two, and suddenly an idea flashed upon his brain. Might not these keys enable him to unlock the door of the mysterious chamber, from which he had heard such strange noises proceed on the first night of his taking up his residence in the old house, and which had remained closed for so many years ? The vague observations that had fallen from the lips of old Matthew Smelton, respecting that room, had excited his curiosity ; and, although he knew not of what interest it could possibly be to him to know, he had ever since felt a most anxious curiosity to penetrate its hidden secrets, without the knowledge of the old man, who might consider such a liberty on his part as most unwarrantable. These keys might afford him the opportunity he wished, and if so, he resolved to avail himself of it.

Matthew and his wife slept in quite an opposite wing of the building, and, from the lateness of the hour, (for it was now past eleven o'clock), he had no doubt that they had long since retired to rest. There was no fear of his being interrupted. In this strange determination he was urged on by unaccountable and powerful feelings which he could not resist, and resolved to lose no time, he took the lamp in his hand, and silently and cautiously proceeded from the chamber, and entered the long and dreary gallery, at the end of which was the place he was anxious to examine. Here he paused for a moment or two and listened; but all was still as the grave; and, inspired with fresh confidence, he advanced on his way, and soon entered the room in which he had slept on the first night of his entrance into the old house, and the door of which was not locked. He found it exactly the same as when he had last been there ; and here he again paused, and reflected upon what he was about to do. He fixed his earnest gaze upon the oaken door of the mysterious chamber, and, in spite of himself, a feeling fast approaching to awe and dread crept over him, and made him hesitate. The number of years, which, according to the account of old Matthew Smelton, that room had been secured against the intrusion of the curious, convinced him that it had been indeed the scene of some fearful tragedy; and that idea rendered him the more anxious to penetrate its mysteries, which, probably had been left by Providence for him to unravel; and, feeling fresh courage and determination, he advanced towards the door, and proceeded to try the different keys contained in the bunch. For some time his efforts were unsuccessful; key after key, after trying each of them several times, proved perfectly useless, and he was about to abandon the attempt in despair and disappointment, when one of them, which somehow or the other had previously escaped his notice, seemed to fit the lock, and, after considerable resistance, it yielded; the heavy door creaked on its rusty hinges, and slowly opened; a strong current of air, followed by a thick cloud of dust, succeeded; the light in the lamp which Evelyn carried was extinguished, involving him in total darkness, and at the same time he imagined that a hollow sound, like a dismal moan, as if from some person in extreme agony, smote his ears.

With a strange and irresistible feeling of superstition and dread, to which he was by no means prone, our hero involuntarily drew back, and, for a moment or two, hesitated ; but, ashamed of what he could not but consider a weakness on his part, and determined, now he had proceeded thus far, not to be diverted from his purpose, especially as there was no one about to observe him ; he groped his way back along the gallery to his chamber, in the grate of which a fire was blazing; and having re-lighted his lamp, once more returned to the spot.

The dust had by this time dispersed, and he was enabled to obtain a rather indistinct view of the interior of the apartment, which, he was led to believe, for so many years, had not been trodden by human foot, and whose mysterious precincts all had feared almost to approach.

Evelyn felt emboldened, and, advancing a step or two into the room, he held the lamp above his head, the better to accelerate his view. Nothing could be more dismal, forbidding, or ruinous, than the scene which presented itself to his

eager observation ;—and what with the singularity of the errand he was upon—
the solemnity of the hour, and the death-like silence which reigned around, he
could not but feel a shuddering sensation take possession of his frame. However,
he hastily conquered that, and then proceeded to his inspection of the apartment.

It was of small dimensions ; the walls hung round with tapestry dropping to
pieces with damp and decay ;—large cobwebs clung to the ceiling, which was
blackened with age;—and the flooring boards were rotten and decayed, and trembled
beneath the feet, threatening to give way with the slightest weight. There was
one small casement placed high in the wall, and secured with strong bars, and
the only articles of furniture the wretched place contained was a small oak table,
an ancient arm chair, and an iron bedstead, on which was a decayed straw
mattress ;—in fact, the room bore all the appearance of having been appropriated
as a place of confinement for some unfortunate being, and for which purpose the
lonely situation of the old house seemed to be very well adapted. The most
dismal thoughts took possession of the mind of Evelyn as these ideas occurred to
him, and he pondered in imagination the dark transactions that had probably
many years since taken place in this miserable chamber. Happening to examine
the flooring-boards more minutely, he perceived that they were deeply stained
in several places, and he started, as he felt convinced, on a closer inspection, that
the marks were those of human blood!

"Gracious powers!" he ejaculated; as various awful thoughts crowded in
rapid succession upon his brain; " what deed of horror has been perpetrated in
this old chamber, and o'er which the veil of mystery has been drawn for so many
years? Am I destined to be the means of bringing to light the hidden secrets
of the past, transacted in this place ? A strange and unaccountable feeling of
mingled awe and dread steals over me at the thought. And yet, why should
I feel myself thus interested in so powerful and extraordinary a manner ?"

Again he started, for he could almost have sworn that at that moment he
heard a hollow, sepulchral voice breathing in his ear, and urging him on to
further investigations, but independent of this, his curiosity was more than ever
excited, and he determined to prosecute his search to the very utmost extent.

After a brief pause, in order in some measure to collect his thoughts, he resumed his examination; and, attracted by a peculiar mark in one of the boards,
and which rather yielded to the weight of his foot, he pressed more heavily upon
it, when, to his astonishment, that portion of the flooring sprang up, revealing a
secret trap, which, on his raising, was succeeded by a thick cloud of dust, and
an offensive effluvia, which, for a few seconds stupified and confused his senses.
Having allowing sufficient time for this to evaporate, he took up the lamp, and
examined that which was beneath more closely. The first thing which met his
gaze, was a black velvet cloak, richly embroidered with gold lace, but exhibiting
evident marks of decay, from the long series of years it had in every probability
been deposited there.

Notwithstanding his efforts to the contrary, Evelyn could not but feel an in-
voluntary dread of removing this relic of the past, doubtful and tenacious as he was
of what might be concealed beneath; but mastering that sensation, and, determined at once to remove his doubts and anxiety, he snatched the cloak, or
mantle away, it mouldering into tatters at his touch, and he started back appalled
and aghast, when the crumbling bones of a human skeleton, with its eyeless
sockets, and distended jaws, met his astonished sight!

Horror-struck and astounded, Evelyn stood and gazed at this ghastly spectacle for a minute or two, and a sensation of awe, not unmingled with dread, took
possession of his senses ; which feeling was strengthened by the solemnity of the
hour, and the gloom of the old chamber, whose long hidden and fearful mysteries
he had thus penetrated. The skeleton was that of a man, and from the decayed

and blackened state of the bones, it was evident that it had been in the secret place where our hero had discovered it, for many years; in fact, the long period which had elapsed since the room had been before entered, according to the statement which Matthew had made, was sufficient to prove that; and that the task of bringing this awful secret to light should have devolved upon him, a complete stranger, excited his especial wonder, and filled his breast with strange emotions.

"Unfortunate man;" he ejaculated;—"thy fate was indeed a terrible one; and even though so many years have passed away, if the inhuman perpetrator or perpetrators of so diabolical a crime be still living, may the just retribution of outraged Heaven yet overtake them."

He started, and let fall the trap-door over the mouldering remains, for, at that moment he could almost have sworn that he heard a low hollow sound, like the painful moan of some poor wretch in his last extremities, close by his side: and

No. 9

he looked hastily around, as if he expected some fearful object to meet his sight; but his own dark shadow, reflected on the wall, was all that his eyes encountered; and, as there was nothing else in the room to excite his curiosity and attention, and, being somewhat agitated by the discovery he had already made, he quitted the place, and securing the door in the same manner in which it had been before, retraced his footsteps to his own chamber.

Here he threw himself in a chair, and reflected deeply and seriously upon the remarkable events of the night. He formed various conjectures upon the subject, and felt a powerful interest in all connected with the awful affair, for which he was at a loss sufficiently to account. He was anxious to question old Matthew more narrowly upon the subject, for he suspected that he knew more than he had thought proper to divulge; but, on more mature consideration, he thought it would be prudent not to do so at present; and above all, not to say anything to the old man of the discovery he had made; though he resolved, when the opportunity should present itself, to consult with Sampson Brayling upon the mysterious business.

Having come to this determination, and passed some further time in rumination, he retired to bed, where his rest was disturbed by frightful dreams, and he was glad when the first blush of day dawned in at his chamber window.

CHAPTER XII.

THE MEETING OF THE LOVERS.—THE VOW OF CONSTANCY.—THE INTERRUP-
TION.—THE DESIGNS OF OLIVER DALTON THWARTED.

WE must now return to Constance, who passed the hours that had to intervene prior to her appointment with Sampson Brayling in the morning, in that state of restlessness and anxiety of mind which may be readily conceived. Sometimes she hesitated to trust herself to the care of the Gipsey, who, she reflected might have some sinister designs in view; but when she remembered that it was to him and his companions that Evelyn was indebted for his escape from prison, and for concealment from his enemies, her doubts were banished, and she reproached herself for having ever entertained them. Besides, what was she not prepared to venture—what risks would she not willingly run to see the unfortunate Evelyn again; and who would be so anxious once more to behold her? It might probably be their last interview, and could she then any longer hesitate? Oh, no, she must consider herself as totally unworthy of his love, if she suffered any scruples to prevent her; and she therefore made up her mind to meet Brayling at the hour appointed, and trust to Providence for the issue. All that she feared was, that her absence from the mansion might become known to her uncle, in which case she would find it a difficult matter to evade the questions he would be sure to put to her on her return. However, hoping for the best, she endeavoured to banish any such apprehensions from her mind, and at length succeeded much better than might have been expected.

Anxious to avoid seeing Sir Milford any more than possible before her departure, lest the agitation of her manner might excite his suspicions, she retired at an earlier hour than usual to her chamber, on the plea of indisposition; and where she was soon afterwards joined by her faithful attendant, Abigail, and they sat conversing together for some time, and before they separated, it was arranged between them that the maid of Constance should arouse her Mistress at an early hour the following morning, and after accompanying her as far as the place where it was appointed she was to meet Sampson Brayling, when she would return to the Grange, so that she might account to Sir Milford for the absence of Constance, in some way or other, should it be discovered.

Abigail having retired from the chamber, our heroine threw herself devoutly upon her knees, and having fervently supplicated the mercy and protection of Omnipotence for herself and Evelyn, she felt much more composed and confident.

At length the eventful morning dawned, and Abigail Allspice, punctual to the hour of appointment, entered the chamber of her Mistress, whom she found already arisen and expecting her.

"My dear lady," remarked Abigail ; "all is silent in the house; your uncle has not yet quitted his chamber, and there are none of the domestics stirring, so that we can depart in safety, and without any fear of being observed."

Constance hesitated, and returned no immediate answer; and now that the critical moment had arrived, it was quite evident that her mind wavered between doubt and fear.

"Alas !" she ejaculated ; "is it not wrong for me to act in this secret and clandestine manner, and in direct opposition to the will of my uncle?"

"It is stern necessity that compels you, Miss ;" returned Abigail;—"and why therefore, should you hesitate. Remember, too, that should you neglect to keep your appointment, how Evelyn Heartwell may consider that you have forgotten him—banished him from your heart, and abandoned him to his fate. Besides, should you not avail yourself of the present opportunity, there is no knowing what may occur to prevent your ever meeting again."

"Ah !" cried Constance ; "that thought at once determines me. Should Evelyn think me unfaithful, I should be one of the most wretched of beings, and never cease to upbraid myself for my neglect and indifference. But the Gipsey ;—think you he is to be depended upon?"

"Why should you doubt him, Miss ?" replied her attendant, "especially after the risks he has run to serve Master Evelyn."

"Most true," observed Constance, "he seems to take a lively interest in the fate of myself and Evelyn, the cause of which I am at a loss to penetrate. But let whatever may be the result, I will trust to him on the present occasion."

"Well spoken, my dear young mistress," said Abigail, "and my word for it, you will have no cause to repent of your confidence. But come, there is no time to be lost ; but ere any of the other inmates of the old Grange are stirring, let us depart on our errand."

Constance nodded assent, and Abigail having wrapped a large cloak around her, the better to conceal her person from observation, they silently quitted the room, and descending the back stairs, Abigail cautiously unlocked a small door which was seldom used, and they were about to issue forth, when they beheld a crowd of persons (most of whom were clad as archers, and were attended by numerous domestics,) advancing along the road, and Constance and her companion drew hastily back in alarm. Presently they heard them pass by the door engaged in busy conversation, and from a few observations that reached their ears, they were satisfied who they were, and the business they were going upon.

"Do you not know, my lady," said Abigail, "that his Grace, the Duke of Shoreditch, gives a grand *fête* to-day ? and these are probably some of the gentlemen archers going to take part in the revels."

Although it may appear strange to the modern readers, it is nevertheless true that there was once a Duke of Shoreditch, but the title has been long since extinct.

His Grace of Shoreditch, together with the Marquis of Islington, Marquis of Hoxton, Marquis of Pancras, and the Marquis of Shacklewell, were gentlemen archers, and got these titles from Henry VIII., in person, at Windsor. The head of the society of bowmen, or archers, held this titular dignity for a long series of years after. His Grace, the Duke of Shoreditch, continued annually to give a grand *fête*, which some of the principal nobility, and even Royalty itself used to honour with their presence. One of the most gorgeous of these entertainments is recorded as having been given by the Duke of Shoreditch, in Smithfield, September 17th, 1583, in which four thousand archers were concerned, above a thousand of them with splended gold chains. And a magnificent spectacle that same *fête* must have been, at which were assembled some of the most celebrated of the English nobility, and a dazzling array of all the most illustrious and peerless damsels of the realm. But, apologizing for this slight digression from the more immediate thread of our story, we will return to Constance and her attendant.

Having listened for a few minutes, till the tramping sounds of the horses, and the noisy hum of the voices of the riders had died away in the distance, they once more ventured to emerge from the door, and finding that the coast was quite clear, and that there was no one to observe them, Abigail took the arm of her agitated mistress, and hurried her on her way without saying a word till they had got to some distance from the mansion.

The morning was fine, and a balmy freshness filled the air, which served to invigorate the spirits of Constance, as they proceeded.

"Heaven knows full well the purity of my motives," she ejaculated, "and will, I trust, pardon me if the step I have taken is imprudent or wrong. Poor Evelyn, surely it would be cruel of me to neglect seeing you, now the opportunity is thus afforded me, and thus to disappoint the only hope you can possibly cherish in this your fearful and torturing situation."

"It would, indeed, Miss," returned Abigail; "nor do I see the necessity of your doing so. But come, my dear young lady, we had better quicken our speed, for it is some little distance to the Wilderness, and you know that Sampson Brayling appointed to meet you at daybreak."

Constance made no reply, but happening for an instant to look back towards the spot they had just quitted, she started, uttered a faint cry, and clung more closely to the arm of her attendant, who, surprised, eagerly demanded the cause of her agitation.

"Surely we are not watched?" replied our heroine; "and yet I am almost positive I just now observed the figures of two or three men hastily turn the corner yonder, who seemed as if they were dogging our footsteps.

"Nay, my dear young lady," said Abigail, "surely these fears are groundless; if you saw any one, they were probably only some casual foot passengers, that were going on their own business. Who is there to watch us? Courage, and let us proceed."

Constance, however, cast another anxious look behind her, and appeared far from satisfied. But she offered no further remark, and they again proceeded in silence.

In a few minutes more they arrived at the extremity of the ancient town of Hogsden, and near the "Old London Apprentice," they were rather startled at beholding the tall form of a female enveloped in a cloak, and who looked as if she was waiting for the appearance of somebody.

Constance whispered fearfully in the ear of her companion, and they were turning hastily aside, with the intention of endeavouring to avoid the curious scrutiny of a stranger at that early hour of the morning, when the woman peremptorily motioned them to stand, and they felt incapable of disobeying her. The woman immediately approached them nearer, and Constance started back with some amazement and alarm when she recognised Mabel, whose mysterious looks, whenever she had previously encountered, and some ambiguous expressions that had fallen from her lips on different occasions, in allusion to Evelyn, had left an unpleasant and torturing impression upon her mind.

And now the earnest looks she fixed upon her, and the general expression of her features were wild and mysterious, and not unmingled with jealousy and malice, and Constance could not help trembling when she thought of the dangerous consequences of which this unexpected meeting might be productive.

"So, lady," observed the Gipsey-girl, after a brief pause, "we have met; though if I may judge from your looks, and the fear your trembling frame evinces, my appearance is as unwelcome as it is unexpected to you."

"Oh, Mabel," ejaculated our heroine, "I pray you do not obstruct or detain me. I go upon an important errand, and——"

"I know thine errand," interrupted Mabel, "and 'tis that which brings me hither. Return to the Grange," she added, authoritively, and addressing herself to Abigail, who was as much surprised and alarmed as her mistress, for she entertained an almost superstitious dread of the gipsies. "Return to the Grange, girl," repeated Mabel, in a still more commanding tone of voice, "I will conduct thy mistress to the place of appointment."

"No, no, Mabel," hastily returned Constance, "I entreat you not to suffer her to leave me."

"I must be obeyed," said the Gipsey-girl, with a determined look; "and there is no time for delay."

"Oh, suffer me then to return with her to the Grange," said Constance; "I fear that I have acted wrong in the step I have already taken. Come, come, Abigail, let us return."

"No," cried Mabel, resolutely; and laying her hand upon the wrist of Constance to arrest her progress; "that must not be. Thou must keep thine appointment with Sampson Brayling. What, is Mabel an object of such suspicion and dread to thee, that thou fearest to entrust thyself with her? Ah!" she added, as a sigh escaped her breast, and a deep expression of melancholy passed over her features; "thou canst little imagine the painful sacrifice she makes to her own feelings in order to gratify the anxious hopes of him *thou* lovest. Oh, that painful thought!"

"Ah! what mean you?" eagerly demanded our heroine, as a sensation of doubt and suspicion agitated her bosom; "but what would you, Mabel? is it money you seek?"

"Money!" repeated the latter, with a look of scorn and indignation; "what do I value the glittering dross? Thinkest thou that Mabel is actuated by any such sordid motives; that her feelings are not as proud and independent as the loftiest and noblest maiden in the universe, although her life is that of the wandering vagrant, as thou wouldst term her? Ah! how little canst thou read my thoughts, Constance of the Grange, or such a question would never have escaped thy lips. But enough of this, we do but waste time, and Brayling will become impatient."

"Your looks and words alarm me," cried Constance; "let me return!"

"Psha!" exclaimed the Gipsey-girl, impatiently;—"no more hesitation;—come, come." And motioning the astonished Abigail to begone, she took the arm of Constance, and hurried her from the spot.

For some few minutes our heroine was so agitated and bewildered, that she scarcely knew where she was, or what she was doing, but at length looking imploringly in the face of her strange companion, she said :—

"Oh, Mabel, you surely do not mean to deceive and betray me?"

"No, Constance," replied her companion; "thou dost me a great injustice if such is the opinion thou dost entertain of me. Though, Heaven knows that I have no cause to entertain any friendly feeling towards thee."

"Ah!" ejaculated Constance, hastily, and with increased surprise and uneasiness at the peculiarity of the Gipsey's manner ;—"what would your words imply? Why should you encourage any other feeling than one of respect, seeing that I never did you any harm?"

"Consciously thou hast not, maiden; but still hast thou injured me in the tenderest part ;—thou hast won the heart of one whom I could freely worship, and for whom I am ready at any moment to sacrifice my life. Thus hast thou stepped in between those fond hopes I had dared to cherish, and blighted them for ever!—Had Evelyn Heartwell never have known such a being as Constance Welborn, even Mabel, the poor wandering outcast of the woods and wilds, might have hoped to have been happy in his love. Ah! me!—mine is indeed a wretched fate!"

"Poor girl! poor girl!" sighed Constance, compassionately; "too well do I now read your feelings, and, from the very bottom of my soul I pity you."

"Pity me!" repeated Mabel, proudly and disdainfully, at the same time hastily dashing away the tears that had involuntarily started to her eyes; "no, no, no; —recall those words, on thy very life. Even thy scorn—thine hatred I could endure, without regret; but thy pity would be as wormwood to my very soul, and I should, indeed, look upon myself as one of the most degraded and despicable of human beings. But enough of this ;—thou knowest my secret, and hate me, despise me for it, if thou wilt; exult in the misery and despair of the lowly and wretched Mabel."

"No, no, Mabel," returned our heroine, in her gentlest accents; "how much you wrong me, if you suppose me capable of such ungenerous, such contemptible feelings toward you. Alas! what better is my fate than yours? What other prospect is there but one of the most unspeakable misery before me? 'Tis true that Evelyn's most devoted affections now are mine, and that, let whatever may occur, his heart will remain faithful to me; but does not fate frown upon us? Are not all our hopes of happiness for ever annihilated; since it is the will of Heaven that we shall never be united; that this may be our last meeting, and that we shall then be separated for ever? Come, Mabel, banish the jealous feelings you entertain towards me from your breast. We are sisters in misfortune, let us then be sisters in sympathy."

The Gipsey-girl seemed moved by her words; she paused a minute or two, and having gazed earnestly in the face of our heroine, she once more sighed deeply, and, as an expression of the most intense emotion passed over her handsome and intelligent features, she said :—

"Well, well, be it so; I do believe thee to be sincere, and will endeavour to calm the wild tempest of my feelings. Enough! we will waive this dismal subject for the present. I have the happiness of the unfortunate Evelyn dearest at my heart, and, though it may only serve to add to the misery of my own breast, I will present no obstacle to your meeting."

"Poor girl," replied Constance, "in those observations, I read the true character of your nature, and—"

"Hold!" interrupted Mabel, hastily and peremptorily; "words of flattery are hateful to me, for I have experienced enough of the hypocrisy of the world to know their hollowness. Let us proceed, for time wanes apace."

Seeing that it was obnoxious to her, Constance uttered no further observations, and inspired with fresh confidence, she increased her speed, and followed her guide in the direction which she took.

They had now arrived to within a short distance of the Wilderness, when

Constance beheld a man suddenly emerge from an opening in the road, and approach towards them.

"Be not alarmed," said Mabel, seeing that her companion hesitated and trembled slightly, "'tis Brayling."

Sampson Braylling had now arrived at the spot, being so disguised that Constance scarcely recognized him, and having greeted her respectfully, he said—

"Thou art punctual, fair lady, and I am glad to find that thou dost possess the good sense and the generosity to place due confidence in the honesty and sincerity of my motives. Thou wilt have no cause to repent of it."

"Brayling," replied Constance, "you must know full well the great risk I run in thus complying with your request; should my uncle discover my absence, what can I say in explanation of my conduct ?"

"We will arrange all that before we part;" returned Sampson.

"But should the place where Evelyn is concealed be discovered, his destruction will be inevitable."

"Oh, fear not; lady," said the Gipsey Chief, "I will be answerable for his safety. But come, any delay here may be fraught with danger. Mabel, retire to our encampment.

"Aye!" returned the latter, with a look of dissatisfaction, " of course I am not permitted to accompany thee on this love errand. Mabel would be a sad intruder at the meeting of Constance Welborn and *her* Evelyn!"

"Dear Mabel," said Constance, with a look of gentle reproach, "surely thou dost not forget thy promise? Farewell, we shall shortly meet again."

"Retire, Mabel, I say again;" sternly commanded Brayling, "thine observations are here out of place. Begone! our companions may require thy presence."

Mabel made no reply, but fixing a haughty look upon the Gipsey, she left the spot, and was soon lost to the sight.

"Thine arm, fair Constance," said Sampson, when she was gone, we have no time for delay; not far from here is a vehicle which will convey us to the place of our destination. Come, let us away."

"Have we far to go?" eagerly asked our heroine, and, at the same time looking timidly around her, still somewhat doubtful, and fearing that they might be watched.

"As far as Finchley," replied Sampson; "on the borders of the Common."

"Ah! such a distance?" ejaculated Constance, "my heart misgives me. I fear the result of this adventure."

"Nay, lady," replied the Gipsey, "pardon me, but this is surely weakness. Dost thou doubt my honesty? I thought thou wert prepared to venture anything to obtain an interview with thy lover."

"Yes, yes," said Constance, with renewed firmness, "I have ventured thus far, and, at any rate, I will not now recede. Lead on, I am prepared to attend you."

Brayling lent her the support of his arm, and they walked as fast as they could from the spot, and turning into a lonely and little frequented part of the neighbourhood, they beheld a vehicle standing by the road-side, and by the side of which was a man to drive it, who looked like one of the gipsies; Brayling having handed Constance in, followed himself, and the vehicle was driven off at a rapid rate.

The thoughts of our heroine were so confused, that for a few minutes she remained wrapped in silence, and Sampson Brayling did not attempt to interrupt her.

"Oh, Brayling," she said at length, "what a bold and hazardous step is this that I have taken, and should it be attended with any unfortunate accidents, it might bring ruin upon the unfortunate Evelyn, and expose me to still greater misery than I even now experience."

"I again urge you, Constance Welborn,'" returned the Gipsey, "to maintain confidence in the issue of this adventure, and not to anticipate the worst."

'But the distance is so great that we have to go," remarked Constance, "and the time which will be necessarily occupied in the interview so long, that it is almost impossible my absence from the mansion can remain concealed from my uncle. How then can I account for it? What excuse can I make that may satisfy his doubts and suspicions?"

"Trust to Providence, lady," answered Sampson, " who knows the purity of your intentions, and will not fail to protect you throughout."

Constance looked at the uncouth Gipsey with surprise; his language and manners were so different from that which she had expected from him. Sampson read her thoughts, and said—

"I see, lady, that my observations amaze thee, but, believe me they are sincere, as thou shalt have reason to acknowledge ere long. I would fain not boast of myself, but rest assured that, though my exterior be uncouth and repulsive, I have a heart that is not insensible to the dictates of humanity and justice. It may be enough to assure thee most solemnly that I am the friend, the honest and fervent friend of yourself and Evelyn, and that I am determined to remain so, even at every hazard."

"Kind, excellent man!" exclaimed Constance, with a burst of gratitude, which she neither could nor attempted to restrain; "pardon me if I ever, even for a moment, appeared to doubt you. I am indeed convinced of the truth and sincerity of your assertions, and rely with every confidence on your friendship. How shall I ever be able to repay the debt of obligation I owe you?"

"Name it not, Miss Constance;" said Brayling, "to know that I have been enabled to perform my duty is all I wish, and that will afford me every gratification for any trouble to which, in my exertions to serve you, I may be put, or any risk which I may run."

"But why should you thus take so extraordinary an interest in the fate of the unhappy Evelyn?" interrogated our heroine.

"Believe me it is no ordinary motive that stimulates me;" answered Sampson, "I feel it is a paramount duty I owe, to see justice rendered to Evelyn Heartwell: I have taken an oath to do so, and thou shalt find that I will not fail to keep my word."

"Generous assurance!" said Constance, " but, alas! what can possibly extricate him from the fearful difficulties by which he is surrounded?"

"Fear not, lady, I can and will, when the fitting time arrives, fully establish his innocence, and will see that the real guilty parties shall not escape that punishment they so justly merit."

"But Oliver Dalton, Brayling," said Constance, "that man to whom Sir Milford is determined to sacrifice me, and whom I cannot, dare not even think upon without an inward and irresistable sensation of fear and shuddering."

"He is a villain, a most consummate villain," said the Gipsey Chief, emphatically, "I know him well, and have him completely in my power. There are circumstances, however, which render it impossible for me fully to secure my ends, by devulging all the black secrets at present."

"Alas! my uncle is inexorable," sighed our heroine, "he has decided my fate, and I am powerless to resist his stern and inflexible decree."

"Fear not, fair Constance Welborn," replied Sampson, "Oliver Dalton shall never become the husband of one who cannot look upon him with any other feelings than those of fear and loathing."

"Vain boast," cried Constance, despairing, "how canst thou prevent it?"

"I have given thee my word, and thou shalt find that I have both the will and the power to keep my promise."

"Mysterious man, your words involve me in doubt and perplexity."

"Be satisfied with what I have said at present, and rest assured that I will not deceive thee.   Courage, courage, Miss Constance, for dark and ponderous as are the clouds that now obscure the horizon of thine happiness, they will in time be dispersed, and the bright sunshine of peace shall once more illumine thy pathway.   But endeavour to banish this painful part of the business from thy mind, and prepare thyself for the trying and affecting scene thou art about to undergo."

"Oh, yes," replied Constance, "I will indeed try to do so.   And yet, dearest Evelyn, anxious though I am for this interview, still do I dread it, for to witness the anguish and despair of your feelings, will be insupportable agony to my soul."

She sobbed bitterly as she gave utterance to those words; and Sampson Brayling, with a delicacy of feeling, which could little have been expected from him, but which did honour to his head and heart, thinking it might better serve

No. 10.

to relieve her, suffered her to give free and uninterrupted indulgence to her various torturing and conflicting emotions.

In this manner they proceeded on their journey, and making no stoppages, but using all the speed they could, at an early hour, and before there were many persons abroad to observe them, they arrived in a by-road not far from the Common. Here the vehicle stopped, and Brayling having stepped from it assisted Constance to alight, and she gazed around with mingled feelings of anxiety and curiosity.

"You will wait here, Saul," said Brayling, to the man who had driven them, "and be careful not to excite the particular attention of any one you may see, any more than possible. Come, Miss Constance, but a few yards farther, and our journey is at an end."

Constance was unable to make any reply. Now that the moment was at hand when she was once more, and for the last time in all probability, her feelings almost overpowered her, and her agitation was so great that she could scarcely contain herself.

Brayling read the thoughts that were passing in her mind, and evidently sympathising with her feelings, he fixed upon her a look of encouragement, and gently and respectfully taking her arm he led her from the spot, and the next moment they stood before the ancient portal of that old house which has been before described to the reader.

There was something particularly solemn and impressive in the aspect of that venerable building, especially as it then appeared, when the grey mists of early dawn had scarcely dispersed before the rising sun; and our heroine, as she gazed upon its moss-covered walls, and ivy-clothed porch, its small and painted casements, and trod its ancient court, now overgrown with tall dank weeds, felt a sensation of awe, not unmingled with dread, stealing over her which she had seldom experienced before. She looked at her companion with an enquiring and doubtful expression of countenance, and he seemed to understand her meaning, for he said :—

"No doubt the appearance of this old house, lady, is not such as to inspire thee with the most lively feelings; but fear not, no danger lurks within its walls, which have afforded a friendly and timely shelter to thy lover in the hour of need. Here no prying eye can watch what passes at this melancholy interview; neither need'st thou apprehend any interruption from those whom thou hast cause to dread."

"And yet," replied our heroine, "anxiously as I have looked forward to, and prayed for this meeting, now that the moment has arrived, my heart almost shrinks from the melancholy task. Oh, Evelyn, that cruel fate should thus present so many obstacles to our happiness."

"Courage, courage, fair Constance," returned the Gipsey, "and endeavour to banish such dismal thoughts from thy mind. Hope for the best, for who knows but this may be the prelude to happier times? How soon may the storms of adversity that now disturb the peace of thyself and Evelyn entirely subside, and be succeeded by a calm and serenity which nothing whatever shall again interrupt."

"Oh, could I indeed encourage such sanguine and cheering hopes, I might then bear the present heavy trials it is now my lot to endure, with some degree of patience and fortitude;" replied Constance, "but, alas! when I view all the fearful and threatening circumstances by which myself and Evelyn are at present surrounded, my heart sinks within me, and I am almost driven to abandon myself to complete despair"

"Nay, Constance," observed Sampson Brayling, "thou must not give way to any such sad and torturing ideas; for, gloomy though thy apprehensions and anticipations may be, I do trust that they will not be realized. But come, we do but delay, and the moments are precious."

"True, true," agreed our heroine, "I—I am ready; now, dear Evelyn, may Heaven give us both fortitude to support with firmness and resignation the painful scene we are about to experience."

She now suffered Brayling to conduct her up to the door of the old house, without making use of any further observation, and raising the massive knocker and letting it fall with a heavy bang, which Sampson thoughtlessly did; the sound startled Constance, and reverberated hollowly through the ancient building.

Old Matthew Smelton, as was his custom, had quitted his chamber for two or three hours, and had been busying himself about the house, in order to wile the time away till somebody else should be stirring.

"So," remarked the old man, "Master Reuben Grangeforth has not yet quitted his chamber, but 'tis early, and I must not reproach him with sluggishness. Poor young man, I fear that the many troubles which beset his mind, do not allow him much repose. I marvel much what can be the secret of his sorrows. It must be a painful one indeed, which can thus sink him to the lowest depths of despair. I am not at all curious, I never was disposed to be so, but now would I give a lifetime to know what it is that preys thus heavily upon his mind, and has reduced him to such a state of misery and despair. It must be something of importance, too, which can cause Sampson Brayling to take such a deep interest in his fate."

How far the old man would have proceeded with his soliloquy, we are not prepared to say, but at that moment he was interrupted by a loud knock at the outer-door, and he started and looked amazed around him.

"Hey-day!" he ejaculated, "visitors so early, who can it be? They must be in a mighty hurry, too, by their knocking so loudly."

Thus saying, Matthew quitted the room, and made his way to the door. In a few minutes he returned, accompanied by Sampson Brayling.

"I'm astonished!" said the old man; "the fair niece of the proud and wealthy Sir Milford Welborn in love with this poor and friendless youth, and in this old dreary house to meet him."

"'Tis even so," answered Brayling, "but restrain thy curiosity and attend to to my wishes. The lady Constance will probably be able to calm her feelings by a few minutes converse with the dame. I must leave thee for about an hour."

"What, before seeing Reuben?" interrogated Matthew, with a look of astonishment.

"Yes," answered Sampson, "business calls me hence, and my presence at the interview of the lovers would be an intrusion. See that thou prepare Reuben for the meeting, and, for the present, farewell; in an hour thou wilt see me again."

Thus saying, and motioning Matthew to be silent and cautious, Brayling hastily quitted the room.

"So," observed Matthew, "the secret is partly out, but there is much more to be divulged. Poor Reuben! but hush, here he comes."

At that moment, Evelyn, whose looks were pale and anxious, from the events of the night, and which have been recorded in the previous pages, entered the room.

"Did I not hear a knock?" he enquired.

"Ye—yes—no—that is—" replied the old man, confused.

"Why this hesitation?" demanded Evelyn, hastily, "is there anything to fear? Speak!"

"Fear!" returned Matthew, "no, Heaven forbid. But I have a surprise for thee, Master Reuben, only thou must be calm. Sampson Brayling has been here."

"Ah!" cried our hero, with a look of surprise and incredulity, "at this early hour, and gone without seeing me? This is strange."

"Business compelled him to do so," said Matthew. "He will return in an hour; in the meantime I have one to introduce to thee, Reuben, whose society will doubtless compensate for his absence."

"What mean you?"

"Nay, now, be calm, be calm, and thou shalt presently see."

And he abruptly retired, leaving our hero in a state of astonishment and perplexity.

"This old man trifles with me," he said, "and yet the throbbings of my heart tell me that—"

Before he could finish the sentence, the room door was thrown back upon its hinges, and with a loud cry of the most painful emotion, the beauteous Constance rushed to his arms.

What a moment of overwhelming excitement was this to the unfortunate lovers; and what pen can possibly do adequate justice to the powerful and various feelings that agitated their bosoms on that trying occasion? For some minutes they could only remain fervently and affectionately locked in each other's arms, and express their feelings by convulsive sobs.

"Beloved Constance," said our hero, at length, partially withdrawing himself from her embrace, and gazing with an intensity of feeling in her pale but lovely countenance, which it would indeed be a most difficult task properly to portray, while the powerful emotions that agitated her gentle bosom, were fully evinced in the anguish of her features, and the humid expression of her eyes; " beloved Constance," he repeated, "and do we then again meet? Do I once more press thy adored form to my throbbing heart, and gaze in reality upon those beauteous features, which, sleeping or waking, have never for an instant been absent from my distracted imagination? Oh, the joy, yet anguish of my bosom on this occasion! Speek to me, dear Constance, let me again listen to the fond tones of thy voice, which are as Heavenly music to my ravished senses."

"Oh, Evelyn!" sighed Constance; and the fervent and affectionate glances which she fixed upon him, fully shewed the sincerity of her observations; " what can I say? How find language sufficiently powerful to give utterance to the feelings that at present rend my heart? And to see thee thus; and to know the fearful difficulties by which thou art surrounded! Oh, with what tenfold severity does it increase my agony!"

"Be calm, my Constance, "said her lover, "and endeavour to support all that cruel fate may yet have in store for us with that fortitude, resignation, and heroism, which his hitherto so nobly distinguished you." "But you are stigmatized as a villain, Evelyn, " she ejaculated;—"execrated and condemned by the more uncharitable of mankind, when I know you to be innocent; scouted from society,—compelled to conceal yourself from your fellow-creatures, and hunted even to the death, as if you were some blood-stained wretch, who merited the most terrible retribution that outraged Heaven could inflict upon you. And think you that I can calmny, patiently endure these agonising thoughts?— Oh, I shall surely go mad!"

"For mercy's sake do not talk thus, dear Constance!" implored Evelyn! " for it drives me to distraction to hear you, and will destroy that manly fortitude and firm reliance upon the merciful interposition of Providence which has hitherto sustained me in the midst of my manifold and almost unparalleled troubles. To know that you still remain faithful to me; that your heart still beats with the fond emotions of love towards me, affords me every consolation, and reanimates my hopes, and full well I am convinced that neither time nor circumstances can alter the sentiments of your heart."

"Oh, Evelyn," she returned; "it is impossible that you could ever for a moment do me the injustice to doubt the fervour, the sincerity, and constancy of my love. No, misfortune does but render you more dear to me;—but, alas!— it appears most improbable, under all the torturing circumstances that my uncle will ever relent, and the importunities of the hated Oliver Dalton add to the misery of my feelings, and the anguish of my despair."

"Ah! the villain!" exclaimed our hero, "it is the thought of him, and the favour he possesses in the estimation of Sir Milford, which distracts me more than all. He, I know full well, is the author of all the misfortunes it is at present my hard lot to endure. And your uncle will compel you to become his bride, and thus doom you to a fate which is by far too horrible for contemplation."

"By Heaven, never!" exclaimed Constance, emphatically; and her fine features became more than usually animated with an expression of determination; "hear me solemnly vow, Evelyn," she added, clasping her hands vehemently together, and raising her eyes fervently towards that Power to which she appealed, "that let whatever may be the consequences to me, even though it should bring every misery upon me that can attend human being; though the heaviest maledictions that my uncle can invoke, may be breathed upon my devoted head, I will never become the wife of Oliver Dalton!"

"Noble-hearted, generous, most self-devoted of women!" cried Evelyn, straining the form of the beauteous maiden still more passionately to his bosom; "that fond, that solemn assurance inspires me with fresh courage; for to know that thou wert sacrificed to such a man as Oliver Dalton, would render me indeed doubly the most wretched of human beings. But why should I exact such a promise from you, Constance, when I know that you cannot struggle against your fate? Strangely infatuated as your uncle is with this bold and unknown adventurer, he will remain inexorable; he will cruelly sacrifice you to one whom he knows you view with scorn, with disgust, and abhorrence; and however repugnant to your feelings, what power can you find to resist his will?"

"Evelyn," returned Constance, and she looked at her lover with a gentle expression of reproach, "you estimate my character, or rather the love I bear you far too lightly, if you imagine that any mortal power shall force me to yield to a fate so monstrous. The more I think of Oliver Dalton, and the dark mystery that is attached to his character and all his proceedings, the greater does my disgust and terror become; and again I solemnly swear, (and Heaven will, I trust, inspire me with firmness and determination to keep my oath,) that there are no sufferings I am not prepared to encouter, nay, even death itself, sooner than such a man as Oliver Dalton shall force me to the altar and compel me to become his wife."

"Alas! alas!" sighed our hero, striking his forehead with his clenched fist, and the intense agony of his looks shewing the fierce tempest of despair and misery which raged within his breast, "what a painful, what an insupportable destiny is ours. In spite of all my efforts to submit to the will of Providence with fortitude and resignation, the thought unmans me, and I could become again a child. Oh, Constance, dear Constance, would to Heaven that we had never known each other, what misery would it have saved us both! But why should I thus selfishly expose you to such suffering, when it is impossible for me to hope that you can ever become mine, poor, wretched outcast as I am? It was presumption in me ever to believe so unworthy as I am, of one so good, so amiable, so peerless as Constance Welborn? Why should I remain here lurking like some guilty miscreant? Why continue thus in degrading indolence, when there are active pursuits that call for the exercise of my energies, and may yet win me honour and distinction? No, I will no longer do so, and become a burden to strangers for a shelter, and the mere means of subsistence. Too long have I already delayed; but now my resolution is fixed, at the earliest period I will enlist myself with the gallant defenders of our country, now risking their life's-blood in the maintenance of right and justice over tyranny and despotism; we will part, dear Constance; I will tear myself away from your presence, and probably you may then cease to remember that there was ever such a wretched individual as Evelyn Heartwell, had a dwelling in the world, or a place in your affections."

"Oh, Evelyn;" sobbed forth our heroine, as though her heart would break, and at the same time fixing upon him a look of such impressive emotion that was sufficient to penetrate to his very soul;—"surely these observations are most cruel and unjust. How have I ever deserved them?—They seem to imply a doubt of my fidelity, and moreover that you repent of the vows you have so frequently given utterance to me, and that you would fain recal them. Alas!—alas!—I fear that I have suffered myself to be flattered by false and delusive hopes, and that the Gipsey-girl, Mabel—"

"Ah! what of her?" demanded Evelyn, eagerly and breathlessly;—"explain yourself, Constance;—what mean you?"—speak, for the love of Heaven, I implore you!"

"She loves you;" replied Constance, with a heart-drawn sigh;—"and probably Evelyn Heartwell may consider her more worthy of his affections than her who would willingly share the humblest lot if it were but with him."

"Oh, Constance;" said her lover in the most melancholy accents; "I thought not to hear such words as these from you; can you then, do you do me that cruel injustice to believe me capable to transfer to another those fond affections which I have so often sworn are yours alone? Oh, this is most severe; 'tis what I never anticipated; a shock to my feelings, in the midst of all my other manifold sufferings, for which I am totally unprepared, and—"

"He was interrupted by the room door being suddenly thrown open, and old Matthew Smelton hastily making his appearance in an evident state of alarm.

"How now, Matthew;" demanded our hero, "why this intrusion?—"

"I fear that there is some treachery abroad;" replied the old man;—"I had occasion to leave the house but a short time since, when I saw two or three men lurking suspiciously in the neighbourhood;—I tried to avoid them, but they watched me narrowly, and—ah!—" he added, with increased alarm;—"see, even now they come across the common towards the house."

Evelyn and Constance hastily approached the window, which commanded a complete view of the common, and the surrounding country, and looked eagerly from it, and they started when they beheld several men, as Matthew had said—approaching the house. As they came nearer, the foremost one more particularly arrested the attention of Constance, and tremblingly clinging to Evelyn, in a voice of terror she exclaimed—

"Oh! see!—by Heaven 'tis Oliver Dalton!—we are lost!—we are lost! Oh, my Evelyn, what will become of you?—"

"Nay, my love;" replied Evelyn; "quiet your alarm. No danger may befal us, in spite of this threatening circumstance. What can bring our enemy here? By what means can he have discovered—"

"There is no time to waste in words," hastily interrupted Matthew; "if this is indeed the man you fear, you have ample cause to apprehend the worst. It is evident he is coming towards the house, and should you remain here, he will at once observe you."

"Oh, what is to be done?" ejaculated the trembling and terrified Constance; "would to Heaven that Brayling had not quitted the house."

"Ah! behold!" cried Evelyn; "they approach nearer; they point suspiciously

unreasonable question to ask, thou wilt condescend to inform me who I have the honour of addressing, and the nature of the business for which I am indebted for this visit at so early an hour in the morning ?"

"It is of a nature that will neither admit of trifling or delay;" answered Oliver, sternly; "so conduct us to an apartment where we can discuss it without any further nonsense."

"Humph!" said the old man, coolly; "rather peremptorily, certainly. However, walk this way, gentlemen—walk this way."

Oliver and his ruffianly companion eyed the old man suspiciously, and following him from the hall, he conducted them into the room where the interview with the lovers had just taken place. Oliver and Will looked anxiously around, and exchanged glances, and then unceremoniously seated themselves.

"Now Sir," interrogated Matthew, addressing himself to Oliver; "may I once more take the liberty of inquiring thy business ?"

"In the first place," replied Oliver, "to whom does this old house belong ?"

"To those who have not inhabited it for many years, and it is not likely that they will do so again in a hurry at any rate;" answered Smelton; "it may be enough to inform thee that I am here in charge of it, and I have no doubt that I shall continue to be so for the remainder of my days."

"And do you mean to say—" demanded Oliver, sternly, and fixing upon the old man a keen and penetrating look—"do you mean to say that you are the only person in the house at the present time ?"

"With the exception of my old dame and yourselves, gentleman," answered Matthew.

"Bah!" exclaimed Will; "art thou going to suffer thyself to be trifled with by this old man, Master Oliver? Dost thou not see that he is attempting to deceive thee ?"

"Aye;" replied Oliver, sternly;—"but he will be puzzled to do that, methinks. Hark ye, old man;—the business which calls us hither is of the most paramount importance, and peremptory description. We have every reason to believe that those whom we seek are at present concealed in this house, although thou hast so boldly and positively asserted to the contrary;—beware, for should it be proved that thou hast connived with them to escape our detection, thou will become involved in such a dilemma as thou wilt find it no easy matter to extricate thyself from."

"Hey-day!" ejaculated Matthew, affecting much surprise, but without evincing any alarm or confusion; "these are strange observations, young gentleman; and I must confess that I am at a loss to understand them. May I be so bold as to inquire what thou meanest ?"

"Dost thou know the niece of Sir Milford Welborn?" asked Oliver, eyeing him narrowly.

"What, the fair Constance Welborn, of the Old Grange, at Hogsden?—Aye, I have often heard of her, and admired her for those amiable qualities for which all who know her give her credit."

"Indeed ?" said Oliver, in a half sarcastic tone; "and is this all thou knowest of her ?"

"Thou puttest extraordinary questions to me, young man;" remarked Matthew; "what more should a poor humble, obscure individual like myself know of the niece of the proud and wealthy baronet, Sir Milford Welborn?"

"Psha!" cried, Will, impatiently; "what a waste of time is this, Master Oliver;—dost thou not perceive the evasive answers with which this old dotard seeks to cajole thee?"

"Aye;" returned Oliver Dalton;—"but by all my hopes they shall not avail him. Hark ye, old man, we have every reason to believe that Constance Welborn

is at this moment in this old house; whither she has come for the purpose of a clandestine meeting with a self-convicted fellon, the villain, Evelyn Heartwell who, for a time, has escaped from the hands of justice, and there are powerful reasons to suspect is concealed here. But a few minutes since, and I am not much mistaken, I saw them both together in this very apartment."

"Mercy on us!" exclaimed the old man; "what strange ideas have taken possession of thee?"

"Bah!" cried Oliver Dalton, passionately "no more trifling, I say again, for I am positive, and determined. Without any further delay, we must search the house, and woe be to thee if thou hast spoken falsely.'

"This insolence is unwarrantable, young man;" replied Matthew, firmly; "I will not be forced into a compliance with thy haughty and unreasonable demands. I have answered thy questions, and I now desire thee to quit the house."

No. 11

" Ah!" cried Oliver; "this resistance confirms my suspicions. Give me up the keys of the different rooms, and do not obstruct us in our search. I feel convinced that those whom we seek are at present concealed in this house, and they must not, shall not be suffered to escape us."

" Oliver Dalton, (for such I now understand is thy name)," said Matthew; " I am an old man, and thou mayest think to take a cowardly advantage of me, but think not that I will submissively yield to thy outrageous demands."

" Then we must e'en enforce compliance," said the villain, Will; and advancing savagely towards Matthew, he grasped him by the collar, hurling him to the other end of the room, and was about to follow up this act by further outrage, when he was suddenly arrested in his purpose by a loud and commanding voice, exclaiming—

"Hold! cowardly villain!"

The door was instantly burst open, and Sampson Brayling, and two or three others of the Gipsies, armed, rushed into the room!

Oliver Dalton and his companion started back confused and astonished, whilst Sampson Brayling, rushing upon Will, with a violent blow from the butt end of his pistol, stretched him stunned and prostrate, at the same time exclaiming :—

" Treacherous knave! I have then discovered thee at thy villainous work, and dearly shalt thou pay for it. Secure the fellow and his worthy employer in separate rooms, for the present. We shall know how to dispose of them anon."

" Sampson Brayling!" exclaimed Oliver, " his features distorted with rage and disappointment;" " Sampson Brayling, beware of what you do. You will not dare to—"

" Not dare!" repeated the Gipsey, scornfully; " what is there that I dare not do with such a miscreant as thou art? But for a few minutes I leave thee to storm to thyself; I have other business just now to attend to. But I have much to say to thee before we part. Away with him, and his ruffianly myrmidon. Matthew, thou wilt conduct them to their temporary lodging."

" Now may the heaviest curses pursue thee for this!" cried Oliver Dalton, fiercly, as the Gipsies seized him ; " confusion! to be thus defeated,—trepanned!"

" Ha, ha, ha!" laughed Sampson, contemptuously; " away with him,—away with him!"

The Gipsies obeyed; Matthew Smelton leading the way, and Oliver Dalton, bursting with rage and indignation, finding it in vain to offer any resistance.

CHAPTER XIII.

THE PARTING OF THE LOVERS.—THE RETURN OF CONSTANCE.—THE RAGE OF OLIVER DALTON.

IN a few minutes old Matthew returned to the room where Sampson Brayling was awaiting him, and seemed much alarmed and disconcerted at what had taken place.

" Well, Matthew," said Brayling; " hast thou seen the rascals safely lodged?" Matthew replied in the affirmative.

" 'Tis well," observed the Gipsey ; " I will see to their disposal anon. The designs of Master Oliver are completely thwarted, and no doubt he is much chagrined and disappointed."

"Yes;" said the old man; "I left him storming with rage, and vowing revenge. But, indeed, Brayling, I like not this business; I am afraid it may be productive of something evil to ourselves, and also the lovers."

"Oh, fear not;" returned the Gipsey; "Oliver Dalton is completely in my power, and he will not dare to oppose my will. It was fortunate that I returned at the time I did to the house."

"True;" coincided Matthew; "but, had you any suspicion that made you hasten your return?"

"Yes;" answered Sampson; "unexpectedly I met Mabel, accompanied by some of the tribe, at a short distance from the house. In opposition to my strict injunctions to the contrary, she had left the encampment, and followed me hither. On the rout she had observed Dalton and the fellow, Will, lurking about; and, suspecting their intentions, she secretly watched them. As matters have turned out, 'tis well she did so. But come, we waste time that is precious. Where have you concealed the lovers?"

"In the secret room of the old gallery, where they are no doubt anxiously awaiting the result of this exciting adventure;" answered the old man.

"Lead the way then," said Brayling; "and I will soon relieve them."

Matthew nodded assent, and they quitted the room together.

The state of suspense and agitation in which the lovers had been during this interval, may be readily conceived. Poor Constance was worked up to a pitch of the greatest excitement, which Evelyn, notwithstanding his own emotion, tried in vain to calm. The certainty that Oliver Dalton had, by some means or the other, become acquainted with their intended meeting, and had traced her footsteps to the old house, and the consequences that were likely to ensue from it, excited her utmost alarm; but the critical situation of that unfortunate youth, to whom she was so fondly, so devotedly attached; the almost certainty of his again falling into the iron clutches of the law—and in which case his fate appeared to her bewildered imagination inevitable, distracted her more than all.

"Alas, Evelyn!" she sighed; "'tis useless attempting to struggle against our fate. Why should we still cherish fond and delusive hopes, when there is nothing but misery and despair before us?"

"Be calm, dear Constance;" replied her lover, in soothing accents, and subduing his own feelings as well as he could; "there is an all-merciful Providence that will yet watch over us, and frustrate the designs of Oliver Dalton, though, for a time, he may seem to triumph."

"Would to Heaven that I could think so;" observed our heroine; "but when I view the dark and ponderous clouds that hover o'er us, portending the fierce tempest which is about to burst upon our heads; when I contemplate the many horrors and dangers that encircle us, and from which we cannot extricate ourselves, my heart sinks within me. But this unexpected arrival of Oliver Dalton here, is a misfortune which distracts me more than all. What may not his dark feelings of jealousy and revenge prompt him to do? It is evident that he must have been aware of my appointment with Sampson Brayling, and traced my footsteps hither; my uncle then will be made acquainted with it all, and how do I tremble when I think of the rage and indignation it will create in his breast."

"Poor girl;" ejaculated Evelyn; "and it is I who have been the cause of exposing thee to such troubles as these. Alas!—wretched, wretched Evelyn."

"Oh, reproach not yourself so unjustly," she replied, "for you are not to blame. I should have been unworthy of your love, and have loathed and despised myself, had I hesitated to brave every danger to meet you, when the opportunity was afforded me. But, oh, Evelyn, can you marvel at the anguish and despair that rack my breast, when I reflect that the place of your conceal-

ment is discovered, and that ere many hours have elapsed, in all human probability you will again be in the hands of your enemies?"

"Oh, fear not for me, my own fond Constance," returned our hero; "for I am
fully prepared to meet with fortitude and resignation any fate that may await me.
Anything is better than this constant state of excitement and suspense. But
why should I, like a cowardly despicable wretch, remain here, while the heartless
miscreant who is the author of all my miseries and misfortunes is now in the
house? Let me at once boldly confront him, and hurl my reproach and defiance
at his head!"

"Hold! hold! Evelyn;" exclaimed Constance, alarmed, and clinging more
affectionately to him. "Would you at once madly precipitate yourself into that
danger which I so greatly apprehend? For the love of Heaven—for my sake—
forbear! But listen."

A loud and confused noise, followed by the hasty closing of doors, now met
their ears, and arrested their particular attention.

"Something particular has happened," said our heroine, with a look of terror.
"And, hark! some persons are approaching this way. Oh, Evelyn! what will
become of you?"

"Courage, courage, Constance," replied her lover, "they cannot discover us
here, unless old Matthew Smelton should betray us; and in his fidelity and
honesty of purpose, I place every reliance. But should we be indeed detected,"
he added, determinedly, and laying his hand on the hilt of his sword, "I will
not yield at least without an effort."

The footsteps now stopped before the secret entrance of the room in which
the lovers were concealed, and hearing the voices of Brayling and Matthew, their
fears were in a great measure dispersed. The next moment the portrait was
pushed back, and the Gipsey and his companion stepped into the room.

"Ah, Brayling," eagerly demanded Evelyn, "what now?"

"Fear not," answered Sampson, "the designs of thine inveterate enemy,
Oliver Dalton, are frustrated, to his dismay and confusion."

"Oh, thank Heaven!" fervently exclaimed our heroine.

"But follow me immediately," said the Gipsey, "there is not any time for delay.
All now depends upon our promptitude. Matthew, I shall see thee again ere
long; see well to the security of the birds we have caged."

Matthew nodded and departed, and Evelyn throwing his arm around the
slender waist of the beauteous Constance, they followed Sampson Brayling
without saying another word.

Having conducted them from the gallery, he led them into the lower apartments.

"I know well thine anxiety," he said, seeing that Evelyn was about to speak,
"and will therefore at once relieve thy suspense as time is precious. The villain,
Oliver, and his companion, are prisoners here, and—"

"But, ah!" interrupted our hero, "thou canst not detain him; and what may
we not have cause to dread from his vengeance?"

"Fear not," replied Brayling, "I have him completely in my power and at
my mercy; and he dare not even attempt to act as his base wishes would prompt
him to do. I shall dispose of him anon, depend upon it. But it is necessary that
Constance should return home without the least possible delay. Thou must
part."

"Part!" repeated the damsel, with a look of the deepest emotion, "oh, that
dismal word. It may be for ever! Evelyn, dear Evelyn!"

"My poor Constance!" returned her lover, fondly embracing her, and imprinting
a fervent kiss upon her lips. "'Tis a hard, a painful trial, but we must submit
to the will of Fate. Be firm, and put thy trust in Heaven, and though we may
never meet again, rest assured that thine image will ever be treasured in the

heart's core of Evelyn Heartwell. Farewell, most amiable, most beloved of woman !"

" Alas !" sighed Constance, and tears gushed to her eyes, " and must I indeed say that melancholy word, adieu ? It chokes me! Evelyn, unfortunate and beloved Evelyn, I will be faithful to the sacred vows which I have uttered, let whatever may be the consequences. Constance Welborn will never become the wife of any other man than Evelyn Heartwell !"

" Bless thee, bless thee for those words," ejaculated our hero; " the remembrance of them will sustain me in every difficulty. Once more, Constance, adieu, and may all good angels watch over thy safety and happiness."

" Come, come," observed Brayling, " the separation must take place, and 'tis useless to delay, for it may be fraught with danger to the lady Constance. In a short time I shall see thee again, Evelyn. I will but see thy lover in safety, and then I will return."

Oh, Brayling," said our hero, cordially pressing the Gipsey's hand ;—" how can I ever sufficiently repay the debt of gratitude I owe thee for the trouble thou hast taken, and the many risks thou hast run for my sake?"

" Say no more about it, Evelyn ; replied Sampson; "I am fully satisfied in being able to serve thee. But enough of this. Be firm, both of you, and rest assured that it shall be no fault of mine if thou dost not shortly meet again."

With one more affectionate embrace, and from which they could with difficulty tare themselves asunder, the lovers now seperated, and Sampson Brayling, encouraging her by a look, led Constance from the room ; and from the casement, Evelyn watched their receding forms across the common till they were hidden from the sight; when he threw himself disconsolately in a chair and abandoned himself to all the anguish of his feelings, till he was rejoined by old Matthew, from whom he elicited all the particulars of what had taken place on Oliver Dalton and his companion, Will, entering the house.

We will now return to Oliver, who, on the orders of Sampson Brayling, had been secured in one of the rooms of the old house, and one of the Gipsies left to watch outside the door, in case he should become violent, and seek to escape.

The reader may well imagine the rage of his feelings when he found himself thus defeated; and, for a few minutes after he was left to himself, he paced the room with disordered steps, in the greatest agitation and excitement of mind, and muttering curses to himself.

" Oh, how completely have my schemes been foiled, and at the very moment when I thought them certain of success," he exclaimed. " Sampson Brayling has quite outwitted me, and here am I caught in my own snare. But I will have an ample revenge; he cannot, he dare not detain me here, and the knowledge I have obtained, I will not fail to take every advantage of. By all my hopes I will not rest till I have worked the complete destruction of that man whom I so mortally detest—Evelyn Heartwell. But to think that him and Constance should have been allowed to meet, and once more to pour their vows of love into each others ears, excites my utmost rage and indignation. And before I can have the opportunity to place him once more in the hands of justice, he will probably have effected his escape from here, and may set at defiance all further attempts to discover him. Oh, curses light on this misfortune, which has thus frustrated my designs."

He paused, and again, with folded arms, traversed the room in the most dis-ordered manner.

" Sampson Brayling, too;" he said at length, " what have I not to fear from him? He knows all my secrets, and can at any moment work my ruin. How unfortunate it is that he should take such an interest in the fate of Evelyn and Constance, for then I might have conciliated his favour, and the success of my schemes would have been all but certain. But now I am indeed at his mercy, nd cannot, dare not act as my feelings would dictate. And shall I suffer myself to be defeated at every point, and allow this hated Evelyn, notwithstanding the black suspicion which at present rests upon his character, ultimately to triumph over me; while I may be denounced to the world as a villain of the deepest die? By all my ambitious hopes, I swear I will not. Oh, how do I envy Evelyn Heartwell! the honeyed accents she no doubt poured into his ears at this meeting; the fond caresses she lavished upon him. For me she has nothing but scorn and hatred. No matter; still am I triumphant. I possess the favours of her uncle, Sir Milford Welborn; he is determined, and although all the circumstances that have recently occurred will necessarily cause some delay, she must ultimately become mine; and with her, what is of far more estimation in my eyes, a wedding portion, which might be sufficient to gratify the avarice of a prince."

Again he paused and reflected, and, as his present critical situation became the more apparent to him, his fears increased.

"What can be the intentions of Sampson Brayling towards me?" he said, as he cast his eyes around the room in which he now found himself a prisoner, "does he mean to detain me here, or at once to denounce me to the world in my true character? Should he do so, I am ruined! Oh, how that thought tortures and distracts me! How unfortunate it was that we should meet again, after the lapse of so many years, and at so critical a moment. Now must I e'en humble. myself to the devil or my destruction is inevitable. My brain is bewildered, and I know not how to act."

He bit his lips as he uttered these words, and his looks shewed the mingled feelings of rage, fear, and disappointment, that agitated his breast. In this state of mind he continued during the time that elapsed since he had been incarcerated in his present place of confinement, and which, to his disordered imagination, seemed an age.

At length he heard some one approaching, and the next moment the room door was unlocked, and Sampson Brayling again stood before him, and fixed upon him a mingled look of malignity and exultation. Oliver inwardly trembled; but he stifled his feelings as well as he could, and met the glances of the Gipsey-chief with a bold and determined air.

"Now, Sampson Brayling—" he said,—"tis time that we came to some understanding. How long dost thou presume to coerce my liberty?"

"Humph!" replied the Gipsey, coolly and disdainfully;—"it seems, then, Oliver Dalton, as I will still, to so suit thy convenience continue to call thee, that thou art truly mortified, and highly indignant at being foiled in thy designs by Sampson Brayling?"

"Beware, Brayling," said Oliver, passionately; "beware what thou dost, for—"

"Hold! fool!—" interrupted Sampson;—"thoud'st better endeavour to control thy passion within the bounds of prudence, or thou mayest find not only thy liberty, but thy life in jeopardy. "Ah! thou wouldst not dare to—"

"*I would not dare!*—and to such a very reptile,—such a cowardly miscreant as thou art?—" retorted Brayling;—"why, have I not thee in my power at my mercy?—could not one breath of mine this moment denounce thee to the world in thy true character,—rob thee, strip thee of all the false feathers with which thou hast taken such pains to fledge thyself, and send thee, bare as a cuckoo, to the hands of the common hangman; and yet thou, knowing all this, as thy blanched cheeks and quivering lips prove thee to do, would affect to dare me!—Bah!"

"Sampson Brayling;" said Oliver, assuming all the firmness he could, though he inwardly trembled at the observations and demeanour of the Gipsey; "this is not the time for idle threats and reproaches. I do not attempt to deny the knowledge thou possessest of my past life, but—"

" Of thy *past* life!" interrupted the Gipsey; " is then thy present character so immaculate that it requires no censure?—' Tis true thou art a squire on sufferance, for is it not in my power to sink thee into the criminal at any moment. Thou knowest this full well, yet it seems thou art madly and obstinately determined to brave my indignation. Beware ! I know thy suspicions, and if it will afford thee any gratification, I do not hesitate at once to inform thee that they are perfectly correct."

" Ah !" exclaimed Dalton ; " Constance then— "

" Has been here," rejoined Sampson, coolly, " and has had an interview with her lover, Evelyn Heartwell !"

" Confusion !" cried Oliver, foaming with rage, " but I will have revenge ; let the proud beauty tremble when her uncle shall become acquainted with this ; as for Evelyn Heartwell, but a few hours more and he shall again be the inmate of a dungeon, awaiting that doom which must inevitably overtake him."

" Hold !" once more commanded Brayling ; "think'st thou that I am not fully prepared to counteract all thy designs ? Thou seem'st to forget that thou art now my prisoner, and that so thou must remain if it so suits my will. As for Evelyn Heartwell, thou knowest full well that he is perfectly innocent of all of which he is accused, and is entirely the victim of thy villany. What if I were to denounce thee as the miscreant who robbed the wretched old miser, Jasper Scrimpe, of his gold, in the Lover's Walk, and made the attempt upon his life ?"

" ' Tis false !" exclaimed Oliver, but at the same time trembling.

" Darest thou deny it ? Fool !—thou art little aware that I could bring forward such damning proof that could not fail to condemn thee."

" No—no—no ;" ejaculated Dalton, fearfully ; " thou talkest erroneously, Brayling ; thou dost but seek to alarm me ! What proof canst thou have of my guilt ?"

" The evidence of those who witnessed the deed ; moreover the assertion of the miser himself !"

Oliver Dalton started and turned pale as Sampson Brayling thus spoke ; and the latter noticed his emotion with evident satisfaction and looks of exultation.

" Ah !" cried Oliver, alarmed, and fixing upon the Gipsey a keen and penetrating look ; "is it even so ? Surely thou canst not have spoken the truth ?

" Thou wilt find to thy cost that I have, if thou art bold enough to put me to the test. But enough of this ; I have not time, neither am I disposed to bandy further words with thee at present. Thou findest to thy utter confusion and dismay that thou art completely frustrated in thy deep laid schemes of villany, and, if thou art wise, thou wilt e'en make the best of a bad bargain, and not exasperate me to proceed to any unpleasant extremities."

" Thou wilt not detain me here ? "

" That all depends upon thyself ; and thou hadst better decide quickly, for I must be gone."

" What wouldst thou have me do ? "

" On ordinary occasions," replied Brayling, "I am fully aware that such a consummate scoundrel as thou art has but little respect for an oath ; but, knowing the power I have over thee, and how easily and speedily I could consign thee to inevitable destruction, I imagine that thou wilt not be rash or imprudent enough to attempt to deceive me. Before I suffer thee to depart, therefore, thou must bind thyself by an oath which I may think proper to dictate, never to divulge to mortal being what thou hast this day discovered. Above all, to utter not a word to Sir Milford Welborn upon the subject ; or to question, reproach, or in any way to annoy the fair Constance.   Art thou prepared to take such an oath ? "

Oliver hesitated, took too or three hasty strides across the room, and muttered curses between his teeth.

"Come, come;" observed Sampson, impatiently; "this is a waste of time. Methinks it should not take thee so long to come to a decision, seeing that thou art so completely at my mercy."

"Oh, curses light upon the misfortune that has made me so;" returned Dalton, bitterly.   "The terms thou wouldst exact from me, Brayling, are severe, and—"

"Thou must comply with them, and that promptly, unless thou wouldst prefer that I should precipitate thy fate, and reveal thee at once to the world in thy natural deformity."

"And what guarantee shall I have that thou wilt not do so after all ?"

"I make thee no promises," answered the Gipsey, sternly and determinedly, "it is my place to demand, thy policy to obey.   It may be sufficient for thee to know that I have designs in contemplation which I am determined to carry out, though it may not answer my purpose to do so immediately.   Wilt thou take the oath ?"

"Thou hast me indeed in thy power, Sampson Brayling," replied the villain, "and I know 'tis useless for me to oppose thee.   But wilt thou then suffer me to depart unmolested ?"

"Aye, and if thou art wise thou wilt avail thyself of the opportunity to fly to some remote part of the country where thou mayest for a time avoid that certain punishment which thy guilt has incurred."

"What," cried Oliver, with an oath, "and abandon all my projects ? relinquish all my hopes of Constance ?"

"True," returned Sampson, "and, if thou art not foolishly obstinate thou wilt not hesitate to do so.   Of this, however, thou mayest rest assured that Constance Welborn shall never be sacrificed to such a villain as thou art."

Again Oliver Dalton muttered a bitter curse between his teeth, and looked at his stern and determined foe with a mingled expression of fear and hatred.

"I will wait no longer," said the Gipsey, decidedly; "thou hast heard   e conditions on which I will suffer thee now to depart; and thou canst form a pretty shrewd guess I should imagine of the consequences that will follow a rejection of my proposals."

"But Will ?" interrogated Oliver.

"Oh, fear not but that I shall know how to dispose of the rascal ;" replied Brayling, "I will not give him the opportunity to do any further mischief, thou mayest depend upon it."

"Confusion !" exclaimed the enraged Dalton, "I am thwarted, defeated at every point."

"Aye, it would be strange indeed, with even all thy cunning and artifice, if thou didst not find Sampson Brayling more than a match for thee.   But the oath, the oath !"

"There is no other alternative, and I must yield," said Oliver, "but, oh, this degradation is even more annoying than all."

Sampson Brayling then drew a pistol from his belt, and presenting it at the head of Oliver, compelled him to repeat word by word after himself, in the most emphatic manner, an oath of the most fearful description.

"'Tis done," said Dalton, in a hoarse voice, when he had concluded; "and now I suppose, Sampson Brayling, thou art satisfied?"

"Aye, for the present," answered the Gipsey; "though, at a future time we shall have to settle the ballance of our accounts.   See that the oath I have just extorted from thee is not broken, or thou knowest the consequences."

Oliver frowned, but made no reply, and Sampson, opening the door, motioned him from the room.

"You will conduct this *gentleman* partly on his journey back;" he said, addressing himself to the two gipsies who had been placed as sentries at the door, "and mind that you answer no questions which he may put to ye. I wish thee good day, Oliver Dalton, and pleasant reflections on thy way back to the Grange."

Oliver Dalton fixed upon Sampson a look of the bitterest malice, as he gave utterance to these sarcastic observations,—but he made no reply, and followed the men from the house; and Sampson having seen him depart, returned to the room in which he had left Evelyn, and whom he found most anxiously and impatiently awaiting him. He eagerly inquired the result of the Gipsey's interview with Oliver, and having heard the particulars, he paused, and reflected for a few minutes.

No. 12.

"Alas, Brayling," he observed at length;" "this is a most unfortunate business, and I deeply regret that it has taken place. Think you that a wretch like Oliver Dalton will value the oath he has taken a straw; and what trouble may not the fond self-devotions of my beloved Constance plunge her into?"

"Fear not," returned Brayling; "no harm shall befal her in consequence of what has taken place, I pledge thee my word for that. Oliver will not dare to break his oath, after the manner in which I have threatened him, for he knows full well that I am determined, and that his immediate destruction would be sure to follow."

"And as thou hast the power, why shouldst thou suffer the villain for a moment to escape that punishment he so justly deserves?" interrogated our hero.

"I have my motives for so doing which I cannot now explain," answered Brayling. "But depend upon it he is powerless to do thee harm. He would not be rash enough to provoke my wrath, and precipitate his own fate, which he knows full well I hold in my hands."

"Alas!" said Evelyn, in the most melancholy accents, "mine is a most wretched fate, to be stigmatised as a villain of the blackest dye; scouted from society as the veriest wretch in existence; compelled to be beholden to strangers for the very food I eat, and the roof that shelters me; oh, how my manly spirit of pride and self-independence revolts at the thought. I can endure it no longer; I will brave the worst, and if Heaven has willed me to become the innocent victim of villainy and injustice, I will meet my fate at once. I had better be dead than thus to drag on this life of misery and degradation."

He threw himself on a seat as he gave utterance to these words, and the agitated expression of his features shewed the wild tempest of passions that raged within his breast. Sampson Brayling stood and gazed at him for a few minutes with looks of the deepest commiseration, and did not offer to interrupt him in his reflections, for he hoped that by allowing him free indulgence of them he would be the more likely to regain his composure.

"Give not way to these wild paroxysms of despair, Evelyn," he said at length, in accents of the deepest compassion. "Thine is, I admit, a cruel fate, and hard to bear; but wait patiently, and mark my words, thou wilt yet live to triumph over all thy difficulties, and to be restored to that proud position in society which thy high merits so justly entitle thee to."

"Oh, how easy it is to advise," replied Evelyn, in the most impatient and disconsolate tones, "but have I not struggled with my fate long enough? And what is there now to inspire me with hope? At any rate I can no longer remain here, but let me at once boldly face my enemies, my base calumniators, and either prove my innocence or meet that destiny which untoward fate may award me."

"No," said Brayling, "that must not be. Again I enjoin thee to wait patiently, and when the fitting time arrives, I will not only make thine innocence manifest to the world, but disclose such facts as shall astound thine enemies."

"Oh, how idle it is to talk thus;" replied our hero, with a look of mild reproach, "thou triflest with my feelings, Brayling."

"Heaven forbid that I should," returned the latter, fervently, "thou wrongest me by the supposition, Evelyn; time will prove to thee how sincerely I am thy friend."

"If thou canst do what thou sayest, why delay it, and thus keep me in this state of insupportable misery and suspense?"

"Believe me I have powerful motives for doing so," answered Sampson, "which I cannot now explain. But rest assured that the time will come, and that shortly; and that all I have promised I am able to and will accomplish. For the present thou art quite safe here; Oliver Dalton will not dare to divulge what he knows of the place of thy concealment."

"But I am sick of remaining in this state of inactivity," said our hero, "had I not better risk that life which is now of such little value to me, in the battles of my country, and seek to win myself an honourable name, than to remain ingloriously at home, a prey to all the miseries and anxieties that can attend the human race ?"

"I admire thy manly spirit, Evelyn," said Brayling, "and believe me I wish not to curb it ; but we will talk further upon this subject on another occasion. At present I must leave thee, and again advise thee to endeavour to calm the excitement which this day's events have naturally created in thy breast. Be satisfied that I have thine interest, thine happiness, and welfare at heart, and will remain true to thee and to the poor girl to whom thine affections are so sincerely devoted through every peril."

"I do believe thee, my friend," said Evelyn, pressing the Gipsey's hand, "and must implore thee to bear with me if my excited feelings should have prompted me to give utterance to anything which may sound harsh or ungenerous. Believe me I fully appreciate thine unexampled kindness to me, a poor friendless youth, and would fain evince the deep feeling of gratitude I bear towards thee."

"I know it, Evelyn," returned the Gipsey, "I know it, and truly estimate thy worth. Be calm, be firm, be patient, and again I promise thee that the time shall shortly arrive when the tempests that have so long poured their violence on thine head shall subside, and peace and happiness, from which thou hast been so long estranged, be once more restored to thee."

Evelyn was about to make some reply when he was prevented from doing so by a knock at the room-door, which being opened, old Matthew made his appearance.

"I beg pardon for this intrusion," observed the old man, "but I was so anxious to know all about Oliver Dalton, and—"

"It is enough for thee to know that he is gone," interrupted Brayling, "and that thou hast nothing to fear from him. I have the villain securely in my power, though for the present I have allowed him his liberty. He will trouble thee no more."

"Ah !" said Matthew, "I am glad to hear that, for I am certain from the very expression of his countenance that he is an arrant scoundrel at heart. But what of the other fellow who accompanied him ?"

"Thou hast him secure," answered Sampson, "and he is powerless to do thee harm. He must remain here probably for a day or two, when I will remove him to the encampment. And now, my friend," he added, addressing himself to Evelyn, "I must depart. I will see thee again as soon as possible ; in the meantime, be satisfied that thy welfare, and that of Constance Welborn, will be my constant study."

"Oh, may Heaven watch over and protect her from the evils by which she is surrounded ;" said our hero, "but to thee, Brayling, how can I express my thanks ? How convince thee of the gratitude I bear towards thee for thy kindness ?"

"Enough," returned Sampson, "I am satisfied, and require no further acknowledgment. Farewell till we meet again."

Evelyn warmly pressed his hand, and expressed his feelings by his looks, and the Gipsey then departed, and left Evelyn and Matthew to themselves.

CHAPTER XIV.

The Interview between Sir Milford and Constance.

WE will not dwell upon the rage and disappointment of Oliver Dalton when the gipsies left him, and as he proceeded on his return home. To be so frustrated in his guilty designs was torturing enough, but the power which Brayling held over him, and the threats he had held out to him, filled him with alarm; and he knew not how to extricate himself from the dangers by which he now found himself so completely surrounded. He thirsted for revenge, but he could see no way by which he could obtain it, and he hesitated rashly to proceed to extremities, knowing full well the critical situation in which he was placed, and how easy it was for Sampson Brayling to carry into effect the threats he had held out to him. Could he by any means contrive to get rid of him, or to silence him effectually, his mind would be at rest, and he felt confident that all his nefarious schemes might be accomplished without much difficulty; but when he reflected upon the utter hopelessness of his being able to do that, and the power which the Gipsey-chief held over his very existence, his uneasiness increased, and his brain was bewildered and distracted, not knowing what course to adopt.

"Now may curses light upon this misfortune," he exclaimed, passionately, as he proceeded on his way, "for, at the very moment when I had flattered myself that my triumph was certain, this last adventure baffles all my plans, and leaves me in the most torturing state of suspense as to what may be the results of what has taken place. Of one thing I am certain, namely, that Brayling is not the man to be trifled with, and should he suspect me of any treachery, he will lose no time to wreak such a vengence on my head as would annihilate me for ever. I now almost wish that I had not discovered the intentions of Constance, for then I might at any rate have been free from the fears, the anxiety, and chagrin that at present distract my mind. The proud and scornful beauty, with what feelings of disgust and loathing does she not view me; while the beggar, Evelyn Heartwell, basks in the bright sunshine of all her favours; and now that so many misfortunes and vicissitudes surround him, he is dearer to her than ever. Oh, how mortifying, how insupportable is that thought! And now that Brayling is acquainted with all my secrets, and has taken her under his protection, what have I not to dread? And shall I suffer her to escape me? By all my hopes she shall not; even though I run every risk to obtain her. Let me arouse all my energies into action, and threatening though my prospects at present appear to be, I may yet triumph."

Such were the various and conflicting thoughts that continued to torture the mind of the villain, Dalton, as he bent his way towards home; but other ideas of an equally painful and perplexing nature haunted his imagination. The fellow, Will, was once more in the power of Brayling, and deprived of his assistance, his other dark designs would be retarded, if not entirely frustrated. The nefarious plot he had had in contemplation to rob the old miser, Jasper Scrimpe, must, for the present, at any rate, be delayed, and it might be some time, if ever, ere the opportunity might again occur to him. Will, too, by threats and intimidations, might be induced to reveal everything to the Gipsey-chief, and thus add to the black list of charges which the latter had to bring against him. Filled with these too probable ideas and apprehensions, Oliver once more uttered the most fearful imprecations on the untoward events of the day ; and, in the same state of doubt and uncertainty in what way to extricate himself from the difficulties by which he now found himself surrounded, he continued on his route, making, at the same time, a powerful effort to recover his composure in some measure, before he should arrive at the Grange.

Return we now to our heroine, the nature of whose feelings on her parting with her lover, and the consequences that might follow the discovery so unfortunately made by Oliver Dalton, may be readily imagined. Her fears pictured the future in the darkest colours, and the probable fate that awaited the unfortunate Evelyn tortured her more than ever. Sampson Brayling exerted himself to the utmost to quiet her alarm ; but though she could not but acknowledge the force of his arguments, and was likewise thoroughly convinced of the integrity of his motives, he succeeded but indifferently, and she dreaded her return to the Grange, and the meeting with her uncle ; for should he have discovered her absence, which it was but too probable he had done, what could she say to quiet the suspicions that would naturally be engendered in his breast ? How sufficiently command her feelings so as not to discover all ?

These fears increased when she had parted with Brayling, who, having accompanied her in the vehicle to some distance from the old house, was compelled to return, and her agitation was but little abated, when the vehicle stopped in a remote part of the town of Hogsden, and having assisted her to alight, the gipsies left her.

The brain of Constance was so bewildered that for a few minutes she stood almost unconscious where she was. The events of the morning were of that exciting, painful, and extraordinary description, that they seemed to her more like a dream than reality. At length she timidly raised her eyes, and looked around her, and then for the first time she recollected where she was, and remembered clearly and distinctly all that had happened. She sighed and trembled, but finding that there was no one near to observe her, and knowing how useless it was any longer to delay her return home, she hastily turned away from the spot, and soon arrived in sight of the Grange. Here she again hesitated, but while she did so, her mind felt some relief when she saw the faithful Abigail issue from the house, and, when she saw her, hasten eagerly towards her.

"Oh, my dear mistress," she ejaculated, "thank Heaven you have returned in safety. I have been so anxious about you. But bless me ! how pale and agitated you look ; has anything happened to alarm you ?"

"I cannot explain here," answered her mistress, "but my uncle ?"

"Do not fear, Miss," returned Abigail, "Sir Milford left the Grange at an early hour this morning, and has not yet come back, so that your absence will be quite unknown to him. Oliver Dalton, too, has not been here, and—"

"Oh, do not name him," interrupted our heroine, with a shudder, "alas, how much have I not to fear from him ?"

"He has not been here this morning, my dear young lady ;" said her attendant, "so he also is in ignorance of—"

"Let us into the house at once," interrupted Constance, in the same agitated tones, "I have much to tell thee, Abigail."

The latter looked at her anxiously, and with no small degree of curiosity, for she could see by the paleness of her countenance and the agitation of her demeanour that something particular had happened, but without saying another word she led the way into the house, and conducted her mistress to her own apartment, where the latter, throwing herself into a chair, gave free indulgence to the feelings that had so long struggled for vent in her bosom, and burst into a copious flood of tears.

It was some time ere she could sufficiently recover herself to reply to the eager questions of Abigail, and make her acquainted with all the particulars that had taken place from the time that herself and Mabel had departed to meet Sampson Brayling, and it may well be imagined with what deep interest and mingled feelings of astonishment, commiseration, disgust, and alarm, Abigail listened to her, but when she had concluded, she tried all she could to quiet her apprehensions, and to persuade her to look forward to a more favourable issue of events than present circumstances seemed calculated to sanction.

"Dear me, Miss," said Abigail, "'tis very unfortunate, and I sincerely feel for yourself and poor Evelyn Heartwell. But by what means could Oliver Dalton have discovered your intentions?"

"I am at a loss to conjecture," replied our heroine, "but, alas! what have I not now to fear from his revengeful and malicious spirit?"

"Compose yourself, Miss," said her attendant, "and everything may turn out better than you now anticipate. To be sure it is alarming enough to know that the villain Dalton should have discovered the place where your lover is concealed, but it is one consolation to find that Sampson Brayling has him completely in his power, and that he is sincerely your friend. Believe me, my dear young lady, however strongly so disposed he may be, Oliver Dalton will not dare to do anything which may be calculated to excite the Gipsey's wrath."

"But, alas!" ejaculated Constance, with a sigh, "how greatly are the dangers that beset poor Evelyn increased; it makes me shudder, and fills my breast with the most torturing and insupportable feelings of anguish and despair when I reflect on them. It will no longer be safe for him to remain where he is; and whither can he go? where fly from the cruel destiny that pursues him? My heart sickens at the thought. Oh, there is nothing but misery and despair for me and that deeply injured youth whose happiness is ever more precious—much more precious to me than my very existence. Providence seems entirely to have deserted us, and abandoned us to our fate."

"Oh, say not so, Miss," remonstrated the compassionate Abigail, "but hope for the best."

Our heroine shook her head mournfully and despairingly, and remained for a few minutes silent, and wrapped in the solitude of her own dismal thoughts. When the conversation was renewed, Abigail again tried to comfort and reassure her, but with very little better effect, and at length Constance requested her to leave her, as she had a wish to be left alone to her own reflections for a short time. The faithful Abigail, who felt as much interest in the welfare and happiness of her mistress as if she had been her own sister, obeyed, and when she was gone, our heroine gave unrestrained indulgence to the feelings that so tumultuously laboured in her breast. Notwithstanding all that Sampson Brayling had said, and the confidence she placed in the honesty and sincerity of his intentions, she could not but entertain the greatest fears for the critical situation in which her lover was now placed; and when she reflected upon the intense agony of mind he must at the present time be enduring, her own care and anxiety was increased tenfold. She pondered deeply over every affectionate word that had escaped his lips at their recent interview—his fond and fervent vows of love and constancy—and when she thought of the little prospect there was of their hopes and wishes ever being realized, but, on the contrary, that the dark clouds of adversity were gathering still faster above their heads, threatening ere long to burst and overwhelm them, her emotions became so powerful that she could with difficulty control them within the bounds of reason. When she thought, too, of the rage and disappointment which Oliver Dalton would experience at what had taken place, and the feelings of revenge to which he would naturally be goaded, her apprehensions were strengthened, and she dreaded to meet him again, however much prudence might induce him to seek to control and conceal the passions that doubtless reigned within his guilty breast. In fact, in whatever direction she turned her thoughts, nothing but the most torturing misery appeared before her, and it required the exertion of all her energies to bear it with any degree of fortitude and resignation. She sank on her knees, and with clasped hands and upraised eyes, she earnestly supplicated the mercy and protection of the Supreme for herself and Evelyn.

She was interrupted by a gentle knock at the room door, and, with mingled feelings of fear and trembling opened it—she felt somewhat relieved when Abigail made her appearance.

"Now, now, my good Abigail," said her mistress, hastily, "what brings you here again?"

"Your uncle has returned, Miss," answered Abigail, "he is in the Grand Saloon, and desires to see you immediately."

"Ah!" ejaculated our heroine, "how my heart trembles. Is he alone?"

"I know not;" answered her attendant, "Oliver Dalton has arrived at the mansion, and—"

"Oliver Dalton!" exclaimed Constance, with increased alarm depicted in her looks.

"Yes, Miss," returned Abigail, "he has been closeted with Sir Milford for about a quarter of an hour."

"Oh, God!" cried our heroine, wringing her hands, "what then have I not to dread?"

"Be firm, my dear lady," replied Abigail, "and all may yet be well. But your uncle waits, and may become impatient. Endeavour to compose your feelings, lest the expression of them should excite Sir Milford's suspicions."

"Oh, would that I could excuse myself from meeting him at present, at any rate," said Constance, "should Oliver have disclosed to him the particulars of this eventful morning, how shall I be able to meet the torrent of my uncle's indignation?"

"Fear not, Miss," replied Abigail, "he will not dare to do that, unless he would bring the immediate vengeance of Sampson Brayling down upon his head. Come, come, courage, my dear lady, courage."

Our heroine did indeed try to tranquilize her feelings, and followed Abigail from the room, and at the door of the saloon, which was standing open, the latter, with an encouraging look, left her.

Constance made a powerful effort to acquire firmness, and to conceal the real emotions that were struggling in her breast, and partially succeeding, she entered the saloon, and she felt somewhat reassured when she found that her uncle was alone.

He was seated in a chair apparently wrapped in thought on her entrance, but he arose on hearing her light footsteps, and advancing with his accustomed tenderness towards her took her hands within his.

"My dear Constance," he observed, "I fear thou wilt think my long absence from home to-day rather strange, and in truth I did much miss thy affectionate greeting at the usual hour; for to thine uncle's heart, child, thy gentle smiles are even as welcome as the light of Heaven. But thou art pale, Constance, and look fatigued, as though thou hadst undergone some unusual mental and bodily exertion. Art thou not well, my love?"

Our heroine felt confused, and trembled, for she fancied that he looked upon her with an eye of suspicion and could almost penetrate her thoughts, but she conquered her feelings as well as she could, and, in a timid voice replied—

"In truth, my dear uncle, I am far from well, and my spirits are depressed. The excitement of the late melancholy events, and—"

"Thou must banish them from thy mind, Constance," hastily interrupted Sir

Milford, and a slight frown passed over his features, which served to increase the emotions of his fair niece, " thou must banish them from thy mind, I tell thee, and turn thy thoughts into a different and more pleasing channel. The boy, Evelyn, must no longer be permitted to occupy them. He has proved himself to be a worthless scoundrel, and it would be criminal to view him with any other feelings but those of disgust and abhorrence. The niece of Sir Milford Welborn," he added, proudly and haughtily, "would indeed degrade herself, could she possibly entertain any emotions of sympathy towards a self-convicted felon."

" Oh, my dear uncle !" sighed poor Constance, with a look of agony, and sinking into a chair, " surely this is most cruel, most uncharitable, and unworthy of you. Oh, how much you wrong the unfortunate Evelyn by these observations, and by entertaining those sentiments of prejudice against him."

" Ah !" exclaimed, the baronet, passionately, " and darest thou plead for him, girl ? Doth the guilty youth still hold the same influence over thine heart which he did when I, believing him good and virtuous, in spite of the disparity of your rank and fortune, gave encouragement to his presumptuous sentiments ?"

" He is innocent, uncle, I will swear by all my hopes of Heaven he is innocent! and therefore do his unmerited misfortunes but serve to increase, to strengthen the love I have always, and must ever, under any circumstances, bear towards him !"

" Constance !" demanded Sir Milford, hastily, and unable to conceal the indignation that swelled his breast, " knowest thou what thou sayest, or art thou mad ? Beware ! thou mayest try my patience too far. Remember the change that is about to take place in thy destiny, and prepare thyself to meet it ; for my determination is fixed, and not all that thou canst do will move me from it ; though any foolish obduracy on thy part may but serve to excite my indignation towards thee. But there is one at hand who may better be able to prevail with thee."

Our heroine heard not the latter words of her uncle, for his previous observations had so alarmed and agitated her, that she had sunk into a temporary state of torpor, but she was suddenly aroused by some one laying their hand upon her wrist, and by hearing the tones of a voice that were too well known and hateful to her, and starting as though a serpent had stung her, she beheld Oliver standing before her, with a bold and confident expression of countenance which she thought it was impossible for even him to have assumed towards her, taking all the circumstances that had recently taken place in consideration.

" Oliver Dalton !" she exclaimed, in tones that shewed at once the feelings of unbounded disgust and resentment the sight of him inspired in her bosom, " is it possible that you have the effrontery to appear before me ? Begone, sir, I dare not, will not hold any converse with you."

" Nay, beauteous Constance," exclaimed the consummate hypocrite, with an assumed look of mild reproach, " these are surely harsh and ungenerous words addressed to one who loves thee with the intensity of passion which glows within my breast, and whose sentiments are sanctioned and encouraged by thine honoured uncle ?"

" Hold, Oliver Dalton !" exclaimed our heroine, rising, and her fine features glowing with the feelings of mortified pride and resentment excited by the boldness of his words. " I know you, and will not suffer my ears to be insulted by your bold advances. I am at a loss for language sufficiently strong to express the sentiments of horror, loathing, and disgust with which you have inspired me, and—"

" How !" cried Sir Milford, passionately, and fixing upon our heroine such a look as made her tremble, while Oliver Dalton, abashed, enraged, and confused

by the firmness and fearlessness of demeanour which our heroine displayed, retired a few paces, muttering curses to himself, "this language so bold and insolent, and that, too, in my presence? Can I believe the evidence of my ears? Beware, girl, beware, girl, lest I forget the link that has hitherto so strongly bound thee to my heart, and aroused to uncontrolable wrath by thy obstinate opposition to my will, invoke the curses of Heaven upon thine head !"

"Oh, my dear uncle, recall those dreadful words !" frantically exclaimed the wretched girl, in the most piteous accents, and tears of unspeakable anguish streaming from her eyes, while, at the same time she sank upon her knees at his feet, "forbear, forbear, and have mercy on me ! I am still your own Constance, whom you have fostered with the hand of affection and benelovence from the earliest days of childhood, and who has ever looked upon you with love and reverence for it. Do not then, I implore you, thus discard me from your heart,

No. 13.

at the house; there can be no doubt as to the designs of the villain. But be firm, Constance," he added, laying his hand on his sword; "I will not yield to such a cowardly miscreant as Oliver Dalton but with my life!"

"Alas! alas!" sighed our heroine, and clinging still closer to him," how vain will be your resistance. You are ruined!"

"How useless is this waste of words and time," remarked Matthew, impatiently.

"What would you advise us to do?" interrogated Evelyn.

"Follow me," replied the old man, "and fear not."

Evelyn threw his arm around the waist of Constance, and fixing upon her a look of encouragement, they followed the old man from the room, and ascending a flight of stairs at the further extremity of the old hall, entered the gallery. The old man conducted them to a large recess in one side of the wall, in which was suspended the half decayed and grim looking portrait of a Knight in a cumbrous frame. To this Matthew applied all his strength, and to the surprise of the lovers, the picture gradually shifted aside, and revealed to them a secret room beyond, which was lighted only by one small dusty casement placed high in the wall.

"Here," said Matthew, stepping into the room, and motioning to them to follow,—"here you may remain safely concealed from discovery. Leave the rest to me, and fear not. I will return to you as soon as possible."

With these words he hastily quitted the place, and drew the portrait back in its place after him.

They looked around with curiosity and astonishment. The room was small, dark, and of the most ancient description, and contained not a single article of furniture. To what use it had formerly been appropriated they were at a loss to imagine. They had not, however, much time for observation, for they were almost immediately startled, by hearing a loud knock at the outer door.

"Ah!" exclaimed Constance, clinging still closer to her lover, and looking timidly up in his face; "they have come. Now all depends upon the firmness and fidelity of Matthew."

"Fear not, dear Constance," returned her lover; "I place every confidence in the integrity and fidelity of the old man."

They endeavoured to wait patiently the issue of this adventure, and listened with the most breathless attention to catch the least sound; but they were in too remote a part of the building to hear anything of what was passing between Matthew Smelton, and Oliver Dalton.

In the meantime, Matthew having mustered all the coolness and firmness he could, without waiting for the knock to be repeated, made his way to the hall, and having opened the door gave admittance to Oliver and his companion, Black Will. Matthew having fully prepared himself for the business, affected to behold them with no small degree of astonishment and curiosity, and inquired their business.

"This is not the place to communicate it;" replied Oliver, haughtily; "of this be assured, old man, that we must be perfectly satisfied upon the business which brings us hither, and that thou wilt act wisely to avoid all equivocation."

"Aye;" observed the ruffian, Will, coarsely; "it will not do for thee to attempt to deceive us, lest thou shouldst have ample cause to repent it."

"Indeed!" returned old Matthew, eying him with a look of the most supreme contempt and defiance. "Thou art rather bold and uncouth in thy speech, methinks, young man. Thou hast e'en forgotten to bring thy civility out with thee this morning; marry, and this is not a very gentle greeting from strangers. But, probably, gentlemen, as it might not be considered a very impertinent or

and consign me to a fate, the bare contemplation of which is even much more horrible to me than death itself."

"Obdurate girl!" returned Sir Milford, sternly, "I will not listen to thee;
my resolution is fixed, and not all thy tears or supplications, I swear, shall move
me to relent. Unless thou becomest the willing bride of the man I have selected
for thee, thou art henceforth an alien from my heart, and the love I now bear
thee will be changed to disgust and loathing;"

"Lost! lost then!" groaned the poor girl, "wretched, wretched Constance!
Oh, Heaven help me!"

Overpowered by her emotions, she sunk back in a chair, and her senses left
her.

CHAPTER XV.

The Storm.—The Man of Mystery.—The Miser.

WHEN Constance Welborn was restored to consciousness she found herself in
her own room, and Abigail in attendance upon her. She looked fearfully and
eagerly around the chamber, as though she expected to meet the angry countenance
of her uncle, as it had appeared when he gave utterance to those harsh and cruel
observations recorded in the preceding chapter; and the hated form of the guilty
Oliver then, as the painful scene she had just experienced rushed vividly upon
her recollection, she burst into tears, and sobbed as though her heart would
break.

Abigail did all that she could to comfort and console her, but for some time
her efforts were completely unavailing, and she therefore offered no further
interruption to her grief, hoping that the free indulgence of it might tend to
alleviate the bitterness of her anguish.

"Alas! alas!" sighed Constance, as the tears still chased each other down
her cheeks, "and has it indeed come to this? Can that aged relative whom I
have ever so highly honoured and revered, so close his heart against me as to
turn a deaf ear to my tears and entreaties, when I would solemnly, firmly, and
energetically protest against his sacrificing me to a man whom I must ever detest
and despise, and who I am too thoroughly convinced is not only a villain at heart,
but the miscreant who has been the author of all the misfortunes that have
befallen my poor Evelyn. Oh, what a truly wretched being am I."

"I pr'ythee calm your feelings," remarked Abigail, "and not to give way to
this intensity of anguish and despair, which will only the more unfit you to
struggle with the numerous difficulties by which you are at present surrounded.
Sir Milford will relent, depend upon it; for the love he bears you, I am convinced,
will never suffer him to compel you to become the bride of one who is so utterly
unworthy of you, and whom he knows you cannot view with any other sentiment
than that of abhorrence."

"Ah, Abigail," sighed her mistress, "in this unfortunate instance I fear that
you judge too charitably and too leniently of my uncle. He is stern and determined in anything to which he has made up his mind, and he will suffer no
opposition to his will. A strange infatuation seems in this instance
to have taken possession of him. Oliver Dalton, by his plausible manners,
and hypocritical assumption of virtues when in his presence, has succeeded in

obtaining a powerful influence over him, and, alas! I have but too much reason to fear that he will remain inexorable."

"Oh, no," returned Abigail, "knowing the kind and affectionate heart of my honoured master, I cannot believe that he will do so. Again I beg of you to remain calm and patient, and to trust to the goodness and mercy of Providence, who will not desert you on this trying occasion."

"Alas!" said our heroine, "how easy it is to advise; but when I view all the wretched circumstances of my fate, I look in vain for consolation or hope. But where are my uncle and Dalton?"

"They both left the Grange together, Miss, immediately after Sir Milford had committed you to my care, on your becoming insensible," answered her maid.

"Ah!" ejaculated Constance, with a look of alarm, "should Oliver reveal to him the events of the morning."

"Do not torture yourself, Miss," observed Abigail, "by giving encouragement to any such ideas, for depend upon it they will prove to be erroneous. Oliver Dalton's fears for his own safety, after the threats that Sampson Brayling has held out to him, and which he will be sure not to fail to carry into execution, should the former provoke him to it, will prevent his doing so. In that respect, believe me, you have nothing to fear."

Our heroine sighed but returned no answer, and after some further conversation Abigail retired from the room, and left her mistress to her own reflections, the melancholy nature of which we need not dwell upon. The day passed gloomily away, and Constance remained confined to her room, and felt some relief that her uncle did not seek to interrupt her seclusion.

In the evening of the day of which we have been writing, there were numerous guests at "The Old Tankard," and the reader may rest assured that the worthy Timothy Tapcan was amongst the number. There were also several of the principal domestics of the gentlemen bowmen who had been in attendance on their masters during the day, at the grand fête given in Smithfield, by his Grace, the Duke of Shoreditch, and, exhilerated in spirits from the excitement of the sports that had taken place on that occasion, the wine-cup and the tankard passed freely round, and racy jests were freely bandied from one to the other. Timothy Tapcan was in his best spirits, and honest old Caleb Cosey, the worthy host, was in his glory, seeing with infinite pleasure the wide-spreading fame of his comfortable hostelrie, and the extent to which it was already patronized.

But there was one among the guests whose presence was indeed extraordinary and unusual, that was the Miser's man, poor Toby Taper, whom Caleb and Timothy had luxuriated with a plentiful meal, and had so liberally plied him with the excellent beverage sold by the landlord, that it began to take a powerful effect on him, and imparted such a rubicund glow to his otherwise pale and cadaverous countenance that had been a stranger to it for many a day.

"Come, come, Toby, my corpulent friend," observed the Tinker, "drink, drink, and refresh thine inward man. They say that strong liquor is man's greatest enemy; but for my own part, I was never afraid to boldly face such a foe, and I defy any one to say that it made Timothy Tapcan sound a retreat yet. Drink, I say again, for methinks thou wilt find this much more invigorating than such beverage as thine old stingy master is in the habit of supplying thee with."

"Aye, aye," chimed in Caleb Cosey, "there's nothing like drinking. Talk about Doctors, why, I flatter myself that I am the best leach for miles around, and I never heard my patients complain of or object to my medicine yet. Come, Toby, thou must e'en repeat the dose, if thou wouldst fain restore thyself to a complete state of convalesence."

"Indeed, good Master Cosey, thou must excuse me," answered Toby, "I am but a weak vessel, and thou hast already plied me with more than I can conveniently contain. I wonder what my old master would say if he was to catch me thus indulging myself. I must begone, for the evening wears apace, and should Jasper return home before me, it would be the loss of two days' food to me at least, though thanks to thy good nature, Timothy, and to thine hospitality, Master Caleb, I am not hungry now."

"And so thy master has been absent from home since the morning, Toby?" said Timothy.

"Yes," replied Toby, "for the first time since the affair in the Lovers' Walk, and I cannot for the life of me conjecture whither he has gone. It must be something of importance that called him forth at so early an hour and has detained him during the day."

"He is a wretched, grovelling, old insect," remarked the tinker, "and I only wish I was in his service for a month, I fancy that he would find me more than a match for him."

"He might," returned Toby, "but thou wilt pardon me, my good friend, if I express my doubts upon that subject. But indeed I must be going, good evening to thee, Master Timothy, farewell, good Caleb. Dear me, what a curious swimming sensation I feel in my head, and my legs, never the strongest at any time, now totter beneath the not over ponderous weight of my body. Good evening, good evening."

And with these words Toby Taper made his exit from the spot, and Timothy and his friends resumed their bacchanalian revelry with increased gusto.

While they were still thus occupied, they were somewhat surprised and startled by the sudden appearance of a stranger amongst them, who seemed as if he had risen from the earth, for no one had observed from what direction he had come, nor had the sound of his footsteps met their ears. He seated himself unceremoniously in the midst of the guests, and drawing from his belt a brace of large pistols, placed them on the table before him.

All eyes were immediately riveted on this mysterious individual, nor did the observations they made of him serve in the least to diminish their curiosity.

He was a man of gigantic stature and muscular frame; clad in a sombre suit of grey russet, which had evidently seen much service, and from the dirt and dust that was accumulated upon it, it would appear that he had travelled far. A long black cloak depended from his shoulders, and a large slouch hat, with two or three raven's feathers, surmounted his head. He appeared to be a man between fifty or sixty years of age; his eyes were dark, restless, and penetrating; his complexion pale, and his features though stern and determined were not exactly repulsive. He gazed keenly upon every person present for an instant without saying a word, then leisurely crossing one leg over the other, he seemed resolved to rest and enjoy himself to his full bent.

"Good evening, friend," observed Caleb Cosey, being the first to speak, "welcome to "The Old Tankark" at Fynesburie, best hostelrie for miles around, although I say it that shouldn't say it. Thou'rt well armed, forsooth," he added, pointing to the formidable looking pistols.

"Aye," answered the stranger, in a careless tone, and playing with one of the pistols, "it saves a waste of time and trouble in case of need. 'Tis my usual way of introducing myself to strangers."

"And allow me to say, Master," returned Caleb, "that it is rather an eccentric and uninviting one."

"Perhaps so," said the unknown, gruffly, "but it pleases myself, and that is all I have to study. Art thou the landlord?"

"Aye, marry am I, good master," replied Caleb Cosey in a bland voice, "and at thine especial service, what shall I have the honour to bring thee?"

"A tankard of the best wine thine hostelrie can produce," said his singular guest, "and be quick, for I'm a-dry, not having slaked my thirst for full half an hour."

"What!" exclaimed Caleb, with a look of astonishment and incredulity, "a whole tankard at once? Surely I must have misunderstood thee, sir."

"No, thou didst not," returned the stranger, "a tankard of wine, I say again, and let it be brimfull, I never take less at a draught or two."

"A tankard of wine at a draught or two," said Caleb aside to Timothy, "here's a customer!"

"Be quick!" said the man, impatiently, "for my throat's parched."

"Serve you directly, sir," said Cosey, making his exit into the house. The guests continued to gaze at the mysterious stranger with looks of wonder and curiosity, but he appeared to take no notice of them, and Caleb quickly returning with the wine, the stranger raised the tankard to his lips and quaffed off one half of the contents at a draught, to the no little astonishment of the beholders. He then placed the measure on the table, smacked his lips, pronounced the wine pretty good, took another draught, and then decided that it was excellent, and paused for a minute or two to take breath.

"Aye, Master," observed Caleb, "it is indeed rare beverage, I warrant you will not find its equal in all England."

"To save trouble and waste of time," said the stranger, "thou mayest as well bring me another tankard, for I shall have disposed of the contents of this in a few minutes,"

"Another tankard, man?" repeated Caleb Cosey, with a look of increased amazement, "surely thou must make a mistake."

"Another tankard, and quick!" ordered the mysterious unknown, peremptorily.

"Dear, dear," muttered the old host, to himself, "what a man! Why he is a perfect wonder. He must be the very devil himself."

He hastened to execute the order, and, on his return, the stranger having finished the contents of the first, and had the second placed before him, said—

"Ah! now I feel somewhat better, and shall do for a short time. Forty years have somewhat changed the aspect of this neighbourhood."

"Aye, marry," replied Caleb, "forty years is a long time master, but "The Old Tankard" stands where it did then, though many of the old inhabitants have yielded to the grim tyrant, Death, in that lengthened period. Thou art then no stranger to this locality, sir?"

"No," answered his guest, "every inch of the ground it covers is known to me. I am deeply, closely associated with it by the most important circumstances."

"You have travelled far apparently, Master?" remarked the landlord, inquisitively.

"True," answered the stranger, after he had taken another hearty drink, "I have but just returned from the world's end."

"In sober truth!" said Caleb, "that is indeed a marvellously long journey, and thou must feel fatigued."

"Ah! but I have been much farther than that!"

"Further than the world's end," said Caleb Cosey, aside, "he must be the very devil himself then, that's certain."

"Psha!" replied Timothy, "thou dost not understand him, he must mean the land's end, in Cornwall."

"Does thine house afford every accommodation?" enquired the stranger.

"Excellent accommodation for man and beast," replied Cosey.

"'Tis well," observed the former, "then I shall probably remain thy guest for a day or two."

"Thou wilt do me honour, good sir," said Caleb.

"Bah!" abruptly returned the unknown, "no flattery, 'tis unpalatable to me. I shall require supper."

"Certainly, sir, with pleasure, what wouldst thou that I should prepare for thee? There is nothing but what my house affords."

"Fish, flesh, and foul, and of that a goodly supply, for my appetite is rather keen."

"I will attend to thy wishes, sir."

"Above all," observed the singular guest, "I must have a brace of capons."

"A brace, sir?"

"Yes," answered the unknown, "or if thou dost cook me three it does not matter, I am not particular to number. Now, shew me to a room, and see that thou dost not annoy me by any impertinent questions."

"This way, if you please, sir," said Caleb, and the stranger, without deigning to notice the rest of the company, who stood by in amazement, rose from his seat, and followed the host of "The Old Tankard" into the house.

Having exchanged a few observations with each other on the singularity of this adventure, the guests slowly departed, and Timothy Tapcan was left alone, but Caleb soon returned from the house, and joined his company.

"Well, Timothy," said Caleb, "what think'st thou of the stranger? Is he not a most extraordinary being?"

"He is," answered the tinker, "and I cannot make him out at all."

"Two tankards of my very best wine," observed Caleb, "and despatched in less time than thou and I could dispose of the contents of a flask. And then the enormous supper he has ordered, why, it is enough to feast half a dozen moderate eaters for a couple of days. He certainly cannot be a human being."

"Why, to tell the truth, Master Caleb," observed Timothy, "I was looking for his cloven foot, but if even thou hast got the devil himself for a guest, I cannot but congratulate thee on having a good customer."

A gathering storm had been threatening for some time, and a loud peal of thunder that seemed to shake the vaulted roof of Heaven, prevented Caleb from making any immediate reply to the observations that had fallen from Timothy.

"His Satanic Majesty generally visits the earth in thunder and lightning, I believe," said Timothy, "so I wish thee much joy of thy guest, Master Caleb. As for myself, I must begone, for I have much more agreeable society waiting for me. I have an appointment with my darling little Abigail this evening, and I would not keep her waiting for all the world. Good night, Cosey, and above all, I would advise thee on no account to offend the gentleman—*from below!*"

Thus saying, with a significant wink, Timothy Tapcan hastened on his way.

"Egad!" said the worthy host, when he was gone, "I am half inclined to think that there is something reasonable in the hints that Timothy has thrown out, and I had much rather that this mysterious stranger had chosen any other hostelrie than mine. But, psha! what a stupid, superstitious old fellow I am. I have got a customer that does not grudge to spend his money liberally, and I ought to be thankful for it. But I must in, and see to his accommodation, or he will become impatient."

Having thus reconciled himself, Caleb entered the house, and to which he was further urged by the loud voice of the stranger calling upon him to attend.

The storm now commenced with much violence, loud roared the thunder, vivid flashed the lightning, fast fell the sheeted rain, and the angry wind howled in fearful gusts around, and in that terrible moment of the elemental strife, the wretched miser, Jasper Scrimpe, arrived at the spot, and hurried for shelter beneath the door-way of the old tavern His features were, if possible, more than usually haggard, and there was an expression in his eyes which shewed that there were thoughts of a torturing nature passing in his mind.

"Confusion light upon this storm," he muttered to himself, in surly tones, "it might have suffered me to reach home before it commenced. It is impossible for me to proceed till it has abated, and now must I seek shelter here, and expose myself to the idle curiosity of those with whom I never care to come in contact. However, it shall not put me to any expence, I am determined. No, no, they shall not get a single farthing out of me for the temporary accommodation."

A ghastly smile of satisfaction passed over the old man's features as this thought occurred to him, and he stood in the door-way and reflected for a minute or two.

" This has been a busy and important day with me," he said at length, "and I have arranged everything with Miles Scrapewell, the old usurer, to my satisfaction. At any rate, I have made the bulk of my property secure, and my mind on that point is at rest; rest!"—he repeated with a shudder, and his countenance appearing more ghastly in the lurid glare of the lightning, "no—no—no!— What hope of rest is there for a wretch like me? My soul shrinks and trembles with fear when I think of the threats of Sampson Brayling. And that paper too;—what were its contents? Fool that I was to be intimidated into signing it! My heart is sad, and my brain distracted. Oh, how the observations of the Gipsey-Chief penetrated my guilty soul! and the overwhelming power of conscience and remorse absorbed all my faculties. Oh, how terrible is the retributive punishment which sooner or later pursues the poor guilty wretch! When will this torment cease? Never, never, never! My doom is sealed. Jasper Scrimpe, thou art accursed of Heaven and man! But away with thought, and let me seek the shelter of the house!" The miser hastily entered the tavern as he gave utterance to these words, and seeing no one about, he made his way along the passage, and entered the first room that presented itself to him. This happened to be the very one in which the mysterious stranger was seated, and he arose abruptly on the entrance of Jasper, annoyed at the intrusion.

At that moment the light from the lamp which was burning upon the table, streamed full upon both their faces, and their eyes met, while the powerful emotions of mingled surprise, terror, and malice that was visible in their features, was of the most extraordinary description.

" Powers of mercy," almost shrieked the miser, starting back a few paces, and trembling in every limb, " what fearful vision is this? Doth the grave thus, after the lapse of so many years, yield up its ghastly tenant to blast and appal mine eyes? or do my distracted senses deceive me? Those well known features that I hoped never more to gaze upon! that too well remembered form! Oh, horror, horror! avaunt, accursed fiend! Begone! nor let me longer sicken and tremble at thy fearful presence! Oh, God!"

With a deep groan of the most indescribable anguish, and covering his face with his hands, the wretched miser rushed precipitately from the room, and left the stranger standing and gazing eargerly after him.

" Can I believe the evidence of my eyes?" he exclaimed, " or is it only some empty delusion got up to mock me? No—no—I could not be deceived! and his words and the agitation which convulsed his frame, convince me that I am not. 'Tis—'tis the bloodstained, guilty miscreant, Gerald Aubrey! to discover whom I have been in search for so many years. Stay, stay, old man, fortune has at last favoured my wishes;—we meet again, and by the infernal host I swear that thou shalt not this time escape me!

He was hastily rushing in pursuit of Jasper, when Caleb entered the room and obstructed him.

" For mercy's sake," said Cosey, " what is the meaning of all this? Old Jasper Scrimpe has left the house like a flash of lightning, and in such a state of alarm and agitation as I have seldom witnessed."

"Ah!" cried the stranger; "he is the wretch I seek, and he must not, shall not be suffered to elude me. Which way did he take? Where does he reside? Quick, quick—on thy life!"

"Bless me!" ejaculated the astonished Caleb; "thou art as much agitated as he was. Well, well, his residence is in Shoreditch; any person will point out to thee the miserable hovel of old Jasper Scrimpe, the miser. But thou surely wilt not venture forth in such a storm as this?"

"Bah!" exclaimed his guest, impatiently, "I heed not the tempest when business of such importance calls me. Detain me not; anon I will return and amply satisfy thee for any trouble to which I may put thee. Here, if thou doubtest me, take this purse as some security for the fulfilment of my promise."

Thus saying, the unknown threw him a well filled purse, and hastily quitted the house.

"Well," observed Caleb, when he was gone, and weighing the purse in his hand, "this is one of the most extraordinary adventures that ever I met with, and I marvel what will be the result of it. Now should I like to know what there is between the old miser and this mysterious stranger. It must be something very particular to excite them both in the manner they were. I wonder if he will return, according to his promise. If he does not, I shall lose a good customer. At any rate he has left me most munificent payment for what he has had, and I have hardly the conscience to take it. No matter, I suppose that I must e'en endeavour to reconcile it to my feelings under the trying circumstances."

With these words the worthy host put the purse in his pocket and walked from the room.

CHAPTER XVI.

A Thrilling Scene.—The Black Deeds of the Past.

The storm still raged with unabated violence, and the streets were almost deserted, for it was not the season for anyone to be abroad who could help it. But, totally regardless of the pelting rain or roaring thunder, the stranger hurried on his way in pursuit of the miser, and just as the latter, trembling with fear, and not venturing to look around him, had reached his own door, the unknown caught sight of him. With an exclamation of satisfaction he bounded across the road, and seizing the old man by the arm, in a voice of exultation he cried :—

"Ah, Gerald Aubrey, I have then overtaken thee. In vain thou seekest to avoid me!"

"Release me, and begone!" exclaimed Jasper, in a hoarse voice, and fixing upon the stranger a look of terror; "let go thine hold, I say—thy touch appals me!"

"Nay, nay," returned the unknown, "indeed we part not so readily. Thou and I have a long account to settle, Gerald Aubrey; for years have I been anxiously looking for this moment—but it has come at last, and I do not part from thee until I have had that ample explanation (satisfaction I can never receive) as I have a right to demand."

"Lost, lost!" groaned the Miser; "Oh, who could have foreseen this? Fearful man, for the present leave me, and I will meet thee on a future occasion, when I shall be better prepared to—"

"Now, now!" interrupted the stranger, hastily, "my impatience will admit of no delay. In with thee, and do not keep me thus standing in the rain, which is by no means calculated to cool my angry feelings, I can assure thee!"

"Oh, God!" exclaimed the wretched old man, striking his forehead, "what will become of me? I am ruined!

With a trembling hand he knocked at the door, which was shortly opened by Toby, and who started back with amazement and some alarm on beholding the stranger. His master snatched the lamp from his hand, and rushed hastily past him, followed closely by his mysterious companion, and having ascended the stairs, entered the room where he usually sat, and, overpowered by the agitation of his feelings, he sank in a chair, and covered his face with his hands.

The unknown gazed around at the miserable room in which he found himself, with feelings of astonishment and disgust.

As for the wretched old Jasper, he quailed beneath the penetrating and

No. 14.

malignant glance which his unwelcome visitor fixed upon him, and trembled in every limb. A pause of some minutes ensued, during which interval the expression of the features of the miser fully evinced the intense agony of mind he was enduring. The stranger folded his arms across his chest, and still continued to fix his earnest gaze upon him, while a grim smile of exultation and contempt passed over his countenance and added to the anguish and terror of the old man. The tempest, too, still raged with increased violence without; peal after peal of thunder rapidly succeeded each other, shaking the dilapidated building to the very foundation; and the vivid lightning glared in at the broken casements, rendering the wretchedness of the place the more apparent.

"So, old man," at length said the stranger, in a tone of irony, "thou hast contrived all these years to cheat the hangman of his due and to escape the gallows; how much longer thinkst thou to be able to elude the punishment thy crimes so justly merit!"

Jasper groaned, and a shuddering sensation came over him which he could not conquer or control.

"Spare me, fearful man!" he at last faltered out, "thy words shock me; and as I gaze upon those well-known features which I had hoped never to behold again, fear palsies my limbs. Oh, I am indeed severely punished. Conscience, conscience!"

"Aye," said his companion, hastily, and grasping his arm, "it should rack thy guilty soul to madness. Art thou not a villain of the blackest dye, and thinkst thou that the blood shall cry to Heaven in vain for vengeance on thine hoary head? Well mayest thou tremble at the sight of me, the living witness of thine hideous crime, and who, now that I have, after the lapse of so many years, again encountered thee, can at any moment consign thee to ignominy and shame. What has thine ill-gotten wealth brought thee? Misery, penury, and the tortures of perdition! Nay, 'tis useless to attempt to deny it, old man; thy trembling limbs, thy wild and restless eyes, and the wretchedness by which thou art surrounded, prove the truth of my words, and afford me some gratification. 'Tis fit that a miscreant like thee, so deeply steeped in crime, should suffer all the earthly torments that can be inflicted on thee."

"The fates conspire against me," said the miser, aside, "was it not enough that Sampson Brayling should have discovered me, and hold me in his power and at his mercy, but that now this additional witness of my guilt should cross my path? Godfrey Malvern," he added, aloud, "I acknowledge thy power, and tremble at thy presence; but I am a miserable old man, and implore thee to forbearance. Would that I could recall the fearful past, or blot it from the tablet of my memory."

"No, no, no!" returned his unwelcome visitor, hastily, "that can never be; the guilty past must ever be present to thy disordered imagination, and harrow up thy soul to madness. Miscreant! and darest thou still to live as a curse and disgrace to humanity? Darest thou to walk abroad in the light of day, with all this heavy weight of crime upon thy conscience? Are not the ghastly features of thy murdered victims ever present before thine eyes, miserable old man, as they appeared in their dying agonies? Hark, how the loud voice of the thunder reverberates throughout thy crazy dwelling; see how the vivid lightning flashes around. Wretch, canst thou remain unmoved in this hour of horror? Dost thou not hear the curses of the dead in the voice of the tempest? Seest thou not the wrath of Heaven in the elemental strife? Hark! that dismal shriek! that—"

"Hold! hold! Godfrey Malvern, I implore thee;" exclaimed the Miser in a hoarse voice; and his cadaverous and unnatural features appearing perfectly frightful in the glare of the lightning; "thou torturest me!"

"I torture thee!" repeated Malvern, with a look of exultation, and again grasping the arm of the wretched old man with fierce violence; "ha! ha! ha! I torture thee!—Oh, how it glads my very soul to hear that. I would rack thy brain to madness;—penetrate the innermost core of thy black and flinty heart; heap accumulated horrors upon thy hoary head, and freeze the blood in thy veins to ice. And I will do so before I leave thee!"

"Horror! horror!" groaned Scrimpe; "I am ruined!—What cursed fate hath caused thee again to cross my path? Thou whom I had hoped never more to behold!"

"Aye, no doubt thou thought'st that thy base designs had succeeded, villain!" replied Godfrey; "and that I was long since dead, but thou seest that I still live to haunt thee to destruction; I, the only witness of thy fiendish crime. For years I have been searching for thee in vain, but now I have found thee I will not fail to take every advantage of it to gratify my revenge, for the many years of misery thou hast caused me. I will constantly blast thee with my presence, old man, and be thy curse, thy terror, making thine hours doubly wretched to thee, and at any moment consigning thee to that fate—the murderer's doom—which sooner or later most assuredly awaits thee!—I—"

"Forbear, forbear those terrible threats," interrupted Jasper; "spare me,—have mercy I entreat,—I do repent me the injustice I have done thee, and would make thee amends—I have the means, Godfrey, thou knowest I have the means!"

"Aye, thou hast the means, miserable, guilty wretch," returned Malvern, with a fearful expression of countenance; "true, thou hast the means, but how acquired? And thinkest thou that I, even guilty as I am, would agree to accept the wages of blood? Darest thou to sue to me for mercy and forbearance, who have such ample cause to view thee with the most deadly feelings of hatred and revenge? Oh, I will yet see thee crouch and tremble at my feet, and as I view thy agonies of fear and remorse, I will laugh aloud in the exultation of my feelings, and mock at thy sufferings."

"Fearful man, begone!" exclaimed the Miser; "I will not listen to thee,—I fear to gaze upon thee."

"And well thou mayest," replied Godfrey, "for thou hast ample cause, and that thou knowest full well. More than a quarter of a century has elapsed since last we met; but no doubt the sight of me recals all thy fearful crimes in vivid colours to thy memory, if indeed thy conscience has for a time been permitted to sleep. On such a night as this, dark, wild, and tempestuous it was, that my eyes beheld thee commit that frightful crime, which—"

"Hush! hush, for mercy's sake!" interrupted Jasper, in accents of increased terror, and looking wildly around the dreary room, as though he fancied and expected to behold some frightful object, "repeat not the dreadful tale I conjure thee. Oh, I am indeed a poor guilty wretch, Heaven help me—Heaven help me?"

And, as he thus gave utterance to the poignant and overwhelming anguish of his feeling, he sunk back in his chair, and covered his face with his hands, fearing to meet the malicious gaze of that man whom he had hoped was long since numbered with the dead, and whom he had so much reason to dread. Godfrey folded his arms across his chest, and contemplated him for a few minutes in silence, and with a mingled expression of triumph, scorn, and hatred. The fury of the fierce tempest was now at its full pitch, and everything was in strict accordance with the nature of the scene and the torrent of passions that raged in the guilty breast of the miser. How the angry elements battled with each other! and unfortunate indeed were those human beings who were exposed to the terrors of such a night.

"So, then, thy guilty conscience does at length smite thee, Gerald Aubrey," said

Godfrey Malvern, at last, "and thy base soul shrinks appalled at the recollection of thy crimes. 'Tis well, 'tis well it should inflict upon thee all the tortures of perdition, and affords me the utmost gratification to witness."

"Forbear! forbear!" again gasped forth Jasper Scrimpe with a convulsive shudder; and looking with a mixture of fear and supplication in the face of his mysterious companion.

"No, thou shalt hear all I have to say, though the tale of blood I have to repeat to thee should strike thee dead," replied Malvern, sternly and determinedly. "Shall I first remind thee of the amiable qualities of thine unfortunate brother-in-law, the husband of thine only sister, the fair lady Agnes? Well did I know his virtues, for I was his domestic, but heaven pardon me, I repaid the favours he so bounteously bestowed upon me with the basest ingratitude."

"Ah!" ejaculated the Miser; "thou art compelled to acknowledge that, and yet thou wouldst fain endeavour to make it appear—"

"Hear me out," commanded Godfrey, in peremptory tones, "for I am determined not to be interrupted. Canst thou deny the truth of the character I have given of thine unfortunate victim? When by a course of the most reckless dissipation, thou hadst squandered the whole of thine own fortune, and reduced thyself to a state of the most absolute poverty; did he not generously pardon thine errors, though he must have known full well that thou hadst ever viewed him with an eye of jealousy and hatred; receive thee into his home as one of his own family, and lavish upon thee riches, luxuries, and all the kindness and affection of a brother! And what was the base return thou didst make for such unexampled benevolence? Didst thou not covet his wealth, and was determined not to shrink from anything, however appalling the deed, to obtain possession of it?"

"Alas! alas!" groaned Jasper, striking his forehead in agony, "'tis too true, I dare not, cannot deny it, miserable wretch that I am; but oh, how bitterly, how sincerely do I now repent it!"

"Repent!" repeated Godfrey; "of what avail is thy repentance now, heartless miscreant as thou art? Can it recall to life those innocent beings who perished by thy accursed hands? Thinkest thou that it will save thee from that just though terrible retribution which sooner or later must overtake thee, and to which it is in my power this very moment to consign thee?"

"Oh, cease! cease!—thy words are as daggers to my heart!'

"They should be as hungry vultures preying upon thy vitals and driving thee to frenzy," returned Malvern, "but the fearful tale is not yet half told, and thou must hear it all. The wealth thou didst covet thou wert determined should be thine with as little delay as possible. Business called thy unfortunate victim from home; he never returned, and all were lost in mystery and consternation to know what had become of him; and who was there that affected so much anxiety as thyself, Gerald Aubrey? Knowest thou the fate of Sir William Milton? Methinks thou shouldst be able to answer that question."

"Spare me, Godfrey Malvern, shrieked Jasper, in a voice of the most uncontrollable anguish; "spare me, and leave me! I do acknowledge my guilt, monster as I am, Heaven, Heaven have mercy on me!" And with clasped hands he sunk upon his knees, and looked the very image of despair and agony.

"Hold, villain!" exclaimed Godfrey sternly; "add not blasphemy to thine other manifold crimes, by daring to appeal for mercy to that Power thou hast so frightfully outraged? Art thou not afraid that the ghastly spirits of the dead should instantly rise before thy terrified eyes, and thunder their curses in thine ears?"

"Oh, horror! horror!" groaned the Miser, glaring wildly round the room, and then again covering his face with his hands, to shut out from his gaze the ghastly forms which the words of Malvern conjured up to his affrighted and tortured imagination.

" Yes," resumed Godfrey, who evidently exulted in the terrors he was inflicting upon the unhappy old man : " e'en such a night as this it was that witnessed the perpetration of thy diabolical crime. Dost thou not remember it, Gerald Aubrey? Methinks it should be imprinted on thy conscience in characters of fire. My poor master was returning to his home, unattended, and in a lonely and un-frequented spot near his residence, thou with another miscreant, in thy pay, were lurking in the darkness of the night, and amidst the furious raging of the tempest to execute thy murderous, thine inhuman purpose. Unconscious of the fate that threatened him, and that from the hand of his own kinsman, Sir William advanced on his way, when thou and thy guilty myrmidon rushed upon him, and plunged thy daggers in his breast ! It was at that fearful moment accident led me to the spot, and my appalled eyes witnessed the foul murder."

" 'Too true, too true," gasped forth Jasper, " oh, it was a fiendish deed ! Why did not Heaven's avenging wrath crush me on the spot ? But why shouldst thou, Godfrey Malvern, now so bitterly reproach me, since thou didst accept my gold to keep secret the terrible crime thou hadst witnessed ?"

" Ah !" exclaimed Godfrey, " and darest thou remind me of that revolting fact ? Beware, beware! 'Tis true, that by threats and the temptation of money thou didst extort an oath of secrecy from me, and what was the manner in which thou didst afterwards reward me ? By thine orders I was forcibly seized at midnight and borne on board a vessel, which conveyed me to a distant country, where I was put on shore on a desolate island and abandoned to my fate. The various vicissitudes and horrors I had to encounter I have not time now to describe. No doubt thou thoughtst that thy villainous ends were accomplished, thy fearful secret safe, and that thou wouldst never behold me again. To thy horror and confusion thou now seest that thou didst deceive thyself, and that, after the lapse of so many years I return to crush thee at any moment I please. Oh, villain, dost thou not even now recall to thy memory the dying looks of thine ill-fated victim, as he sunk bleeding on the earth, the awful glare of the lightning revealing the piteous, the agonising, the ghastly expression of his features more distinctly ; dost thou not fancy thou hearest the last fearful groan which escaped from his breast, while the deafening voice of the thunder pealed a terrific response, and Heaven seemed to hurl its heaviest curses at the head of the murderer ? Canst thou—"

" Silence ! silence, on thy very life !" cried the distracted old man, every muscle of his face frightfully convulsed with the indiscribable anguish of his feelings, " I can hear no more !—horror palsies my very soul !—my brain's on fire !—the tortures of the damned are raging at my heart !—and see !—powers of mercy !—he stands before me !—his hollow eyes are fixed upon me !—and now he points to his gaping wounds !—they bleed afresh !—ah ! horror !—he approaches me nearer !—off ! off, grim phantom !—I cannot bear thine icy touch ! —save me !—save me !—save me !"

Staggering back, the wretched man, with a shriek that reverberated through the house, staggered back a few paces, and sunk insensible on the floor.

For a few moments Godfrey Malvern stood and gazed at the prostrate form of the Miser with mingled looks of malice and exultation, and did not offer to render him any assistance.

" Poor wretch," he at last ejaculated, in tones of contempt, disgust, and abhorrence, " at length thou art reduced to a state of the most abject remorse and degredation. My words have wrung thy guilty soul, and the moment which I have been panting for for so many years has arrived at last. But after the years of turmoil and trouble that I have undergone, sojourning in foreign lands, and experiencing all the perils and dangers of the rover's life, on the broad waters of the ocean, little did I expect that the darling object of my wishes would ever be accomplished. 'Tis well, 'tis well; I will not fail to make good use of the discovery I have made, and of the means afforded me of gratifying my revenge. Oh, how will I torture this hoary miscreant, my heart exults at the thought."

As he thus soliloquised, the most deadly feelings of malice and triumph took possession of the breast of Godfrey Malvern, and imparted their expression to his features. Again he paused for a minute or two, and gazed upon the insensible form of the miser with looks that fully shewed the extent to which he was prepared to carry his intentions into effect.

"Why, what a monstrous libel upon the name of man is this poor guilty creature," he again said, in accents of mingled pity and irony. "Has not his ill-gotten money proved to him a curse, a hourly source of fear, suspicion, and maddening self-reproach? And so it ought: aye, his careworn, haggard features, his wasted form, and the misery and poverty by which he is surrounded, even in the midst of wealth, convince me that his punishment has been severe, though justly merited. Oh, what feelings of satisfaction does this sight excite in my breast. Godfrey Malvern, thy hour of triumph has at last arrived!"

He was interrupted by hearing footsteps ascending the stairs that led to the room, and soon afterwards the door was slowly opened, and Toby Taper, with an anxious countenance, peeped in, but started back in consternation and amazement on beholding the tall figure, and rather repulsive features of the stranger, and the prostrate form of his wretched master on the floor. Godfrey, however, advanced hastily towards him, and grasping him by the collar, hurled him abruptly and unceremoniously into the room; poor Toby sinking on his knees in a state of the greatest alarm, at the same time looking up in the stranger's face with an expression of fear and trembling.

"Who art thou?" Godfrey, sternly demanded

"I—I—I—sir?" stammered out Toby, "I—I—I'm nobody, sir—that is I'm only the butler, cook, nurse, and maid of all work to Master Jasper Scrimpe. Don't hurt me, I beg of thee, for my bones are so marrowless and brittle that they will snap with the slightest touch."

"Humph!" ejaculated Godfrey, with a sarcastic smile, "so, thou art the Miser's man, art thou? Thou livest with him?"

"Live with him!" repeated Toby, with a woe-begone look, "oh, I only wish I did. You would not see me as I am now, so thin and transparent that any one might see to read a letter through my body. No, sir, I starve with him."

"Poor devil!" returned Malvern, "I pity thee, for well do I know the wretched life thou must lead, and the sorry fare thou obtainest from such a master. Here is money for thee, get thee food, and see that this sordid and pernicious old wretch does not share it with thee."

Toby started to his feet with an extraordinary agility that he was not accustomed to display, and stared at his unknown benefactor with amazement and incredulity.

"What!" he cried, turning the cash in his hand, and gloating his eyes upon it, "money! and from a stranger? Oh, sir, I thank thee a thousand times, for thou hast raised such bright visions of food before the eyes of poor Toby Taper as he never experienced before. Oh, won't I have a sumptuous banquet at the very earliest opportunity, when I can give the hungry rats the slip, who would otherwise devour me, victuals and all. Thank thee, good stranger, thank thee."

"Enough of this," replied Godfrey, "I require not thy thanks for such a trifling service as this. See to thy master."

"Dear me," said Toby, "why the old gentleman looks so bad that I am afraid he is dying, and what a terrible loss that would be to me, and to society at large. Whatever is the matter with him?"

"He is the victim of his own guilty conscience, and 'tis meet that he should suffer."

"Thou knowest him then, sir?" said Toby.

"Aye," answered Godfrey, "for a villain of the blackest dye; for a miscreant, who had he had his desserts would have been brought to condign punishment on the gallows years ago."

"Dear me," observed Toby, "how highly flattered my master would feel himself if he only heard the compliment thou hast just now passed upon him, good sir. But I ask pardon, sir, who may you be?"

"One whom he has cause to dread, and who has this night heard a tale of crime and bloodshed from my lips which has harrowed up his feelings. But I must begone."

"What in this storm, sir, and without a word at parting with my master?"

"Oh, I heed not the storm," replied Malvern, "see to old Scrimpe, as he calls himself, and tell him to console himself with the assurance that I will see to his security, and that he shall again behold me anon."

With these words Godfrey Malvern abruptly quitted the room, and left Toby Taper wrapped in amazement.

"Dear me," he said, "here's an adventure; here's another mystery. Who can this stranger be? I'm lost in amazement. But this money he has given me. Oh, what a treasure it is. How shall I expend it? I will never cease eating while it lasts. But how shall I find the opportunity to do it without the knowledge of old Scrimpe? I've a good mind to hasten to "The Old Tankard," and enjoy myself while he remains in this state of insensibility. But no, he would murder me should he recover and find that I was absent; and then this storm rages so violently. Oh, how my mouth waters for the delicious fare that is in store for me. But, hush!—see—the old man revives."

Toby stepped silently aside and watched. The Miser opened his eyes, and raising himself partially on his hands, stared vacantly around the room. The lightning at that moment flashed full upon his face, and startled and appalled him.

"He is not here!" he ejaculated, in a hollow, tremulous voice, "and yet methought but now he stood before me with his malicious looks, recapitulating in words of fire my deeds of blood and horror, and thundering his curses in my ears, his terrible threats of vengeance. But no, it must have been a dream. He is not here now. Oh, if it should have been reality! My blood freezes at the thought. Ah! the truth flashes upon my distracted brain! I was not deceived! I have not been labouring under any wild delusion of my disordered imagination. He has been here; he, the terrible witness of my deed of blood, and whom I had thought was long since mouldering in the grave; and I am ruined! Wretched Jasper Scrimpe, thy career of guilt is nearly run; the crisis of thy fate is approaching. But—but where is he now?" he added, rising to his feet, and gazing eagerly around the apartment. "Ah! thou here, varlet? Hast thou been listening?"

"No, good master," answered Toby, "I have merely been looking after thy welfare, as I always do."

"Hast seen any one? Speak!" demanded the miser, hastily.

"Yes," said Toby, "there was a stranger here, when I first entered the room, and, after passing many handsome and flattering encomiums on thy character—which thy natural modesty would make thee blush to hear if I were to repeat them—he desired me to present his compliments to thee, and to inform thee that he would do himself the honour to wait upon thee again anon."

"Oh, may curses light upon him!" cried the Miser, bitterly, and striking his forehead with his clenched fist, "what fresh feelings of dread and horror has this unexpected meeting with that man, after the expiration of so many years, rekindled in my breast."

"My dear Master," observed the Miser's man, with mock solicitude, "I hope the gentleman has not said anything to wound thy feelings."

"Begone, impertinent knave!" commanded Jasper, sternly. "And mark me, dare but to utter a syllable of what thou mayest have overheard to anyone and thou shalt dearly repent it."

"Yes, dear, kind master," replied Toby, "I will not fail to obey thee," and he retired from the room.

Jasper Scrimpe cast one hurried glance around the room, having locked himself in, and uttering a deep groan of mental agony, he threw himself into a chair, and abandoned himself to his own torturing reflections.

CHAPTER XVII.

A Scene of Excitement.—Destruction of the House of the Miser by Fire.—The Mysterious Disappearance of Jasper.

THE terrors of the night had not at all abated, but, on the contrary, the raging of the tempest seemed to increase in violence every moment. The rain continued to descend in overwhelming torrents; the deafening peals of thunder and the fearful blazing of the lightning, were repeated at shorter intervals, while the wind howled in hollow gusts around, making doors creak on their hinges, and casements rattle in their frames. There were several persons assembled in "The Old Tankard," seeking shelter from the storm, and amongst the rest was our old friend Timothy Tapcan, who had returned from the visit he had been paying, in the early part of the evening to Abigail Allspice, at the Old Grange; and was taking a liberal supply of the worthy host's excellent beverage, in order to drown the effects of the inclemency of the weather.

"Marry!" ejaculated Timothy, "but this is indeed a fearful night; and a man need put plenty of spirits down to keep his spirits up, and in order in some measure to enable him to counteract the effects of the spirits of the storm."

"True, Timothy," coincided Caleb Cosey, "and I say now, as I have ever said, and will always maintain it, there is nothing like drinking, especially for a man placed under such trying circumstances. But I cannot help thinking of that mysterious stranger who honoured me with his patronage this evening; and of the old Miser, who evinced such terror on accidently encountering him, and fled as though he had seen a spectre, followed by my guest, who, I am sorry to say has not returned yet. It was evident to me that they knew each other, and that Jasper Scrimpe was not altogether gratified at the meeting. Hadst thou but seen his countenance of horror, Timothy, and the precipitation with which he fled, thou wouldst never have forgotten him."

"Ah!" said Timothy, "take my word for it, Master Cosey, there is some fearful secret connected with the old miser, which time will bring to light. He never came by all his money honestly; and I am much mistaken if he has not something on his conscience which I would not have for all the gold in the universe."

"No, nor indeed would I, Timothy," returned Caleb. "But didst thou ever meet with such an extraordinary character as my mysterious guest?"

"No, in truth did I not," replied the Tinker, and I should very much like to know something more about him; for he seems to be a man after my own heart, although he is so mysterious in his ways, and no doubt would make a very agreeable companion, when one might become better acquainted with him."

"No doubt of it," said the host, "and, so far as his eating and drinking qualities go, I fancy that there are few, if any, who could surpass him. Only to think now of two tankards of my best wine to himself, and then the meal he afterwards ate was tremendous."

"Aye," observed Timothy, "he was a wonderful man in that way. But I am thinking that we shall not see him again."

"Then, as I said before," returned Caleb, "I shall be extremely sorry for that, for I shall lose an excellent customer. However, whether he returns or not, he has left me a sum sufficient to pay for a week instead of a single evening."

Timothy Tapcan was prevented from making any reply to his companions by
No. 15.

terrific flashes of forked lightning that seemed to threaten universal destruction, and were followed by fearful claps of thunder louder than any yet heard, and which shook the earth to its very centre. To this succeeded a dead silence even more awful than the voice of the tempest in its utmost wrath, and a darkness so intense that it was impossible for the eye to penetrate to any distance. Caleb Cosey and his guests looked at each other with fear and trembling, and neither of them for a few minutes ventured to utter a syllable.

"Dear me," observed Caleb, at length, "that was really very awful. Now I am not at all timid, but I am sadly afraid the storm of this night will be attended with some alarming results. Providence protect us!"

"Aye, so say I, Master Cosey," replied the Tinker, "I am not a man of very serious notions, but methinks that such a night as this is enough to bring any one to their sober senses."

"True," coincided the landlord, who, in spite of himself could not forbear a joke on the occasion, "and I presume, Master Tapcan, that it is thy sober senses that prevents thee from taking thy usual quantity this evening."

They were now startled by a broad glare of lurid light which shot up into the heavens, and illumined all around, making everything appear as clear and distinct as in the day, and presenting a marked and strange contrast to the impenetrable darkness which had before prevailed. The reflection spread, and and it was evident that a terrific conflagration had broken out in some part of the neighbourhood. Dense columns of smoke, and masses of sparks rose to the clouds, and the continued raging of the tempest increased the frightful character of the scene. The guests looked at each other with expressions of surprise and consternation, and for a short time not an observation escaped from either of their lips.

"A fierce fire is evidently raging close at hand," remarked one of them; "Heaven preserve those poor unfortunate creatures who are exposed to its terrors!"

"Ah!" ejaculated the worthy host, "it is as I feared it would be. The lightning has probably struck some old building, and how many hapless beings may now be exposed to a terrible and untimely fate?"

"Very true, Master Cosey," returned the Tinker, "and the flames lead me to imagine that the fire is somewhere in the direction of Shoreditch.—It is a fearful sight."

The reflection every moment became stronger, and it was evident that the conflagration was now at its height, and it appeared that it would be almost impossible to stop its progress until it had done most extensive and fearful damage.

While Caleb and his guests were conversing and deliberating on this exciting subject, an old frequenter of the tavern rushed into the room in a state of breathless excitement, and to the numerous anxious enquiries which were hastily put to him, he said :—

"Oh, my friends, such a shocking calamity; the lightning has struck the old Miser's dwelling, which is burning fiercely; the flames have communicated with some of the adjoining buildings, and God only knows where the fire will end!"

"Ah!" exclaimed two or three of the guests in a breath, "the house of old Jasper Scrimpe! 'tis a judgment on him."

"I must see the result of this," observed Caleb, "come, Timothy, come, my friends."

The whole of the persons assembled rushed eagerly from the house, and hurriedly made their way in the direction of Shoreditch, to which place crowds of persons were running from every quarter, and nothing could surpass the scene of excitement and confusion that prevailed. Having arrived at the spot, the scene which presented itself to the dense masses of persons congregated together, was one of the most frightful description. The wretched hovel of Jasper Scrimpe was burning from the basement story to the roof, and the flames had extended to two or three other houses, threatening their inevitable destruction, while the heat was so intense that every attempt to save them was frustrated, and it seemed utterly impossible to approach them for some distance.

How the burning timbers hissed and crackled, the flames ascending to the sky, followed by clouds of smoke, which seemed to be carried by the wind, (which was bellowing fiercely at the time,) for miles around ; while the mingled shouts of the vast multitude ; the shrieks of the women and children, and the pushing, driving, and hurrying of the crowd, added, if possible, to the horrors of the scene.

The spectators looked on with mingled feelings of awe, curiosity, and breathless anxiety. The inhabitants of the different houses in the immediate vicinity were in a state of the greatest consternation, rushing wildly from their dwellings with such articles of their property as, in their hurry, confusion, and alarm, they could think of preserving ; while others had rushed to the different casements, or on to the roofs of their houses, and wringing their hands, and rushing madly to and fro, rent the air with their piteous cries for assistance.

But the eyes of the principal portion of the crowd were fixed on the house of the Miser with the greatest anxiety. The flames had made their way to the roof, they completely enveloped every part of the building, and, as neither he or his man had yet been seen, it was feared that they had both ere now perished. Suddenly, however, the wretched old man appeared at one of the casements, with frantic gestures, surrounded by the destructive element, wringing his hands and shrieking aloud for help. Everyone gazed on appalled, but to render him any assistance seemed impossible, in his dreadful and critical situation. The next moment poor Toby Taper rushed through the flames into the street, and was immediately surrounded, and conveyed to a place of safety.

With more rapid strides the fiery element worked its destructive ravages ; fiercer and fiercer became the devouring flames, immolating all and every one in their progress, and still did the wretched Miser remain in the same awful situation, not one of the paralyzed mob venturing to attempt to rescue him.

Among the numerous persons congregated together on this most exciting occasion, was one, who with folded arms, and contracted brows, stood and gazed on the appalling scene with mingled feelings of rage, fear, and satisfaction. That one was Oliver Dalton ! At the first appearance of the fire he had hurried from the Old Grange to the spot, and when he discovered that it was the dwelling of Jasper Scrimpe that was being destroyed, his excitement became intense.

" Curses light on this catastrophe !" he muttered to himself, " the burglary I had planned, and determined to accomplish, is frustrated, and the Miser's gold will escape my clutches. Still," he added, " 'tis one consolation to know that Jasper will perish in the flames, and thus will be destroyed one of the principal evidences of the innocence of Evelyn Heartwell and my own guilt."

Suddenly the tall figure of a man was seen elbowing and pushing his way through the crowd towards the Miser's house. He was followed by several others, evidently bent on the same purpose as himself. The people made way for himself and his companions, thinking that they must be rash and fool-hardy fellows to run such a risk as that they seemed to contemplate ; but Caleb Cosey and Timothy Tapcan caught a distinct view of his features as he passed them, and they instantly recognised him to be the mysterious stranger, or, as the readers now know him to be, Godfrey Malvern.

Through the flames, and amidst the burning timbers and falling ruins, Godfrey and his companions fearlessly rushed, and the spectators held their breath in terrible anxiety, and anticipated the result with the most fearful impatience and suspense.   The next moment Godfrey, with two of his daring companions appeared amidst the flames, at the casement where the Miser was standing, and seizing the unfortunate old man, dragged him from the spot. Another minute and the roof of the building fell in with a terrific crash, carrying with it all beneath in one heterogeneous mass. A black cloud of smoke, mingled with sparks, arose from the ruins, and a simultaneous cry of horror escaped from the vast crowd, thinking that all must have perished.

A death-like silence ensued, and the spectators stared at each other aghast, scarcely knowing what to think. It was indeed a painful moment of excitement, and the persons assembled held their breath. But they were not long kept in suspense, for, to their utter astonishment and almost incredulity, when the smoke had in some degree dispersed, the stranger and his companions were seen forcing their way through the ruins, and supporting the fainting form of the exhausted Miser. A part of the mob tried to enclose them; but the stranger and his companions cleared their way, dealing out heavy blows from their cudgels right and left; and when the smoke had in some measure dispersed, they were gone, no one knew how or whither.

CHAPTER XVIII.

The Mystery Thickens.—The Designs of Oliver Dalton.—Escape of Black Will, and his Arrival at the Grange.

For a few minutes the extraordinary circumstance just recorded, seemed to completely paralyze the faculties of the persons assembled, and they gazed at each other with looks of astonishment. But no one was more surprised and bewildered than Oliver Dalton, and he was at a perfect loss to conjecture who the strangers could be, or whither they had so suddenly disappeared with the Miser. He was half inclined to believe that it was Sampson Brayling and some of the Gipsey tribe; but he could not get near enough to recognise them, and he was therefore left in the same state of doubt and uncertainty. Pondering these things in his mind, he left the spot, and slowly bent his way to the Grange.

The sensation caused by the event we have just related, had its due effect upon the crowd, and it was some time before it abated. Nothing now remained of the Miser's house but a heap of smoking and burning ruins; and while the spectators could not but be surprised and feel admiration at the bold and reckless conduct of the men who had, at the imminent peril of their lives, rescued the old Miser from his dreadful situation, when his destruction seemed inevitable, they were lost in mystery as to who they were or whither they had conveyed him. The fire continued to rage with much violence for some time, but at length the by-standers, so long inactive, having exerted themselves to extinguish it, succeeded; it was subdued, and in a short time all fears of its proceeding further were at an end, and nothing now remained of the late fearful scene but a heap of smouldering ruins. The principal portion of the crowd then gradually dispersed, and betook themselves to their homes, and only a few idle gossips remained behind to discuss the stirring events of the night, but above all, the miraculous preservation of Jasper Scrimpe from the very jaws of death, and his no less extraordinary and mysterious disappearance, in the custody of his deliverers.

Caleb Cosey and Timothy Tapcan returned to "The Old Tankard," to refresh their inward man with a cup or two before they separated for the night, and to talk over the remarkable events that had taken place. In fact, they were completely lost in amazement, and there was subject sufficient for them to discuss for a month to come.

"Well," observed Caleb, "I'm quite astounded. This mysterious stranger, as I have said before, must be the very devil himself, and, taking everything into consideration, I am not at all sorry that he has not returned. I do not think I will venture to make use of a coin of the money he has left behind him."

"Oh, well if that's thy determination, Master Cosey," said Timothy, drily ; "thou mayest as well give it to me, for I am not at all superstitious."

"Humph !" ejaculated Caleb ; "I do not think that would be altogether wise on my part either. So, I will e'en take time to consider of it. Seriously speaking, however, Timothy, there is really something very extraordinary about the character and behaviour of that mysterious unknown. He must be perfectly fire-proof, that's certain ; see how he braved the flames, like a salamander; and then, when the old house had fallen, a heap of blazing ruins, did he not, with his companions appear again unhurt, and leading forth the Miser in safety?"

"True," replied the Tinker; "but what was even more wonderful than all, was his sudden disappearance with his companions and old Jasper Scrimpe, notwithstanding the immense crowd that hemmed them in on all sides. Oh, I'm completely bewildered, and that's all about it."

"And so am I," said Cosey; "well the Miser has gone, and it's a chance he has fallen into such hands, if we ever behold him again. But I wonder if his money is gone too."

"Ah !" observed Timothy, "that's a very important fact to ascertain, and no doubt will excite the utmost curiosity. The ruins must undergo a strict search when they have cooled down after the fire. But it is getting late,—give me another jug of the best, Caleb, for these exciting events have upset my nerves, and the heat of the fire has made me thirsty. Another jug, and then I must depart, for the storm has abated, and I may reach home with a dry skin."

"Aye, aye, Master Timothy," replied Caleb; "nothing like drinking; 'tis the universal remedy for all diseases. It's a pleasure to be thy doctor, Timothy, for thou art such an excellent patient."

"Well, well, a truce with thy praises, old Grog-blossom, and attend to my order," returned the Tinker. Caleb obeyed, and quickly returned with the liquor, which Timothy having as quickly despatched, he bade the worthy host good night, and retired. The other guests gradually departed for their homes also, and the old Tankard was quickly hushed in silence.

The ruins continued to smoke and to smoulder the whole of the following day, and crowds of persons thronged to the spot, to discuss the whole of the startling events of the awful night of the conflagration, and in which, unfortunately, there had been a great sacrifice of human life. But the principal topic of the conversation was the marvellous escape of the Miser, and his no less mysterious disappearance, in company with the unknown, and various were the conjectures that were formed upon the subject. Neither he nor the stranger had been seen or heard of from that hour, and Toby Taper, who had been kindly received at the Grange, by Sir Milford Welborn, could afford but little information that was calculated to unravel the mystery, any more than the visit of the stranger to his master, on the evening of the fire; but, of what took place at that interview, he acknowledged himself to be in the most profound state of ignorance.

When it could be done without any particular danger, a number of men, under the superintendence of Sir Thomas Overton, the Magistrate, and Sir Milford Welborn, were set to work to clear away the ruins of the late residence of Jasper Scrimpe, and a vast concourse of persons were attracted to the spot out of curiosity to watch the proceedings. For some time nothing particular was discovered, but at length the labourers came upon an iron-box, well secured, and, from its weight, apparently heavily laden. That was taken charge of by Sir Thomas, and no further discovery of any importance was made among the ruins.

Among the numerous persons assembled on the occasion just mentioned, there was not a more anxious spectator than Oliver Dalton. He watched the progress of the workmen with a greedy eye, and when the chest was discovered, which he had no doubt contained a large portion of the Miser's wealth, a feeling of rage filled his breast which he could not control. He turned away from the spot, and wandering on, he scarcely knew wither, gave free indulgence to the guilty thoughts that raged within his breast.

"Fool that I was,"—he soliloquised,—"fool that I was to delay the execution of my designs against old Jasper Scrimpe so long ; had I not done so, this treasure discovered in the ruins might have been now in my possession, and I could have set the world at defiance, for I should have been independent, and might have purchased the silence of my enemies. But now my plans are frustrated, and I am in the power of Sampson Brayling—completely at his mercy, and he can denounce me to the world in my real character, at any moment he thinks proper, and bring me to ignominy and destruction. Torturing thought ! it drives me to madness as it rises to my fevered brain, and I could curse myself a thousand times for my weak wavering of purpose and the procrastination of my designs. Oh, where is now that devilish cunning and promptitude of action for which I have hitherto prided myself? I have become a mere tyro in artifice and villany. Brayling has sworn that I shall never become the husband of Constance Welborn, and I have too much reason to know that he is not the sort of man to break his word. I am surrounded by difficulties; on every side insurmountable obstacles to the accomplishment of my wishes present themselves ; and I find I am now, at the eleventh hour, entangled in a maze from which I know not how to extricate myself. But, " he added, after a brief pause," let me arouse myself from this lethargy, let me exert all my energies, and gloomy and disheartening though my prospects at present appear to be, I may yet triumph. Shall I suffer the fellow, Sampson Brayling, to hold me in this state of bondage, and to continue to intimidate me, and coerce my ambitious hopes and designs by his threats? Never ! from this moment, I swear to—"

"Nay, thou mayest e'en spare thyself the trouble of an oath, which, if thou studiest thine own safety, thou wilt be compelled to break," said a voice immediately in his ear, and turning hastily round, his surprise, confusion, and discomfiture may be readily imagined, when he discovered Sampson Brayling standing at his elbow.

"Sampson Brayling !" he ejaculated, in a tremulous voice, "hast thou then been listening to me ?"

"Aye," answered the Gipsey, "and the rage and disappointment of thy feelings afford me much gratification."

"And darest thou venture here, in the broad light of day ?" demanded Oliver, with as much firmness as he could assume.

"Dare I !" replied Brayling, with a look of scorn, "what is there that I dare not do, when my motives are just and honest? I dare even accompany thee to the Grange, to pay my respects to Sir Milford Welborn. Doubtless I should receive a hearty welcome, especially for the valuable information it is, as thou knowest, in my power to give him."

"Taunting devil!" exclaimed Oliver, passionately, "what wouldst thou with me more ?"

"Nothing in particular," replied Sampson, coolly, "it was accident that brought me hither; but, since we have met, I would merely remind thee of thine oath, and inform thee that though thou mayest see me not, I do not fail to keep a strict watch upon thine actions. So thou wouldst fain have secured the Miser's treasure ? 'Twas rather covetous of thee truly, and 'tis most unfortunate for thee that this fire has occurred to disappoint thee."

"Leave me," said Oliver, "thy words torture me."

"Well," returned the Gipsey, "I will e'en comply with thy wishes, as I do not covet thy society, having business to attend to. Good day, Master Oliver, and, however painful it may be to thee, I would again advise thee to adhere thy oath, if thou wouldst avert still more unpleasant consequences."

With these words, the Gipsey-chief abruptly quitted the spot, fixing a malicious, ironical, and triumphant look upon Oliver Dalton.

"The villain," he exclaimed, when he was gone, "he knows the power he holds over me, and does not fail to take every advantage of it. With what mingled feelings of fear and rage did his words fill my breast. Would that I could contrive some means to rid myself of him, I might then set every obstacle at defiance, and triumph in all my wishes. I must be firm, and endeavour to accomplish so important a design. Let me but get possession of the hand and fortune of Constance Welborn, and I will boldly risk whatever may follow."

Having come to this determination, Oliver Dalton composed his feelings as well as he could, and slowly made his way to the Grange.

Since the painful interview with her uncle, which has been recorded in a previous chapter, Constance had kept herself secluded as strictly as possible in her own chamber, where she brooded over the melancholy circumstances by which her fate was surrounded, and gloomily anticipated what the future was likely to produce. But, direct her thoughts whichever way she would, she could find nothing that was at all calculated to inspire the least ray of hope in her breast. The stern observations of her uncle convinced her that he would remain unmoved by her tears and supplications, and that, if she remained firmly resolved to oppose his wishes, and reject the hand of Oliver Dalton, he would discard her from his breast, and that she would be cast a poor wretched and friendless being upon the wide world. The thought was dreadful: still was she determined to brave anything, terrible however it might be, rather than submit to a fate so degrading and revolting as a union with that man whom she viewed with so much horror and abhorrence, would be. Sir Milford had not ordered her into his presence since the day of her last interview with him, a circumstance which afforded her much consolation, for she dreaded to meet him, and much more did she fear to encounter Oliver Dalton. But how terrible was the care and anxiety that constantly tortured her mind for the safety of Evelyn, and when she pictured to her disordered and distracted imagination the mental sufferings he must be enduring, notwithstanding all that Sampson Brayling had said, and the confidence which she placed in the sincerity of his friendship, she could not believe that Evelyn could remain safely concealed any longer in the old house at Finchley, and driven forth a wanderer upon the earth, without friends, and unjustly pursued by the myrmidons of the law, what was to become of him? The thought agonised her brain, and made her even more wretched than before. She recalled to her memory every fond word her lover had uttered at their last meeting, and her dreams flowed fast at the melancholy recollection.

"Dear Evelyn," she ejaculated; "under any trial, however severe, that may befal thee, thine heart I am convinced will remain faithful to me. Oh, what a melancholy feeling of consolation does that assurance afford me. And knowing this, is there any danger that I can hesitate to encounter for his sake? No; I should loathe and despise myself if I thought there was. The vows I have so solemnly plighted to thee, dearest Evelyn, I will keep sacred, even by so doing I incur the heaviest wrath of my uncle, and am banished from every happiness, but the certainty of possessing thy love, Evelyn, that the world can bestow."

Inspired with these feelings of affectionate resolution, Constance became more calm and resigned, and endeavoured to await the issue of events with patience and fortitude.

Three days had now elapsed since the fire in Shoreditch, and the mysterious disappearance of the Miser, and the excitement which that extraordinary event had created in the neighbourhood had but little abated. No tidings had yet been heard of Jasper Scrimpe, or the unknown individual who had rescued him from the flames; nor could the slightest probable conjecture be formed as to who the latter was. Poor Toby Taper continued at the Grange, and was an object of much kindly sympathy. He had good reason to feel satisfied with the extraordinary and unexpected change that had taken place, and the poor fellow knew not how to express his gratitude as his feelings prompted. For the first time in his life he knew what it was to enjoy the happiness of a full belly, having a regular and plentiful supply of good and wholesome food, and he thanked his lucky stars which had wrought such a fortunate change in his circumstances.

It was on the evening of the fourth day after the occurrence of the events recorded in the previous pages, Sir Milford Welborn being absent from home, that Oliver Dalton was seated in one of the lower apartments of the Grange, deeply immersed in gloomy thought, when a domestic appeared and informed him that a strange man was waiting in the hall who desired to see him.

"A stranger," said Oliver, aside, "who can it be? However," he added, aloud, and addressing himself to the domestic, "admit him to my presence."

The servant bowed and made his exit, and in a few minutes he returned, ushering in a man of tall figure, and uncouth appearance. Oliver motioned the domestic to retire, and he obeyed, and then turning to his visitor, he demanded:

"Now stranger, who art thou, and what seek'st thou of me?"

"Dost thou not know me, Master Oliver?' said the man, removing the slouch hat from his head which had previously partially concealed his features. Dalton started back with amazement.

"Ah!" he exclaimed, "Will! is it possible thou hast escaped from the clutches of Sampson Brayling?"

"It is true," answered Will, "and I presume it affords thee as much gratification to know it as it does myself?"

"By all my hopes," ejaculated Oliver, "this is most fortunate. Thou art heartily welcome, Will, I much need thine assistance. But tell me, how didst thou contrive to escape from the old house?"

"First let me have some refreshment," said the ruffian, "for I have had such sorry fare for the last week or so, that I am as hungry as a hunter and as dry as a parched pea."

"Well, well," returned Oliver, "I will quickly supply thy wants; but dispatch thy meal with all the expedition thou canst, for I am all impatience to hear the particulars thou hast to communicate to me."

He now rang the bell, and the servant having attended the summons, he ordered him to bring wine and other refreshments. These were promptly supplied and the ruffian voraciously partook of them, Oliver waiting impatiently until he had finished his meal, certain as he was that not till then could he hope to have his curiosity gratified.

"Ah!" said the fellow, smacking his lips, when he had finished, "that was very good, and indeed I stood much in need of it, after the scanty allowance I

have had for some days past at that old house. I never enjoyed anything more in my life. Egad, if this is a sample of the larder kept at the old Grange, I have not the least objection to take up my quarters here altogether."

"Psha!" exclaimed Oliver, impatiently; "this is only idle talk. Now Will, how is it that I see thee here; and how didst thou effect thine escape?—"

"Why,—" returned Will; "the first question is speedily answered. When I found myself again at liberty, I thought the best place I could come to was here;— for I felt certain that thou wouldst be right glad to see me, Master Oliver."

"True;" coincided the latter; "how didst thou know that I also had escaped from the power of Sampson Brayling?—"

"Of course I had no meens of ascertaining that fact;" replied Will; "but I felt confident that Brayling, under all the circumstances, would not venture to detain thee. As for myself, I had made up my mind that I was no better then a dead

No. 16.

man, or, at any rate, that I should never more be suffered to go at large."

"Well, well;" said Dalton, impatiently;—"but proceed to the particulars."

"All in good time, Master;" returned his companion;—"I was thrust into a room in the lone house on the Common. which from its dismal and wretched appearance had evidently formerly been used as a place of confinement for some unfortunate wretch;—and there, after being favoured by a visit from Brayling, during which he heaped the most bitter invectives on my head, and threatened me with his vengence, which I treated with the most stolid indifference, he left me, for the first day in the charge of two of the gipsey tribe, and, as I was led to suppose, quitted the house. Thou mayest be sure, Master Oliver, that I did not much approve of my situation, and many were the curses I invoked upon the defeat we had experienced in our designs. However, I determined to make up my mind to the worst."

"Quick, quick;" said Dalton, "thou art becoming tidious."

"Nay, I must proceed in my own way," answered Will; "and if thou dost thus interrupt me, it will only retard the gratification of thy curiosity. I was supplied with the most scanty fare, and thus two or three days passed away, and I was left in a state of doubt and uncertainty as to the ultimate fate that was in store for me. But at length the Gipseys left the house, and the old man, Matthew Smelton became my only jailor. It was then, for the first time, that the, prospect of escape presented itself to my imagination, He used to visit me twice a day to bring me food, and the better to deceive him, I uttered not a word of complaint, but appeared to submit to my fate with patience and resignation.—Last night he entered the place in which I was confined as usual, and, after a few trifling observations, he was again about to return. His back was turned towards me, when immediately the idea struck me, the opportunity I had been so anxiously looking forward to, now presented itself, and I resolved to avail myself of it. I rushed upon him, and stretching him senseless on the floor, I hastily departed from the room, and made my way from the house, meeting with no obstruction. I did not stop until I had got far away from the neighbourhood, though I had no cause to fear any pursuit, and by a circuitous route I reached town in safety, and thou seest have ventured hither."

"Ah;—" ejaculated Oliver, "thine escape is most fortunate; for I much needed thine aid and advice in the dilemma in which I find myself at present placed. But say, didst thou not see anything of Evelyn Heartwell during the time of thy imprisonment.?"

"No;" answered Will; "though, from the observations that fell from old Smelton, I have reason to believe that he is still in the house."

"Curses light upon him;" said Oliver, "and shall he still be suffered to escape me?"

"It will be thine own fault if he is," answered Will.

"But while he remaines under the protection of Sampson Brayling, is there not everything to fear; Besides, he has me in his power, and has threatened to denounce me and bring me to destruction if I dare to break the oath which he extorted from me before he consented to release me."

"Ah!" demanded Will, "how was that?"

"Listen;" replied Oliver Dalton; and he then related to his ruffianly companion such particulars of the interview that had taken place with himself and Sampson Brayling, on the day when he had attempted to surprise the lovers, with which the reader has been already made acquainted.

"Humph!" muttered Will; "this is rather awkward to be sure;—but I fancy that Oliver Dalton, has not now much more respect for an oath, than he formerly had; or that he is thus going to suffer himself to be so easily intimidated."

"What is to be done?" demanded Oliver "Should I break my oath, Sampson Brayling, thou well knowest, is not the sort of man to fail to carry his threats into execution."

"But, dost thou not see it is to be done without thou compromising thyself in the least?"

'How so?" interrogated Dalton, hastily.

"I have escaped from him;" replied Will;—" and he may rest assured that I shall stand upon no such delicate points. What if I denounce him and his companions, and make known the place where Evelyn Heartwell is concealed?—Brayling and the rest of the tribe may be surprised in their present retreat, and Evelyn secured, the gipsies will be punished as accessorys in his escape from prison, and for having aided him in eluding the hands of justice. Thou then wilt at once rid thyself of all those whom thou hast cause to dread."

"Ah;" ejaculated Oliver; "it would be well indeed if I could do so. But would not Brayling then, goaded on by revenge, be sure to reveal all he knows of me?—And he can, thou knowest, bring forward such facts and witnesses in corroboration of his assertion, that cou'd scarcely fail to condemn me."

"Psha;" exclaimed the fellow, Will; "why shouldst thou hesitate?—Hadst thou not better brave everything rather then be kept in this state of doubt and suspense?;"

"True;" coincided Dalton, after a brief pause;— "and one of his principle witnesses has disappeared in a most mysterious manner."

"Ah!" said Will, eagerly;—"who is that?"

"The old miser, Jasper Scrimpe!"

"Jasper Scrimpe!—is it possible?"

"Tis true;" answered Oliver;— and, he then related to Will the particulars of the awful conflagration in Shoreditch, and the rescue of the Miser from the flames by the unknown, and their subsequent sudden, and extraordinary disappearance; to which account, Black Will listened with the greatest attention and curiosity.

"What thou hast just now related surprises me, Dalton;" he observed;— "tis true that, for the present, thou hast got rid of one whose evidence had he been so disposed, might have proved dangerous to thee, but his gold has escaped our clutches.

"Aye;" said Oliver, passionately;— "curses light upon it. Had we acted with more promptitude in our designs it might have been ours."

"True but tis useless to regret it now. What of the fair Constance?"

"She contrived to return to the Grange before me, on the day of her meeting with Evelyn at the old house on the borders of the Common;" answered Oliver, "and her uncle having left home early in the morning, and therefore knows nothing of her absence, She still treats me with even increased scorn and abhorrence."

"Nevertheless thou wilt not be weak enough to suffer that to divert thee from thy purpose?"

"No;" returned Dalton, determinedly;— "I will hazard anything rather then do so, especially, as her uncle remains inexorable, and even threatened her with his heaviest maledictions if she continues obstinately to oppose his will. Could I rid myself of Brayling before the day fixed for the union, I might entertain the most sanguine hopes in spite of all the obstacles that now present themselves, to finally triumph in my designs."

"That thou mayest do;" remarked Will;—"if thou wilt only follow my advice."

"And what dost thou propose?"

"That I should be admitted to an audience with Sir Milford Welborn;" replied Will;—"when I can reveal to him all the particulars relating to Sampson Brayling, and the place where Evelyn Heartwell is concealed,—and, if thou art over scrupulous upon that point, it will at lease save thy conscience the accusation of having directly broken thine oath with the Gipsey—chief."

"But will not prevent him from seeking revenge against me;"—added Oliver.

"That thou must take the chance of;" remarked Will; "dost thou agree to follow my advice?"

"I do; and there must be no delay in the business; for, as soon as Sampson

Brayling is made acquainted with thy escape, he will be on his guard, and it will probably precipitate his designs against me."

"That must be prevented, at all hazard ; " said Will ; "so, the sooner I see Sir Milford the better."

"He is at present from home. ; " replied Oliver ;— "but doubtless he will soon return. In the mean time, thou hadst better remain here, for it might be dangerous for thee to venture abroad until we have arranged some plan for thy security."

Will was about to return some reply, when a servant entered the room and inform- ed Oliver that Sir Milford Welborn had just returned, and desired to see him in the library.

"Ah !" exclaimed Dalton ; "tis well ;—tell Sir Milford that I will attend him immediately. "

The servant bowed and departed, and Oliver turning to his companion, said. '

"Remain thou here till I send for thee. I will prepare the baronet for the inter- view. But above all, be cautious how thou managest the business with him. "

"Aye; " replied Will ; " leave that to me, and thou shalt have no cause to com- plain. "

Oliver then retired from the room, and made his way to Sir Milford, whom he found awaiting for him in the library.

"So, my dear Sir ; " remarked Dalton, "thou hast returned, and I am glad of it, for I have business with thee. "

"Indeed ? " said the baronet ; "and pray, my young friend, what may that be ? "

"One of the gipsies, belonging to the tribe of which Sampson Brayling is the chief, — replied Oliver ; " having escaped from‘ his companions made his way hither, having, as he said, some important intelligence to communicate to thee."

"Indeed ?" said Sir Milford ; "and is he at present in the house. ? "

"He is ; " answered Oliver ; " and awaits thy permission for an interview."

"Let him be immediately ushered into my presence. Remain thou here, Oliver ; doubtless he has nothing to communicate but what it may be of equal interest for thee to hear. "

A domestic was now summoned and desired to conduct the stranger to the room, and soon afterwards the ruffian Will made his appearance, and bowed obsequiously to the Baronet and Oliver Dalton.

"So, thou art one of the former comrades of Sampson Brayling, the gipsey ? " said the Baronet.

'True, Sir Milford ; " replied Will ; " and having treated me most scurvily, I am determined to have revenge. Thou wilt not need to be informed that to him Eve- lyn Heartwell, who is accused of the robbery and attempted murder of the Miser, Jasper Scrimpe was indebted for his escape from prison. "

"Right ; " coincided Sir Milford ;— " but he and his companions have hitherto eluded the vigilance of those who have been in search of them. Knowest thou where he may be found ? "

"Sampson Brayling and the rest of the tribe,—" answered Will,— " are at pre- sent encamped in the Wilderness near the old Roman Road,—but Evelyn Heartwell,"

"Ah ! " interrupted the baronet,—eagerly !— " what of him ?— It is desirable, if possible, that the ends of justice should not be frustrated by his being suffered to escape, for I believe him to be guilty of all with which he is charged. Hast thou any idea of the place where he is at present concealed ? "

"Yes, Sir Milford ; " answered the villain Will ;—"Evelyn Heartwell ever since his rescue from confinement by Sampson Brayling and the other gipsies has been concealed in an ancient house on the borders of Finchley Common.

"Ah ! " exclaimed Sir Milford,— " hearest thou that Oliver ?—"

"I do, Sir Milford ; " replied the crafty Oliver ;—"but still as I bear no feelings of revenge against him, and in the misery and degradation to which he is now reduced, he must be amply punished, I would much rather that he should not be again apprehended. "

" How ! " ejaculated Sir Milford, with a look of astonishment ; " thou viewest the offences of Evelyn Heartwell much too lightly, methinks, Oliver. Has he not dared to endeavour to fix the foul stigma on thee, and loaded thee with every opprobrious epithet that his malice could dictate ? Besides, while he remains at liberty and Constance is led to suppose him innocent, she will still cherish the fatal passion she now entertains towards him ; to treat thee with scorn and abhorrence, and offer every obstinate resistance to my will ;— but let his guilt once be confirmed, and my word for it he will no longer hold a place in her affections, and she will learn to view thee with that feeling of esteem which, must shortly ripen into love. Evelyn Heartwell, I say again, must no longer be suffered to escape."

"'I will be guided in everything by thy superiour wisdom, Sir Milford ; " observed Dalton, with affected reluctance and submission.

" 'Tis well ; " said the baronet ; then I must decide quickly what is best to done. I thank thee, my good man," he added, turning to Will ; " I thank thee for the valuable and important information thou hast furnished me with. What dost thou suggest shall be done in this business ?—"

"Thou dost me an undeserved honour, Sir Milford, by deferring to my advice ;" answered Will, bowing ;—" it is neassary then, that Brayling and his companions should be surprised, with as little delay as possible, by sufficient numbers in the Wilderness, and no doubt that they will be easily defeated ; at the same time, if officers are despatched to the old house at Finchley, Evelyn Heartwell may be apprehended without much difficulty."

" Good ; " said Sir Milford ; " those suggestions are worthy of every attention. I will immediately to Sir Thomas Overton, and consult with him upon the subject. Remain thou at the Grange, my friend, and Oliver Dalton will see that thou has every thing thou mayest require. Oliver, thou mayest expect me to return in about an hour."

Oliver bowed, and Sir Milford hastly departed from the house.

" By my hopes thou hast managed—this business very cleverly Will ; " remarked Oliver, when the baronet was gone ; " every thing promises as well as I could wish, and I triumph."

" Aye ; " said Will, "I think I may e'en take some credit to myself for having so completely deceived the old gentleman, and at the same time saved thee the embarrassment of appearing to take any immediate interest in the business. I shall expect to be well paid for the trouble I have taken."

" Oh fear not," returned Oliver ; " Sir Milford himself will doubtless handsomely reward thee, and thou mayest rest assured that I shall not forget the obligations I am under to thee."

" Enough ; " observed Will ; " I am satisfied ;—at any rate I shall have my revenge against Sampson Brayling for the trick he played me. In a few hours, and everything is executed with promptitude and ability, both he and Evelyn Heartwell will be in custody, and that, at any rate, will afford me every satisfaction. There must, however, be no more delay than is unavoidable, for, as soon as Brayling shall have discovered my escape, he will be sure to use every precaution to guard against the consequences he may expect to follow."

" True ; " said Oliver ; " but still I cannot help entertaining every dread of Brayling ;— will he not to gratify his feelings of vengeance against me, and to exonerate Evelyn Heartwell, denounce me ?—and, if he possesses the strong proof he boasts of, how can I hope to escape the consequences ? "

" Psha ! " ejaculated his companion, impatiently,— " thou dost alarm thyself without a cause. Sampson Brayling might happen to fall in the engagement which will probably take place beteen the officers and the Gipsies,—for they are sure to offer a desperate resistance; and, should he do so, thou wilt at once be rid of thy greatest enemy, and may then set detection at defiance."

Oliver returned no answer to this, but he appeared anything but satisfied, and they continued to discuss the subject till the return of Sir Milford, who informed them that he had consulted with Sir Thomas Overton, and that gentleman was of opinion that, as it required some mature consideration, it would be better to defer coming to final arrangements till the following day.

"Pardon me, Sir Milford," observed Will, "but that is the very latest moment that the business should be delayed, for should Sampson Brayling discover my flight, he will be on the alert, and both himself and Evelyn Heart-well may contrive to escape."

"Every vigilance shall be used, thou mayest depend upon it," replied the baronet; "in the meantime, as it might not be safe for thee to appear abroad under present circumstances, thou hadst better remain here. If I find that thou hast spoken the truth, fear not but thou shalt be rewarded to thine heart's content."

"I thank thee, Sir Milford," said the Gipsey, "thou wilt find that I have not attempted to deceive thee, and I am willing to abide by the consequences."

"Enough," said Sir Milford, "then thou wilt hold thyself in readiness for to-morrow. Oliver, I place our friend here in thy charge, and see that he lacks not every comfort."

"Thy wishes shall be attended to, sir," answered Dalton; and, motioning to Will, they retired from the room together, and left the baronet to himself.

CHAPTER XX.

The Flight of Evelyn Heartwell.—The Anguish of Constance.—The Scene of Excitement in the Gipsey Encampment.

Our heroine was seated in her own room as usual, immersed in the melancholy thoughts that constantly engrossed her mind, when she was aroused by a hasty tap at the door, and Abigail Allspice entered the apartment, the expression of her features shewing that she had something important to communicate.

"Oh, my dear young lady," she said, "I have such a surprise for you; and I am afraid the news I have to bring you may not be very agreeable."

"Ah!" ejaculated her mistress, starting; "for Heaven's sake what has happened now, Abigail?"

"Nay, Miss," returned Abigail, "I pray you do not alarm yourself; though the circumstance is certainly very suspicious."

"What circumstance?" demanded Constance, hastily, "explain yourself, and do not keep me in suspense."

"Well then, Miss," said her attendant, "Geoffry tells me that an hour or two ago he opened the door to as ruffianly a looking fellow as ever he clapped eyes on, and in whom he immediately recognized one of the gipsies. He requested to see Oliver Dalton, and remained closeted with him till Sir Milford returned home, when he was ushered into his presence. Shortly afterwards the baronet abruptly left the Grange in a state of great excitement, and has only just come back; but I understand that the man is to remain in the house till to-morrow. Is it not strange, my lady?"

"Good God!" exclaimed our heroine, with an agitated look, "some fresh danger surely threatens either to poor Evelyn or myself."

"Ah!" returned Abigail, "I am indeed afraid so; but will you pardon me, Miss, what I am going to tell you? When I heard that this strange visitor was closeted with Sir Milford and Oliver Dalton, I could not resist the curiosity I felt to endeavour to ascertain what they were talking about. So, I silently crept to the door of the library, and applying my ear to the key-hole, I listened with breathless attention. But I could only catch a word here and there, when they raised their voices rather high, but they were sufficient to excite my worst suspicions."

"Ah! and what did you hear, Abigail?" interrogated her mistress, eagerly.

"Why, I heard the names of Evelyn Heartwell and Sampson Brayling frequently mentioned in menacing tones. And more than once they talked about the Wilderness, and the old house at Finchley."

"Alas, then," cried Constance, "it is too evident the place where Evelyn is concealed is betrayed to my uncle, and he is lost!"

"Oh, no, Miss," said Abigail, "that must not be, if it is possible to avoid it. Do not agitate yourself. Brayling must be informed without delay of what has happened and the danger which threatens, and probably there may yet be time to frustrate any designs that may be in contemplation."

"Oh, how can Brayling be apprized of it?" demanded her mistress.

"Why, Miss," answered her faithful attendant, "I have been thinking that the best plan would be for me to endeavour to see my dear Timothy Tapcan immediately, and despatch him with a message to Sampson Brayling at the Wilderness."

"Ah!" exclaimed Constance, eagerly, "could that indeed be done, good Abigail, without exciting the suspicion of my uncle, the Gipsey-chief would be forewarned of the danger that threatens, and the unfortunate Evelyn might yet be saved."

"And it shall be done, my dear young lady," replied Abigail, "and that too without a moment's delay. I am almost sure to find my darling little Timothy at "The Old Tankard," where he always spends his evenings, and there I will go directly. Fear not, my lady, Timothy will execute his mission with his usual ability, and on his return I will make an appointment to meet him near the Grange to hear the result of his errand."

"Thanks, my good Abigail, for your kind and timely suggestions," observed her mistress.

"La, Miss," returned the former, "why should you thank me? I'm sure I am not performing any more than my duty, and so there is an end of the matter. But I will be off to "The Old Tankard" directly."

"Stay, Abigail," said our heroine, "upon better consideration, I think it would be as well for me to address a few lines to Brayling, explaining this alarming business, which your lover, of course, could not so well do."

"True, my lady," said her attendant, that is a very good thought."

Constance then seated herself at the table, and wrote a hasty note to Sampson Brayling, which she delivered to Abigail, who immediately departed on her errand to "The Old Tankard."

Constance awaited her return with the utmost impatience, and in a state of agitation. What her faithful maid had told her had naturally created her greatest alarm, and filled her breast with the most dismal forebodings and apprehensions, and it was not without the greatest difficulty that she could at all tranquillize her feelings.

"Dear Evelyn," she sighed, "for what art thou destined? What melancholy fate is there in store for thee? Alas! I have too much reason to fear the worst! It is evident that thou art betrayed, and driven as thou wilt be from thy present place of concealment, what will become of thee? Whither canst thou go? Where seek a refuge from thine enemies? My heart sickens at the dismal thought. Oh, is there no friendly power to avert the terrible evils with which thou art threatened? Alas! I fear that thou art so surrounded with insurmountable difficulties, that thou wilt find it impossible to extricate thyself."

Thus did she continue to reflect till Abigail returned, which was in a short time, and to the eager questions that were put to her, the latter replied:—

"Oh, yes, Miss, I met my dear Timothy at "The Old Tankard," as I expected to do, and when I told him what had happened, he expressed his regret; for you know Miss, that he is much attached to Master Evelyn and yourself, and would do anything in his humble power to serve you both. So he started off to the Wilderness immediately, and I have got to meet him in about an hour near the Grange, to receive the answer of Sampson Brayling, that is, if he should be fortunate enough to see him."

"I thank you, Abigail," said Constance, "for the zeal you exhibit in my welfare. Oh, may Brayling receive this intelligence in time to save Evelyn from the dangers that threaten him."

"Do not alarm yourself, Miss," said Abigail, "and I trust that everything will turn out better than you now anticipate."

"Heaven grant that it may," fervently ejaculated our heroine; "but when I reflect upon all the dismal circumstances by which myself and Evelyn are surrounded, I find it most difficult to look forward to the future with any degree of hope. The prejudice of Sir Milford against him seems to have increased to vindictiveness, and therefore what have I not to fear?"

"Sampson Brayling, my lady," observed Abigail, "has sworn, you know, to save Master Evelyn at all hazards, and to fully establish his innocence of the foul crime laid to his charge; and I am certain that he is not the man to break his word."

"I have every confidence in the sincerity of the promises of the Gipsey-chief, Abigail," answered her mistress; "but I doubt much his power to fulfil them."

Abigail exerted herself to the utmost to convince her to the contrary, and to inspire her with hope; and at length the time having arrived for her to meet Timothy Tapcan, on his return from the Wilderness, she retired from the room, and quitted the house. It was not many minutes before she returned, and her looks foreboded no very pleasant intelligence.

"Now, Abigail," enquired our heroine, anxiously; "what news? tell me quick?"

"Alas! my lady," answered Abigail, "I fear the information I have to give you, will not only surprise, but grieve you sadly."

"Ah!" ejaculated Constance, in a voice of alarm; "what do your words portend? My heart forebodes the worst. Oh, do not keep me in a state of suspense."

"Be firm, Miss, for after all it may not turn out so bad as it appears to be."

"You torture me, girl," said her mistress, impatiently; "let me know the worst at once, and do not keep me in this state of suspense."

"Well then, Miss," replied Abigail, "Timothy executed his mission with all due celerity and caution, and, on arriving at the place where the Gipsies encamped, he found Sampson Brayling, who had only just returned from the old house at Finchley, in a state of the greatest excitement. But—but these letters which were intrusted to Timothy, to deliver to you, will best explain all."

Our heroine eagerly took the letters, one was from Brayling, but she had no sooner looked at the superscription of the other than she exclaimed, in a voice of extreme agitation:—

"Ah! 'tis from Evelyn, and addressed to me! Dear, dear youth, how do I dread to peruse your epistle, for my heart forebodes some fresh calamity!"

She opened the note of Sampson Brayling first, and, as her eyes glanced hastily over the contents, she turned ghastly pale, and trembled. They ran as follows:—

"Fair lady Constance,—I regret to have to forward you news which I am afraid will cause you pain and anxiety. Your lover, from some cause which he has not clearly explained in the note he left for me, has abruptly and secretly quitted the old house at Finchley, and gone I know not whither, though I strongly suspect that he contemplates entering into the Naval service of his country. While I repeat the noble and independent spirit which has doubtless prompted him, I cannot but think that he has acted rashly and imprudently in the course he has adopted without seeking the advice and counsel of his sincere friend, and yours devotedly, SAMPSON BRAYLING."

A deadly chill fell upon the heart of poor Constance as she perused these few lines; the note fell from her hand; her brain turned giddy, and she almost fainted in the arms of her attendant.

No. 17.

"Gone! gone!" she exclaimed, with a burst of uncontrollable anguish, "and without one last farewell,—one word at leaving me, I fear for ever! Oh, Evelyn, unfortunate idol of my soul, surely this is most cruel, and what I had so little right to expect from thee. But, ah! the letter he left for me! let me muster fortitude to peruse its contents."

She took it from her bosom, where she had hastily thrust it, and as her eyes once more fell upon the well-known characters of her lover, convulsive sobs heaved her afflicted bosom, and scalding tears streamed down her pale cheeks. Again and again she pressed the precious epistle to her lips; but at length she struggled with her emotions as well as she could, and with a trembling hand she opened Evelyn's letter, and with difficulty perused the following affecting lines :—

"Beloved Constance ; the struggle is over ; the die is cast ; I can no longer endure or submit to the humiliating state of dependence to which I have so long been subjected to, and by the time this letter reaches you, most beloved and amiable of women, the unhappy Evelyn Heartwell will be far, far away. Friendless, hopeless, destitute, I cast myself upon the wild waters of my destiny, reckless of what becomes of me, since Constance Welborn is lost to me for ever. I fear that thou wilt blame me, reproach me for this apparent act of precipitation ; but oh, didst thou know the poignant anguish of mind that I am at present enduring, thou would pity and forgive me. We may never more behold each other, but though far distant climes may separate us, and I may still continue to linger out this wretched existence, thy dear form shall ever be present to my imagination ; ever treasured in my heart's warmest affections, until that heart shall have ceased to beat for ever. I dare not trust myself to say more ; bless thee! bless thee, Constance! and oh, in thy prayers, do not forget the unhappy EVELYN."

"Lost! lost!" in frantic accents, exclaimed the distracted maiden ; "he has abandoned me ; left me to dispair and misery, and life is now hateful and insupportable to the wretched Constance !" And overpowered by the violence of her emotions, she fainted in the arms of her attendant.

It may be here necessary to explain briefly some of the particulars connected with the disappearance of Evelyn. The escape of Black Will from the place in which he was confined, had excited his utmost alarm and agitation, for he apprehended that the ruffian in a spirit of revenge, would not fail immediately to reveal all that he knew of the interview Constance had clandestinely obtained with him, and likewise to betray the place of his concealment. Old Matthew in vain tried to quiet his fears; and when Evelyn retired to his chamber for the night it was in such a state of mind that excited considerable alarm in the breast of the old man.

Matthew Smelton arose at his usual time the following morning, and Evelyn had not yet quitted his apartment, but as the hour was early, he did not feel surprised, and bustled himself about in his usual avocations. But when a couple of hours had elapsed, and still Evelyn did not make his appearance, Matthew felt surprised, and became somewhat uneasy, for he feared that he might be prevented by illness. He therefore made his way to his chamber, the door of which he was astonished to find standing wide open, and entering the room, he was still more surprised to find that it was vacated ; Evelyn was not there ; and the undisturbed appearance of the bed fully satisfied Matthew that he had not slept on it the previous night. He was much alarmed, and stood for several minutes in a state of stupefaction, scarcely able to believe the evidence of his senses, but at length his eyes happened to rest upon two letters that were lying on the dressing table. One was addressed to Brayling and the other to Constance, and the whole truth now became sufficiently evident to him—Evelyn had secretly taken his departure from the house. Old Matthew was much agitated at this unforeseen event, and scarcely knew what to do, for that, coupled with the escape of the ruffian, Will, was calculated to excite the worst apprehensions in his breast. He could not but think that our hero had acted with great rashness and imprudence; and, after waiting for some time in the vain hope that he would repent of the course he had taken, and return, the old man had just made up his mind to hasten to Sampson Brayling, and make him acquainted with what had taken place, when the Gipsey opportunely arrived at the house. It is needless to describe the rage and astonishment of Sampson when he became acquainted with the particulars; but he could not help most severely censuring the conduct of Evelyn in departing from the house without previously informing him of his intentions, and after the interest he had ever shewn in his fate, and the trouble he had taken for his security and welfare. Having given old Matthew some necessary instructions, he hurried back to the gipsey encampment, and prepared himself to guard against the consequences that might ensue. With the message of Constance and what followed, the reader has already been made acquainted, but although he took the precaution to see that everything should be in readines to depart immediately, in case of any emergency which might occur, Brayling, with the rest of the tribe, determined to stand his ground in the Wilderness, and to await the result of any attack that might be made upon them.

The dark shadows of evening were fast falling upon the earth; there were but few persons in the streets, and a calm and stillness reigned around that was quite in keeping with the hour. And now the bright moon emerged from behind the clouds that had hitherto obscured her silvery face, and imparted a cheerful aspect to everything upon which her chased beams fell; they penetrated even between the thickly-clustered branches of the tall trees of the Wilderness, which at any time were almost impervious to the light of day, and through an opening might be seen the blackened walls of the ancient gate of the Monastry of Saint John's, standing out in bold relief to the scenery around.

The principal portion of the gipsies were standing or lounging about in sullen silence, or exchanging at intervals, in under tones, some observation with each other. There was an expression of fixed determination upon their swarthy features, that portended some important event—some gathering tempest; and even the women, as well as the men, were armed with pistols and other weapons, to defend themselves in case of necessity. The tents were struck, and with an heterogeneous mass of articles for domestic purposes, were packed up in two or three carts and waggons that were standing close at hand in a convenient spot, ready for an immediate departure, should it be found necessary.

Suddenly Sampson Brayling emerged from behind a cluster of trees, and advanced towards a group of men and women who were standing engaged in earnest conversation close by.

"So," he observed, "thou art all here, and fully prepared, I have no doubt, for anything that may take place?"

"All, all," was the simultaneous reply of the gipsies.

"'Tis well," returned Brayling, "and methinks that the rascals who contemplate us harm, will meet with a much warmer reception than they anticipate."

"Aye," remarked one of the tribe, "but I cannot help thinking, Brayling, now that we have had fair warning of the intentions of our enemies, it would have been much more prudent for us to have departed from this place than to run the risk of an engagement with those with whom we may find ourselves no match in point of numbers."

"How now, Zoah?" sternly demanded the Gipsey-chief, "what means this croaking? Sampson Brayling and his companions never yet were known to shrink from danger, and it is not likely that they are going to do so on the present occasion. I am anxious to give our enemies such a taste of our quality as they little expect, and I have no fear of the result. But where is Mabel ?"

"She is here, what wouldst thou of her ?" said the Gipsey-girl, suddenly starting into the midst of the group. There was a more than usual wild and restless expression in her fine black eyes, and her demeanour was agitated, though at the same time it was not unmingled with an air of determination, which shewed that her mind was occupied with some important design, which she was resolved to accomplish. "What would'st thou with Mabel, Sampson Brayling ?" she again demanded.

"Why hast thou been absent so long from the encampment?" inquired Sampson.

"And what boots it thee to know?" returned Mabel, in sullen accents ; "wouldst thou coerce my liberty, and control all my actions? Thou wilt find that Mabel will submit to no such restraint, even from thee."

"Thou art in one of thy crabbed humours again, girl," said Brayling ; "what has soured thy temper now?"

"And why should I gratify thine idle curiosity?" replied Mabel, in the same sullen and dogged tone ; "but it matters not, if my temper pleases thee not, Sampson Brayling, thou wilt soon cease to be annoyed by it."

"Thy wits are surely abroad, Mabel," observed the Gipsey-chief ; "what meanest thou?"

"Simply," she replied, in accents that told her firm resolve, "that this night, nay, this very hour, I abandon thee and thy tribe ; and it may be that thou wilt never behold me again ! "

"Abandon us ?" repeated Sampson, with a look of astonishment.

"Aye, and canst thou marvel at it? Think'st thou Mabel can continue among ye, while he who holds her heart, her happiness, her every earthly hope in bondage, has committed himself to his fate, and has become a wanderer upon the earth? Think ye that she in her soul's adoration is not most anxious to be near him, to share his fortunes, his troubles, his vicissitudes, nay—to die with him, if it be so willed?"

"Thou dost then, still cherish thy fatal passion for Evelyn Heartwell, in spite of the warning I have given thee of the danger, the criminality of thy so doing?"

"Oh, I heed not thy warning," returned Mabel ; "it cannot stifle the burning sentiments that are indelibly implanted in my breast. I do suspect that thou hast some sinister object in view, in the warning thou hast idly uttered ; if not, why this mystery? Why not at once explain thyself?"

"No, no," returned Brayling; "I tell thee once for all, that the fitting time has not yet arrived, so do not urge me further."

"Then my purpose is fixed," said the Gipsey-girl, firmly, wrapping her cloak more closely around her graceful form, and retreating a few paces ; "farewell, Sampson Brayling ; Mabel, from her very soul, thanks thee for the many kindnesses she hath received from thee, and this instant leaves thee, propably for ever!"

"Hold, girl!" exclaimed Brayling, hastily, "thou art surely mad ; what wouldst thou do?"

"Follow the footsteps of him in whose presence I can only continue to exist," answered Mabel ; "I will pursue him even to the furthest extremity of the globe; the eye of the fond Gipsey-girl shall search him out even though he be concealed in the remotest corner of the earth. The mountain' height, the barren wild, the gloomy forest, or the dark waters of the boundless ocean, shall not impede her in her progress; in calm or storm, in gloom or sunshine, in sickness, or even in death, she will persist in the object she has in view, for which she now alone wishes to live. Evelyn Heartwell, wherever thou goest, the lonely wanderer must in future be thy companion. Farewell Brayling, this is our moment of parting."

"Detain this headstrong girl!" peremptorily commanded Sampson; "her brain is disordered, she knoweth not what she doth. Detain her, I say!"

"Back! back, all of ye!" cried Mabel, determinedly; and standing in an attitude of defiance, she levelled a brace of pistols at the gipsies who were advancing towards her; "the man who dares to obstruct me, only rushes upon instant death! Now, Evelyn Heartwell, I will discover thee wherever thou mayest be concealed."

Astounded by the resoluteness of her manners, the gipsies were arrested in their purpose, and before they or Sampson Brayling could recover from their surprise and confusion, she had turned hastily from the spot, and was out of sight in an instant.

"Rash, impetuous girl!" said the Gipsey-chief; "as ungovernable as the wild tempest. But it is useless to pursue her; when the fierce torrent of her present feelings has exhausted itself, she will probably abandon her designs and return. Now, Zoar, what is the result of the errand I dispatched thee upon? Hast thou seen anything?"

"Yes," answered the Gipsey, Zoah, "a number of armed men, led on by the traitor, Black Will, are advancing rapidly along the road towards this place."

"Ah! then," cried Brayling, "the important moment has arrived; be firm, courage, and the triumph is ours. Back! back!"

Instantly the gipsies concealed themselves among the trees, and immediately afterwards a number of soldiers, with Will at the head of them, arrived in the Wilderness, and were surprised to find that there was no visible enemy to oppose them.

"Be on your guard," observed Black Will, "for, doubtless the rascals are only waiting in ambush to surprise us!"

He had scarcely given utterance to the words, when the correctness of his surmises was confirmed by a sharp volley from the concealed gipsies, which stretched several of their assailants bleeding on the earth, and immediately the whole of the tribe rushed forth, with the fury of wild beasts, and stood prepared for the coming struggle.

"Yield!" cried the officer in command of the men, addressing himself to Brayling, "yield! for resistance is useless."

"Yield!" replied the Gipsey-chief, with a scornful laugh, "never! In a just cause the gipsey tribe know not such a word as submission, even to a superior foe! On, on, comrades, and do your duty with your wonted courage and determination!"

Fierce was the combat which ensued, the gipsies fighting with the most indomitable bravery, and their assailants being thrown into complete confusion by the furious onslaught they made upon them, and the ruffian, Will, taking good care to conceal himself from danger at the commencement of the fray. The struggle did not last long; the gipsies fought desperately, and several of the soldiers having fallen, the rest were compelled to give way, and fled precipitately and in disorder from the spot, pursued by the gipsies, (who committed sad havoc among them in their retreat,) even into the road. Brayling and his companions then returned to the Wilderness.

"Bravely done, my lads, bravely done!" said Sampson; "I fancy we have given our enemies a pretty good taste of our quality. But, come, we have not a moment to lose, for they may quickly return reinforced by overwhelming numbers. Everything is in readiness, so let us immediately depart. The scoundrel, Will, has this time escaped, but I will ensure him his reward by and bye."

In an extraordinary short space of time after the scene of excitement which has just been described, the gipsies were prepared to depart. Some of the women and children seated themselves on the carts, and, in a few minutes the whole tribe were rapidly on their way from the Wilderness,

CHAPTER XXI.

THE PARTING OF EVELYN AND CONSTANCE.—THE DEVOTION OF MABEL.

WHILE these stirring events were going on, the tall figure of a man, closely enveloped in a cloak, and with his hat so slouched down over his brows that it partially concealed his features, cautiously emerged from a dark ally in Shoreditch, and having cast a hasty glance along the street without observing anyone, he crossed the road, and stealthily proceeded on his way towards Hogsden, frequently, however, looking back, as though he was fearful of being watched. This man was Evelyn Heartwell, who had managed to disguise himself in such a manner that it was scarcely possible for even those who knew him well, to have been able to recognize him. But what a sad change had so brief a period wrought in his appearance. His face was pale, his features haggard and careworn, and the expression of his eyes was painfully melancholy and downcast.

After so abruptly leaving the old house at Finchley, which he did in the darkness and stillness of night, he wandered on for some time, not knowing what course to take, and at an early hour the following morning, he found himself in the neighbourhood of Islington, scarcely knowing how he had got there. Although it was so early, finding an old roadside tavern already open for the accommodation of travellers, and not fearing to meet with anyone there who might know him, he ventured to enter, in order that he might obtain some refreshment, of which, being faint and exhausted, he stood much in need. The landlord, he was glad to see, did not eye him with any curiosity, and having ordered what he wanted, which was brought him, he partook of the refreshment, and while he was so engaged, he endeavoured to collect his thoughts so that he might come to some decision as to the course it would now be most prudent for him to adopt. His means were limited, and with which he had been supplied at different times by Sampson Brayling, so that it was necessary he should act with promptitude and energy. He saw no other course open to him but the army or the navy, and he quickly decided upon the latter, though, in his present state of mind, it appeared to him to be a matter of indifference as to what became of him. However, till he could properly arrange his plans, it was necessary that he should find some place of temporary security; and after reflecting upon this for some time, he recollected an old man, who had formerly been in the service of his late adopted father, and on whom he could depend. He resided in an obscure alley in Shoreditch, a place well adapted for concealment, and having hastily despatched his meal, Evelyn departed thither by the most unfrequented route.

On arriving at the miserable dwelling of the old man, the latter beheld him with no small astonishment, but knowing his unmerited misfortunes, he received him with a hearty welcome and the deepest commiseration. Here then Evelyn remained till the night to which we now refer, a prey to those poignant feelings of anguish which the misery of his fate naturally engendered. He had now left the residence of the old man with the intention of making his way to Wapping, where he was most likely to meet with a ship, and, resigning himself to the perils of the deep, for a time at least, if not for ever, bid adieu to his native land, and he was perfectly reckless as to what his fate might be. But could he thus tear himself away without one parting interview with that beloved girl, whom he could never hope to behold again? No, he could not. In spite of the consequences that might follow to himself, he was resolved that, before he finally left the neighbourhood, he would contrive some means to see Constance, to sigh his last adieu on her gentle bosom, and then resign himself to his destiny, let that destiny be whatever it might. It was on that determination he was bent on the eventful night to which we have alluded above; and, as he stole along, fearful of encountering any person that might know him, his heart palpitated with those mingled feelings of doubt, anguish, and despair, which it is usless for us to attempt to describe.

The night was remarkably fine; the bright moon floated in majestic splendour through a sea of fleecy clouds, silvering all around, and imparting an aspect of comparative cheerfulness, even to the grim and unsightly buildings of that ancient locality. The air was calm and serene, inviting persons to walk abroad, yet were the streets nearly deserted, and it was only now and then that a solitary wayfarer crossed the path of Evelyn, who was thus enabled to pass on without any fear of recognition. He paused for a minute or two before the ruins of the Miser's house, and as he contemplated them, the most melancholy thoughts flashed upon his brain, and all the misery of his untoward fate was presented more vividly to his tortured imagination. With a sickly feeling of emotion he turned away from the spot, and was again about to hurry on to the place of his destination, when he was suddenly arrested in his progress by some one laying their hand upon his arm, and starting, his surprise and confusion may be imagined when he beheld the Gipsey-girl standing by his side.

"Ah! Mabel!" he ejaculated, "strange being, hast thou again crossed my path?"

"Aye," returned Mabel, in melancholy accents, "I have discovered thee, Evelyn; the poor Gipsey-girl, goaded by the unconquerable love she bears thee, has abandoned the companions of her childhood, every dear connection and association, to pursue thy footsteps, and to share thy destiny, let that destiny be whatever it may."

"Mabel," replied our hero, "I implore thee not to detain me now, when danger surrounds me. Oh, why wilt thou not seek to stifle that fatal passion in thy breast, which I duly appreciate, but can never return?"

"Ah! there it is," said the poor girl, with a look of the most indescribable anguish, "it is that fatal assurance that renders me the most wretched of human beings, and racks my brain to madness. But though it may entail upon me every misery that can be inflicted, still shall it not divert me from my purpose. My fate is interwoven with thine, dear Evelyn, the only sunshine that crosses the gloom of my path is the light of thy presence; and though I obtain nothing but thy scorn and loathing, wherever thou goest, thither will Mabel follow thee. In the hour of danger she will be at hand to share thy peril; in the time of need she will be present to succour and console thee; and should sickness assail thee, where wilt thou find one to attend to thy necessities so anxiously, so tenderly, as the poor hapless Gipsey-girl? and oh, how amply will she consider herself repaid by one kind look, one word of affection."

"Mabel," replied Evelyn, gently disengaging himself from her hold, "if thou dost indeed regard my feeling, thou wilt cease to talk thus. Hast madness seized upon thy brain? Knowest thou what thou sayest? the rash vows thou hast given utterance? Fate has placed a barrier between us which we cannot remove. Come then, my poor friend, exert thy womanly energy, and learn to conquer a fatal passion that can meet with no encouragement. If thou carest for my safety, eave me, and allow me to pursue my way."

"Leave thee!" repeated Mabel, in a voice of the deepest emotion, "no, no, no, that must not be ; for thy sake, Evelyn, I have already braved, and am still fully prepared to brave everything ; thou art the light of my very soul, the being of my being ; I cannot live without thee, and by all that is sacred we will never part more till death ! Nay, frown not upon me ; spare thy reproaches, for I am determined, from this moment, Mabel, the Gipsey-girl, unites her fate with thine."

"For Heaven's sake unhand me, Mabel," said Evelyn, alarmed, bewildered, and agitated at the extraordinary vehemence and excitement of her manner; "once more I beseech thee do not detain me, for am I not exposed to the most imminent danger every moment that I tarry here ? If thou dost really regard my welfare as thou dost profess to do, thou wilt require no further persuasion."

"Ah !" cried Mabel, still retaining her hold of him, and the expression of her eyes and features becoming still more wild and agitated, "I read thy desperate determination in thy looks; by all my hopes I swear thou shalt not leave me thus. For thy sake I have abandoned the only friends I had on earth; those whose rough fortunes I have shared from the earliest dawn of childhood ; impetuous fate urges me on, and I cannot resist its will. Evelyn, dear Evelyn, for such the poor wandering, outcast Gipsey-girl cannot help calling thee, we part no more !"

"Rash girl, forbear !" exclaimed our hero, "art thou mad ? Return to thy friends, I conjure thee, and abandon the preposterous ideas thou hast suffered to take possession of and to bewilder thy brain. What advantage couldst thou hope to gain by following the fortunes of the forlorn, the wretched Evelyn ?"

"Whither wouldst thou go ?"

"Far, far upon the wild waters of the perilous deep," replied Evelyn, "to meet the enemies of my country in deadly strife, and perfectly reckless of what becomes of me. Hark! I hear the sound of approaching footsteps ! Another moment and I may be discovered ! Release me, Mable ! Nay, nay this obstinate resistance is in vain ! Farewell for ever, should we never meet again, and mayest thou be happier than the wretched Evelyn Heartwell !"

With a desperate effort he tore himself away, and hastily turning in the direction of Hogsden, was immediately hid from the view of poor Mable in the darkness of the night.

For a minute or two the Gipsey-girl was transfixed to the spot, and she gazed vacantly in the direction he had taken.

"He's gone," she observed, in melancholy accents, "but he shall not thus elude me ; I will pursue him, even though it be to death. Ah ! I now read his designs. He goes to endeavour to obtain a parting interview with Constance Welborn. Oh, how that thought tortures me. I will follow him, let the consequences be whatever they may. Farewell, a long and probably last farewell, to all my former scenes and associations; henceforth the hapless Mabel lives for Evelyn Heartwell alone !"

She cast one hasty glance around her, to see that she was not watched by any one, and then rushed precipitately in the same direction that our hero had taken, her mind fully determined and immovable.

In the meantime Evelyn hastily pursued his way, fortunately not encountering any one who knew him, or whom he had any cause to dread, and, at length, breathless with the speed he had made, and the agitation of his feelings, he found himself standing within a few paces of the Old Grange, upon whose ivy-mantled walls the broad light of the moon now fell with silvery radiance. Here he now tried to collect his thoughts, but they were so agitated and distracted, that he had great difficulty in doing so, and it was some minutes ere he could in any degree calm the powerful emotion of his feelings, which his painful meeting with

the Gipsey-girl had only tended to increase. He looked anxiously up at those casements in which he saw lights burning, with the faint and futile hope of catching a glimpse of that beloved being on whom his whole thoughts were fixed, and the rashness, folly, and danger of the course to which he had been impelled in his intense anxiety to behold his adored Constance again, now for the first time occurred to him.

"It is useless for me to hope to see her," he observed to himself, "vigilantly as her actions will doubtless be watched by her uncle. Had I indeed expressed such a wish in the note I left for her, I might indeed have been led to anticipate that melancholy favour. But still, if she was aware that I am so near at hand, I am convinced that she would brave every danger, run every risk, to rush to my arms, and receive my parting embrace, my last fond kiss. Would to Heaven that I could make known to her my presence ; but, alas, how is it possible ?

No. 18.

He paused and reflected deeply, but could not make up his mind in what way to act; and it appeared to him that, after all, he should be compelled to abandon his designs, though the prospect of doing so filled him with the most painful and dismal feelings. While he thus stood and hesitated how to act, Mabel arrived secretly at the spot, and cautiously drew aside to watch unobserved by him. Evelyn walked round the wall that enclosed the gardens of the Grange, and in spite of the danger of his so doing, so great was his anxiety to behold Constance, that he had almost made up his mind to scale it, when he started back alarmed, and hastily concealed himself behind a large tree that grew near the spot, on beholding the door slowly opened, and some one issue forth; but his pleasure and satisfaction may be imagined when he perceived that it was the faithful attendant of Constance, Abigail Allspice. She advanced a step or two into the road, neglecting to close the garden door after her, which Mabel, who was concealed close by, noticing, hastily slipped into the garden, secreted herself in a convenient place, resolved to watch narrowly all that might occur. Observing that Abigail was alone, our hero ventured to reveal himself, and Abigail started with amazement on beholding him.

"Gracious! Master Evelyn Heartwell," she exclaimed; "and is it possible 'tis you? Dear me, how glad, yet how sorry I am to see you. Who'd have thought that you would have ventured here."

"I beseech thee, my good Abigail, to spare thine observations," said our hero; "for I am all anxiety and impatience. Thy mistress, tell me quickly, oh, how is she?"

"Ah! poor young lady," replied Abigail, "sad enough, you may be sure. How can she be otherwise, after receiving your note, and never expecting to behold you again?"

"Oh, would to Heaven that I could see her now," observed Evelyn, "if it was only for a minute, just to say one parting word to her. Good Abigail, do you not think it is possible?"

"Oh, sir," answered Abigail, "I almost tremble at the thought. Sir Milford and Oliver are in the house, closeted together; the ruffian Will is also there, having just returned from an unsuccessful attack on the gipsies in the Wilderness. Should they discover you, your destruction would inevitably follow, and what would then become of my poor young mistress?"

"Nay," returned Evelyn, impatiently; "I am worked up to a pitch of desperation, and am fully prepared to brave everything to accomplish my wishes. Now that I have ventured so far, I cannot, will not depart without seeing my beloved Constance, if there is a possibility. Abigail, will you not assist me?"

"Ah, Master Evelyn," replied Abigail, "that would I most willingly do, as far as in my humble power lies, but,—"

"I pr'ythee do not hesitate," interrupted our hero, with increased anxiety and impatience, "for every moment is precious, and any delay might render all my plans abortive. Sir Milford and Oliver you say are deeply engaged in conversation; Constance surely then, might leave her chamber and meet me here, or in the garden of the Grange, without any fear of discovery. She surely cannot, will not refuse my earnest request, since this night, nay, this very hour I tear myself from her presence for ever."

"Oh, Master Heartwell," observed the kind hearted Abigail, "I pray you do not talk so, for it grieves me to hear you. But tarry here for a minute or two, and I will tell my poor young lady all about your arrival. Be careful that you are not watched by any one, or we shall all be ruined. I will return immediately."

Our hero was about to return his thanks, but Abigail motioning him to silence, re-entered the garden and closed the door after her. The heart of Evelyn now throbbed violently with mingled emotions of hope and fear, and every moment that elapsed before the return of Abigail, appeared to him to be an age. Yet did he almost dread the interview, fully aware as he was of the torturing scene that must ensue. He had not much time, however, allowed him for these reflections; the garden door was again slowly and cautiously opened, and Abigail making her appearance, beckoned him to advance.

"Now, good Abigail," he said eagerly, "what message hast thou for me?"

"Silence!" continued the attendant, "and follow me."

Evelyn did so without uttering another word, and stepping into the garden, Abigail conducted him to a small alcove, which happened to be contiguous to the place where Mabel, violently agitated with mingled feelings of jealousy and expectation, was concealed.

"My poor lady is willing to risk anything to see you, Master Evelyn," observed Abigail, "wait here, and in a minute or two she will join you."

"Sweet condescension," ejaculated Evelyn. "Alas! Constance, that this should probably be our last meeting."

"Be cautious, for Heaven's sake," said Abigail, as she quitted the spot to return to the house, "or all is lost."

Before Evelyn had time to return any answer, Abigail was gone, and with a palpitating heart he looked towards the house, which, by the broad clear light of the moon was revealed to him distinctly. He had not to wait long. Suddenly he beheld two female forms emerge from behind an angle of the building, and having looked cautiously and timidly around them, to ascertain that they were not observed, they stepped quickly and lightly towards the alcove. He knew them immediately to be Constance and Abigail, and the latter having conducted her mistress to within a short distance of the spot, and pointed out to her the place where he was awaiting her, retired, evidently with the intention to keep watch, and prevent their being surprised by those whom they had so much cause to dread.

With trembling footsteps our heroine approached, and Evelyn advancing to meet her, the next moment, with a mingled exclamation of anguish and delight, they were clasped frantically in each others arms. With the most inexpressible emotion, Evelyn led her into the alcove, and there for a few minutes they were unable to give utterance to a word, and could only give vent to their feelings in heartfelt sobs.

"Oh, Constance, beloved Constance," at length sighed Evelyn, partially disengaging himself from her embrace, and looking in her pale but beauteous face with an expression of the most indescribable tenderness and melancholy emotion; "the long dreaded, the torturing moment has at length arrived, and for the last time the wretched Evelyn clasps thy adored form to his heart, and sighs his farewell upon thy bosom. My adverse fate hurries me on; distance must separate us; time must endeavour to blot out the fond remembrance of our hopeless loves, and henceforth we must be as strangers to each other."

"Evelyn, dear, but unfortunate Evelyn, forbear, oh, forbear those fearful words," gasped forth our heroine, tears gushing from her eyes, the lustre of which was now dimmed by the intense, the insupportable anguish of her feelings, "they drive me to madness! Oh, why should cruel fate thus sever two fond and faithful hearts? Thou can'st not, will not leave me, Evelyn, for I feel that I cannot live but in thy presence!"

"And oh, Constance," replied our hero, "and need I attempt to describe to thee the mental agony that this final separation from all that I hold most dear on earth at this moment costs me? But I have no alternative. Fate ordains that we should not come together; that the ardent passions of our hearts should meet with no reward, and every hour that I remain here is only to entail fresh misery upon me, and to be hunted and stigmatized as a felon—a villain of the deepest dye. Let me but once more enfold thy beloved form to my bosom, and press warm kisses of unspeakable affection, of adoration upon thy lips, and then most amiable, most noble hearted, most virtuous of women, farewell, farewell, for ever !"

"No, no, no!" cried the distracted girl in a voice half choked by the power of her emotions, and clinging still more affectionately to him, "recall those torturing words—it must not be—thou must not leave me, Evelyn—I cannot live without thee !—I am ready to yield to any sacrifice for thy sake, to endure the world's scorn, injustice, and opprobrium; to suffer all the privations of poverty, but to part with thee for ever, oh, there is madness in the thought !"

"For Heaven's sake, dear Constance, endeavour to compose thy feelings," remonstrated Evelyn. "Oh, I have acted wrong, I have acted rashly, in subjecting thee to the painful, the agonising trial of this interview. Better had it have been for us both had I torn myself at once away, and resigned myself to that fate which it is useless for me to resist, and which it is madness for me to seek to avail."

"Ah! Evelyn;" she sighed, and looking up in his face with an expression of gentle reproach; "and couldst thou thus have left me without one word at parting? But whither wouldst thou go?"

"Alas!" replied our hero, in the most melancholy accents, "it matters not, all places must be alike to me, wretched, outcast being as I am, and without Constance. But I now go to enter upon the service of my country, to brave the perils of the ocean—the battle and the breeze, and with the melancholy hope that some friendly ball from the cannon of the enemy may shortly lay me low, and thus terminate my career of misery and despair !"

"Oh! cease—cease! I implore thee !" cried Constance, "thy words rack my very soul. Thou must not, shall not expose thyself to such fearful dangers! We will not part, dear Evelyn, I will still cling to thee with all the strength of woman's fondness; let us then boldly continue to battle with our fate, still to cherish the hope that the all-merciful Providence will ultimately smile upon our love; that we may at length, by perseverance, be able to surmount the innumerable difficulties by which we are at present surrounded, and be rewarded at last for the many trials we have experienced in each other's hand."

"Never!" at that moment emphatically exclaimed Mabel, who had been an attentive listener to this interesting conversation, and with feelings of powerful emotion which it is useless for us to attempt to describe. The lovers started at the sound of her voice, and looked at each other with alarm and amazement.

"Ah! what sound was that?" ejaculated our heroine, trembling; "good God! should we be discovered!"

"Nay," said Evelyn, looking forth from the alcove, "do not alarm thyself unnecessarily, sweetest. There is no one nigh; we must have suffered our imagination to deceive us. It could have been nothing more than the sighing of the wind among the foliage."

"Ah, no!" returned Constance, still looking timidly around her, "I am certain it was a human voice which spoke in anger, and one that I have heard before. Oh, Evelyn, dear Evelyn, should we be detected, thy destruction would at least be sure to follow."

"Fear not my love," he returned, firmly, "I will brave everything. But 'tis useless for us longer to delay the painful moment, beauteous, beloved, but unfortunate Constance, one last fond embrace, once more let me press those dear lips; again let me invoke the choicest blessings of Heaven upon thine head, and then we part, part for ever."

"Part! part!" repeated our heroine wildly, and staring vacantly at her lover, "that fearful word! I cannot, dare not listen to it! Evelyn, thou shalt not leave me; can'st thou thus recklessly tear me from thine heart and abandon me to my fate? Cruel, cruel, oh, most cruel! But no, thou shalt not go; I will cling to thee with more than human strength, with more than woman's fervour—Evelyn, I —"

Before she could finish the sentence, they were both startled by the sudden appearance of Abigail, the disordered expression of whose features shewed that some danger threatened them.

"For goodness sake be quick and separate," she said, "but this moment I beheld Oliver Dalton and the ruffian Will coming from the house, and should they approach this way you will be discovered, and I tremble at the consequences that would follow."

"Ah!" exclaimed Evelyn, laying his hand upon his sword, "at least I am armed, and I will defend my beloved Constance from the villians at the hazard of my life!"

"It would be madness to run any such risk," observed Abigail. "Remain you here, Master Evelyn, for a few minutes, till the danger is haply over; I may conduct my mistress by a back way into the house, and she will thus avoid them. Come, come, for Heaven's sake do not delay."

"It must be so;" cried Evelyn, in a voice of the deepest emotion, "the painful moment has arrived! Constance, beloved Constance, bless thee, bless thee! May all good angels watch over and protect thee when I am far away. One fond embrace, and then a long and last adieu!"

"Adieu!" gasped forth the poor girl, clinging more vehemently to him, and sobbing hysterically as though her heart would break; "the word chokes me! Evelyn, my own dear Evelyn, I—"

She could say no more, but overpowered by the insupportable agony of her feelings, she sank in his arms, and hid her pale face in his bosom. He enfolded her in one fervent, one frantic embrace, again and again ardently kissed her lips, her cheeks, her forehead, raised his eyes devoutly towards Heaven and mentally invoked a blessing upon her head; then with a powerful effort, he tore himself from her arms, and resigned her to the care of the faithful Abigail, who led her, almost fainting from the spot. He watched them till they were hidden from his view by an angle of the building, and concluding that they were in safety, and seeing that the coast was clear, he issued from the place, and was hurrying towards the garden door, when two men started from behind a thicket, and crossed his path, and in whom, by the light of the moon, he recognised Oliver and Will.

"Ah!" exclaimed the former with a look of malicious triumph, "daring scoundrel, thou art discovered then. At least this time thou shalt not escape me! Seize him!"

"Villain!" cried our hero, determinedly, and drawing his sword, "think not that I will yield so easily. Thou seest that I am armed; stand back then, for by heaven if thou attemptest to obstruct me, thou shalt pay dearly for it!"

"Hold!" at that moment exclaimed a female voice, in loud and commanding tones, "there is one here who at least is fully prepared to counteract the designs of villainy!"

Evelyn looked up, and to his utter amazement and the confusion of Oliver and his base myrmidon, Mabel, the Gipsey-girl, stood in a menacing attitude before them, and levelling a couple of pistols at their heads.

"Hold, villains!" she cried, in a resolute voice, "there is one who will protect Evelyn Heartwell at the hazard of her life. Dare but to advance a step to obstruct his departure, or to utter the least sound that might alarm the inmates of the house, and these deadly weapons shall do their work of destruction upon ye !"

"Ah !" ejaculated the astonished Evelyn, scarcely able to believe the evidence of his senses, " Mabel here, and at such a critical moment as this ?"

"Confusion !" vociferated Oliver, passionately, "and shall I thus suffer myself to be braved by a woman ?"

"Aye," returned Mabel, "unless thou wouldst madly rush upon thy fate, for thou see'st I am determined. Come, Evelyn, we do but waste most precious time upon those miscreants !"

Oliver Dalton and his companion were completely petrified to the spot with astonishment, and Evelyn unable to utter a word, retreated towards the door, Mabel following him, and guarding him from his enemies, and they at length found themselves outside the house, the Gipsey-girl closing the garden door after them. She urged him a few yards from the spot, when Evelyn paused, and would proceed no further.

"Mable," he said, "how is this ? Didst thou observe the interview between myself and the unfortunate Constance ?"

"Aye," answered Mabel, with a bitter expression of countenance, "and I overheard all the conversation that passed between thee ; the fond vows of love and constancy thou didst exchange with one another. Oh, it was as wormwood to the soul of the Gipsey-girl ; but still she remained firm to her purpose, and so far hath accomplished her purpose. Nay, I know full well what thou wouldst say, Evelyn, and so thou mayest e'en save thyself the trouble of giving utterance to thy feelings. I am resolute ; thou mayest scorn and despise the wretched girl who has abandoned everything for thy sake, but she will nevertheless follow in thy footsteps we will part no more !"

"Mabel," said our hero ; "art thou mad ? Why thus obstinately persist in a course so rash and unreasonable. Return to those with whom thou hast been so long associated, and endeavour to forget that such an unfortunate being as Evelyn Heartwell ever existed, though believe me he will not cease to remember thee in his prayers, and that he will ever cherish for thee the warmest feelings of esteem and gratitude for the kind sympathy thou hast ever evinced in his misfortunes."

At that moment the light from several torches, in the direction of the Old Grange glared upon the air, and seemed to give warning of pursuit.

"Ah !" ejaculated Mabel; "the inmates of the house have been alarmed, and are hurrying hither in pursuit. While we thus tarry, danger increases. Come, Evelyn, let us away !"

"Begone, Mabel," he answered ; "I must away alone. Farewell, and mayest thou be as happy as thy virtues merit."

The Gipsey-girl endeavoured to detain him, but he suddenly burst from her hold, and making his way towards an obscure turning, was immediately hid from the sight by the darkness beyond. Mabel, however, did not pause to reflect, but having marked with a keen eye the course he had taken, precipitately followed in pursuit.

CHAPTER XXII.

GODFREY MALVERN AND THE MISER.—THE JOURNEY AFTER THE FIRE.—THE HAUNT OF VILLAINY AND THE ALARMING DISCOVERY.

WE will now return to the eventful night of the fire at the old Miser's dwelling, and relate extrordinary circumstances that occurred to him after his rescue from the flames by the mysterious man whom he had called by the name of Godfrey Malvern. Straggling in the midst of the awful conflagration, as we have described him, his destruction seemed to be inevitable; and now all the terrors of death and eternity arose with overwhelming force to the distracted imagination of the guilty man, and appalled his very soul. Faster and faster the fierce flames gathered around him, and the burning flooring boards upon which he stood, trembled beneath his weight, threatening every moment to precipitate him into the burning mass below; still no chance of his deliverance from his dreadful situation presented itself. Loudly he shrieked for help, and wrung his hands, in the frenzy of his feelings and the horror of his despair; but no one attempted to come to his rescue; all seemed to mock at his sufferings, and to have abandoned him to his fate. Oh, the agony of that moment! the most eloquent pen must fail to do adequate justice to it. All the black deeds of the past rushed upon his disordered brain; the frightful voices of fiends seemed to thunder in his ears, mocking his sufferings, and loading him with their curses; in the midst of the flames that roared around him, he could almost imagine he saw the grim and ghastly faces of his unfortunate victims, and so great was the effect of the power of his guilty conscience at that fearful moment, that he was several times urged to anticipate the dreadful fate which appeared impending over him, by plunging at once into the midst of the burning ruins.

It was at this frightful and critical juncture that Godfrey Malvern and his companions forced their way through the flames, and arrived at his side, and as Jasper Scrimpe caught sight of the stern features of that man whom he had so much cause to fear, made more awfully distinct to him, in the red reflection of the fire, a shuddering sensation of horror came over him, and he covered his face with his hands. He tried to speak, but he could not, for the smoke almost suffocated him, and, in the next moment he felt himself raised in the powerful arms of Malvern, and carried through the flames from the spot. He had some recollection of the noise of the falling roof of his ancient dwelling, as he was hurried into the street, and the confused shouts of the spectators; his brain then turned giddy; his senses left him, and he remembered no more.

When he was partially restored to consciousness, he found himself in a covered vehicle which was proceeding at a rapid rate, and with Godfrey Malvern, and another man of singularly uncouth appearance, sitting on either side of him. Various were the feelings that rushed with tumultuous rapidity o'er his fevered and distracted brain; but, as he gazed upon the features of Malvern, whose eyes were fixed upon his ghastly countenance with a mingled expression of implacable malice and exultation, fear predominated, and so far gained the ascendancy over every other emotion, that, for a few moments it completely paralized every faculty, and rendered him speechless; but still all the terrible events that had recently taken place ware vividly fresh upon his memory, and added to the horror, the despair, the insupportable anguish that raged within his breast.

Godfrey Malvern seemed to enjoy his agony, and did not offer to interrupt the torturing reflections in which he was evidently immersed; and a sardonic smile overspread his features, which shewed plainly the feelings he was as that moment indulging in. The vehicle still whirled along in the darkness of the night, at the same rapid rate; the course it was taking was wild and dreary, and it was evident, although the unfortunate Miser had no means of judging how far they had journeyed, that they had left London far behind them. They were now preceding across a barren heath, with not the least signs of a human habitation nigh, while in the distance, the eye, at intervals caught the dark shadows of what appeared to be a forest; everything was strange, bewildering, and unfamiliar to the eye of the wretched Jasper Scrimpe; and his disordered mind became lost in labyrinth of fear, doubt, and perplexity, still he could not speak; still he was unable and afraid to question his mysterious enemy as to his intentions, although he had every reason to apprehend the worst, and his blood chilled, and his very heart sunk within him. And now how the power of conscience worked upon his guilty soul, and wrought him up to a pitch of frenzy. All the dark deeds of the past were presented to his distracted imagination, in characters so vivid and so awful from the contemplation, and madness almost seized upon his brain.

Still had the angry elements not exhausted their fury; the thunder roared and the lightning fiercely blazed in the Heavens with unabated violence, the wind howled in dismal gusts across the wild heath, and a fearful deluge of rain descended upon the earth, rattling upon the roof of the vehicle in a manner that frequently made the miserable old Jasper start, and temporarily aroused him from his gloomy and torturing meditations, though Godfrey Malvern seemed to view the fearful scene that was passing around him with the most perfect indifferance.

At length, as a fearful impulse seemed to move him, the Miser suddenly started from his painful reverie, and, as he gazed wildly upon Malvern and his companion, in hoarse and tremulous accents he exclaimed :—

"Where am I? do I still live? or did the fierce flames that consumed my dwelling, and hissed and roared around me perform their dreaded work, and snatch me from that earth I had contaminated by my loathsome presence, to plunge me into an eternity of horror? Ah! what torturing thoughts are these that burn and rack my brain? The voices of fiends thunder in mine ears, and mock at and triumph in my sufferings! Grim and grizzly phantoms rise upon my appalled sight; a thousand hurricans seem to rage around me! I—I am bourne upon the whirlwind to perdition! Save me! Save me! Oh, horror! horror!"

"Bah!" cried Malvern, with a look of contempt and disgust, "no more of this nonsense. So then, thy guilty conscience doth at last torture thee! 'Tis well, 'tis well, it glads me to see it."

"Ah!" gasped forth the wretched Jasper, with wild and distended eyes, "thou here? Am I in thy dreaded power? Then indeed do I fear the worst! I'm lost! I'm lost!"

"Aye, old man," replied Godfrey Malvern, with a malicious look of triumph, "I told thee that we should shortly meet again, and thou seest that I have kept my word. We shall not part again in a hurry, I can assure thee."

"Oh, whither art thou conveying me?" eagerly interrogated Jasper, and trembling violently.

"Thou wilt know anon," answered Malvern, "fear not but that I will provide for thee a safe place of custody."

"Release me, release me, fearful man," ejaculated the Miser, "I read thy dreadful purpose in thy looks; I dare not go with thee. Oh, why didst thou not leave me to perish in the flames?"

"What!" returned Godfrey, with a sarcastic grin, "and send thee to the devil before thy time? Oh, no, that would not have answered my purpose by any means at all."

"Taunting fiend, what cursed fate made thee cross my path, to mock at my sufferiugs, and to add to my tortures? But, my gold! my glittering treasure, oh, where is that?"

"Part of it secure in my possession, as thou seest," replied Malvern, and pointing to a small iron box which he found time to secure when he had rescued the Miser from the flames.

"Ah! my gold!—my gold!" almost shrieked the miserable old man, rising suddenly from his seat, and making an effort to rush towards the box; "'tis there!—'tis there!—let me again clutch it! give me my gold!—give me my gold!"

"Hold! miserable old wretch!" cried Malvern, pushing him back in his seat; "not a single coin of that ill-gotten money shalt thou ever have in thy possession again. I will be thy banker, and will hold it secure, until, perchance, I may meet with those who, if they be still living, have a better claim to it than thou hast."

"Ah!" exclaimed Jasper, wildly; "thou shalt not, dare not hold it from me!"

No. 19.

"Guilty miscreant!" returned Godfrey, "and canst thou still cling to that dross which thou hast purchased by the most atrocious crime, and which has brought upon thee the disgust and hatred of the word?"

"The world!" repeated the miser, in a hoarse voice, and his eyes seeming almost ready to burst from their sockets; "what novice in the various phases of this chequered life, presumest thus to talk to me who have had such long, such woeful years of experience? The world! it is a bitter mockery—a monstrous delusion! It has made me what I am, and therefore do I loathe and despise it. Men point at me the finger of scorn, and call me miser, wretch, grovelling dog; one who knows no other passion but sordid avarice—no other god but gold! And what has made me so? The world, and the hollow sycophants that crawl upon it, under the insidious guise of honour and integrity. The world! oh, there was a time when I looked upon it as one vast garden of sweets and flowers. I found it but a wild desert, full of thorns, and rank and poisonous weeds. My eyes were opened to the light of reason; I looked around me—and what did I see?—the brow of villainy encircled by a jewelled coronet; virtue and integrity without a roof to shelter them from the Winter's blast. Fawning parasytes stalking in silk and velvet, and bedizened with ermine and gold; honest merit clothed in rags. I asked myself the cause of this strange perversion of the laws of nature and of justice, and a voice seemed to thunder in mine ears—'Gold!—'tis gold!—get gold!'—it came like a spell upon me. From that moment the fiend of avarice entered my breast; I cast aside every feeling of honesty, humanity, and virtue; my heart became hard, cold, and sterile as marble; and as I hugged and gloated o'er my precious treasure, I shouted, 'I have the world—the world at my command—for I have gold!—gold!—gold!—' Ha, ha, ha!"

And, with a loud and hysterical laugh, the unfortunate and guilty old man sank back exhausted and insensible in his seat.

"Poor wretch!" said Godfrey, gazing at him for a second or two with a mingled expression of pity and contempt; "at length the horrors of conscience are awakened in thy guilty breast, and thou art justly punished for the dreadful crimes thou hast committed."

He turned from him with a feeling of disgust, and did not attempt to arouse him from the state of unconsciousness into which he had sunk.

The vehicle still pursued its way across the heath, and when it had arrived at its utmost verge, by the direction of Malvern, it was turned off to the right, avoiding the forest, and entered a long and winding lane, overarched with the branches of the tall trees that grew on either side of it, and which, even in the daytime nearly excluded every particle of the light of Heaven. This lane, being of considerable extent, took them some time to traverse, but at length they came to the end of it, and emerged into a more open part of the country, though the scenery that presented itself was wild and dreary in the extreem. Here the Miser once more recovered to a state of consciousness, and looking anxiously at Malvern and his companion, he said, in a voice of agitation :—

"Ah! then, it was no dream; thou art still here, dreaded being, and the fate of Jasper Scrimpe is too evidently approaching."

"Cease!" commanded Godfrey, sternly, "thou wilt have time to indulge in thy soliloquies when thou art alone. I am in no mood to to listen them at present."

"The ambiguity of thy words alarm me," gasped forth Jasper; "what fearful design dost thou contemplate against me?"

"Thou wilt discover that soon enough, no doubt," answered Malvern; "thou mayest, however, be certain that I will not fail to avail myself of every advantage now that I hold thee in my power."

"Lost! lost!" exclaimed the distracted old man, striking his forehead in despair with his clenched fist. "Oh, Heaven!"

"Hold! guilty miscreant!" cried Godfrey, sternly, "darest thou appeal to that Heaven whose laws thou hast so atrociously, so monstrously outraged?"

"Spare me! spare me, Malvern," supplicated the terrified Jasper, with clasped hands; "I do admit the power thou hast over me; I do acknowledge the wrongs I have done thee, and am willing to make thee all the atonement in my power."

"Atonement," repeated Malvern, with a look of contempt; "what atonement canst thou make to me for the miseries, the various trials and vicissitudes, the shame and degradation thy guilt hath brought upon me? Were I at once to consign thee to the hands of the hangman, it would be no more than thou dost justly deserve."

"Oh, mercy, mercy, Malvern," again implored the distracted Miser.

"And what mercy canst thou expect from me, old man?" demanded Godfrey; "thou who wouldst have betrayed me to death; thou who hast made me what I am? But I waste words in talking to thee now. Ere long thou wilt know the fate that is in store for thee, since fortune has accidently placed thee in my power, and that too at the very moment when I least expected it."

"Despair, despair!" groaned Jasper, covering his face with his hands. Malvern contemplated him for a few minutes in silence, but with feelings of satisfaction, and then left him to the miserable indulgence of his own gloomy and racking thoughts.

Through the tempest went the vehicle, and the horses, which performed perfect marvels on that occasion, seemed scarcely ever to slacken their speed. But at length they suddenly came to a dead stand still, and the unfortunate miser was aroused from the deep lethargy into which he had fallen, and looked eagerly from the vehicle. As well as the darkness would permit him, he found that they had stopped before an ancient looking stone building, which had something of the appearance of an inn, though what it had originally been intended for it was difficult to conjecture. It stood alone, and was as wild and dreary a spot as could well be imagined. There was a faint glimmering light in one of the casements, but all the rest of the building was involved in darkness; and Jasper, as he gazed upon it, could not help a shuddering sensation coming over him.

"We stop here for the remainder of the night," observed Malvern; "if I may judge by the light in yonder window, Hugo has not yet retired to rest, so thou mayest as well summons him to the door, Brandon."

The man who had been driving the vehicle, and who was in none of the most amiable humours, being completely drenched to the skin, now alighted, and approaching the door, raised the heavy knocker, and let it fall again with a sound that reverberated loudly through the building and far around.

"What dismal place is this?" anxiously interrogated the Miser; "its gloomy aspect strikes a chill to my heart. I like it not."

"Probably not;" replied Malvern; "but 'tis not my intention to study thy tastes or wishes. Here we tarry for the present; and for my own part, I am not at all sorry to have reached a place of shelter from the storm at last."

Brandon had now repeated the knock, and presently afterwards, the casement in which the light had been seen, was slowly opened, and a man putting his head out, inquired in a gruff voice who was there, and what they could possibly want, disturbing him out of his rest at such an unreasonable hour of the night.

"Be not alarmed or out of temper, good master Hugo;" replied Godfrey, who had now left the carriage and approached underneath the window; "it is only thy friend."

"Ah! Malvern, is it you?" said the man; "Marry, and it must have been something particular that has brought thee here at this time, and in such a storm as this. Wait but a minute and I will attend thee."

Malvern now returned to the vehicle, and assisted the trembling Jasper to aligh, and immediately afterwards the door was opened by Hugo, bearing a lamp, the rays from which fully revealed his features and person to the Miser, who fixed upon him an eager and inquisitive look. He was a middle-aged man of muscular frame, with scowling brows, and harsh, repulsive, and sinister looking features. He eyed the Miser with a look of curiosity; and Godfrey having drawn him aside, and whispering a few words in his ear, he said—

"'Tis well; I will attend. Come, thou hadst better in, for methinkst thou wilt be glad to escape from the inclemency of the weather at last. The fire is not yet extinguished in one of the rooms, and I will see to thy comfort as well as I can."

Godfrey thanked him, briefly; and then turning to the Miser took his arm, and urged him forward; Jasper again shuddered and hesitated, but he knew it was useless to resist, and without saying a word, therefore, though his heart sunk within him, he suffered Malvern to conduct him into the house, Hugo leading the very to a room at the back part of the premises, which was very dark and very dirty, while, in the rusty grate were the scanty remains of a fire. Godfrey mentioned the miser to a seat at the table, and having removed his cloak, and taken off his russets, he sat down himself. Hugo now placed a log of wood upon the fire, and soon kindled it into a cheerful blaze, which imparted some degree of comfort to the room.

"And now, I suppose, Master Malvern," remarked Hugo, "as thee and thy friends have travelled far, and under no very agreeable circumstances, I dare say thou feel'st disposed for some refreshments, so I will e'en place before thee the best that my house at present affords; though had I been aware of thy coming, I would have been better prepared for thy reception."

"Make no apologies, Hugo," said Malvern; " we must be contented with what thou hast got. But be quick, and thou canst doubtless accommodate my companions in another room."

"Aye;" returned Hugo, and motioning Brandon and the others to follow him, he retired from the room, and left Malvern and Jasper Scrimpe to themselves. The miser cast a gloomy and hasty glance around the room, and then once more fixing a look of supplication upon his companion, said,—

"Godfrey Malvern, the whole of this adventure fills me with feelings of doubt and suspicion. What, I pray thee, will be the result of it?"

"Thou must e'en wait patiently, and, doubtless thou wilt see," answered Malvern.

"The aspect of all around makes me tremble," observed Jasper, "this lonely spot is well suited for the perpetration of any deed of darkness."

"Aye," returned Godfrey, with a sarcastic grin, " at least thou shouldst be a good judge of that."

"Forbear, Malvern;" remonstrated the wretched old man, "such observations as those thou hast just now made use of, do but serve to torture me."

"And tharefore does it please me all the better."

"Stern man, hast thou no feeling of pity within thy breast?"

"None for thee;" replied Godfrey, "darest thou plead for it?"

"Alas! alas!" sighed Jasper, and beating his breast with much emotion, "my situation is indeed a terrible one. But tell me, I implore thee, what part of the country are we now in?"

"If it will gratify thy curiosity to know," replied Malvern, "we are now in the county of Essex, and not far from the sea coast."

"Ah!" ejaculated the miser, in accents of astonishment and alarm, "so far, so far from home?"

"Home!" repeated Malvern, with an ironical laugh, "thou hast no home now, old man; thy future destiny is with me. To the world thou art now, for the present, at any rate, dead."

"Ah!" gasped forth Jasper, and fixing upon him a look that was sufficient to penetrate to his innermost thoughts; "what mean those mysterious words?"

"Ask no further questions," returned Malvern, sternly, "for I am not disposed to answer them. All that thou hast to do is to resign thyself to thy fate, whatever it may be, for thou may'st rest assured, so closely as I have thee in my clutches now, thou canst not avert it."

The Miser groaned in the anguish of his terror and despair, and covering his face with his hands. Hugo now returned to the room, bringing with him an ample supply of wine and provisions, which he placed on the table before Godfrey and Jasper.

"There;" he remarked, "although it is not exactly the sort of fare I should have liked to provide thee with, Master Godfrey; thou must e'en take the will for the deed, and I trust that thou wilt find it welcome."

"No apologies, Hugo;" replied his guest, "thou knowest full well that my appetite is none of the dantiest, or most delicate. Thou hast brought plenty of it, and, as I am very hungry, fear not but that I shall do ample justice to it. But how hast thou accommodated my companions?"

"Oh, I have seen to their comfort thou mayest depend upon it," answered Hugo.

"'Tis well;" returned Malvern, "see that you get a chamber ready for my *friend* here as soon as possible, for he requires rest. The room marked No. 3, will do, you understand me?"

"Yes," replied Hugo, "thy wishes shall be promptly attended to."

Jasper was about to speak, but Godfrey, by a significant look enjoined him to silence, and he was constrained to obey.

"Dost thou intend to remain here long?" interrogated Hugo.

"Probably till to-morrow evening," replied Malvern, "bnt certainly no longer."

The Miser looked anxiously but said nothing; for the stern and menacing look of Malvern prevented him. In spite of all his efforts to the contrary, he could not help feeling a powerful sensation of dread stealing over him, and a fearful presentiment that the crisis of his fate was approaching. The lonely situation of the house, the circumstances under which he had been brought there, the uncouth and suspicious appearance of Hugo, but above all, the dark hints and evasive answers of Godfrey, were not at all calculated to quiet these apprehensions and the terrible excitement that shook his frame, and imparted its influence to the expression of his cadavorous and careworn features could not escape the observations of Malvern, who ever and anon eyed him with a look of deadly malice, triumph, and determination.

"Leave us for a time, Hugo," he said, "I will summons thee when myself and my comp—my *friend* here, have a wish to retire."

"Be it so," answered Hugo, and he instantly quitted the room.

"Come, old man," said Godfrey, when he was gone, "why dost thou not eat? 'Tis long, I doubt not, since thou indulged thyself in such a substantial meal as that which is now placed before thee."

"Oh, I cannot eat," answered Jasper, "tell me, Malvern, what is thy terrible purpose, I implore thee? Why hast thou brought me so far away? and what are thine intentions?"

"Need'st thou ask the question?" returned Godfrey, with a frown, "cannot thine own guilty conscience sufficiently answer it? What thinkest thou thou deservest at the hands of that man whom thou hast so deeply injured?"

"Alas! alas!" groaned the old mam, "I know it all, too well, I acknowledge it; but—but—I am an aged man, worn down by anxiety and remorse; spare me, Malvern, in mercy spare me, and suffer me to depart."

"Suffer thee to depart!" repeated Godfrey, hastily, "ha, ha, ha! why what a very fool, a madman thou must deem me. Have I not in vain, in every quarter of the globe; by land and sea, in storm and sunshine, been searching for thee for years. And now that I have found thee, and have thee completely in my power, thinkest thou that I am going to suffer thee again to escape? I have a long account to settle with thee, Gerald Aubrey, and we part not again."

"Oh, on my knees I beseech thee," cried the distracted Scrimpe, in frenzied accents, and sinking at the feet of his inexorable enemy, "I am a ruined man; and the few short months that I may be permitted to live, my punishment will be sufficiently severe, although I do acknowledge, no more than my guilt merits. Thou hast a large portion of my gold, take it, and suffer me to—"

"Cease! cease!" sternly interrupted Malvern, "thou dost supplicate to me in vain. My determination is fixed."

"Oh, God!" groaned the Miser, and throwing himself back in his chair, and burying his face in his hands, he gave himself up to the intense and excruciating anguish and despair of his feelings. He saw at once that it was useless to appeal to Malvern for mercy and forebearance, and all the horrors of the fate that assuredly sooner or later awaited him, rushed with the most overwhelming force upon his disordered brain.

Godfrey now rung the bell, (he having satisfied his own appetite, and amply made up for the abstinence of poor old Jasper,) and Hugo entered the room.

"Now," demanded Malvern, "is all ready?"

"Aye," answered Hugo, "I have made the chamber as comfortable as possible, though I know not whether it will answer the old gentleman's expectations."

"Beggars must not be chosers;" observed Malvern;—and anything is better than being exposed to the tempest of the night, lead the way, Hugo."

Hugo nodded assent, and taking up a lamp, he beckoned Jasper and Malvern to follow him, and led the way. The Miser shuddered, hesitated, and looked imploringly at Godfrey, but the scowling look which the latter fixed upon him, silenced him, and, led by Godfrey, he followed Hugo from the room.

The interior of the house exhibited evident signs of its antiquity, and it had doubtless, at one period been the residence of some distinguished individual, for it still bore the remains of former magnificence. They ascended a staircase of oak, and then found themselves in a gallery of considerable dimentions, and upon which several rooms opened; Hugo led the way to one of those at the further end of the place, and opening the door, ushered Jasper and his companion into the chamber.

The Miser cast his eyes anxiously around the room, and it being small and dark, miserably furnished, and the casements secured with iron bars, it had a cheerless, prison-like appearance, and struck a chill upon his heart. A fire, however, that was burning in the grate, was a welcome sight, and imparted some little degree of comfort to the room.

"I will rejoin thee in a few minutes below, Hugo," said Malvern, "retire."

Hugo bowed and obeyed.

"Now, Gerald," said Malvern, "here is thy apartment for the night, and it strikes me that it is a much better one than thou hast been accustomed to for many years past."

"It is a gloomy place," replied Jasper, "and excites in my breast a sensation of dread as I gaze upon it. Why are the windows secured in such a manner."

"Ask no questions," returned Godfrey, "but be satisfied with the accommodation. There is a bed, so thou canst retire to rest whenever thou think'st proper. Good night, old man," he added, ironically, "and pleasant dreams to thee."

"Stay, stay, Godfrey," exclaimed the Miser, grasping his arm and detaining him, "do not leave me thus in this terrible state of doubt and suspense."

"What, is thy conscience so busy that thou fearest to be alone?" demanded Malvern, with a malicious look.

"Oh, forbear, forbear," returned Jasper, "why delight to taunt me thus?"

"Because it gratifies me to do so," replied Malvern, "now, what wouldst thou?"

"Once more I pray thee to tell me what are thy intentions?"

"To hold thee in safe custody; more thou wilt not know at present."

"Oh, this torturing suspense;" groaned the Miser, "how it racks my brain. Where, oh, where is the place of our destination?"

"Well," replied Godfrey, after a pause, "I do not mind solving that question, if it will afford thee any gratification. Before many hours have elapsed after we quit this house, we shall be on the wide waters of the ocean!"

"The ocean!" repeated Scrimpe, with a look of astonishment and alarm; "ah! thou canst not mean what thou sayest, thou art sporting with my feelings."

"Thy feelings!" said Malvern, in scornful accents, "and has a guilty hardened wretch like thee any sense of feeling?"

"Oh, why expose the poor old man to the terrors of the perilous deep?"

"Dost fear them?" demanded Malvern, with a mysterious look; "dost shudder at the thoughts of the dark waters of the ocean? For years it has been my element, my boundless home, my fate, my fortune has been cast upon it; I have battled with the breeze, braved the shoals and the rocks, and laughed the raging of the angry tempest to scorn."

"Ah! what meanest thou?" eagerly demanded the Miser; "thy words fill me with amazement and curiosity. Explain thyself."

"Listen," said Malvern, taking a chair. "As thou art so anxious, I will e'en gratify thy curiosity, and when thou hearest my recital, methinks thou wilt no longer marvel at the feelings of hatred and revenge I bear towards thee. 'Tis thou, thou that has been the cause of all."

The Miser trembled, but did not attempt to speak, and Malvern proceeded—

"Thy base myrmidons by thine order, having seized me at midnight, in spite of the desperate resistance I made, (for I thought that murder was their intention, and I resolved to sell my life dearly), bore me away to a dungeon, underneath the old ruins, situated near the mansion of thy late victim; there they forced me to swallow some powerful stupifying drug, (at the time I thought it was poison), and I immediately fell into a state of insensibility. How long I had remained so, I had not the least means of judging; but when I was restored to a state of consciousness, I found myself, to my utter astonishment on board a vessel, and out at sea. This ship I soon discovered was a slaver, and bound to the coast of Africa; and the horrors of the fate to which, thou, guilty old man, hadst consigned me, now became apparent to me, and in the fury of my rage, I invoked the lightning of Heaven upon thine head, and called upon the spirit of thy murdered victim to haunt thee to horror and despair!"

"Hold, hold!" cried the terrified, and conscience-stricken Jasper Scrimpe, with a shudder; "hold, I implore thee!"

"Ah!" said Malvern; "it makes thee tremble, and what think'st thou I must have felt who had to endure such unparalled sufferings? Oh, it was a monstrous deed, and it could have been the mind of a fiend alone that could have designed it.

"The captain of this vessel was a brute, and the wretches that composed his crew, a set of blood-thirsty wretches that had long been inured to crime, and who laughed at my sufferings, and who seized every opportunity to annoy and torture me. How can I properly picture the horrors of my fate? the misery, the shame, the degradation to which I was daily, hourly exposed? And this, all this I was convinced, was inflicted on me by thy base instructions."

"Oh, no,—oh, no!—" exclaimed Jasper, "indeed it was not so; by Heaven, Godfrey, thou wrongest me."

"Thou liest!" cried Malvern, passionately, "attempt not to deny it, but do not interrupt me. For weeks I endured this systematic description of torture, and when I ventured to murmur at it, and to remonstrate, what think'st thou, Gerald Anbrey, was the reward I met with? I was lashed to the gratings and flogged,—aye, flogged like a dog! And thou wert the cause of all this! Dost thou marvel that my wounded soul should thirst for a terrible revenge? Every burning lash that entered my quivering, lacerated flesh, drew forth from my parched and feverish lips a fearful curse upon thine head; each drop of blood that oozed from my gaping wounds increased my thirst for vengeance, and I swore that if I lived, and thou shouldst ever again cross my path, that I would have atonement—aye, atonement, even in thy very heart's blood!"

"Horror! horror!" groaned the distracted Miser, wringing his hands; and fixing his blood-shot eyes upon Malvern; "those dreadful words! how they appal me!"

"Aye, and they should do so;" replied Malvern, in tones of the most deadly malice; "the sight of me should freeze thy blood to ice, and death in all its most frightful forms, should present itself to thy disordered imagination. But hear me out, for I am now resolved to gratify thy morbid curiosity to the fullest extent. At length, after we had been about a couple of months at sea, and in sight of a rocky island, at night when I was just about to retire to my wretched hammock, I was surprised and seized by several of the ruffianly crew—bound hand and foot,—tossed into a boat, and rowed away from the ship. A horrible idea of the fate to which the wretches were about to consign me, flashed across my brain; but I viewed it with comparative indifference, for nothing, I thought could surely be worse than the frightful sufferings to which I had been so long and so mercilessly exposed; and I therefore offered not the least resistance, not a word of complaint. The boat having reached the place of destination, I was landed; one small cask of water and a few biscuits were left with me, and the ruffians returned to the boat; and rowing to the ship, abandoned me to that awful fate which seemed inevitable. Gerald Aubrey, if there is still one spark of feeling left within thy sterile breast, thow mayest imagine and feel for my terrible situation. I was alone on a barren rocky island, in darkness, exposed to the piercing cold, and howling wind, without the least means of shelter from the inclemency of the season, no signs of vegitation near, and with no other prospect but that of a horrible death of starvation before my eyes. Still I remained firm, for there was one thought sustained me, and which was never for an instant absent from my mind, it was the hope of living, and to meet with thee, Gerald, that I might ring my curses in thine ears, and hurl my just retribution on thy devoted head."

Jasper again groaned, and averted his gaze from that of Malvern, who, having contemplated him for a second or two with silent feelings of abhorrence and disgust, once more resumed his painfully interesting recital in the following words:

"In a short time my scanty portion of biscuits and water was consumed, and I then found myself in a truly awful situation, without any chance of food, or without the means of slacking my burning thirst. In this deplorable state I remained for a day and a night, greedily devouring such wild herbage as I could find on the island, and which only served to increase the burning thirst that was upon me, when I fortunately picked up a shell fish that had been drifted on the sands beneath the rock, and which I eagerly eat, it appearing to me one of the greatest luxuries that had ever fallen to my lot. A heavy shower of rain fell shortly afterwards, and having repeatedly soaked my handkerchief in it, I was enabled to quench my thirst. After this I crept into a small recess or cavern in the rock, and, worn out with fatigue and anxiety of mind, I sunk into a sound

sleep, from which, as well as I was able to judge, I did not awaken for many
hours afterwards, and not till the sun of another day had just arisen in the
eastern horizon. I felt somewhat refreshed, but the gnawings of hunger soon
again crept upon me, and I had now no means of appeasing it. The whole of
that wretched day and the next passed away without any change for the better,
and I was so weak and exhausted that my trembling limbs could scarce support
my emaciated form. But not the least prospect of relief from my horrible
situation presented itself, and despair fell upon my heart, and madness seized
upon my brain. Several times 1 was upon the point of putting an end to my
sufferings by terminating my wretched existence, but still the thoughts of
revenge witheld me, and I struggled on. On the fourth day I beheld a vessel
in the distance, and which seemed to be steering in the direction of the island.
When she approached nearer, I waved my handkerchief wildly on high, and
shouted aloud for assistance, though of course it was madness to suppose

    No. 20.

that the persons on board could hear my cries. At length I was gratified to find that they saw me or my signal, for a boat put off from the ship, and rapidly made towards the island. As it came swiftly on, I rushed down the rock on to the beach, and in a few minutes afterwards I was released from my perilous situation, and conveyed in the boat towards the vessel!"

"Oh, thank Heaven!" fervently ejaculated the Miser, "it was most fortunate!"

"Nay," hastily observed Malvern, "thou hast no cause to rejoice at my preservation, and the words thou just now uttered, I am convinced, come not from thine heart. But think not that my sufferings were at an end. The ship proved to be a trading vessel bound for Liverpool, and I was received with every kindness on board. We had not proceeded on our voyage, however, many days, when we were chased by a pirate brig, which quickly bore down upon us, and although we made a most determined resistance, it was of no avail; the pirates boarded us, murdered the captain, mate, and several of the crew, taking the rest prisoners, (among whom was myself,) and, after plundering it of everything valuable that it contained, they fired the vessel, and then proceeded on their course. I now found myself in a situation almost as desperate as that from which I had recently escaped. To join the crew of the pirate ship and swear fidelity to their laws, was the only alternative that was offered, or death. Exposed as I had been to the malice and ingratitude of the world, I had not much hesitation in chosing the former, and I soon become as used to the wild and desperate cause of life as if I had been in it for years, and so far ingratiated myself into the favour of the captain and his ruffianly crew, that I was unanimously elected second in command, and was allowed to exercise almost as much authority as the captain himself. Years passed away, I had become innured to crime, but one thought was ever uppermost in my mind, one anxious hope ever occupied it—it was revenge, unmitigated, terrible revenge on thine accursed head, Gerald Aubrey, and that idea continued to haunt me though years flew by ; sleeping or waking, in the battle or the storm, thou wert ever present to my imagination ; and I left scarcely a spot, abroad or at home, unsearched to find thee; but for a time Fortune favoured me not, and thou didst escape me; but the time hath at length arrived, and now, Gerald Aubrey, I have thee at my mercy"

"Oh, horror! horror!" ejaculated the trembling old man, "then there is no hope!"

"Hope!" repeated Malvern, with a savage look, "no, none for thee. But a few words and I have done. The Pirate Captain being slain in one of our desperate engagements, I succeeded to the command of the vessel, and our daring on the broad waters of the ocean became greater than ever. Gerald Aubrey thou must have heard of that fearful man, commonly called the Sea-devil! He whose gallant barque skims the surface of the blue waters like a bird ; whose deeds appear superhuman, and who sets defeat at defiance, and laughs all threats to scorn. The hardiest mariner, who has been accustomed to face danger in every shape, trembles at his name ; and careful nurses use it, but with a shudder, to frighten fractious children into obedience. Would'st see this desperate man, Gerald Aubrey ? Behold, he stands before thee, in the person of Godfrey Malvern, and thy mortal foe !"

"Lost, lost!" exclaimed the Miser, thunderstruck and appalled at the fearful discovery ; and, overpowered by the tumult of feelings that distracted his brain, he sunk senseless on the floor.

Godfrey Malvern gazed at him for a few minutes with an expression of savage triumph, and then, muttering some indistinct observations betwixt his teeth, he retired from the room, taking good care, however, to lock the door after him.

CHAPTER XXIII.

THE TERROR OF JASPER SCRIMPE.—THE JOURNEY RESUMED.—THE PIRATES.

WHEN the Miser recovered his senses he found himself alone; but the exciting recital of Godfrey Malvern, and the alarming disclosure he had made, were as fresh in his memory as if he had but that moment been listening to his observations, and the agitation of his feelings may be readily imagined. What else had he a right to anticipate but the worst, now that he was in the power of Malvern? and from him he could expect no mercy after the deep injuries he had done him. What would in future become of him? Whither was his terrible enemy now conveying him? Was it really his intention to take him on board the pirate ship? He trembled with fear at the thought.

"Oh, why did I not perish in the flames, rather than be subjected to that lingering, torturing fate which seems too surely in store for me? Oh, why, after the lapse of so many, many years, was Malvern again permitted to cross my path? Oh, why has not the wild waves rolled o'er his head long ere now?"

He paused for a minute or two, his eyes were wild and bloodshot, his hands clenched together, and such was the agitation of his feelings that the perspiration stood upon his temples in large drops.

"Miserable old man that I am," he cried; "it is my own crimes that has brought all this upon me, and I merit it, deeply merit the punishment. Such, such is the curse of avarice!"

Again the wretched man groaned as he gave utterance to these words, and sinking in a chair, he abandoned himself to all the anguish of his emotions. Suddenly, as a thought seemed to strike him, he hastened to the door, but finding it fastened he returned to his seat, and once more resigned himself to the most painful thoughts.

The storm had somewhat abated; but the lightning still flashed less vividly, and at longer intervals; the thunder murmured in the distance; the rain came down less violently, and the wind mourned in fitful gusts. The Miser cast a timid glance around the room, and nothing could be more cheerless than the aspect it had at that moment. The fire was nearly burnt out, and the faint reflection it was enabled to cast upon the oaken pannelled wall, only served to make the gloom of the place more striking. The light in the lamp, too, which Malvern had left him, burnt dim, and cast a sickly glare upon the objects around, which the disordered imagination of Jasper Scrimpe distorted into all kinds of frightful and fantastic shapes, and almost trembled to contemplate them. It must be near the morning; but, notwithstanding the fatigue, and the extraordinary exertions he had undergone, Jasper did not feel inclined, or rather he was afraid to retire to rest, and a confused noise from below, which now reached his ears, convinced him that there were other persons in the house who had not sought their beds besides himself. He once more approached the door, and listened attentively, and the voice of Malvern was the first that reached his ears, though he could not distinguish a word that he said. This was succeeded by a song, sung with considerable gusto, by one of the company, and it was followed at its conclusion by loud laughter and applause.

"How these rude sounds shock and alarm me," remarked the Miser; "and especially at such an unseasonable hour as this. These are probably some of the pirate crew come to join their captain, and to conduct me to their fearful vessel. Oh, how my heart throbs at the thought. Alas! what is the fate in store for the wretched Miser?"

The agitation of the old man increased every moment, and despair settled upon his heart. Oh, how painfully fresh was now his memory in recalling the guilty deeds of the past. The black and frightful catalogue of his crimes was presented to his distracted imagination in characters of fire. They seemed to burn, to eat into his very soul, and coil around his heart like envenomed serpents, while strange and appalling sounds rang in his ears, maddening and bewildering his senses. In the intense agony of his feelings he clenched his hands vehemently together till his nails penetrated his flesh, and brought the warm blood from the lacerations thus inflicted. His eyes were blood-shot and wildly glared on vacancy. Imagination could not conceive a more fearful picture of remorse, despair, and abject misery, than that guilty man presented at that moment. Then he partly sank upon his knees, and made a vain effort to pray ;—pray ! could prayers escape the lips of one so utterly accursed of Heaven and man? He started to his feet, terrified at his own presumption.

The voices of the persons below had now ceased, and all was hushed in solemn silence, which was far more painful and impressive than the noise and confusion which had before prevailed, for it was now more fearfully apparent to the wretched Miser that he was alone and in a strange place, with nothing but his own torturing thoughts, and with the dreadful uncertainty of the fate that awaited him, though from the character and feelings towards him of the man in whose power he was, he had every reason to anticipate the worst, and coward fears completely unnerved him, and drove him to distraction. And now an old clock in the house struck in dismal and monotonous tones the hour of three; he started at the sounds—each stroke to him sounded like the knell of death—the awful summons to ignominious execution ; he paused—his mind was wandering, and he scarcely knew where he was. Awhile he stood in a fixed attitude and listened. The low moanings of the wind, as it ever and anon swept around the ancient building, were the only sounds that met his ears, and he made another powerful effort to compose his feelings, and this time he succeeded much better than he had done before. He was exhausted with thinking, and in the hope of gaining a short respite to his mental sufferings, he stretched his weary limbs upon the couch, and closing his eyes, he endeavoured to compose himself to rest; for some time he tried in vain, and tossed about in a nervous state of inquietude, but at length, completely worn out with fatigue and anxiety, he sank into a troubled slumber, which was nearly as torturing to him as his waking moments. Ghostly forms arose to his terrified imigination, and visions of the most frightful description troubled his disordered fancy. How long he had thus slept he had no means of judging, but suddenly a terrific sound, even more awful than the recent warfare of the elements had been vibrated in his ears, and he started wildly from the bed, and glared appalled around the gloomy chamber : was it reality, or only the effects of his disordered imagination and his guilty conscience ? At that moment he could have sworn that he heard a hollow sepulchral voice exclaim—

" Murderer, sleep no more! be thy future hours those of restless torture ; " and as his frenzied eyes still glared upon the spot whence the unearthly sounds seemed to proceed, he beheld, or fancied he beheld, a tall shadowy form glide noiselessly past the foot of the bed, and vanish on the opposite side of the room. The guilty Jasper was transfixed to the spot ! terror palsied all his faculties; large drops of perspiration stood upon his aching temples ; his every limb trembled convulsively ; the hot blood seemed to rush in a torrent to his heart, and for a moment his breath was suspended in horror and fearful expectation. All, however, was hushed in solemn silence, and no object calculated to excite alarm was to be seen in the misty obscurity of the room. The Miser struggled with the overwhelming emotions that had paralyzed his senses, and breathed again.

"It was but my troubled fancy," he ejaculated; "the demon workings of my guilty conscience. Oh, when shall I be released from such dreadful torments? When will peace again descend upon the mind of the wretched Jasper Scrimpe? Peace! the wretched Miser shall never know peace again."

"*The murderer shall never know peace agaim!*" were the fearful words that in the most sepulchral tones now sounded in his ears, and struck upon his soul like the knell of death. This time he was too awfully convinced that he was not deceived; that he was labouring under no delusion of his perturbed imagination. Trembling and appalled, he started to his feet, and glared with terrible expectation through the misty obscurity of the room towards the spot from whence the unearthly sounds seemed to proceed. Merciful Powers! how great was the horror that seized upon his every faculty at the frightful object that now met his sight! Standing before him, in the grey mists of early dawn, and at the further end of the chamber, he beheld a pale shadowy form, clad in the costume of a remote period, and fixed in an attitude of impressive solemnity. It was that of a man. At first it was indistinct, but gradually it seemed to dilate itself, and become too fearfully visible to the appalled gaze of the guilty man. One long, thin, bony hand, was pointed menacingly towards him, the other was diverted to a gaping wound in its side, and from which the purple fluid of life still seemed to flow! For a moment or two the disturbed Jasper could not distinguish the features of this ghastly phantom; but at length they were revealed to him in all their thrilling horror. How his guilty soul quailed at the sight! Clearly revealed to his gaze were the pale and cadaverous features of his murdered victim; the hollow eyes fixed upon him with an expression which made him shudder in every limb.

For a minute or two Jasper stood transfixed to the spot till his eyes were ready to start from their sockets, and still the spectre (for such Jasper could no longer doubt it was,) remained immovable. For a time the tongue of the Miser clove to the roof of his mouth, and terror so completely bound up all his faculties that he was unable to give utterance to a syllable. But at length, worked up to a pitch of complete delirium, he rushed towards the spot where the object of his terror was standing, and in a hoarse voice, he exclaimed:—

"Dread shade of he who fell beneath this accursed hand,—oh, why—oh, why dost thou appear to my appalled sight? Avaunt! avaunt! The terrible vengeance of outraged Heaven is in thy ghastly looks, and my guilty soul shrinks with horrow at the sight! Avaunt! avaunt!"

The lips of the spectre seemed not to move, but these awful words sounded in the Miser's ears:—

"Murderer, prepare to meet thy doom, rest no more! rest no more!"

The Miser, urged on by some inscrutable power, rushed towards his unearthly visitor, he extended his hands as if to clutch it! At that moment a peal of thunder shook the roof of the building. The phantom gradually receded, becoming more and more indistinct, till it faded into thin air, and vanished from the Miser's sight. For a minute he was paralyzed in every limb; the dew of terror bathed his temples; frenzy seized upon his brain; his limbs failed him, and staggering back, with an hysterical laugh, he sunk upon the floor in a state of insensibility.

CHAHTER XXIV.

THE MISER'S AGONY.—THE TRIUMPH OF GODFREY MALVERN.—
THE OPIATE.

To what a state of horror did the wretched man recover. All the awful events of the past hour were impressed upon his memory in characters so appalling that they shook his every nerve; and the more so as the longer he reflected, the more did he become convinced that he had not been labouring under any delusion of his senses. He feared to look around him, and staggering to a seat he buried his face in his hands, and abandoned himself to the maddening thoughts that distracted his brain, and at intervals groans of the most poignant anguish escaped his breast.

He was interrupted by the sound of approaching footsteps ascending the stairs, and presently afterwards the room door was unlocked, and Hugo entered, bringing with him a tray, on which was some provisions, which he placed upon the table, and then turning to Jasper, said:—

"I have brought you your breakfast, which I should imagine you can now eat with a pretty good appetite, having fasted so long. Though, if all that has been told me concerning thee be true, thou hast not been in the habit of indulging thine epicurean propensities for some years past."

"Bah!" exclaimed the Miser, angrily, "thou art lavish of thine insolence, fellow, methinks. Where is Godfrey Malvern?"

"Oh," answered the ruffian, ironically, "the *Captain* is enjoying himself below, and no doubt will do himself the honour of personally inquiring after thine health anon, Master Jasper Scrimpe. He thought, perhaps, the company of his friends might not be agreeable to thee this morning, and therefore allowed thee to breakfast alone. I hope thou slept well, and that thou found everything agreeable in this comfortable chamber."

Jasper frowned, but returned no answer to this coarse speech, and Hugo quitted the room, locking the door after him. Jasper sat for a few minutes in moody thought, and painful were the fears and melancholy forebodings that came over him. He saw at once that there was no chance of escape for him, and that his doom was sealed; it was therefore in vain that he endeavoured to compose the anguish, and to bear up against the misery of his fate with any degree of fortitude or resignation. And what was his future destination? Alas! had not Malvern fully satisfied him upon that point? He was to be exposed to all the perils of the ocean; borne far away from his native land; compelled to be associated with wretches abandoned in crime, and to witness scenes of bloodshed and horror, sufficient to appal the stoutest and most insensible heart. He would hourly have to experience the bitter taunts and reproaches of Godfrey, to be reminded, with feelings of exultation, of the guilty deeds of the past, the terrors of the future, and at any moment when his implacable enemy thought proper, to be sacrificed to his malice and revenge.

In this manner more than a couple of hours passed away, and no one intruded upon him. It seemed that the company below had increased; if so it might be judged from the noise and confusion of their voices, their conversation being carried on in no very minor key, and frequently interspersed with coarse laughter and fearful oaths, which were particularly revolting and disgusting to the Miser's ears, in the state of mind under which he then laboured, and thouroughly convinced him of the brutal and abandoned characters of the men who now formed the companions of Malvern, and with whom in future he should doubtless be compelled to associate. This thought was sufficiently torturing, and the old man clasped his hands together and traversed the room with hasty and disordered steps.

The noise from behind ceased for a brief interval, and Jasper was in hopes that the ruffians had quitted the house; but he was quickly undeceived, for again their loud laughter met his ears, and it was presently succeeded by the following rude song and chorus, which was given in such stentorian tones that he was able to distinguish every word. They ran as follows :—

"O'er the blue sea, o'er the blue sea,
We pirates rove right merrily ;
Reckless of danger, those who dare
To scorn our power, may well beware.
No matter the weather, in day or night,
Though the tempest rages in all its might;

The pirate's barque to seek its prey,
O'er the dark waves still wings its way."

CHORUS.

O'er the blue sea !—o'er the blue sea,
We pirates rove right merrily !

The most tumultuous demonstrations of applause followed this effusion, and then once more a temporary silence ensued. Every word of the song made a powerful impression upon the heart of Jasper, for in it he seemed to read the doom that awaited him, and in the power of such hardened miscreants, what mercy or forbearance could he expect ?

"Oh, better, far better it would have been for me had I perished in the flames that condemned my wretched dwelling," he exclaimed, "than to be exposed to the lingering state of torture that too surely awaits me. Cruel fate has conspired against me, and it is in vain that I may seek to avoid it. Oh, what scenes of horror arise upon my distempered imagination; what harrowing sufferings do I too readily anticipate ! and is there no chance of escape ? None, none!—I am in the power of one who is goaded on by an insatiable spirit of malice and revenge for the wrongs I have done him, and I am powerless as an infant to resist his dreaded will."

He threw himself in a chair, and swaying his body too and fro, in the uncontrollable paroxysm of his agony, groaned aloud. In this deplorable situation he remained for some time, and thus the morning wore dismally away, and the afternoon was far advanced, before anyone again attempted to interrupt him in his misery and solitude, and the silence which now reigned around, so different to the riot and tumult which had recently prevailed, convinced him that most of the ruffians had quitted the house. While these thoughts still occupied his mind, he was aroused by hearing some one ascend the stairs, and he awaited with some degree of anxiety to ascertain who it was. He was not long kept in suspense, the door was unlocked, and the long expected Godfrey Malvern made his appearance. He walked into the room, and folding his arms across his chest, stood and contemplated the Miser for a minute or two with looks of triumph and satisfaction. Jasper Scrimpe could not help shuddering at his presence, and averted his looks with a groan.

"I ask thy pardon, Gerald Aubrey," said Malvern at length, in tones of sarcasm, "I ask thy pardon for obtruding on thy privacy, but I began to fear that thou might'st think mine absence strange and disrespectful, and would be anxious to see me again."

"Oh, hold thine irony, Malvern," said the old man, with a mingled expression of fear and supplication, "I know full well the hatred thou bearest towards me; but is it not enough for thee to know that thou holdest me in thy power, and that thou hast me entirely at thy will and mercy, but that thou must thus seem to take a fiendish delight to torture me ? What wouldst thou with me now ?"

"Merely desire thee to prepare thyself for a speedy departure from this place," replied Malvern; "the evening approaches, and ere the morning dawns, we must be at the end of our journey."

"And whither wouldst thou convey me?" demanded Jasper, with a look of anxiety.

"Have I not already informed thee?" answered Malvern; "thou goest to the home of the daring Rover of the seas;—thy future fate will be upon the dark blue waters of the deep; and when the foaming billows wash the decks of my gallant craft, and the fierce tempest howls around, haply thou mayest fancy that thou hearest the voices of thy murdered victims in the blast, and remorse at length seize upon thy guilty conscience.

The Miser trembled, and almost feared to look upon his dreaded enemy.

"Oh, cease, cease;" he cried, in tremulous accents; "thy words distract me. Oh, surely thou wilt not consign me to such a wretched fate as that which thou hast just so fearfully depictured."

"And darest thou hope that I will relent?" said Godfrey, in tones that shewed the triumph and hatred of his feelings;—"have I not ample cause to despise thy supplications, and to mock at thy sufferings?—Oh, thou canst form no idea of the deep laid scheme of vengeance I have in store for thee. Gerald Aubrey, if years of crime have not rendered thine heart cold and insensible as adamant, I will wring it to its inmost core."

"Fearful man!" groaned the unfortunate Miser; cease those dreadful threats; —implacable as I know full well is the hatred thou bearest me, thou surely wilt not have the heart to put thy terrible threats into execution."

"If thou supposeth that I will for a moment hesitate to perform all that I have promised," returned Malvern; "thou hast sadly miscalculated, Gerald Aubrey, thou formest but an erroneous idea of the man thou hast so deeply, so imparably wronged."

"Alas! alas, then," exclaimed the distracted Miser; "better hadst thou take my life at once;—it would be more merciful of thee to bury thy dagger this moment in my heart, and thus satiate thy feelings of deadly revenge."

"Ah! no;" replied Godfrey; "that would indeed be treating thee with far too much mercy, and would rob me of half my triumph. Thou shalt live to suffer, guilty old man;—live to endure the horrors of remorse and despair; and as I view the maddening agony of thy tortures, it will be my delight to laugh at and revile thee, and to invent fresh schemes to harrow up thy guilty soul to frenzy."

"God of Heaven!" exclaimed Jasper, in a hoarse voice;—"and am I indeed reserved for a fate like this? Oh, Malvern, thou canst not, thou wilt not carry thy diabolical vengeance to such a fiendish extent at that which thou hast described! Already hast thou surely had ample satisfaction in seeing the anguish thou hast inflicted on me; and in witnessing the bitterness of my remorse,—spare me, then, spare me, on my knees I implore thee to spare me!"

With these words, Jasper Scrimpe sank on his knees at the feet of the inexorable Godfrey Malvern, who, however, spurned him from him, and turned away with a look of derision and contempt.

"Bah!" he ejaculated; "miserable old dotard, this is but a waste of time, and thou mayest e'en spare thy prayers and entreaties, for they can make not the least impression on me. My determination is fixed, so thou mayest as well resign thyself to the fate which most certainly awaits thee, and which thou canst not possibly avert. But for the present I leave thee; as soon as darkness shall have veiled the earth we resume our journey."

Jasper, in the despair of his feelings, was about to make some reply, but Godfrey abruptly quitted the room, and left him to the uninterrupted indulgence of his own torturing thoughts. What they were may be readily imagined, and we will not attempt to describe them; and for several minutes after he was gone

Jasper remained in that state of stupefaction, which rendered him almost unconscious as to where he was, and such was the intensity of his emotions that for some time he was deprived of the power of utterance.   At length he started from the seat on which he had powerlessly fallen, and glaring vacantly and wildly around him, he exclaimed in hoarse accents :—

"He's gone, he's gone ! and left the recollection of his threats scorching my brain, and racking my very soul to distraction !—Oh, why did he not stretch me a corpse at his feet?—Why am I still suffered to live, to endure upon earth even more than the torments of the damned ?   Would that I had poison that I might drink oblivion to my anguish !   Oblivion!—No !—that will not be !   Fool !—and dare I hope that my sufferings would end with the termination of my existence ?   No, no,—beyond the grave, for a guilty wretch like me, there is an eternity of horror which I shudder to contemplate.   Oh, shield me, shield me, Heaven, from the dreadful, the hideous doom ! "

No. 21.

Convulsive sobs choked his further utterance; his senses reeled, and he sank once more in the chair, for a time totally unconscious of all around him. Gradually the sombre shades of evening descended upon the earth, and Jasper was aroused from his state of torpidity, by hearing the sound of wheels rolling up to the door of the building. He immediately guessed that it was the vehicle which had conveyed him from London, and therefore prepared himself once more to depart on his dreary journey. He had not to wait long, for Hugo soon afterwards entered the room, and without saying a word motioned to him to follow him. Jasper knew it would be useless to appeal to him, and he therefore followed in silence, and descending the stairs, and entering the parlour he found Malvern, and the same men who had accompanied them from London, ready equipped for the journey. Godfrey drew Hugo aside, and whispered a few words to him in an under tone, to which the latter nodded assent, Malvern then turning to the Miser, said :—

"Thou hast partaken of little, for several hours, old man ;—but if thou art wise thou wilt not now refuse a glass of wine, previous to resuming the journey."

"I require nothing;—" replied Jasper ;--"my mind is too troubled to—"

"Psha !—" interrupted Malvern, forcing a glass upon him ;—" thou must drink I say; for thou wilt need something to counteract the effects of the night air ; and it may be long ere thou hast the same opportunity."

Jasper found it was useless any longer to resist, so, taking the glass from Godfrey's hand, he quaffed off the contents in an instant, and without any further objection. On taking the glass from his lips, he saw, or fancied that he saw, a malicious look of triumph and satisfaction expressed on the features of Malvern, and for the first time a fearful suspicion flushed upon his brain, namely, that he had swallowed poison! and no sooner had the thought occurred to him than a sickly sensation came over him ;—his brain turned giddy ;—a mist seemd to gather before his eyes ;—objects became indistinct to his vision ;—his limbs failed him, and he remembered no more !

CHAPTER XXV.

WAPPING IN THE OLDEN TIME.—EVELYN HEARTWELL DECIDES UPON HIS DESTINY.—MABEL'S AFFECTIONATE DETERMINATION.

GREATLY agitated by the excitement which his feelings had experienced in the last hour, and with the melancholy impression of his affecting parting interview with his beloved Constance, and his scene with Mabel, the Gipsey-girl, still strongly upon his mind, our hero hurried on his way through the dark streets, meeting but with few persons of whom he took no notice, and almost unconscious of the course he was taking. At length having got to some distance, and being out of breath with the speed at which he had been walking, he paused, and looked around him, and for some time his brain was so confused and bewildered that he knew not where he was.

He stood and reflected for a minute or two, and recovering himself a little, he was enabled the more distinctly to observe the locality to which his footeps had wandered, and now for the first time he found himself standing on Tower Hill; and the blackened walls of that ancient fortress arose in massive, bold relief, upon the dim obscurity of the horizon, and seemed to frown upon all beneath.

While Evelyn was thus standing deeply engaged in painful thought, and undecided which way he should go, as his eyes wandered to the opposite side of the way, he suddenly caught a glimpse of a tall form, but whether that of male or female he could not distinguish, lurking under a gateway, and seemingly watching him. His curiosity being excited, and, uncertain whether it might be friend or foe, he laid his hand upon the hilt of his sword, to be prepared to defend himself, in case of necessity, and stepped towards the place; but before he could reach it, the individual, whoever it was, glided swiftly from the spot, hastily turned the corner of an adjacent thoroughfare, and was almost immediately hidden from his view in the darkness of the night. In the hasty glance, however, which he had been enabled to take of its receding form, he had sufficient opportunity to recognise the person of Mabel, and it was therefore evident that she had perseveringly dogged his footsteps from the place where they had before parted, and that she was determined to ascertain whither he was going. The affectionate self-devotion of the poor wanderer could not but move the susceptible heart of Evelyn greatly, and gave rise to many torturing and conflicting emotions in his breast.

"Rash girl," he soliloquised, "alas! what advantage canst thou expect to gain by thus pursuing the footsteps of the wretched, friendless Evelyn? What strange infatuation is it that possesses thee?"

He was interrupted by the sound of rude laughter, and several voices in noisy conversation, and, looking in the direction from whence it seemed to proceed, he beheld several men, habited in the dress of seamen, and apparently half intoxicated, advancing towards the spot where he was standing; and in order to avoid being observed by them, he stepped aside under the gateway which Mabel had lately occupied, and as they passed, he could ascertain from their observations that they were on their way to the neighbourhood of Wapping, and this suggested to him his own course; there he was the most likely, he thought, to obtain a ship, and thither therefore he resolved to go.

"Yes," he said, "there is no other course left open to me, unhappy outcast; persecuted being as I am, and annihilated as now are all my hopes, it matters but little what becomes of me. Oh, Constance, dear Constance, and yet how severe is the pang that tortures my heart at leaving thee, and probably for ever! Poor girl, what sufferings wilt thou not be exposed to when I am far away, and thou art left entirely to the mercy of the villain, Dalton? Alas! that thought alone distracts me."

He drew forth a miniature likeness of our heroine, which he always wore in his bosom, as he thus spoke, and as he gazed upon the dear resemblance his emotions increased, and deep sighs of mental anguish escaped his breast. He pressed the loved treasure again and again to his lips, but at length aroused to the necessity of action he returned it to his bosom, and, having first looked around to be certain that he was not still watched by Mabel, he proceeded on the way that the sailors had taken.

England was at that time engaged in one of the fiercest wars that had raged during the reign of Elizabeth. Some glorious triumphs had been achieved by the matchless and indomitable bravery of her seamen, but not without great losses, and in consequence, men for the navy were in great demand, the more especially as an expedition on a scale of magnitude hitherto almost unprecedented, was being fitted out, with the hope of bringing the enemy to speedy submission. The patriotic blood of every man was aroused, and the enthusiasm of the people was at its highest pitch. All those localities near the water side, at all times and seasons presented, a most animated scene; every tavern was full of sailors, drinking and carousing, indulging in coarse jests, vociferating national songs, eulogizing the prowess of the British Navy, or spinning tough yarns, and recounting various wonderful exploits proformed on the broad waters of the vast deep, for the amusement of their credulous and delighted listeners. In most of those riotous scenes the wives and sweethearts of the sailors took an active part, and mingled their jests and their laughter with that of their rude companions.

In every quarter the cheerful strains of music might be heard, and the merry dance prevailed with the spirit and vivacity so characteristic of British sailors when ashore. To add to the effect of the scene, the Union Jack was flying from every tavern and public building, the sight of which, as they waved proudly in the air, increased the excitement of the persons assembled, and added to the enthusiasm that already glowed within their breasts.

Such was the general aspect of old Wapping, at the time that Evelyn Heartwell arrived there ; and he paused at the entrance, and gazed with mingled feelings of pleasure and astonishment at the novelty of the scene. Several of them decorated with banners and striking devises; the dingy old wooden houses had quite a lively appearance, and the sounds of music, the noise of revelry and laughter, and the bustle and activity that prevailed around, could not but excite the interest of the beholder. Evelyn continued to watch the proceedings for some time, and for a brief period they diverted his thoughts from the melancholy subject which had before so completely engrossed them. At length, however, feeling tired, and likewise requiring some refreshment, he walked towards a tavern, which to him presented a more inviting appearance than the rest, and took his seat at one corner of the table underneath the window, on the outside of the building, and remote from the rest of the company with whom he had no wish to mingle or to be observed by them. He had scarcely taken his seat, and procured some refreshment when the noise which proceeded from within the house aroused him from the lethargy of thought into which he had again fallen, and he could not help listening with some degree of pleasure to the words of the following song and chorus, which were given with considerable spirit, if not with much musical ability :—

The Union Jack flies at the main,
To awe the daring foe again;
The gallant fleet, with fav'ring breeze,
Prepares to brave the dangerous seas.
Britannia's hardy hearts of oak,
Go to break the tyrant's yoke;
And patriot souls with ardour glow,

Their dauntless still to show.
Then, three cheers for the Union Jack,
The gallant Union Jack!
That flaunts on high,
'Neath a smiling sky,
Hurrah for the Union Jack!

This effusion concluded, it was of course rewarded by the heartiest plaudits of the jovial company assembled, and animated by a patriotic feeling, our hero could not help participating in the sentiment of the song.

"Yes," he ejaculated ; "that noble flag which never yet struck to any foreign foe, now waves proudly on high, inviting the brave, and the loyal, and the enthusiastic to arm in defence of our country, our homes, and our queen ;—and is there among those who bear the names of Englishmen one dastard knave who would shrink from the performance of his duty, or hesitate to lend his aid, and even to risk his life in so sacred a cause?"

"Marry, and those are worthy sentiments, my young hero, and speak well for thy spirit of loyalty and patriotism !"

Such were the observations given utterance to immediately in the ear of our hero, who, starting with some confusion at the idea of having being overheard, beheld a man, habited in the dress of a naval officer, standing at his elbow, and eyeing him with no little degree of interest and curiosity.

He was a young man, apparently about his own age, of tall and commanding figure, and as far as Evelyn could distinguish them in the darkness, with handsome and intelligent features ; in fact, his whole appearance was prepossessing in the extreme, and immediately inspired our hero's confidence.

"Thou wilt excuse my freedom, my friend ;" observed the stranger, seating himself without any further ceremony by the side of Evelyn ; "but I am a seaman, and have, young though I am, been long inured to the perils and dangers of the ocean ; and it is a glorious life to lead, which I would not exchange for the most illustrious, enviable, and distinguished station on land. I admire the sentiments thou hast just expressed, sir, and believing thee to be one after my own heart, I should be proud and happy to make thine acquaintance."

" Alas !" replied our hero ; " I fear sir, that thou wouldst meet with but a sorry and gloomy companion in the man of whom thou hast been pleased to take such notice. "

" Thou art unfortunate, I presume, from thine observations ; " said the stranger; " Fate has probably frowned upon thee ;—but what of that ?—Thou mayest yet find ample compensation for the capricious tricks of fortune. Away then with dismal thoughts!—overboard with them I say, and if thy words express the real spirit of patriotism that animates thy breast, enter at once upon the glorious career that now opens upon thee, and invites thee, and in the battles of thy country gain that honour and distinction that should be the ambition of every noble heart."

" Thy words are manly, sir," said Evelyn, with a look of admiration, " and are in perfect unison with my feelings. Thou hast imagined rightly in supposing me to be the victim of untoward fate, and fain would I tare myself away from scenes that now only serve to remind me of my own misery ; gladly would I contribute my humble aid to the service of my country, but, novice as I am in these matters, I am ignorant of the way to accomplish my wishes.

" If then thou wilt accept the friendly offices of Walter Greysham," said the young man ; and, at the mention of that name, Evelyn uttered an exclamation of astonishment, and fixed upon his companion an eager and enquiring look.

" Walter Greysham!" he interrupted, "is it possible? if thou art indeed he whom I once knew by that name, 'tis many years since we last met. Ah ! it is— it is—I now recognise thy features, Walter : dost thou not recollect thine old friend, Evelyn Heartwell ? "

" Evelyn Heartwell !" repeated the young man, in eager tones, and looking more narrowly into his features, " can it be? yes—by all my hopes, it is. Evelyn, my playfellow, schoolfellow, and earliest friend, this is indeed a most welcome meeting, but I much regret to see thee looking so sad and careworn ; I am afraid that sorrow has indeed made sad ravages upon thy constitution. But we cannot converse freely here ; come, let us into the house. Ah ! who is that? dost thou not observe the form of a woman yonder, in the shadow of that old porch ? It appears to me as though she were watching us."

Our hero looked eagerly in the direction to which his companion pointed, and the light from a torch borne by some pedestrian at that moment falling full upon the person of the woman, to his astonishment and confusion, he discovered that it was Mabel. He turned to offer some words in explanation to Walter Greysham, and when he looked again, the Gipsey-girl was gone.

" It is only some curious stranger," he said, trying to conceal his emotion as much as he could from the observation of Walter Greysham; " come, my friend, let us into the house, for I have much to say to thee."

Greysham assented, and having entered the tavern, were shown into a room apart from the other guests, and where they could converse without interruption. No sooner had they disappeared, than Mabel emerging from the place where she had temporarily concealed herself, when she thought she was likely to be observed by Evelyn, once more approached the house, and taking the seat which had recently been occupied by our hero, and avoiding the scrutiny of the persons near her as much as possible, became buried in profound and melancholy meditation. Yes, with the most unshaken determination, the poor girl had followed closely upon the footsteps of Evelyn, and had watched him to the present place. Her countenance was flushed with the excitement of her feelings, but the expression of her eyes and features was firm and resolute, while it was not unmingled with a line of melancholy, which showed plainly the emotion of doubt and fear that agitated her breast.

"Thou thinkest to avoid me, Evelyn Heartwell," she muttered to herself; "thou would'st with cold scorn, neglect, and indifference, abandon the Gipsey-girl to her fate, whilst the image of the beloved Constance Welborn will, in whatever scene thou mayest in future be destined to mingle, be treasured in the inmost recesses of thine heart, and be the constant object of thy thoughts and fondest solicitude. But think not that I will be so easily repulsed, or that I will abandon those hopes I have once ventured to encourage, in spite of all the obstacles that are thrown in my way. No, at every risk, even that of life itself, I will continue to follow thee wherever fate may guide thy footsteps; o'er the boundless waters of the deep, o'er barren wild or sandy desert, through every scene of danger and of difficulty I will continue to pursue thee with that affectionate zeal which now animates me and stimulates all my actions, even though my only reward shall be thy scorn and hatred; my resolution is fixed, and what power is there that can shake it ? "

Her countenance became more expressive of the feelings that held possession of her breast, as she thus soliloquized, and she remained seated in the same attitude of deep thought, and took no notice of the persons near her.

In the meantime Evelyn and Walter Greysham were engaged in a conversation of the most interesting description, and one which they both entered into with equal spirit.

"And how is it, Evelyn," said his companion, "that I now behold thee in this melancholy condition? Alas! I fear that Fortune has lately treated thee most scurvily."

"Thou judgest truly, Greysham;" answered our hero; "I have had that to contend with which would be sufficient to crush even more stubbon spirits than mine. Heaven alone knows what I have suffered, and the wretched state of misery and despair to which I am now reduced. All my brightest prospects blighted, my fondest hopes annihilated. Driven from the pale of society by the most inconceivable villainy, snd branded with the name of felon."

"Is it possible ?" said Greysham, with a look of astonishment and incredulity.

"Alas!" answered Evelyn, "it is too true. Oh, Walter, thou seest now before thee one of the most wretched beings in existence."

"And how is this?" interrogated Walter, "by what strange and untoward circumstances art thou brought to this deplorable condition? For well am I convinced that it has its origin in no misconduct of thine."

"Thou dost me no more than justice by that supposition, my friend," observed Heartwell, "and yet had I been the most consummate villain that ever disgraced society, I could not have been exposed to more indignities and brutal outrages than those which it has been my hard lot to endure."

"Pr'ythee explain thyself," said Walter, "for I feel most anxious to become acquainted with the extraordinary circumstances that have brought about this melancholy change in thy fortunes."

"It is a dismal story," said Evelyn, "but listen, and I will be as brief as I can."

Our hero then related to Walter Greysham, in as few words as he could, all those strange and painful particulars with which the reader has already been made acquainted, and Walter listened to him with the deepest interest and sympathy.

"Thou hast indeed been most unfortunate, Evelyn," he remarked, when he had concluded, "nor do I marvel at the anguish of thy felings. But do not abandon thyself entirely to despair. Conscious of thine own innocence and integrity, thou mayest surely look forward to the future with the most sanguine feelings of hope. Thou wilt yet, depend upon it, to theconfusion of thine enemies, triumph o'er all the difficulties by which thou art at present surrounded, and be able to make the monstrous injustice which has been done thee manifest to the world."

"Would to Heaven that I could think so," ejaculated Evelyn; "but, alas! when I view the unparalleled circumstances of my cruel fate, I find it is impossible to do so."

"Nay, be firm;" said Greysham, "and all will yet terminate much better than thou dost now anticipate. It affords me much satisfaction to think that I have met with thee, for I trust that thou wilt find my friendly services of value to thee in thy present emergency."

"True;" returned our hero;—"it affords me much pleasure to observe, if I may be permitted to judge by appearances, that fortune to thee, at any rate, has been more lavish of her favours than she has been to me."

"Aye," replied Walter; "in sober truth, I have no reason to complain of the fickle dame. My stake has been cast on the bright waters, and although I have had to encounter many a wild tempest, to brave the battle and the breeze, and to steer clear of the shoals, the rocks, and the quicksands of life, thank Providence I have not foundered yet, but have been enabled to weather every danger."

"Thou art apparently an officer of some rank;" said Evelyn.

"Yes, returned Walter, "thanks to Her Most Gracious Majesty, Queen Elizabeth, and ny own untiring perseverance, I have been enabled to attain my present position, and am now appointed to the command of a vessel which is about to sail in the course of a few days to the coast of Spain on secret service; and so Evelyn, if thou thinkest proper to accompany me, thou mayest rest assured that I will study thine interest as carefully as mine own."

"Oh, thanks my kind friend;" said Evelyn, gratefully, and grasping his hand; "most cheerfully do I accept thine offer, and will endeavour to hope, dark even as my prospects are at present, that a brighter future is in store for me."

"Well said;" returned Greysham;—"then that business is settled, and to-morrow, if thou deemest fit, thou shalt be safe on board my gallant craft; to-night thou hadst better remain here, and I will see that the worthy host affords thee every accommodation. I must now leave thee, as I have some little business to attend to; but I will see thee again."

Evelyn again thanked him cordially for the interest he took in his favour, and Walter Greysham departed from the Tavern. Nothing could possibly appear more fortunate to Evelyn than this unexpected meeting, for he well knew the honourable character of his friend, and he was just about to congratulate himself on the subject, when he was startled by a confused noise as if of two persons in stormy altercation near the room in which he was, and before he had time to inquire into the cause the door was burst violently open, and to his embarrassment and surprise Mabel once more stood before him.

The expression of her eyes was melancholy, her countenance was pale, and her whole demeanour wild and agitated.

"Mabel!" ejaculated our hero; "and is it possible that I again behold thee, and in this place so unsuited to thy character and sex?"

"All places are alike to Mabel, where Evelyn Heartwell chooses to go. Her fate is so closely interwoven with his that nothing can again divide them. Thou seestthat I have traced thy footsteps, and am fully aware of thy intentions. In vain thou mayest seek to elude me; I have taken an oath to follow thee wherever thy destiny may be, and no earthly power shall induce me to abandon it. No danger shall appal me, no argument or remonstrance shall move me from my purpose."

"Hold, Mabel," said our hero; "I must not, will not listen to thy rash views. Surely this conduct is little better than madness."

"Thou mayest e'en call it so, and thou wilt," returned Mabel; "and even were I indeed mad, it would be no cause for wonder, fearful as are the trials to which my mind is subjected. Oh, Evelyn, didst thou but know how fondly, how passionately I love thee; even though thine heart acknowledges no other being than Constance Welborn, methinks it would be moved to sympathy and pity."

"I do indeed pity thee, poor girl" replied Evelyn tenderly; "still would it be cruel and unjust of me to give any encouragement to thy fatal passion. Thou knowest full well my desperate situation, and why thou continue to cherish an affection that can never meet with any return? Banish me from thy memory, or, if thou still thinkest of me, let it be only as a dear friend or brother."

"No, no, no," cried Mabel, and her bosom swelled with the power of her emotions, "it is impossible, in vain dost thou advise, thou art all, thou art everything to the poor Gipsey-girl, she hath no eyes for any one but thee, no existence but in thy presence."

"Rash girl," ejaculated Evelyn, "knowest thou not the folly, the uselessness of thy conduct? What can I say to rid thee of these wild thoughts."

"Nothing," she returned, "thou hast no arguments, no persuasions that can have any effect on me. Thou goest to brave the ocean wave, but think not that that shall separate us. Again I tell thee, wherever thou art, there also will Mabel be."

"I cannot, will not longer listen to thee," said Evelyn, in tones of half anger, "this obstinate spirit becomes thee not; leave me, Mabel, I must be alone."

"Enough!" replied the Gipsey-girl, and a strange expression distorted her features, "Mabel alone possesses the scorn and hatred of Evelyn Heartwell, his words have sealed her doom; without his love she hath no wish, no hope to live, but thus hath she at least the courage to die!"

As she uttered these words, she drew a dagger from beneath her cloak, and raising her arm, while a look of frenzied determination flashed from her eyes, she was about to plunge it in her breast, when Evelyn, with the speed of lightning darted towards her, and wresting the deadly weapon from her grasp, exclaimed:—

"Mad woman forbear thy dreadful purpose; wouldst thou then rush unbidden into the presence of thy Maker?"

"Why arrest me in my purpose;" said the unhappy girl, in a voice of the deepest melancholy and regret; "why arrest me in my purpose, since thy decree has rendered life hateful to me? But enough of this," she added haughtily, and moving towards the door; "fondly, devotedly even as she loves thee; willing as she is to make any sacrifice for thy sake, the proud spirit of Mabel will not suffer her to sue to thee. Of this, however, Evelyn Heartwell, thou mayest rest assured that my determination is fixed; henceforth, in spite of all thine opposition, I will be the companion of thy wanderings wheresoever thou goest;—thou mayest loathe me, despise me, nay even heap thy maledictions upon my head, but still will I haunt thy presence; still will I constantly be by thy side, the willing participator in all thy perils, the affectionate sympathizer in all thy sorrows and afflictions. Oh, Evelyn, would to Heaven that thou couldst appreciate the powerful feelings that rack this wretched bosom, would that—but no more; farewell; we shall meet again; in a few hours, *though thou mayest know her not*, Mabel will be with thee again!"

"Hear me, misguided girl—Mabel!" ejaculated Evelyn; but she was gone, and looking from the window as well as the darkness of the night would permit him, he beheld her fine and stately form hastily retreating from the house, and gliding between the numerous persons that thronged the street, it was almost instantaneously hidden from his sight.

THE ESCAPE OF EVELYN HEARTWELL FROM BLACK WILL AT THE OLD
SHIP, AT WAPPING.

"Poor girl! poor girl!" he sighed, as he resumed his seat, "alas! how powerful is the fatal passion that has taken possession of thine heart! Would to Heaven that it was devoted to any other being than the wretched Evelyn."

For a moment or two Evelyn stood amazed and confounded at this extraordinary adventure, and his brain was so bewildered by the strange conduct and persevering devotion of Mabel that he scarcely knew what he was about. Again he looked from the window in the direction she had taken, but he could see nothing of her, and resuming his seat, he abandoned himself to the painful thoughts to which the remarkable circumstance naturally gave rise.

No. 22.

CHAPTER XXVI.

The Hair-breadth Escape of Evelyn Heartwell.—Heroic Conduct of the Gipsey-girl.

For some time, when he was left alone, Evelyn sat lost in gloomy meditation upon the strange change that had taken place in his circumstances within the last few hours, and the stirring scenes upon which he was about to enter; but more than all did the form of his beloved Constance occupy his thoughts; and the certainty of the sufferings to which she would be exposed, and the probable fate which awaited her, alone made him regret the stern necessity which compelled him to quit his native land.

It was not till a late hour that the noisy guests dispersed, and the house and the neighbourhood was in a short time afterwards left in comparative quiet. Our hero then, having previously arranged with the landlord for his temporary accommodation, was conducted to his chamber, and feeling weary, he almost immediately retired to bed. But strange and troublesome dreams disturbed his rest, and continued to haunt his imagination during the night, and when he awoke, which was as soon as the first blush of day appeared in the eastern horizon, he felt but little refreshed, while his spirits were low and desponding. The same riotous description of guests that had thronged the " Old Ship Tavern " (which was the sign of the house,) on the previous night, began to assemble at an early hour in the morning, and to prevent annoyance and idle curiosity, Evelyn remained in the same room which he had occupied with his friend on the previous night, and there anxiously and impatiently awaited his arrival. He had been thus occupied in his own gloomy thoughts for some time, when he was aroused by hearing an unusual noise outside the house, and he was the more startled and alarmed when his own name, mentioned in a familiar voice, distinctly met his ears. Astonished, and immediately suspecting danger, he hastened to the window, which was directly over the doorway of the building, only a few feet from the ground, and commanding an unobstructed view of the street, and his alarm may be imagined when the first object that so unwelcomely met his eyes, was the ruffian, Black Will, in noisy dispute with the landlord, and surrounded by several men, who had doubtless accompanied him to the place.

" Confusion !" exclaimed Evelyn, " I am discovered ! My determined enemies, by some accursed fate, have been enabled to track my footsteps hither, and I am lost ! What is now to be done ?"

There was no time for reflection or hesitation. He saw the landlord yield to the demands of Will; beheld him and his companions enter the house, and heard them ascending the stairs to the room in which he was. Another moment, and his apprehension would be inevitable. He opened the casement, and cast one hasty and anxious glance from it. It was a task of no great difficulty to descend from it to the street, and there were only a few persons about. Will and his companions had just reached the room door; quick as thought, therefore, he stepped from the casement on to the arched roof of the doorway, and leaped from thence into the road, just as Black Will appeared, and shouting aloud to the persons about to arrest him in his flight, discharged the contents of a pistol after him, which, however, fortunately for Evelyn, missed its aim, and drawing his sword, and keeping at bay the persons who might otherwise have molested him, he fled with the rapidity of thought in the direction which first presented itself to him. He could hear the voices of the persons in pursuit of him, and who, in spite of the speed with which he dashed on his way, seemed momentarily to gain upon him. Breathlessly, however, he hurried on, regardless of the course he pursued ; and at length hearing the shouts no more, he began to hope that he had eluded them, when rushing into a narrow street or lane, which seemed to be the most obscure and unfrequented, to his utter confusion and dismay, he beheld Black Will and his companions advancing hurriedly from the other end towards him. With despair our unfortunate hero looked around him, and to his utter alarm beheld a number of other persons approaching him from behind, so that all chance of his retreating in that direction was completely cut off. To escape now seemed impossible ; still was Evelyn firmly resolved not to yield without a desperate resistance.

The ruffian Will, now making sure of his victim, rushed towards the spot on which our hero, sword in hand, and with a bold and determined air was standing, and, as he advanced, exclaimed triumpeantly :—

"So, Master Heartwell, I have thee now secure, thanks to my sagacity which enabled me to track thee from the Old Grange, hither. Yield! resistance thou mayest plainly see is useless!"

"Yield, to a scoundrel like thee," replied Evelyn, resolutely, "never!"

"Obstinate fool!" cried the fellow, "seize him!"

The men advanced to do so, led on by Black Will, and Evelyn having felled two or three of them to the earth, Will was about to rush upon him, when the slight figure of a youth, dressed as a sailor, darted from a corner of the street in between them, and discharging a pistol at the villain, stretched him bleeding from a severe wound on the earth, at the same time exclaiming :—

"Hold! ruffian dog! Here is one who will protect the much wronged Evelyn Heartwell at the hazard of life!"

With astonishment and incredulity, our hero started at the words and the tones in which they were uttered—*it was the voice of Mabel, the Gipsey Girl ;*— and, notwithstanding the disguise which she had assumed, in a moment he recognised her.

Thunderstruck at the intrepidity of the deed and the fall of Will, the men were transfixed to the spot, and were unabled, in there confusion, to offer any opposition.

"Fly!—fly, Evelyn, whilst thou hast the opportunity!" said the heroic girl; Mabel has once more saved thee from destruction, and she is happy !— away !—care not for me in this emergency; we shall meet again !"

Worked up to a pitch of the most unspeakable wonder and admiration, Evelyn was about to reply, but Mabel waved her hand commandingly, and without any farther hesitation he took the road that was open to him, and dashing on with the utmost precipitation, had soon left the scene of the late starting and extraordinary adventure far behind. He paused to take breath in a state of the greatest excitement; and in order to collect his thoughts ; but he had not done so many minutes, when he beheld a man advancing along the foot path, the sight of whom at first excited his suspicion and alarm, but, on his approaching nearer, he uttered an exclamation of astonishment and satisfaction, when he recognised his friend, Walter Greysham.

"Evelyn!—is it possible that I see thee thus, and so far from the tavern, where I was going to meet thee, according to appointment?—" said Walter. "What brings thee hither ; and in such a state of agitation ?"

" My footsteps have been traced by my dreaded enemies to the house where you left me, " replied Evelyn ; " and I have escaped by a complete miracle."

" Ah ! " ejaculated Greysham, with a look of astonishment ;—" is it possible?—explain the circumstances to me."

" This is not the time or place to do so ; " returned our hero ;—" the pursuits is probably not yet abandoned, and those I fear may even now be close upon my heels."

" True, true ; " observed Walter ; " every moment of delay is fraught with danger.   It is fortunate that I have met thee, my residence is close at hand, and there, at any rate, thou wilt be in safety ;—come let us begone."

Evelyn made no reply, but following the footsteps of his friend, they wended their way through several bystreets near the waterside, and at length stopped at the door of a small, but neat house ; and Walter having rang a bell, it was promptly answered by a domestic, and Evelyn was ushered by his companion into a room upstairs, which was handsomely furnished ; here he threw himself into a chair, and for the first time was enabled to obtain some degree of composure.

" Now, Evelyn," said Greysham, " I pr'ythee relate to me the particulars of this singular adventure, for I must confess that I am all impatience to hear them."

Evelyn did so, taking, however, the precaution not to reveal the discovery he had made of Mabel in the person of his courageous preserver.

" By Heaven, it was indeed a most miraculous escape," observed Greysham, when he had concluded, " and the youth who thus so bravely come to thy rescue, Evelyn, in the face of such danger, must be a noble fellow, and proud should I be to own him for one of the crew of the Ariel.   But thinkest thou that thou hadst never seen him before ?"

Evelyn was somewhat confused by this question, and scarcely knew what answer to make.

" His features were indeed somewhat familiar to me," he hesitatingly replied, at length, " but whether I know him or not, I must ever entertain the liveliest feelings of gratitude towards him."

" To be sure thou must do so, brave lad," remarked Walter, " and it does not seem probable that one who knew thee not, would run such a fearful risk in thy defence.   However, thanks to his unexampled intrepidity, thou hast escaped from the clutches of the rascals once more, and thou mayest now consider thyself in perfect safety.   As soon as the shadows of evening have fallen around, we will depart from hence, and go on board the gallant Ariel, which, the day after to-morrow, will weigh anchor from the shores of Old England."

Evelyn thought of Constance, and sighed, and his emotion was observed by Walter.

" Still those vain regrets, and desponding thoughts, Evelyn," he remarked ; " come, come, dismiss them from thy mind, and look forward with hope and confidence to the glorious career upon which thou art about to enter.   The hardy mariner's is a constant life of excitement, and in the spirit-stirring scenes in which thou wilt have to mingle, thou wilt doubtless learn to forget the troubles and the disappointments that now distract thee."

" Forget my faithful Constance!" exclaimed our hero, vehemently, " oh, how I should hate and despise myself if I thought I could.   Walter, thou canst not surely judge so meanly of my passion for that lovely maiden."

" Well, then, Evelyn," returned Greysham, " e'en continue to cherish that passion, and endeavour to encourage the hope that the time may yet arrive when it will be gratified in the possession of the fair being who hath so enslaved thine heart."

Our hero shook his head doubtfully, but anxious to appear as composed and resigned as possible before Walter, he changed the subject to a less painful theme, and even ventured to speculate, with some degree of vivacity, upon the prospects that must shortly open before him in the fresh course of life upon which he was about to enter, and to express a hope that Providence might yet work a favourable change in his destiny; and in which hope, the reader may be sure Walter Greysham did not fail to encourage him. He gave an animated, glowing, and graphic description of a mariner's life, to which Evelyn could not help listening with interest and enthusiasm; and thus the time passed away till the evening set in, and our hero having exchanged his suit for one from the wardrobe of his friend, and which had the effect of completely disguising his person, they left the house together, and making their way to the river's side, entered a boat which was waiting for them, and bent their course, as fast as the tide would permit, towards Woolwich, off which the Ariel was lying.

Many a gallant vessel graced the silvery Thames at that point, and as the eyes of Evelyn eagerly gazed upon each stately ship, their tall masts soaring to the clouds, and their white sails furled, but brightly reflected upon by the chaste moonbeams, he gained a temporary forgetfulness of his sorrows, and became lost in admiration of the novelty of the scene around him. A few minutes more sufficed to place them on board the Ariel, which was, as Walter had represented it to be, a noble vessel, and one in every respect qualified for the important and dangerous service for which it was commissioned. Here then Evelyn, for the the first time, felt himself safe from persuit, and endeavoured to view his destiny with much more calmness and resignation. He sat conversing with Greysham till a late hour, when he was conducted to the cabin set apart for his accommodation, and left to the free indulgence of his own thoughts, the conflicting nature of which we need not attempt to describe. Previous to his retiring to rest, he knelt down and earnestly invoked the protection and the blessing of heaven for his beloved Constance. While he was thus occupied, he was startled by hearing distinctly, a deep sigh near him, and rising suddenly to his feet, he looked anxiously around him and beheld, or immagined he beheld a human form stealing towards the cabin door, which he now perceived, for the first time, he had neglected to fasten. Supprised, and somewhat alarmed, he pursued it; for an instant he caught a glimpse of its dark shaddow, and plainly heard his name repeated in a melancholy, but not unfamiliar voice, but although he had never removed his eyes from the spot where he had seen it, the form had vanished, whither, or in what way, he was at a perfect loss to conjecture. He stood lost in amazement and perplexity for several minutes, when he returned to the cabin, now securing the door after him. This mysterious adventure gave rise to various thoughts in his mind, and he tried in vain to unravel it; and after some time passed in reflection, he retired to rest, and sleep gradually shed its drowsy influence upon his senses.

We will pass over the time that intervened previous to the starting of the gallant Ariel, and during which, nothing particular, or worthy of recording, occurred to our hero. At length the day so anxiously looked forward to on which the vessel was to depart from the shores of Old England, arrived, and all was bustle and activity on board. The novelty of the scene in which he found himself at first diverted the thoughts of Evelyn from other subjects,—but, when the signal gun was fired, the anchor was weighed,—the sails was spread, and, with a favoring breeze, and amid the shouts of the hardy crew, the Ariel gracefully glided on her way. The thoughts that he was now leaving his native land, and that fair being who was far more precious, more valuable to him than his own existence, perhaps for ever, rushed with full force upon his disturbed brain, and he gazed with anxious and despairing eyes upon those objects that so rapidly receded from him, while he abandoned himself entirely to all the anguish and the misery of his feelings.   Walter Greysham had left him for a few minutes, being called to another part of the vessel; and Evelyn was standing in a melancholy attitude on the deck, with his arms folded upon his chest, and his eyes fixed upon the now distant shore, when he was aroused by hearing his name repeated in an emphatic and tender tone by some one immediately behind him, and turning hastily round, he beheld the delicate figure of a young sailor standing near him, but he started with the most powerful emotion, on recognizing the well known features that were fixed so intently upon him. *It was Mabel!*—yes, forgetting the timidity and delicacy of her sex, in the irresistible fervour of the growing passion she entertained for Evelyn Heartwell, the poor girl, true to the solemn vow she had made, had abandoned all thoughts of fear, or the consequences that might follow, and boldly risked every danger, every hardship, to follow his wayward fortunes, and to live alone in the presence of one whom she so fondly loved !

CHAPTER XXVII.

BLACK WILL AND OLIVER.—THE QUARREL.—THE VOW OF VENGEANCE.—THE ALARMING ANNOUNCEMENT.—CONSTANCE MEETS WITH SAMPSON BRAYLING.

IT has been before stated that the men from whom our hero had so providentially effected his escape, through the courageous interposition of Mabel, astounded at the boldness of one who appeared to them to be a mere stripling youth, were completely paralysed, and for the moment, rendered incapable of offering any obstacle to his flight, and the Gipsey-girl, taking advantage of their surprise and confusion, after laughing scornfully and triumphantly, vanished so suddenly from the spot, that her disappearance had almost the appearance of magic, and left them in a state of still greater wonder and bewilderment.

Black Will had only been slightly wounded in the arm, and quickly recovering himself, he started to his feet, and gazed eagerly around him.

"Ah !" he exclaimed, fiercely, "have ye then suffered them both to escape ? Have ye allowed yourselves to be defeated by a boy, and permitted Evelyn Heartwell to slip from your clutches, at the very moment when ye had him at your mercy ?   A murrain seize ye all, varlets, for your cowardice.   And why do ye now thus stand gaping at each other in stupified amazement and inactivity? Continue the pursuit; for by every power I swear he shall not escape !"

Hastily Will bound a handkerchief round his wounded arm, to stay the effusion of the blood, and his companions, aroused by his taunts and reproaches into action, followed him hastily from the spot, and hurried in the direction which they imagined our hero had taken.   Sufficient time, however, had elapsed for him to elude their vigilance ; not the least traces could they discover of him, neither could they meet with any one who could give them such information as was calculated to assist them in the pursuit, and after traversing every street to no purpose in the neighbourhood, they were compelled to abandon their designs, and Black Will returned to the tavern from which Evelyn had effected his escape, muttering curses on the defeat and disappointment he had experienced. From the landlord he could obtain no further information that might assist him, that worthy, for certain reasons best known to himself, neglecting to mention anything of the meeting with Evelyn and Walter Greysham, (with the latter of whom he was well acquainted,) on the evening before, and Will, considering that it would be useless to remain longer where he was, or to prosecute his search further in the neighbourhood, enraged and disappointed, departed with his companions, and separating from them after they had proceeded a little on the road, made his way, in no very agreeable mood towards the Grange.

With a feeling which might be called cowardice, Oliver Dalton had refrained from taking any active part in the pursuit, but waited anxiously at the Grange to hear the result. He was far from easy or satisfied, nay, he almost wished that Evelyn had escaped, for so long as he was out of the way, and was in all probability about to leave the country, he had nothing to apprehend from him, though he had everything to fear from Sampson Brayling, after what had occurred, and he almost regretted that he had anything to do with the ruffian, Black Will, of whose fidelity he entertained the strongest doubts, notwithstanding the many professions he had made. He had already made the most exorbitant demands upon his purse, and when he remonstrated with him upon the subject, it had elicited certain observations from him, which had convinced Oliver he would not hesitate to betray him, the moment he refused to submit to his extortionate wishes. He scarcely knew how to act. It seemed to him almost impossible that the deluded and infatuated Sir Milford could much longer remain in ignorance of his real character, and at times he was worked up to such a pitch of fear, that he was almost tempted to abandon his deep-laid schemes, and to fly to some part of the country where he might escape his enemies, and remain unknown, but then he considered again that he had advanced too far in his villainous projects now to recede; the large marriage portion he was to receive with Constance was a temptation his cupidity could not resist, and he resolved to brave everything in order that he might obtain the gratification of his ambitious wishes, let the consequences be whatever they might.

We need not attempt to describe what were the feelings of anguish which Constance endured after her affecting parting interview with her lover, as described in a previous chapter. The agonising thoughts that she had seen him for the last time continued to haunt her imagination, and drove her to distraction. This emotion was increased when she was informed by Abigail that Evelyn had been detected before he left the gardens of the Grange, and that Will had gone in pursuit of him, and dreadful was the night of anxiety she passed, and the torturing suspense she endured till the following day had far advanced, when she was somewhat relieved by the return of the ruffian to the mansion, and on finding that he had been unsuccessful in his efforts. She breathed a prayer for the safety and protection of the unfortunate Evelyn, and then endeavoured, but with little success, to tranquilize her feelings.

Oliver Dalton was standing at the casement of one of the appartments of the Grange, anxiously watching for the arrival of something to relieve his doubts and apprehensions that beset his mind, when he beheld Black Will approaching across the garden, and he hastened to meet him. The savage expression of disappointment on the villain's features fully prepared Oliver for what had taken place, and without saying a word to him, he motioned him to follow him into the house, and conducted him to the room in which he had been previously seated.

"Now, Will;" he said, when they were alone; "what success?"

"Why need'st thou inquire?" demanded Will, in surly tones; "methinks thou shouldst be able to judge from my appearance Evelyn has escaped, curses light upon him, although we had him securely in our clutches; and I, as thou mayest see, had a narrow escape of my life; and, he added, with a sardonic grin, "what a loss that would have been to society."

"Would that thou hadst perished;" thought Oliver. "Ah!" he said aloud, "I see thou art wounded; how was this? Be quick, and gratify my curiosity."

Will briefly related what had taken place, and again uttered the most fearful maledictions upon the head of Evelyn and his unknown deliverer.

" Base cowardice !" exclaimed Oliver, passionately : " to be thus defeated in thy purpose by a single youth. Thou shouldst be ashamed to acknowledge it, Will."

" Cowardice !" repeated Will, sternly ; " it is a bold word for one to apply to the man who holds his fate in his hands."

" Ah !" cried Dalton, with mingled feelings of rage and alarm ; " darest thou to threaten ?"

" Aye," returned the ruffian, " since the Gipsey, Luke Stanton is so ready to find fault with his old associate. However, I am in no humour to bandy words with thee. I have run every risk to serve thee, and I now expect to be rewarded much more liberally than I have hitherto been."

" Dost thou demand it ?" said Oliver, sternly.

" Aye, I *demand* it, if the term suits thee better," boldly replied Will. " It is no thankful task that I have undertaken for thee ; thy character, thy success, nay, since thou dost compel me to speak out candidly, thy very life, Luke Stanton, are at my mercy, and if thou valuest them, thou wilt not dare to trifle with me. Aye, thou mayest frown, I am a determined man, and am not to be intimidated from my purpose."

" Ay ! so bold and insolent ?" cried Dalton, half quailing beneath the stern and threatening looks which his ruffianly myrmidon fixed upon him, " fool that I was to trust thee. What wouldst thou have ?"

" Money, as I have told thee before," returned Will, " and money I must and will have."

" I will not, I cannot yield to thine extortionate demands," said Oliver.

" Enough," replied Will, coolly, " then thou knowest the consequences. Our connection is at an end, and I wish thee joy of that which is likely soon to follow. Good day, Master Luke Stanton, when next we meet, thou wilt probably have cause to repent what has taken place at this interview."

" Ah ! thou wouldst betray me !" exclaimed Oliver Dalton, rushing towards him as he moved to the door, " villain !"

" Villain in thy teeth, cowardly knave !" cried Will, fiercely, " thou best deservest the title. But a proper tribunal will doubtless shortly have to try that question. Beware, thou hast aroused the vengeance of Black Will, and depend upon it he will not rest until it is fully gratified."

" Miscreant ! traitor ! thou shalt not dare me thus !" exclaimed Oliver, foaming with rage, and grasping Will by the collar as he was moving from the door, " recall thy words, or by the infernal host I swear—"

" Release thine hold ! thou strugglest with one to whom thou art powerless as an infant. Off ! off !" and as the villain thus spoke, he struck Oliver a violent blow, and dashing him to the floor, quitted the room with a fearful malediction just as Sir Milford entered by an opposite door.

The alarm and confusion of Oliver Dalton on beholding the baronet, and at such a moment, may be readily imagined, and, scrambling to his feet as well as he could, he endeavoured to falter out some apology, though he was so abashed and bewildered that he knew not what he said.

" Ah ! Oliver Dalton struck by the man whom I had thought was devoted to his services ?" said Sir Milford, with a look of astonishment and eager curiosity; " what is the meaning of this outrage ?"

" It means, Sir Milford, that he is a villain, whom I regret to have entrusted or employed," replied Dalton, collecting himself in the best manner he could, " estimating the trifling services he has rendered too highly, he made the most extravagant and extortionate demands upon my purse, and because I, properly as I conceive, refused to yield, he dared not only to threaten, but follow it up by the violent and insulting conduct which thou hast witnessed."

"The villain!" said Sir Milford, "to dare to commit such an outrage in my house, and upon one whom I esteem as my dearest friend. But," he added, as he rang the bell violently, "should he not have quitted the place, he shall pay dearly for his insolence."

"Nay, I beseech thee, Sir Milford," said Oliver, whose alarm and confusion increased; "I beseech thee not to degrade thyself by having any altercation with such a brutal scoundrel; though much I fear that—"

"Fear!" interrupted the baronet, with a look of astonishment; "surely Oliver Dalton can have nothing to fear from such a dastardly knave?"

Dalton trembled, and knew not what reply to make, and at that moment a domestic made his appearance, and in reply to the questions that were put to him, informed his master that Will had abruptly quitted the house.

"The rascal!" said Sir Milford, when the servant had quitted the room; "such conduct is most unaccountable, and I dont wonder at thine excitement, Oliver.

No. 23.

But let not the circumstance annoy thee, we are better without his aid, and perhaps we were wrong to have anything to do with him at all. However, thou mayest treat the idle threats of such a fellow with the utter contempt that they merit. Oliver Dalton is too far elevated, too far above him, to have anything to dread from his vengeance."

We need not attempt to describe the feelings of Oliver as Sir Milford thus spoke; too well did he know the power of Black Will, and what he had such good reason to dread, now that the ruffian was exasperated, and he felt abashed, bewildered, and dismayed. He almost feared to meet the glances of the baronet, lest his keen eye should penetrate his thoughts, and deeply did he regret that he should have arrived at such a particular juncture.

"I regret, Sir Milford," he said, at length, "that this scene should have occurred here, and I trust that it will create no false prejudice in thy mind against me."

"Prejudice against thee, Oliver," said the baronet, "what meanest thou? thou speakest in problems. How can it possibly do so, when thou art not to blame? Come, come, unpleasant as this affair unquestionably is, it is unworthy of a serious thought. But what of Evelyn Heartwell?"

"It seems, Sir Milford," answered Oliver, "that Will traced his footsteps to a house in Wapping, that he and his companions pursued him, and having surrounded him, might easily have captured him, but suffered him to be rescued by a complete stripling, a young seaman, whom they also permitted to escape."

"The cowards!" ejaculated Sir Milford.

"True, Sir Milford," coincided Oliver. "But there can now be no doubt that Evelyn Heartwell has made up his mind to go to sea."

"'Tis well," remarked the baronet, "and probably we shall hear no more of him, which is perhaps better than having the excitement of his trial and condemnation. But endeavour to compose thy feelings, Oliver, which I see are much ruffled by this disagreeable adventure, and I will meet thee again in an hour, I have something of importance to impart to thee, something which affects thy future happiness, and the consummation of thy most anxious wishes."

"Oh, Sir Milford," eagerly ejaculated Dalton, "what meanest thou? Tell me, I pray thee—"

"Nay, nay," interrupted Sir Milford, "thou must e'en restrain thine impatience and curiosity till we meet again, when I assure thee that it shall be amply gratified."

With these words he quitted the apartment, and left Oliver Dalton in a state of mingled doubt, astonishment, and apprehension. The whole events of the morning naturally filled him with the greatest alarm, and he could not but look forward to that which seemed to be looming in the future with the greatest fear, for danger appeared to threaten him on every side. His quarrel with Black Will, the threats which he had held out, and his abrupt departure from the Grange, all seemed to portend a coming storm, and how to avoid its overwhelming effects he was perfectly at a loss to imagine.

"How can I act?" he soliloquised, as he paced the room after the departure of Sir Milford, with hasty and uneven strides;—"I am placed in a dilemma from from which I know not how to extricate myself. Better would it have been for me to have prudently endeavoured to conciliate the favour of Will than to provoke this quarrel with him?—To what dangerous and fearful results may it lead?— what may not the vengeance of the ruffian urge him to do?—Fool that I was ever to make a confidant of him. He holds me completely at his mercy, as well as Sampson Brayling, and now that the latter will probably be made acquainted with all that has transpired, and the manner in which I have broken my oath, what have I a right to expect, but the worst that can befall me?—at the very moment when the accomplishment of my ambitious wishes are within my grasp the real villany of my character may be exposed, and Constance Welborn not only escape me, but my destruction be inevitable. In spite of all the sanguine hopes I had so fondly cherished, the crisis of my fate seems to be approaching. But, psha!—away with these gloomy thoughts;—thus far have I boldly ventured, and at every risk I will yet triumph."

In such a state of mind did Oliver Dalton continue for some time,—but at length he succeeded in composing his feelings much better than might have been expected, and when Sir Milford again entered the room he met him with a smile and his usual complaisant demeanor. Having motioned him to a seat, the baronet took one by his side, and then commenced that conversation which Oliver was so anxious to hear. What passed between them on that occasion, it is not necessary at present to divulge;—they remained together for more than an hour, and, when they separated the triumphant expression of Oliver Dalton's features shewed that he had heard something which was highly gratifying to his feelings.

The faithful Abigail had been a careful observer of all that had passed, and by some means, peculiar to her own sagacity, had learned the particulars of Evelyn's escape from the pursuit of his enemies, the subsequent return of Black Will, wounded, to the Grange; his quarrel with Oliver, and hasty departure, no doubt to put some scheme of vengeance into execution. These important facts she hastened to communicate to her young Mistress, who, as has been before stated, had kept herself confined to her own room ever since the eventful evening when she parted with her lover in the gardens of the old Grange. Need we describe her feelings, as she listened to the particulars which Abigail related? But more important than all was the providential escape of Evelyn, the extraordinary way in which it was effected, and his future destination, of which she could no longer entertain any doubts. Tears streamed from her eyes as she gazed upon the miniature likeness of him she so fondly loved, and pressed it again and again to her lips, and clasping her hands together, she fervently returned her thanks to Heaven for his preservation, and invoked its future blessing and protection for him, in the perilous career upon which he had entered. But who could the heroic youth be to whom he was indebted for his safety? She was lost in amazement and perplexity, and a strange feeling arose to her mind, for which she was at a loss to account. The quarrel that had taken place between Oliver Dalton and Black Will afforded her much satisfaction, for she thought it was not unlikely to lead to the most favourable results, but the conference which she was informed was at that moment taking place between Sir Milford and Oliver, caused her some uneasiness, which, however, the kind hearted Abigail endeavoured to the utmost to dissipate, and with considerable effect.

Her mind fully occupied with these remarkable events, Constance passed away the time in conversation with Abigail, till the day was far advanced, and evening was approaching, when she received a peremptory message from her uncle to attend him immediately in the library. With a palpitating and foreboding heart she did so, and found him seated alone, and immersed in deep thought. Her entrance aroused him, and he arose, and greeting her with a faint smile of welcome, conducted her to a seat, and taking a chair by her side, looked earnestly and silently in her face for a few minutes, Constance anxiously, but yet fearfully awaiting for him to begin the conversation.

"Thou art still pale and languid, child," he said, at length, "and the agitation of thy manner shews too plainly thy sadness of heart. Wilt thou never banish these melancholy feelings from thy breast, and re-assume thy former smiles of happiness?"

"Happiness!" repeated our heroine, with a sigh, "alas! I fear that it is never more destined to be my lot. He who alone could——"

" Repeat not his name ; " angrily interrupted Sir Milford ; " polute not thy lips with the name of one who has proved himself to be so great a villain ! "

" Oh, monstrous calumny ! " exclaimed our heroine, her bosom swelling with indignation, and tears starting to her eyes ;—" when will justice be rendered to the unfortunate—the much wronged Evelyn ? "

" Rash, foolish girl ;" exclaimed her uncle ; " thou still doth obstinately cherish that blind passion for him, which was so near bringing disgrace and infamy upon our name ;—still dost pertinaciously endeavour to gloss over his vices. Beware !"

" Nay, " exclaimed Constance, firmly,—" let whatever may be the consequences, I will ever continue to maintain his innocence of the foul charges brought against him."

" Obstinate girl !" cried Sir Milford, sternly ; " I have borne with thy resistance too long ; I have refrained from reproaching thee with disobedience to my will in encouraging secret interviews with the guilty outcast, Evelyn ;—I have given thee more than sufficient time for reflection ; but my patience is now exhausted ; my resolution is formed ; no power of persuasion can move me from it ; in a few days Oliver Dalton shall lead thee to the altar !"

" Become the wife of Oliver Dalton ?" exclaimed Constance, with a look of horror and disgust ;—" by Heaven, never !—sooner would I suffer the most frightful death it is possible for the imagination to conceive. Oh, my uncle, I implore you—"

" No more," he sternly interrupted ; " thou hast heard my final decision, and must abide by it. Prepare thyself on Monday next to depart to my estate near Chalton, where it is my determination the marriage ceremony shall take place without delay."

" Oh, in mercy hear me !"—

" Any appeal to me is useless ; thou hast heard my will, I say again ; thy duty is obedience !" And, without waiting to receive any further reply, he stalked hastily from the room, and left the distracted damsel on her knees, with clasped hands, and giving vent to a wild paroxysm of grief and despair. In this painful condition she was found by Abigail, on her entrance into the room, and by her conducted to her own apartment, where for several hours she suffered all that poignant anguish of mind which the melancholy circumstances of the case naturally created ; though Abigail, with her usual solicitude and attention, sought all that she could to console her.

Sir Milford and Oliver had left the house some time together ; and, as the evening was clear and fine, and the moon shining brightly, Abigail proposed a short walk in the neighbourhood, thinking that it might tend in some measure to alleviate the anguish of her mistress's mind. Constance assented, and in a few minutes afterwards they issued from the house, and crossing the garden, entered the road. All was tranquil around, the air was mild and refreshing, and everything was calculated to soothe the breast of care, but our heroine walked listlessly on, and her mind was too busily occupied to suffer her to pay much attention to anything that was passing around, or to the observations Abigail addressed to her, to divert her thoughts from the dismal subject that engendered them.

The reader may have noticed, in the old Town of Hoxton, and at no great distance from the Whitmore Road, a large wooden building, or rather buildings, (for it has for many years been converted into three separate dwellings, one of which is a tavern,) painted white, and which, in spite of modern improvements, still bears all the traces of great antiquity. It is indeed one of the oldest buildings in that locality, and was formerly known by the name of " The White Farm." At the remote period of which we are writing, it was a place of some importance, with rich pastures, golden corn-fields, and extensive and luxuriant orchards attached, and the fortunate individual who owned the property was generally considered to be a person of no insignificant wealth.

On arriving at this place, Constance paused, and, as she gazed on the old farm in that tranquil hour, with the bright moonbeams reflecting on it, in silvery radiance, melancholy thoughts rushed upon her mind, and tears which she could not restrain, started to her eyes. Oh, how fondly was that old farm associated with her inmost feelings; how numerous were the reminiscences it gave rise to in her breast. It was there that Farmer Heartwell, who had adopted Evelyn, had lived and died; and it was there that that loved, though unfortunate being, had passed all the happy days of his childhood and his youth; days of happiness that Constance feared too sadly, were never more fated to return. It was there that they first met, and that fond passion was engendered, which, through every trial and vicissitude, time had but served to increase, to strengthen, and not diminish, and which could only end with life itself, even though cruel fate ordained that they should never meet again. There was not a spot around that well known place that was not endeared to her by some bright recollection of the past; but, oh how sad was the change that time had wrought in her own circumstances, and those of him who was so dear to her. Where was he now, the former gay, and youthful, and happy tenant of that venerable pile? Alas! echo answered sadly "where?" and the heart sickened at the thoughts of the dangers that too surely surrounded him; the cruel and untimely fate that probably yet awaited him.

While these reflections were passing in her mind, a faint cry from Abigail, and a nudge of the arm, aroused her, and without speaking, for her fears evidently prevented her, she drew the attention of our heroine to two or three dark shadows of human beings, that were moving stealthily towards them, from one corner of the fence that enclosed the farm-yard. Terror seized upon the mind of Constance, but before she could attempt to move from the spot, her arm was rudely grasped by one of the intruders, in whose coarse features, to her surprise and consternation, she recognised those of the ruffian, Black Will. Two other fellows, who accompanied him, at the same time seized poor Abigail, who screamed aloud with terror and dismay.

"Stop her cries," commanded Will; "or we may yet be interrupted in our business. So;" he added, with a savage look of exultation, and addressing himself to our heroine;—"fortune has proved more favourable to me than I anticipated; I hail this unexpected meeting with pleasure and satisfaction, Miss Constance Welborn."

"Unhand me fellow," said Constance, resolutely; "what means this insolent obstruction? What wouldst thou with me?"

"This is not the time to explain," answered Will; "but, since we have so fortunately met, we will not part again in a hurry, thou mayest believe me. Thou must with me."

"With thee, villain?" said the shuddering and indignant young lady; "what wicked designs have you in contemplation? Release me, I say again. or my cries shall alarm the neighbourhood."

"Nay, resistance is useless;" returned the ruffian; and, in spite of the loud cries of herself and Abigail for help, rudely encircling her waist with his arm, he was about to force her from the spot, when he was arrested in his bold and guilty purpose by the sound of approaching footsteps, and eagerly looking in the direction from whence they proceeded, Constance felt some relief on beholding several men advancing rapidly towards the spot. At the sight of them, Black Will gave utterance to a bitter oath, and he and his companions hastily relinquishing their hold of Constance and her attendance, fled precipitately from the spot, in a contrary direction. The next moment our heroine sunk, almost fainting, in the arms of Sampson Brayling.

CHAPTER XXIX.

YES, it was the Gipsey-Chief who had so opportunely arrived at the scene of
danger, and rescued our heroine and her faithful companion from the further
outrage of Black Will and the other ruffians. Constance could not help giving
utterance to an exclamation of satisfaction on recognising him; and Sampson's
astonishment was almost equal to her own on beholding her.

"Miss Constance Welborn!" he observed;—"is it possible that I see thee
abroad at this hour; and am so happy as to be the means of rescuing thee from
danger?—who were the villains that committed this daring outrage?—"

"The one who seized me was the man called Black Will;" answered Constance.

"Is it possible?" said Sampson; "the scoundrel! Oh, it is unfortunate that
he escaped me. But come, lady, let us retire to where we may not be observed
by the prying eye of idle curiosity. Now that we have so fortunately met, I
would a few words of explanation with thee, and then I will conduct thee in
safety to the Grange. Wilt thou attend me, Miss Constance?"

"I will, Sampson," she replied, "but I pray you do not detain me long, for
this adventure has alarmed me, and my uncle, who is from home, knows not of
my absence."

"All that I have to say may be expressed in a few words," observed Brayling,
"and thou art not afraid to trust thyself with me. Come, lady."

Constance nodded assent, and, following him from the spot, Sampson led
the way towards a retired place near the Farm-house, and where they might
converse in safety. Here, in a few words, he explained to her the motives which
had so fortunately brought him to the spot at that hour himself; and two or three
of his most confidential friends, as he said, having, for the last day or two, been
concealed in the old house at Finchley, which had remained undisturbed since
the flight of Evelyn Heartwell had become known.

"Anxious to communicate all I know to thee, lady," continued the Gipsey-
chief, "and hoping that I might contrive some means to see thy faithful attendant,
I ventured to the neighbourhood this evening, and was making my way to the
Grange when thy cries alarmed me."

"My good friend," said our heroine, "how can I ever sufficiently thank you
for the kind interest you take in all that concerns me?"

"I require no thanks, lady," answered Sampson; "I assure thee I feel the
utmost sympathy for thy misfortunes, and would do anything in my power to
serve thee. But I fear from the care and anxiety of thy looks, that thou hast
suffered much during the brief period that has elapsed since we last met. Hast
thou heard anything of the unfortunate Evelyn, since the letter thou hadst from
him, after his hasty flight from the old house?"

Constance briefly related to him the particulars of their parting interview in
the gardens of the Grange, and what had subsequently taken place, and to which
Sampson Brayling listened with the most eager curiosity.

"There can now be no doubt," he observed, "that Evelyn is safe on ship-
board, and I have every reason to believe that Mabel, in disguise, has followed
his footsteps. Ah! an idea strikes me! Could it be to her that he was indebted
for his preservation, disguised as the sailor youth?"

"Infatuated girl!" exclaimed our heroine, "is it possible that she could be so
rash and imprudent? But, oh, Brayling, what is now to become of me, since my
uncle is so determined to sacrifice me to the detested Oliver Dalton; and, on

Monday next I am to be removed to his estate at Chalton, where the dreaded ceremony is to take place. What can possibly rescue me from the fate with which I am threatened?"

"Fear not lady," returned Brayling; "the diabolical designs of the villain, Oliver Dalton, shall be frustrated at any cost. On the day fixed for the unnatural union which you so much and so justly dread, I will be present."

"You, Sampson Brayling," said Constance, with a look of astonishment and incredulity; "you surely cannot be serious. Do you forget the penalty you have already incurred by sheltering and abetting Evelyn Heartwell, and for the affair which so recently occurred in the Wilderness?"

"I know it all," replied Sampson; "and am willing to hazard everything to accomplish my wishes. Fear not, I say again, I entertain not the least doubt as to the result. The miscreant, Dalton, is entirely in my power, and that he knows; I possess such damning evidence of his guilt, as must bring conviction home to the most sceptical mind. Let him then beware ; the termination of his infamous career is approaching; by his own conduct he has precipitated his fate, and let him take the consequences. The villain shall never become the husband of Constance Welborn; I have sworn it, and, believe me, I will not break my oath. I repeat that at the time and the place fixed for the union, I will be present, and, at the very moment when he thinks his triumph secure, Sampson Brayling will tear aside the mask which has so long concealed his real character, and expose his black-hearted villainy to the world."

"Generous man," ejaculated Constance, "and is it possible, that you, almost a stranger, are willing to do all this for my sake, and that of Evelyn?"

"Aye, lady," replied Brayling, "'tis true that I am a rough, uncultivated man, ungifted with brilliancy of speech, but still I trust that beneath this uncouth exterior, there beats a heart that is sensible to every feeling of humanity."

"Oh, yes, Brayling," observed our heroine, extending her hand to him, which he respectfully raised to his lips, "well am I convinced of that, and I honour you for it."

"Thanks, thanks, Miss Constance," I require no more than thy good opinion to urge me on. I will fulfil all that I have promised, thou mayest depend upon it. There is nothing that Sampson Brayling would hesitate to do to defeat the plans of villainy, and in the cause of justice and oppressed innocence."

Constance, overwhelmed by the bluff sincerity of Sampson Brayling, and unable to express her feelings adequately by words, again extended to him her hand, which he raised respectfully to his lips, and fervently repeated his vows of fidelity to her service.

"But, Evelyn," she sighed, "alas! he has gone, and too probably by this time has quitted his native land. Oh, Brayling, how I tremble when I think of the many dangers to which he will doubtlessly be exposed, and the little prospect there is of my ever beholding him again.

"Fear not, lady," returned Sampson; "but put thy trust in Providence, who knowing his innocence, and the foul wrongs that have been inflicted on him will protect him through all the perils and hardships it may be his lot to encounter; it was rash and imprudent of him to take the course he has adopted without first consulting me ;—but I will loose no time in making inquiry about him, and it may not yet be too late to prevent the final accomplishment of his designs."

"From what you have already stated," remarked our heroine,—"I am satisfied that you know more of Evelyn Heartwell, and his origin, than you have hitherto thought proper to divulge."

"True, Miss Constance;" replied Brayling ;—"I am acquainted with such facts as will astonish all who hear them, and will strike confusion and dismay to the hearts of those who have been his most implacable foes ;—but prudence has hitherto restrained my tongue. The time, however, is rapidly approaching, when longer secrecy would not only be impolitic, but an absolute crime; let, then, the guilty tremble, for a terrible day of reckoning will it be for them."

"Your words fill me with astonishment, Sampson;" said Constance, "and excite in my breast the most anxious curiosity. The Gipsey, Mabel, too,—should your surmises be correct, and the infatulated girl followed Evelyn in his dangerous career,—alas!—what sad consequences may it not be productive of."

"Aye;" observed the Gipsey-Chief;—"it is that which excites my anxiety more than all. Headstrong girl;—why did she not listen to my warning?—Did she know the fearful consequences that may arise from her rash conduct, she would shudder at the contemplation of them.

"How torturing is this misery;—" ejaculated our heroine;—"oh, Brayling, what necessity can there possibly be for any further secrecy?—"

"Exercise thy patience but a short time longer, my dear lady," answered Brayling, and all will be explained, I have no doubt to thine entire satisfaction, Everything that I have promised rest assured will be performed, and I have no doubt to thine entire satisfaction."

"But oh, should you fail in your praiseworthy designs;" said Constance, doubtfully.

"Rest confident of my success, Miss Constance;" replied Sampson;—"my motives are founded on truth and justice, and I do not fear the result.

"On the day then appointed for the hated marriage;" remarked our heroine;—"which I cannot think upon with any other feelings than those of disgust and horror—"

"We shall meet again;" said the Gipsey-Chief;—"that day is indeed big with fate, and I shall triumph; Sampson Brayling never yet failed in anything which he undertook to perform."

Abigail, who had stood apart to keep watch, now approached them.

"I beg pardon, Miss, for interrupting you;—" she said;—"but I thought I caught a glimpse of Sir Milford and Dalton, just now, going towards the Grange, so had we not better return?"

Constance replied in the affirmative, and Sampson Brayling having repeated his promises, and watched her and her attendant enter the house by the backway in safety, followed by his companions, took his departure from the spot.

Our heroine passed a sleepless night, so busily was her mind occupied in reflecting upon the startling events that had occurred within the last few days, and in anticipating those, which in all probability were yet in store for her. How conflicting were the hopes, the doubts, and fears she entertained for the future destiny of her lover; and the obstinacy with which the Gipsey-girl persisted in her fatal passion, and in pursuing the footsteps of him whom she evidently so fondly loved, was to her a source of the greatest anxiety and uneasiness, and there was a strange mystery connected with her, which she in vain tried to penetrate. The observations that Sampson Brayling had made to her, were strongly impressed upon her mind, and she looked forward to the day fixed for her unnatural union with Oliver Dalton as one of the most important that had ever occurred to her, though what the result of it might be she almost trembled to conjecture. To appeal any more to her uncle for forbearance she knew would be useless, for that he was obstinately fixed in the determination he had formed, she was fully convinced.

She dreaded to meet Oliver Dalton, for a feeling of terror and disgust came over her whenever she even thought of him, which she in vain sought to control. She avoided his presence as much as possible, but whenever they did meet, the boldness of his manner convinced her that he considered his triumph as certain.

Time fled on rapid wings, and at length the fatal Monday morning arrived

when she was to be taken from the Grange, and conveyed to Milford Hall, near the rural village of Charlton, to be sacrificed by the cruel perversity of her uncle, and adverse fate to that man whom she could not possibly look upon with any other feelings than those of hatred and repugnance. On the evening before she had made a final appeal to Sir Milford, but with no better success than before; he turned a deaf ear to her supplications; enjoined her to obedience on pain of his eternal wrath, and commanded her and her attendant to be in readiness to depart on their journey at an early hour in the morning. Constance left him with a heavy and foreboding heart, and the restless anguish she endured that night, may be far better imagined than we can describe it. To retire to her couch she could not think, and Abigail, (who never left her,) used all her powers of persuasion and expostulation in vain. Oh, how fervent were the prayers she offered up to Heaven for protection for herself and Evelyn, and when she reflected that that persecuted and beloved being was now probably far away, and

No. 24.

exposed to all the perils of the dangerous deep, without one individual near to whisper a word of hope in his ear, her tears flowed unrestrained, and despair took almost entire possession of her heart.

Day had scarcely dawned when herself and Abigail were aroused by the sound of wheels, and hastening to the window they beheld a couple of travelling carriages approaching along the principal avenue towards the house. The heart of Constance sickened at the sight, and she leaned for support upon the arm of Abigail. They had neither of them much time given to them for reflection, for a servant quickly made her appearance with a message from Sir Milford for Constance to attend him immediately below. The painful moment had therefore at length arrived, and Constance making one more powerful effort to regain her fortitude, in which she succeeded far beyond her hopes, committed herself to the care and protection of Providence, took the arm of Abigail, and proceeded down the stairs towards the room in which her uncle awaited her, and, at the door of which Abigail for the present left her. Constance entered the room with a firm step, for her mind was made up, but, on beholding the hateful Oliver Dalton in company with her uncle, and ready dressed for the journey, her heart sunk within her, and she averted her looks with a feeling of abhorrence approaching to horror. Sir Milford addressed a few words to her which she hardly understood, and to which she could make no reply; and Oliver then with a well-affected smile of love and gallantry, attempted to take her hand in order to lead her to the carriage, but, with a look of indignation and contempt, which elicted an angry rebuke from Sir Milford, and confused and abashed Oliver, she spurned him from her, and suffered her uncle to conduct her from the room to the carriage, without saying a word. Here she felt some relief on finding that herself and Abigail were alone to occupy one of the carriages, Sir Milford and Dalton disposing of themselves in the other, and having taken their seats, they were driven off without any further delay. Just as the vehicle in which our heroine was seated, had passed slowly through the garden gates, Constance, happening to look from the window, in order to take a parting glance at the old Grange, as it was revealed in the grey mists of early dawn, beheld the solitary form of a man wrapped in a large mantle, and gliding cautiously from beneath the wall, and suspecting that it was some friend, she thrust her head forward from the window, so that she might satisfy him she was there. The man immediately rushed up to the carriage, which had made a temporary stoppage, and their eyes met, and our heroine could scarcely repress a cry of astonishment when she recognised Sampson Brayling.

"Courage!" he whispered;—and hastily thrusting a note in her hand, was gone in an instant. The sight of the Gipsey-Chief, in some measure relieved the anxiety of our heroines mind, and inspired her with fresh hope and confident It assured her that she had, at least, one faithful friend in the world, and convinced her, if she could indeed, previously, have entertained any feeling of doubt that his motives were pure and disinterested, and that all he had promised he was prepared, and fully determined to perform, to the very letter.

"Kind man;" she observed;—"how much am I already indebted to him; and how much more do I anticipate shall I yet be; alas! I fear that I shall never be able sufficiently to repay the vast obligation I am under to him."

"Ah! Miss;" said Abigail; "Sampson Brayling is indeed an excellent man; a diamond in the rough, as I have often heard my dear Timothy observe; and I only wish that there were many more thousands in the world than there are, like him. But what does he say in his letter?"

Constance opened it, and, as well as the indistinct light would permit her, read the following lines:

"Respected lady, I beseech thee droop not; Sampson Brayling is sincerely thy friend, and will not fail to keep his word. I am active to put my designs into execution, and have every confidence in their success. Oliver Dalton shall be defeated in his villainy, and Sir Milford Welborn, thoroughly convinced of the villainy of the serpent he has so long been nurturing in his bosom. Again I say, lady, fear not, Sampson Brayling will be at Charlton as soon as thou art, and will be always at hand, to receive any information thou mayest have the opportunity to convey to him, through the means of thy faithful maid, Abigail."

"Yes," said our heroine, after she had perused this brief epistle, "I will, notwithstanding the gloomy prospect by which I am at present surrounded, put my trust in Providence, and hope for the best."

"Well said, my dear young lady," returned Abigail, "it glads me to hear you say so, and I feel confident that your hopes will not be disappointed."

This little event re-animated the spirits of Constance, and she became calm and resigned. The morning was dull and heavy, and the way they travelled was anything but pleasant, but she took little heed of it, her mind being so busily occupied with other and more important subjects. Two or three times they stopped on the road, on each of which occasions Oliver Dalton endeavoured to urge her into conversation, but she received his advances with that calm dignity and repelling disdain, that completely abashed him, and only served to strengthen the conviction he had before entertained of the utter abhorrence in which she held him, and, while it mortified his pride, and added to his chagrin, rendered him the more anxious and determined to obtain the gratification of his ambitious and guilty wishes.

Nothing particular or worthy of recording took place on the journey, which was performed with every possible expedition, as regarded the state of the roads at the remote period of which we are writing, and, in due time the carriages stopped at the gothic entrance to Milford Hall.

The old Hall was a noble structure, which had been erected as far back as the reign of William the Conqueror, and had bravely resisted the ravages of time. Its appearance was grand and imposing in the extreme ; and the traveller who passed it could not, in so doing, help gazing at it with feelings of the deepest interest and admiration. It had formerly been a priory, but its holy inmates having abandoned it, it fortunately escaped demolition at the time of the dissolution of Monasteries by Henry the Eighth, and, together with the wide domains attached to it, fell into the possession of the ancestors of the present Sir Milford Welborn, and from which it took the name of Milford Hall. About the year 1710, having been suffered for a long period to fall into decay, it was entirely consumed by fire, so that not a vestige now remains to mark the spot where it formerly stood.

There was a small chapel in the interior of this venerable building which the baronet had had restored, at considerable expense, and it was at this chapel, by his own private chaplain, and without any pomp or ostentation, he had resolved that the ceremony should secretly take place. It was three years before since Sir Milford and his niece had resided for any length of time at the Hall, although it was so much more commodious than the Grange, and only a few miles from London, and little had our heroine anticipated, on their last leaving it, that when they again visited it, it would be under such painful circumstances as the present. Such were the thoughts that arose to her mind, when the vehicles stopped before the ancient edifice, and never had the ancient edifice appeared half so gloomy and cheerless as it did at that moment. The old walls, blackened by time, but stern and stalwart in their age, seemed to frown despair upon her, and she suffered Sir Milford to conduct her into the building, Oliver Dalton following close behind, with many a sigh and a throbbing heart. She reflected, however, upon the promises and the letter of Sampson Brayling, and she regained her firmness and composure, so much so, in fact, that it surprised and gratified her uncle, who argued from it a compliance with his wishes without any further opposition.

On ascending the grand staircase which led to the principal suite of rooms, our heroine, looking round, was pleased to find that Oliver Dalton had not accompanied them, and the baronet having led her into one of the sitting apartments, conducted her to a seat, and stood for a minute or two and contemplated the expression of her countenance in silence.

"Constance," he said, at last, "we have now arrived at the end of our journey, and I trust that, having given thee reasonable time for reflection, you see the folly and imprudence of offering any further resistance to my will. I will be brief with thee, for we have already wasted sufficient argument on the subject, and I am in no mood to discuss it on the present occasion. Everything is in readiness, and thou must therefore prepare thyself to become the wife of Oliver Dalton on Saturday next, at midnight; my friend, Sir Thomas Overton, will be present as a witness of the marriage rites, and his two fair daughters will attend as thy bridesmaids."

"Ah!" exclaimed Constance, as a shuddering sensation, in spite of the fortitude that had hitherto sustained her, came over her ;—"so soon, and at such a solemn hour?"

"Aye,"—replied Sir Milford ;—"under all the circumstances, it is necessary that the ceremony should take place without any more delay, and with as much privacy as possible."

"Oh, my uncle ;" said our heroine, with a look of gentle remonstrance ; "surely this is harsh and unjust, and totally unworthy of you."

"Psha!" returned Sir Milford, impatiently ; "there has been enough of this ; my conduct is guided by motives of prudence, and with a regard to thy future welfare and happiness ; and I am therefore not disposed to listen to thine ill-timed censures ; it is my will, and, if thou wouldst still retain my affection, thou wilt unhesitatingly obey it."

"Sir Milford Welborn ;" replied Constance, regaining her firmness, and rising with calm dignity and determination ; "with all due deference to the authority which I acknowledge you have a right to exercise over me, I would have you pause before you take a step which you may afterwards have such bitter cause to regret ; in the face of high Heaven, and in the name of justice, I solemnly protest against the monstrous sacrifice you would make of my happiness. I repeat that there is no fate, however horrible, that I will not readily submit to, rather than become the wife of such a villian as Oliver Dalton !"

An exclamation of rage in the voice of some person behind, startled her, and, looking round she was somewhat confused on beholding the object of her hatred and indignation standing in the room, his face glowing with passion, and a deadly expression of malice increasing the repulsive aspect of his features.

"Obstinate girl !" cried Sir Milford, passionately, "this behaviour is intolerable, and will do thee no good. Oliver Dalton, I beseech thee to stifle thy feelings of resentment, which the insolent and unprovoked language of my niece is calculated to call forth. We will find the means to crush this turbulent, this obstinate, and disobedient spirit. A servant will conduct thee to the apartments prepared for thy reception," he added, speaking to our heroine, "and I trust by the time we meet again, thou wilt have learnt reason and submission."

He rang the bell as he thus spoke, and a female servant made her appearance. Constance returned no answer to this harsh speech, but curtseying to her uncle, and casting a look of hatred and scorn on Oliver Dalton, she followed the domestic from the room, and was by her conducted to an elegant suite of apartments, fitted up with much taste, and situated in another part of the building.

Here she dismissed the female, and throwing herself in a chair, gave free vent to the feelings that agitated her breast. She was soon afterwards joined by Abigail, who warmly expressed her sympathy with her on the trying occasion, and did all that she could to comfort and console her. That day passed gloomily away, but Constance felt some relief when she found that neither Sir Milford nor Dalton offered to intrude upon her. The following morning, however, she received a peremptory message to attend them below, and what passed at that painful interview, we may safely leave to the imagination of the reader. Our heroine retained her firmness, resisted the importunities of her uncle, with calmness and resolution, and rejected all the overtures and powers of persuasion of Oliver Dalton, with the utter contempt and abhorrence they so justly merited; and when she was permitted to retire from the room, she left them both in a state of the utmost chagrin and disappointment.

Sir Thomas Overton and his too daughters arrived at Milford Hall that day, and they were immediately introduced to our heroine, who was received by them with the utmost cordiality and affability.

The daughters of Sir Thomas were young and amiable, and had ever been on terms of the warmest friendship with our heroine. They deeply sympathised with her in her misfortunes, and when they were alone, she did not hesitate to unburthen her mind to them; and they listened to her with every feeling of compassion and interest, and professed themselves ready to render her all the assistance in their power.

Constance had not forgotten the instructions conveyed by Sampson Brayling in his note, and, at the first opportunity she sent Abigail from the Hall, in the evening, when there was no one likely to observe her, to see whether the Gipsey was true to his appointment, and, on her return, which she had waited for most anxiously, Abigail informed her that she found him waiting, in disguise, according to his promise, at a short distance from the Hall; that she had told him all the particulars of the day and the hour being fixed for the forced marriage to take place; and he had desired her to assure her mistress that he had everything in readiness, and that he would not fail to make his appearance at the critical moment, and make such disclosures as could not fail to create the confusion and dismay of Oliver Dalton, and prevent the union from taking place. With what trembling anxiety, what doubts and fears, did our heroine await the arrival of the time on which hung the crisis of her fate; but she placed every confidence in the integrity and ability of Sampson Brayling to accomplish everything he had undertaken to perform; and the composure and firmness she maintained completely astonished and bewildered Sir Milford and Oliver.

At length the all-important, the fatal day arrived, and the heart of Constance beat high with mingled feelings of fear and expectation. After a trying interview with her uncle and Dalton, she was dismissed in the evening to her own apartments to make her final preparations for the ceremony, and she had but just taken her seat, when Abigail entered, and the expression of her features shewed that she had something of importance to communicate. She did not keep her mistress long in suspense, but, to the eager enquiries she put to her, she informed her that she had seen Sampson Brayling, that by some means or the other, he had secretly contrived to gain access to the Hall, and that he and several of the tribe would remain concealed in the chapel till the proper time arrived for action, when he solemnly promised to accomplish his purpose, or perish in the attempt. The reader may easily conceive the feelings of emotion with which Constance received this intelligence; she sank on her knees, and fervently supplicated the protection of the Supreme, and then awaited the arrival of the momentous period, with calmness, confidence, and resignation.

      *   *   *   *   *   *

Rapidly flew the time; everything gave note of eager preparation in the Hall, and at length eleven chimed from the deep-toned bell of the old clock; another hour and the fate of Constance Welborn would probably be decided;—she trembled and applied to the fair sisters, who had been unremitting in their attendance upon her, for support. The moment came at last when the poor girl was summoned to attend Sir Milford, and the detested Dalton, and a painful moment indeed it was for her;—but she struggled with her feelings as well as she could, and consulted by the young bridesmaid, and followed by Abigail, whose heart palpitated with expectation, she left the room, and descended into that where Sir Milford, Oliver Dalton, and Sir Thomas Overton, were anxiously awaiting to accompany her to the chapel.

We will pass hastily over the scene which followed; but Sir Milford and Oliver, who little suspected the feelings which at that critical moment occupied her breast, were completely astonished at the firmness and self possession of Constance. Again she most vehemently protested against the whole proceedings, and once more supplicated the forbearance of her uncle; but he remained deaf to the appeal, and Constance, assuming an air of haughty defiance, and with a look of ineffable disgust, repelling the attempt of Oliver to take her hand, committed herself to the cure of the sisters and Abigail, and moved in the procession to the chapel.

The ancient chapel was lighted with large wax candles, which cast a sepulchral reflection upon the dark stone walls, and elaborately carved oak panels;—the minister was in waiting; all were arranged before the altar, and, in that dreary hour, when all was hushed in death-like silence, the scene was solemn and impressive in the extreme. And now the minister was about to commence the marriage rites, and all were hushed in breathless silence, all eyes were fixed on Constance, whose cheek was pale, but whose firmness remained unshaken. And the hypocrite, Oliver—how was he at that important moment on which his fate depended?— although he endeavoured to appear firm and confident, he trembled; his lips quivered, and fearful forebodings disturbed his mind. The minister had commenced the ceremony when, at that moment, a loud voice from the farther end of the chapel was heard to exclaim in commanding tones that thrilled the hearts of the hearers—

"Hold!—forbear the unnatural, the unrighteous ceremony!—Heaven and Justice denounce it—forbear!—"

In a moment, Sampson Brayling and a number of the Gipsey tribe arrived, rushed from a remote part of the chapel, and surrounded the altar, to their utter confusion, surprise, and consternation. Overpowered by her feelings, Constance uttered a faint cry, and swooned in the arms of Abigail!

CHAPTER XXX.

THE FINAL DESTINATION OF THE MISER.—THE PIRATE SHIP.—A THRILLING SCENE.

IT is now necessary that we should follow the destiny of the wretched Jasper Scrimpe. The drug which had been administered to him by Godfrey Malvern had the desired effect, and steeped his soul in a complete state of torper for several hours, during which period Malvern and his companions made the best use of their time, and were enabled to complete their journey, and arrive in secrecy at the place of their destination while he still remained in a state of insensibility.

When the Miser did recover to consciousness, he gazed with bewildered looks around him, and was lost in astonishment and alarm at the strange situation in which he found himself. He was reclining on a rude bench in a rocky cavern, which was dimly lighted by a lamp which was placed upon the earth, and which only served to reveal more distinctly the wild and cheerless aspect of the place. His mind was too distracted to allow him to form the least conjecture as to the means by which he had been brought thither, and starting to his feet, for some minutes he continued to gaze vacantly around him, and without the power to utter a syllable. He could hear the dashing of waves against the sides of the rock, and that convinced him he was in some cavernous retreat near the sea-side, and the rapidity of his transport thither seemed to be completely the work of magic. There was a rude door formed at one side of the cavern, which he hurried to as soon as he could, in some degree, collect himself; but he found it securely fastened, and that therefore all retreat that way was effectually prevented. He clasped his forehead in despair, and most agonising were the feelings that racked his mind. Then he called aloud for help, but the dismal echo of his own voice was the only reply he received to his cries. Again he threw himself upon the bench, and the most dreadful thoughts flashed upon and tortured his distracted brain. Was he there alone in that awful place, and had he been brought there and left to perish by a lingering and fearful death of starvation? he shuddered with horror at the thought, and, for the moment, every faculty was suspended. Then again he rent the place with his frantic cries, and beat his breast, and tore his hair in the madness of his feelings. And now all the guilty transactions of his past life rushed upon his conscience with overwhelming force, and added to his tortures. To his disordered fancy strange and hideous forms seemed to hover around him, and to howl their curses in his ears; the effects of these horrible imaginations was too much for the strength of the miserable old man to support, and he once more threw himself upon the bench, and became lost in insensibility.

How long he had thus remained, he knew not;—but at length he was aroused by some one rudely shaking him by the shoulder,—and, looking up, he beheld Godfrey Malvern standing by his side. He started immediately to his feet, and stared at him with trembling anxiety.

"Ah!—dread enemy;" he exclaimed;—"art thou then here?"

"There is no need of the question;" replied Malvern, sternly; "thou seest I am."

"Where am I?" demanded Scrimpe, with fearful impatience;—"what dismal place is this?—"

"Thou art now by the sea shore;" answered Godfrey, "and in the retreat which has often formed a shelter for myself and my daring crew;—in a short time thou wilt be on board my gallant craft which is now anchored only a short distance from the place of thy confinement."

"Oh, God!—oh, God!" groaned the Miser, wringing his hands in despair; "then am I indeed lost. Oh, Malvern, what are thy dark and fearful designs against me? Will nothing whatever move thee to relent, and to view me with some degree of compassion?—"

"Compassion for such a guilty wretch as thou art?" returned Godfrey Malvern, with a look of deadly malice and contempt; "thou seekest it in vain; but, psha! I do but waste words with thee. I must introduce thee to my comrades. Doubtless," he added, with a sarcastic grin, "the amiable Miser, Jasper Scrimpe, will find the society of such bold and reckless fellows most agreeable to him."

"Spare me! spare me, Malvern, I implore thee," ejaculated the old man, clasping his hands vehemently together, and with looks of the most earnest supplication, "thy revenge is guided by the malice of a fiend. Oh, forbear! forbear!"

"No more of this!" returned Godfrey, "thy words can have no effect upon me; I am deaf to thy supplications. This way."

He grasped the arm of the Miser as he spoke, and urged him towards the door, and, abandoning himself to despair, and knowing that it was useless to offer any resistance, in trembling anticipation suffered Malvern to conduct him from the cavern, and to lead him into a winding passage beyond, which seemed to have been the work of nature, and never to have been worked by human hand, out of the solid rock. The wind howled fiercely along this dismal avenue, and Jasper could hear the roaring of the waves as they dashed around, and the sounds seemed to convey despair to his heart. Godfrey, however, hurried him on, and they at length arrived at another roughly constructed door, and Jasper could hear the voices of several men in loud conversation beyond. He shuddered, but he had not much time given him for reflection, for Malvern having knocked three times loudly at the door, the next minute it was opened by a ferocious looking man; the Miser was urged forward, and on looking around him, the scene which met his eyes filled him with feelings of amazement and alarm.

It was a spacious cavern that met his view, lighted by two or three lamps suspended from the lofty roof, and which served to render every object in the place perfectly distinct. In the centre of this place was a long table, around which were seated a number of as determined and savage looking men as could well be imagined, and armed to resist any surprise or attack which might be made upon them. Powder-casks, fire-arms, and other weapons were strewed promiscously about, and everything bespoke the desperate calling of the men whom Jasper Scrimpe gazed upon with so much astonishment and alarm. On their entrance the pirates arose and greeted Godfrey Malvern as their captain most enthusiastically, and all eyes immediately became fixed, with vulgar curiosity, on the trembling Miser. He averted his looks with terror and disgust, and the thoughts which at that moment rushed like a torrent through his mind, were almost sufficient to overwhelm him. Godfrey Malvern quickly aroused him from this lethargy, and taking his arm, and leading him to the foot of the table, and addressing the pirates in exulting and ironical tones, he said :—

"Allow me, comrades, to introduce to ye, my old *friend*, Jasper Scrimpe, otherwise Gerald Aubrey, whom till lately I had not had the honour of meeting for many years ; I trust that thou wilt give him such a welcome as he deserves."

Loud laughter followed this address, and the confusion, the terror and dismay of the wretched Jasper Scrimpe were increased to an almost insupportable degree.

"Godfrey Malvern ;" he said in tones of bitter reproach; "how dost thou unman thyself by conduct such as this; will thine implacable feelings of revenge never be satiated ? thou dost delight to mock at my sufferings. Let me return to the place we have just quitted ;—I cannot—I will not endure the society of ruffians such as these."

"1 would advise thee to be somewhat more choice in thy language ;" observed Malvern;—"these ruffians, as thou hast ventured to call them, will be thy future companions on board my brave barque, and it will be as well for thee to endeavour to accommodate thyself to their manners."

"Heaven help me, then ;" groaned the Miser, with a shudder.

"Darest thou to appeal to Heaven ?" said Godfrey, with a look of hatred and disgust. "But come, thou must join them at the festive board, till the time arrives for us to depart from hence."

"And whither is our future destination ?" eagerly enquired Scrimpe.

"On board the Dare-Devil," answered Godfrey, "which, ere many hours have elapsed, will be far away from these shores."

The unfortunate old man again looked at him with an expression of fear and supplication, and Malvern taking his arm, in spite of the repugnance he evinced, led him to the head of the table amid the mock greeting of the pirates, and

taking his seat, Godfrey placed him at his side, and affecting to treat him with the greatest hospitality and condescension.

The pirates now gave free indulgence to their vulgar mirth and revelry ; rude jokes and songs were passed around, and the brain of Jasper Scrimpe was distracted by the noise and confusion that prevailed around. He gave himself up for lost, and could not but anticipate that which was too probable in store for him, with feeling of the utmost horror.

There was an opening in the rock, at one side of the cavern, through which the open sky was visible, and was ascended to by a short ladder, and seemed to form the only means of ingress and egress to this secret band. More than a couple of hours had passed in the manner that has been described, when a shrill whistle was heard to proceed immediately from below this cavity in the rock, and Malvern, and several of the other pirates, jumped to their feet at the sound, and gazed at aech other with significant looks.

No. 25.

"It is the signal of our comrades;" said Godfrey; "they have come from the ship, and doubtless all is in readiness for our departure. Lower the means of ascent to the entrance to them."

Two of the pirates obeyed this order by lowering a rope ladder outside the cavern, and immediately afterwards two or three men appeared at and descended from the opening, and greeted Malvern and the others.

"How now?—" demanded Godfrey, addressing himself to them;—"have you but just left the ship?"

"We have;" replied one of the ruffians, "and what's the time, enquired Malvern.

"'Tis past eleven o'clock, Captain;" was the answer.

"Ah!" observed the pirate chief; "it is time then, to get on board; the Dare-Devil must be some distance from this coast before daylight. Is all in readiness?"

The man answered in the affirmative, and added that there was no one near to observe them, and that the boats were moored close by to convey them to the ship.

"'Tis well," observed Godfrey, "then let us begone, comrades, it is useless to delay. We shall avoid the suspicions and interruptions of the land-sharks, and the gallant Dare-Devil must once more fearlessly pursue its course o'er the dark blue waters of the ocean, to meet with the same success that has hitherto attended her."

Loud cheers followed this speech, and immediately all was bustle and activity, and the principal portion of the pirates having taken a parting glass of the intoxicating and exhilerating beverage they had been drinking, quitted the cavern.

"And now, Jasper Scrimpe," observed Malvern, "the time for our departure hath arrived. Say, art thou ready?"

"Alas!" sighed the old man, looking dismally around him, "and is there indeed no hope? Godfrey Malvern, art thou still determined to persist in thy guilty purpose?"

"And, after having proceeded thus far," replied the pirate, "thinkest thou it is at all likely that I will abandon my designs at this juncture? Come, we do but waste time in tarrying here."

"And must I, in the decripitude of age and infirmity, be exposed to the terrors and dangers of the ocean?" said the wretched Miser, "and compelled to mingle with miscreants inured to crime and bloodshed?"

"And doth the guilty Jasper Scrimpe dare to murmur against the character of men who are perfectly innocent when compared with him?" demanded Godfrey. "Hypocrite! thy mawkish cant is disgusting. Away with thee! thou canst expect no mercy at mine hands!"

"Forbear! forbear! once more I implore thee!"

"No more," exclaimed Malvern, in a stern voice, "I will no longer listen to thee, my patience is exhausted."

Jasper clasped his hands together, with the most intense and insupportable agony, and Malvern grasping him violently by the arm, led him up the ladder to the opening in the rock, and the next moment they alighted on the beech.

The Miser gazed eargerly around him, and the moon shining clearly, notwithstanding the night was anything but fine, and the wind blew tempestuously from the North, he was enabled to trace every object distinctly. The wide sea was before him, dotted here and there with a distant vessel, and close by he beheld two long boats, in which most of the pirates had already taken their places, whilst the rest were awaiting the arrival of himself and his companion. How terrible and dismal were the fears and forebodings that racked the Miser's mind, as Godfrey Malvern hurried him along the beech towards the nearest boat; the whole appeared to him like some fearful dream, instead of reality, and before he could arouse himself from his state of anguish and terror, he found himself placed in the boat by the side of Malvern, and it was immediately pushed off from the shore and followed by the other. Swiftly the boats glided o'er the surface of the deep, and at length having rounded an angle of the rocks, Jasper beheld at no great distance a stately ship, which he had no doubt was the vessel to which they were bound. He viewed it with a melancholy degree of interest which we need not seek to describe, and as Malvern marked the craft in which he had braved so many perils, and encountered so many dangers, he exclaimed, in tones of pride and admiration :—

"See, how gallantly my noble barque rides on the surface of that ocean, o'er which for years she has spread terror and dismay to the hearts of all those who have encountered her. Never, never will I abandon her but with my life. For weeks has she been anchored off this coast, without exciting the suspicions of the swabs and lubbers, who would give a trifle to get her in their power."

Jasper's heart sunk within him as Godfrey Malvern thus exultingly gave expression to his feelings,—but as the boats came nearer and nearer to the ship, and Jasper Scrimpe gazed eagerly towards it, a convulsive shuddering suddenly seized his limbs, and wildly clutching the arm of Malvern, as he directed his attention to a certain part of the ocean, in a hoarse voice he exclaimed:—

"For the love of Heaven, Malvern,—do not, oh, do not approach that fearful spot !—Hold !—hold !—forbear !—In mercy, I implore thee !—"

"How now?" demanded Godfrey, "art thou mad?—or is it thy guilty conscience that haunts thee with imaginary horrors ?"

"No, no, no ; " almost shrieked the wretched man—"behold !—dost thou not see that ghastly form which glides o'er the waves towards me ?—shield me !—shield me, oh, horror !—"

Surprised, Godfrey Malvern gazed in the direction to which his distracted companion pointed, but he could see nothing. Jasper Scrimpe, however, continued to gaze frenziedly towards the spot, and his terror arrived to an extraordinary pitch. Rising from the bosom of the ocean, surrounded by a supernatural light, and gliding solemnly towards the boat, the Miser imagined he beheld the ghastly, and shadowy form of a man, the head and upper part of the body of which was alone visible above the surface of the waves. Nearer and nearer it approached the boat, till at length it arrived so close, that Jasper had a distinct view of its ghastly features. Horror, horror, they were those of one whose bones had long since mouldered into dust ! The unfortunate being who had perished by his guilty hands. With a wild hysterical cry that rent the midnight air, Jasper Scrimpe sunk insensible at the bottom of the boat, and in that state was borne on board the the pirate vessel.

CHAPTER XXXI.

MABEL AND EVELYN ON THE OCEAN.—THE STORM.—FEARFUL SITUATION OF THE GIPSEY-GIRL.—THE DISCOVERY.

THUNDERSTRUCK at the discovery of the devoted Mabel under such extraordinary circumstances as those we have described in a previous chapter, our hero for a few moments stood speechless, and gazed at her with mingled feelings of pity, regret, and admiration. But there was that expression in her fine dark eyes and handsome features, that shewed the fixed and immovable determination of her soul, and the intensity of that ill-fated passion that glowed within her breast, and which neither time nor circumstances could conquer or subdue.

"Gracious Heaven, Mabel!" at length exclaimed Evelyn; "is it possible that I see thee here?—In this disguise, and—"

"Aye, " replied the Gipsey-Girl in tones of tenderness and self congratulation; "thou see'st I have kept my word. Providence fortunately made me once more the humble instrument of saving thee from thy deadly foes,—and, faithful to the passions my heart owns for thee, dear Evelyn, I am with thee here on the wide waters of the deep, prepared to share with thee in all the dangers it may be thy lot to encounter; to cheer thee on in the moment of trial; to solace, console, and encourage the in thee hour of sickness or of sorrow. Oh, could the proud and peerless beauty, Constance Welborn, give a greater proof of her affection than this?"

"Generous, noble-minded girl," cried our hero, with a burst of enthusiasm and admiration which he could not restrain;—"oh, what a sad and perverse fate thus wildly urges thee on?—why hast thou been tempted to this rash and imprudent step?".

"Thou knowest full well the glowing passion of my heart, and need'st not ask that question;" replied Mabel; and her bright eyes brightened up with even more than their wonted fire as she spoke. "Heaven's brightest sun would be impenetrable darkness to the poor Gipsey-girl; nature's most fertile and luxuriant spots appear to her as deserts wild, without the presence of Evelyn Heartwell. Oh, thou art so deeply ingrafted in my very soul, that that soul would feel accursed, abandoned, if thou wert absent from my sight. I love thee, Evelyn, and though I may never hope for any return, I exalt, I glory in the passion which thine image, thy noble, manly virtues have engendered in my breast."

"Fatal spell that urges thee to conduct so rash, so headstrong, so dangerous," said our hero. "Mabel, heedest thou not the delicate position in which thou hast placed thyself? What if thy sex should be discovered, might it not give rise to suspicions mortifying to me, and insulting and disgusting to the purity of thy feelings to hear?"

"And who would dare," returned Mabel, with an air of dignified confidence, "who would dare to question the purity, the integrity of the Gipsey-girl's motives? Evelyn, dear Evelyn, thou hast obtained an influence over me which it is vain for me to attempt to resist; my hopes, my wishes, my very existence are interwoven with thine; thou mayest call it madness if thou wilt, thou mayest even hate and despise me, but ever, till this poor heart shall ceased to beat, I must love thee, love thee, even to adoration."

The fervour, the excitement of her feelings overpowered her, and sobbing convulsively, she sunk in his arms, and at that moment Walter Grasham arrived at the spot, and started back in amazement at the scene which presented itself to his eyes.

"Aye," he exclaimed, "what do I see? My friend, Evelyn, yard-arm and yard-arm with young Ned Trysail? What's in the wind now? What's the meaning of this?"

Our hero disengaged himself from the fond embrace of the Gipsey-girl in confusion, and vexed at being discovered in such a position by the captain; but Mabel regained her composure and self-possession with remarkable speed, and immediately replied, in a tone and with a demeanour that were sufficient to quiet all suspicions:—

"I ask pardon, your honour; Master Evelyn was merely returning me an acknowledgment for a little service I was fortunate enough to be able to render him lately at Wapping."

"So then;" remarked Greysham;—"thou art the brave lad who so courageously rescued my friend from the land-lubbers, art thou?—Thine hand, my fine fellow;—I add my thanks and admiration to his, and depend upon it, if thou dost continue to merit it, I will be studious of thy future welfare."

"I thank your honour;" returned Mabel, with most perfect coolness and *sang-froid;* and bowing respectfully; "I am satisfied in having been enabled to perform my duty, and as the warmest feelings of my *heart* prompted. That conviction is my most dearly prized reward."

And again bowing to the Captain, and fixing upon Evelyn a look which he could not fail to understand, she retired.

"A brave youth that;" said Walter, when she was gone, "who would suppose that the heart of a lion was enshrined in the breast of such a stripling? Why, the slightness of his form, and the gentleness of his features are almost delicate enough for a female."

Evelyn felt more confused than ever, but he managed to return some evasive answer, and, after a few more observations upon the subject, the conversation dropped.

Day after day flew rapidly by, and the gallant ship proceeded prosperously on its voyage. By degrees the mind of Evelyn became more tranquil and resigned, for the novelty of all that now presented itself to his eyes served to divert him. Still the image of his beloved Constance was never absent from his thoughts, and many were the prayers he offered up to Heaven for her protection and future happiness. He avoided Mabel as much as possible, but she was at his side at every opportunity. Her thoughts, her cares and anxieties were constantly for him.

Hitherto the weather had been favourable, but on the sixth day the vessel had been at sea, the ponderous clouds that had hung low upon the horizon, and the gathering wind, coupled with the wild screeching of the sea-mew, as it just skimmed the surface of the waters, betokened a coming storm. Soon the wind strengthened to a gale, and it blew a perfect hurrican. Night came on, and then the tempest was at its height; the waves rolled to a fearful height, tossing the ship about on their foamy crests like a straw, and washing the decks every instant. The lightning blazed in the heavens with terrific violence, the peals of thunder were frequent and deafening, and the rain fell in overwhelming torrents. Suddenly there was a cry of "A man overboard!" and all was the most powerful excitement in a moment. A fearful idea struck Evelyn, and he looked around for Mabel. But a few minutes before she had been by his side, but she was now no where to be seen. Hastily he rushed to the ship's side, and the lightning's flash confirmed his fears. He beheld the poor girl struggling with the waves, and vainly endeavouring to escape that awful and untimely death which seemed to be inevitable. There was no time to be lost, and our hero, unconscious of fear, acted on the inpulse of the moment. Encircling his waist with a stout rope, he suffered himself to be lowered over the ship's side, and dashed to the rescue of the unfortunate girl. For a minute or two his humane efforts were unavailing, and all hope of saving her appeared to be at an end; but a friendly wave at length dashed her towards him, and desperately he grasped her in his hold, and amidst the cheers of the sailors they were both hauled in safety on the deck. Walter Greysham and the crew gathered quickly round. Mabel was insensible; her long raven tresses floated loose and dishevelled on her shoulders; her fair bosom was uncovered; and unspeakable was the astonishment of all when they discovered that the supposed sailor-boy was a woman!

The poor girl was immediately taken below, and committed to the care of a matronly woman on board, who was there to attend upon the sick, or those who might be wounded in any engagement, in the capacity of nurse; but the wonder and excitement that prevailed among the crew was indescribable.

"Why, how is this, Evelyn?" interrogated Walter Greysham when they were alone; "so then this brave youth, who so nobly risked every danger, nay, even life itself to rescue thee from thine enemies, turns out to be a woman after all, and a lovely one too, and I'm not mistaken."

"Even so, my friend;" replied our hero;—"Poor girl, poor girl, a fatal passion engendered in her breast for me, to which, however, I have never given any encouragement, and can make no other return than the warmest esteem, has urged her to this rash and imprudent step. I knew not of her being aboard till it was too late to induce her to return on shore."

"Egad!" remarked Greysham, with a smile; "this is a most romantic adventure, and thou oughtst to consider thyself highly flattered, Evelyn, in having a young and beauteous woman, thus fearlessly running every risk, braving every peril, in her generous and affectionate devotion to thee. By Jupiter, she is a perfect heroine. This then I presume, is Mabel, the Gipsey-girl, of whom thou hast spoken to me?"

"The same;" answered our hero; "alas! how strange and unfortunate is the infatuation that has taken such powerful possession of her senses."

"Poor girl;" ejaculated Walter, compassionately;—"I pity, and admire her. Conduct such as her's proves a nobleness of mind that is deserving of a better fate."

"True;" coincided Evelyn; but thou wilt treat her with every respect, I know, Walter;—and will not suffer her to be exposed any more than possible to the inconveniences of the position in which she has placed herself?"

"Thou mayest depend on me;" replied Greysham; "I pledge thee my word that poor Mabel shall be treated with all the kindness and deference that are due to her sex, and the eminent virtues that distinguish her character."

Evelyn thanked him, and the bustle and activity that prevailed on deck, requiring his superintendence, the conversation dropped, and they separated.

The storm continued with the greatest violence during the night, and the gallant vessel was exposed to the most iminent peril. The utmost exertions of the captain and crew were kept constantly employed; nor did our hero remain an idle spectator of the exciting scene. Had he been used to such arduous duties from boyhood, he could not have displayed more energy and self possession than he did on this occasion. In skill and activity, he did not yield to even the most experienced seamen on board; and his conduct was such as to elicit the warmest praise and admiration from his friend, Walter Greysham. But in the midst of the greatest danger, when death, in its most awful form seemed to threaten,—all his thoughts were of Constance; and many were the blessings he invoked upon her head.

When the storm was at its height, the scene that reigned around was awful in the extreme, and even the stout hearts of the hardiest seamen could not help shuddering with awe, and a sentiment fast approximating to terror, for who could say, surrounded as they were by such indescribable dangers, how soon every soul on board might be in eternity? Gradually, however, the wind lulled; the peals of thunder became less loud and frequent, and the lightning less vivid. The tempest had exhausted its fury; the danger which had threatened was o'er; with the first blush of morning the storm had entirely subsided, and was succeeded by a dead calm, and the weather-beaten craft still rode proudly and gallantly on those bright blue waters, which had lately threatened to immolate her and her brave crew in their deep bosom.

CHAPTER XXXII.

THE SHIP ON FIRE.—THE LIFE BOATS.—NARROW ESCAPE OF EVELYN AND MABEL.—SEVERE TRIALS.—THE ISLAND.

DURING the raging of the storm, Evelyn had felt the greatest anxiety for Mabel, and he made frequent inquiries after her. He was gratified to learn that she had not suffered so much from the effects of the alarming accident as might have been expected; though she was naturally much excited at her secret being discovered. Every one on board deeply sympathised with the poor girl, and admired the noble, and affectionate feeling that had prompted her to risk everything for the sake of being near that beloved being to whom her very soul was devoted, with a passion so ardent, so intense, that nothing whatever could extinguish its fire, or check its glow. But our hero felt grieved, annoyed, and embarrassed, and he almost dreaded again to meet her, since he well knew that all the arguments or persuasions he could make use of, must fail to banish from her breast the unfortunate passion he had there so fatally created.

In the course of the day she was so far recovered from the severe shock she had sustained as to be able to leave her cabin, now once more attired in the more becoming dress of her sex. Her appearance excited the deepest interest and commiseration; and Walter Greysham, who was much struck with her surpassing beauty, pale and languid though she was, and trembling and blushing with modest diffidence, received her with the greatest respect and kindness, while the expression of his eyes, as he contemplated her handsome features, and the captivating graces of her person, spoke a language far more powerful than esteem or admiration. After the brief conversation, which he would willingly have prolonged, he left her and Evelyn together, and hastened on deck. The scene which followed between the Gipsey-girl and our hero, may be readily imagined. It was of the most affecting description. Mabel sobbed, and wept upon his bosom, pleaded with all the eloquence that passion could impart, the unconquerable love she bore him; implored his pity and consideration, and vowed again and again most solemnly, in spite of his scorn and indifference to cherish that love to the latest moment of her existence. Evelyn's heart bled for the poor girl; he pitied her from his very soul; while her brilliant virtues excited his most enthusiastic admiration and esteem; but he was bewildered and distracted, and knew not how to act. He earnestly assured her of his warmest sympathy, and exerted himself to the utmost to stifle the fatal sentiments she had suffered to obtain such powerful ascendancy in her breast; but all that he could say was completely unavailing; and she left him in a state of mind that shewed her passion was fixed and immovable.

Thus three days elapsed; the weather had become favourable, and swiftly, safely, and majestically the ship sailed on its course over the vast waters of the ocean. There was a bright sky, a favouring breeze, and a tranquil sea, all the terrors of the late storm were forgotten, and the hearts of the gallant crew were light and merry. Alas! what an awful change was in a short time destined to come o'er the scene.

It was about the mid-watch: Walter Greysham and Evelyn had retired to their cabins, and most of the crew had sought their hammocks. The night was dark, but fine, and the only sounds that disturbed the silence which reigned around, was the gentle murmuring of the wind, as it swept the deep, or the undulating waves, as they dashed against the sides of the vessel. Evelyn, on first retiring to rest, had been so disturbed by anxious thoughts that crowded upon his brain, that he had been unable to sleep, and he had scarcely dropped into a doze, when he was aroused by a confused noise on deck, which was almost immediately followed by the fearful cry of "Fire!" In an instant he sprang from his berth, and then to his horror and dismay, saw the red reflection of the destructive element, and found the cabin in which he was filled with smoke, at the same time loud cries of horror and despair assailed his ears from above. Terrified and confused, Evelyn hastily threw on his clothes, and hurried on deck, and there a scene of horror and consternation met his gaze, such as he had never witnessed before. How long the fire had broke out, he knew not; but the wind having arisen, it had got most powerful hold, probably in a brief space of time, and was spreading with fearful rapidity, threatening inevitable destruction to the noble vessel and all on board. He found Walter Greysham wonderfully calm and collected under such frightful circumstances, giving directions to the crew, who were putting forth almost superhuman efforts to extinguish the flames; but, alas! with apparently but little chance of success; for the fiery element seemed to have obtained a complete mastery, and the work of destruction went fiercely on.

Every moment the conflagration spread, the flames and smoke ascending to the Heavens, casting a broad reflection on the deep for miles around, threatening shortly to envelope the ill-fated ship from stem to stern, and roaring and hissing as they mounted to the sky, and played amidst the rigging, which mingled with the wild shouts of the crew, as they hnrried too and fro, added to the excitement of the scene, and rendered it one of the most appaling description the imagination could possibly conceive.

While Evelyn thus stood, and with feelings of despair contemplated the horrors around him, he was somewhat startled by a loud shriek near him, and the next moment Mabel, with a wild and distracted air, and her dark silken tresses flowing in disorder about her shoulders, rushed to his arms.

"Evelyn, dear Evelyn!" she exclaimed, in accents of the deepest emotion, "See! see! the fierce flames gather around us, threatening destruction! Oh, must thou perish thus? No, no, for the love of Heaven endeavour to save thyself while there is yet time. Let us fly, dear Evelyn, I do beseech thee, and try to avoid that dreadful fate which now seems to be impending over us!"

"Unhappy girl!—" replied our hero, in mingled tones of pity, and reproach; "oh, why didst thou suffer thy rash folly to expose thee to such frightful horrors as thee?'

"Reproach me not, Evelyn;" she sighed, with an expression of affection that shone through her fears;—"I do not regret,—Heaven knows that I do not regret; for I am near thee, and oh, 'tis even bliss to die on the bosom of Evelyn Heartwell. Would Constance Welborn have ever ventured thus much for thee?—But, ah!— the fearful element spreads with merciless fury;—the burning timbers yield to its devastating power;—death in its most hideous form stalks before our eyes;—fly, fly, Evelyn, while there is yet time;—save that dear life that is so precious, and leave the hapless Mabel to her fate!"

What language could possibly describe the expression of the noble minded, the heroic girl's features as she thus spoke; the unutterable feeling that lighted up her eyes with tenfold their usual brilliancy, and imparted so grand and overpowering a tone to her whole demeanour? Evelyn was paralysed, riveted to the spot with wonder and admiration, and was unable to speak a word. At that moment Walter Greysham, in a state of the greatest agitation, hurried to the place where they were standing.

"All, all is lost!" he exclaimed, in accents of melancholy and despair, "no human efforts can possibly save my noble craft from the relentless fury of the devouring element. The fierce flames ravaged nearly every part of the ship, and should they reach the powder below, not a soul will escape to tell the dreadful tale. There is not a moment to be lost; the long boats are being launched; hasten, Evelyn, and with this unfortunate damsel, endeavour to escape the frightful fate that otherwise most certainly awaits ye."

In an instant he was gone, and was hidden from the view by the dense smoke around. The confusion and dismay on board the burning ship now increased, and the moment was one of inexpressible terror and excitement. Worked up to a pitch of frenzy, Evelyn seized the beauteous form of the distracted Mabel, and rushed hastily towards the fore part of the vessel, where the flames had not yet reached, but to which they were fast extending. And there a scene of despair met his gaze which was enough to appal the stoutest heart. The boats were

filled, and making their way from the burning ship, others of the crew had
precipitated themselves into the deep, and were clinging, with the madness of
desparation to broken spars, half burning timbers, or anything, which in that awful
moment of peril, they could grapple. Evelyn and the Gipsey-girl looked eagerly
around, and as far as they could see through fire and smoke they were alone, they
were abandoned to their fate in that unfortunate ship, which was so rapidly becoming
a prey to the raging flames. that every instant gathered closer around them, and
already scorched their skin with their intense and overpowering heat.

The boats had proceeded to a short distance from the ship, when Greysham,
for the first time partially recovering himself from the confusion and excitement
under which he had naturally laboured, remembered Evelyn and Mabel, (who
he imagined had followed him, after he had addressed them on the deck) and he
looked around for them, when, to his unspeakable alarm, he discovered that they
were not in either of the boats, and with a shudder of horror he imagined the

No. 26.

dreadful fate which had too probably befallen them. Anxiously himself and his unfortunate companions strained their eyes towards the ship, which was now fast burning to the water's edge, and at that moment they beheld the tall, manly form of Evelyn, bearing the Gipsey-girl in his arms, rush wildly through the flames, and in an instant precipitate himself from the ship's side into the waves beneath. They drew in their breath in terror and anxiety, for that they had rushed upon certain death they had too much reason to fear; but a moment, however, and by the broad reflection of the fire which illumined all around, they beheld them clinging to one of the masts, which had fallen overboard, and struggling towards them. Immediately Greysham ordered the men to hurry the boat to their rescue;—but this was a task of some difficulty, under the circumstances, and every moment of delay was fraught with tenfold danger. Evelyn, with anxious eyes, saw the efforts they were making, and exerted himself with redoubled energy and determination, supporting the insensible form of Mabel with one arm, and battling the waves with the other. But his strength was nearly exhausted, and another instant would probably have decided his fate and that of the Gipsey-girl, when a friendly wave hurried them towards their deliverers, and they were dragged insensible into the boat. The next moment a frightful concussion was felt, which nearly lifted the boat out of the water,—a terrific explosion followed; hugh timbers, splintered into fragments, were blown into the air; the flames had reached the powder magazine, and when the dense black clouds of smoke in some degree dispersed, scarcely any portion of the once stately and noble ship was seen to float upon the glowing surface of the billows!

Walter fixed one despairing look of anguish and regret upon the scene of the frightful catastrophe, heaved a deep sigh, and then covered his face with his hands; the boats hurried on their way, and soon at a considerable distance from the fatal spot.

Evelyn and Mabel in a short time were restored to consciousness; and the state of their feelings on beholding their present deplorable situation, and remembering the frightful fate from which they had so miraculously escaped, may be better imagined than described. With what feelings of intense and unspeakable emotion did poor Mabel gaze upon the pale features of Evelyn; while her heart rose in gratitude to Heaven at least for his preservation.

"Evelyn, beloved Evelyn!" she ejaculated; "thou art saved from the hideous fate with which thy valued life was threatened. We are not yet separated, and I am content."

And hast thou no care for thine own safety, unfortuate girl?" said our hero, in melancholy tones;—"does Mabel value her own existence so little as to feel no gratitude for it's preservation?"

"Oh, yes," replied Mabel, a bright smile irradiating her pale features as she spoke; "could I feel the sweet consolation to know that life was precious to Evelyn Heartwell; the remembrance that through him it was saved, would give it a double value in my estimation; but," she added, and an expression of melancholy and regret again overspread her pale features as she spoke, "I dare not entertain so fond a hope; the life or happiness of Mabel are matters of indifference to Evelyn Heartwell."

"Hold, Mabel," returned our hero, with a look of reproach, "those observations are ungenerous and uncalled for. Thou must indeed think lightly of the mind of Evelyn Heartwell, if, after the sacrifices thou hast made for his sake, he can view thee with less than esteem, though he cannot with love. But this is neither the time nor the place to talk upon so delicate a subject. 'Tis true, we have escaped from the flames that consumed the ill-fated ship, but too probably only to meet with a death more lingering and torturing. Alas! with what horrors are we not still surrounded?"

Mabel shuddered, and heaving a deep sigh, covered her face with her hands, as if to shut out from her gaze the terrors to which Evelyn alluded. The brief dialogue which had passed betwen them had been conducted in a low tone, so that it might not reach the ears of their companions; but Walter Greysham noticed their emotion, and guessed the nature of their observations. He deeply sympathised with and respected their feelings, and while he gazed at the beauteous and intelligent features of the Gipsey-girl, and thought of the noble, the generous and disinterested feelings that guided all her actions, he felt a sensation at his heart which he had never before experienced.

The situation of the unfortunate individuals who had been rescued from the flames was indeed hopeless and fearful. They were upon the wide and open sea; darkness was around them, and they were probably far away from land, or from any prospect of relief from some friendly vessel. So rapid had been the progress of the conflagration, and so great had been their confusion and dismay, that they had been unable to save anything from the ship, with the exception of some biscuits, and a cask or two of fresh water, so that, unless Providence should mercifully send them some speedy aid, nothing but a dreadful fate evidently awaited them. The night air, as it swept over the ocean, was keen and piercing, and many of them being half undressed, shivered with the cold, and were almost perishing. Evelyn sheltered the fair form of Mabel from the inclement blast as well as he could with his cloak, and the tender look she fixed upon him told more than words could have done the grateful feelings of her heart. Sadly they continued on their course, leaving the boats to go as the wind directed them, and anxiously waiting for daylight. It came at last, and imparted no hope to their breasts, no relief to their sufferings. As far as their eyes could stretch they could behold nothing but the misty horizon; not the least signs of land, or any approaching vessel, met their eager sight, and their spirits drooped with misery, disappointment, and despair. The morning was dull and hazy, and the weather continued cold and cheerless. They scarcely knew in which direction, for they were almost ignorant of the latitude they were in, and had nothing whatever to guide them. Throughout that dreary day they continued in the same melancholy and deplorable situation, and they dreaded the approach of darkness. A scanty allowance of the biscuits and water was apportioned out to each of them, for when that was gone, without something came to their relief, nothing but the horrors of starvation stared them in the face.

And now how painful were the thoughts that agonised the bosom of our hero, but which he endeavoured to conceal from the keen observation of Mabel, whose dark eyes were constantly fixed upon him, and seemed to penetrate to his very soul. He pictured to himself the situation of Constance at that moment, and the sufferings she was no doubt enduring for his sake. Probably the crisis of her fate, that revolting fate which she had so ardently tried to avoid, had already arrived, and even now she might be the unhappy wife of the villain, Oliver Dalton. His heart sickened at the thought, and he sought to banish it from his brain. As for his own fate, he was completely careless about that; his hopes were annihilated, and he considered that it was but of little consequence what now became of him. While others, therefore, with feelings of agony, anticipated the doom that awaited them, he gazed upon the misery of all around with an apathetic eye, and resigned himself, with a feeling of calm indifference to whatever might be in store for him.

Night again came on, and it was as dark and cheerless as the previous one had been. It passed away: the morning dawned, and an exclamation of gratitude and joy escaped the lips of the unfortunate sufferers, when the sight of land, at no great distance, on the eastern horizon, met their anxious gaze. A ray of hope now dawned upon their minds and reanimated their spirits, and, the wind being in their favour, they made towards it as rapidly as they could. The island, if such it was, stood high above the sea, and they were anxious to obtain a nearer view of it, that they might endeavour to ascertain what prospects of relief it was calculated to afford them. In about two hours they came within a short distance of it, and they then perceived that it was a rocky island, apparently of some extent, and the approaches to which were by no means difficult, being by the means of two small creeks, where the boats could enter with safety, and the rugged sides of the rock were perfectly accessible. Proceeding through one of these creeks, they moored the boats as well as they could at a convenient spot, and then commenced the ascent; Evelyn and Greysham rendering their assistance to the trembling footsteps of Mabel. They found this rather a more difficult task than they had at first anticipated, especially in the weak and exhausted state in which they were. They succeeded in arriving at the summit, and with eager looks and throbbing hearts they gazed around at the place upon which untoward fate had cast them.

CHAPTER XXXIII.

AWFUL SUFFERINGS OF THE SHIPWRECKED CREW UPON THE DESOLATE ISLAND.
—THE MOMENT OF DESPAIR.—THE FEARFUL RESOLVE OF EVELYN.—HEROIC
CONDUCT OF MABEL.

NOTHING could possibly be more cheerless than the prospect which met the view of the unfortunate crew; and the hopes which had but a few moments before animated their bosoms were as quickly banished, and gave place to all the torturing emotions of misery and despair. As far as their eager eyes could stretch, not the least signs of vegetation or human dwelling met their view. The place appeared to be nothing more than a barren rock, which offered not the smallest means of sustaining life, and on every side seemed to frown horror and death upon them. With feelings of the most unspeakable, the most indescribable anguish, the hapless beings gazed at each other; and many a stout heart, which had often braved danger even its most hideous form, now sunk appalled, forlorn, and desolate.

Evelyn Heartwell anxiously fixed his eyes upon poor Mabel. The noble minded, the heroic girl, who had made so frightful a sacrifice in her unconquerable love for him, was standing, with folded arms, calm and placid; but there was a wild, a torturing expression in her beautiful eyes that told too plainly the tempest of agonising feelings that raged within her breast; and, on beholding the powerful emotions of our hero, which, in spite of all his efforts he found it utterly impossible to restrain, she rushed towards him, and threw herself sobbing on his bosom. Unable to control the passionate feelings of admiration, regard, and gratitude, such unexampled devotion, kindled in his breast, he strained her to his heart, and raising his eyes devoutly to Heaven, silently, but fervently supplicated its mercy and protection, and invoked a blessing on her head. The Gipsey-girl felt the tender pressure; a bright ray of hope dawned upon her mind, and even amidst the horrors by which they were encompassed, a feeling of rapture glowed within her breast, such as she had never experienced before. Evelyn noticed the emotion to which his burst of feeling had given rise, and, fearful that he had gone too far, and had called up delusive visions to her ready imagination which could never be realised, he endeavoured to check it, and, gently disengaging himself from her embrace he looked at her for a moment with a mingled expression of pity and regret."

"Unfortunate Mabel;" he ejaculated, in accents of the deepest sympathy;—"unfortunate Mabel, how doth my heart bleed for thee. Alas! alas! to what a dreadful fate has thine impetuous, thy fatal passion, exposed thee."

"Name it not" she replied; "oh, name it not; I have accomplished the object of my most ardent wishes ;—Mabel has proved the sincerity of her love for thee, Evelyn ; through every danger and vicissitude she hath boldly, fearlessly followed thee, and she is with thee now, to endure all, to die with thee, if it so be the will of Heaven, and, however great her sufferings may be, thou shalt not hear a murmur of complaint or regret escape her lips."

"Noble-hearted girl !" exclaimed Walter Greysham, unable to control his feelings of admiration, "oh, may all-merciful Providence interpose to save thee from the dreadful, the untimely fate which now threatens, and to reward such unexampled virtues as they deserve."

He fixed upon her beauteous countenance a melancholy, expressive look, as he thus spoke, which fully evinced the emotions that glowed within his breast at that moment, and, sighing deeply, turned away, and vainly tried to cheer the spirits of his wretched companions, who were gazing with wild and vacant looks of despair upon each other. But what was there to inspire them with hope ? All around was gloom and misery ; there was the barren rocks on which they had been cast, with its hideous desolation, and freezing sterility ; a bleak, cloudy sky above, and the wide expanse of waters around them, with not the smallest prospect of relief ; an awful, a lingering death staring them in the face on every side ; gaunt and grim despair seeming to mock their sufferings in whichever way they turned their eyes. The day was dull, cold, and cheerless ; a strong wind blew from the N.E., which, being but thinly clad, piérced the limbs of the unfortunate sufferers, and added to the misey of their situation, especially as there was nothing near to afford them the least degree of shelter. As the day advanced it increased in gloom ; the clouds that hung low upon the horizon, became more black and ponderous, and at length burst, discharging a torrent of rain, the thunder rolling in tremendous reverberations, and the lightning flashing its forked fury at intervals around. The sea presented a wild and angry aspect ; the waves rose to a mountainous height, howling frightfully as they dashed and battled against the sides of the rocks, and swept everything before them with their impetuous and irresistable violence. The wild sea-birds screamed dismally as they winged their rapid flight from point to point, and nothing could possibly surpass the infinite terrors of the scene.

Cold, wet, and shivering in every limb, the unfortunate beings sat huddled together, and gazing upon each other with bloodshot eyes, and looks of anguish and despair that were quite frightful to behold. Poor Mabel, whose firmness, resignation, and self-posession were truly wonderful, clung fondly to our hero, who endeavoured as well as he could, from the inclemency of the weather, and by the expression of his features, to shew the deep, the intense solicitude he felt for her. But in the midst of all these horrors, with what indescribable feelings of agony did he think of Constance, whom it now appeared but too probable, he should never behold again. How fervently did he mentally beseech Omnipotence to protect her from the manifold evils by which she was surrounded, and to restore her once more to that happiness from which she had been so long estranged, though that, he feared, was utterly hopeless. With a feeling of emotion, to which no language could do adequate justice, he drew forth the miniature of the beloved girl, which he always carried near his heart, and having gazed at it with melancholy feelings of reverence and devotion, pressed it fervently to his lips, and again invoked a blessing upon her head. But he was suddenly aroused by Mabel grasping his arm vehemently, and the angry expression that flashed from her dark eyes, shewed the powerful feelings of jealousy and anguish that struggled in her breast. With a deep sigh, Evelyn returned the miniature to his bosom, and by a look of mingled pity, gentle remonstrance, and mournful regret, he endeavoured to calm the tempest of violent passions that was raging in the poor girl's breast.

"Tear the hated resemblance from thine heart!" she exclaimed in bitter accents,—"banish her too fondly cherished image from thy memory, unless thou wouldst drive me to madness and despair. Oh, can the proud, wealthy beauty ever love thee, worship thee with the intense passion that glows in the heart of the humble Mabel, the despised Gipsey-girl, who is ready this moment to resign her life to save thee?"

"Forbear Mabel;" replied Evelyn; "thy words torture me!—oh, canst thou, even in this moment of terror, still obstinately persist in a love which nature seems to forbid me to return?"

"Aye, now, and for ever!" cried Mabel, firmly and determinedly;—"hear me, while I solemnly swear that that passion shall cease only with the last pulsation of my heart!—"

Our hero was greatly moved by the vehemence of her manner, and knew not what to say; but at that moment Walter Greysham approached, and thus abruptly brought the too interesting scene to a conclusion.

Fresh miseries rapidly accumulated upon the unfortunate crew of the ill-fated Ariel; all that dreary day the storm continued to rage with unabated violence, and without any intermission, and not the least chance of relief appeared. As night approached, they found a deep cavity in one of the rocks, into which they all crept, to shelter themselves as well as they could from the howling blast, and the pitiless pelting of the rain; and with sad hearts they anxiously awaited the following day, to see what change it might happily effect in their situation. What they endured that night it would be utterly impossible to give an adequate description of, and we must therefore leave it to the imagination of the reader. The next day came, but still no hope, no relief from the anguish of their sufferings. In vain they stretched their eager eyes across the troubled ocean; no signs of any approaching vessel met their sight. It seemed as though they were abandoned by Heaven and man. The tempest had but little abated, and the elements still fiercely battled with each other, spreading dismay and desolation around. And now, unless they were speedily rescued from their dreadful situation, all the horrors of a lingering death of starvation met their appalled view. The whole of the biscuits and water they had saved from the burning vessel were gone; and the gnawing pangs of hunger and thirst already began to prey upon their vitals, imparting an expression of frenzy to their eyes, and the anguish of despair to their pale and ghastly features. But, in the midst of all these fearful trials, it was perfectly astonishing to notice the fortitude, patience, and heroism with which the Gipsey-girl supported herself; not a murmur of complaint; not a word of anguish or despair ever escaped her lips; her demeanour was firm, calm, and resigned; her looks solemn and impressive, though, at times eradiated with a ray of hope; and her thoughts seemed almost constantly fixed on Evelyn Heartwell, whom she watched with the most anxious care. Walter Greysham marked her conduct with the most unqualified feeling of wonder and admiration. Her unassuming virtues had kindled a passion in his breast that must remain fixed for ever.

Unable to contemplate the sufferings of his companions, and his own mind wrought up to a pitch of the wildest and most insupportable anguish, in the course of the day, when he imagined that Mabel was not watching him, Evelyn retired from the spot on which the wretched beings were crouched together, and heedless of whither he went, wandered to another part of the island, he paused on a rocky eminence that overhung the sea, and folding his arms across his chest, he gazed with looks of the most indescribable anguish on the wild scene before him. The storm had but little abated, and nothing could surely surpass the terrors of the scene on which his eyes rested at every side. Fierce lightnings at intervals flashed through the dark and murky clouds, accompanied with peals of thunder which seemed to shake the vaulted roof of Heaven. The ocean presented a wild and angry appearance, and was white with foam, and the rude billows rolled towards the rocks with tumultuous fury, threatening all that came in contact with them with inevitable destruction. As Evelyn thus stood, a deadly feeling came over him that completely absorbed all his faculties, and imparted a morbid sensation to his brain that was as uncontrollable as it was alarming.

"Fate frowns upon me," he soliloquised, "and horror and despair encompass me on every side; all hopes of my ever more beholding my beloved Constance are at an end; cast upon this wretched barren place, without the means of sustenance, what else awaits me but a lingering death of starvation? Why should I prolong this life of misery to witness the increasing sufferings of poor Mabel, and my wretched companions, worse than my own tortures to endure? It is but one bold effort, one desperate plunge, and all is over. Despair urges me on; let me not hesitate, Heaven in its infinite mercy will pardon me the deed. There is nothing now to tempt me to cling to life; all around me is lonely, cheerless, and desolate. I will be firm and resolute. Farewell, dearest Constance, my heart is still with thee, though we are separated by so many dreary miles. Thou wilt never know my fate. Farewell, most faithful, most gentle, most amiable of human beings; may Heaven bless thee, and render thee happier than thou couldst ever have been with the unfortunate Evelyn Heartwell."

As the wretched youth thus spoke, he clasped his hands vehemently together, and raised one solemn glance towards Heaven, then gazed vacantly upon the wild waste of waters. Frenzy was in his eye, despair was in the expression of his distorted, haggard features, and determination nerved him to the rash and awful deed he contemplated. Suddenly, with a loud exclamation of anguish, he raised his arms above his head, and the next instant he was about to precipitate himself from the fearful height on which he stood into the ocean beneath, when a loud shriek arrested him in his deadly purpose, and he was seized with desperate energy by someone behind. He turned, and beheld the reproachful eyes of Mabel fixed upon him, and abashed, confused, and deeply agitated with the variety of conflicting feelings that rushed tumultuously to his brain, he stood paralysed, and powerless as an infant.

CHAPTER XXXIV.

The Horrors of Want.—The Ship in Sight.—The Rescue.—The Suspicious Vessel.—The Chase.—The Engagement with the Pirates.—The Unexpected Meeting.

Unperceived by Evelyn, his mind being too much occupied by his own painful thoughts to suffer him to look round, Mabel had followed him from the spot where he had left his companions in misfortune, determined to watch his actions, for she suspected, from the agitation of his looks, and certain observations that had escaped his lips in her hearing, that he contemplated something desperate, and in that idea she was confirmed, as he hurriedly pursued his way. With what intense agony of feelings did she listen to the melancholy soliloquy to which he gave utterance previous to his attempting the rash act. Every word went like a dagger to the poor girl's heart; but still she remained firm to the purpose which had brought her thither, namely, to save him from self-destruction, or to perish with him; and now that she had succeeded, grasping his wrist with one hand, and with the other elevated, and pointing solemnly towards Heaven, she fixed upon him a look of such intense meaning, that seemed as though it would penetrate to the innermost recesses of his soul. Evelyn shrunk and trembled beneath the expression of her keen glances, and could not utter a word. A silence of two or three minutes ensued, which our hero was the first to break.

"Release me, Mabel;" he ejaculated, in an agitated voice ; "release me, I say, and begone. I am determined ; oh, why should'st thou seek to arrest my purpose, wretched, hopeless being as I am ?"

"Shame on thee, Evelyn," returned the Gipsey-girl, in a tone of mingled pity and reproach ; "is this the manly fortitude thou shoulds't display under difficulties ? Is it worthy of the noble spirit I thought had ever animated thy breast ? Oh, shame on thee, Evelyn Heartwell !"

"And dost thou reproach me, Mabel," he said, in melancholy accents ; "dost thou reproach me because I am driven by madness and despair to that from which my better feelings would, at any other time, revolt ?"

"And can I do otherwise than reproach thee, Evelyn ;" she returned ; "for a weakness so culpable, so inexcusable ? and yet," she added, with a deep sigh, and tears starting to her eyes as she spoke, "Heaven knows that I do so more in sorrow than in anger. Alas !—it is the remembrance of Constance Welborn that guides and urges thee on in all thy rash actions. Not one thought of the humble Mabel has the power to work any favourable influence on thy mind."

"Leave me, Mabel, I implore thee ;" said Evelyn, again trying to disengage himself from her hold ; " I honour, I respect thy motives, and my heart o'erflows with gratitude towards thee for the manner in which thou hast devoted thyself to me ; for the perils and sufferings thou hast encountered for my sake; but life has become a burthen to me, and since all hope is at an end, the world became a wild and cheerless desert to me, I would at once terminate my wretched career, and let it be forgotten that such a miserable being as Evelyn Heartwell ever existed. Leave me, Mabel, I say again ; and may Heaven bless thee, watch over thee, and restore thee to that happiness which thy numerous virtues so richly merit."

"Nay, nay," replied the Gipsey-girl, resolutely, "I will not leave thee thus, Evelyn ; I will cling to thee with more than woman's strength while I have life, and arrest thee in thy deadly purpose. Come, come, let us leave this fearful spot, rendered still more frightful by the awful deed thou didst but just now contemplate !"

With these words the faithful Mabel forced him away, he being so overpowered by his emotions as to be able to offer little or no resistance, and hurried him towards the spot where Walter Greysham, who had been alarmed at his absence, anxiously awaited his appearance.

Still did the horrors of their situation hourly increase, and terrible looks and strange mutterings were exchanged between the men, that seemed to portend something fearful foreboding. They had now been for nearly forty-eight hours without a morsel of food or a drop of water, except such as they had been able to catch from the rain, and all the frightful evidences of hunger and thirst were depictured in their ghastly countenances. Night once more set in dark and dismal, and they again crept to the cavity in the rock to shelter themselves as well as they could from the almost insupportable inclemency of the weather ; and there most of them, worn out with sickness, anxiety, and fatigue, obtained a temporary respite from their sufferings in sleep. But neither Evelyn or Mabel ventured to court rest, for their minds were haunted with strange fears and suspicions, from the looks that the crew had exchanged with one another in the course of the day, and the dark and mysterious observations that had escaped their lips. The night however passed away without anything more particular occurring, and the fourth morning of their dreadful and deplorable situation now dawned upon them, and the sufferings of the whole of the unfortunate beings were terrible in the extreme. The pangs of hunger and thirst that they

experienced were most excruciating and insupportable, and while some drooped low, spiritless, and powerless, others raved with the wild fury of madmen, and gave utterance to the most horrible oaths and execrations. Altogether, it was a scene so frightful, that the imagination alone might conceive it, but any description, however graphic, must fail to pourtray it properly. The storm had ceased, but nothing could be more dull, cold, and cheerless, than the weather continued. Hour after hour passed away, and the sufferings of the ill-fated survivors of the Ariel increased; many stood transfixed, perfect images of despair; while others were lying on the ground exhausted, and helpless as infants. In spite of the unparallelled fortitude and resignation which poor Mabel had hitherto displayed, they now began to fail her; her strength was almost exhausted, and she was obliged to rest for support in the arms of Evelyn, Walter

No. 27.

Greysham hanging over her with looks of agony and solicitude that shewed the powerful feelings she had inspired in his heart.

"This, this is indeed a dreadful trial," sighed the Gipsey-girl, in a faint voice, and with a look that was sufficient to move even the most insensible heart to pity, "but Heaven's will be done. Why should the wretched wanderer, the hopeless Mabel cling to that life, which to her has ever been darkened over with woe? And—and oh, 'twill be sweet, 'twill be bliss unspeakable to die in thy arms, dear Evelyn. Thou—thou wilt not reproach the memory of the poor Gipsey-girl, who loves thee with an ardour her tongue must fail to speak?"

Tortured to the very soul, heart-broken, our hero was about to attempt some reply to this pathetic speech, when he was prevented by the loud and delirious shouts of several men, at a short distance from them, and who had for some time been anxiously straining their eyes over the wide expanse of waters, in the wild hope of seeing some approaching relief. The shouts were repeated with redoubled energy, and then the cries of "a ship! a ship! we're saved! we're saved!" met the eager ears of the wretched beings, and were received with a burst of frantic joy such as no pen could describe. How painfully exciting was the scene that immediately ensued. An unnatural fire seemed to light every eye; those who before had been stretched on the earth, powerless and almost insensible, started with avidity to their feet, and all rushed towards the edge of the rock, and there, sure enough, through the hazy mist of the atmosphere, their eager eyes beheld a vessel in the distance, which seemed steering in the direction of the island.

What a scene now followed: Evelyn, Mabel, and Walter Greysham, sunk on their knees, and with clasped hands, and upraised eyes, returned their thanks to Heaven for this prospect of deliverance from a frightful and untimely death, while others rushed wildly to and fro, shouting, laughing, and crying, by turns. Handkerchiefs, jackets, hats, and everything that could make a signal, now waved in the air, although the ship was too far off at present to observe them, and they watched its progress with alternate feelings of hope and fear. That progress was slow, but they were soon satisfied, beyond a doubt, that it was approaching towards them.

Fortunately, having the means left, their next thought was to kindle a large fire on the rock, which was the more likely to attract the attention of the persons on board, and soon its cheerful flames shot up into the murky air. Several minutes elapsed without any particular result, though the welcome vessel evidently approached nearer and nearer. Again the men renewed their shouts, as though their cries could possibly reach the ears of the persons on board, over the vast waste of waters, and at such a distance. Indeed, so madly impatient were some of them, that they could with difficulty be restrained from leaping into the sea, with the desperate hope of swimming to the ship.

Nearer and nearer the vessel approached, and at length, to the great satisfaction and delight of the unfortunate individuals who were so anxiously watching, it was evident that their signal was observed, for a gun was fired from the ship, and in a few minutes afterwards, a couple of boats were launched, adequately manned, and were rowed with all the speed it was possible towards the island. Quickly the welcome means of relief approached, and as the boats neared the wretched place on which the anxious sufferers were standing, they perceived to their unspeakable gratification, from their costume, that the boats were manned by British sailors, and all doubts and fears of the reception they were likely to meet with on board the ship were at an end. But a few minutes were sufficient to bring the boats into one of the creeks, and the delighted crew, who had so lately been sunk in the lowest abyss of despair, with an energy and agility, that considering the dreadful state of exhaustion to which they were reduced, was truly wonderful, rushed down the side of the rock, eager to escape from the perilous and awful situation in which they had so long been placed. Evelyn, taking Mabel in his arms, and, accompanied by Walter Greysham, followed, and the next instant all had gained the boats in safety, which then put off to the vessel. They learned that the ship was a British frigate, called the Invulnerable, and homeward bound ; a circumstance that Evelyn rather regreted, as he wished not, at present, at any rate, to return to England ; but Mabel heard it with every feeling of satisfaction, and with the hope that Evelyn's restoration to his native land, after so short an absence, might be the precursor of more happy events. In a short time they reached the vessel, where they were received by the captain (with whom Walter Greysham was acquainted) and the crew, with every kindness and respect on board. Every attention was immediately paid to their urgent necessities, and the gallant ship proceeded on her voyage.

How did the hearts of Evelyn and the Gipsey-girl swell with gratitude to Heaven for their almost miraculous preservation from impending death ; and they mingled their feelings together without restraint. But notwithstanding the unequalled fortitude with which Mabel had supported such severe trials, they had the most serious effect upon her constitution, and it was evident it would require the greatest care and attention to restore her to health and strength. She bore up against this illness as well as she could, but was sad and unhappy whenever Evelyn was out of her sight, and the tender looks she constantly fixed upon him shewed that the late dreadful trials to which they had been exposed had but served to strengthen the fatal passion which glowed within her breast. There was one too that watched the conduct of the Gipsey-girl with the most anxious solicitude, and sought her presence at every opportunity ; and that was Walter Greysham, in whose breast she had created sentiments he found it impossible to subdue, and which he was certain he could never eradicate. The fond endearments she lavished upon Evelyn, were torturing to his heart ; but he endeavoured to conceal his emotion as much as possible when in their society, and cherished in secret a passion which neither time nor circumstance could alter.

The weather had now set in fine, and the Invulnerable proceeded on her homeward passage under every favourable circumstance ; and the spirits of those who had lately been exposed to such horrible suffering revived, and they looked forward to the future with hope and confidence. On the sixth day of the rescue of the crew of the Ariel from the desolate Island, a vessel was discovered to the leeward of the Invulnerable, and which seemed to be bearing down upon her with a favouring wind, and from all that could yet be distinguished of it, it carried a very suspicious appearance. The captain knew that the seas they were then navigating were infested by pirates of the most desperate and determined character ; and it therefore behoved him to be upon his guard, particularly as his ship, having been compelled in the late storms to have several of her guns thrown overboard, was not so well prepared for any serious engagement. By the permission of Captain Falkland, Walter Greysham now took the glass, in order to obtain a better view of the stranger, and having watched her for some minutes, said :—

"I fear, Captain, that under all the circumstances, we have no occasion to be anxious for the company of this craft. She is a large and powerful vessel, and, if I may judge from her build, I should say it is not improbable she may carry too much metal for us. Did you ever come athwart the Dare-Devil pirate barque?"

"No," replied Captain Falkland, "though I've often had a wish to have a taste of her quality, though that would not be exactly convenient at the present time. The Dare-Devil, I believe, has often played a desperate game in these seas ?"

"True," returned Greysham, "and I am half inclined to suspect that the ship which is now rapidly bearing down upon us, skimming the surface of the ocean with the quickness of thought, is the very daring buccaneer of which we have just been speaking."

"Ah! sayest thou so, Greysham?" observed the Captain, "then, perhaps, it would be prudent to endeavour to avoid her, though we must be prepared to give her a warm reception, should she overtake us. Stretch every inch of canvas, and make all the way we can, for the stranger, friend or foe, seems to be gaining fast upon us!"

Captain Falkland's orders were obeyed to the very letter, and the Invulnerable sailed swiftly along, making for the nearest harbour, which they knew was at no considerable distance off. Their pursuers, however, gained rapidly upon them, and it soon became but too evident that it would be impossible to avoid her, and her hostile intentions were now pretty nearly shewn, every preparation was made for the action which must inevitably ensue.

All was now excitement and expectation on board the Invulnerable, and, notwithstanding the superior power of the vessel they would have to contend with, the whole of the gallant crew looked forward to the result with the utmost hope and confidence. Mabel was firm and undaunted, and it was with the utmost difficulty she was persuaded to go below, in order to avoid the danger of the action which was about to take place.

In a short time after this, their pursuer had prosecuted the chase with such celerity, that she had got near enough to them to enable them to distinguish her character, and the suspicions of Walter Greysham were then confirmed she hoisted a black flag, bearing all the awful insignia of death, and on it were inscribed, in glaring characters, the dreaded name of "*The Dare-Devil!*" Having arrived within shot, the pirates fired a signal for the Invulnerable to heave too, which salute the latter returned with one of defiance, and then tacked about and fired a broadside into the enemy from all the guns they had on board, and which unexpected act of daring and courage appeared to take the pirates by surprise, and made them wince a little. However the Dare-Devil was not slow in returning the compliment, and did so with such fearful effect, that they committed great destruction on board the Invulnerable. Nothing daunted, the gallant frigate maintained the contest with the most unexampled skill and bravery, and the battle was now at its height, and nothing whatever could equal the excitement of the scene. Notwithstanding the superiority of the pirates' numbers, and the power of their vessel, although they fought with the desperate ferocity of tigers, it soon appeared that the gallant enemy they had to contend with was more than a match for them, and their rage and disappointment were evinced in the dreadful shouts and execrations with which they rent the air, and which might be heard even above the loud roar of the cannon.

Twice the Invulnerable was boarded by the ruffians, who were on each occasion repulsed with frightful slaughter; while their own vessel had already received such serious damage, that she was in a precarious situation. The Invulnerable took advantage of her position, seeing that she was fast filling, from several holes which their guns had made in her hull, and in turn, bravely boarded the Dare-Devil. And now, frightful indeed was the carnage that ensued, the combat being sustained with equal bravery on both sides. The pirate captain in particular, fought with desperate courage, and performing prodigies of valour that were worthy of a better cause; but, covered with wounds he sunk upon the deck, and his comrades, seeing him fall, became disconcerted, and it was now evident in whose favour the sanguinary contest would soon be decided, particularly as loud cries were heard that the pirate ship, which had been rapidly filling for several minutes, was sinking. At that moment, one of the sailors of the Invulnerable, no doubt in the excitement of his feelings, losing sight of that spirit of humanity which ever characterises the British seamen, was about to strike down an aged feeble, unarmed man, who by some strange means had been thrown into the midst of the deadly strife, when Evelyn, who was fortunately near the spot, rushed forward, and arresting the sailors arm, as it was about to inflict the deadly blow, saved the old man's life, at the same time, to his utter astonishment and incredulity, he recognised in his features, those of *the Miser, Jasper Scrimpe!*

Another instant, and the victory was decided in favour of the gallant Invulnerable; the black flag of the pirates was struck, and the frigate had only just time to release itself from the grappling irons, when the Dare-Devil, the long dreaded scourge of the ocean, filled and went down with all on board, Godfrey Malvern, who had staggered to his feet, clinging to the mast, and uttering a loud shout of defiance, as he sunk to his ocean grave!

CHAPTER XXXV.

The Agitation of Jasper Scrimpe.—The Horrors of Remorse.—His Sufferings on board the Pirate Ship.—The Progress of the Invulnerable.

Jasper Scrimpe recognised his preserver at the same moment that he did him, and, had a spectre crossed his path, he could not have evinced greater terror and emotion. His haggard features became distorted; his eyes flashed with an unnatural fire; his lips quivered, and a convulsive shuddering shook his every limb.

"Powers of mercy!" he exclaimed in a hoarse voice; " am I dreaming? or is it some fearful delusion that has taken possession of my senses? Evelyn Heartwell, whom my false accusation would have condemned to death!—and, ah! those features!—what awful remembrances of the guilty past do they recal to my distracted brain?—oh, shield me! hide me!—save me from that avenging form!"

And, overcome with the powerful anguish of his feelings, the wretched old man sunk senseless in the arms of his deliverer, by whom he was conveyed in safety on board the Invulnerable, and borne below, where every attention was ordered to be paid to his recovery.

The victory accomplished, and the gallant Invulnerable steering from the scene of her late triumph, with what eager impatience did Mabel seek the presence of Evelyn, whose heroic conduct throughout the deadly strife, she had watched with feelings of the utmost anxiety and admiration, and the interview that took place was one of the most affecting description. But the extraordinary discovery and meeting with the Miser, under such remarkable circumstances, surprised them more than all, and they looked for an explanation from him with the utmost impatience, though, at present the old man was in too excited a state to be questioned upon the subject.

It may be necessary here, briefly to relate what had occurred to the Miser since the last time we left him, which was after the appalling vision he imagined had been presented to his eyes, when he was being conveyed on board the pirate ship. It was some time ere he recovered his senses, and, when he did so, and discovered the situation he was placed in, his excitement was so great, that it was impossible for him to restrain his feelings within the bounds of reason, and he raved with all the wild fury of a madman, and invoked the most frightful maledictions upon the head of Godfrey Malvern, who, however, only laughed at his observations, and seemed to exult at his terrors and his sufferings. When he was left alone to the solitude of his own dismal thoughts, how torturing were the feelings that laboured in his breast; how harrowing the wild phantasies that arose to his feverish and disordered brain. But the ghastly phantom which he believed he had seen floating on the surface of the ocean, between him and the pirate ship, haunted his imagination more than all, and harrowed up his soul with fear and horror. The torturing remorse of conscience was again awakened, and the miserable old man shuddered to look around him, lest he should again encounter the appalling object of his terror. As he listened to the low moaning sound of the waves, as they dashed against the vessel's sides, he could almost imagine that he heard the sepulchral voices of the dead, breathing curses in his ears, and mocking at the mental anguish he was enduring, and in such moments, frenzy lit his eye, and his every faculty was suspended with the power of his emotions.

"I am accursed," he exclaimed, clasping his burning temples; "the retributive vengeance, the dreadful wrath of Heaven pursues me; the grave yields up the dead to condemn me; man hates, despises me; hunts me like some wild beast; I am loathed, shunned like a pestilence upon the earth. No peace ever enters my guilty soul; there is no rest for me; no sympathy, no pity for the wretch who never felt sympathy or pity for others; all men spurn me like a dog; every one points at me the finger of scorn and dark suspicion, and, in their hearts pronounce me murderer, though their lips may fail to give utterance to the damning truth. And am I not a murderer? Is not my conscience loaded with the weight of bloodshed? Did not these hands commit the fiendish deed that robbed my kinsman of his life? His children, too, oh, where are they? Horror! Horror! My soul shrinks appalled at the contemplation of my hideous crimes!"

With a burst of agony and remorse, he buried his face in his hands; and even the torments of perdition could scarcely be greater than those he was at that moment enduring. In this dreadful state of mind he continued during the night, and sleep never once visited his tortured senses. The pirate ship proceeded on its way, and, when the morning dawned it was far distant from the coast from which it had sailed. The Miser's sufferings continued unabated, and in vain did he supplicate the mercy and forbearance of Godfrey Malvern; who received his appeals with derision, and loaded him with the most galling reproaches. He saw that nothing whatever could move his inexorable heart; that a deadly spirit of malice and revenge goaded him on to further tortures, and he abandoned himself to complete despair. Life had become an insupportable burthen to him, and there were times when he was worked up to such a pitch of frenzy that, if he could have obtained the means, he would have been urged on to the awful crime of self-destruction. And yet did he shudder at the thoughts of death, for the dread Eternity beyond the grave, presented horrors to his mind, which he trembled even to contemplate. Thus the time wore dismally away, till the night of the fearful storm, which the unfortunate beings on board the Ariel had experienced in all its horrors. And, oh, what were the terrible sufferings of the wretched, guilty Jasper Scrimpe on that occasion? The hoarse voice of the thunder, as it reverberated above, seemed charged with the curses of Heaven on his devoted head; the howling wind, and the loud roaring of the angry waves, as they dashed the vessel mercilessly about, bore with them, to his distracted imagination, the dying groans of his innocent and unfortunate victims, while the lurid fire, which ever and anon shot through the clouds, added to the terrors of his guilty soul, and appeared to betoken the awful doom that awaited him. Overwhelmed with remorse and shuddering with fear, he knelt down and tried to pray; but at that moment a deafening peal of thunder shook the Heavens, the ethereal fire flashed vividly into the cabin, he felt a hand, cold and clammy as that of a corpse, and which seemed to freeze his very blood to ice, upon his shoulder, and, looking up with a frenzied eye, by the glare of the lightning, he again beheld that shadowy form, those ghastly features, those unearthly reproachful eyes, that had before haunted his imagination! His every sense was appalled; his eyes were wildly distended; it was no delusion; still did he feel the death grasp congeal his very life's blood; he tried to speak, but his tongue clove to the roof of his mouth, and he could not; once more he endeavoured to shut out the fearful phantom from his sight, but in vain ; there it stood in the lurid reflection of the lightning, with its pale, cadaverous features, and its hollow eyes fixed solemnly upon him! Nature could endure no more, and with a wild yell of frenzy and despair, the Miser fellsenseless on the floor, and became unconscious of every thing around him!

For several days after this terrific event, Jasper Scrimpe was in a state of delirium, and the fearful ravings to which, in this wild paroxysm, he gave utterance, were quite frightful to listen to ; but Malvern, watched him with looks of triumph and satisfaction ; and seemed to glory in the dreadful tortures the unfortunate old man was enduring.

A temporary calm succeeded the storm we have just described, and the Dare-Devil proceeded, on its course, without anything more particular, or worthy of recording occurring, till the weather again changed, and the tempest became more violent than ever, and it was not without the greatest difficulty that the pirate ship was enabled to weather its fury, many a noble vessel falling a prey to the angry elements. During this period of terror and danger, the sufferings of the wretched Miser were repeated, with, if possible, tenfold severity, and he received no sympathy in his misery ; the ruffians on board the ship, on the contrary deriding his anguish, and appearing to take a savage delight in aggravating his fears.

This storm continued for several days, and scarcely had it abated, than a fresh source of alarm presented itself to the distracted Miser. A vessel was observed in the distance, at last offering a chance of booty to the pirates, and seeing that that she was endeavouring to avoid them, consequently evincing some degree of fear, Godfrey detemined to give chase to her, flattering himself, from the superiority of his craft, that she would become an easy prize. During the time of the chase it is needless to attempt to describe the feelings of Jasper Scrimpe, how he shuddered in anticipation of the dreadful scene of slaughter of which he would be compelled to be a witness. From his very soul he prayed that some friendly ball would stretch him a corpse, in the course of the terrible engagement, and thus put an end to his earthly sufferings ; and most fervently he wished that the wretches who held him in their power would be defeated, and that the guilty career they had so long carried on with success, at the cost of their hapless fellow creatures, might thus at last be brought to a termination. The Dare-Devil, was what in these modern times, would be called a clipper ; her sailing powerswere of the first order ; she skimmed the waters like an ocean bird, and, as has been shewn, soon came within gun-shot of the little Invulnerable (little in comparison with the piratical vessel), and from its appearance, they anticipated but a feeble resistance; but, as the result of the engagement proved the ruffians had reckoned without their host. Previous to the commencement of the action, the Miser had been forced below, and there with a palpitating heart, he listened to the dreadful din that prevailed while the work of slaughter was going on. Frequently, as the shots of the Invulnerable pierced the sides of the pirate ship, he had a narrow escape of his life ; but, wrought up to a pitch of frenzy and despair, he sought not to avoid the danger, but, on the contrary, he rather courted such a fate as a fortunate rescue from a state of misery which was beyond all human endurance. And yet was he not without a vague hope that the pirates would be defeated, and that he might at length be rescued from the dreadful situation in which he had so long been placed. It was this idea that impelled him when he found that the Dare-Devil was boarded by its gallant antagonist, and that the vessel was in a sinking condition, to rush from the hold on to the deck in the midst of all the danger, and when his life was so providentially saved by Evelyn Heartwell. What followed has already been related.

For several hours after the scene which has been described in the early par
of this chapter, Jasper Scrimpe remained in a state of insensibility, and our hero
and Mabel anxiously and attentively watched his recovery.   At length the old
man breathed more freely, and opening his eyes, not at first recognising Evelyn
and Mabel, in an agitated tone of voice, and his mind evidently still wandering.
he exclaimed :—

Where am I ? what place is this ?—surely I must have been dreaming or it
must be some wild delusion of the disordered brain, but methought I was rescued
from the power of the wretches who have so long detained me.   But no, no, no.
it cannot be ; it is my wandering, sickly fancy that deceived me, oh, wretched,
wretched Jasper, when will thy troubles be brought to an end ?—"

Calm thy feelings, unfortunate old man ;" said our hero, tenderly ;—" thou
hast nothing to fear; thon art safe, thou art now with friends! "

" Friends ! friends !" repeated the Miser, hastily, "' tis false the guilty Jasper
Scrimpe hast no friends, But,—" he added, and looking with eager curiosity and
amanagement at Evelyn, " who art thou ?   I should know that voice; its tones
strike a thrill of terror to my heart.   Speak, I say, who art thou ?"

" Look up, Jasper Scrimpe," said our hero, " dost thou not know me ?   I am
that unfortunate youth in whose fate thou didst once express such warm and
generous spmpathy; it is the persecuted Evelyn Heartwell who now addresses thee."

The features of the Miser underwent a fearful change, and a convulsive
shuddering seized his limbs, as glaring wildly on the countenance of Evelyn, he
exclaimed :—

" Evelyn Heartwell ! he whom I have so deeply wronged, and might innocently
have doomed to an ignominious death !   Oh, horror ! horror ! I cannot, dare not
encounter thy reproachful looks, thou shouldst blast me with the lightning of
thine hatred and indignation !"

" I pray thee do not give way to this powerful emotion ;" remarked Evelyn,
" it is quite uncalled for.   What thou didst was in error, and in the excited state
of thy mind at the time, was excusable ; I do forgive thee, Jasper."

" Forgive me !" exclaimed the old man, in impatient, melancholy accent, "no,
no, no, thou canst not ; it is a bittter mockery to talk of forgiveness to a guilty
wretch like me.   Ah !" he added, in tones of yet deeper agitation, and again
glaring upon Evelyn; " what features are those that meet my appalled sight! Thou
art there again dread phantom, harrowing up my guilty soul with thy presence !
avaunt ! avaunt ! I cannot bear thy ghostly, withering looks! thy reproachful
eyes ! Dread phantom of my unfortunate victim, avaunt, I say; will the grave
never hide thee from my distracted sight ! oh, horror ! horror !"

And with a loud hysterical laugh, the wretched old man again sunk back in a
state of utter insensibility, and Evelyn and the Gipsey-girl gazed at him with
mingled feelings of pity, regret, and disgust.

" Wretched man," ejaculated our hero, " what a pitiable spectacle does he
present.   Alas ! I fear that the crimes, which so heavily weigh upon his
conscience, are of the most fearful description."

" Most true," replied Mabel, " it is evident that he has committed some dreadful
deed in former years, goaded on by inordinate ambition and the fatal thirst for
gold ; and his punishment now though terrible, is no more than just.   Sampson
Brayling, I have reason to believe, is well acquainted with all the facts of his
former history ; and has also a written confession, signed by his own hand, and
which he extorted from him but a short time before his mysterious disappearance
on the night of the destruction of his miserable dwelling."

" Ah ! is it possible ?" said Evelyn, with a look of astonishment, " why then,
in common justice has Brayling hitherto neglected to denounce him, and make
his crimes known to the world ?"

"I know not, Evelyn," returned Mabel, "but doubtless he has powerful reasons for not doing so; and now that the Miser is once more discovered, and will, if he survives, return to England, probably the whole of the fearful mystery will be unravelled, if the old man in his frenzy does not previously divulge the secret. But come, let us leave him to himself until the excitement of his feelings shall, in some measure, have abated."

Our hero, whose curiosity was greatly excited by the observations that had fallen from the wretched Miser, and especially his emotion on beholding him, returned no answer to this, but reluctantly obeyed, and himself and Mabel quitted the cabin, and left Jasper to the care of those persons who were deputed to attend to him.

It was not till the following day that the old man was restored to anything like a degree of composure, and even then he evinced the greatest emotion on seeing Evelyn and Mabel, and the very tones of their voices seemed to cause a

No. 28

shuddering sensation of some inward and unaccountable dread to thrill through his veins. They had at different times been enabled to elicit from him the particulars of the way in which he had fallen into the power of Godfrey Malvern, and some other facts bearing upon the subject, but he sedulously avoided revealing his real name, or the knowledge he had of him; he evinced the greatest terror when any allusion was made to him, and a feeling of satisfaction when he was assured that he was dead. When, to his anxious inquiries, he was informed that the vessel was bound to England, he betrayed great alarm, and it was a considerable time before he could be in the least degree pacified.

"Attempt not to deceive me;" he exclaimed, and his lips quivered, and his limbs trembled as he spoke; "ye are conveying me to the hands of justice; it is retribution ye seek! oh, I am a miserable, wretched old man; but yet my soul shrinks appalled from the dreadful and ignominious fate to which ye would consign me. Is it not enough that they have plundered me of my gold? that they have left me poor and penniless, but that they would now have my life. Oh, spare my grey hairs, even though they are tainted with crime!"

"Wretched man;" said Evelyn; "great indeed must be thy guilt, that thus the horrors of remorse should goad and distract thy conscience."

"Ah!" cried the Miser, wildly, and glaring fearfully upon our hero; "who art thou, that dare accuse me? Wouldst thou pry into those dark secrets which for so many years have been concealed within the deep recesses of my breast? But," he added, as he fixed his eyes more wildly and vacantly upon the countenance of Evelyn, and his features became distorted with the power of his inward emotion, "what fearful tones are those I listen to, and which appal my very soul? those pale, but too well remembered features, whose lineaments freeze my blood to ice, and paralyse my senses? oh, must I be for ever haunted by this terrible phantom? such—such the very counterpart was he, when youth and vigour animated his noble frame, and every manly virtue glowed within his breast. Speak, speak, who art thou that thus tortures me with thy presence?"

"Thy mind wanders, unfortunate old man," replied Evelyn, looking at the miserable being before him with a feeling of pity and commiseration, which, in spite of his conviction of the heavy weight of crime that rested on his conscience, he could not subdue; "dost thou not remember me? I am that ill-fated Evelyn Heartwell, whom thou didst once befriend."

"'Tis false!" exclaimed the Miser, fiercely, "Jasper Scrimpe perform a friendly action? never! Ha! ha! ha! Go to—go to young man, thou mockest me! The cold, insensible, heartless wretch before ye, never knew a feeling of humanity. For years he has waged war with mankind, and mankind revolt at the mention of his name, and view its guilty enemy with loathing and disgust."

"Old man;" observed Walter Greysham, who was present at this scene, solemnly; "if thou would make atonement to man, and obtain the forgiveness of Heaven, repent, and confess the—"

"Repent! confess!" hastily interrupted Jasper, and his frame became more violently agitated than before. "Repent! confess! for what? to die the death of a felon, on a public scaffold; amidst the yells, the derision, and the execrations of the brutal and gaping crowd? no! no! they shall not force the damning secret from my lips! Confess! what have I to confess? Who dare suspect or accuse me of guilt? Who saw me commit the crime? They are gone; they are dead; ha! ha! ha! I triumph! I triumph! There is no one now lives who can denounce the Miser, Jasper Scrimpe!"

"Miserable old man;" said Mabel, fixing upon him a mingled look of pity, contempt, and disgust, "beware; there is yet one living, who knows well all the awful particulars of thy guilt; who holds in his possession thine own self-condemnation ; and who has it in his power, at any moment, to make thy crimes manifest to the world ; that man is —"

"Who ? who ?" gasped forth the distracted Miser, and his blood-shot eyes glared upon the countenance of the Gipsey-girl, as though they would penetrate to the inmost recesses of her soul, "on thy life, say, who is he who dare to accuse Jasper Scrimpe of that which dark suspicion dare scarce point at ?"

"Sampson Brayling," replied Mabel ; "he still lives, and holds in his possession the black confession of thy crimes, signed by thine own hand !"

The words of the Gipsey-girl seemed to fall like a clap of thunder on the senses of Jasper Scrimpe. A convulsive shuddering seized his limbs ; his eyes appeared almost ready to burst from their sockets ; every feature became frightfully distorted ; and a livid hue like that of death overspread his countenance. He tried to speak, but the words he would have uttered were stifled in his throat, and clasping his hands together, with an hysterical laugh he sank senseless in the arms of Evelyn Heartwell.

"Unhappy man !" exclaimed our hero, "the power of conscience is too much for his distracted brain ! May Heaven pardon him the fearful crimes of which he has too evidently been guilty."

Jasper Scrimpe, in this deplorable state, was removed to the cabin he had hitherto occupied, and left to the care of proper persons, and in the same wretched condition he remained during the rest of the voyage, with at least but few intervals.

The weather continued favourable : the Invulnerable proceeded rapidly on its voyage, and at length the white cliffs of Old England gladdened the anxious eyes of the hardy mariners, who had been so long absent from their native land, and those who were so fondly endeared to them. The ship arrived at Portsmouth ; the sails were furled, the anchor cast, and all hearts were grateful to that allmerciful Providence which had preserved them from the numerous dangers it had been their lot to encounter.

CHAPTER XXXVI.

Evelyn's Secret Departure from the Ship.—An Unexpected and Unwelcome Meeting.—Threatened Danger.—Evelyn once more rescued by the Gipsey-Girl.—The Mysterious Disappearance of the Miser.

It was with mingled feelings of fear, hope, and anxiety, that our hero once more gazed upon his native shores, which he had quitted but a few months since, in the expectation of either being estranged from them for many years, and until Fortune had happily once more smiled upon his destiny, or never to behold again. Alas ! when other hearts on board were glad and buoyant with hope and expectation, how sad and desolate was his. What bright prospects were there to cheer him on his return ?—would he not again tread the shores of his native land a wretched outcast from society, friendless, houseless, and with the foul brand of the felon upon his brow ? What might be the fate he would be destined to hear had befallen Constance ? Unable any longer to resist the stern and inexorable will of her uncle, might she not even now be the wife of the villain, Oliver Dalton, and thus all his hopes be for ever annihilated ? The thought distracted him, and there were moments when he regreted that he had not perished in the many fearful dangers to which he had been exposed, or that he had been prevented in the execution of his rash and deadly purpose of self-destruction by the interference of Mabel. And then, how was he to escape from the fond importunities of that devoted girl ? His heart overflowed with gratitude towards her for the innumerable services she had rendered him ; the immense sacrifice she had made for his sake; and what return could he make her ? even if he could have forgotten Constance Welborn, which was impossible ; a certain instinctive feeling which he could neither control nor understand, he was convinced must prevent him from ever encouraging the fatal passion she entertained for him, and yet she seemed resolved to pursue him with a perseverance as obstinate as it was determined. He would have consulted Walter Greysham upon this important and delicate subject but, under all the circumstances, he hesitated to do so. He had noticed the impression which Mabel had made upon Walter's heart, but still he feared that the Gipsey-girl, in spite of his numerous merits, could never, in her present unhappy state of mind, make any return. After racking his brains for some time with these torturing reflections, the only course which seemed the most advisable for him to pursue was to secretly leave the ship on the first opportunity that presented itself, and once more seek the counsel and assistance of Sampson Brayling, whom he now thought he had better not have quitted so abruptly. He was, he believed, the only sincere friend, with the exception of Constance and Mabel, that he had in the world, and he probably held his future fate in his hands. He felt some anxiety respecting the Miser, but he had no doubt that every care would be taken of him, and that he would be forthcoming at any time when his presence might be required. Having come to this resolution, he hastily wrote notes to Walter and Mabel explanatory of the motives that urged him to this apparently rash and extraordinary step, which he placed where they would be sure to find them, and then anxiously and silently watched the opportunity he sought. It was not long before it presented itself.

The dark shadows of evening had fallen upon the ocean, and all was still around, save the gentle rippling of the waves, or the low murmuring of the wind as it swept around. Walter Greysham and most of the crew had gone ashore in the afternoon, and had not yet returned ; the Miser was in his cabin, lonely and wretched, and as he had not seen Mabel for several hours, he imagined that she had also quitted the vessel. There were only two of the seamen on deck, and they were too busily occupied to observe him ; nothing could be more favourable to his designs than the present moment, and Evelyn, committing himself to the care of Providence, and having secured all the money he possessed about his person, determined to avail himself of it. He silently walked to that part of the deck where one of the boats was hanging over the side of the vessel, and cautiously releasing it from its hold, let it down upon the surface of the ocean, leaping into it himself immediately afterwards. The next moment he dashed away from the ship, and rowed rapidly towards the shore, the darkness that reigned around concealing him from observation. In a few minutes he reached the shore in safety, and, having moored the boat as well as he could, he stepped on land, and for a minute or two he stood, and hesitated what course it would be most prudent for him to pursue, in order that he might not encounter those whom he wished to avoid. Finding that the coast was entirely clear, he took the first path that presented itself, and wrapping his cloak closer around him, in order the better to conceal his person from observation, he hurried on his way. The road he had fortunately selected was lonely and unfrequented, and did not seem likely to lead to any town or village, which he was anxious at that time to avoid, and he therefore walked on with renewed confidence and determination. In this manner he proceeded for about half and hour, when, suddenly turning an angle in the road, to his disappointment he found himself at the entrance to a town, in which an ancient looking tavern was a prominent feature, lights burning in every window, and from which the sounds of noisy revelry saluted his ears. He paused for a moment, undecided what to do, but seeing a waggon standing at the door, the thought struck him that probably for a little money he might be able to obtain a place in it, and thus be conveyed in safety partly on the road. The waggoner was by the side of his team attending to his horses, preparatory to again resuming his journey, and Evelyn walked up to him, and was proceeding to bargain with him, when two men, evidently in a state of intoxication, suddenly emerged from the house, and staggering up to the place where our hero and the waggoner stood, the light of the moon, which at that moment appeared from behind a dark cloud that had before obscured it, fell full upon their faces, and Evelyn started back in alarm and amazement, when in the features of one of them he discovered the ruffian, Black Will, and in those of his companion, another of the Gipsey-tribe, who had abandoned his former associates, and who was known by the name of Zoar.

For a moment or two our hero was so taken by surprise at this unexpected and unwelcome meeting, that he was confused and transfixed to the spot, but Will, who immediately recognised him, uttered a violent oath, and advancing towards him, and laying his hand rudely on his shoulder, exclaimed:—

"Ah! my young adventurer, is it possible, that after so long a time we meet again, and in this place? This is most fortunate. Zoah, the capture of Evelyn Heartwell may repay us for our journey here, and we owe him something for the affair at Wapping. It will be our own faults if we suffer him now to escape us. Let us secure him while we have the chance."

"Hold, ruffians!" exclaimed our hero, drawing his sword, as the fellows approached to seize him, "forbear to obstruct me, or by Heaven ye shall pay dearly for your daring. Stand aside, I say, and let me proceed on my way."

The waggoner stood by in stupified amazement, and offered not to interfere one way or the other; and the conduct of the ruffians became more bold and determined.

"Heed not his threats!" cried Black Will; "at any rate we must be cowards if we are not more than a match for him. On to him!"

Immediately they rushed upon him, and so impetuously that Evelyn was compelled to stand well upon his guard to resist them. The villians giving utterance to the most dreadful oaths, the combat was continued with the most determined bravery, to some short distance from the spot were they had first encountered each other, and Evelyn having severely wounded Zoath, was likely to be triumphant, but at that moment, as illfate would have it, in warding off a desperate blow, which Will was about to deal him, his own sword was broken to the hilt, and sinking on one knee, he was entirely at the mercy of his desperate foe, who, encouraged at the obstinate resistance he had met with, was apparrently about to take advantage of it, when a loud exclamation was heard, and the next instant the ruffian's arm was arrested in its deadly purpose by *Mabel!*

"S'death!—" cried Black Will, with a terrible oath, and starting back a few paces in the utmost state of astonishment, "the Gipsey-girl here again to thwart me in my designs; revenge! revenge!"

As he uttered these words, sword in hand he rushed furiously towards the intrepid girl; but she met him with a laugh of scorn and defiance, and levelling a pistol at his head, held him triumphantly at bay; at the same time, Evelyn having recovered himself, snatched the sword of the wounded Zoah, and the ruffian, in his turn was held completely at their mercy. Another moment, and Walter Greysham, Captain Falkland, and several of the crew of the Invulnerable, who had been seated in the tavern, hastened to the spot, and the scene of astonishment that ensued may be readily imagined.

"Evelyn;" said Walter Greysham; "how is it that I see thee here, so far away from the ship, and equipped as if for travelling a long journey?"

Our hero felt confused by the question, especialy as he saw that the eyes of Mabel were fixed keenly and suspiciously upon him, and at first he scarcely knew how to reply, but at length he said—

" Excuse me, Greysham, for the present ; I fear that I shall incur thy censure for the cause I was impelled to adopt ; but I will explain all at another time, and in another place."

" Be it so," coincided Greysham, " to this heroic girl," he added, turning with a look of fervent admiration to Mabel—" to this heroic girl, then, thou art again indebted for thy preservation ?   But these rascals, who are they ? and what is the meaning of this outrage ?"

" They are the same villains from whom I so narrowly escaped at Wapping," answered Evelyn, " and two of the most inveterate of my enemies."

" Oh, indeed ?" observed Walter, " then we must e'en put a stop to their gambols for a time.   What say you, Captain Falkland, shall we convey the fellows on board the ship, until they have given some explanation of their conduct ?" Captain Falkland assented.

" Aye, aye," said two or three of the sailors in a breath, " away with the lubbers on board, and place them in the bilboes till they shall give a satisfactory account of themselves.   Heave ahead, yer infernal looking swabs !   Heave ahead."

" Beware what you do," said the enraged Will, " or ye may have cause to repent of your conduct."

The only reply this elicited from the seamen was a loud laugh of contempt and defiance, and securing the two ruffians together by a stout rope which they procured from the tavern, amidst the loud and derisive laughter of the sailors, they were hurried along towards the ship, our hero and his companions following in the rear.

Evelyn felt disappointed, confused, and abashed as they proceeded, and shrunk from the piercing and searching glances that Mabel ever and anon fixed upon him, as they proceeded on their way.

" Thou canst not conceal the truth from me, Evelyn," she said at length, in tones of mingled reproach and regret, " thou wouldst have abandoned, without one word at parting, those who have proved themselves to be thy best friends."

" Bear with me, Mabel, I implore thee, and upbraid me not," replied our hero, " and ere long I will endeavour to explain my conduct to thy satisfaction."

Mabel was about to make some further observation, when she was prevented from doing so by Walter Greysham drawing their attention to a dark object moving at a short distance, and which seemed to be endeavouring to avoid them. It was evidently the form of a man gliding stealthily along, and at that moment the moon being obscured by a dense cloud, it was hidden from the sight.   They all gazed in astonishment in the direction of the place whence it had disappeared, but not the least traces of it could they discover, it had vanished as suddenly and as mysteriously as a supernatural being.

" This is very extraordinary and suspicious ;" observed Greysham ; " who could this man have been ; and what could have been his motives for such cautious and remarkable conduct ?"

Every one was lost in conjecture ; and, after a minute or two passed in reflection, without being able to form any satisfactory opinion upon the subject, they continued on their way, and soon afterwards arrived at the ship, where the two ruffians were immediately below, and properly secured.   Walter Greysham and his companions were traversing the deck, and immersed in deep conversation, when the mate approached, and the peculiarity of his looks shewed that he had something important to communicate.

" How now, Elmore ?" interrogated Captain Falkland ; " what is it thou hast got to say ?"

" The old Miser, Jasper Scrimpe—" replied the Mate.

" Ah ! speak ! what of him ?" hastily enquired our hero.

" He is gone—left the ship !" answered Elmore.

"Left the ship!" said the astonished Greysham; "impossible! How is this? explain yourself."

"He was supposed to be safe in the cabin allotted to him;" returned Elmore? "so no one thought it necessary to intrude upon him. About half an hour since, however, a heavy plunge in the sea from one of the port-holes was heard by myself and several of the crew, and looking over the ship's side we beheld, to our astonishment and alarm, by the light of the moon, the gray head of the old man, just about the surface of the waters, and saw him struggling with the waves; but swimming with a strength and dexterity we did not think him capable of. A boat was instantly launched, and myself and two others put off to try to save him; but he had disappeared; and, in the darkness which prevailed at the time, we could discover no traces of him."

"Unhappy man!" ejaculated Evelyn, "the frenzy of despair, and the horrors of a guilty conscience, have doubtless driven him to this rash act. He must have perished."

"Not so," remarked Walter Greysham, "rememberest thou the form we saw on the road, gliding so stealthily from our sight? It must have been him."

"Ah!" said Captain Falkland, "that idea is most probable. Let several of the crew return to the shore, and make strict search for him."

This order was promptly obeyed, everyone waiting with the utmost anxiety and impatience to know the result, but in about two hours the men returned to the ship, not having been able to attain any tidings of the old man, and all were lost in mystery and fruitless conjecture.

CHAPTER XXXVII.

THE FEARFUL JOURNEY OF THE MISER.—THE COTTAGERS.—THE MURDERER'S TABLET.—THE GIBBET ON THE HEATH.—THE GIPSEY SYBIL.—THE PREDICTION.

EXCITED to a state of absolute frenzy by the terrors of his guilty conscience, and scarcely knowing what he did, the unfortunate Jasper Scrimpe had been driven to commit self-destruction, and with that design he had precipitated himself from one of the port-holes of the ship into the sea. But fate had ordained that he should not perish in that way. Clinging to life with the tenacity of most persons in the last extremity, he rose again quickly, and struggled manfully with the waves, and having in his more youthful days been a most expert swimmer, he now put forth all his strength, which the desperate nature of his situation accumulated tenfold, and exerted himself to the utmost to reach the shore, which, however, being at some distance, it was a matter of great doubt whether he would be able to accomplish. He was almost exhausted, he gasped, and panted for breath; every vein was swelled to bursting; each muscle was distended to its utmost limits; another moment, and the wretched man must have yielded to his fate, when his eager eyes fortunately encountered a boat, which had been driven adrift from its moorings, and was floating near him. With frenzied eagerness he clutched at it, and crawling into it it, sunk down for a minute or two quite overpowered. He recovered himself, and looked anxiously around, and to his satisfaction he found that he was not only far away from the ship, but that the boat had been driven by the impetuosity of the waves, very near the land. A few minutes afterwards the old man was safe on shore, and sinking on his knees, in a delirium of wild joy, he laughed aloud. He arose to his feet, and, wet, weary and wretched, he hurried on, heedless of the way he was pursuing, but exulting in the idea that he was again free, though what to do, or whither to go he knew not.

He had proceeded to some distance, when he was startled by the sound of approaching footsteps, and the voices of several persons ; and, trembling with fear, he looked anxiously in the direction from which the sounds proceeded, and, to his alarm, by the light of the moon, he recognised the very individuals whom he wished to avoid. There was no time for reflection; stealing into the shade, and concealed by clustering trees, he pursued his way with all the speed he could, and at length pausing to take breath, and looking around, he found that the coast was clear, and that he had managed to elude those whom, under the present circumstances, he so much dreaded.

He did not lose his presence of mind, however, at this critical moment, neither did he stop to see whether or not he was observed by them, but with cautious footsteps, and avoiding the light of the moon as much as possible, he stole silently aside, and assisted by the shadow which the clustering trees at intervals cast across his path, he was enabled, as has been shown, to elude them, and ultimately to make good his retreat, and after proceeding with all the speed he could for some distance, he once more ventured to pause to take breath, and looking around him, his mind felt somewhat more at rest when he found that there was no person within sight. He now for the first time reflected seriously upon the peculiarity of the situation in which he had placed himself, and endeavoured to collect his ideas sufficiently to come to some reasonable conclusion as to the course it would be most prudent for him to pursue.

But his brain was bewildered, and he could form no definite idea upon the subject. He was a complete stranger in that part of the country in which he now found himself; and wretched and lonely as he was, whither could he go ? where seek a place of refuge ? He wished to hide himself from the eyes of mankind altogether, for the sight of his fellow creatures now created in his breast a sensation of dread. To his disordered imagination, he must be an object of suspicion to all who encountered him; his guilty conscience made him fear that they could read his crimes in the expression of his features, and he dreaded lest they should hand him over to that stern justice which he had for so many, many years escaped, but which, he feared, at last must overtake him. There was but one individual whom he really wished to encounter, and that was the poor fellow who for years had experienced such sorry treatment at his hands—his wretched, half-starved, but faithful attendant, Toby Taper. Harshly, cruelly as he had behaved to that poor simple being, the Miser could not but believe that he would yet sympathize with him in his misfortunes, and assist him with his council and advice, which, although he had always affected to despise and reject, he could now learn to value and receive with gratitude· But Toby he feared had perished on the night of the fire, and he therefore abandoned all hope of ever beholding him again. Still undecided how to act, the old man resumed his dreary way, choosing the road that seemed most lonely and unfrequented.

About his person Jasper Scrimpe had still concealed a considerable sum of money, which he determined to use with the strictest economy ; for still, under all the circumstances that surrounded him, the same sordid spirit, the same pernicious, grasping avarice, that had always characterised him, predominated over every other passion within his breast. With an energy which, considering his age and infirmities, could not have been expected of him, the Miser, all that dark and dismal might continued to wander on, he knew not whither, and meeting only with a solitary traveller now and then, who, like himself, seemed anxious to avoid observation, and plodded on their lonely way without talking any notice of him. And thus he journeyed on till daybreak, when the barking of a dog convinced him that he was near some human habitation ; and, as the light

increased, he saw smoke issue from above a copse of trees.   He made for the spot,
and passing through a gate, entered a serpentine walk, at the end of which was a
neat cottage, standing in the midst of a grass-plot, planted with roses, jessamines,
honeysuckles, and other odoriferous flowers. Weary and miserable as the old
man was, this was indeed a most refreshing and welcome sight, and he was still
more encouraged in his hopes of the assistance he required on observing a young
girl of prepossessing appearance, who was engaged in watering the flowers.
Perceiving Jasper, and struck by his venerable appearance and exhausted condition
she threw aside the machine, and called to her mother, a clean, matronly looking
dame, who was in another part of the garden attending to her bee-hives, to come
and assist her in taking the stranger into the house.   The Miser returned his
acknowledgments for their kindness in terms that were very unusual to him ; but
the humble cottagers checked him with the most benevolent assurances, at the same
time placing before him such homely fare as their dwelling afforded, and of which
    No. 29.

they heartily invited him to partake· The Miser assented, and after he had done so, he felt his strength much recruited. From the old woman he ascertained that he was on the road to London, from which he was distant about fifty miles ; and Jasper felt more satisfied as they evinced none of that inquisitiveness and idle curiousity so characteristic of their sex. Seeing that he had journeyed far, and was very much fatigued, the old woman recommended him to seek a few hours' repose, and he retired to a bed, where sleep soon closed his eyelids, and the black prospect of retrospection and futurity were, for a time, excluded.

Night had again spread her sable mantle o'er the earth, when our fugitive, with a heavy, but grateful heart, bade adieu to his hostess and her daughter, and once more resumed his melancholy journey. The air was serene, and the moon shone in a fine clear sky, when Jasper departed from the cottage, but he had not proceeded far, when the face of the atmosphere became condensed ; the wind whistled, and the flying clouds obscured the planet of night, which lent an intermitting light hardly sufficient to enable him to shun the bogs and precipices which, in the wild front of the country he was traversing, he was likely to meet with.

It was by the side of a clump of trees, whose boughs waved mournfully, that the sight of a white object attracted the Miser's attention, and he advanced to it. It was a stone tablet, and Jasper, with some difficulty, deciphered the following inscription :—

"THIS STONE WAS PLACED HERE,
In commemmoration of a
MOST INHUMAN MURDER!
Committed by
A GANG OF ROBBERS,
Who have long infested this locality,
TO THE TERROR OF ALL TRAVELLERS.
JUSTICE HAS, HOWEVER, OVERTAKEN
THREE OF THE ASSASSINS,
Who have paid the penalty of their crimes !"

A creaking sound prevented his proceeding. Trembling with terror, he turned his eyes towards the heath, and they encountered the view of a triangular gibbet on which were suspended the bodies of three men, whose chains grated in the night breeze !

The accumulated and concurring horrors were too much for the exhausted strength of the old man. His own fearful doom seemed to be foreshadowed in the ghastly objects before him. His brain turned giddy; large drops of perspiration stood upon his quivering temples; his knees smote each other in dreadful trepidation, and with a cry of agony he sank insensible upon the earth.

When suspended animation returned, he looked around him in dismay, and to his utter astonishment, found himself in a spacious vaulted apartment, formed out of the solid rock, but the means by which he had come there were perfectly incomprehensible to him.

Against the sides were suspended swords, shields, cuirasses, helmets, and various implements of war, and in the centre stood a large table, plentifully stored with cold viands and flaggons of wine, and of the last, Jasper, who was faint and exhaused, tasted and found his spirits recruited by it.

All seemed mysterious, he neither heard or saw a human being ; the inscription on the tablet, relative to the murder, and to the robbers who infested the neighbourhood, recurred to him, and he conjectured this to be one of their secret haunts. He took a flambeau, and lighted it by a lamp that was suspended from the roof, and ascended a flight of steps at the opposite extremity of the cavern. At the summit, a massive iron door impeded his passage, and he descended in an agony of despair.

On each side of the cavern were small cabins, and in one part a door much larger than the rest, and rudely formed, which he opened, but the putrid stench which he inhaled caused him to shudder. Nevertheless, as it might be the road to his emancipation, he proceeded, and, after passing though a long passage, found himself in a cemetery, in which several bodies were lying about, in their living apparel, and presented a ghastly spectacle; appalled at the sight, which recalled all the horrors of the guilty past to his memory, a cold shuddering seized the wretched Miser's limbs; his senses reeled; a sickly feeling like that preceding death, came over him, and again he sank inanimate on the humid earth.

CHAPTER XXXVII.

The Designs of Oliver Dalton Defeated.—His Rage and Disappoint-ment.—Attempted Revenge.—Sir Milford Wounded.—Flight of Oliver Dalton.

RETURN we now to the scene in the chapel at Milford Hall, on the eventful night referred to in a previous chapter. To describe properly the excitement and alarm which prevailed on the abrupt and unexpected appearance of Sampson Brayling and his comrades, at such an important and critical juncture, would be impossible; Constance, as has been stated, had fainted; Sir Milford gazed with astonishment and almost incredulity at the Gipsey-chief and his companions; while Oliver Dalton, to whom the tones of Sampson Brayling's voice sounded like the very knell of death, stood overwhelmed with confusion and dismay, and could not articulate a syllable. He saw at once that his plans were defeated;—that his guilt and infamy were about to be exposed, and, while he trembled with fear at the consequenses, he felt ready to burst with rage, disappointment, and despair. Sampson eyed him with looks of malice, triumph and indignation; and, for some minutes remained silent, apparently waiting for him or the baronet to speak.

Sir Milford Welborn was the first to break this painful silence, and fixing upon the Gipsey-chief a haughty and commanding look, he said :—

" Ah! Sampson Brayling, the proscribed Gipsey-chief, who has hitherto aided and abetted the guilty Evelyn Heartwell in his escape from the hands of justice; bold man, what is the meaning of this sacreligious intrusion within these sacred walls ? "

" To save thee, Sir Milford Welborn from committing an act, which would ever afterwards wring thy soul with reproach and shame;" replied Brayling; "and to tear aside the specious disguise which has so long enabled your trembling hypocrite to impose upon thee ! "

" Sir Milford ; " exclaimed Oliver, mustering up all the courage and boldness he could; " I implore thee—surely thou wilt not allow thyself to be prejudiced by any false statement this daring ruffian, the champion, the partizan of the felon Heartwell may think proper to make. ".

" Obstinate idiot !" returned the Gipsey-chief, fixing upon Oliver Dalton a look which made him quail, " hast thou still the shameless audacity to brave my power ! Sir Milford Welborn, my conduct is alone prompted by a love of justice, and I will adduce such facts in corroboration of what I state that may defy any one to counteract. The villain who has so long imposed on thy credulity as Oliver Dalton, whom thou hast hitherto thought to be a very paragon of honour and virtue, and to whom thou wouldst even now sacrifice the hand and fortune of thy fair niece, is no other than the unprincipled adventurer, Luke Stanton, the renegade Gipsey, and the former associate of myself and the ruffian, Black Will, whom he lately did thee the honour to introduce to thee ! "

"Gracious powers!" exclaimed our astonished and agitated heroine, who had recovered her senses, and was gazing with trembling anxiety upon the exciting scene.

"Ah!" cried the baronet; completely astounded; "what is this I have heard? This is a bold charge, Sampson Brayling; but is it possible that thou hast spoken the truth?"

"Oh, Sir Milford, "said Oliver, with the most consummate effrontery; "thou surely wilt not suffer thyself to be deluded by the foul calumny of this daring villain, who, in a spirit of deadly malice and revenge, in consequence of my refusing to yield to his extortionate demands upon my purse, basely seeks my ruin. Thou wilt not credit his ridiculous assertions, which are as false as his heart is black and treacherous!"

"Barefaced scoundrel?" retorted Brayling, "and dost thou still persist in denying my statements, fully prepared as thou knowest I am to substantiate them? Sir Milford Welborn, I brought this young man up from the earliest days of childhood, and there is a secret, a fearful secret connected with his birth which he himself is unacquainted with, and which it is not my intention at the present to reveal. My principal object now is to defeat the diabolical designs of the guilty, and to see justice rendered to the innocent and oppressed; and, with that object in view, I here unhesitatingly proclaim the entire innocence of the unfortunate Evelyn Heartwell of all the foul charges brought against him, and denounce Luke Stanton, alias Oliver Dalton, as not only the real robber, but likewise the attempted murderer of the Miser, Jasper Scrimpe!"

"What proof hast thou, Brayling, in support of this bold accusation?" demanded Sir Thomas Overton, who had hitherto remained a silent observer of all that passed.

"Myself and several more of my tribe was in the Lover's Walk on the evening when it took place," replied the Gipsey, "and secretly observed the whole transaction, though circumstances prevented us coming forward at the time to give evidence as to the fact. But more, I have a confession of the whole of the crimes of the Miser, Jasper Scrimpe, signed by his own hand, and in which he acknowledges the innocence of Evelyn Heartwell; that the pocket-book, with its contents, found upon him, was presented to that much injured youth, by himself, and, moreover, solemnly declares that it was the guilty miscreant who now stands trembling by thy side, that committed the monstrous offence which has been the cause of so much evil and misery."

"Confusion!" muttered Oliver, aside; "can it indeed be true that he possesses the damning proof he speaks of? if so, I am lost!"

"Hast thou that document in thy possession, Brayling?" interrogated Sir Milford, looking at the same time with an expression of doubt and suspicion on Oliver Dalton.

It is here, Sir Milford;" returned Sampson, producing the paper from his bosom; "but I must request thee for the present to peruse only that portion of the confession which refers to the charge at issue."

Sir Milford Welborn eagerly took the paper which Sampson Brayling presented to him, and looking anxiously at the paragraph which the Gipsey pointed out to him, the expression of his countenance underwent a remarkable change.

"This is indeed most convincing;" he observed; "I could swear positively to the signature affixed to this paper being in the hand writing of the Miser, and in it he perfectly exonerated Evelyn Heartwell, whom, he states, he mistook in the excitement of the moment, and solemnly declares that it was Oliver Dalton alone who waylaid and stabbed him in the Lover's Walk!"

Almighty God, I thank thee!" exclaimed our heroine, clasping her hands fervently together, and solemny raising her eyes towards Heaven; "the innocence of the unfortunate Evelyn will at last be firmly established!"

" Of what a monstrous imposture have I suffered myself to be made the dupe;" said the indignant Sir Milford, returning the paper to Brayling ; " wretched, misguided, guilty young man ;" he added, turning sternly to Oliver ; "what answer canst thou possibly have to make to the fearful charge thus brought against thee?"

" Since it seems that thou hast made up thy mind to condemn me ;" replied Dalton, " and to place every reliance upon this shameless forgery, my answer to it, and its detested author shall be brief—tis this !"

With these words the villian hastily snatched a pistol from his belt, and levelled it at Brayling, but at that moment Sir Milford, who had observed the action, rushed suddenly forward to arrest Oliver's arm, and unfortunately receiving the contents of the deadly weapon in his shoulder, to the horror and consternation of Constance, and the other persons present, sunk bleeding in the arms of the attendants ! a simultaneous execration escaped the lips of all assembled, and a loud cry was raised to seize the murderer ; but to the utter astonishment of all, he was nowhere to be seen ; taking advantage of the confusion and excitement that prevailed, Oliver Dalton had suddenly vanished, in a manner as wonderful as it was mysterious ! We can hardly attempt to pourtray the scene which followed this startling catastrophe ; Constance, in a state of distraction, flew to her uncle; and loud shouts were raised to pursue Oliver Dalton, whom it was thought impossible could have escaped from the Hall so suddenly altogether.

" Aye, I will pursue the miscreant immediately ;" exclaimed Brayling ; " he must not be permitted to escape after committing such a monstrous outrage as this. Follow me ! "

With these words, he hastily quitted the chapel, followed by the gipsies ; Sir Milford was conveyed to a chamber, and attended by the agitated Constance and Sir Thomas Overton, the chaplain had retired from the altar some time before ; the lights were extinguished, and all was now silence and darkness in that place, which but a few minutes before had been the scene of such startling events.

A surgeon was in immediate attendance upon Sir Milford, and, on examining the wound he had received, he pronounced it is severe but by no means dangerous ; though there was much to be apprehended from the state of excitement into which events of so extraordinary and alarming a description had naturally thrown him. It would, however, he impossible to do adequate justice to the feelings of our heroine on this occasion ; and it required all the exertions of the two amidable daughters of Sir Thomas Overton to enable her to obtain anything like a degree of composure. The exposure of the infamy of Oliver Dalton's character, and the defeat of his nefarious designs, by the faithful and friendly means of Sampson Brayling, could not but afford her the utmost satisfaction ; the innocence of the deeply injured Evelyn, too, would at last be made manifest to the world ; the foul brand removed from his brow ; but, alas ! where now was that unfortunate youth? What might be the fate that had by this time overtaken him? The thought distracted her, and crushed those fond hopes that might otherwise have been created in her breast. In about an hour Sampson Brayling returned to Milford Hall, he having been unsuccessful in his endeavours to discover Oliver, whose sudden escape was not only extraordinary, but almost incredible.

" But fear not, Miss Constance ;" said the Gipsey, " I will leave no means untried, and it will be strange indeed if the villian should be able to elude my vigilance. It can scarcely be imagined the important and startling facts I have yet to reveal when the fitting time for so doing shall have arrived. But, thank Providence, I have been enabled to defeat his diabolical designs, and to rescue thee from the terrible and unnatural fate which was so long impending over thee."

" Oh, Brayling," said our heroine ; " what a lasting debt of gratitude do I owe you for having so faithfully fulfilled your promise, and for the invaluable service you have rendered me. "

"Name it not, lady;" returned Sampson, "it is an imperative duty I owe to justice; I have solemnly sworn to perform it, even at all hazards; and never shall Sampson Brayling be found to shrink from his word. I deeply regret the accident which has occurred to Sir Milford, but I sincerely hope that it will not be attended with any fatal consequences."

"Oh, Heaven forbid!" fervently ejaculated Constance; "but poor Evelyn; alas! what has become of him? and shall we ever meet again?"

"Oh, yes;" replied the Gipsey; "believe me, lady, that Providence will watch over and protect him, and restore him once more safely to thy presence."

"But oh, Sampson;" said our heroine, "why did you so long delay making this important disclosure, and in removing the base obloquy under which the unfortunate Evelyn rested?"

"Blame me not, Miss Constance;" answered the Gipsey-chief; "there were circumstances that prevented my doing so, and the force of which, I think, thou wilt be ready to admit, when I am allowed more fully to explain. But I must leave thee, lady; there must be no time lost in pursuing Oliver Dalton, and to that duty it is now my intention to devote myself. Farewell, Miss Constance, and assure Sir Milford that he will not find a more sincere or indefatigable friend than in Sampson Brayling."

"Farewell, Brayling," said Constance, extending to him her hand, which he raised to his lips respectfully, "I can but repeat my thanks. But when will you again visit the Hall?"

"Probably in the course of the day, especially if success should crown my efforts," replied Brayling; and he then retired from her presence and quitted the Hall, and Constance returned to the chamber of her uncle, whom she was gratified to find much better that she had expected. He was, however, in a state of great excitement. The fearful disclosures that had been made respecting Oliver, had surprised and shocked him, and he shuddered in the presence of his beauteous niece, when he reflected upon the shameful and revolting fate to which his obstinacy had so nearly consigned her. The scene which passed between them at this interview we will leave to the imagination of the reader.

The news of the extraordinary events that had taken place at Milford Hall soon spread, and caused the greatest sensation in the neighbourhood. Officers were dispatched in every direction by the proper authorities in pursuit of the culprit; but the day passed away without any traces of him being discovered, and the whole affair was involved in the most impenetrable mystery.

CHAPTER XXXVIII.

OLIVER DALTON'S ADVENTURES IN HIS FLIGHT FROM MILFORD HALL.—TOBY TAPER IN A NEW CHARACTER.—THE NARROW ESCAPE.

ACTING with uncommon promptitude, self-possession, and presence of mind, Oliver Dalton had no sooner fired the pistol, and saw Sir Milford fall, than he seized the opportunity which the confusion and distraction of the moment presented, and while all eyes were directed to the wounded baronet, to make good his flight, for, that his game was up it was quite evident. Hastily he glanced around the ancient chapel for the means of retreat, and suddenly his eyes fell upon a private door, by the side of the altar, and which was partly open. To hasten towards it, there being no one near it to obstruct him, was only the work of an instant, and passing quickly beyond, he closed the door silently behind him, and bolting it, effectually prevented any pursuit that way. He now found himself in a long winding passage, which he knew communicated with one wing of the Hall, which, at the present time was not inhabted, and therefore offered him every means of departing unobserved, unless the building should be surrounded, in which case he determined not to be captured without making a desperate and determined resistance. The passage was fortunately lighted by two or three lamps suspended from the arched roof, so that he had no difficulty in finding his way, and in a few minutes he arrived at the extremity, and with little difficulty unfastened a door which there presented itself, and entered a small court-yard that separated the chapel from the building. Here he paused an instant to reflect, and looked up at the casements of that ancient portion of the Hall, but all was involved in complete darkness, and he therefore apprehended no danger from that quarter, and entered the building by a door which was standing conveniently open, the walls of the court-yard being too high for him to scale. He passed through several apartments which had all the dusty and gloomy appearance of having been long neglected; but he had no time to stop to examine; every moment was most precious, particularly as he could now hear the confused buzz of many voices, no doubt proceeding from those who were in pursuit of him, and if he at all delayed his progress, they might probably be enabled to cut off his retreat.

Making his way towards a convenient spot for him to emerge from the hall, Oliver Dalton found his further progress impeded by a massive oak door, strongly barred, locked, and bolted, and which resisted all his efforts, and the exertion of his utmost strength to open it. Vexed and bewildered, he knew not what to do; and his alarm was augmented when he heard the sounds increase, and approach nearer in the direction he had been pursuing, so, that two or thee times he heard his name distinctly mentioned. There was no time for hesitation; it was a matter of life or death, and he therefore hurried up a short flight of steps, which he perceived a little way to the left, and which led him into a small room, in which was a lofty window partly open. He hastened to it, and looked from it, and then perceived that it looked upon a town at the back of the premises, and which was enclosed by a wall of no considerable height, and presented no obstacle to his escape. The window was at no great distance from the ground, so, without any further hesitation, Oliver took a bold leap from it, and alighted in perfect safety on terra-firma; Gathering himself up in an instant, he bounded across the lawn, and scaling the the wall without any difficulty, he found himself at liberty, and at the entrance to a narrow lane, overarched with the wide spreading branches of tall trees, and which afforded every facility for concealment in the event of his being closely pressed; at that moment he heard a distant clock strike the hour of two, and all was darkness and silence around. Presently, however, he saw the light of several torches moving about in the distance, in the vicinity of the Hall, and could hear the murmur of the voices of those persons who were evidently in pursuit of him.

This aroused him into fresh action, and, muttering curses on the desperate change in his fortune, he dashed along the lane at the top of his speed, and soon reached the further end, and crossing a stile, entered upon a range of fields that bounded the main road to some extent, and where he could see no person to intercept his flight. He looked back, and as well as his eyes could penetrate through the darkness, beheld no one in pursuit, so that for the present, at any rate, he imagined he had eluded the danger he had so much reason to apprehend. He now paused for a second or two to gather breath, and collect his thoughts; and a tempest of passions at that moment agitated his mind, at the critical situation in which he found himself, which was almost insupportable. All his ambitious hopes and prospects were crushed, annihilated, and fearful were the maledictions he invoked upon the head of Sampson Brayling, who was undoubtedly the cause of all.

Hitherto he had come to no decision as to whether he should direct his step, but he now determined to make the best of his way to London at once, in one of the obscure localities of which he might probably be better able to conceal himself, until the excitement should in some measure have abated, and he could cautiously arrange his plans for the future. His prospects were anything but cheerful, for he had not more than fifty pounds in his possession, and when that was gone he would be compelled to exercise his wits to the utmost extent to procure more. What a terrible blow had been given to his avaricious and guilty designs, and that too at the very moment when all his wishes were on the eve of being consummated. It was not the loss of Constance he so much regretted, but the splendid fortune his marriage with her would have brought him, and which he considered would fully have enabled him to avoid the penalty of those crimes he had committed.

"But 'psha!" he ejaculated; "of what use is it indulging in idle regret? I will boldly struggle with untoward destiny to the last. What if fortune frowns to-day, to-morrow she may wear again her brightest smiles."

And thus consoling himself, and calming the agitation of his feelings, Oliver Dalton once more proceeded on his way.

At that early hour all was lonely and deserted, and Oliver having now got to a considerable distance from the Hall, felt very little fear of being overtaken However, he thought it advisable not much to abate his speed, and to continue his course by the most unfrequented route, and he had no doubt that he should be able to reach London soon after daylight. Having traversed the fields, he struck into a bye-road beyond, which he knew led to Greenwich, which he was anxious to pass through as quickly as possible, for the Queen and the Court having been staying there for a few days, the town was full of people, amongst some of whom he might happen to be recognized. A very few minutes more brought him on to Blackheath, which at that early hour of the morning looked indeed dreary and cheerless, and was but little calculated to raise the spirits of the fugitive. He crossed it as quickly as possible, and, after traversing the park by an intricate path entered Greenwich. Early as it was, many of the inhabitants were already stirring, but he avoided them as much as possible, and those whom he did encounter took but little notice of him, so that he proceeded with more confidence, and getting beyond the town, hurried on his way to London.

The road he was now pursuing was dreary in the extreem, especially in the shadowy obscurity that still enshrouded the atmosphere; but it was perfectly in accordance with his feelings; and, buried in the gloomy and torturing thoughts that the sudden change in his circumstances and prospects naturally gave rise to, he travelled on, though not with the rapidity as he had done before, as he flattered himself that for the present, at any rate, he had got beyond the reach of danger. The reflections that occupied his mind, as may be expected, were not of the most agreeable nature; and it was in vain that he endeavoured to calm his feelings, and to resign himself to the adverse fate which had so suddenly and unexpectedly overtaken him. At the very moment when his triumph had appeared certain, all his nefarious designs had been defeated; all his golden and ambitious visions banished, and he found himself hurled, as it were, from the very pinnacle of wealth and aggrandizement, to his original nothingness, and driven forth as a branded outcast upon the world. And, to Sampson Brayling he was indebted for all this; he it was who held his hands; and he now, for the first time, saw the impolicy with which he had acted, in not having rather sought to conciliate his friendship and assistance, which he probably might have done by timely sacrifices to his demands, instead of the course he had adopted, and by which he had made him his most powerful and implacable enemy. Still in the midst of his present difficulties and disappointment, Oliver muttered the most deadly feelings of revenge against the Gipsey-chief, and which he was sanguine enough to anticipate he should yet have an opportunity to accomplish. He was fully convinced that Brayling was thoroughly acquainted with all the

secrets of his origin, he having had the sole care of him from the earliest days of childhood; and there was a certain ambiguity in the observations he had at different times made, and what had escaped him in the chapel at Charlton, especially in alluding to the Miser, Jasper Scrimpe, which created strange doubts and surmises in his breast. He would have given anything to become acquainted with the contents of that mysterous confession which the Gipsey had produced, but the whole of which he had been so cautious not to produce, And what had become of that old man? did he still exist? and, if so, where could he be at present concealed; and who was the mysterious stranger that had rescued him from the flames on the night of the fearful conflagration of his wretched dwelling? These were the various subjects that engrossed the thoughts of the guilty Oliver Dalton as he continued his flight; and he in vain tried to form any reasonable or satis-factory conjecture upon them. And many and torturing were the ideas that haunted his mind as to the probable result of the wound he had accidentally

No. 30.

inflicted on Sir Milford Welborn; he shuddered at the thought of its proving fatal to one to whom he realy felt no animosity, but deeply regretted that Sampson Brayling had so providentially escaped the fate which had been intended for him.

He had just arrived at this point in his gloomy ruminations, when, looking up, he perceived a lonely, old-fashioned road-side inn; and seeing that the inmates were already stirring, and thinking that there was no cause to apprehend any danger, he determined to venture into the house in order to procure some refreshment, and obtain a little rest, of which he stood so much in need.   Entering the house, he met the landlord, an old man of about the same rotundity of one of his own butts, with a rubicund visage that seemed to indicate his love of something stronger than water, and even at that early hour of the morning he was evidently in a stupid state of intoxication, and, gazing vacantly at Oliver, began to hiccup his apologies, apparently in the confusion of his ideas that he had detained his visitor.

"I am extre—re—emly sorry, your 'honour," he stammered, "that I have kept you waiting, but what can I do? I have a swarm of idle dogs about the house, who never think of attending to the customers, but snore half their time away. A pla—la—plague upon 'em, I'm never to be at peace. I did think when I buried my wife (I hope she enjoys the rest she denied me), that there was a probability of my enjoying a little quiet, but—"

"Psha!" interrupted Oliver, enough of this nonsense; shew me into a private room for the short time I have to stop here, and let me have refreshments."

"In a minute, your honour," faltered the worthy host, "this way, if you please." And, staggering as he went, he ushered Dalton into a dirty, dark room, at the back of the house.

"Here you are, your honour," said the landlord, "as snug as bottles in sawdust. I warrant me, you will not meet with such ac—ac—accommodation every day as you will at my hostelrie. And now if you will take a little sober advice, you will have a delicate breakfast of cold beef, a glass of wine that cannot be equalled in the queen's cellar, and—"

"As to sober advice," interrupted Oliver, unable to repress a smile, notwithstanding the state of his mind, "I shall have no objection to it, if you have any one at hand to give it. But *you* give sober advice, why you're drunk now, man."

"Come, I like that," said the landlord, "I'm a perfect pattern of sobri—ri—riety, and I'll defy the oldest acquaintance I have in the world to say he ever saw me otherwise than I am at present."

"I believe you;" observed Oliver; "and should any one contradict the assertion, that garnet-studded nose and ruby cheek of thine will give them the lie. But quick, give me the best your house affords."

"I will attend to you directly, Sir;" replied the landlord; "something nice and delicate, though, from your martial air, I presume your honour's a soldier."

Oliver caught at the idea, and replied in the affirmative. "But," he added, what has my being a soldier to do with the refreshments?"

"Why," answered the host; "they tell me you soldiers have the stoutest stomachs of any under the sun."

"And, I trust," returned Oliver, anxious to maintain the character he had assumed; "they will never have cause to say otherwise. We have had some strong dishes prepared for us by our foes, but they have never turned our stomachs, nor will we turn our backs upon them."

"That's just what I say to my friend here;" said the landlord, taking out his flask and drinking; "you have never turned my stomach, and I'll be hanged if ever I turn my back upon you."

Thus saying, he reeled out of the room, and presently re-entered with the refreshments his guest had ordered.

"So," said Oliver, when he was left alone, "this mistake of the landlord's affords me a good suggestion that, with a little addition to my personal appearance, might serve to lull suspicion in a case of emergency, I must think of it."

As Oliver had expected, the refreshments were rascally bad; he therefore partook but sparingly of them, and being most anxious to be on the road again, so that he might reach London before the bustle of the day commenced, he arose from his seat, and prepared to take his departure, when, just as he had approached the room door for that purpose, he was startled by hearing the clattering of horses' hoofs outside, and soon after a bustle in the house; and the buzz of several voices announced the arrival of more travellers at the inn. Oliver felt uneasy, for his ready fears caused him to suspect pursuit, and he wished himself far away from the house, regretting that he had ever entered it, particularly as the landlord was in that state of intoxication that he might not be very cautious or particular what he said. He waited anxiously for an opportunity to present itself when he might leave the house unobserved; and while he did so, to his increased alarm and confusion, he heard the landlord usher his guests into an apartment immediately adjoining that in which he was; but his fears were increased, and his suspicions more strongly confirmed, when he distinctly heard the name of Sir Milford mentioned by one of the new comers, and the tones of whose voice appeared to be familiar to him. The rooms were only separated by a thin partition, and Oliver listened with breathless curiosity and attention to their conversation, so that he might be better able to decide in what way it would be most advisable for him to act at such a critical juncture.

"Bless my soul," he heard the landlord observe, and who appeared to have suddenly become more sober, "bless my soul, how you surprise me! Poor Sir Milford, I knew him well, for I was once in his service, and a more amiable or worthy gentleman never existed. Shot, did you say? Dear me! and is he dead?"

"No," answered the man whom Oliver had before heard speak, "and I trust that the wound he has received is not a serious one, no thanks to the scoundrel who fired the pistol."

"And whom do you say was the author of this most monstrous outrage?" enquired the landlord.

Why," returned the other; "the fellow who called himself Oliver Dalton, and who was at the altar, about to be married to Constance Welborn, when the Gipsey, Brayling, and his comrades, suddenly burst into the chapel, and denounced him. In the confusion, Oliver managed to escape from Milford Hall; but if we continue vigilant, I do not think he can very well elude our pursuit."

The observations that followed were conducted in lower tones, and were indistinct to Oliver; but, in a minute or two the following words in the voice of the landlord met his ears.

"Tall, did you say, and rather good looking?"

"Yes;" was the answer; "but with rather a suspicious and sinister expression of the eyes."

"Ah!" said the worthy host; "my new ostler, Toby, whom I took into my service the other day, and who had been staying for a little time at the house of Sir Milford, in London, after the disappearance of his old master, would know him in an instant, for he has seen him on dozens of occasions, and has good cause to remember him well."

"Confusion!" muttered Dalton, to himself, "the Miser's man, Toby Taper, here! By all that is unfortunate I have accidently entered a very hornet's nest!"

"With a military air, say you?" he now heard the landlord enquire, "with a black velvet hat and feathers, blue doublet, trunk-hose, russet boots, and scarlet mantle?"

"Exactly," replied the man; "marry, and had this same young scoundrel, Oliver Dalton, sat to thee for his portrait, thou couldst not have depictured him more accurately. Have you seen any one answering that description near your house this morning?"

"Not only near my house," answered the loquacious host, "but *in* my house at the present time."

"Ah! is it possible? But where?"

"In the next room."

"Perdition seize thee, babbling old idiot," ejaculated the enraged and terrified Oliver, "he has betrayed me; and another moment's delay will place me in the hands of my enemies. How shall I escape? Ah! that door! I hear them approaching; let me be quick!"

The door he perceived by a window on the same side of the room opened into a yard at the back of the premises, and with the quickness of thought he unfastened it, and closing it hastily after him, perceiving no one to obstruct him, bounded across the yard, taking the side that was overshadowed by some tall trees; and, although he did not stop to look back, he could hear the voices of the persons in pursuit of him.

There was a pair of open doors that had fallen off their hinges in that part of the wall which he reached, and by that means he rushed into the open fields, and was proceeding hastily towards a stack of hay which was close by, when, to his consternation, he beheld the light of a lantern moving towards him, and, before he had time to avoid it, he came full butt upon Toby Taper, in a rather grotesque and outrageous ostler's dress, and who, recognising him in an instant, sunk terrified on his knees, shouting at the very top of his voice, "murder! thieves! fire! an apparition!"

CHAPTER XXXIX.

OLD WESTMINSTER.—OLIVER'S RETREAT.—ANOTHER JOURNEY.—THE HIGH-WAYMAN.—AN UNEXPECTED RECOGNITION AND THE CONSEQUENCES.

SILENCE, knave!" hurriedly exclaimed Oliver, at the same time presenting a pistol at the terrified Toby's head; "mislead my pursuers, or dread my vengeance!"

"Oh, ye—ye—yes, good Master Oliver;" stammered out the trembling Toby; "I will do anything to oblige you, only—"

Dalton waited not to hear more; the sound of his pursuers approached nearer, and extinguishing the light in Toby's lantern with his foot, the better to conceal his person from observation, he made for the stack, were, crouching down, he found the ready means of concealment. He had not been there a second, when his pursuers approached so near that he could plainly distinguish what they said. He heard Toby solemnly declare that he had taken the path to the left, and having seen them hurry in that direction, he rapidly made his way to a dark lane on the right, where, pausing to recover himself from the agitation and excitement into which this adventure had thrown him, he congratulated himself on his narrow and fortunate escape from the clutches of those whom he so much dreaded. He now resumed his journey with increased speed, and in less than another hour and a half he found himself in London, and without meeting with anything more to alarm him. It was now broad daylight, and the busy traffic of the Metropolis had commenced with its usual activity.

Oliver moved quickly on, shunning observation as much as he could, fearing that the news of the outrage at Milford Hall might already have reached London. He carefully avoided all those localities where he was likely to be known and recognized, though, for a time, he was undecided in which way to direct his steps; but at last the thought occurred to him, that some of the low parts of Westminster were likely to afford him every means of concealment, and thither he therefore resolved to direct his progress.

Very different was the aspect of the ancient city of Westminster in those days, to what the memory of "the oldest inhabitant" can recollect it in more modern times. True, the fine old Abbey was there the same as now in its solemn magnificence; but Thorney Island, (the original name of the spot on which it stands), was a wild, marshy place, dangerous to the traveller after nightfall, and presenting but few attractions in the light of day. There were some stately edifices in the vicinity of the Abbey, and the old Palace of Westminster, and immediately adjoining them were miserable streets and alleys of the lowest and filthiest description, the resort of the very off-scourings and refuse of society, and where every species of vice was practised. The Almonry, (corrupted into the "Hamburg,") Tothill Street, and the other rookeries in its boundaries, were infested by the most depraved characters, and who bid open defiance to the law, and remained almost wholly unmolested. What in more modern times was known by the name of York Street, and where the immortal Milton resided, was a quiet, retired spot enough, occupied by quaint, old-fashioned dwellings, and here and there a goodly mansion, occupied by some person of distinction, and imparting something like an air of importance to the immediate locality.

Such was the appearance of Westminster on the morning that Oliver Dalton entered it, and he gazed around him upon its ruined, dirty dwellings, and still more unprepossessing looking inhabitants, with anything but the most pleasurable feelings. Crossing the horse-ferry, he entered upon the open space, now known as Strutton Ground, and here pausing to consider what it would be best for him to do next, he bethought him that his present gay and rich apparel might excite the suspicion and rather too troublesome curiosity of the individuals it would be necessary or prudent for him to associate with at present, and he therefore resolved to endeavour to find out a place where he might exchange it for a more humble and appropriate suit, though he was well aware that in doing so he should be compelled to make a considerable sacrifice. He was not long in finding the place he required, and shortly found himself so completely metamorphosed, that he thought it would be impossible for even those who were most intimately acquainted with him to recognise him. Feeling himself now more secure, he walked on, till after making his way through several bye-ways and courts and alleys, he found himself standing in an ancient-looking tavern in Tothill Street.

The "Cock" Tavern (only recently pulled down, and one of the oldest hostelries in Westminster), was a staunch, goodly-looking building, albeit the persons who frequented it were none of the most respectable order, and kept their midnight orgies with a total disregard to the decorum or the nightly watch. It was, in fact, the resort of all the lowest and most abandoned characters for miles around; and any respectable individual must have been mad, or ignorant of the real character of the house, to have ventured to enter it. It was before this tavern that Oliver Dalton was now standing, and which, even at that early period of the day, was the scene of noisy revelry and dissipation. Oliver, however, had mingled in every grade of society, and knew too well how to accommodate himself to the habits and propensities of the low and reckless portion af the community to feel himself at all daunted, or to hesitate to venture among them. He therefore boldly entered in the house, and, in a short time found himself, hale fellows well met, with as arrant a set of vagabonds and scoundrels as ever came under the cognizance of the Law. Being liberal with his cash in pandering to the bacchanalian propensities, he quickly ingratiated himself in their favour; and so well did he sustain the character he had assumed, that his companions had not the least suspicion, especially as he invented several tales for their especial amusement, of the different adventures he had met with, and the various deeds of rascality he had performed, in the course of his career. They considered him a worthy companion, a devilish merry fellow, and one after their own hearts. Therefore did they give him a cordial welcome, and he joined them in their boisterous mirth and revelry throughout the whole of that day, and long after the hour of midnight, when he was shewn into a rather clean and comfortable chamber, where he retired to rest.

Oliver Dalton remained at the " Cock," for more than a week, and seldom left the house ; but he was getting tired of this monotonous life, and began to think of the course he should adopt to mend his broken fortunes, for his stock of cash was getting exceedingly low, and it was imperatively necessary that he should make a bold effort to replenish his means· Morever, he could not forget the signal defeat of his guilty designs, and his soul thirsted for revenge upon Sampson Brayling, and which he was determined to accomplish at all hazards.

The fellows who frequented the " Cock " gathered, in the course of their perigrinations, a good deal of the current news of the day which they related to each other when they met ; and, amongst other events, the affairs at Milford Hall did not escape their knowledge, and being an event exactly in keeping with their peculiar tastes, they dicussed it freely at their meetings, and by which means Oliver Dalton was enabled to ascertain such partictlars as he was most anxious to know. It was by this means he learned that the wound Sir Milford had received was not of a serious nature, and that he was so far progressing to recovery, that he had accepted the invitation of Sir Thomas Overton to accompany him, with Constance, to Greenwood Abbey, one of his estates in the County of Hampshire. This suggested an idea to Oliver : there were those in Hampshire with whom he had formly been associated in the most lawless pursuits, and who, he had no doubt, would be right glad to welcome him again amongst them ; besides, he might obtain their assistance in furthering his future plans, and thus still have the means of gratifying his wishes, which, for the present, had received so severe and fatal a check. To Hampshire, therefore, he determined to make his way with all possible speed ; and, having added to the disguise of his person, he bade adieu to his dissolute and abandoned companions, and started on his journey· Nothing particular or worthy of recording occurred to him till he reached the county he had been destined for, and found himself on a dark and tempestuous night lost and bewildered in the wild mazes of an almost impenetrable wood, and, at a perfect loss as to which way he should turn in order to extricate himself from it. The farther he proceeded, the more did he become involved in the intricacies of the gloomy place ; and he was about to give up the task in despair, and to make up his mind to remain where he was till the morning, when he was startled by the sudden appearance of a man, enveloped in a dark cloak, from behind a cluster of trees, and who, standing before him in a menacing attitude, seemed inclined to dispute his path. Oliver drew himself back a few paces, and evincing no signs of fear, in a stern voice demanded—

" How now, fellow ; who art thou who thus abruptly cross my path ; and what seek'st thou ?"

" Simply," coolly replied the ruffian, " a ransom which all must pay, when I have the good fortune to encounter, in a convenient spot, thy money, and I must have it without any hesitation.

" Humph!" returned Oliver, with a smile of contempt; " mighty candid, truly; nevertheless, as I am not overburthened with a superfluity of cash, I do not think proper to comply with thy demand. Stand aside, fellow, and, if thou wouldst preserve a whole skin, suffer me to pass on my way without any further hesitation."

" No trifling," said the fellow, producing a pistol from under his cloak ; " thou see'st that I carry with me the most forcible argument in my favour."

"What!" exclaimed Oliver, drawing his sword, and smacking the pistol aside, which exploded in the air; "dog rob dog!—Nay, then, we must e'en have a struggle for it. Look to thyself, daring ruffian!"

With these words he rushed upon the highwayman, who, however, proved to be the most skilful swordsman, and, after a brief combat, Oliver was disarmed, and stumbling, he sunk upon one knee, and was thus at the mercy of his desperate adversary.

"Thou hast staked boldly;" said the robber; but thou seest that the chance is mine; and, if thou valuest thy life, thou wilt make the best thou canst of a bad bargain, and yield what money thou hast about thee, without any further scruple."

Oliver gave utterance to a fearful oath, and, seeing that any further resistance would be madness, was about to comply with this demand, when, at that moment, a flash of lightning distinctly revealed the features of the ruffian to him, and, in a voice of astonishment, he exclaimed—

"Ah! is it possible that I thus again encounter my former associate, Rodolph Brandsby?"

The tones of Dalton's voice now, for the first time, seemed to strike the highwayman, and, looking more narrowly in his countenance, he exclaimed—

"Why, if my eyes deceive me not, 'tis Luke Stanton!"

"The same;" returned Oliver; "and 'tis fortunate that we have met, for thou art just the very man I have wanted to see, though, by my troth, thou went near settling the business of thine old friend."

"Why, Luke," observed Rodolph; "how is it I see thee here?—I thought by this time that thou hadst accomplished thy wishes with the fair niece of Sir Milford Welborn, and that thou hadst forgotten thine old friend."

"No," answered Oliver; curses light upon ill fortune, just on the eve of triumph, my designs have been frustrated by our old companion, Sampson Brayling, and I am now compelled to seek to elude the iron grasp of the Law."

"Is it possible?" ejaculated Rodolph.

"It is true;" replied Oliver; "but I have not time to explain farther here. What has become of your comrades?"

"For some time," answered Rodolph, "those who have not attained the most *elevated* position for gentlemen of their profession, and became martyrs to the gallows, have found a most convenient retreat in the deepest recesses of this forest; our depredations have been so numerous, and we have carried on a most prosperous trade so long, that I'm afraid we shall at last be compelled to shift our quarters to avoid a calamity of a more painful description. But, follow me, and I will introduce thee to them, and I know they will be glad to welcome thee once more amongst them."

Oliver obeyed; exulting in the lucky accident which had led him to encounter the ruffian, Rodolph; and after, with difficulty, forcing their way through the thickest part of the wood, and which was almost impassable, he stopped before an eminence, the base of which was thickly surrounded with brushwood. Walking to a particular spot, Rodolph stooped down, and blew a shrill whistle; which, to the astonishment of Oliver, was answered by another, which seemed to come from the very bowels of the earth. In a moment or two afterwards, some heavy substance was removed from close to where they stood the brushwood was forced away, a glimmering light appeared, and Oliver Dalton was surprised to behold a large opening in the side of the hillock, and the distinct form of a man partly protruding from it.

"Who's there?" demanded the gruff voice of the man.

"All's right;" replied Oliver's companion, "'tis I, your comrade, Rodolph."

The man held up the lamp he carried, and discovering Dalton, ejaculated—

"Ah! thou art not alone; who hast thou with thee?"

"A friend !" returned Rodolph ; "thou needest not hesitate."

The ruffian growled some observation between his teeth, and motioning Rodolph to follow, disappeared below. Brandsby immediately took the hand of Oliver, and leading him into the opening, conducted him down some rude steps, formed out of some earth and small stumps of trees. The entrance widened as they proceeded, and they at length alighted in a long subterranean passage, and followed the footsteps of the ruffian with the light. As they advanced along this passage, which extended far underground, Oliver could hear the voices of several men, and a broad glare of light suddenly burst upon his eyes. The next moment he and his companions stopped at the entrance to a spacious cavern, in which, round a large table, were seated a number of ferocious-looking men, armed to the teeth, and in many of whom Oliver recognised those desperate and lawless men with whom he had at one time been connected. On seeing a stranger, they arose hastily from their seats and rushed towards him ; but quickly recognising his features, they hailed him with boisterous shouts of welcome. Oliver entered the cavern, and the next moment found himself seated in the midst of those whom he wished to see.

CHAPTER XL.

Oliver Dalton in the Robbers' Cave.—The Warning on the Moor.— The Madness of Jasper Scrimpe.

Oliver Dalton could not but consider himself particularly fortunate in meeting so opportunely with those lawless individuals with whom he had formerly been associated, in his present emergency ; and on their part they were disposed to recover one whom they knew to possess that determined, reckless disposition that was so well adapted to their predatory course of life, with every welcome. He recounted to them all the extraordinary adventures he had experienced since they had last met, and they listened to him with much attention and lively interest, and highly applauded the skill and ingenuity with which he had for so long a time contrived to deceive and dupe Sir Milford Welborn, at the same time strongly deprecating the conduct of Sampson Brayling, which had been the means of so completely frustrating all his deep laid schemes at the very moment when their final success seemed so certain.

"Aye, curses light upon his officious zeal in the cause of Evelyn Heartwell, and the fair Constance Welborn," exclaimed Oliver, bitterly, "but for that, my triumph would have been complete, and the ambitious hopes I so boldly encouraged have been realized."

"Sampson Brayling is a dangerous enemy to have to contend with," observed the captain of the desperate horde of ruffians, who had for years spread terror through that part of the country they infested, and set the law at defiance, "and it was an unfortunate thing for you, Luke, that he should again have crossed your path, and that too, at the very time when you had the least cause to wish to renew the acquaintance."

"True," coincided Oliver, "but the time may yet come when I shall have the opportnnity of gratifying my feelings of revenge against him, and I will not rest until I have obtained it. Know you, Reginald, whether it is true that Sir Milford and his niece have accompanied Sir Thomas Overton to the seat of the latter in this neighbourhood ?"

"Yes," replied Reginald, "they arrived but the day before yesterday ; and with an eye to business·(for we have for some time contemplated a midnight visit to the Abbey), we were soon enabled to ascertain that fact. There may be

some booty to be obtained there worth the seeking, and now that you have so fortunately encountered us, Luke, I dare say you will have no objection to join us in the undertaking."

"Your hand, Reginald;" said Oliver, eagerly; "your suggestion has reanimated my hopes, and I am fully prepared for anything that is likely to lead to their accomplishment. The gipsey Luke may triumph yet, and the proud scornful beauty, Constance Welborn, still have cause to tremble at his power. I am all impatience for the execution of this plot; say, when do you propose making the attempt."

"Hold, hold, Luke;" returned Reginald; " we must not be rash or precipitate in this business, if we would make success certain. In a day or two we shall probably be enabled to mature our plans, when we will talk further upon the subject. But come, we are glad of your appearance amongst us, let us then devote an hour or two to that freedom of enjoyment with which these subterranean haunts ever

No. 31.

abounds   Here, in the depths of these forest wilds, we daring bandits have a kingdom of our own, which none have yet been bold enough to venture to invade; so now, comrades, for mirth and revelry !"

With the loudest acclamations of approval the robbers assented to this proposition, and the table was soon again loaded with a most ample supply of every description of refreshments, and ribald jests, loud laughter, and rude songs, in which Oliver Dalton freely joined, made the spacious caverns resound again.   This scene continued for more than a couple of hours, when the ruffians gradually became exhausted by their noisy and tumultuous revels, and Oliver expressing a wish to retire, was shewn into an inner cell, or smaller cavern, in which was a rude bed, and where, being supplied with a lamp, he was left to himself. So remarkable was the change in his situation, that it surprised and bewildered him, and for some time he gave himself up to the busy thoughts that crowded upon his imagination.   He could not but feel gratified, however, at meeting with his former comrades, for he anticipated every assistance from them in his future designs·   His soul thirsted for revenge ; and that revenge he determined yet to accomplish, even at every risk.   He was resolved, if possible, still to get Constance in his power ; and yet, now denounced to the world in his true character, were not his principal designs completely frustrated, and that fortune which had been so nearly within his grasp, was effectually wrested from him·   Again and again did he invoke the most bitter curses on the head of Brayling, who had been the cause of all this, and it was a considerable time before he could at all calm the tempest of angry feelings that raged within his guilty breast.

In this manner Oliver Dalton passed away three days in the robber's cavern, without much progressing in the advancement of his nefarious wishes. 'Tis true, they had nightly watched about the Abbey, which was situated on the borders of the forest in the hopes of being able to obtain some information in furtherance of their lawless designs, and, on two of those occasions, Oliver had accompanied them, but they had hitherto succeeded in obtaining but little information, and Oliver every hour became the more impatient, and began to despair of success. Sir Milford, they learnt, was restored to convalescence, but Constance kept herself entirely secluded in the Abbey, on no account venturing abroad, as though she apprehended some secret danger, and was determined to avoid it by every means in her power.   But little could she imagine that her dreaded enemy was so close at hand.

On one of these occasions, Oliver had accidentally missed his companions, and was endeavouring to find his way to the cavern alone.   The night was dark and tempestuous ; the moon at intervals, 'tis true, emerged for an instant from behind the black clouds that enshrouded the sky, but it was only to cast a sickly and uncertain light upon the cheerless scene, just rendering " darkness visible," and, taking a wrong path, after wandering for some time, Oliver Dalton found himself upon the wild moor, which has been before described, and on which were erected the gibbets of the three murderers who had some time before paid the penalty of their atrocious crimes on that dreary spot.   The gibbets grated harshly in the wind, and Oliver, starting as the mouldering bones of the culprits for the first time met his gaze, shuddered with an indiscribable feeling of horror at the frightful sight, and as his eyes fell upon the inscription on the stone beneath.

"Ah !" he exclaimed, " and such is inevitably the murderer's doom ; such the terrible fate that is too probably in store for me.   What accursed accident has guided my footsteps to this accursed spot ?"

Covering his face with his hands, to shut out the ghastly objects from his appalled vision, he endeavoured to move from the place, when a hollow gust of wind swept around, which having died away in a dismal, moaning sound, the moon again for an instant shewed its pale face, and, by its faint beams he imagined he beheld a shadowy form moving about near the gibbets, and he placed his hand on his sword, to be prepared for any danger that might threaten in so appropriate and lonely a place. He strained his eyes to endeavour to ascertain what it could be, and again he was certain that there was some mysterious object moving near him, and he advanced a few paces towards it, but again the darkness hid it from his view.

"Who goes there?" he demanded, in a stern voice, "speak!"

A strange guttural sound was the only answer he received, and his patience completely exhausted, he drew his sword and darted forward, but started back astonished and somewhat alarmed when he beheld a human form, kneeling beneath the gibbet, and apparently engaged in prayer. The noise he had made aroused it, and starting to its feet, it stood erect before him, and gazed earnestly upon him. As well as the faint light would permit him to distinguish, he perceived that it was the form of an aged woman of singularly repulsive and emaciated features, and whose whole appearance was haggard and wretched in the extreme, while the expression of her eyes was wild and restless. Oliver was much struck by the remarkable character of this miserable being, while she remained fixed in the same attitude, pointing significantly to the blackened and frightful remains that swung dismally in the night wind above her.

"What nocturnal wanderer art thou," at length she said, in a querulous, harsh, and discordant voice, "that thus comest in darkness and silence to this fearful spot? Comest thou to exult o'er these ghastly forms, or art thou some man of crime who in the hideous objects before thee, contemplate the certain fate that awaits thee? Ah! I see the villain stamped upon thy brow; I read the guilty thoughts that hold their empire in thy breast, and even now, beneath the murderer's doom, do I warn thee of the dreadful doom that is impending o'er thee. The measure of thy crimes is nearly full; thy guilty race will soon be run. Heaven's just retribution will no longer be retarded. The fearful day of reckoning is at hand; beware! beware!" She moved quickly from the spot as she uttered the last words, and vanished from the sight of Oliver in a mysterious and unaccountable manner; leaving him petrified to the spot in amazement and terror.

"Can I believe my senses?" he ejaculated, gazing earnestly and anxiously in the direction whence the singular being had disappeared; "or is this only some fearful delusion conjured up by my disordered imagination to mock my inward terrors? Bah! shall I suffer myself thus to become the weak victim of idle superstition? shall I, after all my acts of daring, now allow myself to be intimidated from my purpose by some base imposture, or half crazy woman?—Oliver Dalton, art thou still a man?"

Casting one more timid glance up at the gibbets, he was about to move from the spot, when the sounds of several approaching footsteps saluted his ears, and he beheld human forms at a short distance moving towards him. Fearful of danger, he was about to retire stealthily, when it seemed that, by the dim light of the moon, he was observed, and his fears were removed when the voice of Reginald demanded—

"Who goes there? speak!"

"'Tis I, your friend," replied Oliver, and Reginald and two or three of the other robbers immediately afterwards joined him.

"Why, Luke," said Reginald; "how comest thou to stray from us, and to wander to this not very agreeable spot? But eh, why, man, thou art pale, and thine whole demeanour is agitated. Has the sight of these grim remains alarmed thee?"

Oliver briefly explained.

"Ha! ha! ha!" laughed Reginald;

"Oh, thou must not suffer this little adventure, singular enough though it is, to alarm thee. The woman thou sawest is old Maud, the mother of two of the poor fellows thou seest before thee, their comrades, she formerly resided with us in the cavern, but since the death of her amiable offspring, she has chosen to lead a wandering life, frequently visiting this spot, and uttering her wild plaints and lamentations in the midnight air."

" She spoke words that I own were anything but pleasant to my ears ; " observed Oliver.

" Psha ! " returned Reginald ; " thou shouldst heed them not, for grief hath turned the old woman's brain, and she knows not what she says. But come 'tis not prudent to tarry here. Let us to the cavern."

Oliver offered no observation, and they were about to move from the spot, when they were startled by a low moaning cry, which seemed to proceed from some person in pain close by ; surprised, they moved towards the part from whence it issued, and beheld, stretched face downwards on the earth, the form of a man, who seemed to be either dead or in a state of insensibility.

" Ah ! who have we here ? " said Reginald, stooping down, and examining the person of the man ; " to judge from his miserable garb, he is some poor wretch who has sunk exhausted on the road from fatigue and hunger."

He turned him over on his back as he spoke, and a canvass bag fell from his bosom, the contents of which jingled on the earth.

" Ah ! " cried Reginald, examining the bag, " gold ! by my troth, no unwelcome sight, and one too, which proves that we must not always judge from appearances. He still breathes, but as that is all, perhaps it would be a charity to end his sufferings, before he can return to consciousness."

" Hold ! " exclaimed Oliver Dalton, rushing hastily forward, and arresting the miscreant's arm as he was about to plunge his poinard into the helpless stranger's bosom, " thou wouldst not surely thus recklessly commit murder !"

The moon at that moment reflected strongly on the spot, and plainly revealed the pale features of the prostrate man. Oliver Dalton started back with an exclamation of astonishment and powerful emotion, as if his eyes had encountered some ghastly spectre.

" How now ? " demanded the robber hastily, " what agitates thee thus ? "

" Forbear thy rash hand," answered Oliver, " by all my hopes 'tis he whom I had never expected to behold again—'tis the Miser, Jasper Scrimpe ! "

" Ah ! sayest thou so ? " ejaculated Reginald, " then it may be prudent to spare his life. Away with him to the cavern, this adventure may be of service to us."

The robbers raised the insensible old man from the ground, bore him from the spot, and soon arrived at the cavern, where having strictly examined his clothes, and secured all the money they could find upon his person, they left him to himself.

The reader has already been informed of what happened to the wretched Jasper Scrimpe after the ghastly objects he had beheld in the cemetery of the robbers' cavern. Such an accumulation of horrible events that for some time past so rapidly followed each other, were too much for human nature to support, and no wonder that the long tottering brain of the miserable old man at length yielded to them. When Oliver and the captain of the robbers visited him on the following day, they found him on his knees, with clenched hands and with bloodshot eyes, glaring wildly and vacantly around him. Oliver advanced towards him, but no sooner did Jasper behold him, than he sprang to his feet with a loud yell that resembled nothing human, and in a hoarse voice that made the cavern resound, he exclaimed :

" Off !—off !—foul fiend—there is blood upon thine hands, there is murder in thy looks.—Avaunt, I say,—thy features freeze the purple current of my veins, and add to the tortures of perdition that already rack my guilty soul.—Extinguish those unearthly fires that scorch my brain !—Release me from those galling fetters that bind my limbs !—Off !—off !—thou shalt not bear me to the scaffold !—Oh, save me !—save me from an eternity of horror !—Wretches, they made my sufferings !—Who dare accuse me of murder?—Who dare say that my wealth of which they have plundered me, was purchased by the blood of my dearest kindred ?—'Tis they are mad, not I !—See !—see! —Let them not approach!—Oh, mercy !—mercy !—"

With a wild hysterical laugh, the Miser once more sank upon his knees, and it was evident that the light of reason had left his intellects for ever.

" Poor wretch," said Reginald, " the power of conscience has proved too much for him at last ; would it not have been better to have silenced him for ever, at the moment I suggested."

" No, no, no ;" replied Oliver, with a shudder ; " my soul, hardened and insensible though it is, revolts at the idea of taking his life. It seems to my imagination that he is connected with me in some mysterious manner which I cannot penetrate."

" Psha ! " exclaimed the ruffian ; " this is sheer folly ; what then wouldst thou that we should do with him?"

" For the present, at any rate, let him remain here. His custody may be of every value to us, " replied Oliver. Reginald reluctantly complied, and the Miser staring idiotically around, passively suffered himself to be conducted into a place of security where he was left to himself.

CHAPTER XLI.

CONSTANCE WELBORN AND HER UNCLE.—THE BENIGHTED TRAVELLER.—THE
SURPRISE.—THE STARTLING DISCOVERY.

THE reader will now doubtless be anxious to hear further particulars of the situation of Constance and her friends, and what had happened to them during the period of the occurrences that have been related in the preceding chapters. The excitement caused by the startling events that had taken place at Milford Hall had very little abated, and every exertion was made to discover the retreat of Oliver Dalton, but without success, all traces of him being completely lost after he had so narrowly escaped from the persons sent in pursuit of him, from the old tavern on the London road. All doubts as to the suspicious guest of the drunken host being the man of whom they were in pursuit were removed by poor Toby Taper, who, when he had recovered from his fright, and knew that he was out of the reach of Oliver's pistol, having acknowledged the truth, and his pursuers were greatly vexed and disappointed to think that he should have been so nearly in their power, and yet contrive to affect his escape.

Thus several days passed away, and although Sampson Brayling and his companions, as well as the officers, were most indefatigable, they still failed to discover any clue to him. Sir Milford Welborn, under the unremitting attention of Constance and her friends, progressed much more rapidly to recovery than could have been expected ; but his mind was in a most agitated and excited state, and it required all the exertions of our heroine to console him. To find that he had been so cruelly, so villainously deceived by Oliver Dalton, the man whom he had thought to be the very paragon of honour and integrity, was painful and humiliating enough ; but when he reflected on the injustice he had done the unfortunate Evelyn Heartwell, and sufferings he had inflicted on the gentle Constance, whom he had been so near consigning to an awful and revolting fate, he most bitterly reproached himself, and could not but consider that he had been much to blame ; still he was inclined to believe that Sampson Brayling, notwithstanding the great service he hand rendered them, had acted in a most imprudent and extraordinary manner in delaying to denounce Oliver Dalton, and making Evelyn's innocence manifest before ; and even now he declined to reveal any further particulars for the present, although he asserted that he alone was acquainted with such facts connected with Oliver and Evelyn as would astonish all who heard them. He did not doubt the sincerity of Braylings motives for hesitating to disclose the secret till a future time; still his conduct astonished him, and involved him in the most perplexing mystery and anxiety.

Thus matters stood when Sir Thomas Overton, thinking that the change of air might serve to recruit Sir Milford's strength, invited him and his neice to accompany him and his daughters, on their intended visit to Greenwood Abbey, which it is needless to state, they gladly accepted; and, travelling by easy stages, they arrived in a few days at the place of their destination. The secluded situation, and solemn grandeur of this venerable edifice, was in perfect harmony with their present state of feelings, and they hoped there to be able in some measure to require that tranquillity which the painful and exciting events of the last two or three years had so greatly disturbed. The hours which were not passed by Constance in the society of her uncle and their friends were occupied in her own apartments, where many were the torturing days she passed in brooding upon the probable fate of Evelyn, lamenting the unparalleled misfortunes that had attended him, and the horrible uncertainty that they would ever meet again. Still her heart was, if possible, more fondly devoted to him than ever, and thoroughly convinced she was that, under any circumstances, no other man could supplant him in her affections.

They had not been many days at the Abbey when Sampson Brayling, who was now looked upon by them as one of their most earnest and valuable friends, visited them, and the expression of his features plainly shewed that he had something of importance to communicate, and Sir Milford and our heroine eagerly inquired into the nature of it.

"I must beseech you to be calm, Miss Constance," said the Gipsey, "for that I have to impart to you is of a nature to pain as well as gratify you."

The heart of Constance palpitated violently, and she fixed an earnest and supplicating look upon Brayling as she ejaculated—

"Oh, for Heavens' sakes, my good friend, do not keep us in suspense; say, does that you have to communicate relate to Evelyn?"

"It does;" replied Sampson; "after much trouble and exertion, I have been fortunate enough to succeed in obtaining some news of him which I think may be depended upon."

"Ah!" exclaimed Sir Milford! "is it possible? oh, say does the unfortunate and much injured youth still live?"

"I have every reason to hope so;" answered Brayling.

"Oh, Almighty God. I thank thee!" cried our heroine, clasping her hands together; "dear, dear Evelyn! But proceed, proceed, I implore you;" she added, with breathless impatience.

The vessel he went on board of," continued Brayling, "and which was called the Ariel, was destroyed by fire, and—"

"Oh, Heaven!" gasped forth Constance, with a look of horror, and sinking back in her seat.

"Be calm, lady, and do not unnecessarily alarm yourself, for I trust that Evelyn and Mabel, whom I have reason to believe had followed him on board the same ship, were preserved from the awful fate which threatened them."

"Speak on! speak on!" anxiously urged Sir Milford.

"A ship which hast just arrived in Port," continued Sampson; "spoke to another vessel far out at sea, but homeward bound, the Invulnerable she is called, and was informed that they had pitched up the Captain and a number of the crew of the Ariel from a desolate island, in a most deplorable condition, and that they were conveying them to England."

Constance clasped her hands together and sank on her knees.

"All merciful Father ! she exclaimed, in a voice half choked by the power of her emotions; "grant that loved being may be preserved from all the fearful dangers to which he has been exposed, and that we may again be restored to each other. But, oh, the terrible doubt and uncertainty that still exists : how it racks and tortures my brain ! "

" Be firm, lady, and trust to Providence ; " said the gipsey-chief; " and I hope that a few days will relieve your anxiety and suspense. At any rate, I will lose no time in making all the necessary inquiry, and it shall be no fault of mine if I do not meet with success."

" Oh, thanks! thanks ! " cried our heroine, gratefully pressing the hand of Sampson Brayling who, after about an hour passed in conversation, took his departure from the Abbey, promising to visit them again as soon as possible.

We need not attempt to describe the various feelings that now agitated the breast of our heroine, and in which her uncle so earnestly and warmly participated. Yet was her mind filled with the most painful doubts and apprehensions, and many were the prayers she offered up to Heaven for the safe return of her lover to his native land; and that the unexampled troubles and vicissitudes they had so long experienced, would at last be brought to a termination. But when several days elapsed, and still they received no intelligence, their anxiety and suspense increased to a degree beyond endurance. But important events were about to take place, and there was something " looming in the future" of the most extraordinary description.

The day had been gloomy, cold, and cheerless. The wild scenery which surrounded the Abbey wore a sombre aspect; and the melancholy nature of the weather imported its dismal influence. The night set in stormy and boisterous, and the wind swept in mournful gusts along the different avenues of the ancient building, adding to the utter misery of the hour. It was a night on which to gather round a blazing fire, and while the heart felt grateful to the Supreme for the comforts of a hospitable home and shelter, to sympathise with those less fortunate beings who friendless, houseless, and destitute, were exposed to all the harsh inclemencies of the season.

Constance and her friends were seated in one of the lower rooms, and for some time their spirits drooped, and the conversation had become dull. The tempest was now at its height, and doors creaked on their hinges and casements rattled in their frames, with the violence of the blast.

"It is indeed a fearful night ;" observed Sir Milford; " may Heaven help all those unfortunate creatures, who, deprived of the means of shelter, are exposed to all the fury of such a storm as this."

Constance shuddered ; she thought of Evelyn, who even at that hour might, on the wild waters of the ocean, be exposed to all the horrors of the tempest, and her heart sunk within her.

The wind now for a moment abated, and a dull silence rested on all around, which was, if possible, still more awful than the fiercest raging of the storm. The friends looked at each other wrapped in awe, and without being able to utter a word. Suddenly they started to their feet, and rushed towards the casement, for a loud cry of agony swept across the grounds in front of the Abbey, and gradually died away in the night air, in a low, dull, murmuring sound. The wind again rose and they could hear no more, for the voice of the tempest drowned all other sounds.

"Some poor creature is suffering in the storm," observed Sir Thomas Overton, compassionately, "perhaps perishing from cold and hunger. Let a search be instantly made. Heaven forbid that we should hesitate to perform such a work of charity."

He immediately summoned two or three of the male domestics, and dispatched them with all speed in the direction from whence the cry had proceeded, ordering them to take lanterns with them in order to accelerate their search. They anxiously awaited the result of this adventure, particularly our heroine, in whose bosom a painful foreboding prevailed, for which she could hardly account. The storm increased in violence, and they began to fear lest the servants should be too late to save the sufferer or sufferers whoever they might be.

"Alas!" said Sir Thomas, "should they have been surprised by any of the robbers that infest the forest and the surrounding country, there can be little doubt of the fate which has befallen them."

Constance and her uncle shuddered at this fearful idea, and they awaited the return of the individuals who had been sent on the search with increased impatience.

In the meantime the servants proceeded across the grounds attached to the Abbey, examining every spot minutely, and calling to any one who might be near, as they went. But no object met their sight, and they stood for a minute or two undecided which direction to take. While they still hesitated, the wind again for a brief interval becoming hushed, they fancied they heard a low moaning sound proceeding from a lane a short distance off, but it was only for an instant, and was hardly sufficient to guide them in which way to go. They, however, entered the lane, and by the light of their lanterns, they at length beheld the form of a man stretched upon the earth, apparently dead. Having raised him, they perceived that he was a young man, dressed in the uniform of a naval officer, and who, from the disordered state of his clothes, had evidently had a desperate struggle with his assailants, whoever they might have been. He was wounded, and still breathing had apparently only fainted from loss of blood. Knowing there was no time to be lost, they raised the stranger in their arms, and carried him with all the speed they could towards the Abbey. The anxiety of Constance and her companions had increased from the time they had been gone, and when they beheld, by the light of the lanterns, that they were advancing across the lawn, and carrying a human form, they eagerly made their way into the hall, and gazed with the deepest feelings of interest and compassion on the features of the wounded stranger; while Constance, noticing the naval dress of the young man, felt a strange sensation at her heart which she hardly knew how to express. He was immediately taken into the room they had just quitted, and being placed upon a sofa, a servant was despatched with all speed for the nearest surgeon, while they endeavoured, as well as they could, to staunch the wound.

"Poor fellow;" said Sir Thomas; "it is as I suspected; he has been benighted in the forest, and waylaid by the robbers. I fear he is badly wounded, and it is indeed a miracle that he at all escaped with life from such inhuman ruffians."

"See, he breathes more freely;" cried Constance, eagerly; "Heaven grant that he may not be so badly hurt as we imagine. Ah! he revives."

They moistened his lips with a cordial that one of the servants had procured, and a minute afterwards he heaved a sigh and, opening his eyes, gazed with confused astonishment at the persons around him.

"Where am I?" he said, in a faint voice; "whither has fate guided the footsteps of Walter Greysham?"

"You are with friends who will see to your welfare;" replied Sir Thomas.

"Oh, where are the ruffians, who so sadly maltreated me?" interrogated Walter Greysham, for he indeed it was; "and who are those that now surround me?"

"If it will afford you any satisfaction to know," answered the Baronet; "you are now at Greenwood Abbey, and in the presence of Sir Thomas Overton, Sir Milford Welborn, and his neice."

"Gracious Heaven!" exclaimed Walter, making an effort to raise himself,

and to gaze more narrowly upon them ; "those names! can it be possible ? and I alone ! Oh, God ! what has become of those dear companions of my journey, whom I lost in the mazes of the forest ? "

"Speak, stranger, for the love of Heaven ! " exclaimed our heroine, as a sudden and fearful presentiment darted across her brain ; "whom—whom do you mean ?"

" The unfortunate Evelyn Heartwell, and that fond, devoted being, Mabel the Gipsey girl! " replied Walter Greysham ; and unable to speak another word, and exhausted with the exertion he had already undergone, he fell on the sofa. Constance uttered a frantic shriek of anguish and despair, and sunk in the arms of her uncle, who completely paralyzed by what he had just heard, was scarcely in a better condition than herself. The surgeon now arrived, and Constance was conveyed to her chamber, and attended by Abigail and the daughters of Sir Thomas Overton. The surgeon immediately advised the removal of Walter

No. 32.

Greysham to a bed, so that he might examine the nature of his wound, and Sir Thomas and Sir Milford were for a few minutes left to themselves.

"Gracious Heaven!" cried Sir Milford, "what an extraordinary and unexpected circumstance is this. I fear the shock will be too much for Constance. But the unfortunate Evelyn and Mabel, wandering in the intricate depths of the forest, should they encounter the robbers, I fear the fate which would befall them is certain."

"It may not yet be too late to discover and to save them;" observed Sir Thomas.

"Would that Brayling and his companions were now here. But, at any rate, we must leave no means untried to rescue them from their perilous situation; let a number of the servants arm themselves, and immediately commence the search; Evelyn and his companion may fortunately have avoided the ruffians, but unable to extricate themselves from the mazes of the forest."

This suggestion met with the concurrence of Sir Milford, and the domestics were dispatched without delay, with strict injunctions to prosecute the search with the utmost vigilance.

The surgeon then returned to the room, and informed them that, having examined the hurt the wounded man had received, he was happy to say that it was not so severe as he had at first expected; but that he must be kept perfectly quiet, and free from excitement. Sir Milford then visited the chamber of Constance, whom he found in a state of great agitation which for a time admitted of no consolation, even though she was informed that the strictest search was being made for Evelyn and Mabel. Her fears foreboded the worst; and with feelings of uncontrolable horror she anticipated the dreaful fate which had too probably, even ere now, befallen him. It may be readily imagined the state of anxiety and suspense with which she awaited the return of the domestics; but, when hour after hour passed away, and still they came not, her agony increased to an almost insupportable degree, and every effort to calm her emotions was exhausted in vain.

CHAPTER XLII.

EVELYN AND MABEL IN THE FOREST.—THE ROBBERS.—THE FEARFUL SITUATION.

IT is necessary to account for the occurrence recorded in the foregoing chapter. We left Evelyn Heartwell and Mabel, on their return to the vessel, after the encounter with Black Will, and on finding the escape of the Miser. These events caused them considerable excitement, and it was not for a day or two that they could recover themselves, and Evelyn then seriously began to consider what it was best for him to do. He deeply regretted the flight of Jasper Scrimpe, who was so important a witness of his innocence, and without whose testimony his situation might be as dangerous and precarious as before he quitted England. Anxious as he was to ease the fears and suspense of his beloved Constance, he at first thought of addressing a letter to her to inform her of his safe return; but at length he determined to brave the worst, and returning to London at all hazards to seek an interview with Constance, though it might be the last. It was impossible to conceal his intentions from Mabel, whose penetrating eyes read his every thought, and she expressed her determination to follow him. Walter Greysham also expressed his desire to accompany them, and having seen Black Will and his associates safe in the custody of the proper authorities, they quitted the ship, and commenced their journey. They could only find the means of conveyance for a short distance, and, being anxious not to delay, they resolved to proceed on their journey as far as they were compelled on foot. Nothing particular occurred to them till they were overtaken by the storm in the forest, and wandering through its intricate windings, in the almost impenetrable darkness which prevailed, Evelyn and Mabel became separated from Greysham, and were utterly unable to discover any traces of him again. Their situation was now indeed a most dismal one. The storm raged with terrible violence, and the further they endeavoured to proceed, the more they became lost and bewildered. To add to their dismay, too, the forest, in all probability was infested with robbers, and should they be unfortunate enough to encounter any of them, their fate would be almost certain. But Evelyn felt more for the situation of Mabel than his own.

"Rash girl," he observed, " to what continual perils hast thou exposed thyself, through thine obstinate devotion to one who hath it in his power only to make so poor a return."

"Reproach me not, Evelyn," replied Mabel, "thou dost not hear me murmur one word of complaint, nor wilt thou, even though my life may be in peril. Oh, thou canst but little imagine the melancholy satisfaction it affords me to be permitted thus to share thy troubles and vicissitudes."

"Generous-minded girl," ejaculated our hero, fixing upon her a look of the utmost esteem and admiration, " what can ever repay thee for the many sacrifices thou hast made for my sake !"

"The happiness of being near thee, Evelyn," replied the Gipsey-girl, "and the certainty that I possess at least thine esteem, if I can inspire thy breast with no more tender passion. But thou art now in England, and haply ere long may again behold one who will make thee no longer view me with any other feelings than those of scorn and disgust."

"Again thou wrongest me, indeed thou dost, Mabel, by suppositions such as those to which thou hast just given utterance," returned Evelyn, "but this is not the time or place to discuss this delicate and important subject. How can we possibly proceed ? The difficulties of this forest every moment seem to thicken around us."

"Be patient ;" said Mabel ; "and Providence will probably, presently deliver us from the difficulties of our situation."

"Whichever way we turn," observed our hero, we only seem to get further entangled. If we call for help, there is scarcely a chance of being heard. At any rate, I'll try my fortune."

He shouted as loud as he could ; and then pausing to listen, he heard a shrill whistle from the right, at some distance.

"Providence be thanked ;" he said ; " my cries are heard, some one whistles."

Another whistle from the left, now saluted his ears.

"Ah !" he exclaimed, "answered from the other side ; courage, Mabel, we shall yet be extricated from our present dilemma."

"Be cautious, Evelyn ;" said Mabel ; "I like not these signal, they are more likely to proceed from foes than friends."

Evelyn returned no answer, but hastened a few paces forward towards the right, closely followed by the Gipsey-girl. At that instant a vivid flash of lightning gleamed upon a path which they now perceived was before them, and at the same time revealed the tall figure of a man, masked, and, with a drawn dagger, advancing stealthily towards the trees.

"Ha !" whispered Mabel, grasping his arm ; " dost thou not perceive a ruffian, armed and masked ? We have only our pistols, and were we to discharge one of them, the report might bring overwhelming numbers to his assistance."

The ruffian now advanced nearer, and, in a course but harsh voice, said—

"Who called ?"

"Silence!" again whispered Mabel; "if we return no answer, in the darkness we may retreat unseen."

They crept silently towards the left, as the robbers advanced.

"Speak!" he said, "where are you ?"

They still returned no answer, and at that critical moment another ruffian emerged from the gloom, and in reply to the question said, "Here."

"Die!" cried the robber, raising his arm to strike, as our hero and Mabel stepped behind the large trunk of a tree which was near them.

"Hold!" said the villain, who had last appeared; "'tis I, your comrade."

"Why did you whistle ?" demanded the first robber.

"In answer to your call;" replied the other, "you hallooed to me."

"I never spoke."

"I'll swear I heard a voice;" said the fellow; "it sounded hereabouts, but the thunder roared so violently at the time that I could not clearly distinguish."

"Doubtless 'tis some traveller who may afford us booty;" said his companion; "let us take the left hand path, and, if we hear the call repeated, it will direct us to our prey."

With these words, the robbers retreated from the spot, and Evelyn and Mabel having watched them disappear, came cautiously from behind the place of their concealment.

"Thou wert right, Mabel, in thy suspicions;" observed Evelyn; "there can be no doubt that these fellows are robbers and murderers, and our escape has been most fortunate."

"True;" coincided Mabel; "but doubtless there are more of the villians lurking about, and we have probably not escaped the danger yet. This forest is a likely place for deeds of bloodshed. However, prudence admonishes us to avoid the left hand path, after what we heard the ruffians say. Be cautious, Evelyn, and keep close to me, I am more accustomed to penetrate such wilds as these than thou art."

Our hero assented to this, and following closely upon the footsteps of Mabel, they took the contrary path to that along which the robbers had proceeded, and again sought to grope their way in the darkness. They had not advanced far, when they perceived a glimmering light peeping through an adjacent coppice.

"Ah! thank Heaven," observed Evelyn, "see, yon friendly light probably points to some human habitation."

"It recedes from us;" returned Mabel; "alas! it may only be some goblin of the fen, a Will-o'-the-Wisp, twinkling to deceive us. Do not again venture to call, for thou knowest the danger of that. We will trust to Providence, and follow the light."

They did so, and found the way they were pursuing less entangled, so that they could advance with far less difficulty. And now they perceived several lights moving about in the distance, and which gradually became more distinct.

"'Tis strange" remarked Mabel; "it would seem as though these lights were carried by different persons, perhaps, in search of some friends, lost in the forest. If we still follow them we may probably at last be extricated from our difficulty; but it is advisable to remain silent, for we know not whether they might prove to be friends or foes."

"This suspense is most tantalising," returned our hero; "and I must confess that my patience is almost exhausted. Should we fail to reach some place of shelter, what will become of us in such a storm as this ? and to which we have been already too long exposed. Poor Greysham, too; what can have become of him ? I fear some harm hath befallen him."

All these observations were conducted in the lowest tone of voice and they still continued to follow the lights, which, however, gradually became fainter and fainter, till they faded away altogether, and the unfortunate travellers were again involved in utter darkness, and at a loss what course next to adopt. They did not pause, and after a few minutes they emerged from the greater depths of the forest, and then, through the trees they again beheld lights glimmering at a distance, but these were now stationery, and seemed to proceed from some building.

"Fortune be praised," ejaculated Mabel, "we have surmounted the principal danger at last; we are now upon the borders of the forest."

A few minutes more and they stepped from the gloomy and fearful scene through which they had so long struggled, and found themselves in a lane, at one end of which the lightning enabled them to behold, to their no small relief and gratification, the shadow of a large building, in several windows of which lights were gleaming. The reader will not need to be informed that this was Greenwood Abbey, and the lights that Evelyn and Mabel had seen in the forest had proceeded from the lanterns carried by the persons who had been sent in search of them. They hastened forward and directly afterwards found themselves standing at the entrance to the Abbey.

"This building bears an inviting appearance;" remarked Evelyn; "and should Walter Greysham fortunately have succeeded in reaching here, he will be safe."

Mabel returned no answer, for she had raised the massive knocker, and let it fall with a sound that verberated far around. Soon afterwards they heard footsteps moving along the Hall, and a man's voice inquired who was there?

"Two poor travellers;" replied our hero, "who for some time have been wandering about in the forest, and who now claim the hospitality of a shelter from the storm."

The man uttered an exclamation, which they could not understand; but he immediately opened the door, and examining them by the light of the lamp, he observed—

"Ah! this is fortunate; surely thou must be those of whom myself and my companions have been in search. Say, did ye lose a friend in the forest?"

"We did;" replied Evelyn, astonished at the question; "Captain Greysham, who we fearest had—"

"Enough, enough;" interrupted the domestic; "he is at present in the Abbey, though sadly maltreated by those confounded ruffians with which the forest is infested. Dear me! what a surprise. But this way, my friends, this way."

Evelyn and Mabel were more and more astonished, but without waiting for them to put any further interrogatory to him, the servant motioned them to follow, and ushered them into one of the lower apartments, where he left them abruptly and without saying a word. Completely bewildered at this extraordinary behaviour, and quite at a loss to conjecture to what it all tended, our hero and the Gipsey-girl looked at each other, but before they had time to offer any observation, they heard footsteps hastily approaching, the next instant the room door was thrown open, and the reader may judge of their utter amazement and confusion, when they found themselves in the presence of those, whom of all others, at such a time and in such a place they least expected to see, Sir Milford Welborn, and Sir Thomas Overton, who both advanced to meet them. Quite astounded, and hardly knowing whether he had cause for gratification or for fear, our hero started back a few paces, and bent one knee respectfully before Sir Milford, though, at the same time, an expression of conscious innocence irradiated his features. But the baronet advanced nearer to him, and, in a voice which fully testified the nature of his feelings, said—

"Merciful Heavens, I thank thee; what a fortunate meeting is this. Rise unfortunate youth; it is I who ought to kneel and ask pardon for the numerous wrongs and acts of injustice I have indirectly been the cause of inflicting upon thee. Thine innocence is now made manifest, by a wonderful concurrence of circumstances ; and every atonement for the sufferings thou hast so unjustly endured will be rendered thee."

" What strange, what blessed words are those I hear ? " cried Evelyn, with a look of profound amazement and incredulity;" oh surely, Sir Milford Welborn, thou canst not mock the feelings of the humble Evelyn, and seek to raise delusive hopes in his breast."

" Heaven forbid ; " solemnly returned the baronet ; " my friend, Sir Thomas Overton, here, can testify to the truth of what I assert."

" I am overwhelmed with astonishment ; " ejaculated our hero? " but Oliver Dalton?"

" Name him not, the miscreant, the villain !" answered Sir Milford, warmly ; " Sampson Brayling, that zealous, that indefatigable friend, to whom we all owe an incalculable debt of gratitude, tore away the mask by which he so long deceived me, and exposed the dark, designing hypocrite in his true character, just at the very moment of his expected triumph. He is now flying from the hands of justice."

" Almighty God !" cried Evelyn, clasping his hands vehemently together, while torrents of feelings that rushed to his heart was unspeakable ? " Thy ways are wonderful ! But oh, there is one whose name I dare scarce venture to mention in thy presence, Sir Milford, but whose beloved image, ever uppermost in my thoughts, is dearer to me, oh, far more precious than life itself. Constance—"

" Still lives and loves thee, Evelyn ! " replied Sir Milford.

" Kind Heaven, I thank thee ! " exclaimed Evelyn, sinking on his knees ; " she lives ! my Constance lives, and I am amply rewarded for all the many troubles it has been my lot to encounter!"

" Alas! alas!" sighed the Gipsey-girl, in the most melancholy accents of sorrow and regret ; " and the hopes of Mabel are for ever annihilated. Oh, anguish insupportable ! "

Previous to this the poor girl had stood aside in gloomy silence, and listened to what passed ; and Sir Milford's attention had been too deeply engaged with Evelyn, to take any particular notice of her ; but now recognising her for the first time, the baronet kindly approaching her, said—

" Ah, Mabel ; art thou too here ? pardon me that I did not before recognise thee. Generous, devoted girl ; we are all under an immense weight of obligation to thee for the many services thou hast rendered us."

" Mabel requires no thanks ; " she replied haughtily ; " there is but one object to which her proud ambition soars, but the highborn Constance Welborn presents an insuperable barrier to its accomplishment, and all that is left to her is misery and despair."

" Mabel, for Heaven's sake forbear ; " remonstrated Evelyn ; " if thou dost indeed regard me, and respect my feelings, I implore thee."

He was prevented from finishing the sentence by a loud exclamation of emotion from without ; well did Evelyn know that beloved voice ; his brain swam round ; his heart seemed ready to leap from his breast ; before he could in the least degree recover himself, the door again flew open, Constance, pale and agitated beyond description, appeared ; a simultaneous and frantic exclamation escaped them both ; and the next moment the lovers were locked in each other's arms, and mingling their sobs and tears together. Sir Milford and Sir Thomas stood silently by, gazing with mingled feelings of sympathy and admiration and offered not to interrupt their emotion.

CHAPTER XLIII.

The Happy Meeting.—The Mysterious Visit of the Gipsey-Girl.—
Devoted Love—Affecting Interview—Mabel's Dream.—Her
Departure.—

It would be almost a fruitless task to attempt minutely to describe the scene
which followed; again and again did Evelyn press the beauteous form of the beloved
being whom he had never expected to behold again to his heart; while the power
of their feelings was so intense, that it could not possibly find vent inward. But
at length they both sank upon their knees, and devoutly raised their eyes towards
Heaven; while Sir Milford Welborn, who was greatly moved by the affecting
meeting of those who were so fondly, so faithfully attached to each other, but
whose virtuous passion he had so long opposed, raised his hands above their heads,
and solemnly invoked the blessing of the Almighty.

"Oh, this painful sight;" exclaimed the Gipsey-girl in tones of anguish, and
with looks of mingled jealousy and despair; "tear them asunder! 'tis madness
to the brain of the wretched. Oh, that this poor heart would break—that this
heart would break!"

She covered her face with her hands, sobbed convulsively, and retiring to the
other side of the room, sunk disconsolately in a chair, seemingly unconscious of
everything but the overwhelming agony of her own feelings. Evelyn and Constance
were too much absorbed by their own thoughts and emotions to hear her
observations, or to notice her; but Sir Milford and Sir Thomas kindly approached
her, and, with gentle words and remonstrances, endeavoured to calm the paroxysm
of her unutterable grief. She seemed, however, not to notice them, or to understand what they said, and, after a pause, she looked up at them wildly and
vacantly for a moment, and passively suffering them to conduct her from the room,
the lovers were left to themselves.

Yes, Evelyn and Constance were now alone; they could give free vent,
unrestrained indulgence to their feelings; but, oh, what language could they find
sufficiently eloquent to give full expression to the various passions that struggled
in their breasts? again they had met, but, oh, under what different circumstances
to those they had parted. Then, distraction and despair goaded their hearts; now,
sweet hope and happiness beamed upon them. Then Evelyn was resting under
every odium, scouted from society, and possessing the hatred and scorn of Sir Milford;
while Constance was threatened with a fate she could not contemplate without
horror. Now, the character of Evelyn was exonerated, and the Baronet
received him with the hand of friendship, and smiled upon their love. So great,
so wonderful, so blissful was the change, that they could hardly persuade themselves of its reality. They were too agitated to enter then into the particulars
of all that had happened to them during the time of their separation. That must
be deferred to another occasion; and soon afterwards Sir Milford returned to
the room, and reminding them that the lateness of the hour warned them to retire,
with a fond embrace, and many sweet words of passionate affection, they parted for
the night, and our hero was then conducted to his chamber. And here, when he
was left to himself, he no longer sought to control his feelings, and, with a bounding
heart, he poured forth his gratitude to Heaven for the unexpected happiness which
now brightened his hitherto dark and gloomy prospects. Of so thrilling and
startling a nature had been the events of the last few hours, and by such miraculous
means had his meeting with Constance and her uncle been brought about, that

they appeared to him like the mere illusion of a dream, and he pondered over them again and again in wonder, doubt, and incredulity. But, oh, how greatly was he indebted to Sampson Brayling, and how much he regreted that he had not been there to receive the expressions of his gratitude. So much was his mind occupied by these varied interesting thoughts, that he did not think of retiring to rest; but, at length, while seated in his chair, and reflecting upon all the extra-ordinary circumstances of his chequered life, sleep gradually overpowered his senses. But strange were the visions that were conjured up by his busy imag-nation, from one of which he suddenly started, and a sensation amounting to awe crept through his veins as he heard, or fancied he heard a deep and dismal sigh near him. He sprang from the chair in which he had been reposing, and rubbing his eyes, and looking around him, at first he could not perceive anything, and imagined that he must still have been dreaming; but again he distinctly heard the sound which had before startled him, and hastily gazing towards that part of the room from whence he was certain it proceeded, he started with some degree of alarm, when his eyes rested upon a human form, whose attitude was fixed and solemn. The light from the lamp which was still burning on the table, gleamed so faintly on that part of the room where it was standing, that he could not distinguish it clearly. He therefore boldly advanced towards it, and it did not offer to move in the least as he did so, but, on approaching near it, how great was his astonishment on beholding it was the Gipsey-girl, who, with pale features and wild eyes, was gazing earnestly upon him.

"Mabel!" he exclaimed; "can I believe my senses? For Heaven's sake, what brings thee here at this hour, and in so mysterious a manner?,,

"To gaze upon thee probably for the last time;" replied the poor girl, in a voice of the deepest emotion, and every accent of which thrilled to the heart, and aroused the sympathy of Evelyn; "I fly from the sight of those to whom my presence must now be hateful and repulsive. "

"Strange, infatuated girl;" said our hero; "what mean thy words? What sad, what fatal perversity of mind controls thine actions. Surely thou art mad."

"No, no, I am not mad;" she sighed, "though Heaven knows, that the tumult of passions that constantly rack my drain, should be sufficient to drive reason from its seat. Would that this poor heart might break, and the cold grave give that peace to the hapless wanderer which on earth hath been so long denied her."

"Alas, poor Mabel;" observed Evelyn, deeply moved by the despairing tones in which she spoke; "my heart bleeds for thee; and yet I know not what words to offer thee, that might serve to tranquilize thy feelings, or afford consolation to thy troubled mind. Would to Heaven that thou couldst eradicate this fatal, this unhappy, this hopeless passion from thine heart."

"No, no, no;" again exclaimed the wretched maiden, vehemently; "it is ingrafted in my soul. It is a portion of my very nature; it can terminate only with my existence. Evelyn, the fiat of my doom is sealed. Thou art restored to Constance Welborn; she loves thee still; she will be thine, and the last remaining hope of Mabel is extinguished for ever."

"Ah, Mabel;" said our hero, with a look of gentle reproach; "and canst thou then regret the happy change that Providence hath at length wrought in my cir-cumstances, in my prospects?"

"Heaven forbid;" exclaimed Mabel, fervently; "I rejoice; my heart bounds with gratitude, and yet sinks with despair. Thy happiness is all, is everything to me, yet 'tis her that secures it; she alone will claim thy love and fondest endearments, and therefore am I wretched. Oh, Evelyn, the state of my mind is a problem that even I myself cannot solve. But I will not cast a blight upon thy joys by my presence, and I dare not trust myself to witness the triumph of Constance Welborn. Bless thee, Evelyn, may Heaven's choicest blessings light

upon thine head. I have fulfilled my vow; in all thy dangers, all thy sufferings, thy cares, and thy anxieties I have participated; I have followed thy footsteps through weal and woe; I have seen thee safe to the goal of happiness, and now again I resume my own dreary wanderings, looking anxiously forward to the time when the weary traveller may haply lay herself down in eternal rest."

"Thy words distract me, Mabel;" said Evelyn; "oh, whither wouldst thou go?"

"It matters not;" she replied; "the world is now all alike to me. There is no spot on earth to which I can fly from the deep anguish of a broken heart. Yet could I not leave thee, Evelyn, without at least one sad word at parting, it may be for ever."

"Thou canst not surely think of leaving the Abbey thus abruptly, and at such an hour?"

No. 33.

"Yes, my mind is fixed. I dare not trust myself to see *her* again, and I would not compromise thy welfare or thine happiness. But ere I go, listen for that I have to say, for it may impress itself on thy mind, and at times recur to thy thoughts when I am gone. But last night, when sleep, which only so fitfully comes to me, descended upon my eyelids, I had a dream, a strange, wild fantastic dream; one of mingled joys and sorrow; of wonder and of mystery. Methought that I was again a child, a happy, thoughtless, playful child, such as I first remember myself, when wandering over strange lands, and various places, through wilds and woodland; o'er verdant hill, in forest dell, and daisy-covered meadow, with the rude companions, yet fond protectors of my earliest days, when all around me was joy and sunshine; when all to me was one bright summer's day, and Winter's dreary care was a stranger to my breast, days of unconscious innocence and bliss, never more, alas! fated to return. Suddenly, methought another child, about my own age, joined my artless sports, and merrily gambolled with me in the Summer's sun, light and joyous as were the feelings that animated my own breast. He was a fair boy, whom I fancied that I had often seen before, presented to my imagination in the vision of my slumbers; and towards him methought my heart bounded as though it had lighted on some fresh object to love, and share with me the happiness of my days. How jocund was our laugh, how elastic, how buoyant our steps as hand in hand we tripped it merrily o'er the flower-bedecked earth, until suddenly we came upon a scene, so bright, so lovely, that it dazzled our eyes to gaze upon it. The air was rich and entrancing with the perfume of innumerable flowers; arcades of roses opened to our view from every point of this fairy spot, and birds of every beautiful variety of plumage carroled melodious notes from amidst the emerald foliage of the different trees. While yet we stood entranced at this magic scene, a heavenly form, in robes of transparent white, arose before our wandering eyes, and, lowly, in awe and reverence we bent before it, while raising its hands above our heads, in a voice of unearthly melody which even now seems to thrill in mine ears it said—'Children of mysterious destiny, love each other, for Nature orders it!' We looked up, but the vision was gone, and marvellous was the change that had come over us, and the scenes by which we were surrounded. I likewise imagined in my dream, that, with the rapidity of thought, years had been swept away, and our childhood had ripened into youth, while the spot on which we now stood was wild and barren, and gloom and sadness was on all around. Yet, though manhood was now upon his brow, clearly did I recognize the loved features of the companion of my childhood; they were thine, Evelyn."

"Strange dream;" ejaculated our hero, "No wonder that it should so forcibly impress itself on thy mind, Mabel."

"Nay, hear me out;" said Mabel, "for I have more to relate. Methought that a black and stagnant pool divided us, which I could not cross, and, at every ineffectual attempt that I made to do so, an angry frown contracted thy brows, and and a smile of derision mocked my anguish. Still frantically I persevered, but all my efforts were in vain, some invisible power seemed to hold me back. And now I beheld another form standing by thy side, whose fond blandishments thou didst encourage, and on whom beamed thy brightest smiles of ardent affection. The form was that of Constance Welborn. Oh, the intense agony of my feelings at that moment! Madly I stretched forth my arms towards thee, and appealed to thee for pity and help. But darker became thy frowns, and thou viewdst my sufferings with the bitterest mockery and exultation. And now encircling the waist of my rival with thine arm, gradually didst thou recede from my anxious sight, till a black cloud suddenly descended upon the earth, and hid thee and Constance completely from my view, while, at the same time an appalling voice thundered in mine ears— 'To the woods and the wilds again; thy love is hopeless, Evelyn is not for thee.' I tried to speak, but could not; the blood rushed to my brain; hideous forms danced before mine eyes; and in the horror and agony of my feelings I awoke? Evelyn, already is that fearful dream partly realized; the die is cast; my doom is sealed; to the woods and wilds, to gloom and solitude, I once more hasten, for the bright sunshine is not for me. Oh, Evelyn, farewell, bless thee, bless thee; mayest thou and Constance be happy, even years after the green turf shall have closed o'er the head of the poor, forsaken, wretched Mabel!"

Evelyn was too much affected by the impressive and melancholy tones in which the Gipsey-girl spoke, and the agony of her looks, to return any immediate answer; and for a moment she knelt at his feet, raised his hand fervently to her lips, while her tears flowed fast and unrestrained, and convulsive sobs escaped her bosom. But suddenly she arose, and dashing the tears from her eyes, made a powerful effort to conquer her emotions, and to reassume her usual air of calm dignity and determination, she said—

"'Tis past; the struggle's over; Fate wills it, and I bow to its decree. Evelyn, once more farewell, oh, a fond and fervent farewell; reproach not the memory of the Gipsey-girl, should this be the last time that we may ever meet again; her only fault has been, in the purity and innocence of her heart, loving thee too well. May thy future happiness be as complete as she so earnestly wishes it to be."

"Hold, rash girl!" exclaimed Evelyn, grasping her arm; "reflect, reflect upon the headstrong and imprudent step thou would'st take; by Heaven thou must not, shalt not leave me thus!"

"Detain me not, Evelyn;" commanded Mabel, in a determined voice; and her features agonised with the various passions that struggled in her breast; "it is evil destiny that impels me, and I may not seek to resist it. Adieu, too much loved youth; I will no longer remain an obstacle to thy wishes; doubtless in the fond caresses of the more favoured Constance, thou wilt soon forget that such a humble being as the Gipsey wanderer e'er shadowed thy path, or ever existed. To the woods and the wilds again; the spot where peace and happiness reign is no place for me!"

"Stay! stay! I implore thee, Mabel;" cried our hero, with emotion; but she had quitted the apartment, and, directly afterwards, the closing of one of the outer doors convinced him that she had fulfilled her rash purpose, and left the Abbey.

Evelyn felt sad and melancholy at this circumstance, and was most anxious as to the course which Mabel, in the despair of her feelings might be induced to adopt, sincerely as he pitied her for the hopeless passion which she still so obstinately encouraged; and grateful as he was for the many essential services she had rendered him, and the devoted affection she had evinced towards him; he could not but feel the utmost solicitude for her happiness and welfare; but alas! he feared that her peace of mind was destroyed for ever; and he could not but shudder at the idea of the consequences that were likely to ensue from the annihilation of her hopes. These thoughts, and the extraordinary events of the night, would not suffer him again to court sleep; and impatiently he awaited the time when he should again behold his beloved Constance, of the reality of his restoration to whom he could still scarcely persuade himself. He was also most anxious to ascertain the state of Walter Greysham, but for whose providential discovery after his encounter with the robbers, these events might never have been brought about.

CHAPTER XLIV.

MABEL'S FEARFUL DESIGNS FRUSTRATED BY SAMPSON BRAYLING.—RESCUE
OF THE MISER FROM THE ROBBERS.

UPON leaving the Abbey, Mabel hurried heedlessly on she knew not whither, but made her way once more towards the forest, notwithstanding the dangers that her and Evelyn had previously there so narrowly escaped. Her mind had come to no definite course of action; and, indeed, harrassed as she was by the torturing frenzy of misery and despair, she was perfectly indifferent as to what might become of her. It was now about three o'clock in the morning; it was still impenetrably dark, but the fury of the tempest had greatly abated; though the thunder still at intervals sullenly murmured in the distance, and a faint gleam of lightning every now and then shot across the sky. The brain of the Gipsey-girl was wild and fevered; and there was a dreadful feeling at her heart, which seemed capable of urging her to any deed, however fearful, rash, and desperate. Regardless of danger, fearless of anything that might befall, since every hope was wrecked and stifled within her breast, and life itself plainly presented nothing but a dreary blank, a wide vacuum to her imagination; she wandered on, and being most in unison with her morbid feelings, hastened from the sight of the ancient Abbey, and plunged into the very depths of the forest gloom, only pausing at intervals for a moment, to look wildly and despairingly around her, and to give utterance to some sad lamentation, the cruel destiny which continued to pursue her with such inexorable severity. The wind still moaned dismally among the branches of the tall and sturdy trees, and to her disorded fancy seemed like the ominous voices of evil spirits urging her to death. And now she reached a savage glen where all was darkness and horror. Trees that had been blasted by the lightning's wrath, distorted into every fantastic and unnatural form, stood around, like grim and hideous spectres in the solemn darkness of that dismal place. In some parts of this glen (which was carefully shunned with superstitious dread, even in the broad light of day, by those who knew the locality), the trees were clustered so thickly together, and their giant limbs so closely interwoven, that it was rendered almost impervious; while the thick furze and brushwood that covered the earth, made it difficult and painful to the traveller.

On arriving in this haunt of gloom and horror, a place well adapted to the perpetration of any black and frightful crime, Mabel paused in her progress, and folding her arms across her chest, gazed around her with a look of morbid satisfaction, and an unnatural smile passed over her melancholy features. Her attitude was striking and impressive; it was that of settled deep despair, yet, of calm, stern, inflexible determination. Her keen black eyes shot forth a strange lustre, and spoke a language which revealed the terrible workings of her tortured soul, and her countenance, now pale, almost to cadaverousness, was the very prototype of uncontrolable misery and anguish. Her dark hair, disorderel by the rude wind that swept the glen, sported loose, and dishevelled over her neck and shoulders, added to the general wildness and distraction of her appearance. For a few minutes she stood transfixed as a statue to the spot, and continued to gaze in silence upon the terrors by which she was surrounded; but at length in solemn tones that scarcely resembled anything human in that fearful place, she said—

"Welcome, dark scene of horror, haunt of misery and desolation, welcome to the wretched outcast from the love, the hopes, and happiness of mankind. I hail thee with feelings of melancholy pleasure; for, oh, how well art thou in accordance with the fierce, the black, and unruly passions that hold their empire in my devastated mind. Here let the unhappy Mabel hide herself from the human race, to whom she is an object of scorn, disgust, and loathing. Here can she escape their bitter mockery and brutal taunts; breathe her sorrows to the moaning blast; unseen, unpitied, uncared for, lay herself down and die! die! die! ah! that word; it arouses fresh thoughts and passions within my breast. Why should I continue to live, to bear this insupportable burthen of ceaseless care and anxiety? This is a fitting place for such a deed, and Fate hath surely directed my footsteps hither, that I may at last unseen, uninterruped, terminate my weary pilgrimage, my dismal, hopeless wanderings, and find that eternal peace which is denied me on earth. Why should I hesitate?" she added, after a brief pause, and drawing forth a dagger from beneath her cloak, while terrible determination flashed from her eyes, seemed to nerve her arm; "but one blow, and this friendly weapon will release my troubled soul from its prison-house of cares and anxieties, and leave my cold remains to moulder here at rest. Dark, cheerless, and rugged has been for year the path my footsteps have trod, and death alone points the beacon light to hope and happiness. Yet, fain would I that my ashes should rest where the wild flower blooms, and the yew tree and the willow wave their heads in mournful silence. Ah! hark! what sounds were those?"

She started, for at that moment she fancied she heard a rustling sound among the trees, and the low and indistinct muttering of voices, close by where she stood. Searchingly she cast her eyes around her, seeking to penetrate through the dense gloom of the place; and listened, with breathless attention, though she offered not to move from the spot on which she had been standing. However, she saw nothing to sanction her suspicions and alarm, and the silence was alone broken by the sighing of the wind at intervals; and again the same fearful resolution marked the expression of her features.

"It was but my distempered imagination;" she said; "here there is no prying eye to watch my actions, no busy hand to arrest me in my purpose. Let me be firm, and the dark scene will soon close upon the sorrows of the poor Gipsey-girl."

She pressed her hand upon her forehead, and reflected for a moment. A tear, unbidden, started to her eye, but she dashed it proudly and scornfully away; and solemnly kneeling, as she raised her eyes in earnest supplication, she said—

"Great Father of mercy, pardon, I beseech thee, the deed, and receive the soul of thy wretched creature. Bless thee, bless thee, Evelyn; though on earth we may never more behold each other, in Heaven, I trust, we may be united, never again to part!"

She remained on her knees; for a moment she paused, as she seemed to hesitate, but suddenly she aroused herself, fresh courage appeared to nerve her soul, and animate her features; resolutely she raised the hand that held the deadly weapon, in the air, but, ere it could descend upon her breast, her arm was powerfully arrested in its fatal purpose by some one from behind, and a well known voice, whose tones thrilled through every vain of the unfortunate Mabel, exclaimed—

"Restrain thy rash hand misguided girl, nor by so awful a crime close for ever the gates of mercy to thee, and plunge thy soul in perdition!"

The Gipsey-girl started; uttered an exclamation of agony, and the instrument of death fell from her hand; for it was Sampson Brayling, accompanied by three or four of his tribe, who stood before her. Confounded! appalled, and trembling, Mabel averted her face, and torturing feelings which at that solemn moment swelled her bosom, were too powerful for utterance. Sampson Brayling viewed her with a mingled expression of pity, regret, and reproach, but for a few minutes remained silent.

A few words will suffice to explain the fortunate arrival of the Gipsey-Chief in the forest glen at such a critical juncture. Having received the information, which it has been before stated he communicated to Sir Milford, respecting the destruction of the vessel on which our hero had been aboard, and the part of the crew of which he had ascertained were afterwards rescued from the desolate Island by the Invulnerable, he had lost no time in prosecuting his inquiries further. For that purpose he had made his way to Portsmouth, where he found that the Invulnerable had arrived in safety, and, to his unspeakable satisfaction learned that Evelyn and Mabel were among those who had been rescued, and returned to England, but that they, only a few hours before, had departed, accompanied by the captain of the Ariel, to London. Anxious to remove the suspense of Sir Milford and Constance, Brayling immediately departed to return to Greenwood Abbey with all possible expedition ; and, notwithstanding the unreasonableness of the hour at which he reached there, he would not for a moment delay arousing its inmates. His astonishment at the news he was there destined to hear may be readily imagined, and we will pass over the meeting between him and Evelyn. The sudden departure of Mabel from the Abbey, and the wretched state of her mind at the time, excited his alarm, and, knowing that every moment of delay might be fraught with the most fearful and dangerous consequences, he instantly started in search of her, and the reader has seen with what success he fortunately accomplished his wishes.

"Mabel ; " said the Gipsey-chief in tones of gentle remonstrance ; " and is it thus we meet ? Headstrong girl, dost thou not even now shudder with horror and remorse at the recollection of the frightful crime thou wouldst have committed ? "

"Sampson Brayling ; " returned the Gipsey-girl, looking up with an expression of regret and anguish ; what accursed misfortune sent thee hither at the very moment when my determined hand was about to terminate those sufferings that are now too great for human endurance ? Oh, I could hate thee for arresting me in my deadly purpose."

"Wretched girl ; " ejaculated Brayling ; why wilt thou suffer these fierce, these dreadful, these impetuous passions to get the better of thy reason ? Come—come, leave this gloomy place, and return with me to the Abbey."

"To the Abbey ! " repeated Mabel, with a look of terror ; no—no—no ! Constance Welborn is there ; she basks in the smiles of Evelyn, and holds dominion over his every thought and wish. That—that alone is madness to my brain ; it is no place for the despised, the deserted Mabel ! "

"No more of this," said Sampson, impatiently ; " Mabel, thou disgracest thyself in thus suffering thy worst passions to obtain so fatal and dangerous ascendancy over thee. Arouse thyself, girl, from this weak, degraded—aye, degraded state : I am ashamed of thee. But let us be gone ; our friends at the Abbey will be anxiously awaiting my return."

"Leave me, Brayling, I implore thee ; " ejaculated Mabel, with much emotion ; " abandon me to my fate. Oh, I am weary of life ! "

"Curse those sad thoughts ! returned Brayling. "The clouds that have so long obscured thy prospects, and cast their dark shadows across thy path, are rapidly dispersing ; Mabel shall live for hope, for peace, for happiness.

"For peace ? for happiness ? Alas ! "

"Even so. Oh, Mabel, thou canst but little imagine that which is in store for thee. The hour is rapidly approaching when the important secret of years shall be divulged ; the dark curtain of mystery withdrawn, and Mabel, the wandering Gipsey-girl, claim to take her station amongst the proudest and most peerless maiden in the land."

"Forbear, Brayling ; thou wouldst deceive me. Thou wouldst inspire me with delusive hopes."

"Sampson Brayling scorns to play the deceiver's part, or to mock the troubled mind with fond and dazzling visions that can never be realized ; replied the Gipsey, proudly ; " Mabel shall yet find that she hath no friend more ardent, more sincere, than the rough uncultivated protector of her childhood and her youth." ·

" Oh, what means the strange ambiguity of thy words ? " interrogated Mabel, eagerly ; " explain thyself, Brayling, I implore thee ! "

" Not now—not now ; " he answered ; " the time hath not yet arrived, though it is rapidly approaching."

" Torturing suspense ; " cried Mabel ; " thou mockest me."

" By all my hopes I do not ; " returned Sampson ; " exert thy patience yet a little longer, and thou shalt find that I have not sported with thy feelings, that I have not sought to encourage thy hopes to no purpose.   But come, let us away from this frightful spot, and thank Heaven that my timely arrival prevented thy rash hand the perpetration of a crime, from the bare contemplation of which thy better nature must revolt."

" All merciful Father," exclaimed the Gipsey-girl, solemnly, and raising her fine eyes devoutly towards Heaven ; " guide me how to act.   Sampson Brayling, I yield to thy persuasions ; although I cannot but regret that this hour was not permitted to seal the doom of the wretched Mabel for ever ! "

" Forbear, Mabel ; " observed Sampson, " banish such sad and fearful thoughts from thy breast.   Again I tell thee that there are bright and sunny days of peace and happiness in store for thee ; Sampson Brayling would hate and despise himself, could he hold out hopes and promises to the unfortunate, which he at the same time knows full well can never be fulfilled."

Mabel sighed, fixed upon him an earnest, and searching look ; and extending her hand, and stifling her emotions as well as she could, was about to suffer him to conduct her from the glen, when at that moment they were both startled by a wild and piercing cry that rent the air, and was repeated in dismal echoes far around.

" Ah ! " exclaimed Brayling ; " I fear some unfortunate being stands in need of aid.   Follow me, comrades, this way the sound, so piteous and alarming, seemed to come."

" Probably some fresh victim to the fierce banditti who infest this forest, and from whom myself and Evelyn so narrowly escaped last night ; " observed Mabel, whom this fresh adventure somewhat aroused from the fearful and torturing thoughts in which her mind was before so completely absorbed.

" True ; " returned Sampson ; " and it is necessary, therefore, that we use caution."

The cry was repeated, and, if possible, in a louder and more frantic tone of agony than before.

" There is not a moment to be lost ; " said the Gipsey ; " we are well armed, and therefore have nothing to fear.   Quick, or we may be too late to save the life of some unfortunate fellow creature."

They now made their way through a narrow opening in the glen, Mabel closely following, and as they emerged into a less entangled part of the forest, the shrieks, which were continued, seemed to approach nearer.   The grey dawn of morning was just breaking in the eastern horizon, and rendered surrounding objects more distinct ; but the Gipsies could at first perceive nothing to account for the sounds they had heard ; however, they cautiously advanced in the direction from whence they proceeded, being fully prepared for any sudden surprise which they might have to encounter.   And now they could distinctly hear the shouts of two or three men, and caught a faint glimpse of their forms moving hastily among the trees at a short distance off.   Again that piteous cry resounded in the air, and they had no longer any doubt that a portion of the robbers were in pursuit of some intended victim of outrage.   They had no sooner come to this conclusion than the loud report of a couple of pistols was heard, and the next instant the haggard ·

form of a man, wild with terror and despair, was seen flying with the speed of the wind towards the glen which they had just quitted, and hotly pursued by two others, whose ferocious looks at once revealed their characters. Brayling and his companions suffered the terrified man to approach within a short distance of where they were before they discovered themselves, and no sooner had they done so than, with a loud exclamation, the man rushed forward, and with clasped hands and frenzied looks sunk on his knees before them. Sampson Brayling raised him immediately, for his astonishment may be readily conceived when he found it was the miser, Jasper Scrimpe !

There was no time for explanation at that moment, however, and leaving the unfortunate old man in the care of Mabel, himself and his comrades hastened to meet the ruffians who were in pursuit of him. But no sooner did they behold the superior numbers they had to contend with, than, discharging the contents of their pistols at them, they turned, and taking to immediate flight, were quickly lost to view in the intricacies of the forest. Brayling and his companions now returned to the Miser, whom they found glaring vacantly and idiotically around, and making the air resound again with his wild and frantic exclamations. No sooner did his eyes encounter the form of the Gipsey-Chief than his emotions assumed a more fearful tone than before, and, trembling convulsively in every limb, he shrieked—

"Back ! back, foul fiend ! thou shalt not, darest not approach me ! Thou comest to drag my aged limbs to the scaffold; to denounce me as a murderer ! to consign me to a felon's death ! keep him off, I say ! he has robbed the old man of his gold ! he hath kindled the fires of perdition in his brain, and now would have his life ! see, how he mocks and taunts me ! Back! back ! torturing demon, back !"

"Wretched, guilty man;" observed Brayling, "the power of conscience hath at length done its work, and madness hath seized upon his brain. This strange concurrence of events is most wonderful; and all portend the crisis that is so rapidly approaching. Lead him carefully to the Abbey, where his appearance must greatly heighten the excitement that already prevails there. Come, Mabel; there may be danger in tarrying here, for, should the robbers alarm their comrades, who probably are close at hand, we might find it difficult to escape from their vengeance."

Completely exhausted by the exertions he had undergone, the Miser was now powerless, and quietly suffered himself to be led from the spot, and they moved hastily towards the Abbey.

CHAPTER XLV.

The Design on the Abbey by the Robbers.—A Scene of Excitement.

FINDING that the reason of the wretched Miser had fled for ever, and annoyed by his wild ravings, Oliver Dalton at length reluctantly yielded to the persuasions of Reginald and the other robbers, and consigned him to death. The captain of this lawless and desperate gang proposed to perpetrate the inhuman deed in the place where the unfortunate old man was confined, but Oliver shuddered at the idea, lest his dying groans should reach his ears; and even, though hardened as he was in crime, his soul revolted at the thought ; neither could he find the desperate courage to have any actual hand in the murder himself; for that reason the Miser was committed to the care of two of the most ferocious of the robbers, who seized him in his sleep in the silence of night, and hurried him to the thickest part of the

forest, with the monstrous design there to sacrifice his life, and afterwards to conceal all traces of the deed by burying his body on the spot. In spite of the frenzy of his brain, the poor man seemed to have some vague idea of the design of the ruffians, and made a desperate resistance after they had left the cavern, rending the air with his cries, uttering wild ravings, and at intervals, as the light of reason seemed for an instant to dawn upon his intellect, appealing to them in the most piteous accents for mercy and forbearance. But they mocked at his sufferings, and uttering the most dreadful oaths and imprecations on his head, dragged him along with the most savage violence. With the strength of madness, however, he at last broke from their hold, dashed precipitately forward, and plunging into the most intricate part of the forest, seemed likely to effect his escape. Uttering the most fearful threats and maledictions, the robbers pursued him, and the result is already known to the reader. Cursing the accident that had rescued their intended victim from

No. 34.

their hands, and regretting that they had not at once perpetrated the deed, the robbers made the best of their way to the cavern, where they arrived in a few minutes. Oliver Dalton had been in a great state of agitation during their absence, for his conscience smote him for the frightful crime he had sanctioned, and deeply he regretted that he had not been determined to spare the miserable old man's life, so completely powerless as he was to do him harm. Anxiously and tremblingly he awaited the return of the ruffians, though he dreaded to hear of the accomplishment of their atrocious designs. But when he heard of the escape of Jasper Scrimpe, the excitement of his feelings may be readily imagined. Although he felt a certain degree of relief and satisfaction that the old man's life had not been sacrificed, fresh terrors assailed him. Should his senses be restored he might recollect the events that had recently occurred, and make such a revelation as might lead to the most dangerous results.

"It is an unfortunate affair;" observed Reginald, with an oath; "but thou hast thyself to blame for all; had it not been for thy ridiculous squeamishness, the old man might have been easily despatched, and thou wouldst now have had nothing to fear from him. However, it is useless to regret. What have we to dread from a madman?"

"True;" returned Oliver; "yet there is times when I think of the Miser; strange ideas, misgivings, and forebidings haunt my mind, for which I scarcely know how to account."

"Psha!" exclaimed Reginald; "this is a ridiculous weakness and superstitious feeling unworthy the desperate character of Luke Stanton, or Oliver Dalton, whichever thou pleasest to call thyself. But away with these thoughts; we have far more important subjects to occupy our minds; unless, indeed, thou hast resolved to abandon thy designs against the inmates of the old Abbey, and resign all hopes of the scornful damsel whom thy consummate artifices were so near obtaining possession of."

"Abandon my designs, never!" exclaimed Oliver, resolutely; "the temporary defeat I have met with goads me on to vengeance, and I shall never rest satisfied until I have accomplished my wishes. I will yet gain access to the coffers of the wealthy Sir Milford Welborn, and get the haughty Constance in my power, or perish in the attempt."

"Well spoken;" said the robber; "and to effect that bold task, thou wilt find ready assistants in myself and my comrades."

"Ah! but when shall we make the attempt?" demanded Oliver, eagerly; "I am all impatience for the execution of the desperate task?"

"Hark ye;" replied Reginald; "I am anxious that there should be no unnecessary delay in the business; and for that reason I have set two or three of the most zealous of the band to reconnoitre the Abbey for the last few nights, and they have succeeded in finding the easiest means of access. Let us but once obtain an entrance, and fear not, but should we be disturbed and meet with any resistance, our daggers will accomplish the rest."

"Your words arouse me, Reginald;" said Oliver, "and I feel myself again. When all in the Abbey are hushed in sleep and fancied security, for little can they dream of the danger that threatens them, we may safely effect an entrance, and with determination on our side, and overwhelming superiority of numbers, we have little to apprehend from any resistance that may be offered to us. Still it is a bold venture, and should we fail—"

"Fail?" interrupted Reginald; "it is not possible, if we only act with due precaution and resolution. Our daring band never yet suffered themselves to be defeated in any thing upon which they had fixed their mind. Besides they will be goaded on by a feeling of revenge for the legal murder of their three comrades, whose bones now moulder on the heath."

"True ;" observed Dalton ; "and for that reason we ought to be able to depend upon their determination and fidelity."

"Fidelity !" repeated the robber-chief; "who dare suspect that treachery should lurk among those bold and desperate men, who have for so many years been associated together, and whose daring deeds have stamped their very names with terror ? "

"Enough ;" returned Oliver ; "I am satisfied; and feel most sanguine as to the result. But when shall we attempt to put our designs into execution ? "

"There has already been sufficient delay," replied Reginald ; "and, as we are fully prepared, I propose that to morrow, at midnight, the business should be settled."

"Be it so;" coincided Oliver ;" my impatience can brook no further delay. Constance Welborn, proud, scornful damsel, thou shalt yet have cause to tremble at the power of Oliver Dalton, or, at any rate, he will have a deadly revenge against those who have hitherto thwarted him in his ambitious designs."

"Aye ;" remarked his companion ; "but booty must be our object as well as vengeance; "and I fear not but success will crown our daring efforts. But," he added, after a minute or two's reflection, " an idea strikes me ; I have bethought me of a stratagem which will further our designs, and make our triumph doubly certain."

"Ah !" said Oliver, eagerly, " name it."

"Listen ;" returned Reginald ; "there might still be some difficulty in our gaining an entrance to the Abbey without detection ; now, hospitable as the inmates of the old mansion are, it would be easy to impose upon their credulity. Disguised as a sick and weary traveller, it would not be difficult for one of our comrades to obtain admission to the Abbey in the evening, and to secure a shelter there for the night, and watching his opportunity when the family has retired to rest, and all is hushed in unconscious repose, he could give admittance to the rest of the band, and the business would be accomplished."

"Ah!" exclaimed Dalton, eagerly, " it is an excellent plan, and does thee credit Reginald. But who amongst the band can we trust with such an important task?"

"Myself ;" replied Reginald ; "it is not the first scheme of the kind that I have been engaged in, and fear not but that I shall accomplish it with every success."

"Your hand, Reginald ;" said Oliver ; "I can, I know, depend upon your skill and ingenuity, and this plan inspires me with fresh hopes. Constance Welborn, thou mayest console thyself with the idea of present security if thou wilt ; but little canst thou suspect that thine old enemy hovers so near, and that, if Fate frowns not upon him, thou wilt be securely in his power, and, in spite of thy proud and scornful spirit, and the disgust and horror with which thou viewest him, be compelled to yield to his will. To morrow night then, Reginald—"

"Our well-formed plot shall be put into execution at all hazards ;" rejoined Reginald ; "and, placing every reliance in the courage and determination of our comrades, I entertain no apprehensions as to the result. At the hour of midnight I shall expect thou, Luke, and the rest of our band, to be waiting in readiness for me to admit ye to the scene of action."

"Thou mayest be sure that we will not fail ;" answered Oliver ; "and I am all impatience for the time to arrive."

"Enough ;" said the robber ; "we are fully agreed upon the subject, and to morrow we will finally arrange our plans."

Oliver expressed his assent, and after a few more observations they separated. When alone, Dalton pondered deeply upon his guilty projects, and weighed in his own mind the probability of their success. The undertaking was a desperate one, and, should it fail, his own detection and destination would be likely to follow, and, instead of the gratification of his nefarious and ambitious wishes, that justice which he had hitherto contrived to evade, might overtake him, and he would at last have to pay the fearful penalty of his crimes. In spite of his efforts to the contrary, he could not banish from his mind the certain doubts and misgivings that haunted it, and, every now and then a dismal foreboding of some fearful approaching crisis would obtrude itself upon his imagination, which he in vain tried to dispute, and rendered him anxious and uneasy. The form of the Miser, too, continually occupied his thoughts ; and although he felt some degree of satisfaction to know that the wretched old man had escaped the awful fate intended him, he regretted that he had not remained in his power, and had fallen into other hands, as it might lead to certain discoveries that would be productive of the most serious consequences.

"But, psha !" he ejaculated, "why should I torture and distract my mind with these idle speculations and apprehensions ? Shall I who have proceeded so far, who have hitherto been the bold and reckless villian, but whose situation and circumstances are at present so desperate, now tremble and hesitate when one favourable turn of Fortune's wheel may realize all my wishes ? No, I will be firm and resolute, and, if Oliver Dalton is to fall, at any rate it shall not be without a powerful effort to avert his fate."

Having come to this determination, he became more composed, and impatiently awaited the arrival of the time for the execution of the daring plot.

The following day the robbers completed all their guilty plans for the projected burglary at the Abbey, and the abduction of the fair Constance Welborn ; and all was anxiety and anticipation till the important hour should arrive. It was one of those cold dreary days of which there had been so many of late, with occasional showers, and promised well to give a colouring to the stratagem of Reginald, who was fully prepared to enact the part he had allotted to himself ; and, as soon as the shadows of evening had darkened o'er the earth, he and Rodolphe quitted the cavern, so disguised that it was impossible for any one to have the least suspicion as to their real characters, and made their way towards the Abbey. Oliver, and the rest of the band followed shortly afterwards, in small, detached parties, and by different routes, concealing themselves in various parts near the Abbey till the appointed hour should arrive.

The reader will be able to form a pretty correct idea of the state of Oliver Dalton's mind at this time. He was all upon the tiptoe of expectation ; but still alternate hopes and fears, doubts and misgivings, continued to harass and bewilder his brain. In order to kill the time, which to him appeared particularly tedious, closely enveloped in his dark mantle, so as to conceal his person from observation, he left his companions, and sauntered towards the Abbey, though for what purpose he scarcely knew himself. The hour seemed propitious for any deed of guilt ; all was silent and dark around ; the lights from the different casements of the Abbey being all that broke upon the prevailing gloom. Oliver stood in a convenient spot, where he could command a full view of the venerable building, without any fear of being observed himself, and, folding his arms across his chest, he looked up at the different windows with anxious eyes, and with the vague idea that he might catch a glimpse of Constance Welborn at one of them. How soon did he hope that she would be in his power, and that thought inspired him with fresh courage and determination. Reginald had evidently obtained admission to the Abbey, and so far, therefore, their plot had succeeded, and of its ultimate complete success, there seemed to be very little doubt, considering that the inmates of the Abbey could not be prepared for any such attack, and could offer no effectual resistance to the number of desperate ruffians that would be opposed to them. Yet, in spite of all this, the mind of Oliver Dalton wavered betwixt hope and fear ; and anxious even as he was, he almost dreaded the approach of the critical moment.

He was aroused from these reflections, and awakened to a sense of the caution necessary for him to use, by observing, as well as the darkness would permit him, one of the doors of the old building opened, and the forms of two men, followed by several others issue forth, and advance in the direction of the spot where he stood. He drew himself back in the place of his concealment, and watched them narrowly with feelings of anxious curiosity and suspicion. They drew near, apparently engaged in earnest conversation, and stopped so close to where he was concealed, that he had a clearer view of their persons, and observations that fell from their lips. He listened with breathless attention.

"I am compelled to go ;" said one of them, and Oliver started at the tones of his voice, for they were perfectly familiar to him ; "but probably you will see me again in a few hours. Return you to the Abbey, for doubtless Sir Milford and his fair niece will think it strange that you should withdraw yourself from their society."

"I will obey your wishes, Sampson ;" replied his companion ; "still I cannot to night help feeling a strange sensation of dread, and I shall await your return with the utmost anxiety and impatience."

Had a thunderbolt at that moment struck him, it could scarcely have had a more powerful effect on Oliver Dalton, than at that moment, when he recognised Evelyn Heartwell and Sampson Brayling; and, unable to control his feelings of surprise and emotion, he gave utterance to an exclamation ; but, at the same time alarmed at his own imprudence, he drew himself into the smallest possible compass, and crouched down in his place of concealment, lest he should be discovered.

" What was that?" demanded Brayling, hastily, and looking anxiously round.

" What mean you?" interrogated Evelyn.

" Did you not hear a sound?" said the Gipsey.

" I heard nothing ;" replied his companion. "I could almost have sworn it was a human voice ;" remarked Sampson, opening a small dark lantern, he had with him, and looking cautiously about.

" It could only have been the wind."

" Probably it was ;" returned the Gipsey ; "but knowing the villains that infest this neighbourhood, it naturally makes one suspicious."

" True ;" coincided Evelyn ; "but again I must urge you to return to the Abbey as soon as possible."

" You may be sure that I will make no more delay than is unavoidable ;" answered Brayling ; "farewell, I hope when we meet again that I shall have some favorable news to communicate. Now then, I must begone ; return you into the Abbey, and remember, during my absence, to keep a strict watch over the actions of Mabel."

" I will not fail ;" said Evelyn ; and, pressing the hand of the Gipsey, he retraced his steps to the Abbey, which he re-entered, Brayling watching him cautiously till he had done so ; when, motioning to his companions, followed by them, he departed from the spot in a different direction to that where the robbers were concealed.

Oliver Dalton now ventured from his hiding place, and made his way towards his guilty associates. His astonishment and agitation at what he had seen and heard, may be imagined.

"So," he muttered to himself as he proceeded on his way; "Evelyn and Mabel have escaped the perils and dangers of the ocean, and are now at the Abbey. My rival, whom I had hoped had perished, is restored to his beloved Constance, and doubtless is now received with favour and friendship by Sir Milford, and looked upon as the victim of injustice and a remorseless Fate ; oh, how torturing is his triumph to my soul. But little can he suspect the fresh and overwhelming evils that threaten him. The deep laid scheme that is on the eve of being put into execution to destroy his prospects and his hopes. If Fortune does not turn jilt to me, the moment of my revenge is at hand. It is fortunate that Sampson Brayling and the Gipsies have departed from the Abbey, or, even daring and determined as the robbers are, we might have found our task more difficult of accomplishment than we anticipated. It is not likely that they will return to night, and the success of our plot is therefore the more certain. A short time will decide my hopes and fears, and, till then, let me endeavour to await with patience. My feelings are wrought up to the highest pitch of excitement, and I will remain firm and unshaken."

Thus soliloquising, Oliver Dalton hurried on his way, and soon afterwards rejoined his companions.

Leaving him for a while, we will relate what was passing at the Abbey. The return of Sampson Brayling, accompanied by the unfortunate Miser, and the Gipsey-girl, caused a considerable sensation among the inmates, and the meeting between the faithful Gipsey-Chief and our hero was of the most interesting description. The providential rescue of Jasper Scrimpe from the awful fate with which he had been threatened at the hands of the robbers, caused their greatest wonder and satisfaction ; while his deplorable situation—reason appearing to have abandoned her seat in his brain altogether—excited their deepest commiseration and regret, as so much might still depend upon him to corroborate the disclosures that Sampson Brayling had to make, at what he considered would be a fitting opportunity, and to unravel the strange mysteries that were still to be explained.

On beholding Sir Milford Welborn and our hero for a minute, a faint ray of sanity and recollection seemed to dawn upon the old man's brain ; and, clasping his hands together, and staring vacantly upon them, while a convulsive shuddering shook his limbs, he cried—

" Ah, who are ye who scowl menacingly upon me, and look as though ye would pry into all the dark secrets of my soul, and triumph in my shame and misery ? Away, away ! I know ye now, and will still defy your power ! Who dare accuse me of those frightful crimes, the bare recital of which must make humanity shudder ? — crimes which should since have been buried in the oblivion of the past ! And who art thou, boy, that appal my sight with that fearful resemblance ? Hide, hide those features from my terrified gaze, for they turn my blood to ice, yet seem to scorch my brain with unearthly fires ? Avaunt ?— I mock and defy thee !— Thou darest not accuse me !— Who, who amongst ye dare say ye witnessed the hideous deed ? No, no, no, ye will not, cannot seek to consign the poor old man to the scaffold ! Oh, mercy ! mercy !"

Again he raved in all the frenzy of the most confirmed madness, and unable any longer to witness his sufferings, Sir Milford ordered him to be conveyed to a chamber, and every care and attention to be bestowed upon him which his melancholy situation demanded.

" Wretched old man ;" said Sir Milford, " how terrible must have been that remorse of conscience which could thus lay prostrate an intellect, doubtless once fresh and vigorous."

" True, Sir Milford ;" replied Brayling ; " dark and fearful indeed is the catalogue of his crimes, and terrible should be his punishment."

" But, how is it, Brayling," interrogated Sir Thomas Overton ; " you being in possession of all the facts should still hesitate to reveal them ?"

" Aye," observed Sir Milford ; " surely there can be no just reason for any further delay."

" Pardon me ;" returned Sampson ; " but I have my motives for still deferring the disclosure. But, mark me, when the time shall come, prepare yourselves to hear that which will astound ye all, and will unravel the mystery which has so long enveloped the circumstances immediately connected with Evelyn Heartwell and others."

"Torturing suspense;" exclaimed our hero; "how much longer am I to be subjected to it?"

"I promise you but a short time, Evelyn;" answered the Gipsey; "and believe me thou wilt be amply repaid for this tax upon thy patience.'"

Evelyn and his friends saw that it was useless to urge him farther, and Brayling and Mabel, (who had exhibited the greatest uneasiness while in the presence of Constance) shortly afterwards retired from the room.

Walter Greysham, who was considerably better than could have been expected, after the maltreatment he had received, was informed by Evelyn of all the extraordinary events that had taken place in the prospects of our hero; but when he related the conduct of the Gipsey-girl, and how narrowly she had been saved from self-destruction, he sighed, as a mingled feeling of pity and regret agitated his breast. The powerful impression which the glowing virtues and noble character of Mabel had made upon his heart hourly increased, but it was only to convince him the more that his passion for her was as hopeless as that she so unfortunately entertained for Evelyn.

The day passed over without anything more particular taking place. Evening set in, as has been before described, cold and dreary, and the friends were seated in one of the lower apartments, discussing the extraordinary events that had marked the last two or three years of their lives; and expressing mutual hopes that the time was not far distant when their troubles would be brought to a happy termination. The Miser, who had been placed under the charge of two of the male servants, had, for some hours, ceased his wild raving, and sunk into a state of apathy, or stupor, which was melancholy to behold; and even heartless, mercenary, and repulsive as his character had ever been, it was impossible to view him in his present wretched state; reason destroyed, every faculty prostrated; fallen, wrecked, hopeless and degraded, without feelings of pity, pain and regret.

While the friends were still seated, engaged in conversation, their attention was arrested by a noise which proceeded from the Hall, and Sir Milford ringing the bell to ascertain the cause, Abigail made her appearance, and, in answer to the inquiries of the Baronet said—

"Two poor travellers, and please you, Sir Milford; one an aged man, the other apparently his son, but both of them sinking with fatigue and hunger, have ventured to crave the rights of hospitality. Would it please you to lend a charitable ear to their wishes."

"Certainly, my good Abigail;" said Sir Thomas Overton; "the humble wants of the poor and needy must ever be attended to. Where are these unfortunate men?"

"In the Hall, Sir Thomas;" replied Abigail.

"Conduct them hither;" said Sir Thomas; "we would inquire into their situation."

Abigail curtseyed, and leaving the room, in a few seconds returned with the supposed unfortunate travellers of whom she had spoken. The ruffian, Reginald, was a perfect adept at disguise, and on this occasion he had completely surpassed himself; he and his companion being so entirely metamorphosed that it would have been almost a matter of impossibility to have detected them. They were both dressed in the tattered habiliaments of mendicants; Reginald as a decrepit old man, with long straggling gray hair, pale, careworn, emaciated features, and leaning on a staff. Rodolphe appeared as his son, and looked the very picture of misery, want, and destitution. On being ushered into the room, they made many humble obeisances, and Reginald seemed to be ready to sink with illness and fatigue. They both acted their parts so well that they excited the deepest sympathy among the humane persons present, particularly the gentle Constance, who kindly advancing with the greatest condescension and solicitude towards the apparent wretched old man, conducted him to a seat.

"Heaven bless thee, good young lady," said Reginald, in a feeble and querulous voice; "grace and humanity are in thy fair countenance, and poor old Martin and his son much indeed need the kind consideration of the charitable."

"Thou appearest very ill, old man; observed Sir Thomas; and thou and thy son to be hungry and weary."

"Alas! noble sir;" replied Reginald; "we have both of us travelled many a weary mile, for we are homeless and destitute. It is some hours since we tasted food, and I am so aged and infirm, that I thought I must lie down in the road and die, or I should not have presumed to have obtruded here, with the hope of obtaining some little relief in my terrible distress."

"The deserving poor ever find sympathy and assistance at Greenwood Abbey;" said Sir Thomas; "nor shall it be refused to thee and thy companion, unfortunate old man."

"Oh, thanks, thanks, kind Sir;" cried Rodolphe, apparently overwhelmed with gratitude.

"No thanks;" returned Sir Thomas; "they are uncalled for in the performance of an act which common humanity dictates. My servants will see to your refreshment, and afterwards conduct you to a chamber, where you may obtain that friendly rest of which you seem to stand so much in need."

"Oh, may the blessing of Heaven descend upon thy head, noble Sir, for this act of benevolence to thine humble fellow creatures;" ejaculated Reginald, in tones that were calculated to deceive even the most keen and penetrating observer.

"Enough, old man;" returned Sir Thomas; "accompany the domestic, who will see to thy wants, which are evidently most urgent. In the morning I will see thee again, and talk further upon this subject. Abigail, thou wilt attend to the necessities of these poor people?"

Abigail curtseyed, and the robbers exchanged significant glances, which were not observed by the persons present. They then followed her out of the room.

As they entered the passage, they met Sampson Brayling and Mabel, who were about to rejoin their friends; and, at the sight of them the ruffians could not help starting, and felt somewhat confused and disconcerted.

Brayling and Mabel eyed them narrowly for an instant, and then passed on without making use of any observation. On entering the room, they found the company conversing upon the miserable appearance of the supposed mendicants, and congratulating themselves upon being afforded the opportunity of relieving the wants of those who seemed to be such worthy objects of charity.

"Pardon me, Sir Thomas;" observed Brayling; "far be it from me to seek to check the wishes of benevolence and humanity, but I must be permitted to say, that, in this neighbourhood especially, where there are so many lawless ruffians lurking about, and who adopt such cunning artifices, to accomplish their nefarious designs, it is necessary to use every precaution to guard against them."

"True;" coincided Sir Thomas; "but still I cannot think we have any cause to suspect these poor people."

"Probably not;" returned Brayling, and the conversation upon that subject dropped. Soon afterwards Sampson informed them that business compelled him to leave them that evening, but that he would return as soon as possible; and he then quitted the Abbey, Evelyn following him, as he wished to have a few words with him privately. It was on that occasion that they had been observed by Oliver Dalton, as described in the previous pages.

The pretended beggars having been plentifully supplied with provisions, for which they were unbounded in their expressions of gratitude, were conducted to

a comfortable chamber for the night, and being left to themselves, the robbers gave free vent to their feelings of exultation at the present success of their plot, and laughed heartily at the clever manner in which they had been able to impose upon the credulity of Sir Thomas and the others.

"The success of our designs is now certain;" remarked Reginald.

"Aye;" returned his companion; "though I confess that I felt somewhat alarmed when I found that Sampson Brayling and his comrades were here, for we might have found them more than a match for us, if we had had to contend with them."

"True;" coincided Reginald," and it is a fortunate thing that they have left the Abbey, to which I hope they will not return till we have completed our task. So Mabel and Evelyn Heartwell are restored to their friends. This will indeed be a surprise to Luke Stanton. But, we must still be cautious, and care-

No. 35.

fully watch the time when the family have retired to rest, and all is still in the Abbey."

To this Rodolphe assented, and the two villains waited the arrival of the time with eager impatience.

It was not till nearly midnight that the friends separated, and sought their chambers, and a death-like silence soon reigned throughout the Abbey which seemed propitious to the execution of the guilty scene which was shortly to take place.

There was one individual, however, to whom repose was a stranger, and whose mind was still haunted and distracted by the most wild and ungovernable passions. That hapless being was Mabel, the Gipsey-girl, who, at length unable to tranquillize her feeling, and with no settled purpose, she quitted her chamber, and slowly and silently descended the staircase which led from it. Observing a light in the room where the mendicants were accommodated, and also hearing a muttering of voices, her suspicions and curiosity were excited, and she paused to listen.

"Hist! hist! Rodolphe;" she heard one of them say; "all is now quiet. The inmates of the Abbey have doubtless retired to rest."

"Aye," returned the other, and all is favourable to our designs. By this time no doubt our comrades are waiting outside for admittance."

"'Tis true;" coincided the ruffian; "and we had therefore better not delay. Follow."

Surprised at the discovery she had made, and anxious to frustrate the diabolical designs of the robbers, (for such she now felt convinced they were), Mabel drew herself into a recess in the wall, which fortunately offered the means of concealment, and directly afterwards the door was cautiously opened; and the two ruffians emerged from the room into the galllery beyond; one of them carrying a small lantern, which he held above his head, and looked eagerly around.

"All's safe;" observed Reginald;" the coast is quite clear; now to admit our comrades. This way, Rodolphe."

Reginald now moved stealthily from the spot, closely followed by Rodolphe, and descending the stairs with silent footsteps, immediately disappeared. The Gipsey-girl now issued from the recess, and, advancing on tiptoe to the head of the staircase, and again listened with breathless attention, and could hear the robbers making towards one of the entrances to the Abbey, which was seldom used by the family.

"The designs of the villians do not admit of a doubt;" she muttered to herself; "what is to be done? The danger which threatens is most imminent, and what resistance can be offered to the probable numbers of the robbers? How unfortunate it is that Brayling and the Gipsies have left the Abbey!"

She could now plainly hear the bolts of the door being withdrawn, and the muttering sounds of several voices. There was not a moment to be lost, and Mabel's first impulse was to dart up the staircase at the further end of the gallery which led to that part of the building occupied by the male domestics, and the members of the family, though she feared that they had retired to rest, and would be totally unprepared for the daring attack which was about to be made upon them. She reached the door of the chamber in which she knew that Evelyn reposed; and felt some relief when she saw a light glimmering though the crevices by which she judged that Evelyn had not yet retired to bed, and she ventured to knock.

"Who's there?" hastily demanded our hero, who had been sitting immersed in gloomy mediation.

"'Tis I, Mabel;" she replied, in an under tone; "Quick! quick, Evelyn, for Heaven's sake. There are thieves in the Abbey; the pretended mendicants have betrayed us. Hasten, or all is lost!"

In a moment Evelyn rushed from the chamber in a state of the greatest surprise and bewilderment, and eagerly demanded from the agitated Mabel an explanation.

"The Abbey is beset by villians;" she answered, in breathless haste; "robbery, and probably murder, is intended. And, hark!"

The half-suppressed sounds of several voices were now heard to proceed from below, and it seemed evident that the robbers had entered, and were about to commence the execution of their atrocious plot.

" Ah !" exclaimed Evelyn, in the greatest agitation ; " what is to be done ? Were it possible to arouse the domestics, and apprise them of their danger—but Constance !—she must be protected from the threatened danger. Mabel, for God's sake, lose not a moment's time in endeavouring to alarm Sir Milford and our friends. Hark !—by Heaven the miscreants are ascending the stairs ! "

With the rapidity of thought, and, sword in hand, Evelyn quitted the Gipsey-girl, in the confusion of the moment, scarcely knowing what he did, and rushed into the passage on the right, which he believed led to the suite of rooms occupied by Constance and her attendant. Mabel's presence of mind did not fail her on this important occasion, and knowing no readier means of arousing the family, and daunting the courage of the robbers, she flew to the alarm bell, which she rung violently, and Sir Milford, Sir Thomas, and several of the domestics, half undressed, rushed from their different chambers in a state of the greatest confusion and trepidation. But to return to the robbers. Emboldened by the apparent serenity, and the universal silence which pervaded, Reginald and his companions stole towards the door, by which they had agreed to submit their comrades, and listening attentively, could plainly hear the muttering of voices outside.

" They are there ;" observed Reginald, in an under tone ; "so, now to business. Hist ! Luke, art thou there? "

" Yes ;" answered the voice of Oliver Dalton, in the same cautious tones as those in which Reginald had spoken, " Is all right? "

" Quite safe!" returned Reginald ; " be cautious, and I will admit ye."

Oliver returned no answer, and Reginald and his companion having with some difficulty removed the rusty bolts, admitted them to the Abbey.

" 'Tis fortunate," whispered Oliver ; " so far our plot has succeeded even beyond my expectations. Evelyn Heartwell and Mabel are in the Abbey ! "

" True," replied Reginald.

" Curses light upon him," muttered Dalton ; " but if Fortune desert me not he shall not now escape my deadly malice. Art thou sure all the inmates have retired to rest ? "

" It is not likely that they would be stirring at this unreasonable hour !" returned the robber."

" And yet I thought I observed lights in several of the casements;" remarked Oliver. " Know you the part of the Abbey in which the chamber of Constance is situated? "

" Aye," answered Reginald ; " but it would be advisable first to look to our booty, and the security of those who might venture to oppose us. We waste time ; this way ; be firm, and fear not but we shall succeed."

Dalton returned no answer, though he was all anxiety and suspense, and having pulled the mask down over his face (for he had taken that precaution to conceal his features from observation), he cautiously followed the footsteps of Reginald, and the other robbers did the same. They had, however, only ascended two or three of the stairs, when Oliver started, and grasped the arm of Reginald, in apparent alarm.

" How now ?" hastily and impatiently demanded the latter.

" Did you not hear a noise above ?"

"Bah! I heard nothing;" answered Reginald; "all is as still as the grave. It was nothing but your timid imagination."

"I could almost swear I heard the muttering of human voices;" said Oliver.

"This is sheer folly;" returned Reginald; "there is nothing to apprehend. Let us not delay; our daggers will soon settle any resistance we might chance to meet with."

"Yet would I avoid bloodshed, if possible;" said Oliver.

"Enough;" returned Reginald; "this delay is useless."

Again they proceeded, but in another minute the alarm bell was rung, its deep tones reverberating through the venerable building and far around; lights hurried to and fro, followed by the confused sound of voices, and the opening of doors and hasty closing of doors, and the robbers started back astonished and alarmed.

"Confusion!" cried Oliver; "our plot is detected; we are betrayed!"

"Then our determination must be redoubled," said Reginald; "forward! they must be mad and desperate indeed to attempt to oppose us. Curses light upon that bell! and yet it cannot bring any assistance from the neighbourhood. This way!—this way!—"

Still the bell was rung with increased violence, and the male domestics, who were now aroused to a full sense of the danger which threatened, rushed hurriedly from the different avenues, having armed themselves in the best manner they could. But the superiority of the numbers they had to contend with, and their well-known ferocious character, naturally somewhat intimidated them, and the robbers rushed on furiously, with loud shouts and confident of success. Sir Thomas Overton and Sir Milford now joined the domestics at the head of the staircase, and encouraged them to bolder resistance by their own example. The rage and excitement of Oliver Dalton during this scene may be imagined, and the most fearful curses escaped his lips, as he mingled in the strife, and endeavoured to force his way to that part of the building, which he had every reason to suppose was occupied by Constance, in the hope that in the confusion which prevailed, he might get her in his power, and once outside the Abbey with his fair prize, he considered his success was all but certain. But while he was thus deliberating he abruptly encountered the form of a man, who suddenly made his appearance before him, and his agitation may be well imagined when he recognised Evelyn Heartwell!

CHAPTER XLVI.

The Result of the Attack.—Startling Events.

In the confusion of the struggle the mask of Oliver had been removed, so that his features were fully revealed to our hero at the moment when they met; and, burning with feelings of indignation and disgust; it was impossible for him to help giving expression to them.

"Ah! base traducer! unprincipled miscreant, we meet again. It is then at thy villainous instigation this daring outrage has taken place. At least thou shalt not now escape that justice thou hast so long eluded."

"Vain boaster!" fiercely cried his implacable foe, in accents of the most deadly malice, and rushing upon him; "Oliver Dalton still scorns and defies the hated Evelyn Heartwell."

Worked up to a pitch of desperation at the sight of his rival, Oliver commenced the combat with the utmost fury, and Evelyn being by far the best swordsman, and at the same time cool and collected, had the advantage. Oliver, however, aiming a tremendous blow at the head of our hero, which the latter dexterously warded, in doing so his sword was struck out of his hand, and he staggered back a few paces, being entirely at the mercy of his fierce and revengeful adversary, who did not fail to take advantage of it, and with a loud and fearful oath he rushed forward with the intention to bury his sword in Evelyn's body, when at that instant a loud exclamation in a female voice saluted his ears, and arrested his arm; a door at the back of where Evelyn was placed in such a dangerous situation, flew open, and Mabel rushed before him armed with a pistol, the contents of which she discharged at Oliver Dalton, slightly grazing him as it passed, and inflicting a mortal wound on the villain Reginald when advancing to his assistance, and who, with a fearful oath fell bleeding on the ground. At that moment, Constance Welborn arrived at the spot, and rushed to the arms of her lover; Oliver drawing back in dismay, to shield himself from the imminent danger by which he now found himself surrounded. At this critical juncture, loud shouts where heard from below, followed by the clashing of swords, and a number of men were to be seen, fighting their way up the principal staircase, and the terror of Oliver may be well conceived when he heard the name of Brayling uttered in tones of exultation.

Yes, it was Sampson Brayling and the Gipsies. On their return, they had arrived to within a short distance of the Abbey, when the loud sound of the alarm bell reached their ears, and ther suspicions being excited, they redoubled their speed, and fortunately arrived at the scene of danger at the critical moment when their services were so much required. Aware of the danger by which he was surrounded, and that his only chance of escape was by promptitude of action, Oliver uttered a terrible malediction, and flying from the spot, thrust open a door which he perceived opposite to him, and beyond which was a winding passage that seemed to lead to a different wing of the Abbey. There were fastenings on the other side of the door, and hastily bolting it, to cut off the pursuit of his enemies that way, he fled precipitately along the passage, just as he heard their voices at the door. Here was nothing to impede his progress, and, onward he ran at the top of his speed, and, as he did so, he could distinctly hear the report of fire-arms, the clashing of swords, and loud shouts, yells, and curses, which convinced him that the combat was still being continued with the greatest ferocity by the robbers and their opponents; and he feared that all egress from the Abbey would be effectually cut off. Still he resolved to make a desperate effort to save himself although it was too evident that the chances were against him. He did not wait to hesitate, as he could hear that his pursuers were forcing the door, but, dashing down a flight of stairs which were at the end of the passage, he found himself in a range of stone vaults, which he traversed, until he found his further progress suddenly arrested by an iron door that resisted all his efforts to open it. He now paused, bewildered and dismayed, for, at the moment it seemed that all chances of his escape were at an end.

He could proceed no further, and to retrace his footsteps by the way he had come would be at once to throw himself into the power of those whom he sought to avoid; he was, therefore, as it were, completely caught in a trap, and would at last be forced to yield to the fate which so closely pursued him. And now he could again hear the shouts and the heavy footfalls of the persons above his head, and which convinced him they were close upon his track; and the terrible excitement of his feelings, surpassed all that the power of language could possibly pourtray. In a paroxysm of rage and despair, he threw himself back against the wall, completely bewildered how to act. Another instant, and the place was filled by the Gipsies, led on by Brayling, and followed by Evelyn, Sir Thomas, Sir Milford, and Mabel, and all chances of his escape were now at an end.

With a dreadful oath; he looked for his pistol, resolved to have the life of Evelyn before he yielded, but ere he could remove it from his breast, he was surrounded, and held secure; though it was not without a fierce and resolute resistance on his part, nor until he had received two or three slight wounds, which weakened and disabled him.

"May the tortures of perdition light upon ye all!" furiously exclaimed Oliver, foaming with rage; "and must I at last yield, after all my deeds of daring, without the gratification of my revenge? Evelyn Heartwell, detested rival, thou, whom I so loathe and despise in my very soul, doubtless thou thinkest thy triumph now complete, but, may every curse attend thee, and wither thy future prospects, and—"

"Wretched young man;" interrupted Sir Milford; "these fierce ravings will avail thee not. Thy dark career of guilt is drawing to a close; the avenging wrath of offended Heaven hath at last overtaken thee. Beware, beware then; add not to the heavy weight of sins already upon thy conscience, but rather let thy guilty soul be awakened to a sense of repentance and remorse."

"Repentance! remorse!" repeated Oliver, with an ironical laugh; "the cant of fools and cowards! I scorn, I despise the thought. Ye think that ye have now completely triumphed over me; but I defy ye all. Do with me as ye wilt, no earthly power shall crush the daring spirit of Oliver Dalton!"

"It is but a waste of time to listen to the hardened villain's disgusting language;" said Brayling; "leave him here in this place of security, and—"

"Ah! Sampson Brayling!" cried Oliver, fiercely, and his features became more frightfully distorted than ever with the violence of his passions; "'tis thou who art the accursed cause of all this; and may every misery that can attend the human race, reward thee for it. Coward! I dare thee to meet my just revenge! Release my hands, grant me the means of self-defence, and it shall soon be seen whose turn it is to triumph next."

"Madman!" retorted Brayling, "thine empty boastings and course vituperations excite alone contempt. Integrity and justice have ever prompted the actions of Sampson Brayling, which a few hours will prove, to thine utter shame and confusion; a few hours only, and my lips shall reveal those hidden secrets, and unravel those dark mysteries which will make the guilty tremble, and render at length justice to the innocent and oppressed."

Notwithstanding the bravado and indifference with which Oliver affected to treat everything, the observations of Brayling, and the tones in which he delivered them, made him tremble, and in that gloomy place they left him, and returned to the other part of the Abbey, where the greatly agitated Constance Welborn, and her attendant, Abigail, anxiously awaited to receive them. On hearing the result of the night's alarming adventures, and that Oliver Dalton was not only defeated in his attrocious designs, but was also a prisoner in the Abbey, she clasped her hands together, and offering up her thanks to Providence for the protection it had afforded them, sank in the arms of her lover.

Had it not been for the fortunate arrival of Brayling and the other Gipsies, just at the critical moment, it seemed but too probable the robbers would have succeeded in their guilty plot; but it was, nevertheless, evident that to the wary watchfulness and presence of mind of Mabel, in the first instance, they owed their preservation; and they lost no time in expressing, in the warmest terms, their grateful sense of the great service she had rendered them. She heard them with looks of indifference, and, in her usual melancholy accents, said—

"The Gipsey-girl estimates her own humble deeds too lightly to require thanks. She hath contributed towards the defeat of villainy, and that to her is more than an ample reward."

"My good girl;" observed Sir Milford; "we are much indebted to thee on more than one occasion, and I trust that the time is not far distant when thy numerous virtues will be rewarded by the possession of every earthly prosperity and happiness."

THE MISER OF SHOREDITCH.

"Happiness!" repeated the Gipsey-girl, with a sigh; "ah! no; to Mabel that word is only a bitter mockery!"

"Hold, Mabel;" said Brayling; "this is not the time for vain regrets. I say that thou shalt yet be happy; and thou shalt acknowledge too, the justice of the restraint which the unpolished Sampson Brayling, hath endeavoured to put upon thy wild and wayward passions. The hour so long and so anxiously looked forward to by me hath nearly arrived, and the important secrets connected with thy fate, and that of one most dear to thee, and for whom thou hast made so many noble sacrifices will be revealed to the light of day. Prepare thyself, I say again, for ere to morrow night, I promise that the dark curtain which hath so long concealed the past, shall be withdrawn. Retire, Mabel, and ponder well upon my words."

The poor girl fixed upon him an anxious and inquiring look, glanced fondly, but timidly, towards Evelyn, and, with a respectful demeanour towards Sir Milford and his friends, retired from the room without saying a word.

" And can I believe, Brayling;" said Sir Milford, when Mabel was gone; "that the important crisis, so long expected is at last approaching? Do you really intend to abandon the secrecy you have so long maintained, at the time you have promised?"

" Yes, Sir Milford," answered Brayling, " I will not fail to keep my word. The fitting time for disclosing the truth hath arrived. Oliver, is in our power; the Miser, Evelyn, Mabel, and all connected with the facts, are at hand, and I will not shrink from the performance of the task I have imposed upon myself, and which justice demands. Tax then your patience but a few hours longer, and I promise you that all shall be divulged; the guilty be brought to justice, and the innocent receive that atonement which is due for the wrongs that have been inflicted on them. But, for the present, it is necessary that we should separate for a short time, in order to endeavour to compose ourselves after the startling events that have occurred, and to prepare ourselves for the important task we have shortly yet to perform."

" True;" coincided Sir Milford; " the attempt of Oliver Dalton to escape was a desperate one; but he is now perfectly secure, and his power of doing further mischief is, I trust, at an end."

"Aye, Sir Milford;" remarked Brayling; "his guilty course is run; his presumptuous and nefarious designs are frustrated, and that terrible retribution which is due to his numerous crimes, will at length overtake him."

"Wretched, misguided man;" observed Evelyn, in tones of regret; while a strange feeling took possession of his mind, for which he was at a loss to account; " still, in spite of the manifold wrongs which I have received at his hands, could I freely forgive him, and wish, if he could only be brought to remorse and repentance, he might yet escape the full and ignominious penalty of his crimes."

" These sentiments do honour to thee, Evelyn;" replied Brayling; " it must be the instinct of nature that prompts them. Would that he were worthy of the feeling. But a short time longer, however, and I trust that the dark circumstances of this eventful drama, may be brought to a satisfactory termination."

To this wish every one present heartily responded, after a few more observations, they separated.

CHAPTER XLVII.

THE PRISONER.—THE MYSTERY OF THE PAST.

OLIVER Dalton was conveyed to a small and secure room in that unoccupied part of the old Abbey, which he had traversed in his unsuccessful attempt to escape from his pursuers, and on his being left alone, he threw himself upon a seat, in all the agony of complete despair. He beat his breast, gave utterance to the most dreadful execrations upon the heads of his enemies, and the defeat of his guilty plans, and it was some time before he could at all quell the torrent of wild thoughts and feelings that raged within his breast, and drove him almost to madness. Again he started to his feet, and traversing the room with hasty and uneven steps, and striking his forehead with his clenched fist, in hoarse accents he exclaimed—

"So then, at length it hath come to this; the daring and guilty career of Oliver Dalton is nearly run; his proud and ambitious hopes are crushed, and, secure in the power of his enemies, his doom is sealed for ever. And this is the result of all those bold schemes in which I have hazarded so much, even my soul's welfare. Oh, how great is the triumph of those I so mortally hate and despise, and that thought is even more maddening to my brain than all! And shall I who have hitherto laughed law and justice to scorn, at last be brought to an ignominious fate, and perish amidst the yells and execrations of a vulgar, gaping crowd? Are there no means of escape! none, none! I am in the clutches of those who will keep a wary, watchful eye upon me; will laugh at and exult in my shame and degradation, and seek alone to aggravate my sufferings. Oh, where can I find words sufficiently powerful to curse them as the rage and deadly malice of my heart would dictate? Sampson Brayling, thou hast kept thy word; and thy present triumph adds fresh tortures to my guilty soul! and yet," he continued, after a minute's reflection, "the dark and ambiguous hints that have so frequently escaped him, fill my breast with strange apprehensions; and I feel convinced that he has something to reveal which I am anxious, yet dread to hear. What strange and unaccountable feelings that now obtrude themselves upon me; shake the usual firmness and fortitude that have characterised me, and direct my thoughts to scenes and circumstances that I have never troubled myself to ponder upon before?"

He paused, and strove to divest himself of the extraordinary feeling which seemed every instant to obtain greater influence over him, and with which the persons of Evelyn and Mabel were associated in the most inexplicable way, but he could not. The early days of his childhood among the Gipsies passed in rapid review before his imagination; days when he was a merry, artless boy, a stranger to guilt; and many acts of kindness which he had then experienced from Sampson Brayling, and of innocent affection from Mabel, but which in his future guilty and abandoned career he had learnt to forget and despise, recurred to his memory; and something like a feeling of compunction and regret came across his mind. He reflected deeply upon these subjects for some time, and he found it almost impossible to conquer the emotions they engendered.

"But, psha! away with these foolish thoughts;" he said at length, resolutely; "shall I become a very child in my defeat, and give my enemies fresh cause to exult? No; I have hitherto boldly coped with Fate, and I will continue to do so to the last. Be that fate whatever it may, I will at least meet it like a man; no earthly terrors shall shake the soul of Oliver Dalton!"

Tortured by these conflicting emotions, we will for a short time leave the wretched prisoner, and turn to other particulars which the reader will, no doubt, feel anxious to know. It was now morning, and the excitement that prevailed among the inmates of the Abbey, and the inhabitants in the neighbourhood, at the daring attempts of the robbers on the previous night, was intense. The old building presented many traces of the fray, and shewed the desperate struggle that had taken place; and Evelyn and Constance, together with their friends, could never be sufficiently grateful to Providence for their preservations from the murderous designs of such villains, and which they acknowledged was mainly to be attributed to Mabel and Sampson Brayling. As the latter had intimated, they firmly believed that their troubles and vicissitudes were fast approaching a termination; and they awaited the disclosures

that he had promised to make with the greatest anxiety and suspense. Reginald died shortly after the wound he had received from the unerring aim of the intrepid Mabel; several of his associates were taken prisoners, and the bodies of many that had fled were found in different directions, having perished from their wounds and loss of blood; so that of all the desperate ruffians who had been engaged in the outrage, and which composed the principal portion of the ferocious band that had so long infested the forest, it was very probable but few had escaped. Sir Thomas Overton had communicated with his brother magistrates of the district, and it was arranged, for the better convenience of all parties, that the examination of Oliver Dalton should take place at the Abbey, in the afternoon; and when the overwhelming evidence that would be adduced on the various charges to be brought against him were considered, the certainty of the fate which awaited the wretched man would not admit of a doubt. Walter Greysham, who was sufficiently well to leave his bed, the injuries he had received being even more slight than had at first been expected, expressed the greatest interest in the whole of the extraordinary

No. 36.

and important transactions. The full and complete establishment of the innocence of his friend Evelyn, of the foul offences with which his character had been so unjustly stigmatised, and his restoration to that position in society he was so well formed to adorn, could not but afford him the greatest gratification; but his anxiety was principally for Mabel; he awaited impatiently to hear the mystery connected with that unfortunate girl unravelled; and he could not exactly banish from his mind the idea that it might be the means of leading to some discovery that would realize the fond hopes her transcendent virtues had inspired in his bosom.

While all these exciting events were going forward, there was one important witness, there was one individual in whom a change not less fortunate than remarkable had taken place. This was the Miser, Jasper Scrimpe. The frenzy of madness was calmed; his wild ravings had ceased; and although it was quite evident that nature was nearly exhausted by the manifold sufferings and extraordinary excitement to which he had been so long subjected, and that before long, probably only a few brief hours, his soul would be summoned before the awful tribunal of that Almighty Judge, whose laws he had so monstrously outraged; for a time, at any rate, reason and recollection were restored to his brain, though he abandoned himself to all the anguish of remorse and despair. To Sampson Brayling, who saw him alone, and whom he recognized, he acknowledged the justice of Heaven's retribution for the awful crimes he had committed, and expressed an anxious wish before the final moment arrived, to disburthen his conscience of the heavy weight which had so long pressed upon it, and to offer all the atonement he could; and glad to see this change at the very time when it was so much required, endeavoured to impart to him all the consolation that his deplorable situation would admit of.

"My time is short, "said the miserable old man, with a shudder; "already I feel the hand of death is upon me; but, oh, from what a frightful dream of fancied security have I awakened. Before my appalled eyes a dread eternity opens; and all mankind will shudder at the crimes, and execrate the memory of the guilty being they have known as Jasper Scrimpe!"

"Gerald Aubrey;" said Brayling, solemnly: "Heaven evinces its infinite mercy to thee, in restoring thee to thy senses in time to relieve thy conscience, and to render justice to those who have suffered through thy crimes. This day must reveal the dark secrets of the past, and if thou would'st, even at the eleventh hour, hope for forgiveness, thou wilt confess all, and—"

"This day!" interrupted Jasper, trembling, "confess? acknowledge myself a murderer, and consign myself to a murderer's doom! oh, that thought freezes the very life blood in my veins, and again lights the fire of madness in my brain!"

"Be firm, be firm, old man;" said the Gipsey; "'tis Heaven's will, and thou must submit to it."

"And thou, Brayling;" cried the Miser—fixing upon him a wild and penetrating look—"how wilt thou exonerate thyself? art thou not too implicated in the fiendish work prompted by my accursed avarice? Wert thou not too ready to perform my inhuman bidding, and to sacrifice the innocent lives of those, who—"

"No, no!" exclaimed Brayling, exultingly; "thank Heaven, I peformed not that hideous task; and thy conscience is at least spared that additional weight of crime. They live! they live!"

"Live! live!" gasped forth the Miser, with distended eyes, and limbs convulsed with emotion; "oh, no, no, no, I dare not hope so great a mercy! Thou mockest me, Brayling, and would add fresh tortures to the mind of the wretched culprit."

"By all my hopes I speak the truth;" solemnly and vehemently returned Brayling; "those to whom thou dost allude still live, and this day thou shalt, in confirmation of my assertions, behold them."

Jasper Scrimpe uttered a mingled exclamation of astonishment and satisfaction, and clasping his hands together, and sinking on his knees, raised his eyes gratefully towards Heaven.

"Almighty God!" he cried, "if thou wilt vouchsafe to listen to a wretched sinner like me, oh, receive my thanks for this! My mind is at least relieved from one dreadful burden that was almost too much to bear. Oh, Brayling," he continued, rising from his knees, "thou must indeed have become a monster couldst thou have committed a crime at which humanity shudders. But—but in mercy deceive not the miserable being before thee! Thou wilt convince me that thou hast spoken the truth? Shall I indeed behold those who—"

"Thou shalt," interrupted the Gipsey; "in a few hours thou shalt witness the truth of all I have declared. Be firm, old man, and as thou art truly penitent, and seek to make atonement, may Heaven have mercy upon thy guilty soul!"

"Mercy!" replied the trembling man, and the expression of his furrowed and haggard countenance, as he spoke, was painful to look upon; "I dare not, dare not hope for that mercy which my hardened, callous heart never extended to others. But—but let the consequences be whatever they may to myself, I will speak the truth. God of Heaven grant me my senses to perform the dreadful task which justice demands."

"Enough," said Brayling; "I believe that thy penitence and remorse are sincere, and will leave thee to collect thyself for the momentous time that is approaching."

"Not alone—not alone," gasped forth the Miser, in accents of the most indescribable terror; "oh, leave me not alone to the horror of my own thoughts, lest madness should once more seize upon my brain, and deprive me of the power to do that which the bitter compunction of my soul now dictates. Let me not be alone till the fearful hour arrives."

"Unhappy man," said the Gipsey, in tones of compassion; "thy wishes shall be complied with. Be calm, be firm, and even for so great a sinner as thou art, there may still be hope."

A convulsive emotion agitated the features of Scrimpe, as Brayling thus spoke, and pressing his hands upon his temples, with a groan he sank in a chair, and became lost to everything arround him. In this condition the Gipsey left him, and immediately sought the presence of Sir Thomas and Sir Milford, with whom having consulted on the subject, it was arranged that the Miser should be committed to the care of two confidential domestics, till the time arrived when his presence would be required at the examination of the prisoner. We need not say with what anxiety that time was looked forward to by all the parties interested, but more particularly our hero and Constance. The close of that painful drama in which they had played such active parts was drawing near; the strange and impenetrable mystery which had so long perplexed and tortured their minds was to be unravelled; and upon the important revelations that were expected to take place, and at which Sampson Brayling had so frequently hinted, the future happiness or misery of Evelyn probably depended. And yet, strange though it may seem, notwithstanding the villainy of his conduct, and the miseries he had experienced through his guilty means, Evelyn could not help feeling some degree of pity for the prisoner, and a sensation almost amounting to dread of the ignominious fate which doubtless awaited him. He could not exactly account for these emotions, but he could not banish them from his mind, and in them Constance also participated.

Mabel shunned the presence of every one as much as possible, but did not leave the abbey, and her looks and manners fully evinced the suspense and anxiety with which she awaited the events of that day, on which the destiny of herself and he whose welfare and happiness were far more precious to her than her own existence depended.

And the important hour so big with fate at length arrived.

CHAPTER XLVII.

THE EXAMINATION.—A THRILLING SCENE.

THE examination of the wretched Oliver Dalton was to take place in the great hall of the abbey, which was well adapted for such proceedings; and the magistrates who were to act with Sir Thomas Overton and Sir Milford on the occasion (General Hammersley, and Sir Roland Belmont), having arrived, and all the parties so deeply interested in the important events being present, the doors were thrown open to admit those whom curiosity might attract to the place, though that number amounted to but comparatively few individuals. Evelyn and Constance, who was greatly agitated, occupied a prominent place in the hall, while Mabel, with pale features and disordered demeanour stood apart, near Sampson Brayling, and, as her eyes ever and anon wandered to our hero and Constance, their wild and melancholy expression fully revealed the powerful emotions that struggled in her breast. All was on the tiptoe of expectation, and for a few minutes a breathless silence prevailed, which was at length broken by Sir Roland Belmont ordering the prisoner to be brought in. This was immediately obeyed, and directly afterwards a side door in the hall was thrown open, and Oliver Dalton entered. He advanced to the end of the table at which those who were to examine him were seated, with a bold air and reckless demeanour, and folding his arms across his chest, confronted Brayling, Evelyn, and Constance, with looks of malice and utter defiance. There was no trembling, no faltering in his attitude, and it was evident that he had made up his mind to the worst, and was almost indifferent as to the result. All eyes were fixed upon him, but he met the scrutiny with a manly firmness that was worthy of a better cause; and while the facts of his former offences, and of which Evelyn Heartwell had been so unjustly accused were being deposed to, he fairly smiled in derision and contempt.

"Bah !" he exclaimed, suddenly interrupting the evidence, "and this bitter mockery you call justice; but I scorn and defy ye all! I know full well that ye have prejudiced and condemned me; that ye would doom me to a felon's death; but ye shall not shake the fortitude of Oliver Dalton !"

"Be calm, young man," said Sir Thomas Overton, "more temperate language will better become thy present awful situation. Canst thou deny the charges that have just been brought against thee ?"

"Think not that I am idiot enough to attempt to deny what occurred last night," replied Oliver, "curses light on the accident which frustrated my designs, and prevented the gratification of the revenge I sought. But again I vehemently declare the guilt of Evelyn Heartwell of all with which he was accused, and boldly charge him with the robbery and attempted murder of the Miser."

"Wretched man," said Evelyn, "darest thou still persist in that monstrous, that daring calumny, in the face of all the evidence which has been produced of my entire innocence, and thine unquestionable guilt."

"Pardon me, gentlemen," said Sampson Brayling, "but this is surely little better than a waste of time; the villain knows his guilt, and that I, myself, have the power to prove it beyond the least shadow of a doubt."

"Thou ?" repeated Oliver, with a look of scorn.

"Yes, I, Sampson Brayling, thy former associate;" returned the Gipsey; "I, who reared thee with a parent's care from the earliest days of childhood, rude and wild though was my wandering course of life. Canst thou deny the regard and attention which the humble Gipsey ever bestowed upon thee? And what was thy return for all my kindness? The basest ingratitude. Such was the reward thou didst alone bestow upon thy protector, *the preserver of thy life!*"

"The preserver of my life! Ha! ha! ha!"

"Nay, wretched man," continued Brayling, "mock not my words, for little canst thou imagine the purport of them. Oh, I have that to reveal which should shake thy soul with horror, and yet awaken thine hardened spirit to shame and remorse. Gentlemen, Evelyn, I pray you bear with me, while at last I disclose those awful facts, which, from motives of prudence I have kept locked within mine own breast till the present moment. The time has now arrived, and justice demands the revelation."

The words of Sampson Brayling, and the manner in which he spoke them, created the most powerful sensation in the breasts of all present, and they awaited with breathless impatience to hear that disclosure upon which so much depended Mabel's features became more animated, and she fixed a penetrating look upon Sampson Brayling, eager to catch every word that fell from his lips; even Oliver Dalton evinced some emotion; the expression of his features underwent a remarkable change; his demeanour was less firm and confident, and he drew in his breath, awaiting to hear the statement of Brayling, which he had prefaced in so ominous and mysterious a manner.

"Proceed, proceed;" said Sir Milford, addressing himself to the Gipsey; "we are all attention to listen to what thou hast to state."

Brayling bowed, and commenced in the following words:—

"It is a strange and fearful tale, but Heaven can bear witness that I am about to speak nothing but the truth. And now Oliver Dalton, if every spark of feeling is not entirely extinguished in thy breast, I will appal thy guilty soul. Listen, while I reveal the astounding fact, and defy all earthly power to controvert it. The wretched misguided man, Jasper Scrimpe, whom thou didst rob, and whose blood was shed by thine hand, is thine own uncle,—and in yon deeply injured youth, Evelyn Heartwell, the object of thy deadliest hatred, and whom thou wouldst willingly have consigned to the scaffold, *is thy brother!*"

A thrill of horror and astonishment ran through the hall; an exclamation of emotion escaped the lips of Mabel; and Evelyn clasping his hands together, stood completely paralized, and unable for the moment to utter a word. Oliver Dalton exhibited the greatest agitation; his face became ghastly pale, his lips quivered, and he trembled violently.

"Gracious powers!" at length exclaimed our hero; "how fearful, how astounding is this disclosure. Sampson Brayling, can this be?"

"Be explicit, Brayling," said Sir Milford; "hast thou spoken the truth?"

"I swear it," answered the Gipsey, solemnly; "and have the most unquestionable proofs to substantiate my assertions. The real name of the Miser is Gerald Aubrey. His sister, the amiable Lady Agnes, was married to the wealthy Sir William Wilmot, of the Old Hall, near Finchley Common."

"Sir William Wilmot?" ejaculated Sir Thomas; "I knew him well. He disappeared in a most mysterious manner, and was never heard of afterwards."

"'Tis true," said Brayling; "unfortunate gentleman, dreadful was his fate. Gerald Aubrey coveted his wealth, and after the death of Lady Agnes, which occurred suddenly, he never rested till he had accomplished his guilty and inhuman designs. Business had called Sir William for a day or two from home, and, on his return, which was at night, his unnatural relation waylaid him in a lonely spot, not far from his own mansion, and the unhappy Baronet perished by his hands."

"Horrible!" cried Sir Milford, with a shudder.

"Aye," observed Brayling, "it was a frightful deed; but the murderer's crimes ended not there. The two infant sons of his unfortunate victim were still in the way of his ambitious views, and he resolved to remove them also. At that time

I was a poor, wretched, and desperate man, but thank Heaven, my hands had never yet been stained with innocent blood, nor is that dreadful weight now upon my mind.   Aubrey sought me out, and by the offer of a large reward, prevailed on me to rid him of the two boys.   They were committed to my charge; but when I gazed upon their looks of innocence, my heart recoiled from the monstrous crime, and instead of consigning them to death, one I left at the door of Farmer Heartwell, the other I kept myself.   Soon after joining my present comrades, I brought him up as the orphan, Luke Stanton.   The first of these boys is the lover of thy fair niece, Sir Milford, and the other, his base rival and bitterest enemy, he who so long imposed upon thee in the character of Oliver Dalton !"

"Almighty God !" cried the agitated Evelyn ; " to what tale of wonder have I been listening ? can I believe the evidence of my senses ? Alas ! unhappy, misguided, guilty brother !"

"Hold !" fiercely exclaimed Oliver, who had recovered from his agitation, re-assumed all his wanted recklessness and daring; "I acknowledge not the title; I am not to be imposed upon by any such wild and idle tale.   Detested rival ; my soul holds no kindred with thee.   I still loathe, despise, and curse ye !"

"Remorseless man !" observed Sir Thomas Overton ; " will nothing bring thee to a sense of shame and compunction ?"

"Hear me out ;" said Sampson Brayling ; " for my tale of guilt is not yet complete.   Gerald Aubrey never enjoyed his ill-gotten wealth.   Tortured by the horrors of conscience, he fled his native land, till years had passed away, and the old Hall at Finchley, in one of the chambers of which he had concealed the body of his murdered victim, was for ever deserted."

"Ah ! horror !" gasped forth Evelyn, with the most agonising emotion.

"Shameless slanderer !—liar, hypocrite !" cried Oliver; " what proof hast thou of thy monstrous assertions ?"

"Behold !" returned Brayling, producing the document he had extorted from Jasper Scrimpe; " this written confession, signed by the hand of the Miser himself.   Read—read, Sir Milford, and be convinced !"

Sir Milford took the paper, and read it aloud, and a thrill of horror ran through the breasts of the persons assembled.   But Oliver Dalton remained unmoved, and a smile of derision passed over his features.

"'Tis too true ;" remarked Sir Milford, when he had concluded reading the confession.   "'Tis impossible to resist such evidence as this."

"It is a base forgery !" exclaimed Oliver, firmly; "you will not, cannot surely be deceived by anything so transparent."

"I cannot doubt it, said Sir Milford ; " but," he added, turning to Brayling, "this paper mentions a third child, a girl, the offspring of the ill-fated Sir William Wilmot."

Mabel uttered a faint exclamation, and exhibited the greatest emotion.

"True," answered Brayling ; " a poor little helpless orphan, deserted by all, left to perish, till she was rescued by a friendly hand.   That child also lives, and will be produced anon.   And now, guilty man, since thou wouldst have still greater confirmation of the truth of what I have stated," he added to Oliver,—' 'behold!—what ho, there !"

He advanced towards a door at the farther end of the hall as he spoke, which was thrown open, and the Miser, pale, trembling, and evidently tottering on the verge of eternity, was led forth, supported by the two servants to whose care he had beed confided.   On beholding him, a fearful change took place in the demeanour of Oliver, and his face became ghastly pale as he muttered to himself—

"Ah! the Miser here ! Then I am lost !"

The wretched old. man was led to the centre of the Hall, and all eyes were fixed intently on him, while with difficulty he said—

"The career of the wretched Miser is fast drawing to a close, his days are numbered. The just punishment of accursed avarice is complete. I acknowledge the truth of all the fearful statements made in the document produced by Sampson Brayling. The unfortunate Sir William Wilmot fell by my guilty hands. The mangled remains I concealed beneath the flooring of the old oak chamber, in the old Hall at Finchley, and—"

"Merciful Providence;" interrupted our hero, with a shudder; "then the mouldering remains I so accidently discovered during my concealment in that old mansion, were those of my ill-fated parent?"

"They were! they were!" gasped forth the Miser; "oh, wretch, blood-stained miscreant that I am, I dare not, cannot hope for mercy. Still would I make all the atonement I can for the frightful crimes I have committed. The cash box contained all the papers and title deeds to the estates and property I so unjustly appropriated, but that, alas, was doubtless lost in the fire which took place in my miserable dwelling!"

"No;" observed Sir Thomas Overton; "that box was fortunately discovered, uninjured in the ruins. It is now in my possession."

"Thank Heaven! thank Heaven!" exclaimed the old man, fervently, and clasping his hands together; "then the much injured offspring of my hapless victim will at last obtain the restitution of their rights; but I—oh, horror! how terrible is the future that opens upon my appalled vision! I—I dare not pray! My monstrous crimes have banished me for ever from the pale of mercy! Oh, conscience, how torturing are thy pangs! my soul shrinks with terror; my limbs fail me; my brain turns giddy; support me, I—I—"

Completely overpowered by the intensity of his emotions, the guilty old man sunk exhausted and almost insensible in the arms of the attendants, and was borne to the back of the hall. A pause of a minute or two ensued; every one completely paralyzed by the startling revelations to which they had listened. Terrible indeed were the contending passions that raged within the bosom of the guilty Oliver; he could no longer doubt the fearful truth of what he had heard; his career was now fairly at an end; and fiendish malice, especially towards Sampson Brayling, who had brought about all those important disclosures, agitated his breast, and made him even in that awful moment thirst for revenge. His keen eye quickly saw the means. The attention of the persons present was almost solely diverted to the Miser, and, seizing the opportunity, the villain suddenly snatched a pistol from the belt of one of the men who stood near him, and levelled it at the head of Brayling; at that fatal moment, Mabel, who had observed the action, uttered an exclamation of alarm, and rushing forward to warn the Gipsey of his danger, received the contents of the pistol in her shoulder, and sank bleeding in the arms of Evelyn, Oliver, at the same moment, being seized by the persons standing by.

"Guilty man;" exclaimed Sampson Brayling, solemnly, "the measure of thy crimes is now full, *thou hast slain thy sister!*"

"No, no, no!" cried Oliver, in a voice of terror; "recall those dreadful words! The blow was not intended for Mabel! My sister!—and I her murderer; oh, it is impossible!"

"Wretched youth," ejaculated Sir Milford; "thy soul is now indeed lost for ever! Let us not prolong this revolting scene. Convey him to some place of security," he added, addressing himself to the attendants; "the black catalogue of his crimes is now complete."

Oliver Dalton, who was horrorstruck and subdued, offered no resistance, and he was immediately removed from the hall.

CHAPTER XLIX.

The Miser relapses into Madness.—An Affecting Scene.—Brother and Sister.—The Fearful Discovery.

Suddenly the Miser recovered from the stupor in which he had been for the last few minutes, and starting from his seat, he staggered towards the group that surrounded the fainting Mabel, whom they were about to convey to a chamber, a servant having been dispatched to the nearest place to procure surgical assistance.

"Sister! sister! did they say?" he ejaculated, "that name! but no, surely it cannot be! Madness must again have taken possession of my brain! Poor child! poor child! let me gaze more narrowly upon her!"

The old man stooped down, and with trembling hands parting the ringlets that were floating disordered about the pale but still beautiful face of the unfortunate Mabel, for a moment gazed into her features with the utmost intensity.

"Horror! horror!" he exclaimed, in tones of harrowing emotion, "the dead seems to rise from the grave to appal my sight, and remind me of my fiendish crimes! In those fair gentle features I trace the lineaments of my unfortunate sister Agnes. She is, she must be her child! She's dying! and all this dreadful work is brought about by my accursed deeds! Open earth, and hide such a monster from the shuddering sight of mankind! Drag me to the darkest dungeon! Let me no more be seen in the light of offended Heaven! My brain! my brain's once more on fire! Vultures are gnawing at my heart! See—see that ghastly form that frowns upon me! 'Tis he—'tis the shade of my murdered victim! Avaunt! Avaunt! Oh, horror! Ha! ha! ha!"

Madness had again seized upon the miserable man's brain, and shocked as every one were at his terrible anguish and frenzied ravings, and anxious as they were at the deplorable situation of poor Mabel, he was removed from the hall, from which all strangers had previously been ordered to withdraw.

"Poor girl, poor girl;" said Sir Milford, as he gazed sorrowfully and compassionately in the face of Mabel; "I fear the injury she has received will prove fatal; would that the surgeon would arrive."

My sister;" ejaculated Evelyn, in a voice of the most poignant grief; "and must I loose thee so soon after this discovery? Almighty God, I pray thee avert so terrible a calamity! Oh, it would indeed be hard that one so good and virtuous should meet with so dreadful and untimely a fate. Alas, Brayling, why didst thou not divulge this important secret before?"

"Reproach me not, Sir Evelyn Wilmot," replied Brayling, "for such indeed is thy rightful name and title; I acted for the best, as Heaven is my judge."

"True, true," observed Sir Milford, "and I am certain that my young friend meant no reproof by the words he uttered. Thy conduct has been most noble, Brayling, and for it we owe thee an incalculable debt of gratitude. But see, she revives."

Mabel slowly shewed signs of returning consciousness, and opening her eyes, and finding herself affectionately pressed in the arms of Evelyn, a faint smile of satisfaction passed over her features, and in accents of touching plaintiveness, with difficulty she ejaculated—

"The wanderings of the Gipsey-girl are o'er; her earthly sun has set for ever, so soon, so prematurely after its rising; but—but my path has been the rugged one of care and sorrow, and Death comes as a friend to relieve me from it, and guide me to happier realms. Evelyn—Constance," she added, joing their hands, "thou art worthy of each other—be happy—bless ye!—bless ye!"

"Oh, no!" said our hero, in a voice almost choked with emotion, "it may not yet be too late to save thy life; come, come, dear Mabel,—sister!"

"Sister! sister!" repeated the poor girl, with sudden energy and an expression of joy, "oh, bless thee, bless thee for that word, *brother!* It will light the passage of the poor lonely wanderer of the forest glade to the dreary precincts of the grave. Yet could I wish to live to mingle my heart's fond feelings with thine, dear Evelyn. But no, I will not murmur! Oh, that pang! The dark curtain of death is closing on the vision of the Gipsey-girl; yet—yet there is light and joy beyond. Brayling—Evelyn—Constance—farewell—I am happy! —I am happy!"

She sank back in the arms of Evelyn. Constance, who had sobbed aloud with the poignancy of her anguish at the pathetic scene, sunk on her knees by her side, and taking the fine hand of Mabel in her own, and looking with painful emotion in her face, she exclaimed—

No. 37.

"She is gone! poor, noble-hearted, affectionate girl, she is no more!"

"No, no, dear Constance, be calm;" returned Evelyn; "her heart still throbs; she has but again fainted from the loss of blood."

At that moment the surgeon arrived, and having hastily examined the wound and stopped the effusion of blood, ordered her to be immediately conveyed to a chamber, whither he followed, attended by Constance, Evelyn, and the daughters of Sir Thomas Overton, who had been present during the whole of the startling proceedings, and had evinced the deepest interest in all that had taken place.

When the news of the shocking calamity which had befallen the Gipsey-girl reached the ears of Walter Greysham, and all the extraordinary revelations that had taken place at the examination of Oliver Dalton, his agitation and alarm was extreme; and, notwithstanding his own weak state, he persisted in hastening to the apartment to which the poor girl had been conveyed, and met Evelyn and Sir Milford coming from it, they having left her in the care of the surgeon, Constance, and Abigail. Breathlessly Greysham inquired into the condition of that unfortunate being who had made so powerful an impression upon his heart, and which was strengthened, and his hopes in a great measure revived, on learning that she was proved, beyond all shadow of a doubt, to be the sister of his friend Evelyn Heartwell, or rather Sir Evelyn Wilmot, as he in future must be recognised. He felt as though a mountain had been removed from his breast, when he was informed that the surgeon had given it as his opinion that the wound which she had received was far from dangerous, and that the present torpid state in which she was lying, being quite unconscious, was owing more to loss of blood, and the shock her system had received, than anything else; and that a few hours only might work a favourable change, and enable him to form a better opinion as to the probable result.

The extraordinary and thrilling events of that ever-memorable day, filled them all with wonder and a certain degree of awe; and the disclosures which Sampson Brayling had made were of such a remarkable character that, in spite of the unquestionable proofs that had been brought forward to corroborate them, Evelyn and his friends could not without great difficulty persuade themselves of their reality. Our hero reflected with horror upon the melancholy circumstances that had attended the fate of his father, and shuddered with horror when he thought of the immense weight of crime that loaded the soul of Jasper Scrimps; and sincerely did he implore the mercy of Heaven for the wretched man, whose remorse was now evidently so intense. He also shuddered at the awful situation of Oliver, and in spite of the heinousness of his guilt, the generous instincts of his nature could not allow him to feel otherwise than pity and regret towards him. But the principal anxiety of all was for Mabel, and many were the inquiries they made respecting her. She still remained in a state of insensibility, assiduously watched by Constance, who could not be prevailed upon to leave her bedside even for a minute. At length, however, she breathed more freely, and opening her eyes, looked anxiously around her. On observing Constance, a faint smile of satisfaction overspread her pale features, and she extended her hand gratefully towards her. Her first words, however, were to inquire for Evelyn, and to express an ardent wish to see him. This request the surgeon did not consider it prudent to comply with, as he feared the excitement might be too much for her, and she submitted patiently to his decision. She complained of but little pain, and expressed herself happy at the presence of Constance, for whom she now evinced all the affection of a sister. At length, calm and undisturbed, she gradually sunk into repose, and experienced several hours of refreshing sleep, and when she awoke, she was so much better that the surgeon was more sanguine than ever as to her ultimate recovery, and now granted her the interview which he had refused her on the previous night; considering that it was perfectly safe for him to do so. Grateful for the quick and favourable change which had taken place in the poor girl, Evelyn hastened to her chamber, and the scene which took place between the newly-discovered brother and sister, and Constance Welborn, who, at the request of Mabel, remained present, was of the most affecting and impressive description. Most earnestly did poor Mabel implore the forgiveness of Evelyn, for the frequent annoyances she feared she had caused him; and that of Constance, for the feelings of jealousy she had entertained towards her, though she had ever esteemed her virtues, and the unshaken constancy of her affection for Evelyn; and again she invoked the blessings of Heaven on their future destiny, and prayed that they might realise that happiness, which after the fortitude and resignation with which they had supported so many painful trials they were so justly entitled to. Upon the awful fate of her father, Sir William Wilmot, she scarcely dared trust herself to speak; but she mingled her tears with those of Evelyn to his memory, and fervently invoked the mercy of the Almighty Judge for that unhappy man, whom sordid avarice had led to the perpetration of so horrible a crime; and no less charitably did her amiable heart urge her to express her feelings towards the guilty Oliver, who, hurried on by his ungovernable passions, had been the cause of so much trouble and misery to them all. The interview had the most beneficial effect upon her, contrary to the doubts and apprehensions of the surgeon; she became composed, and comparatively happy, and continued to mend from that hour.

Nor must it be supposed that Sampson Brayling was forgotten; he had indeed proved himself to be an ardent and sincere friend; and they all felt that they could never sufficiently evince their sense of gratitude for the great service he had, with no little risk to himself, rendered them. Black Will, the ruffian who had taken such a prominent part in the nefarious designs of Oliver, Brayling, on his leaving the Abbey on the night of the attempted burglary and abduction, had seen placed in a position to be conveyed to London, there to meet the several heinous charges that were to be preferred against him; and thus everything was in a fair way to bring the persons inculpated in this eventful drama to commensurate punishment, and render justice to the injured and oppressed.

The awful situation of Oliver, and the ignominious fate that unquestionably awaited him, annoyed and tortured the mind of our hero more than anything else; not that he could for one moment attempt to deny the justice of the retribution which had at length overtaken him, so great had been his guilt; but the feelings of nature predominated over those of vindictiveness and revenge; he could freely forgive him, and would have felt gratified could his fearful doom with any reason and consistency been averted, and he have been suffered to live to repentance. In a few hours, the unhappy prisoner was to be removed to the County Goal, there to await that trial which must inevitably take place; and it was with those charitable and humane feelings that Evelyn determined to visit him before his departure, hoping that he might happily be enabled to make some favourable impression upon his stubborn mind, and awaken him to a sense of the awful position in which he stood. Sir Milford Welborn, who also felt the deepest interest in the fate of the wretched young man, proposed to accompany him, and they accordingly made their way to that part of the Abbey in which Oliver had been confined, after the exciting scene in the hall on the day of the examination.

On arriving there they were astonished and somewhat alarmed at finding the room door standing partially open, and, their suspicions being excited, they advanced, and entering the room, started back aghast on beholding the poor fellow who had been set to watch and attend upon him stretched upon the floor, and weltering in his blood from a frightful wound in the back of his head, and the prisoner gone. They immediately raised an alarm, and assistance being procured, the wounded man was removed, it being found that he still breathed, though it appeared impossible, from the horrible nature of the injury he had received, that he could ever recover his senses, or long survive.

This fearful crime excited an universal feeling of horror; the proper authorities were speedily apprised of the dreadful circumstance, and a pursuit commenced without delay; as it was impossible to leave any means untried to prevent the escape of so hardened and atrocious a criminal.

CHAPTER XLVIII.

The Pursuit.—The Hour of Doom.—The Fate of Oliver Dalton.

It may here be as well to mention that an iron bar was discovered in the prisoner's place of confinement, which had either fallen, or been forced from the window, and with which the murder (for the unfortunate man was now no more), had no doubt been committed. A large bunch of keys had been taken from his belt, so that the assassin had secured every means of egress from the Abbey. But we will proceed to explain such facts as the reader may be anxious to know.

For some hours after the examination, Oliver Dalton abandoned himself entirely to mingled feelings of rage, astonishment, terror and despair. It was impossible for him, though he tried hard to do so, to entertain the least doubt of the truth of all the extraordinary and astounding statements that had been made, and at times something like remorse entered his guilty breast, when he thought of the ties of consanguinity that existed between himself and those who had suffered so much, and so unjustly through his villainy. But that feeling was only transient, and gave way to one of rage and deadly malice, at the utter destruction that had overtaken him, and the triumph of those whom he had so heartlessly and relentlessly persecuted, and at the shameful death which was inevitably impending o'er his head.

"And must I, after all," he passionately exclaimed, as with disordered steps he traversed his gloomy room, "must I meet the ignominious doom of the most atrocious criminal, and finish my bold career beneath the hands of the public executioner? No, better that I myself should terminate my existence than leave this last scene of triumph for my detested enemies to accomplish. But I have not the means; and is it not possible for me yet to effect my escape? That thought again arouses me into action, and forbids me to abandon myself entirely to despair."

He looked anxiously around the room as these ideas occurred to him, and partially revived his hopes; but nothing there met his observation to encourage them. It was a stone apartment of small dimensions, and had all the appearance of having, in former days, been appropriated to a place of confinement, probably for the unfortunate victims of monastic cruelty. The oak door was strongly bolted on the outside, and there was only one window, placed high in the wall, and strongly barred. A sudden thought struck Oliver, and standing on the stone bench beneath the window, he was not only able to reach it, but to see from it; and found that it looked on to the roof of one of the smaller wings of the building, which might be easily reached from thence.

"Could I only succeed in forcing those bars from their sockets, I might yet regain my liberty, in the darkness and stillness of night."

He tried them. They were rusted with age, and two or three of them were so loose, that he thought, if he had any instrument with which he could further destroy the stone work, he might remove them, though, they resisted all his efforts to force them with his hands alone. He re-seated himself on the bench, and considered what was best to be done. There was a heap of rubbish in one corner of the room, probably the accumulation of years, and the thought struck him to search among that. For some time he did so without any successful result; but at length he came upon a large rusty nail, which, by sharpening the point, he thought he might make answer the purpose. With this, then, he immediately commenced operations; but his progress was necessarily slow, as he could only work during those intervals when he was not likely to be interrupted, or discovered by the visits of the man who was appointed to act as his gaoler. It was not till the following day that he had succeeded in removing one of the bars, and he had no sooner done so than he heard the man at the door, and he had only just time to resume his seat and conceal the bar behind him, when he entered the room, bringing him an allowance of provisions. Oliver now noticed more particularly than he had done before the bunch of keys suspended from his belt, and a desperate idea flashed upon his brain. If he could only obtain possession of those keys, his tedious and uncertain labours at the window would be at an end, and he might easily effect his escape; but how to do so? Guilty as Oliver Dalton had been, his heart had ever revolted at the idea of murder; but his situation was a desperate one, and he saw no other than desperate means by which he could accomplish his wishes. There was no time for hesitation, or the opportunity which now presented itself might never occur again. The unfortunate man's back was towards him as he was about to leave the room, and Oliver, acting upon the impulse of the moment, rose hastily, but cautiously from his seat, and seizing the iron bar which he had forced from the window, he dealt the poor fellow such a tremendous blow on the head, that he sank senseless on the floor, almost without a groan.

Oliver looked for a moment, with a shudder, on the dreadful work of his hands; and he could not but regret the awful crime he had committed in thus taking the life of an innocent man; but this was no time for compunctious feelings, and stifling them as well as he could in his breast, he took the keys from the side of the unfortunate man, and silently left the room, neglecting to bolt it after him. It was now the dusk of evening, and he thought it not unlikely that he might be able to pass from the Abbey without being observed by any of the domestics, who it was most probable would not be about. He listened at the head of the staircase, which ascended to the room wherein he had been confined; all was still, it being, as we have before stated, in a remote and unoccupied part of the Abbey, and that emboldened him. However, a thought occurred to him which might better ensure his safety, and returning to the room, he stripped the murdered man of his cloak, in which he enveloped himself, and putting on his hat in the place of his own, considered himself sufficiently disguised to escape immediate recognition, and, with more confidence descended the stairs with stealthy steps; and, arriving at the bottom, hesitated which way to proceed. It was, however, to him, all a matter of chance, and he therefore took the first way that presented itself, moving on as quickly as possible, well knowing that his only chance of escape was by quickness of action; for should his flight be discovered before he could emerge from the Abbey, his retreat would be certain to be cut off. He met with few impediments; most of the doors were standing open, and those that were fastened readily yielded to the keys he had secured, so, that in a few minutes he found himself in the open air, and standing on a spot which seemed to offer him every facility of escape. During these few minutes, however, Evelyn and Sir Milford had made the fearful discovery of the murder of the gaoler, and the alarm being given, the pursuit had already commenced. Oliver imagined that he could hear a confused noise in the Abbey, and, his fears and suspicions being excited, he plunged into an opposite thicket, which was the likeliest place to conceal his receding form from observation, and hurried forward as fast as possible, for the glimmering of lights between the trees now confirmed his worst suspicions. The wretched guilty man felt that this was the most desperate moment of his life; in fact, that it was a race for life or death, and fear lent him wings. Not that he could encourage the hope that he would ultimately be able to escape the penalty of his crimes ; he was convinced that his guilty course was nearly run, that the crisis of his fate was approaching, but he shuddered at the idea of dying by the hands of the public executioner, and he was resolved when driven to the extremity, sooner than be taken, to terminate his own miserable existence.

Such were the terrible thoughts of Oliver Dalton as he pursued his way, and added to them the whole of the extraordinary and fearful revelations that had taken place at his examination, rushed with overwhelming force upon his brain, and drove him almost to madness. Strange and frightful noises seemed to vibrate in his ears, and ghastly phantoms to flit before his eyes, and cross his path ; shapeless airy forms, murmuring despair, and deriding the agony of his guilty soul.

But it was not long before he had got some distance from the Abbey ; indeed he was soon buried among the trees, for he had plunged into a path that was just practicable, though not without the greatest difficulty, and many disagreeables; but then it had this advantage,—it led immediately from the spot, through a covered and hidden track, to a cross-road—one that would lead him clear from the neighbourhood without much fear of meeting with any body.   All too was ushed in silence, save the fitful gusts of wind that moaned sullenly among the branches of the trees; and he imagined that he had eluded his pursuers for the present, at any rate, if they had ever been upon his track.   After proceeding for some time with unabated speed, he arrived at the end of the wood, where he had to descend a steep bank, and cross a ditch, which, having accomplished, he found himself on the hard, firm roadway, a cross road, but which by traversing still at the top of his speed, which he could now do without observation, he would now enter the main road, which he would much rather he could have avoided, as it would offer, he knew, but few facilities for concealment, if he should chance to be overtaken.   And then he had no means of resistance ; nothing to defend himself with excepting a clasp knife, which he found about his person, having previously forgotten that it was in his possession.   The night was perfectly fine, but there was but little moon, and that had not made its appearance.   There was a white mist that hung low on the ground, heavy and wet, and made everything look gloomy and dark.   Now and then, as he came to a more elevated part of the road, he would rise above the mist, and could then see across the ocean of white vapour that lay upon the earth.   The tree tops could be seen plainly, while their lower halves were completely and entirely lost to the eye ; even the road itself could not be clearly distinguished.

Oliver, however, what with the excitement of his feelings and the haste with which he had hitherto proceeded, now began to feel weary.   He was compelled to slacken his speed, which he imagined he might now do with some degree of safety, but he had scarcely come to this conclusion when he was startled by imagining he heard the distant sound of several hasty and heavy footsteps behind him.   He listened attentively for a few seconds, and then he could distinctly hear the sound of footsteps, and the voices of men.   These sounds came clear and distinct on the night air ; though Oliver could not see them he could hear ; but his eyes could not pierce the darkness and mist that floated around him.   Everything was dim and doubtful beyond the hedge rows as he passed them, and the tall trees, when any appeared.   He heard the sound increasing, and they were evidently fast gaining upon him, while, almost exhausted by the previous rapidity of his flight, his limbs failed him, and, although he exerted himself to the utmost, he could only move at a very slow pace indeed, and which would not at all enable him to outstrip those who were advancing so rapidly upon him.

"Some infernal spell is upon me;" he exclaimed; "and my strength fails me, just at the very time when I most require it. Hark! they are close upon me, and I can just discern the forms of several men through the mist. The alarm has been given, and I feel convinced that these persons are in pursuit of me. I shall yet be captured; but no, this knife, at any rate, will save me from the hangman's hands. What's to be done? I cannot avoid them, and—ah! this tree promptly offers to me the means of shelter till they have passed!"

Quick as thought he climbed into the closely interwoven branches of a sturdy oak that grew by the road-side, and scarcely venturing to breathe, he awaited the arrival of the individuals who had so greatly excited his alarm. He had not to wait long, for they quickly approached the spot, and he then perceived that they were several of the Coast-guard, who from their bustle and activity seemed to be upon some important expedition. They were talking loudly, and certainly not with that due precaution they might have been expected to adopt, as they advanced; and Oliver, by listening, could find no difficulty in distinguishing what they said. His suspicions were at once confirmed when he heard his own name mentioned, and he crouched still closer into the branches of the tree, scarcely venturing to move, lest the noise should attract their attention and betray him: and now they had arrived at the spot.

"Ah! I thought thou wert deceived by the darkness and the mist, Harden," said the foremost one; "this tree, no doubt, was the form which thou thought'st thou didst observe moving stealthily along. They assume all kinds of extravagant shapes in the distance on such a night as this."

"True, Harold," coincided one of his companions, "and for my own part, I think our search should have been principally confined to the wood, where the rascal would be more likely to fly for concealment, than to seek the open road."

"Well;" remarked the first speaker, "there is something reasonable in that; however, you know what our instructions are, and we have only to obey them. This Oliver Dalton as he is called is an artful fellow, but I think he will find it difficult to escape this time. However, let us proceed."

They now resumed their way, and Oliver eagerly watched them from the tree, till their forms were hidden from the sight in the dim obscurity beyond. He then felt as though the weight of a mountain had been removed from his breast, and breathed more freely. He lingered in the tree for a few minutes, and endeavoured to collect his ideas, and to consider what it was best for him to do. It would be most imprudent he thought for him to continue to pursue the main road, especially as he perceived a wide range of fields that were seperated from the road by the bank from which the tree he was in grew; and, across them therefore, he determined to bend his course, and take his chance as to whither they might conduct him. Descending the tree, he alighted safely in the field on the other side, and, having first looked cautiously forward, to ascertain whether the coast was clear, he crept cautiously by the bank, so that he might the better crouch down and conceal himself should any one appear.

In this manner he proceeded across two or three fields without meeting with any obstruction, and was about to cross a stile into another, when he was alarmed by the short sharp bark of a dog, and hastily looking in the direction from whence it came, he beheld through the darkness, the outlines of some building a short distance off, and which was probably a farm house; but ere he had time to think what to do, he perceived a large mastiff dog bounding towards him, and barking furiously as he came. To attempt to run Oliver knew would be useless, and he had no other alternative, therefore, but to brave the threatened danger. Muttering a dreadful oath between his teeth, he drew forth his knife, and fixing himself in a firm attitude, he awaited the nearer approach of the dog, which no sooner beheld him distinctly than, leaping over the stile, he bounded furiously towards him. It was a fearful moment for Oliver, and with a boldness which could only have been caused by the desperate nature of his situation, with his knife in one hand, in a moment he closed with the dog which, as might have been expected, in an instant laid hold of him. The struggle was brief, but terrific, while it lasted; and several were the frightful wounds inflicted upon Oliver by the ferocious brute's teeth before he could get the hand, in which was his knife, sufficiently at liberty to use it. But when he did so, he plunged it repeatedly into the side of the dog and withdrew it again, reeking with blood.

In a few moments the poor animal relaxed his hold, and with a piteous wailing cry, sunk dead at the feet of Oliver, who panted for breath from the remarkable exertions he had undergone. He wiped the perspiration from his forehead, and then excited by the acute pain he felt from the different lacerations he had received, he uttered several fearful curses, and then glared around, undecided which path to take, now that he had delivered himself from his ferocious antagonist. But he had no time to hesitate, he saw lights moving from the building in the direction where he stood, and that was sufficient to convince him that the inmates were aroused by the barking of the dog, and his danger of apprehension was the more imminent, as he felt so faint from loss of blood that to move from the spot with anything like speed was extremely difficult, if not impossible. There was no time to be lost, however, and therefore watching the movements of the lights, by dint of great exertion, he struck hastily into a contrary direction, and stealing along under the shadow of a row of trees, he turned an abrupt corner, and suddenly came upon a narrow lane, which seemed to offer him all the means of persuing his flight unobserved, which he needed, and he proceeded with more courage and desperate determination, though with increased pain.

Oliver Dalton, singularly enough, had not quitted the spot where he had had such a fierce encounter with the dog many minutes, when Sampson Brayling and several of the gipsies, and accompanied by Evelyn, who felt anxious to witness the result of this painful adventure, arrived in the field, having accidently fallen upon the track of the guilty fugitive. Seeing the lights, which had now become stationary, they hastened towards them, and found a small group of persons who had come from the farm house, busily engaged in examining the mangled carcase of the dog.

"What is the meaning of this, my friend?" enquired Evelyn, of one of the persons assembled, "there seems to have been some foul work here."

"Marry, and thou mayest well say that, young gentleman;" replied the stranger; "and my poor faithful Nero hath met with a sad fate; a murrian seize the scroundrel who did it, say I; we were alarmed by the barking of the dog, but could not get here in time, or we might have secured the rascally trespasser, who no doubt is lurking about here for some villainous purpose."

"Ay," said another of the men; "and no doubt the fellow did not succeed in killing Nero before he had himself met with severe punishment, for he would find him an awkward customer to deal with. See, there are large stains of blood, which doubtless mark the direction which the man hath taken, and shew that he has been desperately wounded. And ah! what is this? a portion of a doublet, of rich material, and which was probably torn from the dress of the intruder in the struggle."

"Let me look at it," said Evelyn; and taking it from the hand of the rustic, and examining it minutely, he exclaimed—

"It is a portion of the very dress Oliver wore; I'll swear to it! He hath directed his flight this way, and it must have been him who had the fierce encounter with the dog. Unhappy man, to what terrible fate is he hurrying himself? We can trace the way he has gone, by the marks of blood and the trodden grass."

"Let us hasten then," said Brayling, "for there is no time to be lost."

Borrowing one of the lanterns from the men, they proceeded to follow the footsteps of Oliver as nearly as they could guess, and at length found themselves in the lane which he had entered a short time before, and which they also traversed. Two or three times they imagined they beheld the shadow of a retreating form at a distance, but it was quickly gone, and they concluded that they might have been mistaken. Still they hastily and impatiently pursued their way, and had nearly arrived at the further end of the lane, when they were startled by the loud report of fire-arms, and hurrying forward, and emerging from the lane, they came upon a few of the coast-guard, who had been dispatched in the pursuit.

" Did the firing proceed from you?" eagerly inquired our hero.

" It did ;" replied the man; " we saw the villain hastening this way, and as he refused to stop when we ordered him, we fired, and I'm much mistaken if we did not hit him too."

" Heaven forbid !" ejaculated Evelyn, with emotion; " wretched, guilty brother, I would that thy life might yet be spared for repentance."

" He has doubtless taken the way to the rocks that overhang the sea, yonder," observed the officer; " if he is wounded, which I have every reason to believe he is, and that too, severely, he cannot possibly proceed far." They hurried on towards the rocks, which were only at a short distance. and at length stood in a singularly wild and romantic spot, which opened to the sea, bounded on either side by stupendous rocks, whose bases were washed by the ocean spray. The moon had risen and cast a gentle light upon the scene. The deep blue vault of heaven was studded with stars; the whole firmament was spangled with these transparent and sparkling luminaries.

" He is not here," observed the officer, " unless he has sunk exhausted, or concealed himself somewhere among the rocks. Ah ! behold !" he added, pointing to a lofty projection of one of the rocks, which overhung the ocean, and on which the wretched Oliver appeared, with ghastly and haggard features, and fast sinking with loss of blood. On beholding Evelyn, Brayling, and the others, a malicious expression of revenge distorted his features ; and with difficulty he moved forward, until he stood on the very verge of the rock. At the command of the officer of the coast-guard, the men levelled their muskets, and were about to fire, when Evelyn rushing hastily forward, exclaimed:—

" Hold!—take not his life !—Oliver, unfortunate, misguided man ;—'tis madness to seek to offer any resistance; yield—yield, I implore thee, and mercy may yet be extended towards thee."

" Yield, to thee, whom I still hate and despise, and to die on a scaffold ?" returned Oliver, in a fierce and determined voice ;—"never ! Oliver Dalton's hour is come, and thus he courts his fate—Fire !"

Before Evelyn could again interpose to prevent it, a volley was discharged at Oliver, as he stood, dauntless and with an air of defiance, his arms elevated above his head, on the brink of the rock. One frightful cry escaped him, half exulting, half agonizing; he gave a slight convulsive bound in the air, and then plunged headlong into the waste of waters that opened to receive him.

A simultaneous exclamation of horror burst from the lips of Evelyn and Sampson Brayling, and they rushed forward. The moon shone bright in the vault of heaven ;—and twice the form of the guilty Oliver was seen partly to rise above the waves—the ghastly paleness of the countenance, discoloured only by the blood which streamed from a gaping wound in his forehead, and the fixed and unnatural glare of the eyes, plainly revealed in the moonlight—it was dashed along for some distance with the speed of the whirlwind, and the waves closed over the guilty Oliver Dalton for ever !

No. 38.

CHAPTER XLIX.

THE MISER'S DEATH.—CONCLUSION.

SAD was the fate of the man who had played so prominent a part in this eventful drama, the wild, the daring, the reckless adventurer, Oliver Dalton, otherwise Alfred Wilmot. He had kept his word; he had escaped an ignominious death upon the public scaffold; but the retribution of heaven had overtaken him in a scarcely less terrible and awful manner. Evelyn heaved a sigh of the most heart-felt regret, as he and Sampson Brayling turned away from the spot, and slowly retraced their footsteps to the abbey, indescribably shocked at the fearful scene they had witnessed.

Sir Milford, Sir Thomas, and those so deeply interested, had anxiously awaited the return of our hero and Brayling, and it may readily be imagined the feelings of horror with which they listened to the apalling particulars which were related to them. Great as the guilt of the wretched Oliver had been, and the misery he had caused them, all rancorous, all revengeful feelings were stifled in their breasts, and earnestly they prayed the mercy of the Supreme for his guilty soul. With melancholy and painful feelings they separated for the night, having resolved to quit the abbey where the recent fearful events had taken place, as soon as possible, and return to London. But a fresh scene of excitement was preparing for them—the last sad scene in the painful tragedy, which we will proceed to relate.

They met at rather an earlier hour than usual the following morning, and were seated in the breakfasting room, discussing the important events of the last few days, and the remarkable change that was effected in their future prospects, when they were disturbed by an unusual noise in the corridor leading to the room in which they were assembled, and before they had time to inquire into the cause, the door was thrown unceremoniously open, and the man who had been deputed to keep watch over the unfortunate Miser, staggered into the room pale and agitated, and sunk exhausted in a chair. Astonished and alarmed, they eagerly inquired the cause of his emotion, but the only answer they could elicit from him was:—

"The Miser!—oh, quick!—he's escaped from his room, and—"

Before he could finish the sentence, a wild and terrific shriek rang through the abbey, such as they well knew it was impossible for any one but the unfortunate maniac to utter, and they immediately rushed from the room in the direction from whence the cry proceeded.

We will now explain what the man had not the power to do. The Miser had for some hours been more calm than usual, and there seemed to be no probability of his relapsing, for the present, into one of those violent paroxysms which were so painful to witness. Towards morning, his attendant, overcome by fatigue, had insensibly fallen into a sound sleep in his arm-chair—having neglected to take the key out of the lock on the inside. From this he was aroused by a loud cry, and starting to his feet, he beheld the Miser standing in a fierce and frenzied attitude before him, with his fists clenched, his features frightfully distorted, and his eyes glaring wildly upon him, like balls of fire. The poor fellow being thus aroused from his sleep, was of course, astounded and alarmed, and before he could recover himself, with another terrific cry, the maniac sprang upon him like a tiger upon his prey, and grasping him by the throat, so fiercely, as nearly to strangle him, dashed him to the floor, and opening the door, bounded like lightning from the room, and up the first staircase that presented itself to him. It was then that the man recovered somewhat from his consternation and confusion, but fearful to pursue him alone, he hastened, as has been described, to the room in which his master and his friends were seated, to raise the alarm.

The loud shouts of the unfortunate old man, directed their footsteps, and convinced them that in the wild delirium of madness, instead of attempting to make his way into the open air, he was making his way to the upper part of the abbey. Still, so rapid was his flight, that they could not overtake him; and by the time they got to the top story, they found to their dismay, that he had made his way through a trap-door on to the roof. They could still hear his wild and frantic shrieks, and as quick as possible, they emerged on to the roof. And there, on the parapet, at that dizzy height from the earth, stood the form of the aged man, erect, waving his arms above his head, and laughing hysterically. They beheld him with bated breath, and trembling horror, and for a moment knew not how to act; but at last fancying that his attention was diverted another way, Evelyn and Sampson Brayling rushed hastily forward to seize him; but he had seen them, and in an instant, before they could reach him, with a fearful laugh, that re-echoed far around, he precipitated himself from the parapet, on to the earth below.

A cry of horror escaped the breasts of all those who witnessed this frightful catastrophe, and for a minute they were unable to move; but at length, with breathless haste they hurried below, and to the lawn in front of the abbey. And there, huddled up in a mis-shapen mass, lay the mangled form of the old man. They raised him, and the expression of his features was frightful to gaze upon. He still breathed, but it was only for a moment; one deep, one fearful groan escaped his lips, a convulsive emotion slightly shook his limbs, then gurgling sound was heard in his throat, and all was still—the guilty soul of the Miser, Jasper Scrimpe, was summoned to its dread account.

* * * * * *

It would be painful to dwell unnecessarily upon these startling events, or the impression which they left for some time on the minds of the persons most deeply nterested. A week after the exciting occurrences, they quitted the abbey, and returned to London; and our hero now, by so singular a reverse of fortune, found himself the welcome guest of Sir Milford Welborn, at the old Grange, and the love of himself and Constance sanctioned and approved by him who had formerly been so strongly opposed to it.

The documents preserved in the cash-box of the Miser, fully established the claims of our hero to the title and estates of Sir William Wilmot, and he took possession of them accordingly. His first solemn act was to exhume the remains of his unfortunate parent from the unhallowed place where they had for so many years lain, and to have them consigned to the family vault of the old church-yard at Finchley, with all that pomp and solemnity that were due to his rank and virtues while living. The old hall at Finchley was ordered to be put in thorough repair as Sir Evelyn and his sister, much to the joy of the tenants and dependants, resolved to make it their occasional place of residence.

The beauteous Mabel was soon restored to convalescence, and that noble heart which for so many years had been a prey to sorrow, now throbbed and bounded with happiness and content. Almost the first thought that suggested itself to Sir Evelyn and his sister, was how they could ever sufficiently testify their gratitude to that excellent man, Sampson Brayling, who had proved such an inestimable and dis-interested friend to them all. They questioned him upon the subject, and the Gipsey was much affected, and could not speak for some time.

" Oh, Sir Evelyn," he said at length, " am I not sufficiently rewarded in seeing thee and Miss Mabel happy, and in knowing that, in performing an act of justice, and restoring thee to thy rights, I have performed my duty?—But yet there is one favour I would fain ask."

" Name it, name it?" eagerly demanded our hero and his sister, in a breath.

" I am getting old;" replied Brayling; "and the wanderer's life is no longer suited to me. Ever treat the companions, whom I intend to leave, with kindness, for they have rendered thee good service, and suffer me to pass the remainder of my days beneath thy roof."

"Gladly, cheerfully, do I grant thy request, my best, my dearest friend;" said Sir Evelyn, warmly pressing his hand; "while thou livest we will never part."

Brayling bent one knee to the ground, and raising the hands of Sir Evelyn and Mabel to his lips, was overpowered by his emotions.

Nor did Evelyn forget poor Toby Taper, he took him into his service, and that faithful creature never had reason again to complain that he was "so hungry."

Months rolled on, and the rude tempest of the past was lulled into a beautiful calm, bright augury of the happiness which was in store for them. And now that every obstacle was at an end, the time was fixed for the union of Sir Evelyn and his faithful Constance to take place, and for weeks before, preparations on the most extensive scale were put in operation, and all was on the tiptoe of joyful expectation. No one evinced greater happiness than Mabel. She was almost constantly with her brother and Constance, to the latter of whom she ever showed the most affectionate attention, and again and again expressed her regret for the feelings of jealousy she had formerly entertained towards her. Need we say how warmly Constance reciprocated those sentiments? They already loved each other with the ardent affection of sisters, and were only happy when in each other's society. They looked back upon the dismal past with mingled feelings of regret and satisfaction, for though the troubles to which they had been exposed were great, Omnipotence had in His own wise time released them from their sorrows, and the future presented a bright, a cheerful, and hopeful prospect. Mabel and Constance had both been sisters in misfortune, and therefore, can it be wondered that they should feel such a mutual sympathy towards each other? In fact, assimilating as they did in every grace and virtue of the mind, and now that every cause of jealousy or regret was removed, they could not be otherwise than contented and happy. And need we say with what feelings of delight Sir Evelyn viewed the harmony that so happily existed between his newly discovered sister and that fair, that faithful, and beloved being with whom his fate was so shortly to be united? It was indeed to him a source of the purest satisfaction and gratification, and greatly added to the sanguine hopes he so fondly entertained of the future. Bright and sunny were the prospects that now presented themselves to his vivid imagination; and what a happy contrast did they offer to the painful ordeal of the past, which it had been the fate of them all to pass through. They felt that they were indeed now amply rewarded for all the numerous trials and vicissitudes it had been their lot to encounter, and which they had supported with that patience, fortitude, and resignation which had thus at last enabled them to surmount every difficulty.

Most warmly did Sir Milford Welborn participate in those joyful feelings, and he looked forward to the union of Sir Evelyn and his amiable and beauteous niece with every hope and confidence. Nature had formed them for each other. The fervour and sincerity of their love had indeed been put to a severe test, and it seemed impossible that the union of two such worthy beings could be productive of anything but the greatest bliss.

To the noble-minded Mabel too, the baronet shewed the most marked attention, honouring her as the sister of Evelyn; but more so for those brilliant qualities of the mind which so greatly distinguished her, and which could not fail to excite the love and admiration of all who were acquainted with her strange and romantic history. Simple, bland, and kind to all, Mabel was indeed the pure child of nature; the beloved of all, and shedding a bright halo of happiness around every one who had the pleasure of her society and friendship.

The happy day, the wedding-day, at length arrived, and Sir Evelyn led his beautiful Constance to the altar, Mabel being the principal bridesmaid on that auspicious occasion, in conjunction with the five daughters of Sir Thomas Overton.

On the same day the faithful Abigail became the wife of the honest-hearted, though eccentric Timothy Tapcan ; her mistress presenting her with a handsome wedding portion, as a reward for her long tried fidelity, and retaining her in her service, Timothy being taken into that of Sir Evelyn.

A happy day indeed, was that at the old Grange, and in the surrounding neighbourhood ; for young and old, rich and poor, were invited to share in the festivities, Sampson Brayling, and those with whom he had for so many years been associated being amongst the most favoured guests.

The old Tankard at Fynesburie was full of company, who were very jovial, and Caleb Cosey was full of spirits ; and there was merry dancing round the old maypole till a late hour ; but even a whole week had elapsed before the revels ceased altogether, and many and fervent were the prayers that rose from honest hearts for the future welfire and happiness of Sir Evelyn Wilmot, his beauteous bride, and his noble-minded sister, Mabel, whose romantic history, extraordinary adventures, and exemplary virtues became the future theme of many a poet's song.

Walter Greysham continued at the old Grange for some weeks, the magnet that attracted him there we need not say was Mabel ; nor could he leave the mansion until he had confessed to that fair and amiable girl, the ardent passion with which she had inspired him. Mabel listened to him with every sympathy and respect, but firmly declined his overtures. Her resolution was fixed : she would never marry, but would find her whole happiness, by living with her brother and his fair bride, for the rest of her days, and in exerting herself to contribute to theirs. Walter was hurt and disappointed, but he submitted with the best grace he could ; and endeavoured to forget his hopeless passion in the bustle and activity of his profession.

The fervent wishes of Mabel for the happiness of those whom she valued above all earthly beings, were fully realised ; the union of Sir Evelyn and Constance was crowned with every human felicity, and, together with Mabel, they shed a lustre upon all who came within the circle of their acquaintance, and were looked up to with reverence and esteem by the humblest of their dependants. In due time their happiness was completed by the birth of a daughter, who, as a mark of affection, received the name of Mabel, who cherished the little innocent with the same unbounded love as if it had been her own offspring.

And with what tender, what assiduous care, was it the chief delight of the former gipsey-girl to watch and nurture this beautiful child, and the future offspring of that brother to whom her heart's finest affections had ever been so warmly attached before she knew the ties of nature that existed between them. How ardently did she exert herself to sow the seeds of virtue, to instil into their young minds all those noble precepts with which herself and their parents were so richly endowed. It was indeed to Mabel a task of love, and amply was she rewarded for it. The children viewed her with the fondest regard and veneration. Apt scholars were they, and under the affectionate and vigilant eye of so able a tutoress, their young mind daily and hourly expanded, and their virtues, " growing with their growth, and strengthening with their strength," fully realised all the fond anticipations their parents and relations had ventured to encourage.

Mabel, whose personal and intrinsic charms seemed to increase with her years, continued to be the admired of all beholders, especially of the opposite sex, from several of whom she received many tempting overtures ; but adhering to her original resolution, she declined them all : thus, with feelings of regret, disappointing the hopes of many a worthy youth, but still returning their most ardent regard and esteem.

It may, perhaps, not be uninteresting to state, that, after several years of active service, in which he had arrived at the greatest distinction, Walter Greysham returned to his native country, in which, for a time, he was resolved to rest himself, after the arduous duties he had to perform. The passion he had formerly entertained for Mabel had mellowed into a feeling of respect, which she returned with equal sincerity. In due time a mutual sentiment of love sprang up between him and one of the daughters of Sir Thomas Overton, which meeting with his warmest approval, their fates were indissolubly united in the holy bonds of matrimony.

The old Hall at Finchley, the family mansion of Sir Evelyn Wilmot, which his ancestors had inhabited for many successive generations, having undergone all the necessary repairs, and some of the most dilapidated portions of the stately building completely restored, it reassumed its original cheerful and hospitable aspect. That portion in which the remains of the late unfortunate baronet had been deposited, was entirely removed, and a finely executed monument to his memory, erected on the site. In fact, our hero devoted much of his time and study to the improvement of the estate, and received a commensurate reward in the blessings of his humble but numerous tenantry, whose social comforts it was ever his anxious care to watch over and enhance.

Having thus rendered ample justice to all the various actors in our eventful drama, we have little more to add. Those amiable beings who had born their numerous trials and vicissitudes with such unexampled fortitude, patience, and resignation, had at last met with their due reward; while justice had overtaken the guilty—truly realising the beautiful words of the poet, namely:—

> " Heaven is just,
> And, when the measure of man's crimes is full,
> Will bare its red right arm, and launch its lightnings."

Sir Milford Welborn lived to see a numerous family of children bless the hopes and wishes of Evelyn and Constance, emulating as they did the virtues of their parents, and then calmly sunk to the tomb, stricken with years of honour and integrity. Sampson Brayling too, who acted as steward to the estates of Sir Evelyn, lived to a good old age, venerated by Mabel and her brother as a second parent, and universally beloved by all who knew him.

A new building was shortly erected on the site of the residence of the Miser; but for many years the spot was pointed out to the anxious inquirer, and people shuddered as they listened to the history of JASPER SCRIMPE, THE MISER OF SHOREDITCH!

FINIS.

PRINTED BY R. BEARD, CRAVEN BUILDINGS, CITY ROAD.